I0831361

GORGIAS REPRINTS IN ARCHAEOLOGY

Volume 5 / I

Explorations in Bible Land

The Excavations at the Temple Court in Nippur

EXPLORATIONS

IN

BIBLE LANDS

During the 19th Century

BY

H. V. HILPRECHT

Clark Research Professor of Assyriology and Scientific Director of the Babylonian Expedition, University of Pennsylvania

WITH THE CO-OPERATION OF

LIC. DR. BENZINGER, Formerly University of Berlin
PROF. DR. HOMMEL, University of Munich
PROF. DR. JENSEN, University of Marburg
PROF DR. STEINDORFF, University of Leipzig

Volume I

With Nearly Two Hundred Illustrations and Four Maps

GORGIAS PRESS
2002

First Gorgias Press Edition, 2002.

 Published in the United States of America by Gorgias Press LLC, New Jersey. This edition is a facsimile reprint of the original edition published by A. J. Molman and Company, Philadelphia, in 1903.

ISBN 1-931956-51-0 (Volume 1)

ISBN 1-931956-52-9 (Volume 2)

GORGIAS PRESS

46 Orris Ave., Piscataway, NJ 08854 USA

www.gorgiaspress.com

Printed and bound in the United States of America.

TO

H. CLAY TRUMBULL

THE REDISCOVERER OF KADESH-BARNEA

AS A SMALL TOKEN OF HIGH ESTEEM AND
LOVING AFFECTION

THE EDITOR

PUBLISHER'S NOTE

The owner of the original copy from which this facsimile edition was made had inserted in the book a newspaper clip announcing the marriage of Hilprecht which we reproduce below. The name of the newspaper and the year of publication are unknown.

LEARNED MAN IS MARRIED.

Professor Hilprecht, the Assyriologist, Takes a Bride.

PHILADELPHIA, April 24.—If it had been announced that he had discovered another Nippur, the friends of Prof. Hermanus V. Hilprecht, professor of assyriology and semitic philology and archæology at the University of Pennsylvania, would not have been more startled than when they learned that he was married last night to Mrs. W. H. Robinson, of 1932 Locust street.

Dr. Hilprecht is known the world over as the man who has turned back the clock of history three thousand years. He discovered the oldest library in the world, which was collected at least ten thousand years ago.

PREFACE

NEARLY ten years ago Messrs. A. J. Holman & Co. approached me with a request to prepare, for the close of the century, a brief historical sketch on the explorations in Bible lands, which would convey to the intelligent English-reading public a clear conception of the gradual resurrection of the principal ancient nations of Western Asia and Egypt. After much hesitation, I consented to become responsible for the execution of their comprehensive plan, provided that I be allowed to solicit the coöperation of other specialists for the treatment of those subjects which did not lie directly within the sphere of my own investigations, as most of the books dealing with this fascinating theme suffer from the one serious defect that their authors are not competent authorities in every part of that vast field which they attempt to plough and cultivate for the benefit and instruction of others. Several well-known German specialists, whose names appear on the title-page, were therefore accordingly invited to join the editor in the preparation of the volume, and to present to the reader sketches of their respective branches of science, with the historical development of which they have been prominently connected during previous years. At the close of 1900 the entire MS. was ready to be printed, when the results of a series of excavations carried on by the Babylonian Expedition of the University of Pennsylvania began to attract more than ordinary attention on both sides of the Atlantic. In view of the growing demand for a popular and authentic report of these important archæological researches, the publishers deemed it necessary to modify their former plans by asking the editor to make the exploration of Assyria and Babylonia the characteristic feature of the uncompleted book, and, above all, to incorporate with it *the first full account of the American labors at Nuffar.* Thus it came about that the opening article of this collective volume, intended to give but a brief survey of a subject which at present stands in the centre of general interest, has grown far beyond its original limits.

As the results of Koldewey's methodical excavations and topographical researches at the vast ruin fields of the ancient metropolis on the Euphrates, belong chiefly to the twentieth century and, moreover, are not yet fully accessible to other scholars, their omission in these pages will scarcely be regarded as a serious deficiency, since the object of the present book was to set forth the work of the explorers of the previous century. If, however, the public interest in the material here submitted should warrant it, they will find their proper treatment in a future edition.

In preparing the first 288 pages of my own contribution I have had the extraordinary assistance of my lamented wife and colaborer, who, with her remarkable knowledge of the history of Assyriology and her characteristic unselfish devotion to the cause of science and art, promoted the work of the Babylonian Expedition of the University of Pennsylvania (in charge of her husband) in many essential ways unknown to the public. The best passages in the following chapter on the "Resurrection of Assyria and Babylonia" are likewise due to her. She laid down her pen only when the approaching angel of death wrested it from her tired hand on March 1, 1902. The Board of Trustees of the University of Pennsylvania has since honored the memory of this great and gifted woman by resolving unanimously that the famous collections of tablets from the temple library at Nippur shall be known henceforth by her name. In view of her very extensive contributions to the present book, it was my desire to have her name associated with mine on its title-page. But when I asked for her consent the day previous to her final departure, — immediately after she had completed her last task, and had arranged with me for the next twenty years the details of the scientific publications of the American Expedition to Nuffar, — I received the memorable reply: "Why should the world learn to discriminate between your work and my work, your person and my person? Was not your God my God, your country my country, your labor my labor, your sorrow my sorrow, your name my name? Let it remain so even at my coffin and tomb." In the light of this sacred legacy, my reviewers will pardon me for appearing to appropriate more than is due to me.

More rapidly than I could have anticipated I was placed in a position to carry out my wife's lofty ideas with regard to the strictly scientific publications of the Philadelphia expedition. It seems therefore eminently proper for me in this connection to express publicly my deep gratitude to Messrs. Edward W. and Clarence H. Clark of Philadelphia, the two widely known patrons of American explorations in Babylonia, who by their recent munificent gift of $100,000 have enabled the Board of Trustees of the University of Pennsylvania to establish the "Clark Research Professorship of Assyriology," the only chair of its kind in existence. As its first incumbent I am authorized to devote the rest of my life to the study and deciphering of those remarkable results which through the generosity and energy of a few

Philadelphia citizens were obtained at the ruins of Nuffar, and which through the liberality and personal interest of Mr. Eckley B. Coxe, Jr., will be printed and submitted to the public more rapidly than was hitherto possible.

From the very beginning I have been connected with the various Babylonian expeditions of the University of Pennsylvania. The farther we proceeded with our researches, the more it became necessary for me to spend my time almost regularly every year in three different parts of the world and to surrender completely the comfort of a fixed home. In consequence of this nomadic life I was often out of contact with my well-equipped library, — a disadvantage especially felt when certain passages were to be examined or verified from the earlier literature dealing with my subject. With warm appreciation of all the friendly assistance received, I acknowledge my great indebtedness to Messrs. Halil Bey, Director of the Imperial Ottoman Museum; Leon Heuzey, Director of the Louvre; L. King of the British Museum; Dr. A. Gies, First Dragoman of the German Embassy in Constantinople; F. Furtwaengler, H. Gebzer, F. Hommel, R. Kittel, V. Scheil, Eberhard Schrader, F. Thureau-Dangin, Karl Vollers, and not the least to my friend and assistant, A. T. Clay, who not only read a complete set of proofs, and improved the English garment of all the articles here published, but in many other ways facilitated the preparation and printing of the entire volume.

As it was not always advisable to ship valuable photographic material to his temporary abode, the editor found it sometimes difficult to illustrate the articles of his colaborers in an adequate manner. In several instances it would have been almost impossible for him to obtain suitable illustrations had he not profited by the material kindly placed at his disposal by Mrs. Sara Y. Stevenson, Sc. D., Curator of the Egyptian Section of the Archæological Museum of the University of Pennsylvania; Miss Mary Robinson, daughter of the late Professor Edward Robinson of New York; Mrs. T. Bent and Mrs. W. Wright of London; Mr. C. S. Fisher, of the Babylonian Expedition of the University of Pennsylvania; Mr. T. Grotefend of Hanover; Professor J. Halévy of Paris; and Count Landberg of Munich; to all of whom are due his cordial thanks.

It is the hope of both authors and publishers that the present volume may help to fill a serious gap in our modern literature by presenting in a systematic but popular form a fascinating subject, equal in importance to the Bible student, historian, archæologist, and philologist. The rich material often scattered through old editions of rare books and comparatively inaccessible journals has been examined anew, sifted, and treated by a number of experts in the light of their latest researches. It was our one aim to bring the history of the gradual exploration of those distant oriental countries, which formed the significant scene and background of God's dealings with Israel as a nation, more vividly before the educated classes of Christendom. May the time and labor devoted to the preparation of this work contribute their small share towards arousing a deeper interest on the part of the public in excavating more of those priceless treasures of the past which have played such a conspicuous role in the interpretation of the Old Testament writings.

THE EDITOR.

JENA, December 27, 1902.

CONTENTS.

INDEXES.

LIST OF ILLUSTRATIONS.

The asterisk (*) indicates that the illustration has been added by the Editor to the material furnished by the contributors.

ASSYRIA AND BABYLONIA.

PALESTINE.

EGYPT.

ARABIA.

THE HITTITES.

MAPS.

(IN THE POCKET AT THE END OF THE BOOK.)

THE RESURRECTION
OF
ASSYRIA AND BABYLONIA

2

G. F. Grotefend

THE RESURRECTION OF ASSYRIA AND BABYLONIA

BY PROFESSOR H. V. HILPRECHT, PH.D., D.D., LL.D.

THE history of the exploration of Assyria and Babylonia and of the excavation of its ruined cities is a peculiar one. It is a history so full of dramatic effects and genuine surprises, and at the same time so unique and far-reaching in its results and bearings upon so many different branches of science, that it will always read more like a thrilling romance penned by the skilful hand of a gifted writer endowed with an extraordinary power of imagination than like a plain and sober presentation of actual facts and events.

In the Trenches of Nuffar

Nineveh and Babylon! What illustrious names and prominent types of human strength, intellectual power, and lofty aspiration; but also what terrible examples of atrocious deeds, of lack of restraint, of moral corruption, and ultimate downfall! "Empty, and void, and waste" (Nah. 2 : 10); when "flocks lie down in the midst of her" (Zeph. 2 : 14); when "the gates of the rivers shall be opened, and the palace shall be dissolved" (Nah. 2 : 6) — was the fate of the queen in the North; and "How art thou fallen from heaven, O Lucifer, son of the morning! how art thou cut down to the ground, which didst weaken the nations" (Is. 14 : 12) — rings like a mourning wail through Babylon's crumbling walls, and like the mocking echo of the prophetic curse from the shattered temples in the South.

Ignorant peasants draw their primitive ploughs over the ruined palaces of Qoyunjuk and Khorsabâd; roaming Bedouins pasture their herds on the grass-covered slopes of Nimrûd and Qal'at Shirgât; Turkish garrisons and modern villages crown the summits of Erbîl and Nebî Yûnus. Nothing reminds the traveller of the old Assyrian civilization but formless heaps and conical mounds. The solitude and utter devastation which characterize Babylonia in her present aspect are even more impressive and appalling. The whole country from 'Aqarqûf to Qorna looks "as when God overthrew Sodom and Gomorrah" (Is. 13 : 19; Jer. 50 : 40). The innumerable canals which in bygone days, like so many nourishing veins, crossed the rich alluvial plain, bringing life and joy and wealth to every village and field, are choked up with rubbish and earth. Unattended by industrious hands and no longer fed by the Euphrates and Tigris, they are completely "dried up" — "a drought is upon the waters of Babylon" (Jer. 50 : 38). But their lofty embankments, like a perfect network, "stretching on every side in long lines until they are lost in the hazy distance, or magnified by the mirage into mountains, still defy the hand of time," bearing witness to the great skill and diligent labor which once turned these barren plains into one luxuriant garden. The proverbial fertility and prosperity of Babylonia, which excited the admiration of classical writers, have long disappeared. "Her cities are a desolation, a dry land, and a wilderness" (Jer. 51:43). The soil is parched and the ground is covered with fine sand, sometimes sparingly clad with *'arid* and *serîm*, *qubbâr*, and *tarfa*, and other low shrubs and plants of the desert.

And yet this is but one side — and not the most gloomy — of Chaldea's present cheerless condition. "The sea is come up upon Babylon: she is covered with the multitudes of the waves thereof" (Jer. 51:42), says the Old Testament

The 'Afej Marshes near Nuffar

seer, in his terse and graphic description of the future state of the unfortunate country. In the autumn and winter Babylonia is a "desert of sand," but during spring and summer she is almost a continuous marsh, a veritable "desert of the sea" (Is. 21:1). While the inundations prevail a dense vegetation springs from the stagnant waters. Large flocks of birds with brilliant plumage, "pelicans and cormorants sail about in the undisputed possession of their safe and tranquil retreats." Turtles and snakes glide swiftly through the lagoons, while millions of green little frogs are seated on the bending rushes. Ugly buffaloes are struggling and splashing amongst the tall reeds and coarse grasses, "their unwieldy bodies often entirely concealed under water and their hideous heads just visible upon the surface." Wild animals, boars and hyenas, jackals and wolves, and an occasional lion, infest the jungles. Here and there a small plot of ground, a shallow island, a high-towering ruin, bare of every sign of vegetation, and towards the north large elevated tracts of barren soil covered with fragments of brick and glass and stone appear above the horizon of these pestiferous marshes. Half-naked men, women, and children, almost black from constant exposure to the sun, inhabit these desolate regions. Filthy huts of reeds and mats are their abodes during the night; in long pointed boats of the same material they skim by day over the waters, pasturing their flocks, or catching fish with the spear. To sustain their life, they cultivate a little rice, barley, and maize, on the edges of the inundations. Generally good-natured and humorous like children, these Ma'dân tribes get easily excited, and at the slightest provocation are ready to fight with each other. Practicing the vices more than the virtues of the Arab race, extremely ignorant and superstitious, they live in the most primitive state of barbarism and destitution, despised by the Bedouins of the desert, who frequently drive their cattle and sheep away and plunder their little property during the winter.

Restlessly shifting nomads in the north and ignorant swamp dwellers in the south have become the legitimate heirs of Asshur and Babel. What contrast between ancient civilization and modern degeneration! The mighty kings of yore have passed away, their empires were shattered, their countries destroyed. Nineveh and Babylon seemed completely to have vanished from the earth. Hundreds of years were necessary to revive the interest in their history and to determine merely their sites, while the exploration of their principal ruins, the deciphering of their inscriptions, and the restoration of their literature and art were achieved only in the course of the nineteenth century. The road was long, the process slow, and many persons and circumstances combined to bring about the final result.

I

THE REDISCOVERY OF NINEVEH AND BABYLON

NINEVEH

Nineveh, the capital of the Assyrian empire, owed its greatness and domineering influence exclusively to the conquering spirit of its rulers and the military glory and prowess of its armies. As soon as the latter had been routed, her influence ceased, the city fell, never to rise again, and its very site was quickly forgotten among the nations. When two hundred years later Xenophon and his ten thousand Greeks fought their way through the wilderness and mountains to the Black Sea, they passed the ruins of Nineveh without even mentioning her by name. But a vague local tradition, always an important factor in the East, continued to linger around the desolate region between Mosul and the mouth of the Upper Zâb, where the final drama had been enacted.

Benjamin of Tudela, a learned Spanish Jew, who travelled to Palestine and the districts of the Euphrates and Tigris in the twelfth century, about the time when Rabbi Pethahiah of Ratisbon visited Mesopotamia, had no difficulty in locating the actual position of Nineveh. In speaking of Mosul he says: "This city, situated on the Tigris, is connected with ancient Nineveh by a bridge. It is true, Nineveh lies now in utter ruins, but numerous villages and small towns occupy its former space."[1]

[1] Comp. *Itinerarium Beniamini Tudelensis* (*ex Hebraico Latinum factum Bened. Aria Montano interprete*), Antwerp, 1575, p. 58.

The German physician, Leonhart Rauwolff, who spent several days in Mosul at the beginning of 1575, writes [1] in his attractive quaint style with reference to a high round hill directly outside the city (apparently Qoyunjuk): [2] "It was entirely honeycombed, being inhabited by poor people, whom I often saw crawling out and in in large numbers, like ants in their heap. At that place and in the region hereabout years ago the mighty city of Nineveh was situated. Originally built by Asshur, it was for a time the capital of Assyria under the rulers of the first monarchy down to Sennacherib and his sons." [3]

Sir Anthony Shirley, who sailed to the East at the close of the sixteenth century, is equally positive: "Nineve, that which God Himself calleth That great Citie, hath not one stone standing which may give memory of the being of a towne. One English mile from it is a place called Mosul, a small thing, rather to be a witnesse of the other's might-

[1] In his *Itinerarium* or *Rayssbüchlein*, which appeared in Laugingen, 1583, the author writes his name either Rauwolf, Rauwolff, or Rauchwolff, the middle being the most frequent of all. Interwoven with *allerhandt wunderbarliche geschicht und Historien, die den gutherzigen leser erlustigen und höheren sachen nach zudenken auffmundtern sollen*, this book contains much valuable information as to what Rauwolff has seen in the Orient during the three years of his perilous journey, which lasted from May 15, 1573, to February 12, 1576. Of especial importance are his observations on the flora of the regions traversed, a subject on which he speaks with greater authority.

[2] Comp. the statement of Tavernier, quoted on p. 10.

[3] P. 244: *Sonst ersahe ich auch ausserhalb gleich vor der Stadt ein hohen runden Bihel, der schier gantz durchgraben und von armen leuten bewohnet wirt, wie ichs dann offtermals hab in grosser anzahl (als die Ohnmaysen in irem hauffen) sehen auss und einkriechen. An der stet und in der gegne hierumb, ist vor Jaren gelegen die mechtige Statt Ninive, welche (von Assur erstlich erbawet) unter den Potentaten der ersten Monarchi, eine zeitlang biss auf den Sennacherib und seine Söne die Hauptstatt in Assyrien gewesen*, etc. Comp., also, p. 214: *Mossel so vor Jaren Ninive gehaissen.*

inesse and God's judgement, than of any fashion of magnificence in it selfe."[1]

From the beginning of the seventeenth century we quote two other witnesses, John Cartwright, an English traveller, and Pietro della Valle, an Italian nobleman, the latter being satisfied with the general statement: "Mousul, where previously Nineveh stood,"[2] the former entering into certain details of the topography of the ruins, which, notwithstanding his assurance to the contrary, he cannot have examined very thoroughly. As a first attempt at drawing some kind of a picture of the city on the basis of personal observation, legendary information from the natives, and a study of the ancient sources, his words may deserve a certain attention: "We set forward toward Mosul, a very antient towne in this countrey, . . . and so pitched on the bankes of the river Tigris. Here in these plaines of Assiria and on the bankes of the Tigris, and in the region of Eden, was Ninevie built by Nimrod, but finished by Ninus. It is agreed by all prophane writers, and confirmed by the Scriptures that this citty exceeded all other citties in circuit, and answerable magnificence. For it seems by the ruinous foundation (which I thoroughly viewed) that it was built with four sides, but not equall or square; for the two longer sides had each of them (as we gesse) an hundredth and fifty furlongs, the two shorter sides, ninety furlongs, which amounteth to foure hundred and eighty furlongs of ground, which makes three score miles, accounting eight furlongs to an Italian mile. The walls whereof were an hundredth foote upright, and had such a breadth, as three Chariots might

[1] Comp. "His Relation of His Travels into Persia," London, 1613, p. 21, partly quoted by Felix Jones in "Journal of the Royal Asiatic Society," vol. xv., p. 333, footnote 3; and the Dutch edition, Leyden, 1706, p. 10.

[2] I quote from the German translation in my library (*Reise-Beschreibung*, Geneva, 1674), part 1, p. 193, b: *Mousul, an welchem Ort vorzeiten Ninive gestanden.*

passe on the rampire in front: these walls were garnished with a thousand and five hundreth towers, which gave exceeding beauty to the rest, and a strength no lesse admirable for the nature of those times." [1]

Tavernier, who justly prides himself in having travelled by land more than sixty thousand miles within forty years, made no less than six different excursions into Asia. In April, 1644, he spent over a week at Mosul, and most naturally also visited the ruins of Nineveh, which were pointed out to him on the left bank of the Tigris. "They appear as a formless mass of ruined houses extending almost a mile alongside the river. One recognizes there a large number of vaults or holes which are all uninhabited," — evidently the same place which, seventy-five years before him, Rauwolff had found frequented by poor people, and not unfittingly had compared to a large ant-hill. "Half a mile from the Tigris is a small hill occupied by many houses and a mosque, which is still in a fine state of preservation. According to the accounts of the natives the prophet Jonah lies buried here." [2]

During the eighteenth century men of business, scholars, and priests of different religious orders kept the old tradition alive in the accounts of their travels. But in 1748 Jean Otter, a member of the French Academy, and afterwards professor of Arabic, who had spent ten years in the provinces of Turkey and Persia for the distinct purpose of studying geographical and historical questions, suddenly introduced a strong element of doubt as to the value and continuity of the local tradition around Mosul.[3] He dis-

[1] "The Preacher's Travels," London, 1611, pp. 89, *seq.* Comp., also, Rogers, "History of Babylonia and Assyria," vol. i., pp. 94, *seq.*

[2] Comp. *Herrn Johann Baptisten Taverniers Vierzig-Jährige Reise-Beschreibung*, translated by Menudier, Nuremberg, 1681, part 1, p. 74.

[3] In his *Voyage en Turquie et en Perse*, Paris, 1748, vol. i., pp. 133, *seq.* Comp., also, Buckingham, "Travels in Mesopotamia," London, 1827, vol. ii., p. 17.

criminates between the statement of the Arabian geographer Abûlfedâ, claiming the eastern bank of the Tigris for the true site of Nineveh, and a tradition current among the natives,[1] who identify Eski-Mosul, a ruin on the western side and considerably higher up the river, with the ancient city, himself favoring, however, the former view. For, "opposite Mosul there is a place called *Tell Et-tûba*, *i. e.*, 'Mound of Repentance,' where, they say, the Ninevites put on sackcloth and ashes to turn away the wrath of God."

The old tradition which placed the ruin of Nineveh opposite Mosul was vindicated anew by the Danish scholar Carsten Niebuhr, who visited the place in 1766. Though not attempting to give a detailed description of the ruins in which we are chiefly interested, he states his own personal conviction very decidedly, and adds some new and important facts illustrated by the first sketch of the large southern mound of Nebî Yûnus.[2] Jewish and Christian inhabitants alike declare that Nineveh stood on the left bank of the river, and they differ only as to the original extent of the city.

Two principal hills are to be distinguished, the former crowned with the village of Nunia (*i. e.*, Nineveh) and a mosque said to contain the tomb of the prophet Jonah (Nebî Yûnus), the other known by the name of Qal'at Nunia ("the castle of Nineveh"), and occupied by the village of Qoyunjuk. While living in Mosul near the Tigris, he was also shown the ancient walls of the city on the other

[1] Also reported (and favored) by the Italian Academician and botanist Sestini, who in 1781 travelled from Constantinople through Asia Minor to Mosul and Basra, and in the following year from there via Mosul and Aleppo to Alexandria. Comp. the French translation of his account, *Voyage de Constantinople à Bassora*, etc., Paris, vi. (year of the Republic = 1798), p. 152.

[2] Comp. *C. Niebuhrs Reisebeschreibung nach Arabien und andern umliegenden Ländern*, Copenhagen, 1778, vol. ii., p. 353, and Plates xlvi. and xlvii., No. 2.

side, which formerly he had mistaken for a chain of low hills. Niebuhr's account was brief, but it contained all the essential elements of a correct description of the ruins, and by its very brevity and terse presentation of facts stands out prominently from the early literature as a silent protest against the rubbish so often contained in the works of previous travellers.

To a certain degree, therefore, D'Anville was justified in summing up the whole question concerning the site of Nineveh, at the close of the eighteenth century, by making the bold statement in his geographical work, "The Euphrates and Tigris":[1] "We know that the opposite or left bank of the river has preserved vestiges of Nineveh, and that the tradition as to the preaching of Jonah by no means has been forgotten there."

BABYLON

The case of Babylon was somewhat different. The powerful influence which for nearly two thousand years this great Oriental metropolis had exercised upon the nations of Western Asia, no less by its learning and civilization than by its victorious battles; the fame of its former splendor and magnitude handed down by so many different writers; the enormous mass of ruins still testifying to its gigantic temples and palaces; and the local tradition continuing to live among the inhabitants of that desolate region with greater force and tenacity than in the district of Mosul, prevented its name and site from ever being forgotten entirely. At the end of the first Christian century the city was in ruins and practically deserted. But even when Baghdad had risen to the front, taking the place of Babylon and Seleucia as an eastern centre of commerce and civilization, Arabian and Persian writers occasionally speak of the

[1] *L'Euphrate et le Tigre*, Paris, 1779, p. 88.

two, and as late as the close of the tenth century, Ibn Hauqal refers to Babel as "a small village." [1]

The more we advance in the first half of the second millennium, the scantier grows our information. Benjamin of Tudela has but little to say. His interest centred in the relics of the numerous Jewish colonies of the countries traversed and in their history and tradition. Briefly he mentions the ruins of the palace of Nebuchadrezzar, "to men inaccessible on account of the various and malignant kinds of serpents and scorpions living there." [2] With more detail he describes the Tower of Babel ("built by the dispersed generation, of bricks called *al-ajûr* " [3]), which apparently he identified with the lofty ruins of Birs (Nimrûd). Other travellers, like Marco Polo, visited the same regions without even referring to the large artificial mounds which they must frequently have noticed on their journeys. Travelling to the valleys of the Euphrates and Tigris, in those early days, was more for adventure or commercial and religious purposes than for the scientific exploration of the remains of a bygone race, about which even the most

[1] A brief summary of the different ancient writers who refer to the gradual disappearance of Babylon, and of the more prominent European travellers who visited or are reported to have visited the ruins of Babylon (with extracts from their accounts in an appendix), is found in the introduction to the "Collection of Rich's Memoirs," written by Mrs. Rich. It rests upon the well-known dissertation on Babylon by De Ste. Croix, published in the *Mémoires de l' Académie des Inscriptions et des Belles-Lettres*, 1789. Of more recent writers who have treated the same subject, I mention only Kaulen (*Assyrien und Babylonien*, 5th ed., 1899) and Rogers ("History of Babylonia and Assyria," vol. i., 1900). Much information on the early writers is also scattered through Ritter's *Die Erdkunde von Asien*, especially vol. xi. of the whole series.

[2] *Itinerarium Beniamini Tudelensis*, p. 70, *seq.*

[3] The Latin translation has Lagzar (לאגזר). *Al-ajúr* (comp. *lâjûr* in the Maghreb dialects) is used also by the present inhabitants of Babylonia as another designation for "baked brick" (*tâbûq*). The word is identical with the Babylonian *agurru*, as was recognized by Rawlinson, "Journal of the Royal Asiatic Society," vol. xvii., p. 9.

learned knew but little. In the following sketch I quote, in historical order, only those travellers who have actually furnished some kind of useful information concerning Babylon or other Babylonian sites.

From the latter part of the sixteenth century we have three testimonials, that of Rauwolff, the adventurous physician of Augsburg (travelling 1573–76), that of the Venetian jeweller, Balbi (1579–80),[1] and that of the English merchant Eldred (1583), a contemporary of Queen Elizabeth, who descended the Euphrates in a boat, landed at Fallûja (or Felûja, according to the popular Arabic pronunciation), and proceeded across 'Irâq to Baghdad. In vague terms they all speak of the ruins of "the mighty city of Babylon," the "Tower of Babel," and the "Tower of Daniel," which they beheld in the neighborhood of Fallûja or on their way to Baghdad or "New Babylon." Their words have been generally accepted without criticism.[2] It is, however, entirely out of question that a traveller who disembarked at Fallûja, directing his course due east, and arriving at Baghdad after one and a half days' journey, could possibly have passed or even have seen the ruins of Babylon. From a comparison of the accounts given by Rauwolff, Eldred, and others with what I personally observed in 1889, when for the first time I travelled precisely the same road, there can be no doubt that they mistook the various ruin heaps and the many large and small portions of high embankments of ancient canals everywhere visible [3] for scattered re-

[1] Not having been able to examine his statement in the author's own book, I profited by the brief résumé of his travel given by Mrs. Rich in her edition of her husband's "Collected Memoirs," p. 55, footnote *.

[2] Rogers, in his "History of Babylonia and Assyria," vol. i., pp. 89, *seqq.*, asserts that Eldred confused Baghdad and Babylon. But this is incorrect, for Eldred says plainly enough: "The citie of New Babylon [Baghdad] joyneth upon the aforesaid desert where the Olde citie was," *i. e.*, the desert between Fallûja and Baghdad which our author crossed.

[3] Possibly they included even the large ruins of Anbâr, plainly to be recog-

'Aqarqûf, the "Tower of Babel" of Early Travellers

mains of the very extended city of Babylon, and the imposing brick structure of 'Aqarqûf for the "Tower of Babel" or "of Daniel." For 'Aqarqûf, generally pronounced 'Agargûf, and situated about nine to ten miles to the west of Baghdad, is the one gigantic ruin which every traveller crossing the narrow tract of land from Fallûja to Baghdad must pass and wonder at. Moreover, the description of that ruin, as given by Eldred and others after him, contains several characteristic features from which it can be identified without difficulty. We quote Eldred's own language: "Here also are yet standing the ruines of the olde Tower of Babell, which being upon a plaine ground seemeth a farre off very great, but the nearer you come to it, the lesser and lesser it appeareth: sundry times I have gone thither to see it, and found the remnants yet standing about a quarter of a mile in compasse, and almost as high as the stone work of Paules steeple in London, but it showeth much bigger. The brickes remaining in this most ancient monument be half a yard [in the sense of our "foot"] thicke and three quarters of a yard long, being dried in the Sunne only, and betweene every course of brickes there lieth a course of mattes made of canes, which remaine sounde and not perished, as though they had been layed within one yeere."[1]

Master Allen,[2] who travelled in the same region not

nized from Fallûja, and only a few miles to the north of it. For all these travellers had a vague idea that ancient Babylon was situated on the Euphrates, and that its ruins covered a vast territory. Eldred's description is especially explicit: "In this place which we crossed over stood the olde mightie citie of Babylon, many olde ruines whereof are easilie to be seene by daylight, which I, John Eldred, have often beheld at my goode leisure, having made three voyages between the New citie of Babylon [*i. e.*, Baghdad] and Aleppo."

[1] Hakluyt, "The Principal Navigations, Voiages, and Discoveries of the English Nation," London, 1589, p. 232.

[2] Comp. "Purchas his Pilgrimage," London, 1626, p. 50 (quoted in Rich's "Collected Memoirs," pp. 321, *seq.*, footnote *).

many years afterwards, gives as his measurement of those bricks twelve by eight by six inches. Eldred's statement, however, is more correct. While visiting 'Aqarqûf, I found the average size of complete bricks from that ruin to be eleven inches square by four inches and a quarter thick.[1] The layers of reed matting, a characteristic feature of the massive ruin, are not so frequent as stated by Eldred. They occur only after every fifth to seventh layer of bricks, at an average interval of nearly three feet. What is now left of this high, towering, and inaccessible structure, above the accumulation of rubbish at its base, rises to a little over a hundred feet. If there is still any doubt as to the correctness of the theory set forth, a mere reference to the positive statement of Tavernier,[2] who visited Baghdad in 1652, will suffice to dispel it.

Shirley's and Cartwright's references to Babylon, or rather to the locality just discussed, may be well passed over, the former delighting more in preaching than in teaching, the latter largely reproducing the account of Eldred, with which he was doubtless familiar. Of but little intrinsic value is also what Boeventing, Taxeira, and a number of other travellers of the same general period have to relate.

[1] Chesney, "The Expedition for the Survey of the Rivers Euphrates and Tigris," vol. ii., p. 605, practically gives the same measures ($11\frac{1}{4}$ inches square by 4 deep).

[2] I quote from the German edition before me (*Vierzig-Jährige Reise-Beschreibung*, translated by Menudier, Nuremberg, 1681, part 1, p. 91): *Ich muss noch allhier beyfügen, was ich wegen dessjenigen, das insgemein von dem Rest des Thurns zu Babylon geglaubet wird, in acht nehmen können, welcher Name (Babylon) auch ordentlich der Stadt Bagdad gegeben wird, ungeachtet selbige davon über 3 Meilen entfernet liget. Man siehet also . . . einen grossen von Erden aufgehäuften Hügel, den man noch heut zu Tage Nemrod nennet. Selbiger ist in mitten einer grossen Landschafft, und lässet sich ferne schon zu Gesichte fassen. Das gemeine Volk, wie ich bereits gedacht, glaubet, es seye solcher der Überrest des Babylonischen Thurns: Allein es hat einen besseren Schein, was die Araber ausgeben, welche es Agarcouf nennen.* Comp., also, *C. Niebuhrs Reisebeschreibung*, Copenhagen, 1778, vol. ii., p. 305.

The first to examine the real site of ancient Babylon with a certain care was Pietro della Valle, who sent the first copy of a few cuneiform characters from Persepolis to Europe, at the same time stating his reasons why they should be read from the left to the right. This famous traveller also carried with him a few inscribed bricks — probably the first that ever reached Europe — from Bâbil, which he visited towards the end of 1616, and from Muqayyar (Ur of the Chaldees), which he examined in 1625 on his homeward journey. His description of Bâbil, the most northern mound of the ruins of Babylon, while not satisfactory in itself, stands far above the information of previous travellers. He tells us that this large mound, less ruined at those days than at the beginning of the twentieth century, was a huge rectangular tower or pyramid with its corners pointing to the four cardinal points. The material of this structure he describes as "the most remarkable thing I ever saw." It consists of sundried-bricks, something so strange to him that in order to make quite sure, he dug at several places into the mass with pickaxes. "Here and there, especially at places which served as supports, the bricks of the same size were baked."

Vincenzo Maria di S. Caterina di Sienna, procurator general of the Carmelite monks, who sailed up the Euphrates forty years later, like Pietro della Valle even made an attempt at vindicating the local tradition by arguing that the place is situated on the banks of the Euphrates, that the surrounding districts are fertile, that for many miles the land is covered with the ruins of magnificent buildings, and above all, that there still exist the remains of the Tower of Babel, "which to this day is called Nimrod's tower," — referring to Birs (Nimrûd) on the western side of the Euphrates.

More sceptical is the view taken by the Dominican father Emmanuel de St. Albert,[1] who paid a visit to this remark-

[1] In D'Anville's *Mémoire sur la Position de Babylone*, 1761, published as a paper of the *Mémoires de l'Académie des Inscriptions et des Belles-Lettres*, vol. xxviii., p. 256.

able spot about 1700. In sharp contrast to the earlier travellers, who with but few exceptions were always ready to chronicle as facts the fanciful stories related to them by Oriental companions and interpreters in obliging response to their numerous questions, we here find a sober and distrustful inquirer carefully discriminating between "the foolish stories" current among the inhabitants of the country and his own personal observations and inferences. Near Hilla, on the two opposite banks of the river and at a considerable distance from each other, he noticed two artificial elevations, the one "situated in Mesopotamia," containing the ruins of a large building, "the other in Arabia about an hour's distance from the Euphrates," characterized by two masses of cemented brick (the one standing, the other lying overturned beside it), which "seemed as if they had been vitrified." "People think that this latter hill is the remains of the real Babylon, but I do not know what they will make of the other, which is opposite and exactly like this one." Convinced, however, that the ruins must be ancient, and much impressed by the curious "writing in unknown characters" which he found on the large square bricks, Father Emmanuel selected a few of the latter from both hills and carried them away with him.

Travellers, whose education was limited, and missionaries, who viewed those ruins chiefly from a religious standpoint, have had their say. Let us now briefly discuss the views of such visitors who took a strictly scientific interest in the ruins of Babylon. In connection with his epoch-making journey to Arabia and Persia, Carsten Niebuhr examined the mounds around Hilla in 1765. Though furnishing little new information as to their real size and condition, in this respect not unlike the French geographer and historian Jean Otter, who had been at the same mounds in 1743, Niebuhr presented certain reasons for his own positive conviction that the ruins of Babylon must be located in the neighborhood of Hilla.[1] He regarded the designation of "Ard Babel" given to that region by the natives, and the apparent remains of an ancient city found on both sides of the river, especially the numerous inscribed bricks lying on the ground, which are evidence of a very high state of civilization, as solid proof for the correctness of the local tradition. He even pointed out the large ruin heaps, "three quarters of a German mile to the north-northwest of Hilla and close by the eastern bank of the river [El-Qasr]," as the probable site of Babylon's castle and the hanging gardens mentioned by Strabo, while Birs (Nimrûd), "an entire hill of fine bricks with a tower on the top" he regarded as Herodotus' "Temple of Belus," therefore as lying still within the precinct of ancient Babylon.

Our last and best informed witness from the close of the eighteenth century, who deserves, therefore, our special attention, is Abbé De Beauchamp. Well equipped with astronomical and other useful knowledge, he resided at Baghdad as the Pope's vicar-general of Babylonia for some time between 1780 and 1790. The ruins of Babylon, in which he was deeply interested, being only sixteen to eighteen hours distant from Baghdad, he paid two visits to the famous site, publishing the results of his various observations in several memoirs,[2] from which we extract the following noteworthy facts: "There is no difficulty about the position of Babylon." Its ruins are situated in the district of Hilla, about one league to the north of it (latitude 32° 34′), on the opposite (left) side of the Euphrates, "exactly under the mound the Arabs call Babel." There are no ruins of Babylon proper on the western side of the river, as D'Anville in his

[1] Comp. *Reisebeschreibung*, Copenhagen, 1778, vol. ii., pp. 287, *seq.*: *Dass Babylon in der Gegend von Helle gelegen habe, daran ist gar kein Zweifel.*

[2] In *Journal des Savants*, Mai, 1785, and Dec., 1790. For extracts see Rich's "Collected Memoirs," pp. 301, *seq.*

geographical work assumes, making the Euphrates divide the city. The mounds which are to be seen "on the other side of the river, at about a league's distance from its banks, are called by the Arabs Bros [meaning Birs]." Among the ruins of Babylon, which chiefly consist of bricks scattered about, "there is in particular an elevation which is flat on the top, of an irregular form, and intersected by ravines. It would never have been taken for the work of human hands, were it not proved by the layers of bricks found in it. . . . They are baked with fire and cemented with *zepht* [*zift*] or bitumen; between each layer are found osiers." Not very far from this mound, "on the banks of the river, are immense heaps of ruins which have served and still serve for the building of Hillah. . . . Here are found those large and thick bricks imprinted with unknown characters, specimens of which I have presented to the Abbé Bartholomy. This place [evidently El-Qasr] and the mound of Babel are commonly called by the Arabs *Makloube* [or rather *Muqailîba*,[1] popularly pronounced *Mujêlîba*], that is, overturned." Further to the north Beauchamp was shown a thick brick wall, "which ran perpendicular to the bed of the river and was probably the wall of the city." The Arabs employed to dig for bricks obtained their material from this and similar walls, and sometimes even from whole chambers, "frequently finding earthen vessels and engraved marbles, . . . sometimes idols of clay representing human figures, or solid cylinders covered with very small writing . . . and about eight years ago a statue as large as life, which was thrown amongst the rubbish." On the wall of a chamber they had discovered "figures of a cow and of the sun and moon formed of varnished bricks." Beauchamp himself secured a brick on which was a lion, and

[1] In the Arabic dialect of modern Babylonia the diminutive (*fu'ail*) is frequently used instead of the regular noun formation. Comp. Oppert, *Expédition en Mésopotamie*, vol. i., p. 114.

others with a crescent in relief. He even employed two laborers for three hours in clearing a large stone which the Arabs supposed to be an idol, apparently the large lion of the Qasr [1] recently set up again by the German expedition.

Imperfect as the report of Beauchamp must appear in the light of our present knowledge, at the time when it was written it conveyed to the public for the first time a tolerably clear idea of the exact position and enormous size of the ruins of Babylon and of the great possibilities connected with their future excavation. It was particularly in England that people began to realize the importance of these cylinders and bricks covered with cuneiform writing "resembling the inscriptions of Persepolis mentioned by Chardin." The East India Company of London became the first public exponent of this rapidly growing interest in Great Britain, by ordering their Resident at Basra to obtain several specimens of these remarkable bricks and to send them carefully packed to London. At the beginning of the nineteenth century a small case of Babylonian antiquities arrived, the first of a long series to follow years later. Insignificant as it was, it soon played an important rôle in helping to determine the character of the third system of writing used in the Persian inscriptions.

There were other travellers at the close of the eighteenth century, who, like Edw. Ives [2] and the French physician G. A. Olivier,[3] also visited the ruins of Nineveh and Babylon, occasionally even contributing a few details to our previous knowledge. But they did not alter the general conception derived from the work of their predecessors, especially Niebuhr and Beauchamp. The first period of

1 Also the opinion of Rich, "Collected Memoirs," pp. 36, 64, *seq.*

2 Comp. "Journal from Persia to England," London, 1773, vol. ii., pp. 321, *seq.* (Nineveh), etc.

3 Comp. *Voyage dans l'Empire Othoman, l'Egypte et la Perse*, 6 vols., Paris, 1801–07, especially vol. ii.

Assyrian and Babylonian exploration had come to an end. Merchants and adventurers, missionaries and scholars had equally contributed their share to awakening Western Europe from its long lethargy by again vividly directing the attention of the learned and religious classes to the two great centres of civilization in the ancient East. The ruins of Nineveh, on the upper course of the Tigris, had been less frequently visited and less accurately described than those of Babylon on the lower Euphrates. The reason is very evident. The glory of the great Assyrian metropolis vanished more quickly and completely from human sight, and its ruins lay further from the great caravan road on which the early travellers proceeded to Baghdad, the famous city of Hârûn-ar-Rashîd, then a principal centre for the exchange of the products of Asia and Europe. But the ascertained results of the observations and efforts of many, and in particular the better equipped missionaries and scholars of the eighteenth century, were the rediscovery and almost definite fixing of the actual sites of Nineveh and Babylon, which, forgotten by Europe, had seemed to lie under a doom of eternal silence, — the Divine response to the curses of the oppressed nations and of the Old Testament prophets.

II

EXPLORING AND SURVEYING IN THE NINETEENTH CENTURY

The close of the eighteenth and the dawn of the nineteenth centuries witnessed a feverish activity in the workshops of a small but steadily growing number of European scholars. The continuous reports by different travellers of the imposing ruins of Persepolis, the occasional reproduction of sculptures and inscriptions from the walls and pillars of its palaces, the careful sifting and critical editing of the whole material by the indefatigable explorer Niebuhr, had convinced even the most sceptical men of science that there were really still in existence considerable artistic and literary remains of a bygone nation, whose powerful influence, at times, had been felt even in Egypt and Greece. Strong efforts were made in Denmark, France, and Germany to obtain a satisfactory knowledge of the ancient sacred language of the Zend-Avesta, to discover the meaning of the younger Pehlevi inscriptions on Sassanian seals and other small objects so frequently found in Persia, and to attempt even the deciphering of these strange wedge-shaped characters on the walls of Persepolis. Names like Anquetil-Duperron, Eugène Burnouf, Sylvestre de Sacy, Niebuhr, Tychsen, Münter, and others will always occupy a prominent position in the esteem of the following generations as the pioneers and leaders in a great movement which ultimately led to the establishment of the great science of cuneiform research, destined as it was to revolutionize our whole conception of the countries and nations of Western Asia. This new science, though the final result of many combined forces, sprang so suddenly into existence that when it was actually there, nobody seemed ready to receive it.

In the year 1802 the genius of a young German scholar, Georg Friederich Grotefend, then only twenty-seven years old, well versed in classical philology but absolutely ignorant of Oriental learning, solved the riddle, practically in a few days, that had puzzled much older men and scholars apparently much better qualified than himself. Under the magical touch of his hand the mystic and complicated characters of ancient Persia suddenly gained new life. But when he was far enough advanced to announce to the Academy of Sciences in Göttingen the epoch-making discovery which established his fame and reputation forever, that learned body, though comprising men of eminent mental training and intelligence, strange to say, declined to publish the Latin memoirs of this little known college teacher, who did not belong to the University circle proper, nor was even an Orientalist by profession. It was not until ninety years later (1893) that his original papers were rediscovered and published by Prof. Wilhelm Meyer, of Göttingen, in the Academy's Transactions — a truly unique case of *post mortem* examination in science.

Fortunately Grotefend did not need to wait for a critical test and proper acknowledgment of his remarkable work until he would have reached a patriarchal age at the close of the nineteenth century. Heeren, De Sacy, and others lent their helping hands to disseminate the extraordinary news of the great historical event in the learned world of Europe. Afterwards it became gradually known that far away from Western civilization, in the mountain ranges of Persia, an energetic and talented officer of the British army, Lieutenant (later Sir) Henry Rawlinson (born on April 11, 1810), had almost independently, though more than thirty years later, arrived at the same results as Grotefend by a similar process of combination.

Niebuhr had already pointed out that the inscriptions of Persepolis appeared always in three different systems of writing found side by side, the first having an alphabet of over forty signs, the second being more complicated, and the third even more so. Grotefend had gone a step farther by insisting that the three systems of writing represented three different languages, of which the first was the old Persian spoken by the kings who erected those palaces and inscribed their walls. The second he called Median, the third Babylonian. The name given to the second language, which is agglutinative, has later been repeatedly changed into Scythian, Susian, Amardian, Elamitic, Anzanian, and Neo-Susian. The designation of the third language as Babylonian had been made possible by a comparison of its complicated characters with the Babylonian inscriptions of the East India House in London, published, soon after their arrival in 1801, by Joseph Hager. This designation was at once generally accepted, and has remained in use ever since.

For the time being, however, little interest was manifested in the last-named and most difficult system of writing, which evidently contained only a Babylonian translation of the corresponding Persian inscriptions. More material, written exclusively in the third style of cuneiform writing, was needed from the Babylonian and Assyrian mounds themselves, not only to attract the curiosity but to command the undivided attention of scholars. This having been once provided, it would be only a question of time when the same key, which, in the hands of Grotefend, had wrought such wonders as to unlock the doors to the history of ancient Persia, would open the far more glorious and remote past of the great civilization between the Euphrates and Tigris. But in order to obtain the inscriptions needed, other more preparatory work had to be undertaken first. The treasure-house itself had to be examined and studied more carefully, before a successful attempt could be made to lift the treasure concealed in its midst. A survey of Babylon and Nineveh and other prominent ruins in easy access, and more authentic and reliable information concerning the geography and topography of the whole country in which they were situated, was an indispensable requirement before the work of excavation could properly begin.

So far England had been conspicuously absent from the serious technical work carried on by representatives of other nations in the study and in the field. And yet no other European power was so eminently qualified to provide what still was lacking as the "Queen of the Sea," through her regular and well-established commercial and political relations with India and the Persian gulf. The sound of popular interest and enthusiasm, which had been heard in Great Britain at the close of the eighteenth century, never died away entirely. Englishmen now came forward well qualified to carry out the first part of this scientific mission of the European nations in the country between the Euphrates and Tigris, where for many years they worked with great energy, skill, and success.

CLAUDIUS JAMES RICH

The first methodical explorer and surveyor of Babylonian and Assyrian ruins and rivers was Claudius James Rich. Born in 1787 near Dijon, in France, educated in Bristol, England, he developed, when a mere child, such a decided gift for the study of Oriental languages that at the age of sixteen years he was appointed to a cadetship in the East India Company's military service. Seriously affected by circumstances in the carrying out of his plans, he spent more than three years in the different parts of the Levant, perfecting himself in Italian, Turkish, and Arabic. His knowledge of the Turkish language and manners was so thorough that while in Damascus not only did he enter the grand mosque "in the disguise of a Mameluke," but his host, "an honest Turk, who was captivated with his address, eagerly entreated him to settle at that place, offering him his interest and his daughter in marriage." From Aleppo he proceeded by land to Basra, whence he sailed for Bombay, which he reached early in September, 1807. A few months later he was married there to the eldest daughter of Sir James Mackintosh, to whom we owe the publication of most of her husband's travels and researches outside of the two memoirs on Babylon published by himself. About the same time he was appointed Resident of the East India Company at Baghdad, a position which he held until his sudden and most lamented death from cholera morbus in Shiraz, October 5, 1821.[1]

The leisure which Rich enjoyed from his public duties he spent in pursuing his favorite historical, geographical, and archæological studies, the most valuable fruits of which are his accurate surveys and descriptions of the ruins of Babylon and Nineveh. In December, 1811, he made his first brief visit to the site of Babylon. It lasted but ten days, but it sufficed to convince him that no correct account of the ruins had yet been written. Completely deceived "by the incoherent accounts of former travellers," instead of a few "isolated mounds," he found "the whole country covered with the vestiges of building, in some places consisting of brick walls surprisingly fresh, in others merely a vast succession of mounds of rubbish of such indeterminate figures, variety, and extent as to involve the person who should have formed any theory in inextricable confusion and contradiction." He set to work at once to change this condition.

His two memoirs on the ruins of Babylon (especially the first) are a perfect mine of trustworthy information radically different from anything published on the subject in previous years. He sketches the present character of the whole country around Babylon, describes the vestiges of ancient

[1] Rich's first "Memoir on the Ruins of Babylon" was written in 1812 in Baghdad, and published (with many typographical errors and unsatisfactory plates) in the *Fundgruben des Orients*, Vienna, 1813. To make it accessible to English readers, Rich republished this memoir in London (1816), where also his second memoir appeared in 1818. Both memoirs were later republished with Major Rennel's treatise "On the Topography of Ancient Babylon," suggested by Rich's first publication, and with Rich's diaries of his first excursion to Babylon and his journey to Persepolis, accompanied by a useful introduction and appendix, all being united by Mrs. Rich into a collective volume, London, 1839. His widow also edited his "Narrative of a Residence in Koordistan and on the site of Ancient Nineveh," London, 1836.

canals and outlying mounds, and "the prodigious extent" of the centre of all his attention,— the ruins of Babylon itself. And to all this he adds his personal observations on the modern fashion of building houses, and the present occupations and customs of the inhabitants of 'Irâq, interwoven with frequent references to the legends of the Arabs and the methods of their administration under Turkish rule, correctly assuming that "the peculiar climate of this district must have caused a similarity of habits and accommodations in all ages." But valuable as all these details are, they form, so to speak, only the framework for his faithful and minute picture of the ruins of Babylon,[1] which we now reproduce, as far as possible with his own words: —

"The whole of the area enclosed by the boundary on the east and south, and the river on the west, is two miles and six hundred yards in breadth from E. to W., and as much from Pietro della Valle's ruin [*i. e.*, Bâbil in the north], to the northern part" of the southern city wall, "or two miles and one thousand yards to the most southerly mound of all. This space is again longitudinally subdivided into nearly half, by a straight line of the same kind with the boundary, but much its inferior in point of size. . . . These ruins consist of mounds of earth, formed by the decomposition of buildings, channelled and furrowed by the weather, and the surface of them strewed with pieces of brick, bitumen, and pottery."

The most northern mound is Bâbil, called by the natives *Mujêlîba.*[2] "Full five miles distant from Hilla, and nine hundred and fifty yards from the river bank, it is of an oblong shape, irregular in its height and the measurement of its sides, which point to the cardinal points. The elevation of the southeast or highest angle, is one hundred and

[1] Comp. Map, No. 2 (Plan of Babylon).

[2] Like Beauchamp, Rich states correctly that this term is sometimes also applied to the second mound, El-Qasr.

forty-one feet.[1] The western face, which is the least elevated, is the most interesting on account of the appearance of building it presents." Rich regarded this conspicuous mound as part of the royal precincts, possibly the hanging gardens.

"A mile to the south of Bâbil is a large conglomeration of mounds, the shape of which is nearly a square of seven hundred yards[2] in length and breadth." It was designated

El-Qasr, East Face

by Rich El-Qasr ("the palace") from a very remarkable ruin, "which being uncovered, and in part detached from the rubbish, is visible from a considerable distance. . . . It consists of several walls and piers, eight feet in thickness, in some places ornamented with niches, and in others strengthened

[1] The height as measured by Rich differs considerably from that given by the later surveyors. This difference, while doubtless to a large extent the result of Rich's inaccurate estimation, must also be explained by the fact that in course of time the Arab brick-diggers have reduced the height of Bâbil.

[2] Most of the numbers given by Rich have been later on more or less modified by the different surveyors, who had more time and were better equipped with instruments.

by pilasters and buttresses, built of fine burnt brick (still perfectly clean and sharp), laid in lime-cement of such tenacity, that those whose business it is to find bricks have given up working on account of the extreme difficulty of extracting them whole." Here stood, as we now know, the palace of Nebuchadrezzar, in which Alexander the Great died after his famous campaign against India.

Separated from the previous mound by a valley of five hundred and fifty yards in length, "covered with tussocks of rank grass, there rises to the south another grand mass of ruins, the most elevated part of which is only fifty or sixty feet above the plain. From the small dome in the centre dedicated to the memory of a spurious son of 'Alî, named 'Omrân ('Amrân), it is called by the Arabs, Tell 'Omrân ibn 'Alî. It has been likewise considerably dug into by peasants in search of bricks and antiquities.

The most southern point is connected with the large embankment here traceable and with a flourishing village, near which the luxurious date groves of Hilla commence. Both are called Qumquma (Sachau), now generally pronounced Jumjuma (regarded by Rich as original, meaning "skull") or Jimjime. Here terminate the ruins of ancient Babylon.

It was to be expected that Rich, in connection with his topographical work on the ruins of Babylon, would also examine "the most interesting and remarkable of all the Babylonian remains," *viz.*, Birs (Nimrûd), of which he likewise left us an accurate description, in several details soon afterwards supplemented by that of Buckingham. Like his successor he recognized the general character of the ruins as a stage tower, doubtless influenced by his endeavor to identify it with the Tower of Belus, and by the deep and lasting impression which this gigantic ruin, still one hundred and fifty-three feet high,[1] made upon him at his first visit. I

[1] According to Felix Jones's survey of 1855, this is the exact vertical distance of Birs (Nimrûd) from the water level of the plain to the highest point of

quote his own language: "The morning was at first stormy, and threatened a severe fall of rain, but as we approached the object of our journey, the heavy clouds separating, discovered the Birs frowning over the plain, and presenting the appearance of a circular hill, crowned by a tower, with a high ridge extending along the foot of it. Its being entirely concealed from our view, during the first part of our ride, prevented our acquiring the gradual idea, in general so prejudicial to effect, and so particularly lamented by those who visit the Pyramids. Just as we were within the proper distance, it burst at once upon our sight, in the midst of rolling masses of thick black clouds partially obscured by that kind of haze whose indistinctness is one great cause of sublimity, whilst a few strong catches of stormy light, thrown upon the desert in the background, served to give some idea of the immense extent and dreary solitude of the wastes in which this venerable ruin stands."[1]

The impression which the ruin left upon the mind of an otherwise sober observer and unbiassed man of facts was so profound that it deflected his judgment and blinded his eyes as to the great incongruity between his favorite theory and all the topographical evidence so minutely and accurately set forth by himself, — another illustration of the truth how detrimental to scientific investigation any preconceived opinion or impression must be.

In addition to all his valuable topographical studies Rich directed his attention to other no less important subjects of an archæological character. We refer to his remarks on the hieratic and demotic styles of cuneiform writing ("Memoirs," pp. 184, *seqq.*); his observation that inscribed bricks, when found *in situ*, are "invariably placed with their faces or written sides downwards" (pp. 162, *seqq.*), a fact which he

the ruin at the summit of the mound, as over against the 235 feet strangely given by Rich.

[1] Comp. Rich's "Collected Memoirs," edited by his widow, p. 74.

at once employed skilfully against his opponent, Rennell, to vindicate the Babylonian origin of the "surprisingly fresh" looking ruin of the Qasr; furthermore, his discussion of the different kinds of cement (bitumen, mortar, clay, etc.) used in ancient and modern Babylonia (pp. 100, *seqq.*), later supplemented by Colonel Chesney;[1] and his endeavor "to ascertain in what particular part of the ruin each antique is found" (pp. 187, *seqq.*), — the fundamental principle of all scientific excavations, against which later excavators have sinned only too often.

He spared neither personal exertion nor expenses to acquire every fragment of sculpture and inscribed stone of which he had got information. To his efforts we owe the barrel cylinder, with Nebuchadrezzar's account of his work on the famous canal, *Lîbil-khegal.* It was Rich who collected the first contract tablets and account lists discovered in the lower parts of the Qasr (*l. c.*, p. 187), and it is Rich again who obtained the first fragment of a clay tablet from Ashurbânapal's library at Nineveh.[2]

But in mentioning the latter, we have approached another field of the indefatigable explorer's labors and researches, which we now propose to sketch briefly.

In 1820 and 1821, on his return from a trip to Persia and Kurdistân, Rich made an exploring tour to some of the most prominent ruins of ancient Assyria, Erbîl (ancient Arbela), Qoyunjuk, Nebî Yûnus (Nineveh), and Nimrûd. The modern town of Erbîl is situated partly on the top and partly at the foot of an artificial mound "about 150 feet high and 1000 feet in diameter." A Turkish castle, which up to the present day has been the chief obstacle to systematic excavations, crowns its flat top. Rich spent two and

[1] In "The Euphrates and Tigris Expedition," vol. ii., pp. 625, *seqq.*

[2] Whoever has had one of these finest specimens of cuneiform tablets in his hands will readily recognize the character and origin of Rich's fragment from his short description (*l. c.*, p. 188).

a half days at the place taking measurements, and trying hard to obtain satisfactory information as to the contents of these ruins and their early history. But he could learn very little beyond the fact that some time before his arrival a man by the name of Hajji 'Abdullah Bey had dug up a sepulchre, in which was a body laid in state, that fell to dust after it had been exposed to the air, and that large bricks without inscriptions had been taken by another man from a structure below the cellar of his house standing inside the castle.

He was more fortunate at the ruins of Nimrûd, which he visited in March, 1821. Though he could devote but a few hours to their examination, he was able to sketch and measure the chief mounds, to furnish a brief description of their actual condition, and to determine their general character from scattered fragments of burnt bricks with cuneiform inscriptions. In the large village of Nimrûd, about a quarter of a mile from the west face of the platform, he even procured a whole brick covered with cuneiform writing on its face and edge, and containing the name and title of King Shalmaneser II., as we now know, since the deciphering of the Assyrian script has long been an accomplished fact.

Of still greater importance and of fundamental value for the archæological work of his successors was his residence of four months in Mosul. It fell between his visits to Erbîl and Nimrûd, and was only interrupted by an absence of twelve days, during which he paid a visit to the Yezîdi villages and the Christian monasteries of Mâr Mattî and Rabbân Hormuzd, to the northeast and north of Mosul, surveying the country, gathering Syriac manuscripts, and studying the manners and customs of the people. The great facilities and freedom of movement which he enjoyed in consequence of his official position and the pleasant relations established with the Turkish authorities at three previous visits to this neighborhood were now utilized by Rich to satisfy his curiosity and scientific interest in the large mounds on the eastern side of the Tigris, opposite Mosul.

Tradition identified them with ancient Nineveh, as stated above (pp. 7–12). Yet doubts as to the correctness and continuity of the local tradition, as already expressed by Jean Otter, were justified, as long as the latter had not been corroborated by convincing facts. They were first adduced by Rich, who, by a careful topographical survey of the ruins here grouped together and by a close examination of all the large hewn stones, inscribed slabs, burnt bricks, and other smaller antiquities accidentally found by the natives, demonstrated beyond doubt that all these vestiges were of the same general age and character; that they belonged to a powerful nation, which, like the Babylonians, employed cuneiform script for its writing; and that the original area of the ancient city, represented by the two large mounds, Qoyunjuk and Nebî Yûnus, and enclosed by three walls on the east and by one wall each on the three other sides, was "about one and a half to two miles broad and four miles long" — strong reasons, indeed, in support of the local tradition and the general belief expressed by so many travellers.

Twenty-eight years later his famous countryman, Layard, was enabled to excavate this site methodically and to make those startling discoveries which restored the lost civilization of the Assyrian empire to the astonished world. But it will always remain the great merit of Rich to have placed the floating local tradition upon a scientific basis, to have determined the real significance of the large Assyrian mounds in general, and to have prepared the way for their thorough exploration by his important maps and accurate description.

In returning from Mosul to Baghdad Rich used the *kelek*,[1] as on two previous occasions, in order to obtain more

[1] A native raft composed of goat-skins inflated with air, and by reeds or

exact bearings of the frequent windings of the river, to fix the situations of ruins and other places on its embankments, and to correct and supplement his former measurements. On the basis of the rich material thus brought together personally, he drew the first useful map of the course of the Tigris from Mosul to a point about eighteen miles to the north of Baghdad, a map in every way far superior to that of Carsten Niebuhr, which rests entirely upon information, and that of Beauchamp, which in all essential features must be regarded as a mere copy of the latter's.

Kelek or Native Raft composed of Goat-Skins

Previously he had surveyed a considerable portion of the Euphrates, *viz.*, from Hît to about the thirty-third degree north latitude. All his material was later incorporated into the results obtained by the British Euphrates expedition, and in 1849 edited by Colonel Chesney, its commander, as sheets VI. and VII. of his magnificent series of maps of the Euphrates and Tigris valleys.

After the untimely death of Rich in the fall of 1821, his Oriental antiquities, coins, and an extraordinary collection of eight hundred manuscripts[1] were purchased by the English

ropes fastened close together to a frame of rough logs. On one part of this very ancient means of navigation a kind of hut covered with matting is generally raised as a necessary shelter against rain and sun.

[1] According to Forshall, 3 of these are in Greek, 59 in Syriac, 8 in Carshunic, 389 in Arabic, 231 in Persian, 108 in Turkish, 2 in Armenian,

Parliament for the use of the British Museum. The fragments of clay and stone which he had gathered so scrupulously from Babylonian and Assyrian ruins filled a comparatively small space, and for the greater part at present have little but historical value. But these small beginnings contained in them the powerful germ which in due time produced the rich treasures now filling the halls of the London Museum.

After the fundamental work of Rich little was left for the average European traveller to report on the ruins of Babylon and Nineveh, unless he possessed an extraordinary gift of observation and discrimination, combined with experience and technical training, archæological taste, and a fair acquaintance with the works of the classical writers and the native historians and geographers. Among the men to whom in some way or other we are indebted for new information concerning the geography and topography of ancient Assyria and Babylonia at the very time when Rich himself was carrying on his investigations, the two following deserve our special attention.

J. S. BUCKINGHAM

It was in the year 1816, when, on his way to India, after a long and adventurous journey from Egypt through Palestine, Syria, and the adjacent districts east of the Jordan, Buckingham had arrived at Aleppo. Soon afterwards he joined the caravan of a rich Moslem merchant, with whom by way of Urfa and Mardîn he travelled to Mosul, "adopting the dress, manners, and language of the country" for the sake of greater safety and convenience. A few days before the caravan reached the Tigris, it was overtaken by two Turkish Tartars in charge of papers from the British ambas-

and 1 in Hebrew. A list of the Syriac MSS., accompanied by a brief description, is given by Forshall on pp. 306–311 of vol. ii. of Rich's "Narrative of a Residence in Koordistan."

The Euphrates above Dêr, with the Ruins of Zelebîye on the Left

sador in Constantinople to Mr. Rich, then English Resident at Baghdad. Buckingham decided at once to profit by the opportunity, so unexpectedly offered, of travelling in comparative safety through a country in which he had met with so much lawlessness and interference. Sacrificing, therefore, his personal comfort to speed and safety, he completed his journey in the company of the two Tartars. In consequence of the new arrangement, however, he could spend only two days at Mosul, and devote but a few morning hours immediately before his departure to a hasty inspection of the ruins of Nineveh, which for this reason contributed nothing to a better understanding of the site of this ancient city. In the oppressive heat of a Mesopotamian summer, and deserted on the road by one of his Tartars, he finally arrived at Baghdad, where, in the congenial atmosphere of Rich's hospitable house, he found the necessary encouragement and assistance in executing his plan of paying a visit to some of the principal mounds of ancient Babylonia.

Accompanied by Mr. Bellino, the well-informed secretary to the Residency, he at first examined the ruins of 'Aqarqûf, of which he has left us a more critical, correct, and comprehensive account than any of the preceding travellers, even Niebuhr and Olivier not excluded. From the numerous fragments of brick and pottery and other vestiges of former buildings scattered around the shapeless mass of the detached ruin he recognized with Olivier that near this so-called "Tower of Nimrod"[1] there must have stood a city to which a large canal (the 'Îsâ), uniting the two great rivers,

[1] One of the designations commonly given to this ruin by the Arabs (comp. above, p. 16, note 2, and Rich's "Memoirs," p. 80). 'Aqarqûf has no satisfactory etymology in Arabic. Possibly it is only the badly mutilated old Babylonian name of the city. Comp. Buckingham, "Trav.," vol. ii., p. 226, footnote, and Ker Porter, "Travels," vol. ii., pp. 276, 279. A learned Arab of Baghdad, whom Buckingham consulted (*l. c.*, p. 239), did not hesitate to explain it as "the place of him who rebelled against God." Two other etymologies are quoted by Yâqût in his geographical dictionary.

conveyed the necessary supply of water. To judge from the materials and the style of the principal building the whole settlement is of Babylonian origin. Accordingly, the theory of Niebuhr, who believed the lofty ruin to be an artificial elevation on which one of the early caliphs of Baghdad, or even one of the Persian kings of El-Madâ'in, had erected a country house, to enjoy from such a height a breeze of cool and fresh air during the sultry summer months in the Babylonian plain, is improbable. It was rather Buckingham's firm conviction that the building represents the "remains of some isolated monument either of a sepulchral or religious nature." From the fact that the "present shapeless form having so large a base, and being proportionately so small at the top, seemed nearer to that of a much worn pyramid than any other,"[1] and from his observation that a much larger mass of the fallen fragments of the top would be visible around the base if it had been a square tower, he inferred correctly that the often described ruin was originally a step pyramid similar to that found at Saqqâra in Egypt.[2] Though the interior of the solid ruin of 'Aqarqûf is composed of unbaked bricks, "its exterior surface seems to have been coated with furnace-burnt ones, many of which, both whole and broken, are scattered about the foot of the pile." The real character of Babylonian stage-towers at that time having not yet been disclosed by the excavations, it was only natural that Buckingham, well acquainted with the pyramids of Egypt as he was, and once having recognized the original form of the structure at 'Aqarqûf as a step-pyramid or stage-tower, should have regarded the latter as an ancient royal tomb rather than as the most conspicuous part of a Babylonian temple. According to inscribed bricks later discovered all around

[1] Comp. the four different views given by Ker Porter on p. 227 of his richly illustrated work quoted below, and the illustration facing p. 15 above.

[2] See the illustration given below under Egypt.

the central ruin by Sir Henry Rawlinson, the city whose stage-tower is represented by ʻAqarqûf was called Dur-Kurigalzu.[1]

Two days later Buckingham and Bellino — the former in the disguise of a Bedouin acting as the guide of the latter — were on their way to the ruins of Babylon. As soon as the Mujêlîba came into view, they turned away from the regular caravan road to Hilla, subjecting the whole complex of mounds along the eastern bank of the Euphrates to a care-

Bâbil. West Face, as it appeared in 1811

ful examination. In every detail Buckingham was able to corroborate the description and measurements of Rich, also sharing his view that this most northern pile of ruins could never have represented the tower of Belus, as had been so vigorously maintained by Major Rennell. He pointed out that the appearance of walls and portions of buildings on its summit apparently constructed at different periods, the small quantity of rubbish accumulated around its base, and the

[1] For a brief sketch of the history of exploration of the ruins of ʻAqarqûf, see Ritter, *Die Erdkunde*, vol. xi., pp. 847–852.

remains of brickwork and masonry visible near the surface on the northern and western sides at the foot of the heap, proved beyond doubt that this mound "was never built on to a much greater height than that at which its highest part now stands," and for this very reason could not in any respect correspond to the famous tower for which it had been frequently taken. These features just mentioned, "added to the circumstance of its being evidently surrounded by ditches, and perhaps walls, with its situation within a quarter of a mile of the river, are strong arguments in favour of its being the castellated palace described" by Diodorus Siculus.

After a satisfactory inspection of all the details connected with the second mound, called El-Qasr, Buckingham came to the conclusion arrived at by Rich that this ruin represented the remains of an (other) "extensive palace;" but differing somewhat from the view of his predecessor, he was inclined to identify the hanging gardens with a part of the ruins of El-Qasr, or possibly even 'Omrân ibn 'Alî. The neighborhood of the river, a peculiar brick here discovered by Rich,[1] and the famous single tree called Athla[2] standing close to the broken walls and piers of El-Qasr, seemed to him favorable to his theory of locating the hanging gardens not very far from the latter.

Not satisfied with a mere examination of the principal mounds of Babylon, the two companions set out towards the east to search for the original walls of the great metropolis. In order to fully understand their efforts and to judge Buckingham's final and serious mistake in the proper light

[1] Engraved with a certain religious symbol, a kind of upright pole with pointed top, often found in bas-reliefs and seal-cylinders, but by Buckingham and others mistaken for a spade. Comp. Rich's "Memoirs," p. 60, note *, and Ker Porter, "Travels," vol. ii., pl. 77, c.

[2] If not a distinct species, at least a beautiful variety of *Tamarix Orientalis* (*tarfa*) according to the Arabic *Materia Medica* of Ibn Kibtî, the Baghdâdî (A. H. 711). Comp. Mignan, "Travels," p. 258; Sonini, "Travels in Egypt," pp. 247, *seq.*; Forskâl, *Flora Ægyptiaco-Arabica*, p. 206.

of his period, we must remember that the two most able geographers — D'Anville and Major Rennell — who had previously ventured to express an opinion on the original size of Babylon, as described by the classical writers, had differed so radically in their conclusions that new material was required to establish the entire correctness of Herodotus's measures, in which Rennell and Buckingham firmly believed. In favor, therefore, of giving to Babylon the full extent assigned to it by its earliest historian, Buckingham found no difficulty in reclaiming the great network of ancient canals to the east of Babylon, flanked by very high embankments and often filled with mud and sand far above the level of the surrounding plain, as "the remains of buildings originally disposed in streets, and crossing each other at right angles, with immense spaces of open and level ground on each side of them."

For more than two hours, in pursuit of their phantom, the two travellers had been riding over the parched and burning plain covered with burnt brick and pottery and an occasional detached heap of rubbish. The heat of the atmosphere had meanwhile become so intense and the air so suffocating and almost insufferable that Bellino, completely exhausted with thirst and fatigue, declined to proceed any farther. Buckingham left his companion in the shade of a Mohammedan tomb, himself pushing ahead, determined to reach a pyramidal mound called El-Ohêmir,[1] and previously visited only by Dr. Hine and Captain Lockett, of the British Residency at Baghdad, which he regarded as of the most

[1] Differently rendered by the travellers as *Al Hheimar* (Rich, Buckingham), *Al-Hymer* (Ker Porter), *El-Hamir* (Mignan), (*El-*) *Ohemir* (Frazer), *Uhaimir* (lit. transl.), in accordance with a more or less successful endeavor to reproduce the present Arabic pronunciation of the word. The name, derived from Arabic *ahmar*, "red," designates the hill as "the reddish one" (diminutive) from its most characteristic feature, the deep red brickwork crowning its summit. A similar name is El-Homairâ (dimin. of the fem. *hamrâ*), one of the smaller mounds of Babylon, east of El-Qasr.

importance for the final solution of his problem. Half an hour after quitting Bellino he reached the foot of the steep mound of which he had been so eagerly in search. But he could remain only a few minutes. Clouds of dust and sand filling his eyes, mouth, ears, and nostrils, and rendering it difficult and painful to look around, drove him soon from the summit, which he judged to be seventy to eighty feet high. Yet this brief examination of the conical red mound and its surroundings had sufficed to enable him to furnish a general description of the size and character of the ruins and to state his conviction that this elevated pile, though nearly eight miles distant from the Euphrates, was the extreme eastern boundary of ancient Babylon, and itself a portion of its celebrated wall. In support of his extraordinary theory, which rested entirely upon the partly misunderstood statements of Herodotus, he endeavored to show that the peculiar white layers of ashes, occurring at certain intervals in the principal ruin of baked bricks, corresponded precisely to "the composition of heated bitumen mixed with the tops [rather stems !] of reeds," so particularly mentioned by the Greek historian as the characteristic cement used in the construction of the ditch and walls of Babylon.

After their late arrival at Hilla, the two travellers presented a letter of introduction received from Rich to a powerful Arab residing in the same town. Through his assistance they were enabled to pay a visit to the lofty ruins on the western side of the Euphrates, which had been "identified" by Niebuhr and Rich with the "Tower of Belus," so often described by the classical writers. With regard to the name of this ruin Buckingham states correctly [1] that,

[1] As I personally have been able to verify repeatedly in that neighborhood in recent years. Comp., also, Abbé De Beauchamp, above, p. 20. The same name, El-Birs, is the only one given by Mas'ûdî in the chapter where he describes the course of the Euphrates. Similarly the Qâmûs gives Birs as the name of a town or district between Hilla and Kûfa still known.

though generally referred to as Birs Nimrûd by the different travellers, it should properly be called only El-Birs. "Whenever Nimrûd is added, it is merely because the inhabitants of this country are as fond of attributing everything to this 'mighty hunter before the Lord,' as the inhabitants of Egypt are to Pharaoh, or those of Syria to Solomon." Both Rich and Buckingham assumed with good reason that the word *Birs* has no satisfactory etymology in Arabic, — the latter, for very apparent reasons, proposing to regard it as a corruption of "Belus, its original name," which of course is out of the question. Since the extensive ruins of El-Birs have been identified with the remains of the Babylonian city of Borsippa, we can safely assert that Birs or Burs — as it is pronounced occasionally — is nothing but a local corruption of Borsippa,[1] just as the first half of the modern Egyptian village of Saft el-Henne has preserved the name of the ancient Egyptian god Sopt, whose sanctuary, Per-Sopt, was situated there.

On the basis of a careful study of the memoirs of Rich and Rennell, and after a close personal inspection of the ruins, Buckingham at once recognized the original building represented by the mound, on which the vitrified wall occupies such a conspicuous place, as a stage-tower. He went even farther than Rich by pointing out that four stages, "receding one within another, are to be distinctly traced, on the north and east sides, projecting through the general rubbish of its face." Determined as he was to prove the accuracy of Herodotus' account of the enormous area of Babylon, and not less influenced than Rich by the magnitude of the lofty ruin, which, according to his idea, could not possibly have been excluded by the walls from the territory of the ancient city, he did not hesitate for a moment to take the ruin of El-Birs for its western extreme, as he had

[1] Already recognized as such by Captain Mignan, "Travels in Chaldæa," London, 1829, pp. 258, *seq.*

taken the ruin at El-Ohêmir for its eastern. At the same time he accepted and strengthened the theory of Rich, who had identified El-Birs with the famous Tower of Babel, however contrary to the very explicit statement of Arrian: "The Temple of Belus is situated in the heart of Babylon."

SIR ROBERT KER PORTER

One of the greatest mines of information concerning the life and manners of the people of Western Asia at the beginning of the last century, and also with regard to the monuments, inscriptions, and other antiquities then known to exist in Persia and Babylonia, is the magnificent work of Sir Robert Ker Porter, "Travels in Georgia, Persia, Armenia, Ancient Babylonia, etc., etc., during the years 1817–20,"[1] equally remarkable for the "truth in what the author relates," and the "fidelity in what he copies" and illustrates by his numerous drawings, portraits, and sketches. From childhood loving and practising the arts, he had become a famous painter of international reputation, whose eminent talents, striking personality, and final marriage with a Russian princess had secured for him a social standing which enabled him, by his pen and brush, to reach circles hitherto but little influenced by the books of ordinary travellers and the scientific and often dry investigations of men of the type of Otter, Niebuhr, Beauchamp, and Rich. In his popularization of a subject which so far had stirred the minds of only a limited class of people, and in appealing, by his religious sentiment, the manner of his style, and the accurate representation of what he had observed, not less to the men of science and religion than to the aristocratic circles of Europe, on whose interest and financial support the resurrection of Assyria and Babylonia chiefly depended, lies the significance of Ker Porter as a Babylonian explorer.

[1] Two volumes, London, 1821, 1822.

After extensive travels through Georgia and Persia, in the course of which the great monuments of Naqs-i-Rustam and Persepolis had received his special attention, Porter arrived at Baghdad in October, 1818. About two years previously Buckingham had visited the same region, though by reason of peculiar circumstances [1] the latter's work could not be published until eleven years later. Compared with the clear statements and sober facts presented by his predecessors, Porter's book is sometimes deficient in definite information, — pious meditations and personal speculations occasionally becoming the undesirable substitutes for an intelligent description, judicial discrimination, and logical reasoning. Yet, with all these defects, due less to his lack of good will and personal devotion than to his unfamiliarity with the Oriental languages and the absence of a proper technical training, Porter will always hold his distinct place in the history of Babylonian exploration.

During the six weeks which he spent under the inspiring influence of Rich at the British Residency in Baghdad, he examined the four Babylonian ruins at that time standing in the centre of public interest: 'Aqarqûf, El-Birs, Bâbil, and El-Ohêmir. As in the case of Buckingham, Bellino became his regular companion on his excursions to the ruins just mentioned. What his description of 'Aqarqûf lacks in new elements and successful combination is made good by the four excellent drawings which he has left us of the four different sides of that conspicuous landmark at the northern boundary of ancient Babylonia. Of interest also is his remark as to the original purpose of the ruin in question, as coming nearer to the truth than that of any previous traveller: "I should suppose the mass we now

[1] Arising from the scandalous and malicious accusations of Buckingham's former travelling companion, W. J. Bankes, who in the most contemptible manner prevented the publication of his book, at the same time endeavoring to ruin the literary character of the author, as he had ruined him socially and financially in India.

see to be no more than the base of some loftier superstructure, probably designed for the double use of a temple and an observatory ; a style of sacred edifice common with the Chaldeans, and likely to form the principal object in every city and town devoted to the idolatry of Belus and the worship of the stars."

Protected by more than a hundred well-armed horsemen of the Turkish army against any possible molestation from the marauding Bedouins, who were at open war with the governor of Baghdad, Porter had the rare opportunity of inspecting the huge mass of buildings known as El-Birs or Birs Nimrûd, with a feeling of absolute security and comfort. Rich and Buckingham having described the more essential features of this grandest of all Babylonian ruins before, our traveller had nothing to add, but the more to speculate on the probable age and cause of the destruction of this "Tower of Belus," of which again he left us four fairly good drawings, though in certain prominent details decidedly inferior to the pen-and-ink sketch published by Rich. It was Porter's firm conviction that the extraordinary ruin as it now stands, "and doubtless representing the Tower of Babel," is the work of three different periods and builders. As over against the fundamental investigations of his two contemporaries, who by their accurate description and sober judgment of Babylonian ruins so favorably contrasted with the uncritical method of the early travellers, we find in Porter's account of Birs (Nimrûd) a certain inclination to fall back into the outlived fashion of previous centuries. According to his view, the original tower built by Nimrod and "partially overturned by the Divine wrath," is still to be recognized in the four lowest stages of the present remains. "In this ruinous and abandoned state most likely the tower remained till Babylon was refounded by Semiramis, who, covering the shattered summit of the great pile with some new erection, would there place her observatory and altar to Bel." Nebuchadrezzar, finding "the stupendous monument of Babel" in the manner in which it was left by the "Assyrian queen," and "constituting it the chief embellishment of his imperial city," restored the temple "on its old solid foundations." But as "it can hardly be doubted that Xerxes, in his destruction of the temple, overturned the whole of what had been added by the Babylonian monarchs, it does not seem improbable that what we now see on the fire-blasted summit of the pile, its rent wall, and scattered fragments, with their partially vitrified masses, may be a part of that very stage of the primeval tower which felt the effects of the Divine vengeance." Not many years afterwards poor Porter's fantastic speculations were reduced to what they were really worth by the discovery that most of the vitrified bricks bear the common inscription of Nebuchadrezzar.

Ten days later, when Ker Porter paid a second visit to the Birs, he had the unique spectacle of seeing "three majestic lions taking the air upon the heights of the pyramid" — a veritable illustration of Isaiah's prophetic word: "Wild beasts of the desert shall lie there; and their houses shall be full of doleful creatures" (13:21). But this time his stay did not last very long. While leisurely surveying the boundless desert from the sublime eminence on which he stood, a dark mass came up like a cloud from the horizon. It was soon discovered that a body of Bedouins was rapidly moving towards their place of observation, which they now hastily left, chased by the Arab pursuers to the very walls of Hilla.

Quite different from what he has to relate of Birs (Nimrûd) is Porter's account of the ruins of Babylon. His eye seems sharpened to discover the slightest peculiarity; with a judicious discrimination he sets forth all the characteristic features of the bewildering mass; his expression is clear, his language precise, and yet betraying all the enthusiasm with which he approaches his subject. In this regard and in his earnest endeavor to define the enormous extent of these ruins on both banks of the river with accuracy, his graphic description may well be placed alongside those of Rich and Buckingham, which in several details our author even supplements. Like his predecessors he adduces ample proof that the Mujêlîba can never be taken for the remains of the "Tower of Babel." The absence of any trace of a sacred enclosure on its southern side, and of any considerable rubbish to represent the remains of the temple and residences of the priests around its base, the comparatively low elevation of the whole platform, the ruins of extensive buildings on its summit, the discovery of certain subterranean passages and objects in its interior, its very commanding position and strategic importance for the defence of the city, — in fact the whole situation and peculiar style of this gigantic mass of brick-formed earth "mark it out to have been the citadel of the fortified new palace of the ancient authors."

He traced Nebuchadrezzar's ancient embankments to a considerable length along the steep eastern shore; he noticed the peculiarities of the edge-inscribed bricks on the lofty conical mound of El-Homairâ; he dwelt upon the remarkable changes which had recently taken place in the appearance of the Qasr "from the everlasting digging in its apparently inexhaustible quarries," and he expressed his strong belief that this latter mound with its adjoining ridges contained nothing else than the "more modern and greater palace" and the hanging gardens.

With Rich and Buckingham, Porter believed Babylon to have extended considerably on the western side of the Euphrates, as far as Birs (Nimrûd). In the expectation of finding traces of the "lesser palace," he spent a whole day in examining the ground to the north and west of Hilla, finally inclined to regard a group of mounds half-way between El-Qasr and the Birs as the possible remains of Alexander the Great's temporary abode, from which in the course of his illness he was removed to the palace on the other side, only to die.

In order to ascertain, if possible, the exact boundary line of the metropolis on the eastern side of the river, he visited El-Ohêmir and a number of mounds in its neighborhood. Accompanied by Bellino and his usual strong escort, and provided with all the necessities of life, he set out on a fine November morning and examined the whole district at his leisure, so that he could leave us a much more satisfactory description than that of Buckingham, who had been at the same ruins but a few minutes under the most trying circumstances. To Ker Porter we are likewise indebted for the first inscribed brick[1] taken from the pyramidal mound of El-Ohêmir, from which we learn that the god Zamâma had his temple here restored by a Babylonian king, probably Adad-ap[al-]idinnam of the Pashe dynasty, who lived about 1065 B. C. The principal ruin, covered with a mass of red brickwork, and exhibiting "four straight faces, but unequal and mutilated, looking towards the cardinal points," apparently represents the original stage-tower or *ziggurrat* of this temple. From a marble fragment picked up by Bellino, it becomes evident that the place must have occupied a prominent position as early as the time of Hammurabi, about one thousand years earlier. There can be little doubt that the city buried here is no other than Kîsh, with its famous sanctuary, playing such an important rôle at the very beginning of Babylonian history. Though at the time unfamiliar with the details mentioned, which are but the product of subsequent investigations, Porter clearly recognized the general character of El-Ohêmir and its neighboring ruins, and, contrary to Buckingham's untenable theory, regarded it as entirely out of question to suppose that these

[1] Published in his "Travels," vol. ii., pl. 77, a.

mounds "could have ever stood within the limits of Babylon or even formed any part of its great bulwarked exterior wall."

Ker Porter had spent nearly a fortnight in examining the ruins of Babylon and their environments. After his return to Baghdad he illustrated what he had seen, not only by drawings of the most interesting mounds visited and objects discovered, but, profiting from the assistance of Bellino, by several plates of cuneiform inscriptions, among them the fragment of a large barrel-cylinder, which he had found in the ruins of the Qasr.[1]

It is not within the scope of our present sketch to mention all the different travellers who during the first half of the last century visited the sites of Nineveh and Babylon and a few other prominent mounds of the two ancient empires on the Tigris and Euphrates. As a rule their accounts are little more than repetitions of facts and conditions even then well established. Men like Colonel Macdonald Kinneir (1808 and 1813)[2] and Edward Frederick (1811) had formed the necessary link between the old school of travellers in the eighteenth century and the accurate observers and topographical students of the nineteenth century. The time was now drawing rapidly near when instead of the text of the classical writers so ably interpreted by Rennell and others, or the measuring rod and compass so well used by Rich and his immediate successors, to whom we

[1] Now in the British Museum. In its preserved portions it is a Neo-Babylonian duplicate of certain sections (col. iii., 15–63, and col. vi., 44, to col. vii., 20) of the so-called East India House Inscription of Nebuchadrezzar, giving a summary of his building operations in Babylon and Borsippa.

[2] "Geographical Memoir of the Persian Empire," together with Frederick's "Account of the present compared with the ancient state of Babylon," published in the "Transactions of the Bombay Society," Bombay, 1813, pp. 273–295, and pp. 120–139 respectively. Comp., also, Kinneir's "Travels in Asia Minor, Armenia, and Kurdistan," the account of his journey from Constantinople to Basra, in the year 1813.

may still add Captain Keppel (1824),[1] spade and pickaxe would be called upon to speak the final word and settle those much discussed topographical questions. At the threshold which separates this last chapter of Assyrian and Babylonian exploration from the earlier period just treated, stand two men, who while properly speaking they added but few positive facts to our knowledge of ancient Babylonian ruins, yet instinctively felt the pulse of the coming age, and through their own personal courage and enterprising spirit entered upon the very road which ultimately led to success.

CAPTAIN ROBERT MIGNAN

In the years 1826–28, when Major Taylor was the East India Company's political representative at Basra, Captain Robert Mignan, in command of the escort attached to the Resident, made several archæological excursions into the little known districts of Persia, 'Irâq el-'Arabî, and northern Mesopotamia. While each of these little expeditions claims the attention of the historian of ancient geography to a certain degree, in this connection it will be sufficient to sketch briefly his share in the exploration of ancient Babylonia.[2]

In consequence of the constant quarrels which the different Arab tribes were carrying on among themselves or against their common enemy, the Turkish government, only few travellers had ventured to leave the regular caravan road and to extend their researches beyond a very limited radius around Baghdad and Hilla. Kinneir and Keppel had thrown some light on certain remarkable vestiges on the banks of the Lower Tigris, but the whole

[1] "Personal Narrative of Travels in Babylonia, Assyria, Media, and Scythia," 3d ed., London, 1827, 2 volumes.

[2] Comp. his "Travels in Chaldæa," London, 1829.

region adjoining the two rivers between Qorna and Babylon on the one side, and Ctesiphon and Seleucia on the other, needed a much closer investigation, before it could lay claim to another title than that of a *terra incognita*. Determined to prosecute his studies on a line different from those previously followed, Mignan decided to proceed on foot from Basra to Baghdad and Hilla, "accompanied by six Arabs, completely armed and equipped after the fashion of the country, and by a small boat, tracked by eight sturdy natives, in order to facilitate his researches on either bank of the stream." Accordingly he set out on his novel tour towards the end of October, 1827. Many years afterwards, when exploring the interior of Southern Babylonia, though then still unacquainted with Mignan's travels, I adopted the same method of alternate walking and riding in a native canoe (*turrâda*). On the basis of my own past experience, I am convinced that the method described is the only one which in the end will accomplish a thorough exploration of the marshy interior of Babylonia.

The independence which Mignan thus enjoyed in all his movements was utilized especially to satisfy his curiosity concerning the early remains occasionally met on both sides of the Tigris. Often, when an old wall or an especially promising mound attracted his attention, he stopped a few hours to investigate the place or to cut a trench into the ruin, with a view of ascertaining its age or discovering its character. Sixteen days after his departure from Basra, and unmolested on his way by the Arabs, he reached the city of the caliphs. Under the heavy showers of an early November rain, he examined the tower of 'Aqarqûf, in a few subordinate points even correcting the accounts of previous travellers. Then he turned his attention to the ruins of Babylon, Birs, and Ohêmir, to which he devoted nearly a week of undivided attention. After all that had been written on them, we cannot expect to find extraordinary new discoveries in his description. Once more he summed up the different reasons, from which it may be safely concluded that the great metropolis stood in the place assigned to it, referring particularly to "the distances given by Herodotus from Is or Hît, and by Strabo and the Theodosian tables from Seleucia." With Buckingham he believed that Birs and Ohêmir are probably to be included in the original territory of Babylon; but contrary to the generally expressed opinion of his predecessors, he asserted emphatically that Birs (Nimrûd) cannot be identified with the Tower of Belus, as "all ancient authors agree in placing it in the midst of the city;" and with good reason he disclosed as the real cause for the universal mistake the fact that "it more nearly resembles the state of decay into which we might suppose that edifice to have fallen, after the lapse of ages, than any other remains within the circumference of Babylon." Yet while thus judiciously protesting against a serious topographical error of his predecessors, he himself fell into another. Notwithstanding all the strong evidence presented against an identification of the Mujêlîba with the famous tower, he clung to the exploded theory of Rennell, at the same time transferring the so-called lesser palace to the reddish mound of Homaîrâ. He agreed with his predecessors only in the identification of the Qasr with the castellated palace of Nebuchadrezzar.

But Mignan's new departure from the method of research hitherto employed was not so much due to the circumstance that he again went on foot over the whole field from the Birs to Ohêmir, in order to comprehend all the topographical details more thoroughly, as rather to the fact that he endeavored by actual small excavations at the principal mounds to discover their contents and to find new arguments for his proposed identifications. Sometimes he was successful beyond expectation. At the Qasr, *e.g.*, he employed no less than thirty men to clear away the rubbish along the western face of a large pilaster. A space of twelve feet square and twenty feet deep was soon removed, when he suddenly came upon a well-preserved platform of inscribed bricks, each measuring nearly twenty inches square — the largest which so far had been discovered. From the same clearing he obtained four seal-cylinders, three engraved gems, and several silver and copper coins, one of Alexander the Great being among them; while in a small recess near a well-preserved wall of an unexplored passage on the eastern side of the Qasr, he even found a large and beautiful inscribed barrel cylinder *in situ*, the first thus excavated by any European explorer.

What Mignan had done with regard to our knowledge of the eastern border of ancient Babylonia was attempted for the interior of the country by another Englishman.

G. BAILLIE FRASER

In connection with his travels in Kurdistân and Persia, which in no small degree helped to shape the future life and career of a Layard, Fraser made a hasty tour through the unexplored regions of the interior of Babylonia. The whole trip, on which he was accompanied by Dr. Ross, physician of the English Residency at Baghdad, lasted but one month, from December 24, 1834, to January 22, 1835. Naturally the information gathered and the impression gained had to be one-sided and inaccurate; but nevertheless his vivid account was of considerable value for the time being, as the greater part of the country traversed had never been visited by any European before. Names of ruins now so familiar to every student of Assyrian are found for the first time in Fraser's "Travels in Koordistan, Mesopotamia, etc." [1]

[1] London, 1840, two volumes. For Babylonia comp. vol. ii., pp. 1–165.

After a brief visit to the ruins of Ctesiphon and Seleucia, the little cavalcade, numbering fifteen persons, all the servants included, proceeded to Babylon and Birs (Nimrûd), whence by way of El-Ohêmir they turned back to the Tigris, which they reached not very far from Tell Iskharîe, a peculiar and most interesting group of stone-covered mounds extending for about two miles on both sides of the bed of an ancient canal. With the assistance of two ill-qualified Arab guides, they pushed from there through the Babylonian plain, to-day often included in the general term of Jezîre ("island"), passed Tell Jôkha and Senkere at some distance, crossed the Shatt el-Kâr, and, soon afterwards, the Euphrates with considerable difficulty, examined the conspicuous mounds of Muqayyar, which had attracted their attention as soon as they reached the western bank of "the great river" (the so-called Shâmîye), and finally arrived at Sûq esh-Shiyûkh, the most southern point of their remarkable travels. After an unpleasant stay of several days with the shaikh of the Muntefik(j), the party returned to Baghdad in nine days, for the greater part nearly following their old track, but stopping at Senkere for a little while, passing Warkâ on their left, and observing the lofty ruin of Tell (J)îde far away in the distance. Before his final departure from Baghdad, Fraser also paid a visit to the imposing ruin of ʻAqarqûf, which had been so often described by previous travellers.

Fraser was the first who boldly entered the then unknown regions of the Babylonian marshes and pasture grounds occupied by roaming Bedouins and the half-settled thievish and uncouth Maʻdân tribes. In this fact lies his importance for the history of Babylonian exploration. From his graphic account of the character and manners of the present Arabs and the nature of their desolate country, from his constant references to the many ancient canals often interfering with his progress, and the numerous sites of former cities, towns, and villages, of which he found important traces everywhere, we gained a first general idea of what ancient Babylonia must have been in the days of her splendor, and also what had become of this small but fertile country in the course of two millenniums. The picture which he draws is anything but pleasing. Where apparently a dense population and a high grade of civilization had formerly existed, there prevails at present nothing but utter ruin, lawlessness, and poverty. Even the characteristic virtues of the Arabs of the desert, proclaimed by so many songs and noble examples, seemed almost unknown or regarded as a mere farce in the interior of Babylonia. What wonder, then, that Fraser, little acquainted as he had been with Arab life and manners before, and suffering considerably from cold and exposure, lack of food and water during a severe Babylonian January, sums up his description of the country and of "all Arabs and Shaikhs, jointly and severally," with the words of Burns, *mutato nomine:* —

> "There 's nothing here but Arab pride
> And Arab dirt and hunger;
> If Heaven it was that sent us here,
> It sure was in an anger!"

So far the exploration of Assyria and Babylonia had been exclusively in the hands of private individuals who possessed great courage and the necessary means for travelling in districts which through their geographical position and the notoriously lawless habits of their inhabitants had offered most serious obstacles to an accurate scientific investigation. It is true, since the time of Niebuhr and Beauchamp a number of valuable geographical and topographical data had gradually been gathered, and careful measurements, trigonometrical angles, and astronomical calculations had more and more taken the place of former vague statements and general descriptions. A few attempts had even been made at drawing maps of the countries traversed, with the courses of rivers, the ranges of mountains, and the relative positions of the places and ruins examined. But no two maps could have been found which agreed with each other even in the most essential and characteristic features. It was therefore very evident that government support was needed, and the methodical survey by a well-equipped staff of experts required, in order to change this unsatisfactory condition. Most naturally the eyes of all who were interested in the resurrection of Assyria and Babylonia turned to England, where at this very moment peculiar constellations had arisen which were prognostications of systematic action.

THE EUPHRATES EXPEDITION

Under the especial patronage of King William IV., in the years 1835–37, an expedition was organized by the British government, in order to survey the northern part of Syria, to explore the basins of the rivers Euphrates and Tigris, to test the navigability of the former, and to examine in the countries adjacent to these great rivers the markets with which the expedition might be thrown in contact. The Suez Canal not yet existing, England, jealously watched by France and Russia, advanced this important step, apparently in the hope of stirring the national energy and enterprise by the results to be achieved to such an enthusiasm as to lead to establishing regular railway or steamer communications with the far East by way of the Euphrates valley, and to restoring life and prosperity to a region renowned for its fertility in ancient times and generally regarded as the seat of the earliest civilization.

This expedition, then, owed its origin mainly to commercial and political considerations, with the ultimate view of securing the Euphrates valley as a highway to India. But though its purpose was a practical one, it deserves a more prominent place in the history of Babylonian exploration and surveying than is generally accorded to it in Assyriological publications, alike for the novelty and magnitude of the enterprise, for the grand scale upon which it was got up, for the difficulties it had to encounter, and for the importance of the scientific results obtained.[1]

Fifteen officers, including Captain H. B. Lynch and William F. Ainsworth, surgeon and geologist to the expedition, formed the staff of this great military undertaking commanded by Colonel (afterwards Major-General) Francis Rawdon Chesney, who had travelled extensively in Western Asia before. The members of the expedition left Liverpool in February, 1835. Large provisions and the material of two iron steamers accompanied them to the bay of Antioch, whence under the greatest difficulties they were transported over land to the Upper Euphrates. Somewhat below the ferry and castle of Birejik (but on the west bank of "the great river") light field works were thrown up, and a temporary station established under the name of Port William. Long delays in the transport of the material, carried by 841 camels and 160 mules from the seashore to the Euphrates, heavy rains and consequent inundations, the difficult task of putting the boats together, and the severity of the fever, which seized so many of the party, consumed almost the whole first year. As it was found impossible to descend the river during the winter, the greater portion of this season was spent in reconnoitring the Taurus and the country between the Euphrates and the river Balikh-Su as

[1] Comp. Chesney, "The Expedition for the Survey of the Rivers Euphrates and Tigris," 2 vols., London, 1850; Chesney, "Narrative of the Euphrates Expedition," London, 1868; and a volume of twelve sections of a large map, and two additional maps of Arabia and adjacent countries, London, 1849. Also W. F. Ainsworth, "Researches in Assyria, Babylonia, and Chaldæa, forming part of the Labours of the Euphrates Expedition," London, 1838, and the same author's "A Personal Narrative of the Euphrates Expedition," 2 vols., London, 1888.

far north as Sammosata, the ancient capital of Commagene, and including Urfa (Edessa) and the ruins of Haran.

About a year after the expedition had left England, the descent of the Euphrates was commenced, on the 16th of March, 1836. It was a memorable day when the first two steamboats brought to these regions, "Euphrates" and "Tigris," left their moorings. The whole Christian and Mohammedan population of the small town had turned out "to see an iron boat swim, and, what was more, stem the current of the river." For according to Chesney and Ainsworth, there was a tradition familiar at Birejik, which

The Steamers "Euphrates" and "Tigris" descending the Euphrates

accompanied the expedition down the whole river, that when iron should swim on the waters of the Frât, the fall of Mohammedanism would commence.

The descent was made in the following manner. The day before the steamers started, a boat was sent ahead to examine and sound the river for a distance of twenty to thirty miles. "The officer who had accomplished his task became the pilot on the occasion of the first day's descent, while another was despatched in advance to become the pilot on the second day. Thus the naval officers took it by turns to survey the river and tc pilot the vessel." The detailed bearings of the river were taken by Colonel Chesney from the steamer itself. At times exploring tours and explanatory missions were sent to the neighboring districts of the Arabs, while at the same time the survey was carried on ashore by a chain of ground trigonometrical angles across the principal heights as they presented themselves.

In the early afternoon of May 21, 1836, the expedition suffered a most serious loss, almost at the same spot where many centuries before the apostate emperor Julian had met with a similar misfortune. The weather suddenly changed, "accompanied by a portentous fall of the barometer. . . . In the course of a few minutes dense masses of black clouds, streaked with orange, red, and yellow, appeared coming up from the W. S. W., and approached the boats with fearful velocity." Not far below the junction of the river Khâbûr (the biblical Habor) with the Euphrates, during a brief but fearful hurricane or simoom of the desert, which, turning day into night, struck the two boats with terrible force, the "Tigris," for the time being the flagship of the little squadron, was capsized, and rapidly went to the muddy bottom of the foaming river. Twenty men, including Lieutenants Cockburn and R. B. Lynch (brother of the commander of the "Tigris"), were drowned in the Euphrates. Only fourteen of the crew were washed by the high waves over the bank into a field of corn, Colonel Chesney, the gallant leader, fortunately being among the survivors. Few of the bodies, mostly disfigured by vultures beyond recognition, were recovered and buried. Among other things picked up "was Colonel Chesney's Bible, to which great interest attached itself, as it had already gone to the bottom of the river when the Colonel

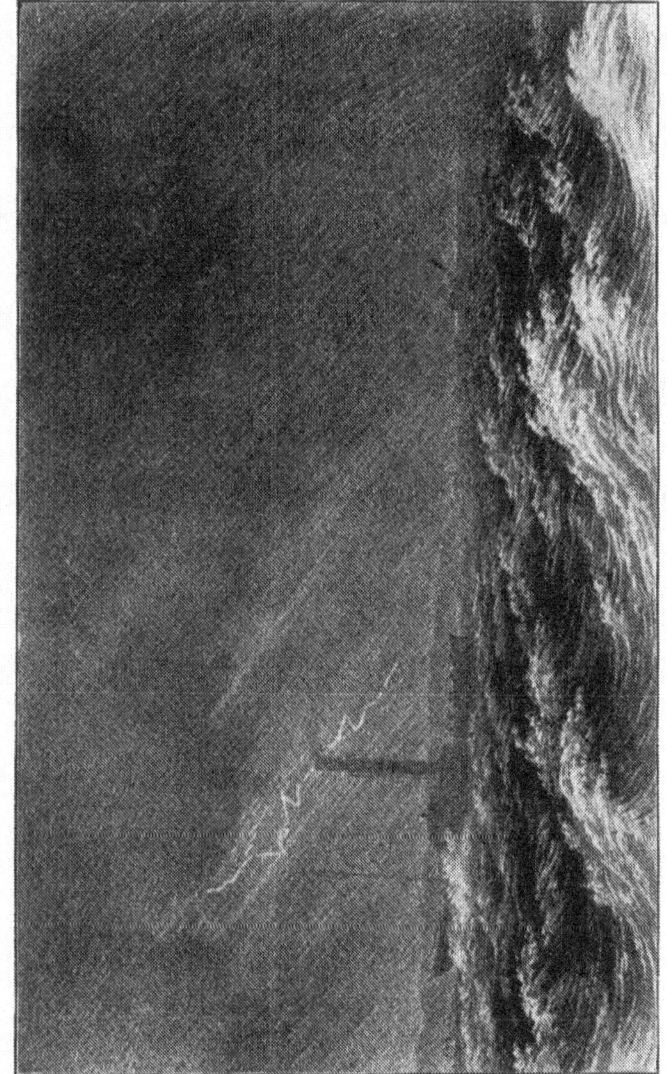

Loss of the "Tigris" during a Hurricane

was first navigating the river on a raft, and had been washed ashore in a similar manner."

The "Euphrates" having descended the rest of the river alone, ascended also the Tigris as far as ancient Opis. But on October 28, in connection with an attempt to ascend the Euphrates, — the second part of the task assigned to the expedition, — upon entering the Lamlûn marshes of Babylonia, the engine of the steamer broke down; and the crew, after making every possible effort to repair it temporarily, was obliged to drop down the river with the current, occasionally assisted by the sails. This breakdown was the beginning of the end. The funds of the expedition were exhausted; and Russia having reproached the Porte "for allowing steam navigation in the interior rivers of the empire to a nation whose policy was avowedly opposed to her own," the British government gradually lost its interest in an undertaking begun with such energy and enthusiasm, and the results of which up to that time had been fully adequate to the money and labor spent.

At the close of the nineteenth century, the old scheme of connecting the Persian Gulf with the Mediterranean by rail or boat has been vigorously taken up again by Germany, with an apparently greater prospect of ultimate success. A regular steamboat line, however, as it seems at present, will scarcely ever be established on the Euphrates, because of the enormous outlay of capital necessary to secure a certain depth of water at all seasons within a well-regulated channel, and to prevent the Arabs from building their dams into the stream or digging new canals for the purpose of irrigation.

Among the incomplete scientific results obtained by the Euphrates Expedition, the series of twelve maps, published by Colonel Chesney twelve years later (1849), ranks first. Even to-day, when for some time more accurate maps of certain sections of the Euphrates and Tigris basins have been in our hands, it is still of inestimable value, forming, as it does, the only source of our topographical knowledge for by far the larger part of the course of the two rivers. Naturally the accuracy attainable for any map prepared from a survey by water can only be relative. Rich's survey of the middle course of the Tigris, carried on from a primitive raft on a "swift-flowing" river,[1] afterwards incorporated in Colonel Chesney's fundamental work, must therefore be even less accurate than that of the staff of the Euphrates Expedition, conducted from a well-equipped steamer on a river with considerably less current.

The great influence which these maps exercised upon future archæological explorations in the countries between the Euphrates and the Tigris, lies in the fact that for the first time they showed the enormous wealth of ancient ruins, canals, and other remains of former civilizations along the entire embankment of both rivers. Ainsworth, who manifested a particular interest in the archæology and history of the country, described carefully what he saw on his daily excursions, thus enabling us to form a first correct idea of the difference between the numerous barren hills crowned with the ruins of extensive castles, temples, and towers, along the upper course of the Euphrates, and the thousands of ancient and modern canals, numberless mounds of baked and sun-dried bricks, half buried under the sands of the desert or submerged under the encroaching water of the rivers, turning the country into immense swamps for many miles, along the lower course of both the Euphrates and Tigris. Through his "Researches in Assyria, Babylonia, and Chaldæa" the same scholar added not only considerably to our knowledge of the general features of Mesopotamia and 'Irâq el-'Arabî (climate, vegetation, zoölogy, and natural history), but he also furnished the first scientific treatment of the latest deposits by transport, of the physical geography and geology of the alluvial districts of Babylonia,

[1] The name of the Tigris signifies "swift-flowing."

and of the geological relations of the bitumen and naphtha springs characteristic of the adjacent regions.

The work of the Euphrates Expedition had been practically confined to a survey of the two great rivers. The next step needed for the exploration of Babylonia and Assyria proper was to proceed from the base established by Colonel Chesney and his staff into the interior of the neighboring districts, of which little or nothing was known, surveying section after section until all the material was gathered for constructing a trustworthy map of the whole country. This preliminary task has not yet been finished, even at the close of the nineteenth century. The most essential progress so far made in this regard is closely connected with the first great classical period of Assyrian and Babylonian excavations, during which Sir Henry Rawlinson, equally prominent as a soldier and explorer, decipherer and linguist, comparative geographer and archæologist, occupied the influential position of British Resident and Consul-General in Baghdad, to the greatest advantage of the scientific undertakings carried on in the regions of the Euphrates and Tigris during his administration (1843–55).[1]

JAMES FELIX JONES

Among the technically trained men of that time who in no small part assisted by their work and interest in building up the young science of Assyriology, Commander James Felix Jones will always hold an especially conspicuous place. His excellent topographical material, for the greater part unfortunately buried in the "Records of the Bombay

[1] After a residence of five years in Persia, Rawlinson had spent the greater portion of 1839 in Baghdad, when in consequence of the great war in Afghanistan he was appointed Political Agent at Candahar, where he distinguished himself greatly until 1843, when he was sent back to Baghdad as "Political Agent and Consul-General in Turkish Arabia."

Government,"[1] from which twenty-five years later Heinrich Kiepert excavated it for the benefit of Oriental students, deserves a few words also in this connection.

Being stationed with his armed boat "Nitocris" at Baghdad, Jones naturally made this city the base of his operations. His attention was first directed to a re-examination of the course of the Tigris above the point where the Shatt el-Adhêm empties into the former. In April, 1846, when the annual rise of the river had provided the necessary water for his steamer, he advanced northward. Notwithstanding the increased force of the current, which at times almost equalled the power of the machine, seriously interfering with his progress, Jones reached the rapids of the Tigris above Tekrît, and by his measurements and triangulations greatly improved the earlier map of Rich and furnished considerable new information.

In the years 1848–50, during the months of March and April, when the lack of water and the absence of a settled population did not yet prove too great an obstacle to topographical work in regions where every accommodation was wanting, he made three exploration tours into the districts to the east of the Tigris. His intention was to determine the tract of the ancient Nahrawân Canal, which, leaving the Tigris about halfway between Tekrît and Sâmarrâ, had once brought life and fertility to the whole territory as far down as Kûd(t) el-'Amâra, to-day almost entirely covered with the sand of the desert or with large brackish water pools.

Of even greater importance from an Assyriological standpoint are his "Researches in the vicinity of the Median Wall of Xenophon and along the old course of the River Tigris," carried on in March, 1850, shortly before he closed

[1] It was with great difficulty and only after long searching that I finally procured a copy of his "Selections from the Records of the Bombay Government," No. xliii., 1857, for my own library.

his investigations on the eastern side of the river just mentioned. Although he succeeded as little in discovering the "Median Wall" as his predecessors, Ross and Lynch (1836), or his successor Lieutenant Bewsher, all of whom endeavored in vain to locate it, yet, in addition to all the valuable discoveries of Babylonian and later Mohammedan ruins and canals which he carefully fixed and described on this journey, Jones proved conclusively that, contrary to previously held opinions, the site of the influential and powerful Babylonian city of Opis, better known from Xenophon's and Alexander's campaigns, is identical with the enormous Tell Manjûr, on the southern or right side of the present bed of the Tigris; and that, moreover, this location is entirely in accordance with ancient tradition, which places it on the northern or left bank of that river, in so far as the ancient bed of the Tigris, still called by the natives "the little Tigris" (Shtêt and Dijêl),[1] with numerous traces of canals once proceeding from the latter, could be established by him beyond any doubt to the S.W. of Opis.[2]

But the crowning piece of Jones's numerous contributions to the general and comparative geography of the countries adjacent to the Tigris was his excellent plan of Nineveh and his survey of the whole district intermediate between the Tigris and the Upper Zâb.[3] The new impulse given to science by the epoch-making discoveries of Botta and Layard in the Assyrian mounds had turned the eyes of the civilized world again to the long-forgotten country in which those historical places were situated. Yielding to a general desire of seeing a complete picture of Assyria in her present desolation, the East India Company, at the request of the

[1] In June, 1900, when I examined that whole region, I heard both names from the Arabs.

[2] Comp. on this whole question Kiepert, *Begleitworte zur Karte der Ruinenfelder von Babylon*, Berlin, 1883, pp. 24, *seq.*

[3] Comp. his report in the "Journal of the Royal Asiatic Society of Great Britain and Ireland," vol. xv. (London, 1855), pp. 297–397.

Trustees of the British Museum, despatched Commander Jones in the spring of 1852 to proceed with the construction of the necessary map. Assisted by Dr. Hyslop[1] of the British Residency in Baghdad, chiefly interested in the flora of the Nineveh region, the work was accomplished within a month and a half, at that great time when Victor Place was still excavating at Khorsabâd, and Rawlinson inspecting the work of the Assyrian explorers, while Fresnel and Oppert had just arrived in that neighborhood from Paris, previous to their excavations in Babylon.

In three large sheets, which up to this day are the standard work for the geography of ancient Assyria, the results of the survey were published. Before closing his interesting report on the topography of Nineveh, Jones paid a warm tribute to the work of Rich, "the first real laborer in Assyrian fields," by writing the following memorable words: "His survey (of Nineveh and Nimrûd) will be found as correct as the most diligent enthusiast can desire; indeed, were it not for the renewed inquiry into Assyrian subjects, the present survey we have the honor of submitting to the public might have been dispensed with, for its value chiefly consists in corroborating the fidelity of his positions, and otherwise, though quite unnecessary, stamping his narrative with the broad seal of truth."

LYNCH, SELBY, COLLINGWOOD, BEWSHER

In the mean while the way was being gradually prepared for a similar kind of work in Babylonia. Fraser,[2] Loftus,[3] and Layard[4] had boldly entered the swamps of 'Irâq and examined the interior of the country, the former two traversing this great alluvial plain almost its entire length, and

[1] Who had succeeded Dr. Ross as physician, after the former's untimely death.

[2] Comp. above, pp. 54, *seqq.*

[3] Comp. below, pp. 139, *seqq.*

[4] Comp. below, pp. 157, *seqq.*

bringing back the startling news that the whole surface was literally covered with large towers, extensive mounds, and numerous smaller ruins, with frequent traces of ancient canals, fragments of bricks, statuary, and many other objects of a high antiquity. Fully convinced of the character and age of these remains of a former civilization, Sir Henry Rawlinson at once conceived the idea of having the whole of Babylonia surveyed after the manner so admirably followed by Jones and Hyslop in Assyria. Prior to his return to England (1855), he requested the two last-named experienced men, assisted by T. Kerr Lynch, to make an accurate survey also of the ruins of Babylon and its environments, an order which they executed in 1854-55. Finally, after the lapse of some time, through Rawlinson's efforts a special committee was appointed by the British government of India for the purpose of carrying out his more comprehensive plan. It consisted of Commander William Beaumont Selby and Lieutenants Collingwood and Bewsher. But notwithstanding the fact that this commission spent the years 1861-65 in Babylonia executing the orders received, and that the most difficult part of the work, the surveying of the swampy district from Musayyib to Shenâfîye, on the west side of the Euphrates, was finished in the very first year (1861), yet at the end of the period mentioned only about the fourth part of the entire area was on paper.

When contrasted with the large amount of work done by Jones within such a short time and often under trying circumstances, one cannot but realize that the old fiery enthusiasm, which inspired the first Babylonian and Assyrian explorers willingly to risk everything, in order to break unknown ground and recover an ancient country, was strongly on the wane. And the American Expedition of the University of Pennsylvania had not yet demonstrated that, notwithstanding the excessive heat and the often almost incredible swarms of vermin and insects, it was possible to work ten to fourteen hours every day during the whole year at the edge of one of the most extensive Babylonian swamps, infested with unruly Arabs and troublesome deserters from the Turkish army, without any considerable increase of danger to the health and life of its members. Commander Selby and his party, however, spent only a few weeks out of every twelve months in actual work in the field, so that in 1866 the Indian government suspended the slowly proceeding and rather expensive work. In 1871 the results obtained by the commission of three were published under the title "Trigonometrical survey of a part of Mesopotamia with the rivers Euphrates and Tigris" (two sheets), comprising the land between 33½ and 32 degrees north latitude. Even in its incomplete condition this map of Babylonia, thoroughly scientific, denotes a new epoch in the study of ancient Babylonian geography. A third sheet gives the regions west of the Euphrates, as mentioned above, while a fourth contains a most accurate survey of the city of Babylon. From all the material which since the time of Rich had been gathered together, in 1883 Heinrich Kiepert constructed his own excellent and much consulted map of Northern Babylonia,[1] until the present day our only trustworthy guide through all the ruins to the south of Baghdad. No attempt has as yet been made to survey Central and Southern Babylonia.

How long will this unsatisfactory condition last? A single man, or even two or three, while in charge of an expedition at one of the Babylonian ruins, cannot survey the remaining three quarters of the whole land to the south of Nuffar within a reasonable space of time. An especial expedition must be organized to execute the work properly and scientifically, under a firmân which should grant the members of this expedition the necessary right to dig enough at

[1] *Ruinenfelder der Umgegend von Babylon*, Berlin, 1883.

the most prominent ruins to identify the early Babylonian cities buried below them.

In the year 1893, when the organization of the Babylonian Section of the Imperial Ottoman Museum was entrusted to the present writer, he was also requested to submit a report to the Minister of Public Instruction on the steps necessary for an effective preservation of the Babylonian ruins and their future methodical exploration. The report was written and certain measures proposed. A serious effort was even made to have the plan as outlined above adopted and executed by the Ottoman government, at whose disposal were a number of excellent officers trained in Germany and in France. For several years I had hoped to carry out the work myself with Halil Bey, Director of the Ottoman Museum, a high Danish military officer, and a number of engineers and architects from England and America. But pressing duties in Philadelphia, Constantinople, and Nuffar prevented me from realizing the long cherished plan.

The time, as it seemed, was not yet ripe for such an enterprise. It has considerably matured since. In connection with the preliminary survey for the recently planned railroad from Baghdad to Quwait, an accurate map of Central and Southern Babylonia could be easily prepared by Germany without any great additional expense. At a time when fresh zeal and activity for the organization of new expeditions to the land of the earliest civilization are manifested everywhere, may this grand opportunity, almost providentially given to Germany, not be lost but be seized with characteristic energy and perseverance and utilized for the benefit of Babylonian research at the dawn of the twentieth century.

III

EXCAVATIONS AT THE PRINCIPAL SITES OF ASSYRIA AND BABYLONIA

In the fall of 1843, after a distinguished service in Afghanistan (1839–42), Rawlinson, as we have seen above (p. 63, note 1), was transferred to Baghdad as "British Political Agent in Turkish Arabia." The young "student-soldier," then occupying the rank of major, had requested Lord Ellenborough, Governor-General of India, to appoint him to this particular post (just about to be vacant) rather than to the much more dignified and lucrative "Central India Agency" offered him, because of his strong desire "to return to the scene of his former labors and resume his cuneiform investigations, in which he had found the greatest pleasure and satisfaction."[1] In accepting a far inferior position with its lighter political duties, which allowed him ample leisure for his favorite studies, Rawlinson, with great perspicacity, chose a life for which he was peculiarly fitted, and entered upon a road which soon brought him fame and recognition far beyond anything that he could ever have achieved in governing half-civilized tribes or fighting victorious battles. The twelve years during which Rawlinson held his appointment in Baghdad mark the first great period of Assyrian and Babylonian excavations. It is true he undertook but little work in the trenches himself, but he influenced and supervised the excavations of others, and personally examined all the important ruins of Assyria and Northern Babylonia. His advice and assistance were sought by nearly all those who with pick and spade were engaged in uncovering the buried monuments of two great

[1] Comp. "A Memoir of Major-General Sir Henry Creswicke Rawlinson," by his brother, Canon George Rawlinson, London, 1898, pp. 139, *seqq.*

empires. While Continental explorers won their laurels on the mounds of Khorsabâd and Nimrûd, Rawlinson forced the inaccessible rock of Behistun to surrender the great trilingual inscription of Darius, which, in the quietude of

The Rock of Behistun with the Great Trilingual Inscription

his study on the Tigris, became the "Rosetta Stone" of Assyriology, and in his master hand the key to the understanding of the Assyrian documents.[1]

So far the leading explorers of Assyrian and Babylonian ruins in the nineteenth century had been British officers and private travellers. In no small degree, the East India Company, through its efficient representatives at Baghdad and Basra, had promoted and deepened the interest in the

[1] The two fundamental and epoch-making publications in which Rawlinson submitted the first complete copy and his decipherment of the second (Persian) and third (Babylonian) columns of the Behistun inscription to the learned world, appeared in the "Journal of the Royal Asiatic Society of Great Britain and Ireland," vols. x. (1846–47), xi. (1849), xii. (1850), and xiv. (1851).

ancient history and geography of the Euphrates and Tigris valleys; and as long as this company existed, it never ceased to be a generous patron of all scientific undertakings carried on in regions which, through their close connection with the Bible, have always exercised a powerful influence upon the mind of the English public. Under Rawlinson's energetic and tactful management of British interests in "Turkish Arabia," the old traditional policy of the company was kept alive, and such a spirit of bold progress and scientific investigation was inaugurated in England as had never been witnessed before in the Oriental studies of that country. And yet, through a peculiar combination of circumstances and events, the first decisive step in the line of actual excavations was made not by an English explorer, but by an Orientalist of France, Professor Julius von Mohl, one of the secretaries of the French Asiatic Society, who, born and educated in Germany, had gained the firm conviction that those few but remarkable bricks which he had recently seen in London were but the first indication and sure promise of a rich literary harvest awaiting the fortunate excavator in the mounds of Babylonia and Assyria. No sooner, therefore, had the French government established a consular agency in Mosul and selected a suitable candidate for the new position, than Mohl urged him most strongly to utilize his exceptional opportunity in the interest of science, and to start excavations in the large mounds opposite Mosul.

1

THE DISCOVERY OF ASSYRIAN PALACES

FRENCH EXCAVATIONS AT KHORSABÂD BY BOTTA AND PLACE

The man whom France had so judiciously sent as consular agent to Mosul in 1842 was the naturalist Paul Emil Botta, a nephew of the celebrated historian of Italy, and himself a man of no small gifts and of considerable experience in the consular service at Alexandria. A long residence in Egypt, Yemen, and Syria, "undertaken regardless of difficulties or the dangers of climate, solely to further his scientific pursuits, had eminently adapted him for an appointment in the East. He could assimilate himself to the habits of the people; was conversant with their language; possessed energy of character; and was besides an intelligent and practised observer. With such qualifications, it was obvious that his residence in the vicinity of a spot that history and tradition agreed in pointing out as the site of Nineveh could not but be productive of important results."[1] Botta was then only thirty-seven years of age. Though very limited in his pecuniary resources, he commenced his researches immediately after his arrival at Mosul with the full ardor of youth, yet in the cautious and methodical manner of the scholar. He first examined the whole region around Mosul, visited the interior of many modern houses, and tried to acquire every antiquity in the hands of dealers and other persons, with the fixed purpose of tracing the place of their origin, and selecting if possible a suitable ruin for the commencement of his own operations. He soon came, however, to the conclusion that, unlike Hilla and other Babylonian places, Mosul had not been con-

[1] Comp. Joseph Bonomi, "Nineveh and its Palaces," London, 1852, p. 7.

structed with ancient Assyrian material.[1] Of the two conspicuous mounds on the other side of the Tigris, which alone seemed to indicate a higher antiquity, the southern one, called Nebî Yûnus, and partly covered with a village of the same name, attracted his first attention; for it was there that Rich had reported the existence of subterranean walls and cuneiform inscriptions. But the religious prejudice of the inhabitants, and the large sum necessary for their expropriation, excluded from the beginning any attempt on his part at excavating here. There remained, then, nothing else for him but to start operations at the northern *tell* Qoyunjuk (generally written K(o)uyunjik, and meaning "Lamb" in Turkish), which doubtless was an artificial mass, and, to all appearance, contained the remains of some prominent ancient building.[2] Here Botta commenced his researches on a very moderate scale, in the month of December, 1842. The results of his first efforts were not very encouraging. Numerous fragments of bas-reliefs and cuneiform inscriptions, through which the Assyrian origin of the mound was established beyond question, were brought to light, but "nothing in a perfect state was obtained to reward the trouble and outlay" of the explorer. Though greatly discouraged by the absence of striking finds, he continued his excavations till the middle of March, 1843.

During all the time that Botta was occupied at Qoyunjuk, superintending his workmen, and carefully examining every little fragment that came out of the ground, the curious natives of the neighboring places used to gather around his trenches, gesticulating and discussing what this strange proceeding of the foreigner meant, but realizing that apparently he was in quest of sculptured stones, inscribed bricks, and

[1] As Rich had regarded as very likely.

[2] Comp. the Plan of the Ruins of Nineveh, published in a subsequent chapter, "Temporary Revival of Public Interest in Assyrian Excavations" (*sub* "George Smith").

other antiquities which he eagerly bought whenever they were offered. One day, as far back as December, 1842, an inhabitant of a distant village, a dyer of Khorsabâd, who built his ovens of bricks obtained from the mound on which his village stood, happened to pass by Qoyunjuk and to express his astonishment about Botta's operations. As soon as he had learned what was the real purpose of all these diggings, he declared that plenty of such stones as they wanted were found near his village, at the same time offering to procure as many as the foreigner wished. Botta, accustomed to the Arab endeavor of appearing as bearers of important and pleasing news, did not at first pay much attention to what the man had reported, even after the latter had been induced to bring two complete bricks with cuneiform inscriptions from Khorsabâd to Mosul. But finally, weary with his fruitless search in the mound of Qoyunjuk,

Mound and Village of Khorsabâd, from the West

he abandoned the scene of his disappointing labors, and remembering the Arab dyer with his bricks and his story, he despatched a few of his workmen to Khorsabâd on March 20, 1843, to test the mound as the peasant had advised.

The village of Khorsabâd, situated about five hours to the northeast of Mosul, on the left bank of the same little river Khôsar which flows through Nineveh, is built on the more elevated eastern part of a long-stretched mound. The gradually descending western half of the same *tell* ends in two ridges which are both unoccupied. It was in the northern ridge of the latter section that Botta's workmen began to cut their trenches. They came almost immediately upon two parallel walls covered with the mutilated remains of large bas-reliefs and cuneiform inscriptions. A messenger was despatched to Mosul in order to inform their master of the great discovery. But well acquainted with the rich phantasy and flowery speech of the Arab race, Botta seriously doubted the truth of the extraordinary news so quickly received, and at first ordered a servant to the scene of excavations with instructions to inspect the work and bring him a more intelligent account of the actual finds. The required evidence was soon in Botta's possession. There could be no longer any doubt that this time the Arabs had spoken the full truth, and that most remarkable antiquities of a genuine Assyrian character had been brought to light. He now hastened at once to Khorsabâd himself. His consular duties allowed him to remain only one day. But the few hours which he could spend in the trenches were well employed. Though the first sight of these strange sculptures and witnesses of a long-forgotten past which, out of the depth of a buried civilization, suddenly rose like the *fata morgana* before his astonished eyes, must have filled his soul with great excitement and rare delight, yet he could calm himself sufficiently to sit down among his Arab workmen, and sketch the most important reliefs and inscriptions for his friend in Paris.

On April 5, 1843, Botta wrote the first of a series of letters to Mohl,[1] in which he briefly described what he had

[1] Published in *Journal Asiatique*, series iv., vol. ii., pp. 61–72 (dated

just seen, and expressed the hope that some way might be found for the safe transport and final preservation of the excavated treasures. His ardent desire was soon to be realized beyond expectation. It was a memorable day when his letter was submitted to the members of the *Société Asiatique*, and the explorer's statement was read: "I believe myself to be the first who has discovered sculptures which with some reason can be referred to the period when Nineveh was flourishing." What could have appealed more strongly to the French nation! The impression which these simple and yet so significant words created in the scientific circles of France was extraordinary. The Academy of Paris at once requested the minister to grant the necessary funds for a continuation of the excavations (so far chiefly carried on at Botta's personal expense), and for the transport of all the objects recovered to Europe. With its old traditional spirit of munificence, and always ready to encourage and support undertakings which by their very nature were to shed new lustre upon the name of France, the government granted the required sum, and a few months later despatched E. Flandin, well prepared by his work in Persia, to the assistance of Botta, in order to sketch all such monuments as could not safely be removed from Khorsabâd. But half a year elapsed before the artist arrived at the ruins, and in the meanwhile Botta had to fight his way, blocked with numerous obstacles, to the best of his ability.

Many of the excavated sculptures had suffered considerably at the time when the great building was destroyed by fire. Resting only on the earth of the mound, they began to crumble as soon as the halls were cleared of rubbish and

April 5, 1843), with 12 plates; pp. 201–214 (May 2, 1843), with 9 plates; vol. iii., pp. 91–103 (June 2, 1843) and pp. 424–435 (July 24, 1843), with 17 plates; vol. iv., pp. 301–314 (Oct. 31, 1843), with 11 plates. Comp., also, his report to the Minister of the Interior (March 22, 1844) in vol. v., pp. 201–207.

exposed to light. He ordered large beams to prevent the collapse of the walls. But scarcely had he turned his back when the unscrupulous inhabitants of the village, always in need of wood, pillaged his supports, thus causing destruction. The heat of the summer and the rains of the winter interfered seriously with his progress, often damaging beyond recognition what with great labor and patience had just been rescued from the ground, sometimes even before he was able to examine the sculptures. The malarious condition of the whole region caused illness and death among his workmen, proving nearly fatal to his own life. The peasants of Khorsabâd, suspicious beyond measure, and unwilling to aid his researches, refused to work and sell him their houses, which occupied the most important part of the ruins. In addition to all these constant worriments, necessarily affecting his mind and body, the governor of Mosul, with ever-increasing jealousy and cunning, tried in many ways to dishearten the explorer. He shared the general belief of his people that the foreigner was searching for treasures. Anxious to appropriate them himself, he frequently threw Botta's workmen into prison in order to extract a confession, or he appointed watchmen at the trenches to seize every piece of gold that might be discovered. When all this failed to have the desired effect, he closed the work altogether, on the pretext that Botta was evidently establishing a military station to take the country by force of arms from the sultan.

At Paris and Constantinople everything was done by the French government and its representative to counteract these miserable machinations, and to prove the utter baselessness of the malicious accusations. Finally, well-directed energy, tact, and perseverance triumphed over all the obstacles and animosity of the native population. Botta gradually induced the chief of the village to abandon his house on the summit of the mound temporarily for a reasonable price, and to move down into the plain, where later the rest of the inhabitants followed, after the explorer's promise to restore the original contour of the mound as soon as the latter had been fully examined. Even before this agreement was entered into with the villagers, Botta had found it necessary to fill his trenches again after he had copied the inscriptions, drawn the sculptures, and removed those antiquities which could be transported, as the only way in which the large mass of crumbling reliefs could be saved for future research from their rapid destruction by the air. But it was not until the beginning of May, 1844, after the excavations had rested almost completely[1] during the winter, that Flandin finally brought the necessary firmân from Constantinople allowing the resumption of the excavations. Notwithstanding the approaching heat, no more time was lost. Three hundred Christian refugees were gradually engaged to excavate the unexplored part of the mound, Botta copying the inscriptions and Flandin preparing the drawings of the sculptures as soon as they had been exposed. Both men worked with the greatest harmony, energy, and devotion during the whole oppressive summer, until, in October, 1844, after most remarkable success, the excavations were suspended temporarily.

A large mass of material was packed for shipment by raft down the Tigris to Basra, whence the Cormorant, a French man-of-war, in 1846, carried it safely to Havre. Flandin was the first to leave Khorsabâd (November, 1844) and to return to Paris. His large portfolio of beautiful sketches and drawings had fairly prepared the way for the arrival of the originals. But when now these extraordinary monuments themselves had found a worthy place in the large halls of the Louvre, constituting the first great Assyrian museum of

[1] Only interrupted by a short visit to Khorsabâd in company with a few travellers, among them Mr. Dittel, sent by the Russian Minister of Public Instruction to inspect the excavations. In connection with this visit Botta even made a slight excavation in order to satisfy the curiosity of his guests.

Europe; when these gigantic winged bulls, with their serene expression of dignified strength and intellectual power, and these fine reliefs illustrating the different scenes of peace and war of a bygone race before which the nations of Asia had trembled, stood there again before the eyes of

Bas-Relief from the Palace of Sargon, Khorsabâd

the whole world, as a powerful witness to the beginning of a resurrection of an almost forgotten empire, the enthusiasm among all classes of France knew no bounds. By order of the government, and under the auspices of the Minister of the Interior, the most prominent members of the Institute of France were at once appointed a commission, under whose advice and coöperation Botta and Flandin were enabled to publish the results of their combined labors in a magnificent work of five large volumes.[1]

The excavations of the two explorers had penetrated into the interior of the mound of Khorsabâd until all traces of walls disappeared. But a careful study of the plan drawn by Flandin had enabled them to infer that the great structure which yielded all these bas-reliefs and inscriptions must formerly have extended considerably farther. From certain indications in the ground it became evident that a part of the monumental building had been intentionally destroyed in ancient times, but it was to be expected that another considerable part was still preserved somewhere in the unexplored sections of the mound. Stimulated by the hope of finding the lost trace again, Botta himself opened a number of trial trenches at various points. But all his exertions having failed, he came to the conclusion that everything that remained of the palace at Khorsabâd had been excavated, and therefore he put a stop to the work on this ruin.

In the year 1851 the French Assembly voted a sum of money for an expedition to be sent to Babylonia (which we shall discuss later), and another for the resumption of the suspended excavations at Khorsabâd, to be directed by Victor Place, a skilful architect and Botta's successor as French consular agent at Mosul. Technically well prepared for his task, and faithfully supported in the trenches by Botta's intelligent foreman, Nahushi, who with many other former workmen had gladly reëntered French employment, Place completed the systematic examination of the great palace and restored its ground-plan during the years 1851–55. Under his supervision the excavations exposed all the remaining buildings and rooms attached to the sculptured halls, — a space about three times as large as that explored by his

[1] *Monument de Ninive découvert et décrit par M. P. E. Botta, mesuré et dessiné par M. E. Flandin*, 5 volumes with 400 plates, Paris, 1849–50.

Wall Decoration in Enamelled Tiles, Khorsabâd

predecessor, and successfully extended even to the walls of the town. In these outlying mounds he unearthed four simple and three very fine gates, flanked by large winged bulls and other sculptures, and their arches most beautifully decorated with friezes of blue and white enamelled tiles representing winged genii and animals, plants and rosettes, in excellent design and execution. At the angle[1] formed by two of the walls of the palace he made an especially valuable discovery in the form of an inscribed box serving as corner-stone, and containing seven tablets of different size, in gold, silver, copper, lead, lapis lazuli, magnesite, and limestone. They all bore identical cuneiform records pertaining to the history of these buildings.

It was not always very easy for Place to trace the rooms of the "harem" and the other smaller structures, as no sculptures like those discovered by Botta had adorned their walls and sustained the crumbling mass of unbaked bricks. But gradually his eyes became sharpened and were able to distinguish the faint outlines of walls from the surrounding earth and rubbish. Though his excavations did not yield

[1] Comp. Oppert, *Expédition en Mésopotamie*, vol. i., p. 349, note 2.

anything like the rich harvest in large monuments of art reaped by his predecessor, as we have just seen, they were by no means deficient in them. But they were especially productive in those small objects of clay and stone, glass and metal, which in a welcome manner supplemented our knowledge of the life and customs and daily needs of the ancient Assyrians. Place discovered no less than fourteen inscribed barrel cylinders with historical records. He found a regular magazine of pottery, another full of colored tiles, and a third containing iron implements of every description in such a fine state of preservation that several of them were used at once by his Arab workmen. He unearthed even the water-closets, the bakery and the "wine-cellar" of the king, the latter easily to be identified by a number of pointed jars resting in a double row of small holes on the paved floor, and discharging a strong smell of yeast after the first rain had dissolved their red sediments.

Unlike Botta, who, after his great discovery, most naturally had concentrated all his energy upon a systematic exploration of the mound of Khorsabâd, Place made repeated excursions into the regions to the east and south of Mosul, examining many of the smaller mounds with which the whole country is covered, and excavating for a few months without success at Qal'at Shirgât, the large Tell Shemâmyk (about halfway between the Upper Zâb and Erbîl, to the southwest of the latter) and even in the neighborhood of Nimrûd, which had yielded such extraordinary treasures to Layard.[1] About the same time English excavations were carried on by Rassam, in the ruins just mentioned, under Rawlinson's direction, the Ottoman firmân having granted to both the French and British governments the right of excavating "in any ground belonging to the state." In consquence of this

[1] Comp. *Lettre de M. Place à M. Mohl sur une Expédition faite à Arbèles* (dated Mosul, Nov. 20, 1852) in the *Journal Asiatique*, series iv., vol. xx. (1852), pp. 441–470.

peculiar arrangement, the interests of the two European nations threatened frequently to clash against each other, a pardonable rivalry existing all the while between the different excavators, accompanied by a constant friction and ill-feeling among their workmen. This was particularly the case at Qal'at Shirgât, where Rawlinson "made a distinct and categorical assertion of the British claims," and at Qoyunjuk, where, at Place's request, he had apportioned the northern half of the mound to the French representative — a compact which was later entirely ignored by Rassam on the ground that this mound was not state property, and that Rawlinson accordingly had no power to give away what did not belong to him.[1]

Unfortunately, a large part of the antiquities excavated by Victor Place at Khorsabâd met with a sad fate. Together with sixty-eight cases of the finest bas-reliefs from Ashurbânapal's palace at Qoyunjuk, which Rawlinson had allowed him to select for the Louvre, and including all the results of Fresnel's expedition to Babylon, they were lost on two rafts in the Tigris on their way from Baghdad to Basra in the spring of 1855. But notwithstanding this lamentable misfortune, Place was enabled to submit to the public all those results which he had previously brought on paper in another magnificent work published by his liberal government.[2]

The importance of all the discoveries at Khorsabâd, brought about by the united efforts of Botta, Flandin, and Place, cannot be overrated. The mounds under which the monuments had been buried for twenty-five hundred years represented a whole fortified town, called after its founder,

[1] Comp. the interesting story of these quarrels as told by Rassam, "Asshur and the Land of Nimrod," New York, 1897, pp. 7, 12–27; and George Rawlinson, "Memoir of Major-General Sir Henry Creswicke Rawlinson," pp. 178, *seqq.*

[2] Victor Place, *Ninive et l'Assyrie, avec des essais de restauration par F. Thomas*, 3 volumes, Paris, 1866–69.

The Palace of Sargon, Conqueror of Samaria, according to the Restoration of Victor Place

Sargon, the conqueror of Samaria (722 B. C.), Dûr-Sharrukên or "Sargon's Castle." The walls by which the town was protected were found intact at their bases. They constituted a rectangular parallelogram, or nearly a square, pointing with its four corners to the cardinal points, and enclosing a space of a little over 741 acres. Its northwest side was interrupted by the royal palace, which, like a huge bastion, protruded considerably into the plain, at the same time forming part of the great town-wall. The latter was provided with eight monumental gates, each of which was named after an Assyrian deity.

The royal residence was erected on a lofty terrace, nearly forty-five feet high and built of unbaked bricks cased with a wall of large square stones. At the northern corner of this raised platform, covering an area of nearly twenty-five acres of land, was an open place; near the western corner stood a temple, and at the centre of the southwest side rose the stage-tower belonging to it and used also for astronomical observations; the rest was occupied by the palace itself. This latter was divided into three sections, the seraglio occupying the centre of the terrace and extending towards the plain; the harem, with only two entrances, situated at the southern corner, and the domestic quarters at the eastern corner, connected with the store and provision rooms, the stables, kitchen, and bakery, at the centre of the southeast side. The seraglio, inhabited by the king and his large retinue of military and civil officers, like the other two sections of the extensive building, consisted of a great many larger and smaller rooms grouped around several open courts. The northwest wing contained the public reception rooms, — wide halls, elaborately decorated with winged bulls, magnificent sculptures and historical inscriptions, glorifying the king in his actions of peace and war. We see him hunting wild animals, doing homage to the gods, sitting at the table and listening to the singers and musicians, or attacking strong cities and castles, subduing foreign nations, punishing rebels, and leading back thousands of captives and innumerable spoil of every description. The private apartments of the monarch, which were much smaller and simpler, occupied the southeast wing, close to the harem or women's quarter. The latter was entirely separated from the other two sections, even its single rooms, as the traces of discovered hinges indicate, being closed by folding doors, while everywhere else the entrances appear to have been covered with curtains.

The floor of the different chambers as a rule was only stamped clay, upon which in many cases doubtless precious rugs had been spread. Here and there it was overlaid with tiles or marble blocks, which were especially employed for pavements in connection with courts and open spaces around the palace. The walls of the rooms, serving to exclude the intense heat of the summer, and to protect against the severe cold of the winter, were exceptionally thick. They varied between nine feet and a half and sixteen feet, and in one case reached the enormous thickness of even twenty-five feet and a half. Apart from the large reception rooms and gateways, which displayed all the splendor that Assyrian artists were able to give them, the inner walls were generally covered only with a white plaster surrounded by black lines, while the women's apartments were adorned more tastefully with fresco paintings and white or black arabesques. Marble statues as a decorative element were found exclusively in the principal court of the harem. The exterior of the palace walls exhibited a system of groups of half-columns, separated by dentated recesses or chasings, — the prevailing type of ancient Babylonian external architecture, as we shall see later.

It is impossible to enter into all the characteristic features which this remarkable complex must have presented to Sargon and his people, and as a careful study of the whole monument allowed Place and others gradually to restore it. The Assyrian architecture, previously completely unknown, appeared suddenly before us in all the details of a sumptuous building, adorned with sculptures and paintings which lead us back into the midst of Assyrian life during the eighth pre-Christian century. We get acquainted with the occupations of the king and his subjects, their customs, their pleasures, their mode of living, their religion, their art, and part of their literature. With great astonishment, artists and scholars began to realize how high a standard this people in the East had reached at a time when Europe as a whole was still in a state of barbarism. With extraordinary enthusiasm, students of philology and history welcomed the enormous mass of authentic material, which, in the hands of Rawlinson, Hincks, and Oppert, was soon to shed a flood of new light upon the person and reign and language of that great warrior, Sargon, so far known only by name from a statement in Isaiah (20 : 1), and upon the whole history and geography of Western Asia shrouded in darkness, and which, by its constant references to names and events mentioned in the Bible, was eagerly called upon as an unexpected witness to test the truthfulness of the Holy Scriptures. There have been made other and even greater discoveries in Assyrian and Babylonian ruins since Botta's far-reaching exploration of the mounds of Khorsabâd, but there never has been aroused again such a deep and general interest in the excavation of distant Oriental sites as towards the middle of the last century, when Sargon's palace rose suddenly out of the ground, and furnished the first faithful picture of a great epoch of art which had vanished completely from human sight.

ENGLISH EXCAVATIONS AT NIMRÛD, QOYUNJUK, AND QAL'AT SHIRGÂT BY LAYARD, RASSAM, AND LOFTUS

The eagerness and determination of the scholar to decipher and understand those long cuneiform inscriptions which, like a commentary, accompanied the monuments of Khorsabâd, could be satisfied only after the whole material had arrived and been published. In the meanwhile the new impulse given to archæological studies by the announcement of Botta's success manifested itself at once in influencing a young Englishman to imitate the latter's example, and to start excavations at one of the most prominent Assyrian mounds, which, even two years before Botta's arrival at Mosul, he had viewed "with the design of thoroughly examining them whenever it might be in his power." The man who now, as England's champion, stepped forth into the international contest for great archæological discoveries was so exceptionally qualified and prepared for his task by natural gifts and the experience of his past life, and at the same time so eminently successful in the choice of his methods and men, in the overcoming of extraordinary obstacles and difficulties, in the rapid obtaining of the most glorious results, and in the forcible and direct manner with which through the remarkable story of his rare achievements he appealed to the heart of his countrymen and to the sentiment of the whole educated world, that he at once became, and during the whole nineteenth century remained, the central figure of Assyrian exploration.

Sir Austen Henry Layard, the descendant of a Huguenot refugee who had settled in England, was born in Paris on March 5, 1817. In consequence of his father's illness, which frequently necessitated a change of climate, he spent much of his boyhood in France, Switzerland, and Italy, where, with all the deficiencies of a desultory and highly cosmopolitan education, he acquired a taste for the fine arts and archæology, and that characteristic love for travel and adventure which prepared him so well for his later nomadic life and career as an explorer. When about sixteen years of age he was sent to the house of his uncle in London to study law. But, to quote his own words, "after spending nearly six years in the office of a solicitor, and in the chambers of an eminent conveyancer, I determined for various reasons to leave England and to seek a career elsewhere." From his childhood well acquainted with several European languages, and familiar with the manners of men in various European lands, he now longed to see the fascinating Orient itself, the land of the "Arabian Nights," which had often inflamed his youthful mind. With the greatest eagerness he had devoured every volume of Eastern travel that fell in his way. The reading of the works of Morier, Malcolm, and Rich, and the personal acquaintance with men like Baillie Fraser (comp. pp. 54, *seqq.*, above) and Sir Charles Fellowes, favorably known from his discoveries among the ruined cities of Asia Minor, had inspired him with an ardent desire to follow in their footsteps. In order to prepare himself for his journey, he had mastered the Arabic letters, picked up a little of the Persian language, taken lessons in the use of the sextant from a retired captain of the merchant service, and even hastily acquired a superficial medical knowledge of the treatment of wounds and certain Oriental diseases.

In the company of another enthusiastic traveller, E. L. Mitford, who, like Layard himself,[1] has left us a narrative

[1] Comp. Layard, "Early Adventures in Persia, Susiana, and Babylonia, including a Residence among the Bakhtiyari and other Wild Tribes before the Discovery of Nineveh," 1st ed., London, 1887, 2 vols. The second edition (London, 1894, 1 vol.), an abridgment of the first, and omitting a description of the countries through which Layard and Mitford travelled together, has an introductory chapter on the author's life and work by his surviving friend, Lord Aberdare.

of this first interesting journey,[1] the latter finally set out upon his "Early Adventures" in the summer of 1839, "with the intention of making his way through Turkey, Asia Minor, Syria, Persia, and India to Ceylon," where he expected to establish himself permanently. Not without difficulties and troublesome incidents the two associates reached Jerusalem in January, 1840, where they separated for a little while, Mitford declining to join in the perilous excursion to the ruins of Petra, Ammon, and Jerâsh, which Layard, passionately fond of adventures, undertook alone. Two months later he reached Aleppo, whence, together with Mitford, he travelled to Mosul and Baghdad. During their brief stay at the former place, the two travellers met Ainsworth, a prominent member of the British Euphrates Expedition,[2] and Christian Rassam, brother of the later faithful friend and assistant of Layard, with both of whom they visited the ruins of Nineveh, Hammâm ʿAlî, Qalʿat Shirgât, and El-Hadhr. It was in the month of April, 1840, in connection with this excursion down the western bank of the Tigris, that Layard, from an artificial eminence, for the first time looked upon the line of lofty mounds on the other side of the river, called Nimrûd, where but shortly afterwards he was to raise "a lasting monument to his own fame."

Mitford and Layard travelled together as far as Hamadân, whence on August 8 of the same year they finally parted, the former to continue his long and difficult journey to Kandahar, and the latter to engage in his adventurous life and perilous wanderings among the wild tribes of Persia and ʿIrâq, until two years later, when we find him again at Mosul,

[1] Edward Ledwich Mitford, "A Land-March from England to Ceylon Forty Years Ago, through Dalmatia, Montenegro, Turkey, Asia Minor, Syria, Palestine, Assyria, Persia, Afghanistan, Scinde, and India," London, 1884, 2 vols.

[2] Comp. pp. 57, *seqq.*, above.

stopping there for a little while on his way from Baghdad to Constantinople. Botta had meanwhile been appointed French consular agent, and tentatively cut a trench or two in the mound of Qoyunjuk. The two famous explorers met then and there — June, 1842 — for the first time, the one on the fair road to a great discovery, the other so far disappointed in his efforts to raise the necessary funds for similar excavations. Brief as this first meeting was, it formed the beginning of a friendly intercourse between the two great men, Layard, free from envy and jealousy, always encouraging Botta in his labors, and particularly calling his attention to Nimrûd, the one place above others which he himself so eagerly desired to explore, when the paucity of results at Qoyunjuk threatened to dishearten his lonely friend.

Robbed as he frequently was, and exposed to hardships and dangers of every kind, repeatedly even at the point of losing his life, Layard never ceased to "look back with feelings of grateful delight to those happy days when, free and unheeded, we left at dawn the humble cottage or cheerful tent, and lingering as we listed, unconscious of distance and of the hour, found ourselves as the sun went down under some hoary ruin tenanted by the wandering Arab, or in some crumbling village still bearing a well-known name. No experienced dragoman measured our distances and appointed our stations. We were honored with no conversations by pashas, nor did we seek any civilities from governors. We neither drew tears nor curses from villagers by seizing their horses, or searching their houses for provisions: their welcome was sincere; their scanty fare was placed before us; we ate and came and went in peace."

At a time when every moment the chronic dispute as to the actual boundary line between Turkey and Persia threatened to lead to a serious war which might prove detrimental to British interests in those countries, Layard's intimate knowledge of the territory in dispute proved of great value to Sir Stratford Canning (afterwards Lord Stratford de Redcliffe), then British ambassador at the Porte in Constantinople, whither our traveller had hastened. Though for apparent political reasons the Russian point of view was finally accepted by England, much against Canning's protest and his own very decided conviction, Layard had found in this man of influence a liberal patron, who during the following years entrusted him with many important missions, endeavoring all the time to have him definitely attached to his staff. While thus waiting at the shore of the Bosphorus for a much coveted position, Layard remained in regular correspondence with Botta, whose reports and drawings he received before they were published. The latter's unexpected brilliant success at Khorsabâd brought him new encouragement for his own plans, and increased his hope and desire to return on some future day to Mesopotamia and excavate the ruins of Nineveh. With his mind firmly fixed upon this one object of his life, he commenced "the study of the Semitic languages, to which I conjectured the cuneiform inscriptions from the Assyrian ruins belonged."[1] But when he saw Sir Stratford making arrangements for a temporary return to England, he became tired of waiting longer for his promised attachéship, and one day spoke to the latter of his ardent desire to examine the mounds near Mosul. To his great delight, his generous patron not only approved of his suggestion, but offered £60 (=$300) towards the expenses which would be incurred in making tentative

[1] Comp. "Early Adventures," 2d edition, p. 409. We quote the above statement literally, in order to show that Layard, with his well-known intuition, divined the truth later established, even before Löwenstein expressed the same thought in his *Essai de déchiffrement de l'Écriture Assyrienne pour servir à l'explication du Monument de Khorsabad*, Paris and Leipzig, 1845, pp. 12, *seq.*

The Ruins of Nimrûd

Layard removing a human-headed winged bull to a raft on the Tigris

excavations. Who was happier than Layard! Without a servant, and without any other effects than a pair of large saddle-bags, but with a cheerful heart, and, above all, with this modest sum in his pocket, increased by a few pounds from his own meagre resources, he started in October, 1845, to excavate Nineveh. How eagerly Layard turned his face towards the place in which all his hopes had centred for the past five years we may easily infer from the fact that, like a Tartar, he travelled by day and night without rest, crossing the mountains of Kurdistân and galloping over the plains of Assyria, until he reached Mosul, twelve days after his departure from Samsûn.

First Expedition, 1845–1847. Profiting by the experience of Botta, Layard deemed it best for the time being to conceal the real object of his journey from the ill-disposed governor and the inhabitants of Mosul. On the 8th of November, having secretly procured a few tools, he left the town with "guns, spears, and other formidable weapons," ostensibly to hunt wild boars in a neighboring district. Accompanied by Mr. Ross, a British resident merchant, who in many ways facilitated the work of our explorer during his long stay in Assyria, and by a mason and two servants, he floated down the Tigris on a small raft, reaching Nimrûd the same night. With six untrained Arabs, he commenced work at two different points of the ruins on the following morning. Like the mounds of Khorsabâd, the ruins of Nimrûd represent a clearly defined rectangular parallelogram, rising above the ground as a plateau of considerable height and extent, and pointing with its two smaller sides to the north and south respectively. A lofty cone, from the distance strikingly resembling a mountain of volcanic origin, and constituting the most characteristic feature of this conglomeration of furrowed hills, occupies their northwest corner. During the early spring the whole mound is clothed with a luxuriant growth of grass and many-colored flowers. Black Arab tents and herds of grazing sheep, watched by the youngest members of some Bedouin tribe, are scattered over the ruins, relieving the monotony of the region for a few months. But when the rays of the sun and the scorching winds from the desert have turned the pleasant picture of a short but cheerful life again into a parched and barren waste, the human eye wanders unobstructed over the whole plateau, meeting numerous fragments of stone and pottery everywhere.

The absence of all vegetation in November enabled Layard to examine the remains with which the site was covered without difficulty. Following up the result of this general survey, which convinced him "that sculptured remains must still exist in some part of the mound," he placed three of his workmen at a spot near the middle of the west side of the ruins, and the other three at the southwest corner. Before night interrupted their first day's labors, they had partly excavated two chambers lined with alabaster slabs, all of which bore cuneiform inscriptions at their centres. The slabs from the chamber in the northwest section of the mound were in a fine state of preservation, while those from the southwest corner evidently had been exposed to intense heat, which had cracked them in every part. Remains of extensive buildings had thus been brought to light within a few hours. Soon afterwards it became apparent that Layard had discovered two Assyrian palaces on the very first day of his excavations.

Exceedingly pleased with these unexpected results, Layard established his headquarters at once in the least ruined house of a deserted village which was only twenty minutes' walk from the scene of his labors. On the next morning he increased his force by five Turcomans from Selâmîye, situated three miles farther up the river, a place to which he had soon to remove himself in consequence of the hazards of the region around Nimrûd. On the third day he opened a trench in the high conical mound at the northwest corner, but finding nothing but fragments of inscribed brick, little appreciated in those early days of Assyrian exploration, he abandoned this section again, and concentrated his eleven men for the next time upon the southwest corner of the ruins, "where the many ramifications of the building already identified promised speedier success." A few days later he hurried to Mosul to acquaint the pasha with the object of his researches. A tiny piece of gold-leaf, recently discovered at Nimrûd, had already found its way into the writing-tray of the latter, and roused his suspicion. Other signs indicated that a formidable opposition was gradually forming to prevent English excavations. Layard, not protected by a firmân from the Sultan, recognized what was coming. But as the governor, whose greediness had reduced the whole province to utter poverty and lawlessness, had not as yet openly declared against his proceedings, our explorer lost no time to push his researches as much as possible. He sent agents to several conspicuous ruins between the Tigris and the Zâb, "in order to ascertain the existence of sculptured buildings in some part of the country," at the same time increasing his own party to thirty men at the southwest corner of Nimrûd. It was soon found that the inscriptions on all the slabs so far exposed were identical with those unearthed in the northwest building, and that in every case a few letters had been cut away at the edges in order to make the stones fit into the wall. "From these facts it became evident that materials taken from another building had been used" in the construction of the one which Layard was exploring. No sculptures, however, had so far been disclosed.

Winter rains were now setting in, and the excavations proceeded but slowly. The hours given to rest in the miserable hovel at Selâmîye were spent most uncomfortably. The roofs of the house were leaking, and a perfect torrent descended on the floor and the rug on which the explorer was lying. "Crouched up in a corner, or under a rude table," which was surrounded by trenches to carry off the accumulating water, he usually passed the night on these occasions. Finally, on the 28th of November, after he had ordered to clear the earth away from both sides of newly exposed slabs, the first bas-reliefs were discovered. Layard and his Arabs were equally excited, and notwithstanding a violent shower of rain, they worked enthusiastically until dark. But their joy did not last very long; the next day the governor of Mosul closed the excavations at Nimrûd. French jealousy, Mohammedan prejudices, and the pasha's own ill-will were equally responsible for this unfortunate result. There remained nothing for Layard but to acquiesce. At his own request, however, a *qawwâs* was sent to the mounds as representative of the Ottoman government, while he pretended only to draw the sculptures and copy the inscriptions which had already been uncovered. It was not difficult for him to induce this officer to allow the employment of a few workmen to guard the sculptures during the day. In reality, they were sent to different sections of the mound to search for other sculptures and inscribed monuments. The experiment was very successful. Without being interrupted in his attempt, Layard uncovered several large figures, uninjured by fire, near the west edge, a crouching lion at the southeast corner, the torsos of a pair of gigantic winged bulls, two small winged lions, likewise mutilated, and a human figure nine feet high, in the centre of the mound. Though only detached and unconnected walls had been found so far, "there was no longer any doubt of the existence not only of sculptures and inscriptions, but even of vast edifices, in the interior of the mound of Nimrûd." Nearly six weeks of undivided attention and constant exposure to hardships had been devoted to the exploration of the ruins. Layard now decided to lose no more time in opening new trenches, but to inform Sir Stratford Canning how successfully the first part of his mission had been carried through, and to urge "the necessity of a firmân, which would prevent any future interference on the part of the authorities or the inhabitants of the country."

Towards the end of 1845 — about the time when this letter was written — one of the chief obstacles to archæological research in Assyria for the time being was suddenly removed. The old governor was replaced by an enlightened, just, and tolerant officer of the new school. With a view of quietly awaiting the beneficial result of this radical change in the administration for the province as a whole, and for his own work at Nimrûd, Layard covered over the sculptures brought to light, and withdrew altogether from the ruins. He descended the Tigris on a raft, and spent Christmas with Major Rawlinson, whom he desired to consult concerning the arrangements to be made for the removal of the sculptures at a future period. The two great English pioneers met then for the first time. "It was a happy chance which brought together two such men as Layard and Rawlinson as laborers at the same time and in the same field, but each with his special task — each strongest where the other was weakest — Layard, the excavator, the effective task-master, the hard-working and judicious gatherer together of materials; and Rawlinson, the classical scholar, the linguist, the diligent student of history, the man at once of wide reading and keen insight, the cool, dispassionate investigator and weigher of evidence. The two men mutually esteemed and respected each other, and they were ready to assist each other to the utmost of their power."[1]

At the beginning of January, 1846, Layard returned to Mosul. The change since his departure had been as sudden as great. A few conciliatory acts on the part of the new

[1] Comp. George Rawlinson, "A Memoir of Major-General Sir Henry Creswicke Rawlinson," London, 1898, p. 152.

governor had quickly restored confidence among the inhabitants of the province. Even the Bedouins were returning to their old camping grounds between the Tigris and Zâb, from which for a long while they had been excluded. The incessant winter rains had brought forward the vegetation of the spring, and the surface and sides of Nimrûd were clothed in a pleasing green. Security having been established in this part of the country, the mound itself now offered a more convenient and more agreeable residence to Layard than the distant village of Selâmîye. Accompanied by a number of workmen and by Hormuzd Rassam, an intelligent Chaldean Christian and brother of the British vice-consul at Mosul, who henceforth acted as his reliable agent and overseer, he therefore moved at once to his new dwelling-place at Nimrûd. The polite governor had offered no objection to the continuation of his labors, but another month elapsed before he could venture to resume his excavations. For the *qâdi* of Mosul once more had stirred up the people of the town against the explorer, so that it was found necessary to postpone work until the storm had passed away.

It was near the middle of February before Layard could make some fresh experiments at the southwest corner of the mound. Slab after slab was exposed, by which it was proved that "the building had not been entirely destroyed by fire, but had been partly exposed to gradual decay." But in order to arouse the necessary interest in England, he needed much better preserved sculptures. Abandoning, therefore, the edifice, which until then had received his principal attention, he placed the workmen at the centre of a ravine which ran far into the west side of the mound, near the spot where he had previously unearthed the first complete monuments. His labors here were followed by an immediate success. He came upon a large hall, in which all the slabs were not only in their original position, but in the finest state of preservation. It soon became evident that he had found the earliest palace of Nimrûd, from which many of the sculptures employed in the construction of the southwest building had been quarried.

On the morning following these discoveries he rode to the encampment of a neighboring shaikh, and was returning to his trenches, when he observed two Arabs of the latter's tribe "urging their mares to the top of their speed. On approaching him they stopped. 'Hasten, O Bey,' exclaimed one of them; 'hasten to the diggers, for they have found Nimrod himself. Wallah, it is wonderful, but it is true! we have seen him with our eyes. There is no God but God;' and both joining in this pious exclamation, they galloped off without further words in the direction of their tents." On reaching the ruins, he ascertained that the workmen had discovered the enormous human head of one of those winged lions which now adorn the British Museum. An equally well preserved corresponding figure was disclosed before nightfall about twelve feet away in the rubbish, both forming the southern entrance into a chamber. Unfortunately "one of the workmen, on catching the first glimpse of the monster, had thrown down his basket and run off towards Mosul as fast as his legs could carry him. . . . He had scarcely checked his speed before reaching the bridge. Entering breathless into the bazaars, he announced to every one he met that Nimrod had appeared." The result of this unexpected occurrence became quickly apparent. The governor, "not remembering very clearly whether Nimrod was a true-believing prophet or an infidel," sent a somewhat unintelligible message "to the effect that the remains should be treated with respect, and be by no means further disturbed, and that he wished the excavations to be stopped at once." This was practically the last interference with Layard's work on the part of the Mohammedan population. In accordance with the official request, the operations were discontinued until the general excitement in the town had somewhat subsided. Only two workmen were retained, who by the end of March discovered a second pair of winged human-headed lions, differing considerably in form from those previously unearthed, but likewise covered with very fine cuneiform inscriptions. Not many days afterwards, the much desired firmân was finally received from Constantinople. It was as comprehensive as possible, "authorizing the continuation of the excavations, and the removal of such objects as might be discovered."

One of the greatest difficulties so far encountered had now disappeared completely. Still, the necessary financial support was wanting, and Layard had to pursue his researches as best he could with the rapidly decreasing small means at his disposal. But bold as he was, and thoroughly enjoying the newly obtained privilege, he began at that very time to cut his first tentative trenches into the mound of Qoyunjuk, opposite Mosul. Notwithstanding all his poverty, and regardless of the French consul's unwarranted opposition, he continued his excavations on the southern face, where the mound was highest, for about a month, until he had convinced himself, from fragments of sculptures and inscribed bricks, "that the remains were those of a building contemporary, or nearly so, with Khorsabâd, and consequently of a more recent epoch than the most ancient palace of Nimrûd." Meanwhile, the almost intolerable heat of the Assyrian summer had commenced. Hot winds and flights of locusts soon destroyed what had been left of the green plants of the desert and the few patches of cultivation along the river. Yet Layard felt little inclined to yield to circumstances which drove even the Bedouins into more northern districts. He was still under the refreshing influence of a brief visit which, with a cheerful party of Christian and Mohammedan ladies and gentlemen from Mosul, he had paid to the principal shaikh of the Shammar and to the lonely ruins of El-Hadhr, on the west side of the Tigris, during the recent suspension of his work. No wonder, then, that, after his excavations at Qoyunjuk, he returned to Nimrûd again, and with about thirty men resumed his examination of the contents and extent of the large northwest building, which had previously furnished the well-preserved monuments. His Arabs, standing completely under the spell of his personal magnetism, seemed to feel as much interest in the objects disclosed as their enthusiastic master. As each head of all these strange figures was uncovered, "they showed their amazement by extravagant gestures or exclamations of surprise. If it was a bearded man, they concluded at once that it was an idol or a *jin*, and cursed or spat upon it. If a eunuch, they declared that it was the likeness of a beautiful female, and kissed or patted the cheek."

By the end of July so many fine bas-reliefs had been discovered in this building that Layard decided to make an effort to send a representative collection to England. Rawlinson's attempt at despatching the small steamer Nitocris, commanded by Felix Jones, directly to Nimrûd for their embarkation to Baghdad, failed. Layard was therefore obliged to follow Botta's example and forward the smaller sculptures, the weight of which was reduced by cutting from the back, on a raft to Basra, which they reached safely some time in August. The explorer's health began now visibly to suffer from continual exposure to the excessive heat. A week's stay at Mosul, during which he discovered a gateway flanked by two mutilated winged figures and cuneiform inscriptions with the name of Sennacherib in the northern boundary wall of Qoyunjuk, seemed to have refreshed him sufficiently to warrant his return to Nimrûd. He uncovered the tops of many more slabs, bearing either similar sculptures or having only the usual inscription across them; but before August was over it was very evident that he required a cooler climate to regain his former vigor. Leaving, therefore, a few guards at the mound to protect his antiquities, and accompanied by Rassam and a few servants and irregular soldiers, he departed to the Tiyâri Mountains, to the north of Mosul. The next two months were given entirely to rest and to his old favorite wanderings among the mountains and valleys of Kurdistân. The beautiful scenery and the exhilarating climate of these romantic districts, in which Kurdish tribes, Chaldean Christians, and the remarkable sect of the Yezîdis or "Worshippers of the Devil," followed each their peculiar habits and interesting customs, soon completely restored him to health.

Towards the end of October, after his return from an expedition into the Sinjâr Mountains, on which he had accompanied the pasha of Mosul and his soldiers, we find him again in the trenches of Nimrûd. Important changes had taken place during his absence with regard to the character of his excavations. So far they had been conducted as a private undertaking for the account of Sir Stratford Canning. Letters were now received from England advising him that the latter had presented the sculptures discovered in Assyrian ruins, together with all the privileges connected with the imperial firmân, to the British nation. In consequence of this generous act of the ambassador, a grant of funds had been placed at the disposal of the British Museum "for the continuation of the researches commenced at Nimrûd and elsewhere." This part of the news was encouraging, but, alas, the grant was very small, considerably smaller than the sum given by the French government to Botta for the exploration of Khorsabâd. And the British grant was to include even "private expenses, those of carriage, and many extraordinary outlays inevitable in the East." But though the funds were scarcely adequate to the objects in view, Layard accepted the charge of superintending the excavations, and made every exertion to procure as many antiquities as possible. In the interest of science it remains a cause of deep regret that after his great discoveries, Layard did not at once find the same hearty support in England as his more fortunate French colleague so speedily had obtained in Paris. Not even an artist was despatched to draw the sculptures and copy the inscriptions, though many of the monuments "were in too dilapidated a condition to be removed," and though Layard "had neither knowledge nor experience as a draughtsman, — a disqualification which he could scarcely hope to overcome." He was thus practically prevented by his own government from making a methodical exploration of Nimrûd. And this lack of method, system, and thoroughness unfortunately remained a characteristic feature of most of the following English excavations in Assyrian and Babylonian ruins, — a lack felt by nobody more keenly than by Layard, Loftus, and all the other great British explorers. Let us hear what Layard himself has to say on this system of unscientific pillage, justified to a certain degree only at the beginning of his excavations, but entirely to be condemned as soon as they were carried on under the auspices of a great nation. "The smallness of the sum placed at my disposal compelled me to follow the same plan in the excavations that I had hitherto adopted — *viz.*, to dig trenches along the sides of the chambers, and to expose the whole of the slabs, without removing the earth from the centre. Thus, few of the chambers were fully explored, and many small objects of great interest may have been left undiscovered. As I was directed to bury the building with earth after I had explored it, to avoid unnecessary expense I filled up the chambers with the rubbish taken from those subsequently uncovered, having first examined the walls, copied the inscriptions, and drawn the sculptures." From many other similar passages in his books we quote only the following two, in which he complains: "As the means at my disposal did not warrant any outlay in making more experiments without the promise of the discovery of something to carry away, I felt myself compelled, much against my inclination, to abandon the excavations in this part of the mound, after uncovering portions of two chambers." Or again: "If, after carrying a trench to a reasonable depth and distance, no remains of sculpture or inscription appeared, I abandoned it and renewed the experiment elsewhere."

In view of the unsatisfactory manner in which the excavations at Nimrûd were now conducted, it would be an exceedingly unpleasant task to follow Layard into all the different trenches which he cut at many parts of the mound for no other purpose than to obtain the largest possible number of well-preserved objects of art at the least possible outlay of time and money. The winter season was fast approaching. In order to protect himself sufficiently against the dangers of the climate and the thievish inclinations of the marauding Bedouins, he constructed his own house in the plain near the ruins, and settled the Arab workmen with their families and friends around this temporary abode. Fifty strong Nestorian Christians, who wielded the pickaxe in the trenches, were quartered with their wives and children in a house on the mound itself. By the first of November the excavations were recommenced on a large scale at different sections: at the northwest and southwest buildings, in the centre of the mound, near the gigantic bulls mentioned above; in the southeast corner, where no walls as yet had been discovered, and in other parts of the ruins hitherto unexamined. The first six weeks following this new arrangement "were amongst the most prosperous and fruitful in events" during all his researches in Assyria. Scarcely a day passed by without some new and important discovery. The trenches carried to a considerable depth in the southeast corner yielded at first nothing but inscribed bricks and pottery and several clay coffins of a late period; but those in the southwest palace brought to light a number of very valuable antiquities. Among other relics of the past, Layard found a crouching lion in alabaster, a pair of winged lions in a coarse limestone, the bodies of two lions carved out of one stone and forming a pedestal; the statues of two exquisite but crumbling sphinxes, and several interesting bas-reliefs uniting the head of an eagle or a lion with the body and arms of a man. He could now definitely prove that the slabs hitherto found in this section of the mound, and originally chiefly brought from the northwest edifice, were never meant to be exposed to view in the later palace. "They were, in fact, placed against the wall of sun-dried bricks, and the back of the slab, smoothed preparatory to being resculptured, was turned towards the interior of the chambers." In order to ascertain, therefore, the name of the king who built this palace, he had to dig behind the slabs. By continuing his researches in this new light, he soon found cuneiform inscriptions which bore the name of Esarhaddon, king of Assyria (2 Kings 19:37).

Important as all these discoveries turned out to be, they were far surpassed by his finds in two other sections of the ruins. In the largest room of the northwest palace, which apparently had served as the royal reception hall, a series of the most beautiful and most interesting sculptures were brought to light, glorifying King Ashurnâsirapal (885–860 B. C.) in war and peace. All the scenes are realistic and full of life, executed with great care and spirit. Here the monarch is followed by his warriors, himself standing in a chariot and discharging arrows, while enemies are tumbling from their horses or falling from the turrets of a besieged city; there, in a boat, he is crossing a river full of tortoises and fishes, and lined with date-groves and gardens; then, again, he receives the prisoners, led by warriors and counted by scribes, or he is returning victoriously in procession, followed by his army and preceded by musicians and standard-bearers, while above them fly vultures with human heads in their talons. In other smaller chambers close by the principal hall, Layard found a number of bottles in glass and alabaster, bearing the name and titles of Sargon, who lived 150 years later, and, furthermore, he rescued from the rubbish sixteen copper lions, having served as weights, and a large quantity of iron scales of Assyrian armor and several perfect helmets in copper, immediately falling to pieces, which in a welcome manner helped to interpret the sculptures on the walls.

It was in the central building, however, that one of the most remarkable and important discoveries awaited the explorer. From a brick which apparently contained the genealogy of the builder,[1] he concluded correctly at once that this third palace had been constructed by "the son of the founder of the earlier [northwest] edifice." He next came upon slabs with gigantic winged figures, and upon the fragments of a large winged bull in yellow limestone. The trench had reached the considerable length of fifty feet without yielding any valuable antiquity, and Layard was already planning to abandon his researches in this part of the mound as fruitless, when suddenly an obelisk of black marble, nearly seven feet high, lying on its side, but in admirable preservation, was unearthed by his workmen. It was the famous obelisk of King Shalmaneser II. (860–825 B. C.), who had erected this stele of victory in his palace to commemorate the leading military events of his government. Sculptured on all four sides, it shows twenty small bas-reliefs, and above, below, and between them 210 lines of cuneiform inscription, containing the interesting passage above the second series of reliefs: "I received the tribute of Jehu, son of Omrî, silver, gold, etc." (comp. 1 Kings 19:16, *seq.;* 2 Kings, chaps. 9 and 10).

[1] As Layard was able to determine from the repeated occurrence of the two cuneiform signs for "son" and "king," which even then had been recognized as such by the decipherers.

The Black Obelisk of Shalmaneser II.

Until the present day this black obelisk has remained one of the choicest historical monuments ever rescued from the mounds of Assyria. Layard was not slow in recognizing the exceptional value of this precious relic. It was at once packed carefully, and a gang of trustworthy Arabs were placed near it at night, until shortly afterwards, on Christmas day, 1846, with twenty-two other cases of antiquities, it could be safely sent to Rawlinson, who, a few months later, wrote the first tentative exposition of the contents of its inscription.[1]

The first four months of 1847 were devoted principally to the exploration of the large northwest palace of Ashurnâsir-apal, where the sculptures and inscriptions, not having been exposed to a conflagration, as a rule were found in admirable preservation. By the end of April, Layard had explored twenty-eight halls and chambers, sometimes painted with figures and ornaments on a thin coating of plaster, but more frequently cased with alabaster slabs representing the monarch's wars and hunting expeditions, large winged figures

[1] In a letter addressed to the Royal Asiatic Society, dated June 19, 1847.

separated by the sacred tree, various religious ceremonies, and elaborate scroll-work. Besides these larger monuments, he discovered numerous smaller objects of art, such as ivory ornaments betraying Egyptian origin or influence, three lions' paws in copper, different vases in clay and metal, and many baked bricks elaborately painted with animals, flowers, and cuneiform characters, which apparently had decorated the walls above the sculptures.

In the ruins of the central edifice, which, with the northwest palace, had been used as a quarry to supply material for the southwest palace, he uncovered over one hundred sculptured slabs "packed in rows, one against the other," and "placed in a regular series, according to the subjects upon them." Nearly all the trenches which he opened in different parts of the mound, particularly, also, in the southeast corner and near the west edge, exposed to view traces of buildings, brick pavements, remains of walls and chambers, and fragments of sculptures. In his endeavor "to ascertain the nature of the wall surrounding the inner buildings," he found it to be nearly fifty feet thick, constructed of sun-dried bricks, and in its centre containing the first Assyrian arch ever discovered.

Until the end of April, thirteen pairs of the gigantic winged bulls and lions and several fragments of others had rewarded his labors. The authorities in London, not contemplating the removal of any of these enormous sculptures for the present, had determined that they "should not be sawn into pieces, to be put together again in Europe, as the pair of bulls sent from Khorsabâd to Paris," but that they were to remain at Nimrûd covered with earth, "until some favorable opportunity of moving them entire might occur." But Layard was not the man to leave behind the most imposing of all the monuments unearthed, without making a serious effort to ship them. Accordingly he selected one of the best-preserved smaller bulls and a similar lion, and strained his brain and resources to the utmost to move them. With infinite toil and skill he succeeded.[1] On the 22d of April, the two large monuments, with the finest bas-reliefs and above thirty cases of smaller objects found in the ruins, as a third cargo, left the mound on rafts for Basra, where they arrived safely, and were transshipped later to England. According to the instructions received from the trustees of the British Museum, the Assyrian palaces, which for a short while had been exposed to the light of day, as the last remains of the Biblical city of Calah (Gen. 10 : 11), telling their wonderful stories of human glory and decay, were soon reburied.[2]

By the middle of May, Layard had finished his work and left Nimrûd. But he did not quit the banks of the Tigris without having opened trenches at two other ruins. In the course of the first months of 1847, he had found an opportunity to visit the mound of Qal'at Shirgât, notoriously dangerous as "a place of rendezvous for all plundering parties." A first general description of the ruins had been given by Ainsworth,[3] with whom he had explored this neighborhood seven years before. The large extent of the mounds, which in size compare favorably with those of Nimrûd and Qoyunjuk, and "a tradition current amongst the Arabs that strange figures carved in black stone still existed among the ruins," had excited his curiosity anew. He therefore sent a few gangs of Arab workmen down the river to excavate at the most promising points. Shortly afterwards he himself followed, spending two days at the ruins in company with a shaikh of the Jebûr, who was in search of fresh pastures for the flocks of his tribe. The hasty excavations, carried on

[1] Comp. the illustration facing p. 93.

[2] "The present surface of Nimrûd is a picture of utter destruction," many of the slabs and sculptures which could not be removed being only half buried. Comp. Sachau, *Am Euphrat und Tigris*, Leipzig, 1900, p. 105.

[3] In the "Journal of the Royal Geographical Society," vol. xi.

principally on the western side of the mound, brought to light only a mutilated but very interesting sitting figure in black basalt, of life size, and on three sides covered with a cuneiform inscription of Shalmaneser II., inscribed bricks of the same ruler, bits of boundary stones, fragments of slabs with cuneiform characters, and a few tombs with their usual contents belonging to a late period. Layard tried to have researches at this much exposed site continued under the superintendence of a Nestorian Christian, even after his departure, but repeated attacks from the Bedouins forced his workmen soon to withdraw. The sitting figure, as the first Assyrian statue discovered, was later sent by Mr. Ross, whom we have mentioned above, to London.

A small sum of money still remained after Layard had closed his trenches at Nimrûd. He proposed, therefore, to devote it to a renewed personal search for the ruins of Nineveh in the mounds opposite Mosul. The prejudices of the Mohammedan population forbidding explorations at Nebî Yûnus, as we have seen in connection with Botta's attempts, he devoted a month of concentrated attention to the mound of Qoyunjuk, where he had cut a few trenches in the previous year. His Arab basket men pitched their tents on the summit of the mound, the Nestorian diggers at its foot, while he himself spent the nights in the town and the days in the field. Well acquainted with the nature and position of Assyrian palaces as he was from his experience at Nimrûd, he now set to work at first to discover the platform of sun-dried bricks upon which large edifices were generally constructed. At a depth of twenty feet he reached it, as he had expected. His next move was to open long trenches to its level in different directions near the southwest corner, until one morning the workmen came upon a wall, and following it, found an entrance formed by winged bulls, and leading into a hall. After four weeks' labor, nine long and narrow chambers of a large building destroyed by fire had been explored. In consequence of the conflagration most of the bas-reliefs, about ten feet high and from eight to nine feet wide, and four pairs of human-headed winged bulls, all of which had lined the walls, were reduced to lime. Perfect inscriptions were not very numerous, except on the bricks. But enough of the writing remained to show that Layard had discovered the first Assyrian palace in the long-forgotten and ruined city of Nineveh. The monuments were too much destroyed to think of their removal. "A fisherman fishing with hook and line in a pond" was almost the only fragment of sculpture which Layard could send home as a first specimen of Assyrian art from Sennacherib's palace at Nineveh. Two more chambers, several other slabs, and a fairly preserved boundary stone with a long inscription were soon afterwards discovered by Ross in another wing of the same building.

On the 24th of June, 1847, Layard, accompanied by Rassam, left Mosul to return to Constantinople and England. The ruins which he had examined were, to quote his own words, "very inadequately explored." But with all his enthusiasm, energy, and constant exposure to dangers, he could do no better, considering the very small means at his disposal and the demands made upon him. After nearly two years of solid labor the tangible results were enormous. He had identified the sites of the Biblical Calah (Nimrûd) and Nineveh, the capital of the Assyrian empire (in part represented by Ḳoyunjuk), as the inscriptions unearthed soon taught us. Moreover, he had discovered remains of no less than eight Assyrian palaces. At Nimrûd, he found the northwest palace constructed by Ashurnâsirapal I. (885–860 B. C.), and, in part at least, restored and reoccupied by Sargon (722–705 B. C.); the central palace erected by Shalmaneser II. (860–825 B. C.), and rebuilt almost entirely by the Biblical Pul or Tiglath-Pileser III. (745–727 B. C.); [1]

[1] The great inscribed bulls and the black obelisk belonged to the older

between these two, at the west edge of the mound, a smaller palace of Adadnirâri III. (812–783 B. C.); in the southwest corner the palace of Esarhaddon (681–668 B. C.), who largely employed older materials from the northwest and central palaces; and in the southeast corner the insignificant remains of a building of Ashuretililâni (after 626 B. C.), grandson of Esarhaddon and one of the last rulers of the Assyrian empire. And in addition to these seven palaces at Calah, he had discovered and partly excavated the large palace of Sennacherib (705–681 B. C.) at Nineveh. Indeed, he had accomplished a glorious work — and a munificent gift from the British nation awaited him at home. "As a reward for my various services and for my discoveries, I was appointed an unpaid attaché of Her Majesty's Embassy at Constantinople."[1]

It was not until the spring of 1848 that Layard received orders to proceed to his new post in Turkey. The half-year immediately preceding his departure for the Bosphorus was principally devoted to the preparation of the narrative[2] of his first expedition, and to supervising the printing of the illustrations of the monuments[3] and of the copies of the inscriptions[4] recovered. These books, published during his absence from England, created an extraordinary impression throughout Europe, far beyond anything he could ever have dreamed of. It was in particular his popular narrative,

king, while the series of over one hundred slabs, representing battles and sieges, and arranged as if ready for removal (comp. p. 108), formed part of the decorations of the palace of Tiglath-Pileser III.

[1] Comp. Austen H. Layard, "Early Adventures in Persia, Susiana, and Babylonia," 2d ed., London, 1894, p. 426 (the closing words of the whole book).

[2] Layard, "Nineveh and its Remains, a Narrative of a First Expedition to Nineveh," London, 1848.

[3] Layard, "The Monuments of Nineveh, from Drawings Made on the Spot," series i., 100 plates, London, 1849.

[4] Layard, "Inscriptions in the Cuneiform Character from Assyrian Monuments," 98 plates, London, 1851.

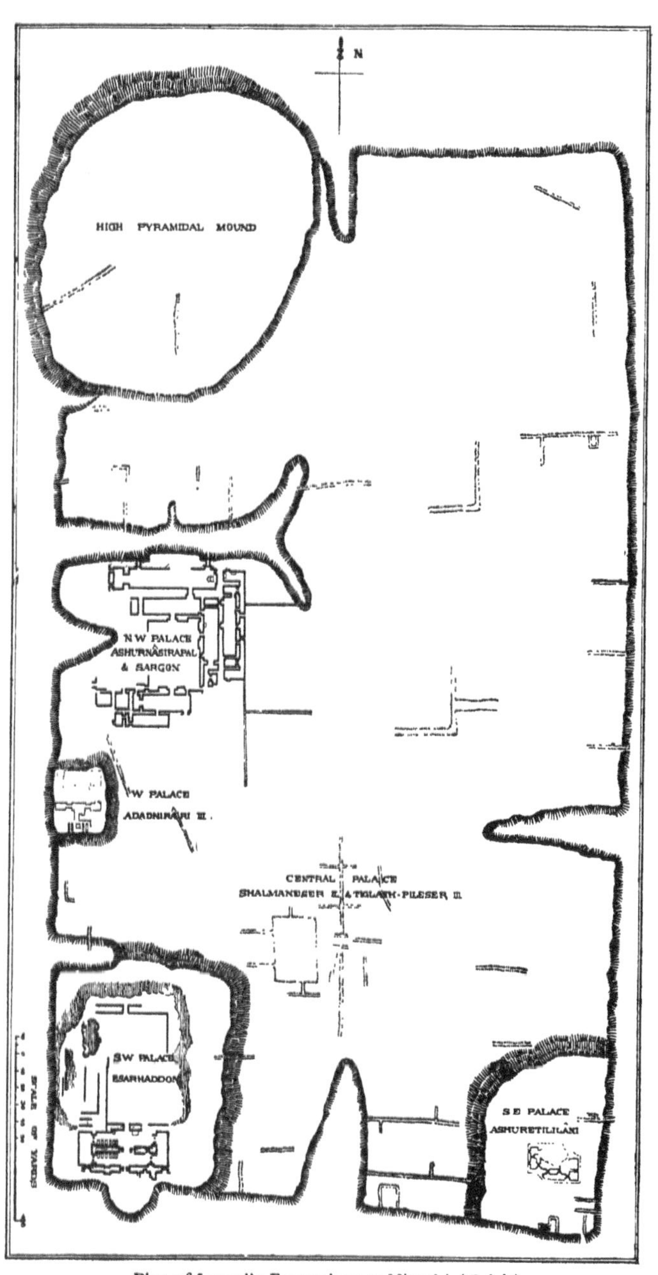

Plan of Layard's Excavations at Nimrûd (Calah)

written almost in the style of a fascinating novel, enlivened by the numerous stories of his difficulties and adventures, and interwoven with faithful accounts of the habits and customs of many different tribes, which had a marvellous success with the public. Though entirely unfamiliar with the contents of the cuneiform inscriptions, he had a rare gift of combination, and he understood in a masterly manner how to interpret the sculptures on the walls of the Assyrian palaces, and to illustrate the Scriptures and profane writers from these long-buried sources. The pressure of public opinion was now brought to bear upon the British government. Before many months had passed, Layard received an urgent request from the British Museum to lead a second expedition to Nineveh, and he readily consented to go.

Second Expedition, 1849–1851. This time, Layard was better assisted and equipped with funds than previously. F. Cooper, a competent artist, had been selected to draw those bas-reliefs and sculptures which injury and decay had rendered unfit for removal, and Dr. Sandwith, a physician, who was on a visit to the East, was soon induced to join his party. Accompanied by these two Englishmen and by Hormuzd Rassam, his former faithful companion, he left Constantinople on the 28th of August, 1849, by a British steamer bound for the Black Sea. Three days later they disembarked and took the direct land route to Mosul *via* Erzerum and Lake Wan. On the first of October they were at Qoyunjuk again. Since Layard's return to Europe in 1847, little had been done at these ruins. For a short while Mr. Ross, an English merchant of Mosul, had conducted excavations on a small scale, as mentioned above, and after his departure from the town, Christian Rassam, the British vice-consul, had placed a few workmen in the abandoned trenches at the request of the trustees of the British Museum, "rather to retain possession of the spot, and to prevent interference on the part of others, than to carry on extensive operations." By the middle of October, Layard had finished the necessary preparations and resumed active work at the mound with a force of about one hundred men. In order to save time and labor he changed the method of excavating formerly employed. Instead of carrying away all the rubbish from the surface down to the platform, he began to tunnel along the walls, sinking shafts at intervals to admit light, air, and the descending workmen, and "removing only as much earth as was necessary to show the sculptured walls." It is clear that under such circumstances the examination of the buried halls and chambers was even less thorough than it had been previously at Nimrûd, as their centres had to be left standing to prevent the narrow subterranean passages from collapsing under the pressure from above. Small objects of art were accordingly found very rarely, their discovery being due more to a fortunate accident than to a methodical search.

As soon as the excavations in the mounds opposite Mosul had been fairly started, Layard and Hormuzd Rassam hurried to Nimrûd, where operations were simultaneously conducted until the end of spring, 1850. Work was resumed in the four principal sections of the mound which had yielded so many antiquities during the first expedition, but trenches were now also opened in the remaining parts of the ruins. It was particularly the high conical mound at the northwest corner and the adjacent northern edge of the large plateau which received greater attention than had hitherto been possible. One morning, shortly after his arrival, while ascending the mound, Layard found an unexpected visitor in his trenches. In glancing downward from the summit of the ruins, he discovered Rawlinson on the floor of an excavated chamber, "wrapped in his travelling cloak, deep in sleep, and wearied by a long and harassing night's ride." After an absence of more than twenty-two years from England, this gallant officer was on his way home. Accompanied by a single servant, he had made the trip from Baghdad to Mosul, generally counted eight to twelve days, in less than seventy-two hours, a feat reminding us vividly of his famous ride between Poonah and Panwell,[1] when still a young and ambitious lieutenant in India (1832). Unfortunately, in the present case, Rawlinson's extraordinary exertion, at a time when his health had suffered considerably from hard mental work and the effect of a semi-tropical climate, proved too much for his weakened constitution. For several days he was seriously ill at Mosul, unable to do more than to pay a hasty visit to Layard's excavations before his departure.

The work at Qoyunjuk and Nimrûd proceeded regularly under the supervision of efficient native overseers. No longer embarrassed by those difficulties and molestations from the governor and the inhabitants of the country which had taxed their patience and energy so often during the previous campaign, Layard and Rassam spent their time generally between the two places, unless absent on one of their numerous exploration tours to the Sinjâr and the banks of the Khâbûr, to Khorsabâd and Bâviân, to the rock sculptures of Gunduk, and the cuneiform inscriptions of Wan, to the ruins of Babylon and Nuffar, or to any of the different Assyrian sites in their immediate neighborhood. Following the example of Layard, who wisely abstained from relating, day by day, the further progress of his labors, we will now sketch briefly the principal discoveries which characterized the English operations in the two great ruins of Nineveh and Calah during the years 1849–51.

The ruins of Qoyunjuk had practically been only scratched by Botta and Layard in their nervous attempts at disclosing sculptured remains in some part of the large mound. It was now decided to submit the whole complex to an

[1] Distance, 72 miles; time occupied, 3 hours, 7 minutes.

examination by experimental shafts and trial trenches, and to make the excavation of the southwest palace of Qoyunjuk the chief object of the present campaign. Like the southwest edifice at Nimrûd, the latter had been destroyed by fire, when the Median armies, murdering and pillaging, entered the gates of Nineveh (606 B. C.). Consequently, hundreds of the most elaborate sculptures were found cracked and broken, or almost entirely reduced to lime. Yet many had more or less escaped the results of the great conflagration, thus allowing the explorer to determine the spirited scenes which once adorned the walls of the principal chambers. Battles and victories, sieges and conquests, hunting scenes and sacrifices to the gods, were again the leading representations. But in the general conception of the subject, in the treatment of the costumes worn by the Assyrian

The Ruins of Nineveh, from the North

warriors, as well as by the subdued nations, in the character of the ornaments, in the arrangement of the inscriptions, and in many other important details, there is a marked difference between the bas-reliefs in the palace of Sennacherib and those of the older palaces at Nimrûd. There the sculptured slabs showed large figures or simple groups, divided into two friezes, an upper and a lower one, by intervening inscriptions, "the subject being frequently confined to one tablet, and arranged with some attempt at composition, so as to form a separate picture." Here the four walls of a chamber were generally adorned "by one series of sculptures, representing a consecutive history, uninterrupted by inscriptions, or by the divisions in the alabaster panelling." Short epigraphs or labels, as a rule placed on the upper part of the stones, give the names of the conquered country, city, and even of the principal prisoners and historical events pictured below. Hundreds of figures cover the face of the slabs from top to bottom. We become acquainted with the peculiarities, in type and dress, of foreign nations, and the characteristic features and products of their lands; we are introduced into the very life and occupations of the persons represented. The sculptor shows us the Babylonian swamps with their jungles of tall reeds, frequented by wild boars, and barbarous tribes skimming over the waters in their light boats of wicker-work, exactly as they are used to-day by the inhabitants of the same marshes; or he takes us into the high mountains of Kurdistân, covered with trees and crowned with castles, endeavoring even to convey the idea of a valley by reversing the trees and mountains on one side of the stream, which is filled with fishes and crabs and turtles. He indicates the different headgear worn by female musicians, or by captive women carried with their husbands and children to Nineveh. Some wear their hair in long ringlets, some platted or braided, some confined in a net; others are characterized by hoods fitting close over their heads, others by a kind of turban; Elamite ladies have their hair in curls falling on their shoulders, and bound above the temples by a band or fillet, while those from Syria wear a high conical headdress, similar to that which is frequently found to-day in those regions. It is impossible to enter into all the details so faithfully represented. Without the knowledge of a single cuneiform character, we learned the principal events of Sennacherib's government, and from a mere study of those sculptured walls we got familiar with the customs and habits of the ancient Assyrians, at the same time obtaining a first clear glance of the whole civilization of Western Asia.

How much the interpretation of the Old Testament books profited from Layard's epoch-making discoveries, we can scarcely realize fully after we have been under the powerful influence which went forth from the resurrected palaces of Qoyunjuk since the earliest days of our childhood. Being written in a language closely akin to Assyrian, and compiled by men brought up in the same atmosphere and surroundings, they frequently describe the very institutions, customs, and deeds so vividly portrayed on the alabaster slabs of Nineveh. But it was not only through analogy and comparison that so many obscure words and passages in the Scriptures received fresh light and often an entirely new meaning, — sometimes the very same persons and events mentioned in the historical and prophetical books of the Bible were depicted on those monuments or recorded in their accompanying inscriptions. We refer only to the fine series of thirteen slabs adorning the walls of a room nearly in the centre of the great southwest wing of Sennacherib's palace. Seated upon his throne in the hilly districts of Southern Palestine, and surrounded by his formidable army, is the Assyrian king, attired in his richly embroidered robes. In the distance severe fighting is still going on, archers and slingers and spearmen attack a fortified city, defended by the besieged with great determination. But part of the place has been taken. Beneath its walls are seen Assyrian warriors impaling their prisoners or flaying them alive, while from the gateway of a tower issues a long procession of captives, camels and carts laden with women and children and spoil, advancing towards the monarch. Above the head of the king we read the inscription: "Sennacherib, king of the Universe, king of Assyria, sat upon a throne and reviewed the spoil of the city of Lachish."[1]

The discovery of so many priceless sculptures in more than seventy rooms, halls, and galleries of the palace of one of the greatest monarchs of the ancient East forms a most striking result of Layard's second expedition to Nineveh. Indeed these bas-reliefs alone would have sufficed to make his name immortal, and to place his work in the trenches of Ḳoyunjuk far above the average archæological explorations in Assyrian and Babylonian mounds. And yet they represent only half of what was actually obtained. No less remarkable, and in many respects of even greater importance for the founding and developing of the young Assyriological science, was another discovery, which at first may have seemed rather insignificant in the light of those magnificent sculptures. We know from the cuneiform inscriptions of Sennacherib's grandson, Ashurbânapal, that the southwest palace of Nineveh, which thousands of captives from all the conquered nations of Western Asia, under the rod of their merciless taskmasters, had erected on the gigantic platform at the confluence of the Tigris and the Khôsar, was largely repaired and for some time occupied by this last great ruler of a great empire. So far as Layard's excavations, however, went to show, there remained very few complete sculptures of this monarch[2] which escaped the general destruction, while many fragments of inscribed slabs testified to his extensive work at that building. But though

[1] Comp. 2 Kings 18 : 13, *seq.*, 19 : 8, and the parallel passages, Is. 36 : 1, *seq.*, 27 : 8.

[2] Prominent among them are six fossiliferous limestone slabs adorned with scenes of his Elamitic war. These slabs, however, belonged originally to the older palace, as the name and titles of Sennacherib on the back of each bas-relief indicate. Ashurbânapal therefore adopted the same method in repairing his grandfather's building as was followed by his father, Esarhaddon, with regard to his own palace at Calah, almost entirely constructed of older material. Comp. Layard, "Nineveh and Babylon," p. 459.

the bas-reliefs which once announced his battles and victories to the people have long ago crumbled away, there were found in another section of the same southern wing of Sennacherib's palace those precious relics which will hand down from generation to generation the name of Ashurbânapal as that of a great patron of art and literature, and as the powerful monarch "instructed in the wisdom of the god Nebo."

One day Layard came upon two small chambers, opening into each other, and once panelled with sculptured slabs, most of which had been destroyed. But in removing the earth and rubbish from their interior he recognized that "to the height of a foot or more from the floor they were entirely filled with cuneiform tablets of baked clay, some entire, but the greater part broken into many fragments." He had discovered part of the famous royal library of Nineveh founded and maintained by the kings of the last Assyrian empire (about 720–620 B. C.), the other half being later unearthed by Rassam in Ashurbânapal's north palace at Qoyunjuk. It was especially the last-mentioned king (668–626 B. C.) who "enlarged and enriched the collection of tablets which his predecessors had brought together, in such a way as to constitute them into a veritable library, by the addition of hundreds, even thousands of documents . . . dealing with every branch of learning and science known to the wise men of his day."[1] These tablets, when complete, varying in length from one inch to fifteen inches, were made of the

[1] Comp. Bezold, "Catalogue of the Cuneiform Tablets in the Kouyunjik Collection of the British Museum," vol. v. (London, 1899), p. xiii. The statement made by Bezold on p. xiv. of this volume, "that in 1849 and 1850 Layard discovered the palace of Ashurbânapal," though found in other Assyriological publications, is as erroneous as another view found, *e. g.*, in Delitzsch's writings (comp. *Mürdter's Geschichte Babyloniens und Assyriens*, Calw and Stuttgart, 2nd ed. 1891, p. 5, or *Ex Oriente Lux*, Leipzig, 1898, p. 6) that it was only Rassam who discovered Ashurbânapal's library. This library was stored in two palaces and discovered by both Layard (southwest palace) and Rassam (north palace).

finest clay, and inscribed with the most minute but singularly sharp and well defined cuneiform writing. Their contents are as varied and different as the forms and sizes of the fragments themselves. There are historical records and chronological lists which make us acquainted with the chief events and the number of years of the governments of many Assyrian kings; there are astronomical reports and observations, mathematical calculations, tables of measures of length and capacity, which reveal to us a branch of science in which the Babylonians and Assyrians excelled all other nations of the ancient world; there are hundreds of hymns and psalms, prayers and oracles, mythological texts and incantations, in their poetical expression and depth of religious feeling often not inferior to the best Hebrew poetry; there are letters and addresses from kings and ministers, officers, and private persons, which deal with military expeditions, the revolts of subdued enemies, the payment of tribute, the administration of provinces, the repairing of buildings, the digging of canals, the purchase of horses, the complaints of unjust treatment or taxation, the transport of winged bulls, the calling in of a physician to prescribe for a lady of the court, and many other interesting details. By far the larger mass of the tablets discovered treat of astrology, and of the subjects of medicine and religious observations so closely connected with this pseudo-science. Not the least important tablets in the whole collection are those lists of cuneiform signs and syllabaries, lists of months, plants, stones, animals, temples, gods, cities, mountains and countries, etc., lists of synonyms, verbal forms, and other grammatical exercises, and a large number of bilingual texts which formed and still form the chief source for the reconstruction of the Assyrian and Sumerian grammars and lexicons. In view of such important and startling discoveries, the many smaller results which crowned Layard's archæological researches at Nineveh — I refer only to his large collection of fine seals and seal-impressions,[1] to his determination of the northwest city gate, and to his accidental discovery of chambers of Esarhaddon's palace at the southern mound of Nebî-Yûnus[2] — may well be passed over.

The excavations at Nimrûd, started at the high conical mound in the northwest corner, were also accompanied by results of considerable interest and value. By means of tunnels the workmen had soon reached a part of solid masonry, forming the substructure for the upper part of a massive building. From a comparison of this ruin with the similar high-towering mounds at Khorsabâd, El-Birs, and other Babylonian sites, it is evident that Layard had found the remains of the *ziggurrat* or stage-tower of Calah, at first wrongly regarded by him and Rawlinson as "the tomb of Sardanapalus." Immediately adjoining this tower were two small temples erected by Ashurnâsirapal II., and separated from each other by a staircase or inclined passage leading up to the platform from the north. They were built of sun-dried brick coated with plaster, and besides clay images and fragments of other idols contained a number of valuable sculptures, bas-reliefs, and inscribed slabs, which had adorned their principal entrances. One of the recesses at the end of a chamber was paved with one enormous limestone slab measuring no less than 21 feet by 16 feet 7 inches by 1 foot 1 inch, and completely covered with cuneiform inscriptions recording the wars and campaigns of the ruler, and full of geographical information, but also of disgusting details of the cruel punishments inflicted upon the unfortunate conquered nations. A similar great monolith was found in the second

[1] The well-known Hittite, Egyptian, and Aramean seal-impressions on clay being among them. Comp. Layard, *l. c.*, pp. 153–161.

[2] Where he had offered to a Moslem property owner to dig underground summer apartments for him, through one of his agents, on condition that he should have all the antiquities discovered during the excavations.

temple, and in the earth above it the entire statue of the monarch, with the following self-glorifying inscription, running across his breast: "Ashurnâsirapal, the great king, the powerful king, king of the Universe, king of Assyria, son of Tuklat-Ninib, the great king, the powerful king, king of the Universe, king of Assyria, son of Adadnirâri, the great king, the powerful king, king of the Universe, king of Assyria, the conqueror from beyond the Tigris to the Lebanon and the Great Sea [Mediterranean] — all the countries from the rising of the sun to the setting thereof he subdued under his feet."

Of no less importance, though of a different character, was a discovery in the northwest palace. Near the west edge of the mound the workmen came accidentally upon a chamber built by Ashurnâsirapal, which probably served as a storeroom. In one corner was a well nearly sixty feet deep, while in other parts of the room there were found twelve huge copper vessels partly filled with smaller objects. Beneath and behind these caldrons were heaped without order large masses of copper and bronze vessels, arms (shields, swords, daggers, heads of spears and arrows), iron implements, such as picks, saws, hammers, etc., glass bowls, ivory relics, and several entire elephants' tusks. In another corner of this interesting chamber had stood the royal throne, carved in wood and cased with elaborate bronze ornaments. It was badly decayed, but enough remained to ascertain that it resembled in shape the chairs of state represented on the slabs of Khorsabâd and Qoyunjuk, and particularly that on which Sennacherib is seated while reviewing the captives and spoil of the city of Lachish. About one hundred and fifty bronze vessels of different sizes and shapes, and eighty small bells in the same metal, could be sent to the British Museum. As many of the former were in a fine state of preservation and remarkable for the beauty of their design, being ornamented with the embossed or incised figures of men, animals, trees, and flowers, they constitute a most valuable collection of representative specimens of ancient metallurgy. A great many of the objects discovered are doubtless of Assyrian origin; others may have formed part

Bronze Plate from Nimrûd (Calah)

of the spoil of some conquered nation, or perhaps they were made by foreign artists brought captive to the banks of the Tigris.

Omitting an enumeration of the numerous fragments of interesting sculptures and of other minor antiquities [1] excavated at Nimrûd during the second expedition, we mention only the fact that in the southeast corner of the mound

[1] *E. g.*, a weight in the shape of a duck discovered in the northwest palace, and bearing the inscription: "30 standard mana, palace of Erba-Marduk, king of Babylon" — a king otherwise unknown.

Layard disclosed the remains of an earlier building[1] and a solitary brick arch beneath the palace or temple constructed by Ashuretililâni, while in the ramparts of earth marking the walls of Calah, he traced fifty-eight towers to the north, and about fifty to the east, at the same time establishing the existence of a number of approaches or stairways on the four different sides of the enclosed platform.

In addition to his successful excavations at Nineveh and Calah, and to his less fortunate operations at Babylon and Nuffar, about which we shall have to say a few words later, Layard, either himself or through one of his native agents, cut trial trenches into various other mounds, extending his researches even as far west as the Khâbûr. Most of these examinations were carried on too hastily and without method, and therefore have little value, while others, like those carried on in the mounds of Bahshîqa, Karamles, Lak, Shemâmyk, Sherîf Khan, Abû Mârya, and ʻArbân, yielded inscribed bricks or slabs from which the Assyrian origin of these ruins could be established. At Sherîf Khan, on the Tigris, three miles to the north of Qoyunjuk, he discovered even remains of two Assyrian temples and inscribed limestone slabs from a palace which Esarhaddon had erected for his son, Ashurbânapal, at Tarbisu; at Qalʻat Shirgât he gathered fragments of two large octagonal terra-cotta prisms of Tiglath-Pileser I. (about 1100 B. C.); and at ʻArbân, on the Biblical Habor, he conducted personal excavations for three weeks, bringing to light two pairs of winged bulls, a large lion with extended jaws, similar to those found in one of the small temples at Nimrûd, and pieces of carved stone and painted brick — all belonging to the "palace" of a man otherwise unknown, who, to judge from his style of art, must have lived about the time of Ashurnâsirapal II.

[1] Constructed by Shalmaneser II., as was proved by George Smith more than twenty years later. Comp. his "Assyrian Discoveries," 3d ed., New York, 1876, pp. 76–79.

During this second expedition Layard and the other members of his staff suffered from fever and ague considerably more than previously. Before the first summer had fairly commenced, both Dr. Sandwith and Mr. Cooper were seriously ill and had to return to Europe. Another artist was sent by the British Musem, but a few months after his arrival he was drowned in the Gômal at the foot of Sennacherib's sculptures at Bâviân (July, 1851). Layard and Rassam alone braved and withstood the inhospitable climate until their funds were exhausted. More than one hundred and twenty large cases of sculptures, tablets, and other antiquities had been sent down to Baghdad, awaiting examination by Rawlinson previous to their shipment to England. Finally, on April 28, 1851, the two explorers themselves turned from the ruins of Nineveh, rich in new honors and yet "with a heavy heart." Two years later Layard submitted the results of his latest researches to the public,[1] and for the first time was able to interweave the fascinating story of his work and wanderings with numerous quotations from the Assyrian inscriptions so admirably interpreted by Rawlinson and by Hincks. His nomadic days had now come to an end. He did not visit again the mounds of Nineveh and Babylon. The enthusiastic reception of his books all over Europe, and the extraordinary services which he had rendered to the cause of science and art in his own country, secured for him at last that recognition from his government to which he was entitled. But though no longer active in the field of Assyrian exploration, where he occupies the foremost position, he never lost his interest in the continuation of this work by others, and twenty-four years later (1877), as Her Majesty's ambassador at Constantinople, he supported Rassam with the same

[1] Comp. Layard, "Discoveries in the Ruins of Nineveh and Babylon," London, 1853; and the same author's "The Monuments of Nineveh," series ii., 71 plates, London, 1853.

sympathy and loyalty which once, when an unknown adventurer, he himself had experienced there at the hand of his predecessor and patron.

During the two years which Rawlinson spent in England (1850–51) for the restoration of his health and to superintend the publication of his famous second memoir "On the Babylonian Translation of the Great Persian Inscription at Behistun," through which he announced to the world that the deciphering of the Babylono-Assyrian cuneiform writing was an accomplished fact, he entered into closer relations with the British Museum. The trustees of this large storehouse of ancient art-treasures were anxious to resume their researches in the ruins on the banks of the Tigris and the Euphrates, which hitherto had been conducted with such marvellous success by Layard. Who was better qualified to carry out their plans and to take charge of the proposed excavations than Rawlinson, with his unique knowledge of the cuneiform languages, his rare experience as a soldier and traveller, and his remarkable influence in the East as the political representative of a great nation at Baghdad! And he was at once ready to add the labors of an explorer and excavator to those of a diplomat and decipherer. Before he departed from England, he was entrusted with the supervision of all the excavations which might be carried on by the British Museum in Assyria, Babylonia, and Susiana, and was authorized to employ such agents as he thought fit in excavating and transporting the best-preserved antiquities to the national collections in London.[1] Well provided with the necessary funds furnished by the government and private individuals, he entered upon his second official residence in Baghdad in the fall of 1851. But intelligent men who could be relied upon, and at the same time were able to manage the work properly in the

[1] Comp. George Rawlinson, "A Memoir of Major-General Sir Henry Creswicke Rawlinson," London, 1898, pp. 172, *seqq.*

trenches, far away from the place to which he was generally bound by his principal duties, were very rare in those regions. He was about to send Loftus, of the Turco-Persian Boundary Commission, who had excavated for him at the large mound of Susa, to the Assyrian ruins, when the trustees of the British Museum came unexpectedly to his assistance. The manifest interest among the religious and scientific circles of England in the historical and literary results of Layard's discoveries, daily increased by Rawlinson's own letters and instructive communications on the contents of the unearthed cuneiform inscriptions, influenced that administrative body to despatch a third artist[1] to the scene of the old excavations, soon followed by Hormuzd Rassam, as chief practical excavator. Their choice could not have fallen upon a better man. In the school of Layard excellently trained and prepared for his task, as a native of Mosul entirely familiar with the language and character of the Arabs, through his previous connections deeply interested in the undertaking, and after a long contact with Western civilization thoroughly impregnated with the English spirit of energy, he was an ideal explorer, the very man whom Rawlinson, the scientific leader and real soul of all these explorations, needed to carry the work in the Assyrian ruins to a successful conclusion. But Rassam's position was not very easy. For several years his predecessor, profiting by every hint which the appearance of the ground afforded, had tunnelled through the most promising spots of the Assyrian mounds, and what remained unexplored of Qoyunjuk had been transferred by Rawlinson to Victor Place, in generous response to the latter's request. Yet Rassam was shrewd and determined, and knew how to overcome difficulties.

[1] By the name of Hodder, to succeed the lamented Mr. Bell, who was drowned in the Gômal. Hodder remained in Mesopotamia until the beginning of 1854, when he fell seriously ill, and was supplanted by William Boutcher.

Rassam's Excavations, 1852–54. In the fall of 1852 operations were commenced under his superintendence, and continued till the beginning of April, 1854. Following Layard's example, he placed his workmen at as many different sites as possible, anxious also to prevent his French rival from encroaching any further upon what he regarded as the British sphere of influence. But more than a year elapsed without any of those startling discoveries to which the English nation had got accustomed through Layard's phenomenal success. At Qal'at Shirgât, where he excavated twice in the course of 1853, he obtained two terra-cotta prisms, inscribed with the annals of Tiglath-Pileser I. They were only duplicates of others unearthed by his predecessor two years before;[1] but, unlike those, they were complete and in a fine state of preservation, found buried in solid masonry, about thirty feet apart, at two of the corners of an almost perfect square, which originally formed part of the large temple of the city of Ashur. Soon afterwards their long text of 811 lines played a certain rôle in the history of Assyriology, being selected by the council of the Royal Asiatic Society of Great Britain and Ireland for a public test as to the correctness of the deciphering of the Assyrian cuneiform writing.[2]

At the southeast corner of Nimrûd, Rassam discovered Ezida, the temple of Nebo, and six large statues of the god, two of which had been set up by a governor of Calah "for the life of Adadnirâri [III.], king of Assyria, his lord, and for the life of Sammurâmat [generally but wrongly

[1] Comp. p. 126. The real facts concerning the discovery of these important prisms as set forth above are generally misrepresented, their discovery being ascribed either to Layard or Rassam.

[2] The inscription was sent to four prominent Assyrian scholars, Rawlinson, Hincks, Oppert, and Talbot, at the latter's suggestion, for independent translations, which in all essential points agreed, and were published in the journal of that society, vol. xviii., pp. 150–219, London, 1857.

identified with Semiramis], lady of the palace, his mistress." In another room of the same building he came upon the well-preserved stele of Samsi-Adad IV. (825–812 B. C.), father of the former and son of Shalmaneser II.;[1] while among heaps upon heaps of broken sculptures in the so-called central palace he unearthed fragments of an inscribed black obelisk of Ashurnâsirapal II., which when complete must have exceeded any other Assyrian obelisk so far discovered in size. But his principal work was carried on at Qoyunjuk. Shaft after shaft was sunk in the ground to find traces of a new palace — the one *desideratum* above others in those early days of exploration. As Victor Place never excavated in the northern half of the mound, so liberally allotted to him by Rawlinson,[2] Rassam profited by his absence, and placed some of his Arabs very close to the line of demarcation drawn by his chief, in order to obtain some clue as to the probable contents of that forbidden section. But his endeavors did not prove very successful. Meanwhile he had also opened trenches in the English southern half of the mound, which yielded a white obelisk nearly ten feet high, covered with bas-reliefs, and an inscription of Ashurnâsirapal II., the upper half of a similar monument, and the torso of a female statue from the palace of Ashurbêlkala, son of Tiglath-Pileser I.

Valuable as all these and other recovered antiquities were in themselves, they shrank almost into insignificance when compared with the character and mass of Layard's accumulated treasures. Rassam felt this very keenly, and was dis-

[1] That even Shalmaneser II. himself built at the temple of Nebo was shown later by George Smith, "Assyrian Discoveries," 3d ed., New York, 1876, pp. 73, *seq.*

[2] Who, after Botta's and Layard's fruitless attempts, very evidently did not regard that section worth keeping. For on other occasions he took quite a different attitude both against Place and Loftus in his vigorous defence of the interests of the British Museum.

satisfied, particularly as the time rapidly drew near when the funds available for his work would cease. His only hope lay in the northern part of Qoyunjuk, over which he had no control, but which he longed to examine. How could he explore it "without getting into hot water with Mr. Place"? If anything was to be done, it had to be done quickly. He decided upon an experimental examination of the spot by a few trustworthy Arabs at night. A favorable opportunity and a bright moonlight were all that was required for his nocturnal adventure, and they presented themselves very soon. Let us hear the story of this daring attempt, and of his subsequent discovery, in Rassam's own language.

"It was on the night of the 20th of December, 1853, that I commenced to examine the ground in which I was fortunate enough to discover, after three nights' trial, the grand palace of Ashurbânapal, commonly known by the name of Sardanapalus. When everything was ready I went and marked three places, some distance from each other, in which our operations were to be commenced. Only a few trenches had been opened there in the time of Sir Henry Layard; but on this occasion I ordered the men to dig transversely, and cut deeper down. I told them they were to stop work at dawn, and return to the same diggings again the next night. The very first night we worked there, one of the gangs came upon indications of an ancient building; but though we found among the rubbish painted bricks and pieces of marble on which there were signs of inscriptions and bas-reliefs, I did not feel sanguine as to the result. The next night the whole number of workmen dug in that spot; and, to the great delight of all, we hit upon a remnant of a marble wall, on examining which I came to the conclusion that it belonged to an Assyrian building which had existed on that spot. The remnant of the bas-relief showed that the wall was standing in its original position, and, though the upper part of it had been destroyed, I was able to judge, from experience, that it had not been brought thither from another building. The lower part of the slab, which contained the feet of Assyrian soldiers and captives, was still fixed in the paved floor with brick and stone masonry, intended to support it at the back. To my great disappointment, after having excavated round the spot a few feet, both the remnant of the bas-relief and the wall came to an end, and there was nothing to be seen save ashes, bones, and other rubbish. . . . This put a damper on my spirits, especially as I had on that day reported to both the British Museum authorities and Sir Henry Rawlinson the discovery of what I considered to be a new palace, as I was then fully convinced of its being so. I knew, also, that if I failed to realize my expectations I should only be found fault with and laughed at for my unrewarded zeal. However, I felt that as I had commenced so I must go on, even if only to be disappointed. The next night I superintended the work in person, and increased the number of men, placing them in separate gangs around the area, which seemed the most likely place for good results. The remnant of the sculptured wall discovered was on a low level, running upward, and this fact alone was enough to convince an experienced eye that the part of the building I had hit upon was an ascending passage leading to the main building. I therefore arranged my gangs to dig in a southeasterly direction, as I was certain that if there was anything remaining it would be found there. The men were made to work on without stopping, one gang assisting the other. My instinct did not deceive me; for one division of the workmen, after three or four hours' hard labor, were rewarded by the first grand discovery of a beautiful bas-relief in a perfect state of preservation, representing the king, who was afterwards identified as Ashurbânapal, standing in a chariot, about to start on a hunting expedition, and his attendants handing him the necessary weapons for the chase. . . . The delight of the workmen was naturally beyond description; for as soon as the word *suwar* ('images') was uttered, it went through the whole party like electricity. They all rushed to see the new discovery, and after having gazed on the bas-relief with wonder, they collected together, and began to dance and sing my praises, in the tune of their war-song, with all their might. Indeed, for a moment I did not know which was the most pleasant feeling that possessed me, the joy of my faithful men or the finding of the new palace." [1]

After this unmistakable success had rewarded his clandestine efforts, Rassam was no longer afraid of French or Turkish interference, and accordingly ordered the work to be continued in broad daylight. For "it was an established rule that whenever one discovered a new palace, no one else could meddle with it, and thus, in my position as the agent of the British Museum, I had secured it for England." The large edifice once having been discovered, one cannot help wondering how Botta and Layard could have missed coming upon some of its walls, which in many places were only a foot below the surface, and indeed in one or two instances so close to it that "a child might have scratched the ground with his fingers and touched the top of the sculptures." Before the first day was over, Rassam had cleared the upper parts of all the bas-reliefs which adorned the long but narrow hall, known as the "lion-room," because the subject here represented is the royal lion-hunt. The sculptures gathered from this and other chambers of the palace belong to the finest specimens of Assyrian art. The change from the old school of the tenth century to that of the later period referred to above (p. 117), both in the design and in the execution of single objects and persons and of whole groups,

[1] Comp. Rassam, "Asshur and the Land of Nimrod," New York, 1897, pp. 24, *seqq.*

is even more pronounced in the sculptures of the palace of Ashurbânapal than in those from the reign of his grandfather. They are distinguished by the sharpness of the outline, their minute finish, and the very correct and striking delineation of animals, especially lions and horses, in their different motions and positions. In looking at these fine bas-reliefs we gain the conviction that the artist has carefully studied and actually seen in life what he has reproduced here so truthfully in stone on the walls. The furious lion, foiled in his revenge, burying his teeth in the chariot wheels; the wounded lioness with her outstretched head, suffering agony, and vainly endeavoring to drag her paralyzed lower limbs after her; or the king on his spirited horse with wild excitement in his face, and in hot pursuit of the swift wild ass of the desert, — all these scenes are so

King Ashurbânapal Hunting

realistic in their conception, and at the same time so beautifully portrayed, that from the beginning they have found a most deserved admiration.

This lion-room was a picture gallery and library at the same time. For in the centre of the same hall Rassam discovered the other half of Ashurbânapal's library, several thousand clay tablets, mostly fragmentary, in character similar to those rescued by Layard, and including the Assyrian account of the Deluge. It is impossible to follow Rassam into all the chambers which he laid open, and which were generally lined with bas-reliefs illustrating the king's wars against Elam, Babylonia, the Arabs, etc. While breaking down the walls of one of these rooms, he found a large terra-cotta prism, unfortunately crumbling to pieces when exposed to the air, but soon afterwards replaced by the fragments of a second. They were duplicates, and contained the annals of Ashurbânapal, equally important for our knowledge of the history and for a study of the language and grammar of that prominent period of Assyrian art and literature.

During the first three months in 1854 the fortunate explorer was busy in excavating the palace as far as he could. But his funds were limited and quickly exhausted. At the beginning of April he was obliged to dismiss the different gangs of workmen employed at Qoyunjuk and Nimrûd and to return to England. The acceptance of a political appointment at Aden prevented him from going out to Nineveh again in the same year, as the British Museum had planned. His place was filled by Loftus and by Boutcher, who acted as the artist of the former. They had been for some time in Southern Babylonia, carrying on excavations at a moderate rate on behalf of the Assyrian Excavation Fund. This was a private society organized for the purpose of enlarging the field of English operations in Assyria and Babylonia, as the parliamentary grant secured by the British Museum was considered quite inadequate for the proper continuation of the national work so gloriously initiated by Layard. The thought and spirit which led to the founding of this society were most excellent and praiseworthy, but the method and means by which its representatives endeavored to reach their aim were neither tactful nor wise, and finally became even prejudicial to the very interests they intended to serve. Instead of placing their contributions and funds with a statement of their desired application at the disposal of the British Museum, that great national agency for all such archæological undertakings, the managers of the new corporation proceeded independently. The expedition which they sent out appeared as a competitor rather than as a helpmate of the other, and was about to risk serious collisions between the rival workmen of the two parties by occupying the same mound of Qoyunjuk after Rassam's departure, when upon the energetic representation of Rawlinson, who naturally did not look very favorably on the proceedings of this new society, an arrangement was concluded in London which placed matters on an entirely satisfactory basis. The Assyrian Excavation Fund transferred its remaining property to the British Museum, and decided that Loftus and Boutcher should henceforth receive their directions from Rawlinson.

The examination of the north palace of Ashurbânapal at Nineveh was resumed with new vigor under these two men, who had gathered considerable experience in the trenches of Warkâ and Senkere. While Boutcher drew the numerous sculptures and copied the monumental inscriptions, Loftus continued the excavations where Rassam had left them, trying first of all to determine the precise extent of the new building. But he also cleared a portion of its interior, and laid bare the whole ascending passage and a portal with three adjoining rooms at the western corner. Being deeply interested in the edifice as a whole, and in the determination of its architectural features, somewhat neglected by his predecessor, he did not confine himself to digging for new sculptures, though appreciating them whenever they were found. The bas-relief representing the king in comfortable repose upon a couch under the trees of his garden, and the queen sitting on a chair beside him, both drinking from cups while attendants with towels and fans stand behind them, was with many other interesting monuments discovered by Loftus. Unfortunately, however, the British Museum had not the means or did not care to continue the excavations at Nineveh and Calah after Rawlinson's final departure from Baghdad, for Loftus and Boutcher were soon recalled. Repeated attempts have been made since to resume the work at Qoyunjuk, but a Layard was not found to remove the obstacles in the field and to stir the masses at home to provide the financial support. Neither of the two large buildings which occupy the platform of Qoyunjuk has as yet been thoroughly explored, and much more remains to be done before the grand palace of Ashurbânapal with its hidden treasures will rise before our eyes as completely as that excavated in a methodical manner by Botta and Place at Khorsabâd.

2

FIRST SUCCESSFUL ATTEMPTS IN BABYLONIA

During the first four years of the second half of the last century the proverbial solitude of the Babylonian ruins seemed to have disappeared temporarily under the powerful influence of some magical spell. Fraser's intrepid march across the desolate plain and extensive swamps of 'Irâq, followed by his intelligent report of the innumerable mounds and other frequent traces of a high civilization which he had met everywhere in the almost forgotten districts of the interior of Babylonia, had directed the general attention again to the vast ruins of ancient Chaldea. Botta's and Layard's epoch-making discoveries in the royal palaces of Khorsabâd and Nimrûd had created an extraordinary enthusiasm throughout Europe. As a result of both, scholars began to meditate about the possibilities connected with a methodical exploration of the most conspicuous ruins in Babylonia. The earlier accounts and descriptions of Rich and Ker Porter and Buckingham were eagerly devoured and reëxamined with a new zeal, stimulated by the hope of finding other indications that the soil of the country in the south would contain no less important treasures than those which had just been extracted from the Assyrian tells in the north.

But neither scientific nor religious interest was the immediate cause of these tentative but fundamental researches in Babylonia with which we will now occupy ourselves in the following pages. The first successful explorations and excavations in the interior of Babylonia were rather the indirect result of certain political difficulties, which in 1839–40 threatened to lead to serious complications between Turkey and Persia. The chief trouble was caused by the extensive frontier between the two Mohammedan neighbors continually changing its limits as the strength of either government for the time prevailed. Under the influence of the cabinets of England and Russia, which offered their friendly mediation in order to maintain peace in regions not very far from their own frontiers in India and Georgia, a joint commission with representatives from the four powers was finally appointed and instructed "to survey and define a precise line of boundary between the two countries in question which might not admit of future dispute." The work of this "Turco-Persian Frontier Commission," after meeting with extraordinary difficulties and delays, lasted from 1849 to 1852.

WILLIAM KENNETT LOFTUS

To the staff of the British commissioner, Colonel Williams, "the Hero of Kars," was attached, as geologist, William Kennett Loftus, who utilized the rare facilities granted to him as a member of that commission to satisfy "his strong desire for breaking new ground" in an unexplored region, "which from our childhood we have been led to regard as the cradle of the human race."

After a short trip to the ruins of Babylon, El-Birs, Kefil (with "the tomb of the prophet Ezekiel"), Kûfa, famous in early Moslem history, and the celebrated Persian shrines of Meshhed 'Alî and Kerbelâ, — all but the first situated on the western side of the Euphrates, — Loftus decided to examine the geology of the Chaldean marshes and to explore the ruins of Warkâ, which, previous to the discovery of the Muqayyar cylinders, on the basis of native tradition, Sir Henry Rawlinson was inclined to identify with Ur of the Chaldees, the birthplace of the patriarch Abraham. An opportunity presented itself towards the end of December, 1849, when the representatives of the four powers, for nearly eight months detained at Baghdad, were at last ordered to proceed to the southern point of the disputed boundary line. While the other members of the party were conveyed to Mohammera by the armed steamer Nitocris, under the command of Captain Felix Jones, mentioned above in connection with his excellent maps of Nineveh, Loftus, accompanied by his friend and comrade, H. A. Churchill, and a number of irregular Turkish horsemen, took the land route between the Euphrates and Tigris, hitherto but once trodden by European foot.

Notwithstanding the great difficulties and dangers then attending a journey into Babylonia proper, the two explorers, "determined on being pleased with anything," overcame all obstacles with courage and patience, reaching the camp of the frontier commission on the eastern bank of the Shatt el-'Arab safely after an absence of several weeks. They had crossed the unsafe districts of the Zobaid Arabs and their tributaries, regarded as perfectly wild and uncontrolled in those days; they had visited the filthy reed huts of the fickle and unreliable 'Afej tribes, inhabiting the verge and numerous islands of the immense swamps named after them; and riding parallel with the course of the ancient bed of the Shatt el-Kâr, they had established friendly relations with the wildest and poorest but good-natured Ma'dân tribes in Southern Babylonia. Everywhere, like Fraser, they had found traces of an early civilization and a former dense population, and for the first time they had closely examined these lofty and massive piles covered with fragments of stone and broken pottery, which loom up in solitary grandeur from the surrounding plains and marshes of ancient Chaldea. The ruins of Nuffar, Hammâm, Tell

Ruins of Tell Hammâm

(J)îde, Warkâ, Muqayyar, and others became at once centres of general interest, and were rescued forever from the oblivion of past centuries.

Loftus' enthusiastic report of all the wonderful things which he had seen, illustrated by careful sketches and plans and by a number of small antiquities picked up on the surface of the various mounds, or purchased for a trifle from the neighboring Arabs, impressed Colonel Williams so favorably that he readily listened to the suggestions of the bold explorer "that excavations should be conducted on a small scale at Warkâ." After a few days' rest, we find

Loftus again on his way to the ruins, supplied with the necessary funds by his patron, and "with instructions more especially to procure specimens of the remarkable coffins of the locality, and seek objects as might be easily packed for transmission to the British Museum." His whole caravan consisted of four servants, three muleteers, two Arab guides, and fifteen horses and mules.

Under the protection of the powerful Muntefik(j) shaikh Fah(a')d (" Leopard," " Panther"), Loftus proceeded to the Arab encampment nearest to the ruins of Warkâ. It was fully six miles away from the scene of his labors, a distance soon afterwards increased even to nine miles, when, in consequence of the frequent desertions of his Tuwaiba workmen, he was forced to decamp to Durrâjî on the Euphrates, in order to ensure greater safety to his little party.

His work of three weeks was harassing in the extreme. " At sunrise," to quote his own words, " I set out with the Arabs for the mounds, . . . and never left them during the whole day. The soil was so light that, in walking from trench to trench, my feet were buried at each step. The Arabs required constant directions and watching. It was usually long after sunset ere we returned to camp, stumbling every instant over the broken ground. A few minutes sufficed for me to swallow the food my cook had prepared, when, almost tired to death, I was obliged to lay down plans from my rough notes, write my journal, and pack the objects procured in the course of the day. On many occasions it was two o'clock in the morning before I retired to rest, perfectly benumbed from the intensity of the cold, which even the double walls of my little tent could not exclude."

After many fruitless trials and the demolition of perhaps a hundred specimens, Loftus succeeded in finding a method by which some of the fragile but heavy slipper-shaped coffins so abundantly found at Warkâ could be removed

Tuwaiba Arabs carrying the First Coffin from the Ruins of Warkâ

without breaking. The surface of the coffin having been carefully cleaned, inside and out, thick layers of paper were pasted on both sides. When thoroughly dried, this hard mass became like a sheath, strengthening and protecting the enclosed coffin, which now could be lifted and handled without difficulty. Many years later, in connection with the University of Pennsylvania's excavations at Nuffar, the same method was often employed with the same general result, and more than fifty coffins were carried away "whole" to Europe and America. Yet after a long experience I have definitely abandoned this method as unsatisfactory and most damaging to the blue enamel of the object thus treated. It is by far wiser to save and pack all the fragments of glazed coffins separately and to put them together at home in a strictly scientific manner. Yet for the time being Loftus might well feel proud of having been able to secure the first three complete Babylonian coffins, then still unknown to European scholars. Under the dances and yells of his Tuwaiba Arabs, frantic with delight and excitement, they were carried with numerous other antiquities to the river, whence they were shipped to the British Museum.

Towards the end of 1853 Loftus returned to the ruins of Babylonia for the last time, in charge of an expedition sent out by the "Assyrian Excavation Fund" of London and accompanied by his two friends, W. Boutcher and T. Kerr Lynch. In order to secure him greater facilities, he was soon afterwards appointed by his government an attaché of the British Embassy at Constantinople. It was his intention to commence operations at the conspicuous mound of Hammâm, where in connection with a former visit he had found the large fragments of a fine but intentionally defaced statue in black granite. But the utter lack of water in the Shatt el-Kâr interfered seriously with his plans. Compelled, therefore, to seek another locality, he decided at once to resume the excavation of Warkâ, where he had won his first laurels. And it was in connection with this last visit to the place so dear to him that he effected the principal discoveries which established his name as a Babylonian explorer.

The first three months of the year 1854 he devoted to his difficult task. Conditions around Warkâ had completely changed during his absence. The Tuwaiba tribe had been driven out of Mesopotamia, and it was no small matter to obtain the necessary gangs of workmen from his distant friends and the exorbitant shaikh of El-Khidhr. In consequence of the river having failed to overflow its natural banks in the previous years, extreme poverty prevailed among the Arabs of the Lower Euphrates, and it became necessary to order all the supplies for men and beasts from Sûq esh-Shiyûkh, a distance of sixty miles, while every day a number of camels were engaged to carry water from the river to the camp, which he had pitched halfway between El-Khidhr and the ruins, and to the Arabs working in the trenches of Warkâ, nine miles away. To make the situation even more disagreeable, frequent sand-storms,[1] especially characteristic of the regions of Warkâ and Jôkha and Tell Ibrâhîm (Cuthah), at the slightest breath of air enveloped the mounds "in a dense cloud of impalpable sand," driving from their places the workmen, who often lost their way in returning to camp. Loftus, however, was not to be discouraged by all the difficulties, and with determination he tried to accomplish his task.

The ruins of Warkâ, the largest in all Babylonia, are situated on an elevated tract of desert soil slightly raised above a series of inundations and marshes caused by the annual overflowing of the Euphrates. When this inundation does not occur, the desolation and solitude of Warkâ are even more striking than at ordinary seasons. There is then no life for miles around. "No river glides in grandeur at the base of its mounds; no green date groves flour-

[1] At least twice or thrice a week.

ish near its ruins. The jackal and the hyæna appear to shun the dull aspect of its tombs. The king of birds never hovers over the deserted waste. A blade of grass or an insect finds no existence there. The shrivelled lichen alone, clinging to the withered surface of the broken brick, seems to glory in its universal dominion upon these barren walls." No wonder that of all the deserted pictures which Loftus ever beheld, that of Warkâ incomparably surpassed them all.

The ruins represent an enormous accumulation of long stretched mounds within "an irregular circle, nearly six miles in circumference, defined by the traces of an earthen rampart, in some places fifty feet high." As at Nuffar, a wide depression, the bed of some ancient canal, divides this elevated platform of débris into two unequal parts, varying

Tell Buwêrîye at Warkâ

in height from twenty to fifty feet, above which still larger mounds rise. The principal and doubtless earliest edifices are found in the southwest section, and to this Loftus very naturally directed his attention. Most conspicuous among them is a pyramidal mound, about a hundred feet high, called by the Arabs Buwêrîye, *i. e.*, "reed matting," because at certain intervals reed mats are placed between the layers of unbaked brick. It represents the stage tower or *ziggurrat* of the ancient Babylonian city Uruk or Erech (Gen. 10 : 10), forming part of the famous temple *E-anna*, sacred to the goddess Ninni or Nanâ. The mass of the structure, which, unlike the similar towers of Muqayyar and Nuffar, at present [1] has no external facing of kiln-baked brickwork, is at least as old as King Ur-Gur (about 2700 B. C.), whose name is stamped upon the baked bricks of the water courses [2] built in the centre of its sides. Singâshid, a monarch living somewhat later, left traces of his restoration at the summit of the Buwêrîye. The lowest stage was apparently not reached by Loftus, who after a fruitless attempt to discover a barrel cylinder in the west corner of the building, and unable to carry on any extensive excavation, left this mound to future explorers.

Another interesting structure at Warkâ is a ruin called Wuswas, said to be derived from a negro of this name who hunted here for treasures. It is situated less than a thousand feet to the southwest of the Buwêrîye, and, like the latter, though much smaller in size, contained in a walled quadrangle, including an area of more than seven and a half acres. Its corners again are approximately toward the four

[1] From a number of indications and details in Loftus' description it follows almost with certainty that the stage tower of Erech originally also had the usual facing of brickwork. It evidently, however, furnished welcome building material to the later inhabitants of Erech. More extensive and deeper excavations would doubtless reveal traces enough in the lower stage.

[2] Mistaken by Loftus for buttresses "erected for the purpose of supporting the main edifice" (p. 167). Comp. Hilprecht, "The Babylonian Expedition of the University of Pennsylvania," series A, vol. i., part 2, p. 18. I doubt whether Loftus examined all the four sides of the building ("on the centre of each side"). As the tower must have had an entrance, possibly on the southwest side, it is impossible to believe that this side should have had a drain on its centre. My own view is that, like the *ziggurrat* at Nuffar, the tower at Warkâ had such "buttresses" only on two sides (the number "three," given in my publication, p. 18, was due to Haynes' erroneous report).

cardinal points. The most important part of this great enclosure is the edifice on the southwest side, which is 246 feet long and 174 feet wide, elevated on a lofty artificial platform fifty feet high. This building at once attracted Loftus' attention. By a number of trenches he uncovered a considerable portion of the southwest façade, which in some places was still twenty-seven feet high. The peculiar style of exterior decoration here exhibited afforded us the first glimpse of Babylonian architecture. On the whole, this façade shows the same characteristic features — stepped recesses with chasings at their sides, repeated at regular intervals — as the exterior of Sargon's palace at Khorsabâd, excavated by Victor Place about the same time, or the ancient southeast wall of the temple enclosure at Nippur, uncovered during our latest campaign in 1899–1900, and many other Babylonian public buildings examined by various explorers.

Loftus found an entrance to this remarkable complex at its northeast side, leading into a large outer court flanked by chambers on either side. He also traced and partly excavated a number of halls and smaller rooms along the southwest façade, which had neither door nor window; he could ascertain the extraordinary thickness of the walls as compared with the size of the enclosed chambers, and the lack of uniformity in size and shape noticeable in the latter, — another characteristic feature of Babylonian architecture; he found that the bricks used in the construction of this edifice were either marked with a deeply impressed triangular stamp on the under side — something altogether unknown from early Babylonian ruins — or were stamped with "an oblong die bearing thirteen lines of minute cuneiform characters," which has not yet been published. But Loftus was unable to determine the real character of this structure. In consideration of the small funds at his disposal, and apparently disappointed by his failure to discover sculptured bas-reliefs and other works of art, similar to those which had repaid the labors of Botta, Place, and Layard in the Assyrian mounds, he abandoned his trenches at Wuswas, as he had done at the Buwêrîye, trying another place where he might find the coveted treasures. From all the indications contained in Loftus' description of his work at Wuswas we may infer that the remaining walls of the excavated building cannot be older than 1400 B. C., and possibly are about 800 to 1000 years later, apparently being a temple or the residence of some high-ranked person.

To the south of Wuswas there is a second immense structure, resembling the former in area and general disposition of its plan, but having no court and being more lofty and therefore more imposing in the distance. The bricks bearing the same peculiarities as those of Wuswas, it seems to be of about the same age. Loftus accordingly abstained from examining this edifice, turning his attention rather to a doubtless earlier building situated nearly on a level with the desert, close to the southern angle of the Buwêrîye. He unearthed part of a wall, thirty feet long, entirely composed of small yellow terra-cotta cones, three inches and a half

Terra-Cotta Cone Wall at Warkâ

long. They were all arranged in half circles with their rounded bases facing outwards. "Some had been dipped in red and black color and were arranged in various ornamental patterns, such as diamonds, triangles, zigzags, and stripes, which had a remarkably pleasing effect." Large numbers of such cones, frequently bearing votive inscriptions, have been found in most of the early Babylonian ruins where excavations were conducted, thus proving the correctness of Loftus' theory that "they were undoubtedly much used as an architectural decoration" in ancient Chaldea.

Another extraordinary mode of decoration in architecture was found in a mound near Wuswas. Upon a basement or terrace of mud-brick there rose a long wall entirely composed of unbaked bricks and conical vases, fragments of the latter being scattered all about the surface in its neighborhood. The arrangement was as follows: "Above the foundation were a few layers of mud-bricks, and superimposed on which were three rows of these vases, arranged horizontally, mouths outward, and immediately above each other. This order of brick and pot work was repeated thrice, and was succeeded upwards by a mass of unbaked bricks. The vases vary in size from ten to fifteen inches in length, with a general diameter at the mouth of four inches. The cup or interior is only six inches deep, consequently the conical end is solid." One can easily imagine the very strange and striking effect produced by these circular openings of the vases, the original purpose and age of which Loftus was unable to ascertain.

On the east side of the Buwêrîye he excavated a terrace paved with bricks "inscribed in slightly relieved cuneiform characters" containing the name of Cambyses, while half a mile southeast of the former, in a small detached mound, he found a large mass of broken columns, capitals, cornices, and many other relics of rich internal decoration — all belonging to the Parthian period.

Important portable antiquities of early Babylonian times were unfortunately not disclosed by the explorer. Yet his excavations were by no means entirely lacking in literary documents and other valuable archæological objects, though mostly of a comparatively late period. As most conspicuous among them may be mentioned less than a hundred so-called contract tablets of the Neo-Babylonian, Persian, and even Seleucide dynasties, the latter at the same time proving that at least as late as the third pre-Christian century cuneiform writing was in use in Babylonia; a few syllabaries and two large mushroom-shaped cones of baked clay covered on their flat tops and stems with cuneiform legends; an interesting small tablet in serpentine with pictures on the one side and four lines of early cuneiform characters on the other; a limestone slab with an imperfect inscription in South-Arabian writing — the first of the kind discovered in Babylonian ruins; a brick with stamp in relief of an elevated altar surmounted by a seven-rayed sun; several terracotta figurines; a thin silver plate embossed with a beautiful female figure; fragments of a bivalve shell (*tridacna squamosa*), the exterior of which shows fine carvings of horses and lotus flowers, etc.

The chief results of our explorer's rather superficial diggings at Warkâ being for the greater part due to a fortunate accident rather than to a clearly defined method and logical planning, were of real importance only for the history of architecture and for a study of the burial customs prevailing during the Persian, Parthian, and later occupations of Babylonia. Loftus is therefore correct in summing up his labors with the statement that "Warkâ may still be considered as unexplored." Within the three months at his disposal he scratched a little here and there, like Layard at Babylon and Nuffar, filled with a nervous desire to find important large museum pieces at the least possible outlay of time and money. Warkâ, however, is not the place to yield them readily. Objects of art and business archives and libraries with precious literary documents are doubtless contained in the enormous mounds. But in what condition they will be found is another quite different question. As we know from cuneiform records, the Elamite hordes invading Babylonia towards the end of the third pre-Christian millennium sacked and looted the temples and palaces of ancient Erech above others, establishing even a kingdom of their own in those regions. The large stratum of intentionally broken inscribed vases, statues, reliefs, and other objects of art of the earliest Babylonian period surrounding the temple court of Nippur, which I have shown to be the results of revengeful Elamite destruction, indicates what we may expect to find in the middle strata of Warkâ. In order to reach these deeper strata, a heavy superincumbent mass of rubbish and funereal remains, representing a period of about one thousand years after the fall of the Neo-Babylonian empire, has to be examined and removed.

In itself, any ancient city continuously inhabited for at least 5000 years, and repeatedly occupied by hostile armies, as Erech was, must be regarded as a site most unfavorable to the discovery of large and well preserved earlier antiquities. As a rule these latter, if escaping the vicissitudes of war, have been transferred from generation to generation until they were consumed or damaged in their natural continued use, while others, perhaps intact at the time when they were hidden under collapsing walls, have been frequently afterwards brought to light in connection with the thousands of later burials. No longer understood or appreciated by the inhabitants of a subsequent age, and frequently also of another race and religion, they were often intentionally broken and employed in a manner quite different from their original purpose.

In addition to the points just mentioned, the natural conditions around Warkâ are even worse than at Nuffar. From February or March to July the inundations of the Euphrates extend frequently almost to the very base of the ruins. The swamps thus formed are swarming with innumerable mosquitoes, which, with the even more dreaded sand-flies of the surrounding desert, render the life of the explorer extremely miserable. Towards the latter part of the summer the waters recede. The human system, being worn out by the heat and fatigue of the summer, is liable to fall a victim to the severe fevers now following, which have constantly proved to be the greatest real danger to our own expeditions at Nuffar. At other times, particularly when the Euphrates fails to inundate those regions, fresh water is not to be had for miles in the neighborhood, while at the same time the frequent sand-storms, of which Warkâ is one of the most characteristic centres, increase the general discomfort and render work in the trenches often absolutely impossible. No expedition should ever resume excavations at Warkâ unless it fully understands all these difficulties beforehand, and, in contrast with the superficial scratchings of Loftus, is prepared to excavate these largest of all Babylonian mounds in a strictly methodical manner for a period of at least fifty years, assured of a fund of no less than $500,000. By the mere "digging" for a few years at such an important place as Warkâ, Assyriology would irreparably lose more than it ever could gain by the unearthing of a number of antiquities, however valuable in themselves.

After three months of brave battling against odd circumstances Loftus instinctively began to realize the grandeur of the task with which he was confronted, and the utter insufficiency of the means at his disposal and the methods hitherto employed. Accordingly he decided to quit Warkâ, leaving its thorough exploration to an adequately equipped future expedition. Under the protection of a friendly shaikh of the Shammar Bedouins, then encamped near the ruins of Warkâ, he moved to Senkere, on the western bank of the Shatt el-Kâr, situated about fifteen miles southeast of the former and plainly visible on a clear day from the summit of the Buwêrîye. These mounds had previously been visited only by Fraser and Ross in the course of their hasty journey through the Jezîre, briefly described above (pp. 54–56).

As over against the lofty ruins of Warkâ, covering a city

which continued to be inhabited for centuries after the commencement of the Christian era, Senkere, rather smaller in height and extent than the former, shows no trace of any considerable occupation later than the Neo-Babylonian and Persian periods. From the very beginning it was therefore evident that Loftus' labors at this site would be repaid by much quicker and more satisfactory results than at Warkâ. The two principal mounds of the ruins, which measure over four miles in circumference, were first examined. They contained the remains of the temple and stage-tower of the Sun-god, as was readily ascertained by a few trenches cut into their centre and base. The stage-tower, about four hundred paces to the northeast of the temple ruins proper, shows the same peculiarities as the Buwêrîye at Warkâ and other similar buildings. From inscribed bricks taken from this mound it was proved that Hammurabi, of the so-called First Dynasty of Babylon (about 2250 B. C.), and Nabonidos, the last king of the Neo-Babylonian dynasty (556–539 B. C.), were among those who repaired this very ancient structure.

It was of course out of the question for Loftus to make an attempt to uncover the temple of the Sun-god completely, in order to restore its original plan, within the few weeks which he was able to devote to the excavations at Senkere. However, he showed that upon a large platform or terrace constructed six feet above another larger one, from which the former receded seventy-four feet, there stood a large hall or chamber entirely filled with rubbish. The walls of this building, which doubtless formed the main feature of the whole oval mound, were in part preserved, being still four feet high. While cleaning its characteristic entrance, formed by ten stepped recesses, Loftus was fortunate to discover two barrel-shaped clay cylinders. They were duplicates, bearing the same inscription. A third copy was soon afterwards discovered at a distant part of the ruins. From these cuneiform records and from numerous bricks taken from the upper building and the enclosing temple wall, it was ascertained that, in accordance with a reference on the cylinder brought by Rich's secretary Bellino from Babylon, Nebuchadrezzar had devoted considerable time and labor to the restoration of this ancient sanctuary. It became furthermore evident that the ancient Babylonian city buried under the ruins of Senkere was no other than Larsam, sacred to Shamash and identical with the Biblical Ellasar (Gen. 14 : 1). From a single brick of sixteen lines, also taken from these ruins, Sir Henry Rawlinson obtained the name of a new king, Burnaburiyash (about 1400 B. C.), one of the powerful rulers of the Cassite dynasty, while the lower strata of the mound furnished ample evidence that King Ur-Gur of Ur (about 2700 B. C.), the great builder of Babylonian temples, had also been very active at Larsam.

In addition to these very important discoveries, by which the name of the ancient city was identified and the first glimpses of its long history obtained, Loftus furnished material for us to show that in later years, when the temple was in ruins, the ground of the destroyed city of Larsam, like the other more prominent mounds of Babylonia, was used as a vast cemetery. Contrary, however, to the views of Loftus and other writers who followed him without criticism, the numerous clay tablets, which he continually found scattered through the upper layers partially burned, blackened and otherwise damaged by fire, and disintegrating from the nitrous earth composing or surrounding them, in most cases have nothing to do with the tombs in and around which they occur. Belonging to the period of about 2400 to 500 B. C., these tablets as a rule considerably antedate those burials. It has not yet been proved that in real Babylonian times Larsam was a cemetery, and in fact many strong reasons speak against such an assumption. On the other hand it is only natural to infer that when Larsam finally was no more, later grave-diggers, frequently disturbing the deserted mounds to a considerable depth, should accidentally have struck hundreds of clay tablets and seal-cylinders, which they moved out of their original resting places to an upper stratum, thus filling the burial ground with the literary and artistic remains of an older period, and creating the impression upon the uninitiated or careless observer that the burials are contemporary with those antiquities, and that the latter furnish us a real clue for determining the age of the former. In the first years of our own excavations at Nuffar I was frequently misled by the positive statements of those in the field, occasionally quoting Loftus and Taylor as their authorities, until by personally taking charge of the expedition, I definitely determined that with but few exceptions, which can easily be explained, the large mass of tombs at Nuffar is later than 400 B. C., though often found thirty feet and more below the surface.

Many of the tablets discovered by Loftus were wrapped in thin clay envelopes, similarly inscribed, and like the enclosed document covered with the impressions of seal cylinders. Others, also bearing the impressions of cylinders, were triangular in shape. From the fact that at their corners there are holes through which cords must have passed, it became evident, even without deciphering their inscriptions, that they were used somewhat like labels attached to an object. As a rule I have found Babylonian documents of this class to belong to the second half of the third pre-Christian millennium. Of especial value and interest was a certain tablet which proved to be a table of squares from one to sixty, both numbers

Clay Tablet with Envelope, Nuffar

1 and 60, being rendered by the same perpendicular wedge, thus confirming the statement of Berosus that the Babylonians employed a sexagesimal system of calculation.

Among the stray clay reliefs taken from the upper layers of Senkere, but doubtless belonging to a much earlier period of Babylonian civilization, are some tablets with a religious representation, others showing persons employed in their every-day life. One of the latter, for example, exhibits two persons boxing, while two others are occupied over a large vase; another reproduces a lion roaring and furiously lashing his tail because of being disturbed in his feast of a bullock by a man armed with a hatchet and a club.

Larsam is one of those mounds easily excavated and sure to repay the labors of the systematic explorer quickly. Representing one of the earliest and most famous Babylonian cities, with a sanctuary in which the kings of all ages down to Nabonidos were prominently interested, it will furnish literary and artistic monuments of importance for the early history and civilization of Babylonia.

While engaged in his work at Senkere, Loftus sent a few gangs of workmen to the ruins of Tell Sifr and Tell Medîna, on the east of the Shatt el-Kâr. The trenches cut into the desolate mound of Medîna, situated on the border of extensive marshes and inhabited by lions and other wild animals, yielded no results beyond a single stray clay tablet, a number of tombs, and the common types of pottery. But the excavations carried on for a few days at Tell Sifr ("Copper") were most encouraging, bringing to light about one hundred mostly well-preserved case tablets, dated in the reigns of the kings of the First Dynasty of Babylon (Samsu-iluna, previously unknown, being among them), and a large collection of caldrons, vases, dishes, hammers, hatchets, knives, daggers, fetters, mirrors, and other instruments and utensils, all in copper, and evidently likewise belonging to the second half of the third pre-Christian millennium.

Unfortunately the excavations so successfully begun at Senkere and Tell Sifr came to a sudden end. The continued advance of the marshes from the overflowing of the Shatt el-Kâr indicated very plainly that in a few weeks the whole of Southern Babylonia would be covered with inundations. The Arabs, who for several successive years had terribly suffered from lack of water and food, and therefore were anxious to cultivate their patches of land, rapidly decreased the necessary forces in the trenches by their frequent desertions. In order not to be finally left alone with his excavated treasures on an isolated mound surrounded by the Chaldean swamps, Loftus was forced to sacrifice his personal wishes and return to the Euphrates, much to his regret quitting the South Babylonian mounds, the real character and contents of which he had been the first to disclose to the public.

SIR AUSTEN HENRY LAYARD

The next to appear on the unexplored ground in the South was Henry Layard. A long experience in the trenches of Nimrûd and Ḳoyunjuk had qualified him above others for the exploration of the mounds in ancient Babylonia. Besides, he was well acquainted with the life and manners of the Arabs, and not unfamiliar with the peculiarities of ʻIrâq el-ʻArabî as a whole. For in connection with his early adventures in Lûristân and Khûzistân he had visited Baghdad repeatedly, and in Arab or Persian disguise he had travelled even among the lawless tribes of the districts adjoining the two rivers to the east and west as far down as Ḳorna and Basra. Prevented hitherto by lack of means from carrying out his old and comprehensive scheme of "excavating many remarkable sites both in Chaldea and Susiana," he was finally enabled to gratify his ardent desire to a limited extent. Apparently influenced in their decision by the encouraging results of Loftus' first tentative work at

Warkâ, the trustees of the British Museum granted him permission to excavate some of the more prominent Babylonian mounds.

Accompanied by his trusted comrade Rassam and by about thirty of his most experienced workmen from Mosul, he descended the Tigris on a raft, reaching Baghdad October 26, 1850. But the time was ill chosen for his exploring tour. His old friend Dr. Ross had died a year before; Colonel Rawlinson, the British resident, was on a leave of absence in England; Hormuzd Rassam fell seriously ill soon after their arrival, and the whole country around the city was swarming with Bedouins in open revolt against the Ottoman government, so that it was next to impossible to leave for the ruins of Babylon.

Not to lose time, he began operations at Tell Mohammed, a few miles to the southeast of Baghdad, where Captain Jones' crew had discovered inscribed bronze balls, from which it became evident that at some previous time a royal Babylonian palace (of Hammurabi) had occupied this site. Beyond several insignificant finds Layard's excavations proved unsuccessful. After a delay of nearly six weeks he moved to Hilla. Owing to the disturbed state of the country he could do no more than pay a hurried visit to the conspicuous mound of El-Birs, which, like his predecessors, he recognized at once as the remains of a stage tower, "the general type of the Chaldean and Assyrian temples."

As soon as he had established friendly relations with the most influential inhabitants of the town, he commenced excavations at Bâbil. The subterranean passages opened by Rich forty years previously were quickly discovered and followed up, but without results. By means of a few deep trenches he arrived at the doubtless correct conclusion that the coffins here found must belong to a period subsequent to the destruction of the edifice which forms the centre of the mound, and that in all probability long after the fall of the Babylonian empire a citadel had crowned its summit. He exposed at the foot of the hill enormous piers and buttresses of brickwork, frequently bearing the name of Nebuchadrezzar, but he could find no clue as to the original character of the gigantic structure which had left such vast remains.

Next he turned to the shapeless mass of shattered walls, known since the time of Rich under the name of El-Qasr ("The Palace"), but like Bâbil also frequently called Mujêlîba ("Overturned") by the Arab population. Again his labors were deficient in positive results. He gathered nothing but a few specimens of the well-known enamelled bricks of various colors, and excavated some rudely engraved gems and the fragment of a limestone slab containing two human figures with unimportant cuneiform characters.

No better antiquities were discovered at Tell 'Omrân ibn 'Alî and several smaller mounds included in the territory of ancient Babylon. After a month of nearly fruitless digging in the extensive ruins of the famous metropolis he decided to leave a small gang of workmen at these disappointing mounds and to depart with his Mosul Arabs for Tell Nuffar, the only place in the interior of the country to which he devoted a few weeks of concentrated attention. At the head of a good-sized caravan of fifty men he arrived at the marshes of Nuffar on January 17, 1851. He was received in the most friendly manner by the shaikh of the 'Afej, whose protection he had solicited before he left the banks of the Euphrates. But much to his disappointment and personal discomfort he felt obliged to comply with the shaikh's request and to pitch his tent at Sûq el-'Afej, "the market place" of the tribe and the residence of his newly acquired patron. The conglomeration of filthy reed huts which had received this high-sounding name was situated at the southeast edge of the unhealthy marshes and nearly three miles away from the ruins of Nuffar. In order to reach the latter with his Arabs of Mosul and a number of 'Afej, it was necessary to cross the swamps every

'Afej Reed-Huts near Nuffar

day by means of the *turrâda*, a long narrow and shallow boat of the natives consisting of a framework of bulrushes covered with bitumen.

The imposing ruins of Nuffar, with Babylon and Warkâ the largest in Babylonia, are situated at the northeastern boundary of these marshes, which vary in size according to the extent of the annual inundations of the Euphrates. A large canal, now dry and for miles entirely filled with sand and rubbish, divides the ruins into two almost equal parts. It is called by the surrounding tribes Shatt en-Nîl, supposed to be a continuation of the famous canal which, branching off from the Euphrates above Babylon, once carried life and fertility to the otherwise barren plains of Central Babylonia. On an average about fifty to sixty feet high, the ruins of Nuffar form a collection of mounds torn up by frequent gulleys and furrows into a number of spurs and ridges, from the distance not unlike a rugged mountain range on the banks of the upper Tigris.

In the Babylonian language the city buried here was called Nippur. Out of the midst of collapsed walls and broken drains at the northeastern corner of these vast ruins there rises a conical mound to the height of about ninety-five feet above the present level of the plain. It is called Bint el-Amîr ("The Princess") by the Arabs of the neighborhood, and covers the remains of *Imgharsag*, the ancient stage-tower of *Ekur*, the great sanctuary of Bêl. An almost straight line formed by two narrow ridges to the northeast of the temple towards the desert indicates the course of *Nîmit-Marduk*, the outer wall of the city. The surface of this whole mass of ruins is covered with numerous fragments of brick, glazed and unglazed pottery, stone, glass and scoria, which generally mark the sites of Babylonian cities.

Layard spent less than a fortnight at these ruins, to examine their contents, devoting considerable time to the fruitless search of "a great black stone" said by the Arabs to exist somewhere in the mounds of Nuffar. But a last time his hopes and expectations connected with the ruins of Babylonia were bitterly disappointed. Though opening many trenches in different sections of the ruins, and especially in the conical mound at the northeastern corner, where forty years later the present writer still found their traces, he discovered little of the true Babylonian period beyond massive walls and stray bricks inscribed with a cuneiform legend of King Ur-Gur. All the mounds seemed literally filled with the burials of a people inhabiting those regions long after the ancient city was covered with rubbish and the sand of the desert. He unearthed and examined nearly a hundred slipper-shaped clay coffins similar to those which Loftus had recently sent from Warkâ to England. Frequently they contained small cups and vases with blackish deposits of unknown liquids and crumbling remains of dates and bones, occasionally a few beads and engraved stones, but in no case ornaments of gold and silver.

Somewhat disheartened by this lack of success which everywhere characterized his brief and superficial work among the Babylonian ruins, differing from those in Assyria by the natural conditions of the soil, their long and varied occupation and the peculiarity of the material employed in constructing palaces and other large edifices, Layard's opinion of the character of the mounds examined was naturally faulty and colored by his unfortunate experience. "On the whole I am much inclined to question whether extensive excavations carried on at Niffer would produce any very important or interesting results," was the verdict of the great explorer at the middle of the last century. "More than sixty thousand cuneiform tablets so far rescued from the archives of Nippur, temple library definitely located, and a large pre-Sargonic gate discovered below the desert," was another message which fifty years later the present writer could despatch to the committee of the Philadelphia expedition from the same mounds of Nuffar. In consequence of the state of anarchy which prevailed everywhere in Babylonia, and influenced by what has been stated above, Layard abandoned his original plan of visiting and exploring the ruins of Warkâ. His physical condition had also suffered considerably during his brief stay among the 'Afej. The dampness of the soil and the unwholesome air of the surrounding marshes had brought on a severe attack of pleurisy and fever. It was therefore with a feeling of joy and relief that soon after the arrival of Rassam, who had just recovered from his long and severe illness at Baghdad, Layard quitted the unhospitable and malarious regions around Nuffar forever.

We cannot close the brief description of Layard's fruitless efforts in Babylonia without quoting a remark which, on the authority of Fresnel,[1] he is said to have made to his English friends after his return to Baghdad. "There will be nothing to be hoped for from the site of Babylon except with a parliamentary vote for £25,000 (= $125,000), and if ever this sum should be voted, I would solicit the favor of not being charged with its application."

THE FRENCH EXPEDITION UNDER FRESNEL, OPPERT AND THOMAS

The continued activity of the English explorers among the ruins of Assyria and Babylonia, the encouraging news of the results of Loftus' first tentative work at Warkâ, and the general conviction of European scholars that the kings of Babylon must have left similar and even earlier monuments than those excavated by Botta and Layard in the Assyrian mounds moved the French government to a decisive step. In August, 1851, Léon Faucher, then minister of the interior, laid a plan for the organization of "a scientific and artistic expedition to Mesopotamia and Media" before the National Assembly, accompanied by the urgent request for a credit of 70,000 francs (=$14,000). The necessary permission was soon granted. On October 1, the members of the expedition left Paris, and Marseilles eight days later. Fulgence Fresnel, formerly French consul at Jidda and thoroughly acquainted with the language and manners of the Arabs, was the director, ably assisted by Jules Oppert as Assyriologist, a young naturalized German scholar of great talents and independence of judgment, and Felix Thomas as architect.

[1] In *Journal Asiatique*, Series v., vol. vi. (1856), p. 548.

Adverse circumstances and unavoidable delays kept the members of the expedition three months on their way from France to Alexandretta, a time which they employed to the best of their ability in examining the ancient remains at Malta, Alexandria, Baalbek, and the Nahr el-Kelb above Beirût. With forty mules they finally left Aleppo, and after an interesting journey via Diarbekr, Mardîn, and Nisibîn, on March 1, 1852, reached Mosul, where Victor Place had succeeded Botta as vice-consul and archæological representative of France, while Layard, having finished his second successful campaign at Qoyunjuk, had returned to Europe in the previous year. The very next day after their arrival on this historical ground the enthusiastic French commission visited Place at Khorsabâd, who had but recently commenced his operations there. For three weeks they remained at Mosul, occupying themselves with a study of the history of the city, examining the ruins of Nineveh on the other side of the river, taking squeezes, copying cuneiform inscriptions, and preparing themselves in many other ways for their impending task at Babylon. As soon as their large raft of three hundred goat-skins was finished, they embarked and descended the Tigris, arriving at Baghdad five days later.

As we have seen above in connection with Layard's visit to Babylonia, there prevailed at the middle of the last century a general state of anarchy in the northern part of that country. Large parties of roaming Arabs, defying the authority of the Turkish governor, were constantly plundering pilgrims and caravans, and even made the neighborhood of Baghdad very unsafe. The French expedition was not slow in recognizing its unfavorable position. Men like Rawlinson, who were thoroughly familiar with the country and its inhabitants, advised the three members strongly to devote their first attention rather to the Median ruins, Oppert himself proposing to explore the site of ancient Ecbatana. But the cool political relations then existing between France and Persia seemed to Fresnel a serious obstacle to any successful work in that direction. After a repeated discussion of the whole situation, it was decided to remain at Baghdad, waiting for the first opportunity to proceed to Hilla.

This decision did not turn out to be very wise; for it soon became evident that the dangers had been greatly exaggerated, in order to keep the expedition from the ruins. Over three months the members were thus practically shut up within the walls of the city.[1] Spring passed away, and it was summer when a foolish rumor of the discovery of the golden statue of Nebuchadrezzar at Babylon, which spread rapidly all over Asia Minor, finding its way even into the American papers, finally roused Fresnel to new activity. In the company of two regiments of soldiers, who happened to leave for Hilla, the French expedition quitted Baghdad, established its headquarters at Jumjuma[2] or Jimjime, and began actual excavations at the Qasr on July 15, 1852.

The commencement of their work was most discouraging. The mass of masonry and rubbish to be removed was enormous and far beyond the time and means at their disposal. Owing to the great danger connected with cutting trenches into the loose fragments, they had to confine their labors to certain sections of the large ruin. The results, accordingly, were as modest as possible. Like Layard, they found the ordinary bricks inscribed with the well-known legend of Nebuchadrezzar, of which Oppert made

[1] Shortly before their final departure for Babylon, Oppert and Thomas made a brief excursion by water to the ruins of Ctesiphon and Seleucia (June 23), and also paid a visit to Kâdhimên, a little above Baghdad.

[2] While in his recent publication, *Am Euphrat und am Tigris* (p. 37), Sachau regards *Qumquma* as the original word, Oppert (*Expédition en Mésopotamie*, vol. i., p. 141), following Rich (comp. p. 30, above) and the Turkish geographer (Rich's "Collected Memoirs," p. 61), retained *Jumjuma*, meaning "Skull, Calvary."

the best by showing that nearly forty different stamps had been employed in their manufacture. They gathered a large number of varnished tiles representing portions of men, animals, plants, ornaments, and cuneiform characters, as often noticed before, and they discovered even some fragments of a barrel cylinder of Nebuchadrezzar, a duplicate of the complete cylinder published by Rich.

Of no greater importance were the excavations conducted in Tell 'Omrân ibn 'Alî (to the south of the Qasr), which Oppert firmly believed to represent the site of the famous hanging gardens, and which he examined alone, as his two companions Fresnel and Thomas had fallen ill. He showed that the whole upper part of the ruin contained tombs of a very late period. They were particularly numerous at the extreme ends and in the ravines of the mound, but in no case were found at any great depth in the centre, which contained many inscribed bricks of Nebuchadrezzar. These tombs clearly betrayed their Parthian origin. They were generally constructed in the form of coffins of Babylonian bricks, which sometimes bore cuneiform inscriptions of Esarhaddon, Nebuchadrezzar, Neriglissar, and Nabonidos. Though for the greater part previously pillaged, these burial places yielded a quantity of smaller antiquities, such as terra-cotta vases, simple and ornamented, clay figurines and playthings, glass vessels, instruments in copper and iron, and a few gold objects. As the lower strata, apparently concealing structures from the time of Nebuchadrezzar, could not be examined satisfactorily, unfortunately no definite information was obtained as to the character of the large edifice which once occupied this prominent site. Oppert's theory as set forth above, and defended by him with much vigor, has recently been proved by Dr. Koldewey's researches to be erroneous.

The most imposing mound of the ruins of the ancient metropolis is Bâbil, situated at the extreme northern end of the vast complex. Its summit, forming an irregular plateau of considerable extent, had been described by Rich, Buckingham, Porter and other earlier explorers as covered with numerous remains of buildings. When Oppert examined this site, all these walls had disappeared under the industrious hands of the Arab brick-diggers, who had begun to start excavations even in the interior of the enormous tumulus. Since then Bâbil has again completely changed its aspect,

Bâbil, South-East Face, as it appeared in 1853

so that if three pictures of the same mound taken at the beginning, middle and end of the last century were placed alongside of one another,[1] nobody would recognize one and the same ruin in them. The French excavations undertaken on a very limited scale at the top and base of this mound brought to light only the common bricks and fragments of stone and glass and part of a Greek inscription, without furnishing any clue as to the building which originally stood here. Interpreting the classical writers in the light of his

[1] Comp. Rich's sketch of 1811 (see page 39, above) with that made by the French architect Thomas in 1853, and reproduced on the present page.

own theories concerning the topography of Babylon, Oppert came to the conclusion that Bâbil represents the ruins of the pyramid called by Strabo the "Sepulchre of Bêl," which according to his view was a building entirely distinct from the "Temple of Bêl" with its stage-tower.

Considerable time was devoted to tracing the ancient quay of the river and the different walls of the city. Fully convinced that the capital of Nebuchadrezzar was about twenty-five times as large as the ancient city of Babylon[1] (previous to the fall of Nineveh), and that the latter was reserved exclusively for the royal quarter under the kings of the Neo-Babylonian dynasty, Oppert followed Buckingham's example and included El-Birs and El-Ohêmir in the enormous territory of his "Greater Babylon." He examined these two extreme quarters and the territory lying between them personally, supplementing or correcting the statements of his predecessors in certain details. While himself occupied with the excavations at 'Omrân ibn 'Alî, he even ordered a few trenches to be cut in Tell Ibrâhîm el-Khalîl, a large mound adjoining El-Birs, and with the latter forming the principal ruins of an ancient city. The finds were insignificant, with the exception of a small dated tablet found in a tomb and bearing the name of the place, Barsip, at the end. In the light of Sir Henry Rawlinson's fundamental discoveries at the Birs made a few years later, but published several years before Oppert's work appeared, this document, though as a stray tablet of little importance for the whole question in itself, could be claimed as the first cuneiform witness in support of the proposed identification of these ruins with ancient Borsippa.[2] Having once set

[1] According to Oppert, the great outer wall of Babylon enclosed a territory as large as the whole department of the Seine, or fifteen times as large as the city of Paris in 1859, or seven times the extent of Paris in 1860. Comp. Oppert, *l. c.*, vol. i., p. 234.

[2] Comp. Oppert, *l. c.*, vol. i., p. 204.

forth his theory on the enormous extent of the city of Babylon and having failed to find any trace of Herodotus' "Temple of Belus" among the ruins on the left side of the Euphrates, it was only natural that with most of the former travellers Oppert should decide upon the gigantic remains of the tower of Borsippa as the ruins of that great sanctuary.

In October, 1852, Fresnel and Oppert excavated for a week at the group of mounds generally called El-Ohêmir, and including the tumulus of El-Khazna ("The Treasure"), El-Bandar ("The Harbor") and a number of lower elevations, several hours to the east of Babylon, near the old bed of the Shatt en-Nîl. They uncovered a brick pavement of Nebuchadrezzar close by El-Ohêmir, and a piece of basalt bearing an archaic cuneiform inscription with many smaller antiquities in the other two principal mounds just mentioned. The identification of this whole group "with one of the two cities of Cuthah" referred to by Arab writers was proposed by Oppert, but cannot be accepted. For the brick found and published by Ker Porter says clearly that Zamâma, the chief deity of Kîsh, had his sanctuary, *E-me-te-ur-sag-ga*, there,[1] while the god of Cuthah was Nergal.

The French explorers worked at Babylon and its environment for almost two years, extending their topographical researches on the west side of the Euphrates as far as Kerbelâ and Kefîl, and locating and briefly describing a number of Babylonian and Mohammedan ruins previously unknown. At the beginning of February, 1854, after a visit to the ruins of 'Aqarqûf, Oppert finally left Babylonia, while Fresnel remained in Baghdad until his early death in November, 1855. The former returned to France by way of Mosul, where in the company of Victor Place he devoted six weeks to a thorough study of the ruins of Nineveh and Khorsabâd, and their exposed monuments, many of which he could decipher at the places of their discovery before they were

[1] Comp. p. 49, above, with ii. *R.* 50, 12.

removed to Europe. On July 1, 1854, Oppert arrived at Paris alone with his notes and plans and a few antiquities, waiting for the bulk of the results of his expedition, which had been ordered to be sent home by a French boat from Basra. But unfortunately they never reached their destination. It was about a year later when Oppert, while in London, learned the first news of the disaster from Sir Henry Layard. All the collections excavated and purchased, including even the valuable marble vase of Narâm-Sin (about 3750 B. C.), the first and for a long while the only monument of the ancient Sargonides discovered, went down in the muddy waters of the Tigris, a few miles above its junction with the Euphrates, on May 23, 1855.

It was a long series of difficulties and adverse circumstances which the French expedition had to encounter from the beginning to the end. Owing to the very limited means at their disposal, Fresnel and Oppert had not been able to do much more than to scratch the surface of the vast mounds, without contributing anything of importance to our knowledge of the ancient topography of Nebuchadrezzar's metropolis. "The great city of Babylon" was practically still unexplored when the French expedition quitted the ruins. But notwithstanding all that has been said to the contrary, scientific results were by no means lacking. In a general way first communicated by Fresnel in the *Journal Asiatique*,[1] they were methodically and neatly set forth by Oppert, the real soul of the whole undertaking, in a work of two volumes,[2] illustrated by a number of sketches from the

[1] Comp. Fresnel's two letters to J. Mohl, published in the *Journal Asiatique*, Series v., vol. i. (1853), pp. 485–548, dated Hilla, December, 1852, and continued in vol. ii. (1853), pp. 5–78; and vol. vi. (1856), pp. 525–548, dated Hilla, end of June, 1853.

[2] Authorized by ministerial order in 1856, it appeared under the title *Expédition Scientifique en Mésopotamie*, two volumes, Paris, vol. ii. (published first), 1859: "Decipherment of the Cuneiform Inscriptions" (part

hand of Thomas.[1] This publication, written by one of the founders of the young Assyriological science, will always hold a prominent place in the history of exploration, alike for the manifold information it conveys on various archæological topics, for the boldness with which our author attacks difficult topographical problems, and above all for the skill and brilliancy with which Oppert — in many cases for the first time — translates and analyzes the historical inscriptions from Assyrian and Babylonian palaces, thus contributing essentially to the restoration of the eventful past of two powerful nations.

J. E. TAYLOR

At the beginning of 1854, when Petermann, of Berlin, was studying the language and life of the Sabean Christians at Sûq esh-Shiyûkh, and Loftus was engaged at Warkâ for the "Assyrian Excavation Fund," at the request of Sir Henry Rawlinson excavations were also undertaken at Muqayyar for the British Museum by J. E. Taylor, Her Majesty's Vice-Consul at Basra. The ruins of Muqayyar[2] ("Bitumined" or "Cemented with Bitumen") are situated upon a slight elevation six to seven miles southwest from the modern town of Nasrîye. The country all about is so low that frequently during the annual flood of the Euphrates, *i. e.*, from March till June or July, the ruins form practically an island in the midst of a large marsh, unap-

iii. including inscriptions discovered by the French expedition); vol. i. 1863: "Report of the Journey and Results of the Expedition" (pp. 287–357 containing a description of Assyrian ruins, illustrated by a translation of the largest and most important inscriptions then discovered).

[1] Published as part of an Atlas (21 plates) accompanying Oppert's two volumes.

[2] To-day generally pronounced *Mugayer* by the Arabs. The various writers, with more or less success endeavoring to reproduce the name as it was heard by them, write it in many different ways, *Muqueijer*, *Mughyer*, *Mugeyer*, *Mughair*, *Megheyer*, *Meghaiir*, *Umghyer*, *Umgheir*, etc.

proachable on any side except in boats. The ruins are then sometimes occupied as a stronghold by the Dhafir, a lawless tribe of the desert, which at certain seasons extends its camping-grounds far into the districts of the Jezîre. Travellers who in recent years desired to visit Muqayyar were often obliged to do so at their own risk,[1] the Turkish officials not only declining a military escort, but demanding even a written declaration in which it is stated that the person in question does not hold the Ottoman government responsible for any accident that may befall him in a region outside of their real jurisdiction.

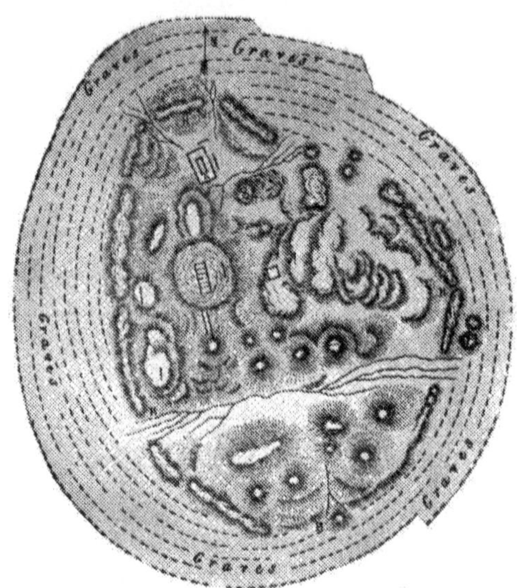

Plan of the Ruins of Muqayyar
(*Ur of the Chaldees*)

The ruins of Muqayyar consist of a series of low mounds of oval form, their whole circumference measuring nearly 3000 yards, and their largest diameter from north to south a little over 1000 yards. Previous to Taylor, they had been examined by Pietro della Valle (1625), who took one of the inscribed bricks with him, and

[1] A French professor from Bordeaux, who had been my guest at Nuffar in March, 1900, and whom I had advised to visit Muqayyar also, reported the same experience to me. The Dhafir allowed him only to walk around the ruins hurriedly. Since the fall of 1900, after the great troubles among the Arabs of those regions and to the south of them have been settled temporarily, conditions have improved somewhat.

gathered some inscribed seal cylinders on the surface,[1] by Baillie Fraser (1835),[2] and by Loftus (1850), who again visited them shortly before he quitted Babylonia forever (1854).[3] But our real knowledge of the character and contents of the ruins is based upon the excavations of the first-named explorer, who worked there in the beginning of 1854, and who opened a few additional trenches, in connection with a second visit, about a year later.

Near the north end of the mounds stands the principal building of the whole site, about seventy feet high. It is a two-storied structure having the plan of a right-angled parallelogram, the largest sides of which are the northeast and southwest, being each 198 feet long, while the others measure only 133 feet. As in all other similar Babylonian buildings, one angle points almost due north. The lower story, twenty-seven feet high, is supported by strong buttresses; the upper story, receding from thirty to forty-seven feet from the edge of the first, is fourteen feet high, surmounted by about five feet of brick rubbish. The ascent to this remarkable stage-tower, perforated with numerous air-holes, like those at ʻAqarqûf and El-Birs, was on the northeast side. By driving a tunnel into the very heart of the mound, Taylor convinced himself first that "the whole building was built of sun-dried bricks in the centre, with a

[1] Pietro della Valle (comp. p. 17, above) not only gave the correct etymology of the name of the ruins, but recognized even the peculiar signs on the bricks and seal cylinders as *unbekannte und uhralte Buchstaben. Unter anderen Buchstaben habe ich iher zween an vielen Orten wahrgenommen, worunter der eine wie eine liegende Pyramid oder Flamm-säule* (▷), *der andere aber wie ein Stern mit acht Strahlen* (✳) — the sign for "God" — *gewest.* Comp. the German translation of his work, *Reiss-Beschreibung*, Geneva, 1674, part 4, p. 184.

[2] Comp. his "Travels in Koordistan, Mesopotamia," etc., vol. ii., pp. 90–94, and p. 55, above.

[3] "Travels and Researches in Chaldæa and Susiana," pp. 127–135. Comp., also, p. 141, above.

thick coating of massive, partially burnt bricks of a light red color with layers of reeds between them, the whole to the thickness of ten feet being cased by a wall of inscribed kiln-burnt bricks." Next he turned his attention to the four corners. While excavating the southwest corner of the upper story, he found, six feet below the surface, a perfect inscribed clay cylinder, standing in a niche formed by the omission of one of the bricks in the layer. A similar cylinder having been discovered in the northwest corner, the fortunate explorer naturally concluded that corresponding objects would be found in the remaining two corners. A shaft sunk in each of them proved his theory to be correct, at the same time bringing out the important fact that the commemorative cylinders of the builders or restorers of Babylonian temples and palaces were generally deposited in the four corners. Fragments of another larger and even more interesting barrel cylinder were rescued from the same mound and from a lower elevation immediately north of it.

The massive structure thus examined by Taylor turned out to be the famous temple of the Moon-god Sin.[1] It is "the only example of a Babylonian temple remaining in good preservation not wholly covered by rubbish." [2] From the fine barrel cylinders and the large inscribed bricks differing as to size and inscription in the two stories, Rawlinson established soon afterwards that the site of Muqayyar represents the Biblical Ur of the Chaldees (Gen. 11:28; 15:7). The temple was constructed by King Ur-Gur (about 2700 B. C.), repaired by his son Dungi, and more than 2000 years later was for the last time restored by the last king of Babylon, Nabuna'id (Nabonidos), who deposited the account of his work inscribed upon these clay cylinders in the corners of the stage-tower.

[1] After him Mount Sinai is called, the name meaning "Sacred to Sin."

[2] Comp. Loftus, *l. c.*, p. 128.

The discovery of these documents was of the greatest importance for Biblical history in another way. The inscriptions upon all of them closed with a poetical prayer for the life of the king's oldest son, Bêl-shar-usur, who is no other than the Biblical Belshazzar (Dan. 5), appointed by

Ruins of the Temple of Sin at Muqayyar

his father as co-regent, defeated by Cyrus near Opis, and murdered soon after the conquest of Babylon.

In a small hill close to the southeast corner of the large ruin Taylor unearthed a regular house built of large inscribed bricks upon a platform of sun-dried bricks. Some of the burnt bricks were remarkably fine, having a thin coating of enamel or gypsum on which the cuneiform characters had been stamped, — the first example of this kind known. From the northwest corner of the mud wall he obtained a small black stone inscribed on both sides, from which it can be inferred that the building dates back to the third millennium.

At a depth considerably below this building, he came upon a pavement consisting of bricks fourteen inches long, eight and a half wide, and three and a half thick, " most of them having the impressions of the tips of two fingers at the back; none were inscribed, the whole imbedded in bitumen." From what the present writer has pointed out in 1896 as a characteristic feature of the earliest Babylonian bricks,[1] it is very evident that here Taylor had reached the pre-Sargonic period (about 4000 B. C.).

He mentions other interesting bricks found upon the same mound, which were " painted red, and had an inscription over nearly the whole length and breadth in a small neat character," while "on one portion of them was the symbol of two crescents, back to back." But his statements here and in other places are so vague that our curiosity is only raised without any chance of being satisfied.

The rest of the mounds of Muqayyar, so far as Taylor was able to dig into them, seemed to represent a vast cemetery of the early Babylonians, yielding clay coffins and

Clay Coffin from Muqayyar

vases of different size and shape, numerous drains, and many smaller objects in stone, metal, and clay valuable for illustrating the life and customs of the former inhabitants, especially those of the later periods.

All around the graves in the different parts of the ruins

[1] Comp. Hilprecht, "The Babylonian Expedition of the University of Pennsylvania," Series A, vol. i., part 2, p. 45.

he came across many fragments of inscribed cones. In the long west mound he found two whole jars filled with clay tablets placed in envelopes of the same material, and frequently bearing seal impressions, in addition to over thirty stray tablets and fragments.

Notwithstanding the insignificant funds and the short time placed at the disposal of our explorer, and notwithstanding the lack of a proper archæological training so seriously felt by himself, and through which a large portion of the scientific results have been lost, Taylor's patient labors and attempts at disclosing the contents of Muqayyar were successful beyond expectation. Different travellers have since visited the ruins, taking measurements and picking up a few objects here and there on the surface; but they all have added practically nothing to our knowledge of those mounds, which is derived exclusively from the reports of Loftus and Taylor written nearly fifty years ago. The methodical exploration of Muqayyar and a complete restoration of its history belong still to the desirable things expected from the future. There is hope, however, that even before the German railroad line from Baghdad to Basra has been constructed, an American expedition will start excavations at these ruins in the beginning of the twentieth century.[1] Owing to the lawlessness of the Arab tribes roaming over that part of the desert, and no less to the swampy condition of the neighborhood of Muqayyar during the annual inundations, there are peculiar difficulties to be overcome here, similar to those prevailing at Nippur and Warkâ. But with the necessary tact and determination they can be overcome, and the mounds, considerably smaller in extent than either of the two ruins mentioned, can be thoroughly

[1] According to information received by cable from Dr. Banks, the director of the planned Expedition to Ur, at the beginning of October, 1901, the Ottoman Government has declined to grant him a firmân for the excavation of Muqayyar.

explored at an expense of $200,000 within a period of twenty-five years. The results, though scarcely ever furnishing a document referring to the life and person of Abraham, — as has been expected, — will doubtless add many fresh stones to the rising building of the early history of Babylonia.

Previous to his second visit to Muqayyar, early in 1855, Taylor excavated for a few days at two other ruins, called Tell el-Lahm and Abû Shahrain. The former ruin, consisting of two mounds of some height surrounded by a number of smaller ridges and elevations, is situated three hours to the south of Sûq esh-Shiyûkh, near the dry bed of an ancient canal, and does not exceed half a mile in circumference. Nothing of especial interest was discovered. But Taylor exhumed numerous coffins formed of two large jars joined together by a bitumen cement, traced several pavements constructed of baked bricks, occasionally bearing defaced cuneiform characters, and found a perfect clay tablet, so that the Babylonian origin, though not the early name of the site, could be established beyond any reasonable doubt.

Of greater importance were Taylor's excavations at Abû Shahrain, situated in the desert beyond the sandstone bluffs which separate it from Ur and the valley of the Euphrates, but — strange to say — very generally placed wrongly by Assyriologists on the left side of "the great river," somewhere opposite Sûq esh-Shiyûkh,[1] though its correct situa-

[1] With whom this error started I do not know. We find it in Ménant, *Babylone et la Chaldée* (1875), and Delitzsch, *Wo lag das Paradies?* (1881) — notwithstanding Taylor's very explicit statements to the contrary. George Rawlinson, "Five Great Monarchies," 4th ed., London, 1879, vol. ii., ("Map of Mesopotamia," etc.) places Abû Shahrain correctly, on the right side of the river, but too far to the south. About where Tell el-Lahm is situated is Abû Shahrain, and where he has Abû Shahrain is Tell el-Lahm. The ruins of Abû Shahrain, situated as they are in a deep valley, cannot be seen from Muqayyar, nor are they identical with Nowawis,

tion might have been inferred from several cuneiform passages in which Eridu is mentioned. "The first aspect of the mounds is that of a ruined fort, surrounded by high walls with a keep or tower at one end," placed on an eminence nearly in the centre of the dry bed of an inland sea. They are half concealed in a deep valley about fifteen miles wide, and only towards the north open to the Euphrates. For the greater part this depression is "covered with a nitrous incrustation, but with here and there a few patches of alluvium, scantily clothed with the shrubs and plants peculiar to the desert." To the northwest and southeast of the principal mounds are "small low mounds full of graves, funeral vases, and urns." Faint traces of an ancient canal, six yards broad, were discovered at no great distance to the northwest of the ruins.

These latter, which are considerably smaller than those of Muqayyar, "rise abruptly from the plain, and are not encumbered with the masses of rubbish usually surrounding similar places." Consisting of a platform enclosed by a sandstone wall twenty feet high, the whole complex is divided into two parts of nearly equal extent. As in most of the larger Babylonian ruins so far examined, the northern part of Abû Shahrain is occupied by a pyramidal tower of two stages, constructed of sun-dried brick cased with a wall of kiln-burnt brick, and still about seventy feet high.

The summit of the first stage of this building is reached by a staircase fifteen feet wide and seventy feet long, originally constructed of polished marble slabs, now scattered all over the mound, and at its foot flanked by two columns of an interesting construction. An inclined road leads up to

as assumed by Peters ("Nippur," vol. ii., pp. 96 and 298, *seq.*) Scheil's recent statement concerning them (*Recueil*, vol. xxi., p. 126) evidently rests on Arab information. It is correct, but only confirms facts better known from Taylor's own accurate reports, which, however, do not seem to have been read carefully by Assyriologists during the last twenty-five years.

the second story. "Pieces of agate, alabaster, and marble, finely cut and polished, small pieces of pure gold, gold-headed and plain copper nails, cover the ground about the basement" of the latter — sufficient to indicate that a small

Temple Ruin at Abû Shahrain from the South

but richly embellished sacred chamber formerly crowned the top of the second stage. Around the whole tower there is a pavement of inscribed baked brick placed upon a large layer of clay two feet thick.

From several trenches cut in various parts of these remarkable mounds, Taylor reached the startling conclusion that all the ruined buildings he met with, including the ponderous mass of the stage-tower, rested on the fine sand of the desert confined by a coating of sun-dried brick, upon which the above-mentioned sandstone wall rises. In contrast to all the other Babylonian ruins, where natural stone is almost entirely unknown as building material, we find sandstone and granite and marble liberally employed in Abû Shahrain, a fact which illustrates and proves the correctness of the theory that the extensive use of clay in ancient Babylonia is due only to the complete absence of any kind of stone in the alluvial ground of the country.

A number of chambers, which the explorer excavated, yielded but little. But the inscribed bricks gathered from the temple enclosure told us the important news that the city here buried was Eridu, sacred to the early inhabitants of Babylonia as the seat of a famous oracle so frequently mentioned in the inscriptions of the third pre-Christian millennium and later. A peculiar structure partly unearthed at the south-east section of the ruins, the precise character of which has hitherto not been recognized, also testifies to the great age of the place. The uninscribed bricks were laid in bitumen, and by their curious shape ("thin at both ends and thick in the middle, as in the margin, the under part perfectly flat") naturally attracted the attention of Taylor. From what we now know about the history of Babylonian brick-making, it becomes evident that Taylor had hit a pre-Sargonic structure of about 4000 B.C., the southern gateway of the large temple complex. If instead of "a few feet" he had dug about fifteen to twenty feet on either side along the stone wall adjoining it, he probably would have found another similar pair of bastions, thereby obtaining the characteristic three divisions of a Sumerian gateway with a central passage for beasts and chariots and two narrower side entrances, reached by means of steps, for the people.

With regard to portable finds, Taylor's work at Abû Shahrain was unproductive of important results. But the discovery and brief description of those large ruins and of so many inscribed bricks, through which it was possible to restore the old Babylonian name of the city buried there, was in itself a most valuable contribution to our knowledge of ancient comparative geography, especially when it is remembered that, owing to the seclusion of the spot and the insecurity of its neighborhood, Abû Shahrain has never been visited again by any European or American explorer.[1]

[1] Taylor's reports are published in the "Journal of the Royal Asiatic Society of Great Britain and Ireland," vol. xv. (1855), under the titles

SIR HENRY RAWLINSON

The first period of Babylonian excavations was well brought to an end by Sir Henry Rawlinson himself. For a long while the Birs (Nimrûd) with its high towering peak had been the one ruin above all which he desired to subject to a more careful examination than had been hitherto the case. During the months of September and October, 1854, shortly before he closed his memorable career in the Orient entirely, his desire could be finally gratified.

On behalf of the British Museum, he sent an intelligent young man, Joseph Tonietti, apothecary in the Ottoman army, to the ruins of Birs with instructions to ascertain the general features of the building through a number

El Birs, Northwest Face

of specified trenches, and in particular to run a trench along the whole line of one of the walls "until the angles were turned at the two corners, so as to expose the complete face of one of the stages" of which Rawlinson had no doubt the

"Notes on the Ruins of Muqeyer," pp. 260–276, and "Notes on Abu Shahrain and Tel-el-Lahm," pp. 404–415.

original building had been formed. His orders were carried out "with care and judgment" within a little more than two months, when the director, who had been encamped for ten days at the foot of the ruins of Babylon, occupied with questions of their topography, appeared personally on the ground, in order to apply his knowledge and critical discrimination to the partly exposed structure.

Having satisfied himself from an inspection of the various trenches in progress that the outer wall of the southeastern face of the third stage had been completely uncovered, he "proceeded on the next morning with a couple of gangs of workmen to turn to account the experience obtained from the excavations of Qal'at Shirgât (in Assyria) and Muqayyar (in Babylonia) in searching for commemorative cylinders. Accordingly he "placed a gang at work upon each of the exposed angles of the third stage, directing them to remove the bricks forming the corner carefully, one after the other," until "they had reached the tenth layer of brick above the plinth at the base." Half an hour later Rawlinson was summoned to the southern corner, where the workmen had reached the limit which he had marked out for their preliminary work. On reaching the spot, he was first "occupied for a few minutes in adjusting a prismatic compass on the lowest brick now remaining of the original angle, which fortunately projected a little," and he then ordered the work to be resumed. The excitement which immediately followed we describe better in his own language.

"No sooner had the next layer of bricks been removed than the workmen called out there was a *Khazeneh* [*khazna*], or 'treasure hole;' that is, in the corner at the distance of two bricks from the exterior surface, there was a vacant space filled half up with loose reddish sand. 'Clear away the sand,' I said, 'and bring out the cylinder;' and as I spoke the words, the Arab, groping with his hand among the débris in the hole, seized and held up in triumph a fine cylinder of baked clay, in as perfect a condition as when it was deposited in the artificial cavity above twenty-four centuries ago. The workmen were perfectly bewildered. They could be heard whispering to each other that it was *sihr*, or 'magic,' while the greybeard of the party significantly observed to his companion that the compass, which, as I have mentioned, I had just before been using, and had accidentally placed immediately above the cylinder, was certainly '*a wonderful instrument*.'"

Soon afterwards an exact duplicate of the cylinder was discovered near the eastern corner of the same stage, while a search for the remaining cylinders at the northern and western corners proved fruitless, because the greater portion of the wall at these angles had been already broken away. But from the débris which had rolled down from the upper stages, Rawlinson gathered two more fragments of a third cylinder with the same inscriptions, and a small fragment of a much larger new cylinder. All these documents are commemorative records of the time of Nebuchadrezzar, by whom they were placed there after his restoration of the old tower of Borsippa, called *E-ur-imin-an-ki*, *i. e.*, "Temple of the Seven Directions (Spheres) of Heaven and Earth," while the last-mentioned fragment "in some detail contains a notice of Nebuchadrezzar's expedition to the Mediterranean and his conquest of the kings of the West."

In entire accordance with the peculiar Babylonian name of the tower which formed the most conspicuous part of the temple Ezida, dedicated to Nebo, son of Merodach, were Rawlinson's remarkable findings in the trenches. There could not be any doubt that the six or seven stages of the huge temple tower still to be recognized had been differently colored, and that "the color black for the first stage,[1] red

[1] The bricks of this stage are the only ones laid in bitumen, and the face

for the third,[1] and blue for what seemed to be the sixth, were precisely the colors which belonged to the first, third, and sixth spheres of the Sabæan planetary system . . . or the colors which appertained to the planets Saturn, Mars, and Mercury."

Down to the present time the large vitrified masses of brickwork on the top of the Birs have given rise to much speculation and to the wildest theories concerning their origin, prominent among which is the common belief that they are fragments of the upper stage of the original "Tower of Babel," destroyed by lightning from heaven (Gen. 11),[2] which rather must have formed a prominent part of Babylon proper on the other side of the Euphrates. While examining these upright and scattered remains of ancient walls on the summit of the mound, the present writer, with other explorers, often recognized the well preserved name of Nebuchadrezzar on many of the clearly defined bricks which had undergone this vitrification.

Among all the theories proposed to explain this remarkable phenomenon at such an elevation, that of Sir Henry Rawlinson, though not entirely removing all the difficulties, seems still to be the most plausible. He assumes that previous to the erection of the culminating stage, of which the remains exist in the solid pile at the summit, by the action of fierce and continued heat the bricks of the second highest stage of the temple were artificially vitrified, in order to give them the color of the corresponding sphere of Mercury by the solid mass of dark blue slag thus obtained. And "it was owing to the accidental use of an imperishable material like slag so near the summit of the Birs, that we are

of the exposed southeastern wall "to a depth of half an inch was coated with the same material, so as to give it a jet-black appearance."

[1] Built of bricks of red clay and only half burned. They were laid in crude red clay, mixed up with chopped straw.

[2] Comp., *e. g.*, Ker Porter, pp. 46, *seq.*, above.

indebted for the solitary preservation of this one building among the many hundreds of not inferior temples which once studded the surface of Babylonia."

After a careful study of all the details offered by the trenches, the inscriptions, and other outside facts, Rawlinson gave a tentative picture of the original design of the temple at Borsippa: "Upon a platform of crude brick, raised a few feet above the alluvial plain, and belonging to a temple which was erected probably in the remotest antiquity by one of the primitive Babylonian kings, Nebuchadrezzar, towards the close of his reign, must have rebuilt seven distinct stages, one upon the other, symbolical of the concentric circles of the seven spheres, and each colored with the peculiar tint which belonged to the ruling planet." The first stage was black, sacred to Saturn; the second red-brown or orange, sacred to Jupiter; the third, red, belonged to Mars; the fourth, gold-plated, to the sun; the fifth, yellowish white, to Venus; the sixth, dark blue, to Mercury (Nebo); the seventh, silver-plated, to the moon. The entrance to this grand structure was on the northeast side, as in the temple of Sin at Ur. The lowest stage was two hundred and seventy-two feet square, and probably twenty-six feet high. As the successive stages rose to the height of about one hundred and sixty feet, they gradually receded, becoming smaller and smaller, the seventh stage being occupied by the richly decorated shrine of the god Nabû (Nebo), "The Guardian of Heaven and Earth," to whom the temple was dedicated.[1]

[1] Rawlinson's first paper "On the Birs Nimrûd, or the Great Temple of Borsippa," was published in the "Journal of the Royal Asiatic Society," vol. xvii. (1860), pp. 1–34.

The Tower of Babel

According to the model prepared by Sir Henry Rawlinson

3

TEMPORARY REVIVAL OF PUBLIC INTEREST IN ASSYRIAN EXCAVATIONS

A large amount of cuneiform material had been gradually stored in the halls of the Louvre and of the British Museum towards the middle of the last century. Before other funds were likely to be granted by governments and liberal-minded individuals for the continuation of the excavations in Assyrian and Babylonian mounds, it became necessary to satisfy the learned, and to prove to the public at large that the numerous monuments and broken clay tablets unearthed could really be read, and that their intrinsic value or the contents of their inscriptions were well worth the capital and time spent in their rediscovery. The number of scholars ready to make the study of cuneiform inscriptions their chief occupation, or at least part of their life's work, was exceedingly limited, and those who had manifested any deeper interest in their interpretation were concerned more with the Persian inscriptions than with those of Assyria. Grotefend had tried repeatedly to elucidate the meaning of the most complicated of all cuneiform writings, — the so-called third system of the Persian monuments, but he had made little progress. In 1845, Loewenstern of Paris had guessed the Semitic character of the Assyrian language correctly. Soon afterwards De Longpérier had recognized a few proper names often occurring in the titles of the Khorsabâd inscriptions. Botta had published important collections of the different cuneiform signs found in the same texts, from which it was proved beyond doubt that the Assyrians could never have employed an alphabet. And following in the footsteps of his predecessors, De Saulcy had even gone so far as to undertake boldly the translation of an entire Assyrian inscription. But valuable as all these attempts were as public expressions of the growing interest in Assyrian literature and civilization, and of the constant efforts made to solve a difficult problem, the positive gain derived from them was very moderate. There was too much chaff mixed with the few grains of wheat which remained after sifting. To have finally accomplished the gigantic task in all its essential features, and at the same time to have laid that solid grammatical foundation upon which the young science of Assyriology gradually rose like a magnificent dome, and as a grand monument of the penetrating acumen and the conquering force of the human mind, is the lasting merit of Edward Hincks, an Irish clergyman, and of Colonel Rawlinson.

The combined labors of these two great British geniuses shed a flood of light upon a subject where previously nothing but darkness and utter confusion prevailed. But the results at which they had arrived by strictly scientific methods and through sound reasoning, appeared so extraordinary and strange even to those who were occupied with the study of ancient nations, and their manner of thinking and writing, that twenty-five years were necessary to secure for Assyriology the general recognition of the educated classes of Europe.

The detailed investigations of the many new questions raised by the successful determination of the numerous polyphone characters which constitute the Assyrian writing were, however, carried on vigorously by a few enthusiastic scholars of England and France, until, in 1857, a peculiar but impressive demonstration on the part of the Royal Asiatic Society[1] led to a public acknowledgment in England of the correctness of the principles of Assyrian deciphering and to a general acceptance of its startling conclusions. Soon afterwards (1859) Oppert's fundamental discussion of the whole problem, accompanied by a thorough

[1] Comp. p. 130, above.

analysis and a literal translation of representative inscriptions,[1] produced a similar effect in France, while it took ten to twenty years longer before German scepticism was fully overcome through Eberhard Schrader's renewed critical examination of the elaborate system of Assyrian writing, and his convincing proofs of the perfect reliability of the achieved philological and historical results.[2]

Meanwhile the rich cuneiform material previously gathered began to be made accessible to all those who were eager to participate in the fascinating researches of the newly established science. Rawlinson himself became the originator of a comprehensive plan, the execution of which was entrusted to him, in 1860, by the trustees of the British Museum. Ably assisted by Edwin Norris, Secretary of the Royal Asiatic Society, to whom we are indebted for the first attempt at compiling an Assyrian dictionary, and by George Smith, a talented engraver, who "was employed to sort the fragments, and tentatively to piece together such as seemed to him to belong to each other,"[3] the "father of Assyriology"—as Rawlinson has been well styled—undertook to publish the most important texts of the English collections in an accurate and trustworthy edition. In the course of twenty-four years five large volumes of "The Cuneiform Inscriptions of Western Asia"[4] were prepared by the united

[1] Comp. Oppert, *Expédition Scientifique en Mésopotamie*, vol. ii., p. 1859, and p. 171, above.

[2] Comp. E. Schrader, *Die Basis der Entzifferung der assyrisch-babylonischen Keilinschriften*, in *Zeitschrift der Deutschen Morgenländischen Gesellschaft*, vol. xxiii., Leipzig, 1869, and *Die assyrisch-babylonischen Kerlinschriften. Kritische Untersuchung der Grundlagen ihrer Entzifferung, nebst dem Babylonischen Texte der Trilinguen Inschriften in Transscription samt Übersetzung und Glossar, ibidem*, vol. xxvi., Leipzig, 1872, and furthermore, *Keilinschriften und Geschichtsforschung*, Giessen, 1878.

[3] Comp. George Rawlinson, "A Memoir of Major-General Sir Henry Creswicke Rawlinson," London, 1898, p. 240.

[4] Vol. i., London, 1861; vol. ii., 1866; vol. iii., 1870; vol. iv., 1875;

efforts of these three men and of Theophilus Pinches, who later took the places of Norris and Smith. Notwithstanding the numerous mistakes occurring on its pages, which must be attributed as much to the frequently unsatisfactory condition of the originals as to the defective knowledge of the laws of palæography and philology in these early days of Assyrian research, this English publication has remained the standard work from which our young science has drawn its chief nourishment until the present day.

GEORGE SMITH (1873–76)

In connection with his duties as Rawlinson's assistant George Smith manifested a decided gift for quickly recognizing the characteristic peculiarities of the many and often very similar cuneiform signs, which soon enabled him to acquire an extraordinary skill in finding missing fragments of broken tablets. Natural talents and personal inclinations, fostered by the frequent intercourse and conferences with the acknowledged master in the field of Assyriology, encouraged him to make strong efforts to overcome the disadvantages resulting from the lack of a proper education, and to occupy himself seriously with the language and writing of a people whose relics he was handling daily. It was particularly his earnest desire to contribute something towards a better understanding of the Old Testament which influenced him to devote his whole time to the study of the Assyrian monuments. After he had gone over the originals and paper casts of most of the historical inscriptions, especially of Ashurbânapal, whose annals he was the first to edit and to translate entirely, he began a methodical search for important texts among the thousands of fragments from the famous library of the same monarch.

2d edition (prepared by Pinches), 1891; vol. v., Part 1, 1880 (Pinches); Part 2, 1884 (Pinches).

While unpacking the numerous boxes, and cleaning their contents, his eye used to glance over the cuneiform characters, as they gradually appeared under his brush upon the surface of each tablet. To facilitate his later studies, he divided the whole material into six divisions. Whenever anything of interest attracted his attention, he laid the fragment aside, endeavoring to find the other parts and trying every piece that seemed to join or to throw some light on the new subject. One day, in the fall of 1872, he picked up a very large fragment of the "mythological division," which occupied his mind completely as soon as he commenced to decipher. He read of a destructive flood and of a great ship resting on the mountain of Nisir. A dove was sent out to try if the water had subsided. A swallow came next; but it found no resting place, and returned likewise. A raven followed, which noticed the receding waters, discovered something to eat, flew away and did not return.

Smith had discovered the Babylonian account of the Deluge, which in salient points agreed most strikingly with the Biblical narrative. He immediately made a brief announcement of what he had found. The general interest was roused. With renewed zeal he began to search for the missing pieces. After infinite toil he discovered portions of two other copies and several minor parts of the first fragment, at the same time recognizing that the Babylonian account of the Deluge formed the eleventh chapter of a series of probably twelve tablets containing the legends of the great national hero Gilgamesh, commonly known by the name of Izdubar from Smith's first provisional reading, and regarded as identical with the Nimrod of the Bible (Gen. 10). On December 3 of the same year Smith gave a public lecture before a large meeting of the Society of Biblical Archæology at which Rawlinson presided, while Gladstone and other prominent men took part in the discussion. He sketched the principal contents of the Gilgamesh legends, accompanied by a first coherent translation of the fragmentary account of the Deluge. The sensation created by this paper in England and elsewhere was extraordinary. Scientific and religious circles were equally profuse in their comment upon the value of the new discovery, and loud voices were heard pleading for the early resumption of the excavations in the mounds of Nineveh.

Before the government could act, the proprietors of the London "Daily Telegraph" seized this opportunity to make themselves, through Edwin Arnold, their editor-in-chief, the eloquent interpreters of the public sentiment. They offered to advance one thousand guineas for a fresh expedition to the East, if Smith would go out personally to search for other tablets of the interesting legends, and from time to time would send accounts of his journeys and discoveries to their paper. The British Museum accepted the generous proposition and granted the necessary leave of absence to its officer. On the 20th of January, 1873, George Smith left London, reaching Mosul, "the object of so many of his thoughts and hopes," six weeks later. But on his arrival in Assyria he learned that no firmân had yet been granted in Constantinople. Unable to obtain any favors from the local government, he started for Baghdad, on his way down the Tigris examining the mounds of Nimrûd and Qal'at Shirgât, as far as winter storms and rains would permit. He could spend only a fortnight in northern Babylonia, but it was profitably employed in buying antiquities and visiting the mounds of Babylon, El-Birs, Ohêmir and Tell Ibrâhîm in rapid succession. The more he looked upon these enormous heaps of rubbish gradually formed by the crumbling works of former generations, the more he realized the necessity of their methodical exploration. He would himself have preferred excavating in "the older and richer country" to searching for the fragmentary copies of Babylonian originals in the palaces of Assyrian kings. But it may well be doubted whether he would have been so successful in the South as he was with his clearly defined task and his limited time in the North. Most curious is his attempt at rearranging the principal ruins of Babylon in accordance with his own notions of the topography of the ancient metropolis. Notwithstanding his superior knowledge of the cuneiform inscriptions, and though contrary to all evidence adduced by the early explorers of the nineteenth century, he revived the old theory of Rennell and Mignan, believing the lofty mound of Bâbil to represent the remains of the temple of Belus. The hanging gardens were placed on the western side of the Qasr, between the river Euphrates and the palace of Nebuchadrezzar, and the fine yellow piers and buttresses of the latter regarded as part of them; while 'Omrân ibn 'Alî, "which promises little or nothing to an explorer," only marks "the spot, where the old city was most thickly inhabited." It was fortunate for Smith and for science that he had no time to imitate Layard's example at Babylon and Nippur, the final grant of the firmân calling him away to the mounds of Assyria.

On the 3d of April he was back in Mosul. Six days later he started his excavations at Nimrûd, which he continued for a whole month. There was no longer a chance of lighting on any new sculptured palaces or temples like those discovered by Botta and Layard. The "day of small things," announced long before by Rawlinson as "certain to follow on the rich yield of the earlier labours," had commenced. "New inscriptions and small objects of art are all that I expect to obtain from continual excavations either in Assyria or Babylonia," he had written to Sir Henry Ellis in 1853,[1] and the proceeds of the later operations fully justified his prediction. Smith opened trenches at nearly all the

[1] Comp. George Rawlinson, "A Memoir of Major-General Sir Henry Creswicke Rawlinson," London, 1898, pp. 117, *seq.*

different places of Nimrûd, where Layard and Rassam had won their laurels, but on the whole he found nothing but duplicates of texts and other antiquities previously known. His entire fresh harvest from the ruins of Calah consisted in part of an inscribed slab of Tiglath-Pileser III.; three terra-cotta models of a hand embedded in the walls — one of them bearing a legend of Ashurnâsirapal II.; fragments of enamelled bricks representing scenes of war; and a receptacle discovered in the floor of a room of the S. E. palace and filled with six terra-cotta winged genii. These figures apparently were placed there to protect the building and to secure fertility to its inmates.[1] From the ornamentation of the palace, the nature of the few objects gathered from its chambers, and inscribed bricks taken from the drains surrounding it, Smith was enabled to conclude that it originally must have been a private building for the wives and families of King Shalmaneser II. (later restored by Ashuretililâni).

On the 7th of May he moved to Qoyunjuk to begin his search for the remaining tablets of the royal library. He superintended the work in person, with the exception of a brief absence caused by his visits to the ruins of Hammâm 'Alî and Khorsabâd. The excavations proceeded but slowly. The whole ground had been cut up by former explorers and by the builders of the Mosul bridge, who extracted their materials from the foundation walls of the Assyrian palaces. Many of Layard's subterranean passages had collapsed, and small valleys and hills had been formed, changing the old contour of the mound entirely. Wherever the eye glanced, it saw nothing but pits and gulleys partly filled with rubbish, crumbling walls of unbaked clay threatening to fall at the slightest vibration, heavy blocks of stones peeping out of the ground, large pieces of sculptured slabs jammed

[1] Not merely "to preserve the building against the power of evil spirits;" Smith, "Assyrian Discoveries," 3d ed., New York, 1876, p. 78.

in between heaps of fragments of bricks, mortar, and pottery — a vast picture of utter confusion and destruction. To secure good results it would have been necessary to remove and to sift this whole mass of earth. All that Smith could do was to select the library spaces of the two ruined buildings and to examine that neighborhood once more for fragments of tablets, leaving their discovery chiefly to good luck and to fortunate circumstances. But after all, the mission for which he had been sent out was accomplished more quickly than he could have expected. On the 14th of May, on cleaning one of the fragments of cuneiform inscriptions from the palace of Ashurbânapal, the result of that day's digging, he found to his surprise and gratification "that it contained the greater portion of seventeen lines of inscription belonging to the first column of the Chaldean account of the Deluge, which

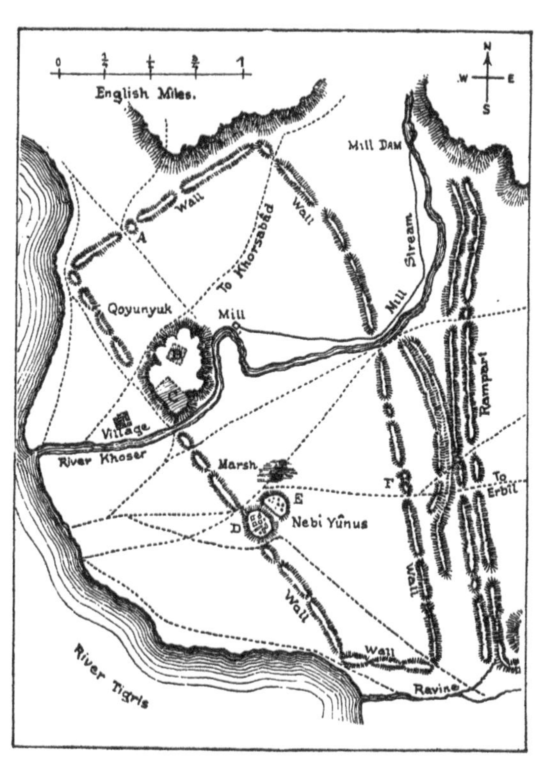

The Ruins of Nineveh

A North gate. B North palace (of Ashurbânapal). C South-west palace (of Sennacherib). D Village of Nebî Yûnus. E Burial ground. F Large east gate. Roads are marked thus: - - - - - - - -.

fitted into the only place where there was a serious blank in the story."[1] The cheerful news was soon cabled to London, in the expectation that the proprietors of the "Daily Telegraph" would feel encouraged to continue the excavations still longer. But considering "that the discovery of the missing fragment of the deluge text accomplished the object they had in view," they declined to authorize new explorations. Disappointed as Smith felt at the sudden termination of his work, he had to obey. On the 9th of June he withdrew his Arabs from the mound, leaving the same day for England, which country he reached forty days later, after his antiquities had been seized by the custom house officials in Alexandretta.

Through the representations of the British ambassador at Constantinople, the precious fragments of the library, which formed the principal result of his expedition, were soon released. Upon their arrival in London they received Smith's immediate attention. Before long he could report on the variety and importance of their contents. The trustees of the British Museum, realizing the value of the recent additions, decided to profit by the old firmân as long as it lasted, and, setting aside a sum of £1000, directed their curator to return to Nineveh at once and search for other inscriptions at the mound of Qoyunjuk. On the 25th of November, 1873, Smith was on the road again, arriving at Mosul on the first day of the new year. During the few months of his absence from the field things had changed considerably. Another governor, to whom the pasha of Mosul was subordinate, had been appointed at Baghdad. He now issued orders to watch the movements of the foreigner, to question his superintendents, and to place a scribe as spy over his excavations. Greatly annoyed as Smith naturally felt by constant false reports and many other im-

[1] The divine command to construct and to fill the ark with all kinds of living creatures.

pediments thrown in his way, he conducted his labors with characteristic determination, gradually increasing the number of his workmen to almost six hundred. The peculiar task of his mission requiring, as it did within the short period of two months, the examination of as wide an area as possible and the removal of an enormous amount of rubbish thrown upon the surface of the mound by the former excavators, explains sufficiently why he employed such a large body of men over which it was impossible to exercise a proper control. About the middle of March his firmân ceased. A few days previously he closed his researches. But a new embarrassment appeared. The local authorities refused to let him go, unless he delivered half of all the antiquities found as the share of the Ottoman Museum. Telegraphic communications were opened with the British ambassador at Constantinople, which subsequently led to a satisfactory arrangement with the Porte. Leaving only half of the duplicates in the hands of the Turkish officials, Smith could finally depart from Mosul on the 4th of April, 1874.

In examining the fruit of our explorer's two visits to the East, we are forcibly reminded of a word of Rawlinson. The immediate results of his excavations were "not such as to secure popular applause, or even to satisfy the utilitarian party;" they had to be studied at first to prove that they constituted a very decided gain for science. Under peculiar difficulties Smith had worked only three months altogether in the rich mines of antiquities at Ḳoyunjuk. But in this limited space of time he had obtained over 3000 inscriptions from the royal library of Nineveh, including mythological, astronomical, chronological, and grammatical texts, prayers, hymns, and litanies, syllabaries, and bilingual tablets of the utmost importance. Moreover, the majority of the fragments rescued formed parts of inscriptions, the other portions of which were already in the British Museum, thus completing or greatly enlarging representative texts of nearly all the different branches of Assyrian literature. Among the new inscriptions which he brought home, there were fragments of the Chaldean stories of the Creation, of the Fall of Man, of the Deluge, and portions of the national epics of Gilgamesh; the legend of the seven evil spirits; the mythical account of the youth of Sargon of Agade; a "tablet for recording the division of heavens according to the four seasons and the rule for regulating the intercalary month of the year"; the report of an eclipse of the moon and its probable meaning for Assyria; an officer's communication to the king as to repairs necessary at the queen's palace at Kabzi (=Tell Shemâmyk); a beautiful bilingual hymn to Ishtar, as "the light of heaven"; an invocation to the deified hero Gilgamesh; explanations of the ideographs of prominent Assyrian and Babylonian cities; directions to the workmen as to what inscriptions are to be carved over the various sculptures in the palace, and many other tablets of equal interest and importance. His new acquisitions added no less to our knowledge of the general history of Assyria and its neighboring countries. I mention only the fine stone tablet of Adadnirâri I. (about 1325 B. C.),[1] purchased from the French consul at Mosul; the votive dishes and bricks of his son, Shalmaneser I., from a palace and temple at Nineveh; the first inscription of Mutakkil-Nusku (about 1175 B. C.); the Assyrian copy of the genealogy and building operations of the Cassite king, Agumkakrime (about 1600 B. C.); a new fragment of the synchronous history of Assyria and Babylonia in the thirteenth century; the expedition of Sargon against Ashdod (Is. 20:1) from a new octagonal prism; a large number of texts to complete the annals of Sennacherib, Esarhaddon, and Ashurbânapal, and part of a barrel cylinder of Sinsharishkun, the last Assyrian ruler — all of which were discovered at the mound of

[1] Which had been discovered in the ruins of Qal'at Shirgât on the Tigris.

Qoyunjuk. Compared with former expeditions the excavations of Smith furnished but little on the subject of art and architecture. This cannot surprise us, for he was sent out not to find sculptures and palaces, but to search for those small fragments of inscriptions which others had neglected to extract from their trenches.

After his return to England in June, 1874, George Smith was occupied for some time with a renewed examination of the Qoyunjuk collection of tablets, in order to gather and to translate all those texts which dealt with the earliest Babylonian legends, and through their frequent remarkable coincidence with similar stories in the Old Testament were likely to throw new light upon the first chapters of the Pentateuch, and to illustrate the origin and development of ancient Hebrew traditions. In rapid succession he published his "Assyrian Discoveries" (London, 1875), which gave the history and principal results of his two expeditions, and "The Chaldean Account of Genesis" (London, 1876), containing the translations of Babylonian legends and fables from the cuneiform inscriptions discovered by Layard, Rassam, and himself. Both books were received enthusiastically by the public, the latter witnessing no less than five editions within a few months. It was doubtless in no small part due to this great popularity, which the researches of Smith found again in consequence of their bearing upon the Bible, that, in the fall of 1875, the British Museum decided to resume its excavations at Nineveh. In March, 1876, after the necessary firmân had been granted again, Smith could start for the East a third time. A collection of antiquities unearthed by the Arabs at Jumjuma the previous winter, and offered for sale to Rawlinson, led him at first to Baghdad. But on his arrival he found himself seriously embarrassed. The whole population was in a state of great excitement. Cholera and plague had appeared and played terrible havoc among the inhabitants of the towns and the wandering tribes of the desert. Order and discipline had become words without meaning, the regular channels of communication with the officials were frequently interrupted, and the laws of hospitality were no longer respected. Smith tried in vain to fight against unfortunate circumstances and superior forces. As long as the dreaded maladies kept their iron rule in the country, there was no possibility for him to begin excavations. Unmindful of the dangers from climate and constant exposure, working too much and resting too little, often without food and finding no shelter, he gradually broke down on the road. With difficulty he dragged himself to Aleppo, where on the 19th of August he died[1] in the house of the English consul, having fallen a staunch fighter in the cause of science.

In looking back upon the short but eventful life of George Smith as a scholar and as an explorer, we cannot but admire the man who by his extraordinary zeal and power of will became one of the most remarkable interpreters of cuneiform inscriptions whom England has produced. Without the advantage of a well directed instruction, and in his early days debarred from those beneficial associations with inspiring men which essentially help to color our life and to shape our character, he was left to his own inclinations until he attracted the attention of Rawlinson. With the latter as a guide, and supported by natural gifts, he worked hard to train his mind and to fill out those gaps which separated him from the republic of letters. But notwithstanding all his serious exertions, he did not succeed entirely in effacing the traces of a desultory self-education, and the obnoxious influences of an unguarded youth. As an explorer he did not possess that linguistic talent, that

[1] Comp. the notices of his death in "The Academy," vol. x., pp. 265, *seq.*, and "The Athenæum" of Sept. 9, 1876, p. 338. Extracts from Smith's last diary were published by Delitzsch, *Wo lag das Paradies?* Leipzig, 1881, pp. 266, *seq.*

congenial manner of adapting oneself to the customs and laws of the East, that loving sympathy with the joys and sorrows of the children of the desert, which won for Layard the respect and confidence of the natives, and made him a welcome guest at every camp-fire and tent of the Arabs. And as a scholar he did not acquire that depth and extent of knowledge, that independence of judgment and bold self-reliance which permeate the writings of Rawlinson, nor could he ever boast of Hinck's mental brilliancy and that subtle understanding of grammatical rules which characterize the latter's works. But stern in the conception of his duties, always thinking of his task and never of his person, provided with an astonishing memory, and a highly developed sense for the differences of form, he stands unexcelled in his masterly knowledge of the cuneiform inscriptions of the British Museum, while his numerous contributions to science testify to that rare intuition and gift of divination which enabled him often to translate correctly where others failed to grasp the meaning.

RASSAM (1878–82).

Upon the sudden death of George Smith the trustees of the British Museum requested Hormuzd Rassam to take charge again of the excavations in the Assyrian mounds. Although in 1869 the latter had resigned his political appointment at Aden and retired to private life in England, after many hardships experienced as prisoner of King Theodore of Abyssinia, he accepted the proffered trust at once and started for Constantinople in November, 1876, in order to obtain a more satisfactory firmân than had been granted to his predecessor. But all his efforts in this direction proved without result. Certain grave political complications which soon led to the Turco-Russian war, and the unexpected termination of the International Conference at Pera which tried to prevent it, had created a situation most unfavorable to the resumption of archæological researches in the Ottoman empire. Edhem Pasha, father of Hamdy Bey, the present director-general of the Imperial Museum at Stambul, was then Grand Vizier. He was not ill disposed towards England, but as one of Turkey's most eminent and enlightened statesmen, he considered it his first duty to protect and promote the interests of his own country. Accordingly, he suggested that "a convention should be entered into between the British government and the Porte, giving the sole privilege to England of making researches in Turkey, similar to that which had been agreed upon between Germany and Greece." Such an arrangement, however, was to be based upon the condition that Turkey retained all the antiquities discovered, with option of giving only duplicates to the British Museum. But Rassam did not consider himself authorized to spend public money without the prospect of some material compensation. Looking upon the mere right of publishing the scientific results as "an empty favor," for which he had little understanding, he declined the proposition of the Grand Vizier as a one-sided agreement, and returned to England after having waited nearly four months in a vain effort to accomplish his purpose.

All the ambassadors had left Constantinople before, as a last protest against Turkey's stubborn and most unfortunate attitude towards the conciliatory measures proposed by the great European powers. But England deemed it soon necessary to dispatch a special representative to the Turkish capital, who was well versed in Oriental matters and publicly known as a warm friend of the Ottoman empire. The choice of the British government fell upon Sir Henry Layard, who at that time occupied a similar position at the court of Spain. No better appointment could have been made for realizing the plans of the British Museum. Two months after Layard's arrival at Constantinople (April, 1877), we find Rassam again on the shore of the Bosphorus, inspired with fresh enthusiasm by the hope of attaining the object of his mission under the more favorable new constellation. Deeply interested as the ambassador still was in the Assyrian researches of his nation, which more than thirty years previously he had inaugurated so successfully himself, he addressed the Sultan personally for a renewal of the old concessions repeatedly accorded to the British Museum. The request was granted at once, but before the official document could be signed, Rassam "received orders from Sir Henry Layard, under direction of the Foreign Office," to visit the Armenians and other Christians in Asia Minor who were reported to be maltreated and in danger of being massacred by their fanatic Kurdish neighbors. About the time when this diplomatic mission was completed, — towards the end of 1877, — Rassam was informed by cable that the Sublime Porte had formally sanctioned the resumption of his excavations in Assyria. A few weeks later he commenced that series of explorations which, with several short interruptions, generally caused by the ceasing of the necessary funds at home, were carried on with his well-known energy, in four distinct campaigns, for a period of nearly five years, from January 7, 1878, to the end of July, 1882.[1]

[1] *First Expedition:* He leaves England June, 1877, Constantinople a month later, begins operations at the Assyrian mounds Jan. 7, 1878, departs from Mosul May 17, returns to London July 12 of the same year.

Second Expedition: He leaves England Oct. 8, 1878, arrives at Mosul Nov. 16, descends the Tigris for Baghdad Jan. 30, 1879, excavates and explores Babylonian sites during February and March, returns to Mosul April 2, departs for Europe May 2, reaches London June 19 of the same year.

Third Expedition: He leaves London April 7, 1880, arrives at Hilla May 24, superintends the excavations at Babylon and neighboring ruins for eight days, spends a week in Baghdad, leaves this city June 9, reaches Mosul a fortnight later, departs for Wan July 15, reaches the latter July 29, for a month resumes the excavations at Toprak Kale, which at his request an American missionary, Dr. Reynolds (later in conjunction with Captain Clayton,

As long as Layard occupied his influential position at the Turkish capital (1877–80) there was no difficulty in obtaining new grants, and the special recommendation of his excavator to all the local authorities in the different provinces of the Ottoman empire. The first firmân lasted only one year. It gave Rassam the right to explore any Assyrian ruin not occupied by Moslem tombs, and allotted one third of the antiquities discovered to the British Museum, one third to the owner of the mound, and the rest to the Archæological Museum at Constantinople, the share of the latter naturally being doubled in case the site was crown property. An imperial delegate, who was appointed at first to guard the interests of the Ministry of Public Instruction in the trenches, was soon afterwards withdrawn on the representation of the British ambassador. The second firmân, written in the name of Layard, must be regarded as a gracious compliment paid to him by the Sultan. It was granted for two years (until Oct. 15, 1880), with the promise of a further term (till 1882), if required, and invested Layard with the exceptional power of carrying on excavations simultaneously in the various ruins of the vilayets of Baghdad, Aleppo, and Wan (Mosul being included in the first-named pashalic),

the newly appointed British consul), had carried on for him since 1879. He leaves Wan Sept. 10, returns to Mosul Sept. 27, superintends the Assyrian excavations for six weeks, leaves Mosul by raft Nov. 11, excavates at Babylon and El-Birs during the first three weeks in December. Then he proceeds northward to explore other Babylonian ruins and to search for the site of ancient Sippara, begins his excavations at Abû Habba and tries Tell Ibrâhîm and other neighboring mounds during the first four months of 1881, departs from Abû Habba for the Mediterranean May 3, 1881, reaching England about two months later.

Fourth Expedition: He leaves England March 7, 1882, reaches Baghdad April 21, superintends the excavations at Abû Habba until the end of July, waits nearly three months longer at Baghdad for a renewal of the firmân, but, disappointed in his hopes, departs for Basra Oct. 22, 1882, leaves the latter port Nov. 11 by steamer, reaching London again in December, 1882.

giving him, in addition, the privilege of retaining all the antiquities found except duplicates, after their mere formal inspection by an imperial commissioner.

It was a comparatively easy task for Rassam to excavate under such favorable conditions and supported by a powerful friend. The remarkable results which accompanied his labors in Babylonia will be treated later. The method followed was everywhere the same. Owing to the large geographical area included in his permit it was impossible for him to superintend all the excavations in person. As a rule he directed them only from the distance, sometimes not visiting the same ruin for weeks and months, and in a few cases even for a whole year. During his absence from 'Irâq, the British Resident at Baghdad undertook a general control of his excavations in Babylonia, while at Mosul his nephew, Nimrûd Rassam, acted most of the time as his agent in connection with the operations conducted on several Assyrian sites. A number of intelligent native overseers, among whom a certain Dâûd Tômâ played a conspicuous rôle as his representative at Babylon, carried on the work as well as they could and as far as possible in accordance with their master's instructions. One can easily imagine how unsatisfactory such an arrangement must prove in the end, as diametrically opposed to all sound principles of a strict scientific investigation and in part as contrary to the very explicit instructions received from the British Museum. It was the old system of pillage in a new and enlarged edition. Nobody recognized and felt this more than Hamdy Bey, to whom we must be truly grateful for sparing no efforts to stop this antiquated and obnoxious system immediately after the termination of Rassam's concession in 1882. Through his energetic measures, which led to a complete reorganization of the Ottoman laws of excavation, henceforth no person received permission to explore more than one ancient ruin at the same time, and this only with the express stipulation that all the antiquities recovered became the exclusive property of the Imperial Museum in Constantinople.

Before Rassam left England in 1877, his duties had been clearly defined by the trustees of the great London Museum. In continuing the work of his lamented predecessor, he was ordered to concentrate his activity upon the mounds of Nineveh, and to try to secure as many fragments as possible from the library of Ashurbânapal. But such a task was very little to the liking of Rassam, whose personal ambition was directed to sensational finds rather than to a careful search for broken clay tablets which he could not read, and the importance of which he was not educated enough to realize. We cannot do better than to quote his own words: "Although that was the first object of my mission, I was, nevertheless, more eager to discover some new ancient sites than to confine my whole energy on such a tame undertaking. . . . My aim was to discover unknown edifices, and to bring to light some important Assyrian monument."[1] His ambition was soon to be gratified.

A year before he was commissioned to renew the British explorations in Assyria, a friend of his, employed as dragoman in the French consulate at Mosul, had sent him two pieces of ancient bronze adorned with figures and cuneiform signs, in which Sayce recognized the name of Shalmaneser. Upon the latter's advice, Rassam endeavored to determine, immediately after his return to the banks of the Tigris, where these relics had been found. It did not take him long to learn that the two pieces presented to him were part of a large bronze plate accidentally unearthed by a peasant in the mound of Balawât(d), about fifteen miles to the east of Mosul. On examining this ruin he observed that the whole site had been largely used as a burial ground by the native population of that district, and was therefore excluded from the

[1] Comp. Rassam, "Asshur and the Land of Nimrod," New York, 1897, p. 200.

sphere of his firmân. But feeling that the exceptional character of the desired monument "was well worth the risk of getting into hot water with the authorities, and even with the villagers," he troubled himself concerning the restrictions imposed upon him by law or etiquette just as little then, as he had done twenty-four years previously, when he tore down the barrier erected by Rawlinson, and occupied the French territory of Qoyunjuk. However, it cost him considerable time and anxiety and frequent disappointment before he obtained the much coveted prize. The excitement and disturbance among the Arabs of the neighboring tribes subsequent to his first attempts at cutting trenches in the promising mound were extraordinary, and at times threatened to end in serious conflicts and bloodshed. There even were moments when he himself lost all hope of ever reaching the object of his desire and efforts. But by profiting from every temporary lull in the storm, by distributing occasional small gifts among the dissatisfied workmen, and by superintending the excavations, as far as possible, himself, he overcame the chief opposition, and the strong prejudices of the owners of graves, so far as to enable him to ascertain the general contents of the mound, and to make some most valuable discoveries.

Shortly after the commencement of their operations the workmen came upon several scrolls or strips of bronze, in form and execution similar to those in his possession. Originally about four inches thick, they had suffered greatly from corrosion and other causes, and no sooner had they been exposed to the air, when they began to crack and to crumble, offering no small difficulty to their safe removal to Mosul. Within five days the whole twisted and bent mass was uncovered and packed in proper cases large enough to take in the full length of this remarkable monument. Sixty feet away to the northwest a second set of bronze strips was disclosed, half the size of the former, and in several other characteristic features differing from it. It was, however, so much injured from the dampness of the soil in which it had been hidden for more than 2500 years, that it fell to pieces immediately after its discovery. These ornamented bronze plates had once covered the cedar gates of a large Assyrian building. Each leaf of the first-mentioned better-preserved monument consisted of seven panels eight feet long, and

Part of a Bronze Panel from the Great Palace Gate of Balawât

richly embossed with double rows of figures surrounded by a border of rosettes. The plates represent a variety of subjects taken from the life and campaigns of a king, who according to the accompanying inscription was no other than Shalmaneser II.[1] The ancient town buried under the rub-

[1] The publication of this important monument was undertaken in 1881 by the Society of Biblical Archæology, but for some reason it has never been finished. Comp. "The Bronze Ornaments of the Palace Gates of Balawat," edited, with an introduction, by Samuel Birch, with descriptions and translations by Theophilus G. Pinches, parts i.–iv., 72 plates, London.

bish heap of Balawât was called Imgur-Bêl. It had been chosen by Ashurnâsirapal II. as the site for one of his palaces, restored and completed by his son and successor, Shalmaneser.

By means of tunnels Rassam extended his excavations to various sections of the interesting mound, at one place coming upon the ruins of a small temple, at the entrance of which stood a huge marble coffer. The latter contained two beautiful tablets of the same material covered with identical inscriptions of Ashurnâsirapal; a similar third tablet was lying upon an altar in its neighborhood, and fragments of others were scattered among the débris. Exaggerated rumors of this "great find" spread rapidly. Some credulous people insisted that a treasure-chest full of gold had been brought to light, while others believed that the very stone tablets of Moses inscribed with the Ten Commandments had been discovered. Great excitement was the result in the trenches, and new riots broke out in the villages. The large quantity of human bones constantly unearthed tended only to increase the general irritation, and to inflame all slumbering passions. After a little while Rassam found it useless to contend longer against ignorance and fanaticism. As soon as he had cleared the little chamber entirely, he abandoned his trenches at Balawât, convinced that a thorough examination of the whole remarkable site was an absolute impossibility for the time being.

The discovery of such a unique specimen of ancient metallurgy as the bronze gates of Imgur-Bêl had well inaugurated the resumption of Rassam's researches in the Assyrian mounds. Neary 500 workmen were occupied at the same time, to continue the British excavations at Qoyunjuk and Nimrûd. The most promising space of the palaces of Sennacherib and Ashurbânapal, practically stripped of only their bas-reliefs and larger objects of art by the early explorers, had been subjected by Smith to a more careful examination. The quick results of his labors have been treated above. To extricate more of the precious fragments from the royal library, it became necessary to remove all the débris thrown in the excavated halls, or without system heaped upon some unexplored part of the ruin. The large pillars of earth left untouched by Layard and Rassam in the centres of the different rooms (comp. p. 115) and every enclosing wall likely to contain relics of the past were torn down. The number of tablets obtained in the end were not as great as Smith had expected. Instead of the 20,000 fragments calculated by him to remain buried in the unexcavated portions of the palace of Sennacherib, scarcely 2000 were gathered by Rassam from the two buildings after five years' labors.[1] But an important and nearly perfect decagon prism in terra-cotta inscribed with the annals of Ashurbânapal[2] was found in a solid brick wall of the north palace, and no less than four fine barrel-cylinders of Sennacherib,[3] covered with identical records, were taken from the southwest palace in rapid succession.

The results from the trenches of Nimrûd were rather meagre. In resuming the exploration of the two temples discovered by Layard near the northwest edge of the elevated ruin, Rassam unearthed a marble altar, and several inscribed marble seats still standing in their original positions; he gathered a few bas-reliefs, a number of carved stones, and clay tablets, and filled more than half a dozen baskets with fragments of enamelled tiles. But here as well as in other

[1] All the tablets and fragments so far obtained by the British Museum from the royal library of Nineveh were made accessible to scientific research through C. Bezold's fine "Catalogue of the Cuneiform Tablets in the Kouyunjik Collection of the British Museum," 5 vols., London, 1889–99.

[2] Two fragmentary and crumbling copies of this important monument had been discovered by Rassam in the same palace as early as 1854. Comp. p. 136, above.

[3] One of them is preserved in the Imperial Ottoman Museum at Constantinople.

parts of the country his work bore more the character of a gleaning following the rich harvest which he with Layard had gathered from the same ruin fields a quarter of a century before. Notwithstanding all his serious efforts to make other startling discoveries like that which had crowned his first year's labors at Balawât, and notwithstanding the fact that the excavations at Nimrûd and Qoyunjuk, at Qal'at Shirgât, and other Assyrian mounds, never ceased entirely during the five years which he spent again in the service of the British Museum, his great expectations were not to be realized. For a little while, in 1879, it had seemed as if Rassam would be able to accomplish what all the great Assyrian excavators before him had tried in vain — the partial exploration of Nebî Yûnus. Layard had managed through one of his overseers to dig for a few days in the courtyard of a Moslem house, proving the existence of buildings and monuments of Adadnirâri III., Sennacherib and Esarhaddon in the interior of this second large ruin of Nineveh. In 1852, Hilmi Pasha, then governor of Mosul, had excavated there eight or nine months for the Ottoman government, discovering two large winged bulls, several bas-reliefs, and an important marble slab, commonly known among Assyriologists as "Sennacherib Constantinople." [1] But since then nobody had made another move to disclose the secrets of Nebî Yûnus. Rassam went quietly and cautiously to work by making friends among the different classes of the inhabitants of the village, which occupied nearly the whole mound. With infinite patience and energy he gradually overcame the opposition of the most

[1] This monument disappeared suddenly from the collections of the Imperial Museum between 1873 and 1875 under Déthier's administration. Comp. Hilprecht in *Zeitschrift für Assyriologie*, vol. xiii., pp. 322–326. Within the last few months I have been able to trace the lost marble slab to the shores of England, where at some future day it may possibly be rediscovered in the halls of the British Museum.

influential and fanatic circles, succeeding even in winning the confidence and assistance of the guardians of the holy shrine dedicated to the memory of the prophet Jonah. Well-to-do landowners began to offer him their courtyards for trial-trenches without asking for an indemnity or remuneration; others, who were in poorer circumstances, were ready to sell him their miserable huts for a small sum. If he had possessed money enough, he "could have bought half of the village for a mere trifle." Many of the laborers whom he employed at Qoyunjuk had been prudently chosen from Nebî Yûnus. It was only natural, therefore, that they should faithfully stand by their master, strengthening his hands in the new undertaking at their own village. One morning operations were hopefully started at the great ruin. In the beginning everything went on very well. But before his tentative examination could have yielded any satisfactory results, the jealousy and intrigues of some evil-disposed individuals, who brought their influence to bear upon the local authorities of Mosul and upon the Minister of Public Instruction at Constantinople, caused the temporary suspension of his excavations, soon followed by the entire annihilation of all his dreams.[1]

With Rassam's return to England, in 1882, the Assyrian excavations of the nineteenth century have practically come to an end. E. A. Wallis Budge of the British Museum has since paid repeated visits to the East (1888, 1889, 1891), looking after English interests also at Qoyunjuk and neighboring mounds. Other scholars and explorers (the present writer included) have wandered over those barren hills, meditating over Nineveh's days of splendor, gazing at Calah's sunken walls, resting for a little while on

[1] Comp. Hormuzd Rassam, "Asshur and the Land of Nimrod," New York, 1897. This book contains a narrative of his different journeys in Mesopotamia, Assyria, and Babylonia, and the account of his principal discoveries in the ruins which he excavated.

Ashur's lonely site. But no expedition has pitched its tents again with the roaming tribes between the Tigris and the Zâb; the sounds of pickaxe and spade have long ago died away. Only now and then a stray cuneiform tablet or an inscribed marble slab, accidentally found in the mounds when a house is built, or a tomb is dug, reminds us of the great possibilities connected with methodical researches in those distant plains. Much more remains to be done, before the resurrection of ancient Assyria will be accomplished. Hundreds of ruins scarcely yet known by their names await the explorer. It is true, not all of them will yield magnificent palaces and lofty temples, gigantic human-headed bulls and elaborate sculptures. But whether the results be great or small, every fragment of inscribed clay or stone will tell a story, and contribute its share to a better knowledge of the life and history, of the art and literature, of that powerful nation which conquered Babylon, transplanted Israel, subdued Egypt, even reached Cyprus, and left its monuments carved on the rocky shores of the Mediterranean.

4

METHODICAL EXCAVATIONS IN BABYLONIA

The large number of fine monuments of art which through the efforts of a few determined explorers had been sent from the districts of the Euphrates and Tigris to the national collections in Paris and London, came almost exclusively from the mounds of Assyria proper. Marble, so liberally used as a decorative element and building material in the palaces and temples of the empire in the North, seemed but rarely[1] to have been employed by the inhabit-

[1] Marble, sandstone and granite as building materials in ancient Babylonia were found to any great extent only in the temple ruin of Abû Shahrain

ants of the alluvial plain in the South, where from the earliest times clay evidently took the place of stone. The tentative excavations of Loftus and Taylor in ancient Chaldea had indeed been of fundamental importance. They gave us a first glimpse of the long and varied history, and of the peculiar and interesting civilization of a country of which we knew very little before; they even revealed to us in Babylonian soil the existence of antiquities considerably older than those which had been unearthed at Nimrûd and Qal'at Shirgât; but, on the whole, they had been unproductive of those striking artistic remains which without any comment from the learned appeal directly to the mind of intelligent people. The decided failure of Layard's attempts at Babylon and Nuffar, and the widely felt disappointment with regard to the tangible results of the French excavations under Fresnel and Oppert did not tend to raise the Babylonian mounds in the public estimation, or to induce governments and private individuals to send new expeditions into a country half under water, half covered with the sand of the desert, and completely in the control of lawless and ignorant tribes.

But however seriously these and similar considerations at first must have affected the plans and decisions of other explorers, the chief obstacle to the commencement of methodical excavations in Babylonian ruins was doubtless the brilliant success of Botta, Layard, and Rassam in the North, which for a long while distracted the general attention from ancient Chaldea. Moreover, the epoch-making discovery of the royal library of Nineveh provided such a vast mass of choice cuneiform texts, written in an extremely neat and regular script on well-prepared and carefully baked

(Eridu) situated in a depression of the Arabian desert, where stone apparently was as easily obtained as clay. Comp. pp. 178, *seqq.*, above. In the Seleucidan and Parthian periods under foreign influence, stone was used considerably more all over Babylonia.

material, and at the same time representing nearly every branch of Assyrian literature — precisely what the first pioneers of the young science needed to restore the dictionary and to establish the grammatical laws of the long-forgotten language — that the few unbaked and crumbling tablets from the South, with their much more difficult writing and their new palæographical problems, with their unknown technical phrases and their comparatively uninteresting contents, naturally received but little attention in the early days of Assyriology.

It is true, the increasing study of the thousands of clay-books from Nineveh demonstrated more and more the fact that the great literary products with which they make us acquainted are only copies of Babylonian originals; and the subsequent comparison of the sculptured monuments of Assyria with the seal-cylinders and other often mutilated objects of art from the ruins and tombs of Chaldea again led scholars to the neighbourhood of the Persian Gulf as the real cradle of this whole remarkable civilization. But a new powerful influence was needed to overcome old prejudices entirely and to place the Babylonian mounds in the centre of public attention. The well-known archæological mines in the North, which had seemed to yield an almost inexhaustible supply of valuable monuments, began gradually to give forth less abundantly and even to cease altogether. The sudden death of George Smith, who had stimulated and deepened the interest of the religious communities of his nation in cuneiform research, and thereby temporarily revived the old enthusiasm for British excavations at Qoyunjuk, marked the beginning of the end of that brief but significant period which bears the stamp of his personality as the great epigone of the classical age of Assyrian exploration.

FRENCH EXCAVATIONS AT TELLÔ UNDER DE SARZEC

It was the French representative at Mosul who in 1842 had successfully inaugurated the resurrection of the palaces and temples of Assyria; and it was another French representative at Basra who thirty-five years later made a no less far-reaching discovery in the mounds of Chaldea, which opened the second great period in the history of Assyrian and Babylonian exploration, — the period of methodical excavations in the ruins of Babylonia proper. In January, 1877, Ernest de Sarzec, a man of tall stature and expressive features, then about forty years old, combining an active mind and sharp intellect with a pronounced taste for art and archæology, and through his previous service in Egypt and Abyssinia well versed in Oriental manners and to a certain degree familiar with the life of the desert, was transferred to Basra as vice-consul of France.

This city, situated on a rich alluvial soil of recent formation and surrounded by luxuriant gardens and palm-groves, which for sixty miles on both sides accompany the grand but muddy river until it empties into the Persian Gulf near the light-house of Fâo, is one of the hottest and most unhealthy places in the whole Turkish empire. The population is almost exclusively Mohammedan. The few European merchants and representatives of foreign governments, who live as a small colony by themselves along the west bank of the Shatt el-'Arab, outside the city proper, suffer more or less from fever and the enervating influence of the oppressive climate. An occasional ride into the desert, with its bracing air, and the hunting of the wild boar, francolin, and bustard are the general means by which the members of the European colony try to keep up their energy and vitality in the hot-house atmosphere of this tropical region. But such an aimless life was very little to the liking of De Sarzec, who longed for a more serious occupation to fill out the ample time left him by the slight duties of his consular position. Being stationed near the ruins of some of the great centres of ancient civilization, he decided at once to visit the sites of Babylon and El-Birs, and to devote his leisure hours, if practicable, to the exploration of a section of Southern Babylonia.

He was very fortunate to find a trustworthy councillor in J. Asfar, a prominent native Christian, and the present hospitable representative of the Strick-Asfar line of steamboats plying regularly between London and Basra. The latter had formerly dealt in antiquities and was personally acquainted with several Arab diggers, who continued to keep him well informed as to the most promising ruins between the Euphrates and the Tigris. The name of Tellô had recently become a watchword among them in consequence of the discovery of inscribed bricks and cones and the partly inscribed torso of a fine statue of Gudea in diorite,[1] said to have come from these ruins.[2] It is Asfar's merit to have first directed the attention of De Sarzec to this remarkable site and to have urged him to lose no time in examining it more closely and in securing it for France.[3] In order to avoid undesirable public attention, the French vice-consul deemed it wise for the present not to apply for the necessary firmân at Constantinople, but to begin his

[1] Published by Lenormant, *Choix de Textes Cunéiformes inédits*, Paris, 1873–75, p. 5, no. 3, and in George Smith, "History of Babylonia," edited by A. H. Sayce, London, 1877.

[2] No sufficient reasons have been brought forward, however, to show that this torso actually came from Tellô. Mr. Leonard W. King, of the British Museum, whom I asked for information as to its place of origin, was unable to throw any light on this question. Comp. p. 221, note 1, below.

[3] For valuable information as to the immediate causes which led to De Sarzec's great discovery, I am obliged to his friend, Mr. Asfar, who had preserved his deep interest in Babylonian excavations as late as 1900, when the present writer spent nearly three weeks at Basra and its neighborhood, frequently enjoying his unbounded hospitality.

operations as quietly as possible, somewhat in the manner followed by the first explorers of Assyria. Moreover, the whole of Southern Babylonia was then in a kind of semi-independent state under Nâsir Pasha, the great chief of the Muntefik(j), who built the town of Nasrîye called after him, and was appointed the first wâli of Basra. It was therefore necessary to secure his good will and protection for any scientific undertaking that might be carried on in regions where the law of the desert prevailed, and Nâsir's power was the only acknowledged authority. Immediately after his arrival on the Persian Gulf, De Sarzec entered into personal communication with the latter and established those friendly relations by means of which he was able to travel safely everywhere among his tribes and to excavate at Tellô or any other ruin as long as Nâsir retained his position.

In March of 1877, after a brief reconnoitring tour along the banks of the Shatt el-Haï, we find De Sarzec already in the midst of his work, commencing that series of brief but successful campaigns which were soon to surprise the scientific world, and to make Tellô, previously scarcely known by name in Europe, the "Pompeii of the early Babylonian antiquity."[1] For very apparent reasons De Sarzec did not write the history of his various expeditions extending over a considerable part of the last twenty-four years of the nineteenth century, so that it becomes extremely difficult for us to gather all the facts and data necessary to obtain a clear conception of the genesis and maturing of his plans, of the precise results of each year's exploration, of the difficulties which he encountered, and of the methods and ways by which he overcame all the obstacles, and in the end accomplished his memorable task.

[1] Thus styled by Heuzey in the introduction to his *Catalogue de la Sculpture Chaldéenne au Musée du Louvre*, Paris, 1901, the galley-proofs of which he kindly placed at my disposal in January, 1901, long before the book itself appeared.

His excavations were carried on in eleven distinct campaigns, generally lasting from three to four months in winter and spring. With regard to the three great intervals lying between them, they might be grouped together into four different periods, each of which is characterized by some more or less conspicuous discovery: I. 1877, 1878, 1880, 1881; II. 1888, 1889; III. 1893, 1894, 1895; IV. 1898, 1900. But as the excavations conducted by De Sarzec at Tellô in the later years consisted mainly in deepening and extending the trenches previously opened at the two principal elevations of the ruins, a mere chronological enumeration of all his single discoveries would neither do justice to the explorer, nor enable us to comprehend the importance of the results obtained in their final totality, as well as in their mutual relation to each other. It will therefore be preferable to consider the excavations from an historical and a topographical point of view at the same time. In this way we shall be enabled to preserve the unity of the subject and to avoid unnecessary repetitions. Accordingly we distinguish three phases in the excavations of De Sarzec: 1. His preliminary work of determining the character of the whole ruins by trial trenches, 1877–78; 2. The excavation of a Seleucidan palace and of ancient Babylonian remains, especially a fine collection of large statues at the principal mound of Tellô, 1880–81; 3. The unearthing of constructions, sculptures and inscriptions of a still earlier civilization in another prominent mound of the same ruins, 1888–89, 1893–95, 1898, 1900.

1. The ruins of Tellô, or more correctly Tell-Lô,[1] are situated in a district which is half the year a desert and the other half a swamp, about eight miles to the northeast of Shatra, a small Turkish town and the seat of a *qâimmaqâm*,

[1] The meaning and etymology of Tellô is obscure. An attempt by the late Dr. Schéfer of Paris to explain the name is found in Heuzey, *Découvertes en Chaldée par Ernest de Sarzec*, p. 8, note 1.

or sub-governor. They include a number of higher and lower elevations stretching from northwest to southeast for about four English miles along the left bank of a large dry canal that represents either the ancient bed or a branch of the Shatt el-Haï, from which in a straight line they are distant a little over three English miles. The two principal mounds of the whole site are designated as mounds A and B in the following sketch. The former and smaller one (A) rises only fifty feet above the plain at the extreme northwest end of the ruins, while the latter (B) is nearly fifty-six feet high and about 650 feet to the southeast of it. These and the many other smaller mounds constituting the ruins of Tellô consist as a rule of an artificial massive terrace of unbaked brick, upon and around which the scattered remains of one or more ancient buildings once occupying the platform are mixed with the sand of the desert into one shapeless mass.

In January, 1877, at his very first ride over the ruins, De Sarzec recognized the value of this large archæological field, scarcely yet touched by the professional Arab digger, from the many fragments of inscribed cones and bricks, sculptures and vases which covered the surface. Among other objects of interest he picked up the magnificent piece of a large statue in dolerite inscribed on the shoulder. After a few minutes he had gathered evidence enough to convince him that he stood on a prominent site of great antiquity. The fragment of the statue was interpreted by him as having rolled down from Mound A, at the foot of which it was discovered, thus serving as the first indication of an important building which probably was concealed in its interior. This starting point for his excavations once being given, he hired all the workmen whom he could obtain from the wandering tribes, and set to work to determine the character and contents of the hill in question. A few weeks of digging revealed the fact indicated above, that the whole mound consisted of a platform of unbaked bricks crowned by an edifice of considerable size and extent. But he was not satisfied with this general result. Though the lack of drinking water in the immediate vicinity of the ruins and the proverbial insecurity of the whole region did not allow him to pitch his tents anywhere near the mounds, he was by no means discouraged. During all his several expeditions to Tellô he established his headquarters at Mantar-Qaraghol, in the midst of the green fields embellishing the left bank of the Shatt el-Haï, whence he walked or rode every morning to the ruins, to return in the evening to the waters of the river. After seven months of successful excavations conducted during the springs of 1877 and 1878, he obtained a leave of absence from his duties at Basra, and sailed to France as the bearer of important news and with the first fruit of his archæological researches.

By following a ravine ending at the point where the fine sculptured fragment was discovered, he had reached a kind of deep recess in the outer northeast wall of the building which stood on the platform. No sooner did the workmen begin to remove the débris with which it was filled, when the lower part of a great statue in dolerite, partly covered with a long cuneiform inscription, rose gradually out of the depth. It became at once evident that the shoulder piece bearing the name of Gudea, referred to above, was a portion of this extraordinary monument. De Sarzec having no means at his disposal to remove the heavy torso, took a squeeze of the inscription and buried the precious relic again for a future occasion. Two years later, when Rassam visited Tellô, he found its upper part exposed again by the Arabs.[1]

[1] Comp. Rassam, "Asshur and the Land of Nimrod," New York, 1897, p. 276, on the one side, and De Sarzec and Heuzey, *Découvertes en Chaldée*, p. 5, on the other. The British explorer asserts that this first statue unearthed by De Sarzec is identical with the one previously discovered and mutilated by the natives, who sold the bust and arm to George Smith. But this statement

After the French consul had ascertained the general character of Mound A and its probable contents, he devoted the rest of his time to an investigation of the other parts of the ruins by placing his workmen in long rows over the whole surface of the enormous site. This peculiar method, which would have utterly failed at Babylon, Nuffar, Warkâ, and other similar mounds, produced important results at a ruin as little settled in later times as Tellô subsequently proved to be. De Sarzec unearthed many fragments of inscribed vases and sculptures, several inscribed door-sockets, a large number of cuneiform tablets, the bronze horn of a bull in life-size, etc. He exposed large columns of bricks of the time of Gudea, and found not a few peculiar cubical brick structures generally concealing a votive tablet of Gudea or Dungi. The latter was placed over a small copper or bronze statue of a man or a bull, which often terminated in the form of a nail. Above all, he brought to light one of the earliest bas-reliefs

Votive Statuette in Copper
Inscribed with the name of Gudea, about 2700 B. C.

is wrong, as the inscription on the back of De Sarzec's statue is complete. In fact, it must be regarded as doubtful if the torso obtained by Smith belongs to any of the statues or fragments discovered by De Sarzec at Tellô, as long as this question has not been settled by means of casts of the pieces in the British Museum sent to Paris for examination.

of ancient Chaldea so far known,[1] the first two fragments of the famous "stele of vultures" erected by King Eannatum, and two[2] large terra-cotta cylinders of Gudea in tolerably good preservation. Each of the latter is nearly two feet long and a little over one foot in diameter, and is inscribed with about 2000 lines of early cuneiform writing, thus forming the longest inscriptions of that ancient period so far known.

On his arrival at home (July 28, 1878), De Sarzec was most fortunate in finding the precise man whom he needed in order to see his work placed upon a permanent basis. Waddington, well known in scientific circles for his numismatic researches, was then Minister of Foreign Affairs. Deeply interested as he was in the enthusiastic reports of his consul, he referred him for a critical examination of his excavated treasures to Léon Heuzey, the distinguished curator of the Department of Oriental Antiquities at the Louvre, who at once recognized that here were the first true specimens of that original, ancient Chaldean art to which De Longpérier tentatively had ascribed two statuettes previously obtained by the National Museum of France. From this moment dates the archæological alliance and personal friendship between De Sarzec and Heuzey which in the course of the next twenty years bore the richest fruit for Assyriology and was of fundamental importance for the gradual restoration of a lost page in the history of ancient Oriental art and civilization.

On the recommendation of Heuzey the antiquities already discovered at Tellô were deposited in the Louvre with a view of their final acquisition by the nation, while De Sarzec was requested to return quietly to the ruins and to develop

[1] Comp. Heuzey, *Découvertes*, pl. 1, no. 1.

[2] The third one, the existence of which was divined by Amiaud from certain indications contained in the cuneiform texts of the first two cylinders, has been found since by the Arabs. Comp. Scheil in Maspéro's *Recueil,* vol. xxi (1899), p. 124.

his promising investigations at his own responsibility and expense, until the proper moment for action had come on the side of the government. At the same time the necessary steps were taken in Constantinople to secure the imperial firmân which established French priority over a ruin soon to attract a more general attention. As we shall see later in connection with the contemporaneous British excavations in the vilayet of Baghdad, this cautious but resolute proceeding by a few initiated men, who carefully guarded the secret of De Sarzec's great discovery, saved Tellô from the hands of Rassam, long the shrewd and successful rival of French explorers in Assyria and Babylonia.

2. On the 21st of January, 1880, De Sarzec was back again at his encampment near the Shatt el-Haï, this time accompanied by his young bride, who henceforth generally shared the pleasures and deprivations of her husband in the desert. During this and the following campaign (November 12, 1880, to March 15, 1881) he concentrated his energy on a thorough examination of the great building hidden under Mound A and of its immediate environments, discovering no less than nine[1] large statues in dolerite, besides several statuettes in stone and metal, fragments of precious bas-reliefs, an onyx vase of Narâm-Sin, and numerous inscriptions and small objects of art. It is true, all the statues hitherto unearthed were previously decapitated, and in some instances otherwise mutilated, but three detached heads, soon afterwards rescued by De Sarzec from different parts of the ruins, enabled us to gain a clearer conception of

[1] According to Heuzey, in the introduction to his *Catalogue de la Sculpture Chaldéenne au Musée du Louvre*, Paris, 1902. De Sarzec, in his brief description of his first four campaigns (*Découvertes en Chaldée*, p. 6) mentions the discovery of a tenth (or including the lower part of a statue unearthed in 1877, an eleventh) statue, and speaks of only two detached heads then found by him. This difference in counting is due to the size and fragmentary condition of some of the statues and objects discovered.

the unique type of these priceless specimens of ancient Babylonian art.

With the exception of the six hottest months of the year, which he spent in the cooler *serdâbs*[1] of Baghdad, to restore his health affected by the usual swamp fevers of 'Irâq, he continued his labors at Tellô until the spring of 1881, finding even older remains below the foundations of the abovementioned palace, when the threatening attitude of the Muntefik(j) tribes, and the growing insecurity of his own party drove him away from the ruins. At the end of May in the following year he arrived at Paris a second time with a most valuable collection of antiquities, which by special *irade* from the Sultan he had been allowed to carry away with him as his personal property.

The first announcement of De Sarzec's fundamental discovery before the French Academy,[2] and Oppert's impressive address at the Fifth International Congress of Orientalists at Berlin,[3] opening with the significant words: "Since the discovery of Nineveh . . . no discovery has been made which compares in importance with the recent excavations in Chaldea," had fairly prepared the scientific world for the extraordinary character and the rare value of these ancient monuments. But when they were finally unpacked and for the first time exhibited in the galleries of the

[1] Subterranean cool rooms which are provided in every better house of Baghdad in order to enable the inhabitants to escape the often intolerable heat of the daytime during the summer months.

[2] Published in *Revue Archéologique*, new series, vol. xlii, Nov., 1881, pp. 56 and 259–272: *Les Fouilles de Chaldée; communication d'une lettre de M. de Sarzec par Léon Heuzey.*

[3] *Die französischen Ausgrabungen in Chaldäa*, pp. 235–248 of *Abhandlungen des Berliner Orientalisten-Congresses.* A useful synopsis of the early literature on De Sarzec's discoveries was given by Hommel in *Die Semitischen Völker und Sprachen*, Leipzig, 1883, p. 459, note 104, to which may be added an article by Georges Perrot in *Revue des Deux-Mondes*, Oct. 1, 1882, pp. 525, *seqq.*

Louvre, the general expectation was far surpassed by the grand spectacle which presented itself to the eyes of a representative assembly. This first fine collection of early Babylonian sculptures was received in Paris with an enthusiasm second only to the popular outburst which greeted Botta's gigantic winged bulls from the palace of Sargon thirty-six years previously.[1] On the proposition of Jules Ferry, then Minister of Public Instruction, the French Assembly voted an exceptional credit to the National Museum for the immediate acquisition of all the monuments from Tellô, while the *Académie des Inscriptions et Belles Lettres* added a much more coveted prize to this pecuniary remuneration on the side of the government, by appointing the successful explorer a member of the Institute of France. An Oriental section was created in the Louvre, with Léon Heuzey, the faithful and energetic supporter of De Sarzec's plans and endeavors, as its director. Under the auspices of the Minister of Public Instruction, and assisted in the deciphering of the often difficult cuneiform inscriptions by Oppert, Amiaud, and lately by Thureau-Dangin, Heuzey began that magnificent publication[2] in which he made the new discoveries accessible to science, and laid the solid foundation for a methodical treatment of ancient Chaldean art, by applying fixed archæological laws to the elucidation of the Assyrian and Babylonian monuments.

The palace excavated in Mound A does not belong to the Babylonian period proper. But in order to understand the topographical conditions and certain changes which took place in the upper strata of Tellô, it will be necessary to include it in our brief description of the principal results obtained by De Sarzec at this most conspicuous part of the ruins. The massive structure of crude bricks upon which

[1] Comp. pp. 79, *seqq.*, above.

[2] *Découvertes en Chaldée par Ernest de Sarzec*, published by Léon Heuzey, large folio, Paris, 1884, *seqq.* The work is not yet complete.

the building was erected forms an immense terrace over 600 feet square and 40 feet high. As certain walls discovered in it prove that this lofty and substantial base was not the work of one builder, we have to distinguish between an earlier *substratum* and later additions. The crumbling remains of the large edifice lying on the top of it form a rectangular parallelogram about 175 feet long and 100 feet wide. Only two of its sides, the principal and slightly curved northeast, and the smaller but similar northwest façade, exhibit any attempt at exterior ornamentation, consisting of those simple dentated recesses and half-columns with which we are familiar from Loftus' excavations at Warkâ. As to its ground plan, the building does not essentially differ from the principle and arrangement observed in the Assyrian palace of Khorsabâd, or in the Seleucido-Parthian palace recently completely excavated by the present writer at the ruins of Nuffar. Here as there we have a number of different rooms and halls — in the latter case thirty-six — around a grouped number of open courts[1] and around as many different centres.

The walls of this edifice, in some places still ten feet high, are built of ancient Babylonian bricks, laid in mortar or bitumen and generally bearing the name and titles of Gudea, a famous ruler of that Southern district, who lived, however, about twenty-five hundred years prior to the days when his material was used a second time. Each of the four exterior walls, on an average four feet thick, has one entrance, but no trace of any window. The northeast façade originally had two gates, the principal one of which, for some unknown reason, was soon afterwards closed again. The inscribed bricks used for this purpose, and similar ones taken from certain constructions in the interior, are modelled after the

[1] The palace of Tellô has three courts of different dimensions. The smallest is nearly square, measuring about 20 by 18½ feet, the second is 27 by 30 feet, while the largest is about 56 by 69 feet.

pattern of Gudea's material, but bear the Babylonian name Hadadnâdinakhe(s) in late Aramean and early Greek characters, from which the general age of this building was determined to be about 300 – 250 B. C., a result corroborated by the fact that numerous coins with Greek legends of the kings of Characene[1] were found in its ruins.

Both the inside of the palace and the open space immediately before its principal façade were paved with burned bricks of the same size and make-up as those in the walls of the palace. These bricks did not rest directly upon the large terrace of crude bricks, but upon a layer of earth two to three feet deep mixed with sculptured fragments of an early period. In the centre of the platform before the palace there stood upon a kind of pedestal an ancient trough or manger, in limestone, about eight feet long, one foot and a half wide, and one foot deep. Being out of its original position it had apparently been used by the later architects to provide water for the guards stationed near the northeast entrance of the palace. Its two small sides had preserved traces of cuneiform writing of the style of the time of Gudea, to whom this unique monument doubtless must be ascribed. The two long sides, once exquisitely adorned with bas-reliefs, had likewise suffered considerably from exposure. But enough remained to recognize in them a living chain of female figures, a "frieze of veritable Chaldean Naiads through their union symbolizing the perpetuity of water."[2] A number of women, in graceful attitude, hold, in their outstretched hands, magical vases which they evidently are passing one to another. A double stream of water gushing forth from each of these inexhaustible receptacles represents the two sacred rivers, the Tigris and the Euphrates, which, on

[1] A district situated on the east bank of the Tigris, not very far from its junction with the Euphrates.

[2] Thus in his usual masterly manner characterized by Heuzey, *Découvertes*, p. 217 (comp. p. 43, note 1, of the same work).

another fine sculptured fragment rescued from the rubbish below the pavement of the same palace,[1] are indicated with even greater detail by a plant growing out of the vase and by a fish swimming against the current in each river.

Close to the middle of the southwest wall of the palace just described, and extending considerably into its principal courts, there rose two massive structures, or terraces of baked bricks laid in bitumen, above the remains of the Parthian building. Both joined each other at one corner, but they were reached by separate stairs and differed from each other also as to their height. As they interfered greatly with the general plan and arrangement of the interior of the palace, it was evident from the beginning that they belonged to an older building, lifting, so to speak, its head out of a lower stratum into the post-Babylonian period, as the last witness of a by-gone age. The fact, however, that the inscribed bricks, so far as examined, bore the name of Gudea on their upper [2] sides, was in itself a proof that the visible portion of this ancient structure had in part been relaid and otherwise changed in accordance with its different use in the Seleucidan times. The two terraces, affording a grand view over the surrounding plain, must have been important to the late inhabitants from a military standpoint, while at the same time they served as a kind of elevated gallery or esplanade where the residents of the palace could enjoy a fresh breeze of air in the cooler evening hours of a hot Babylonian summer.

No sooner had De Sarzec commenced to examine the ground around the vertical walls of these peculiar structures than, to his great astonishment, he came upon other remains of the same building imbedded in the crude brick terrace. Unfortunately, the rebellion breaking out among the Muntefik(j) tribes, in 1881, brought the explorer's work to a sudden

[1] Comp. *Découvertes*, pl. 25, no. 6.

[2] Comp. the end of p. 31, above.

end, so that he was then unable to arrive at a definite conclusion concerning its true character. But in connection with his later campaigns he also resumed his excavations at the lower strata of Mound A, discovering that the remains which had puzzled him so much before belonged to the tower of a fortified enclosure. In digging along its base, he established that one side of the latter showed the same simple pattern as the two façades of the Parthian building, — in other words, those peculiar architectural ornaments which the ancient Babylonians and Assyrians reserved exclusively for exterior decoration. Soon afterwards he excavated a large gate with three stepped recesses, which on the one hand was flanked by the tower, while on the other side its wall was lost in the later building.[1]

All the bricks taken from this fortified enclosure were in their original position, and bore the inscription : "To Nin-Girsu, the powerful champion of Bêl, Gudea, patesi of *Shir-pur-la*, accomplished something worthy, built the temple *Eninnû-Imgig(-ĝu)barbara*[2] and restored it." This legend and similar statements occurring on the statues in dolerite and on other votive objects rescued from the same part of the ruins, the fact that Mound A represents the most extensive single hill of Tellô, and several other considerations, lead necessarily to the conclusion that the ancient structure lying below the Seleucidan palace and partly worked into it can only be *Eninnû*, the chief sanctuary of the Babylonian city, sacred to Nin-Girsu or Nin-Su(n)gir, the tutelary deity of Lagash.

[1] Comp. Heuzey in *Comptes Rendus de l'Académie des Inscriptions*, 1894, pp. 34–42.

[2] The name of the temple appears either as *E-Ninnû*, "House of God Ningirsu" (Ninnû, "50," being the ideogram of the god), or as *E-Imgig-(-ĝu)bara*, *i. e.* the temple called *Imgig(-ĝu)bara* ("Imgig is shining"), or as *E-Ninnû-Imgig(-ĝu)barbara* (a composition of these two names). The divine bird Imgig was the emblem of the God Ningirsu and of his city *Shir-pur-la* (*Z.A.* xv, pp. 52 *seq.*, xvi, p. 357), according to Hommel, originally a raven (*shir-pur(-ĝu)* = *âribu.*)

This temple existed at Tellô from the earliest times.[1] But an examination of the inscription on the statue of Ur-Bau, and the results of De Sarzec's explorations in the lower strata, would seem to indicate that this ruler abandoned the old site of Eninnû altogether, and rebuilt the temple on a larger scale at the place where its ruins are seen at present. However, it must not be forgotten that the displacement of a renowned sanctuary involved in this theory is something unheard of in the history of ancient Babylonia. It is contrary to the well-known spirit of conservatism manifested by the ancient inhabitants of Babylonia in all matters connected with their religion, and directly opposed to the numerous statements contained in the so-called building inscriptions and boundary regulations of all periods.[2]

Unfortunately very little of the temple of Nin-Su(n)gir seems to have been left. De Sarzec had previously discovered a wall of Ur-Bau under the east corner of the palace. But besides it and the tower and gate of Gudea he brought nothing to light except layers of crude bricks from the artificial terrace. In the light of these negative results, how can the continuity of the sanctuary at one and the same place be defended? On the ground that in order to secure a stronger and larger foundation for his own new sanctuary, Ur-Bau may have razed the crumbling terrace of the old temple entirely, as many other Babylonian and Assyrian monarchs

[1] The *E-Ningirsu* of Ur-Ninâ is practically the same name as *E-Ninnû*, both meaning "temple of Ninib." As far as I can see, the name *E-Ninnû* occurs for the first time in the inscriptions of Entemena, great-grandson of Ur-Ninâ, and in a text of Urukagina.

[2] That in the earliest days of ancient Babylonia practically the same spirit prevailed as in Semitic times with regard to the inviolable character of sacred enclosures, boundary lines, agreements (especially when made with gods, *i. e.*, their territory, income, gifts) is clear from certain instructive passages engraved upon "the historical cone of Entemena," which doubtless came from Tellô (comp. *Revue d'Assyriologie*, vol. iv, pp. 37, *seqq.*), and from the long curse attached to Gudea's inscription on Statue B.

did afterwards in other cities. And no less on the ground that according to all evidence furnished by the excavations,[1] the present terrace, on which the local rulers of the Seleucidan age erected their castle, is considerably smaller than the platform of the patesis of Lagash. There can be no doubt therefore that a considerable part of the earliest temple ruins, which in all probability included even those of a stage-tower,[2] was intentionally demolished and removed by Ur-Bau, or, if not by him, surely by the Parthian princes of the third century, who built their palace almost exclusively of the bricks of Gudea's temple. We have a somewhat similar case at Nippur. For it is a remarkable fact that the characteristic change from a Babylonian sanctuary into a Seleucido-Parthian palace observed at Tellô is precisely the same as took place in the sacred precinct of Bêl at Nuffar, so that the evidence obtained in the trenches of the latter, better

1 And in a recent letter to the present writer expressly confirmed by Heuzey.

2 From the analogical case of Nippur (Fourth Campaign, below), where a central kernel of the huge *ziggurrat* descends far down into the pre-Sargonic stratum, and from certain passages in the earliest inscriptions from Tellô, I feel convinced that a stage-tower, the most characteristic part of every prominent Babylonian temple, must also have existed at Lagash — however modest in size — at the time of the earliest kings. Traces of it may still be found somewhere in the lowest strata of Mound A. For the pre-Sargonic *ziggurrat* at Nippur comp. Helm and Hilprecht, *Mitteilung über die chemische Untersuchung von altbabylonischen Kupfer- und Bronze Gegenständen und deren Altersbestimmung*, in *Verhandlungen der Berliner anthropologischen Gesellschaft*, Febr. 16, 1901, p. 159. As to a stage-tower probably mentioned in the Tellô inscriptions, comp. Gudea D, col. ii, l. 11: *E-pa e-ub-imin-na-ni mu-na-ru*, and Jensen in Schrader's *Keilinschriftliche Bibliothek*, vol. iii, part 1, pp. 50, *seq.* Comp. also Ur-Ninâ's inscription published in *Découvertes*, pl. 2, no. 2, col. ii, l. 7–10, where *uruna-ní mu-ru*, "he built his (Ningirsu's) observatory," is immediately preceded by *E-pa mu-ru*, so that in view of the Gudea passage, we probably have to recognize a close connection between the *Epa* and the *uruna*, the latter being situated upon the top of the former. For stage-tower and observatory cannot be separated from each other in ancient Babylonia.

preserved ruin [1] goes far to explain the detached walls unearthed in the lower strata of Tellô.

With the exception of the Seleucido-Parthian building just described, the few but important remains of Eninnû and the ingeniously constructed brick columns of Gudea above (p. 222) referred to, De Sarzec's excavations had so far been comparatively unproductive of noteworthy architectural results. They were more interesting and truly epoch-making in their bearing upon our knowledge of the origin and development of ancient Babylonian art. For the rubbish which filled the chambers and halls of the palace not only contained the ordinary pottery, iron instruments, perforated stone seals in the forms of animals,[2] and other objects characteristic of the last centuries preceding the Christian era, but it also yielded numerous door-sockets of Gudea and Ur-Bau re-used later in part, inscribed vases and mace-heads, a large quantity of seal cylinders,[3] principally

[1] Comp. my "Report from Nuffar to the Committee of the Babyl. Exped. in Philadelphia," April 21, 1900, from which I quote: "The building described by Peters and Haynes as the temple of Bêl is only a huge Parthian fortress lying on the top of the ancient temple ruin, and so constructed that the upper stages of the *ziggurrat* served as a kind of citadel."

[2] Found under the alabaster threshold in the inner gate of the southwest side of the palace, where, in accordance with a custom frequently observed in Assyrian buildings, they evidently had been placed as talismans. The fine Sommerville collection of talismans in the Archæological Museum of the University of Pennsylvania contains a large number of similar Parthian stone seals.

[3] Likewise serving as talismans against demons and their obnoxious influences. This interesting use of ancient Babylonian seal-cylinders, cuneiform tablets, and other inscribed objects by the later inhabitants of the country explains why they occur so frequently in Parthian tombs (comp. my remarks on pp. 154, *seq.*, 168, above, and De Sarzec and Heuzey, *Découvertes*, p. 73, note 1). But it also illustrates how impossible it is to use such finds without criticism as material for determining the age of tombs in Babylonian ruins, as unfortunately was done by Peters in his "Nippur," vol. ii, p. 219. Peters' classification of Babylonian coffins and pottery cannot be taken seriously,

taken from the mortar uniting the different layers of brick in a furnace, and not a few of those priceless fragments of bas-reliefs, statues, and statuettes which will always form the basis for a systematic study of earlier Chaldean art. The most valuable discoveries, however, awaited the explorer in the débris filling the large open court and the rooms and passages grouped around it, and in the layer of earth separating the pavement of the Parthian edifice from the crude brick terrace below it. No less than eight decapitated statues — four sitting and four standing — lay on the court in two distinct groups scarcely more than ten yards apart from each other. A detached shaved head, doubtless originally belonging to one of them, was found in their immediate neighborhood.

Among the many valuable antiquities which came from the adjoining halls and from the earth below this whole section we mention one of the largest bas-reliefs discovered in Tellô,[1] representing a procession of priests and a musician playing a peculiarly decorated harp of eleven chords dating from the time of Gudea; a little fragment of sculpture of the same epoch, which rapidly gained a certain celebrity among modern artists for the exquisite modelling and fine execution of a naked female foot;[2] a mutilated and half-calcined slab showing a humped bull carved with a rare skill and surprising fidelity to nature;[3] a small but well preserved head in steatite reproducing the type of the large shaved head with a remarkable grace and delicacy;[4] a new piece of

because it ignores the established laws of archæology and the principles of historical research.

[1] Over four feet high, and, according to Heuzey, probably belonging to a four-sided altar, stele, or pedestal (*Découvertes*, pl. 23).

[2] Comp. *Découvertes*, pl. 25, no. 6, identical with the fragment quoted on p. 229, above.

[3] Comp. *Découvertes*, pl. 25, no. 4.

[4] Comp. *Découvertes*, pl. 25, no. 1.

the "stele of vultures" previously mentioned;[1] and the first fragment of an inscribed tablet of Ur-Ninâ, exhibiting the lion-headed eagle with outspread wings victoriously clutching two lions in its powerful talons, — the well-known coat of arms of the city of *Shir-pur-la*.[2]

The last-named monument enabled Heuzey to bring the earliest remains of Chaldean art, so scrupulously gathered by De Sarzec, into closer relation with the ancient kings of Tellô. He ascertained that, contrary to what we know of the first princes of Assyria, the rulers who style themselves "kings of *Shir-pur-la*" are older[3] than those who bear the title *patesi*, *i. e.*, "priest-king," or more exactly "prince-priest," in their inscriptions, — a result which allowed him at once to establish an approximate chronology for the newly discovered rulers of Southern Babylonia in accordance with the progress in style to be traced in their sculptures and bas-reliefs. Furthermore, the French archæologist determined a number of general facts,[4] on the basis of which he successfully defended the two following theses, — (1) that the style of the monuments of Tellô is not a style of imitation, but a real and genuine archaism; (2) that quite a number of the monuments discovered antedate the remote epoch of King Narâm-Sin (about 3750 B. C.[5]), and lead us back to the very

[1] Comp. *Découvertes*, pls. 3 and 4, B.

[2] Comp. *Découvertes*, pl. 1, no. 2. A very similar fragment is in the Imperial Ottoman Museum at Constantinople (no. 420).

[3] This statement has reference only to the two principal groups of rulers of Lagash then known. In all probability there was still an earlier dynasty at Tellô, the members of which bear the title *patesi*. Comp. Thureau-Dangin in *Zeitschrift fur Assyriologie*, vol. xv, p. 403.

[4] Comp. Heuzey's subtle observations on Chaldean art in *Revue Archéologique*, new series, vol. xlii, 1881, p. 263, and in *Découvertes*, pp. 77–86, 119–127, 186, *seq*.

[5] The date of Narâm-Sin's government was obtained from a cylinder of Nabonidos excavated by Rassam at Abû Habba about the same time. Comp. p. 273, below.

beginning of Chaldean art. These fundamental deductions and historical conclusions, so quickly drawn by Heuzey after his study of the archæological details of the monuments, found their full corroboration through the deciphering of their accompanying inscriptions by Oppert and Amiaud, and through the present writer's palæographical and historical researches in connection with the Nuffar antiquities, which afforded a welcome means of controlling and supplementing the results obtained at Tellô.

The magnificent collection of statues in diorite, or more exactly dolerite, will always remain the principal discovery connected with De Sarzec's name. With the exception of but one erected by Ur-Bau, they bear the name of Gudea, patesi of *Shir-pur-la* or Lagash, as the city at some time must have been called. Famous as the choicest museum pieces so far recovered from Babylonian soil, and remarkable for their unity of style and technique, and therefore occupying a most prominent place in the history of ancient art, they appeal to us no less through the simplicity and correctness of their attitude and through the reality and power of their expression, than through the extraordinary skill and ability with which one of the hardest stones in existence has here been handled by unknown Chaldean artists. The mere fact that such monuments could originate in ancient Babylonia speaks volumes for the unique character and the peculiar vitality of this great civilization, which started near the Persian Gulf thousands of years before our era, and fundamentally influenced the religious ideas and the intellectual development of the principal Semitic nations, and through them left its impression even upon Europe and upon our own civilization.

All the statues represent a human ruler — generally Gudea — whose name is found in a kind of cartouche on the right shoulder or in a long inscription engraved upon a conspicuous part of the body or garment; and they all

Gudea, Priest-King of Lagash, as Architect

Statue in dolerite, about 2700 B. C.

have the hands clasped before the breast in an attitude of reverence. As over against the typical sobriety and conventional style of the early Egyptian sculptures, the Chaldean artist endeavors to express real life and to imitate nature within certain limits set by the peculiar material, "the routine of the studios and the rules of sacred etiquette." The swelling of the muscles of the right arm, the delicately carved nails of the fingers, the expressive details of the feet firmly resting on the ground, the characteristic manner in which the fringed shawl is thrown over the left shoulder, and the first naive and timid attempt at reproducing its graceful folds betray a remarkable gift of observation and no small sculptural talent on the part of these ancient Sumerians. Two of the sitting statues show Gudea as an architect with a large tablet upon his lap, while a carefully divided rule and a stylus are carved in relief near its upper and right edges. The surface of the one tablet is empty,[1] while on the other the patesi has drawn a large fortified enclosure provided with gates, bastions and towers.

The great number and the artistic value of the monuments of Gudea point to an extraordinary prosperity and a comparatively peaceful development of the various resources of the city of Lagash at the time of his government (about 2700 B. C.). This natural inference is fully confirmed by the vast remains of his buildings at the ruins and by the unique contents of his many inscriptions. The latter were greeted by Assyriologists as the first genuine documents of a period when Sumerian was still a spoken language, however much influenced already by the grammar and lexicography of their Semitic neighbors and conquerors. But aside from their linguistic and palæographical importance these inscriptions, though even at present by no means fully understood, revealed to us such a surprising picture of the greatness and extent of the ancient Sumerian

[1] This is the tablet seen in the illustration facing this page.

civilization and of the geographical horizon of the early inhabitants of Lagash that at first it seemed almost impossible to regard it as faithful and historical. Gudea fought victorious battles against Elam and sent his agents as far as the Mediterranean. He cut his cedars in Northern Syria and Idumea and obtained his dolerite in the quarries of Eastern Arabia (Magan). His caravans brought copper from the mines of the Nejd (Kimash), and his ships carried gold and precious wood from the mountains of Medina and the rocky shores of the Sinaitic peninsula (Melukh).[1] What an outlook into the lively intercourse and the exchange of products between the nations of Western Asia at the threshold of the fourth and third pre-Christian millenniums, but also what an indication of the powerful influence which went forth from this little known race of Southern Babylonia, irresistibly advancing in all directions and affecting Palestine long before Abram left his ancestral home on the west bank of the Euphrates. And yet De Sarzec's excavations at Tellô and the Philadelphia expedition to Nuffar were soon to provide ample new material by means of which we were enabled to follow that remarkable civilization a thousand years and even further back.

3. De Sarzec's careful description of the many ancient remains unearthed by him, and Heuzey's admirable exposition of the age and importance of the new material, prepared the way for an early resumption of the excavations at Tellô. But in view of certain fundamental changes recently

[1] Comp. Hommel's article "Explorations in Arabia," in this volume. Iron, however, was not among the metals brought by Gudea from Melukh, as was asserted by Hommel and (following him) by myself (in *Verhandlungen der Berliner anthropologischen Gesellschaft*, session of 16 Febr., 1901, p. 164). So far no iron has been discovered in the earliest strata of either Nuffar or Tellô. Indeed, I doubt whether it appears in Assyria and Babylonia much before 1000 B. C. The earliest large finds of iron implements known to us from the exploration of Assyrian and Babylonian ruins date from the eighth century B. C. and were made in Sargon's palace at Khorsabâd (comp. p. 83,

made in the archæological laws of the Ottoman empire[1] at Hamdy Bey's recommendation, the French minister deemed it wise at first to ascertain the future attitude of the Porte with regard to the ownership of other antiquities which might be discovered, before he sanctioned any further exploration in Southern Babylonia. After frequent and protracted negotiations a satisfactory understanding was finally reached between the two interested powers. De Sarzec had meanwhile been appointed consul at Baghdad. In 1888 he was authorized to proceed again to the scene of his former labors, which henceforth were deprived of their private character and conducted under the auspices and at the expense of the French government.

Certain scattered fragments of sculptures and a few inscriptions[2] previously gathered had made it evident that the mounds of Tellô contained monuments considerably older than the statues of Ur-Bau and Gudea, and reaching back almost to the very beginning of Babylonian civilization. The question arose, Which of the numerous elevations of the very extensive site most probably represents the principal settlement of this early period and is likely to repay methodical researches with corresponding important discoveries? Remembering the very numerous ancient constructions which ten years before had been brought to light by his trial trenches in Mound B, De Sarzec now directed his chief attention

above) and in Ashurnâsirapal's northwest palace at Nimrûd (comp. p. 124, above). As we know, however, that Sargon (722–705 B. C.) also restored and for a while occupied the latter palace (comp. pp. 106 and 111, above) the iron utensils found in it doubtless go back to him and not to the time of Ashurnâsirapal.

[1] Comp. pp. 205, *seq.*, above.

[2] Among them inscribed monuments of Ur-Ninâ, Eannatum, Entemena, and Enannatum. Comp. the fragments of the bas-reliefs of Ur-Ninâ and "the stele of vultures" previously referred to; furthermore *Découvertes*, pp. 59 and 68; and Heuzy, *Les rois de Tellô et la période archaïque de l'art chaldéen*, in *Revue Archéologique*, Nov., 1885.

to the exploration of this section of the ruins, at the same time continuing his examination of the lower strata of Mound A, as indicated above.

It was a comparatively easy task for the explorer to determine the character of the latest accumulation which covered the top of this tumulus. Upon a layer of crude bricks he found part of a wall which constituted the last remains of a building of the time of Gudea (2700 B. C.), whose name was engraved on a door-socket and upon a small copper figurine discovered *in situ*. Another figurine of the type of the basket-bearers had a votive inscription of Dungi, king of Ur, who belonged to the same general epoch. But his greatest finds from this upper stratum of Mound B were two exquisite round trays in veined onyx and half-transparent alabaster,[1] which, with the fragment of a third, bore the names of as many different patesis of Lagash, Ur-Ninsun, otherwise unknown, Nammakhani, the son-in-law and successor of Ur-Bau, and (Ga)lukani, a vassal of Dungi.

As soon as De Sarzec commenced to deepen his trenches, he came upon older walls constructed of entirely different bricks laid in bitumen. They were baked and oblong, flat on their lower and convex on their upper side, and without exception had a mark of the right thumb in the centre of the latter. A few of them bearing a legend of King Ur-Ninâ in large linear writing, it seemed safe to assume that here there were architectural remains which went back to the earliest kings of Lagash. With great care and expectation De Sarzec examined the whole building and its environment in the course of the next twelve years. Everywhere at the same level characterized by a large pavement of bricks and reached at an average depth of only thirteen feet from the surface, he found inscribed stone tablets and door-sockets,

[1] Now in the Museum of Archæology at Constantinople, where with other Babylonian antiquities they were catalogued by the present writer.

Silver Vase of Entemena, Priest-King of Lagash, decorated with the Emblem of his God
About 3950 B. C.

weapons, — including a colossal spear-head[1] dedicated to Ningirsu by an ancient king of Kish, and the elaborately carved mace-head of the even earlier King Mesilim of the same city, — figurines in copper, the magnificent silver vase of Entemena, lion heads and bas-reliefs, — among them the famous genealogical bas-reliefs of Ur-Ninâ and three new fragments of "the stele of vultures," — besides many other precious antiquities which about 4000 B. C. had been presented as votive offerings to their gods by Ur-Ninâ, Eannatum, Entemena, Enannatum, etc., and several contemporaneous rulers of other Babylonian cities with whom this powerful dynasty of Lagash fought battles or otherwise came into contact.

But even Ur-Ninâ's edifice did not represent the earliest settlement of Mound B. In examining the ground below his platform, De Sarzec disclosed remains of a still older building imbedded in the crude bricks of the lofty terrace which served as a solid basis for the great king's own construction. Its ruined walls rose to the height of more than nine feet, and were made of bricks similar to those from the next higher stratum, but somewhat smaller in size and without their characteristic thumb marks. This very ancient building rested upon a pavement of gypsum, lying nearly sixteen feet and a half below the platform of Ur-Ninâ and a little over twenty-six feet above the surrounding plain, occupying therefore about the centre of the whole artificial mound. The unknown ruler of Lagash who erected it must have lived towards the end of the fifth pre-Christian millennium. A number of votive statuettes in copper of a very archaic type, and fragments of sculptured stones, including the lower part of a large military stele, which, owing to its weight and its unimportant details, remained on the ground,[2]

[1] In copper, over two feet and a half long.

[2] In limestone, over six and a half feet long, almost three feet high, and half a foot thick. Comp. *Découvertes*, pp. 195, *seq.*, and pl. 56, no. 2.

repaid De Sarzec's researches in the rubbish that filled the interior of the structure and covered the adjacent platform.

A new interruption in the French excavations at Tellô was caused in 1889 by the explorer's failing health and his temporary transfer to a higher and more lucrative position in Batavia. When four years later he returned once more to Southern Babylonia, soon afterwards (1894) to be appointed consul-general, he extended his trenches in all directions around these enigmatic architectural remains, and resumed his explorations at the other points previously attacked. In order to ascertain especially, whether perhaps the lower strata of mound B concealed monuments of even greater antiquity than hitherto disclosed by him, he ordered his workmen to cut a trench through the solid mass of bricks which had formed the basis for the different buildings once crowning its summit. At a depth of a little over twenty-six feet he reached the virgin soil, where he discontinued his researches. With the exception of a number of empty receptacles made of bitumen in the shape of large jars and similar to others which had been found in the walls of the archaic building, this experimental cutting yielded only a few rude mace-heads, hammers, small stone eggs, probably used by slingers in warfare,[1] and the like, and fragments of ordinary pottery, all apparently contemporaneous with the first edifice for which the terrace had been erected.

On the west slope of Mound B De Sarzec excavated two wells and a water-course of the time of Eannatum. In a manner peculiar to the earliest period of Babylonian history, the two former were constructed of plano-convex bricks marked with the impressions of two fingers — thumb and

[1] According to De Sarzec and Heuzey, *Une Ville Royale Chaldéenne*, Paris, 1900, p. 63, these eggs were commonly found at Tellô, but their use is regarded as unknown. They occur frequently also at Nuffar. Comp. Fourth Campaign, Temple Mound, Section 6, below.

index—and in some instances bearing a long legend of the monarch just mentioned. After a brief reference to his reign and principal military expeditions, this ruler glorifies in having constructed "the great terrace of the well," *i. e.*, in having extended the crude brick terrace of his predecessor so far as to include in it the mouths of these two water supplies which he raised from the plain up to the level of Ur-Ninâ's buildings.[1] From the neighboring débris came some fine pieces of carved or incised shell, showing spirited scenes of men, animals and plants, and doubtless belonging to the same general epoch. A good many similar specimens of this important branch of ancient Chaldean art, a few of them colored, have been recently obtained from various other central and south-Babylonian ruins by the present writer.[2]

A rectangular massive building, remains of a gate, and several artificial reservoirs differing greatly in size and form were brought to light to the southeast and northeast of Enannatuma's wells. A few inscribed bricks and a number of copper figurines carrying alabaster tablets upon their heads indicated sufficiently that most of these structures were the work of Entemena, nephew of the last-mentioned patesi of *Shir-pur-la*. Some of them may have been rebuilt in subsequent times, but preceding the governments of Ur-Bau and Gudea. Not without good reason Heuzey proposed to identify the terrace to the southeast with the substructure of the *Ab*(*Esh*)-*gi*[3] mentioned on some of the inscribed bricks taken from the former, and the sacred enclosure to the northeast, which in part at least can be still defined by means of the copper figurines found *in situ*, with the *Ab-bi-ru*[4] of the alabaster tablets.

[1] Comp. De Sarzec and Heuzey, *Une Ville Royale Chaldéenne*, Paris, 1900, pp. 69–75, especially p. 74.

[2] Comp. Hilprecht, "The South-Babylonian Ruins of Abû Hatab and Fâra" (in course of preparation).

[3] Comp. De Sarzec and Heuzey, *Une Ville Royale Chaldéenne*, p. 79.

[4] Comp. De Sarzec and Heuzey, l. c., pp. 87, *seqq*.

Though the precise meaning of both of these names is obscure, Heuzey is doubtless correct in trying to explain the significance of the two structures represented by them from the nature of the principal building occupying Mound B, from the character of the numerous antiquities excavated in their neighborhood, and from certain other indications furnished by the inscriptions. The large oval reservoir and three smaller rectangular ones, discovered within the enclosure marked by Entemena's figurines, have probably reference to the (temporary) storing of dates [1] and to the preparation of date wine. Even to-day the date-growing Arabs of Babylonia, who have not been influenced by certain changes recently introduced in connection with the increased export of dates to Europe and America, use similar elevated receptacles, — the so-called *medibsa*,[2] — which have all the characteristic features of the ancient (oval) basin with its inclined pavement and outlet.

There are architectural remains which were unearthed in other parts of these ruins close to the large brick terrace erected by Ur-Ninâ and enlarged by his successors. But being too fragmentary in themselves and valuable chiefly as providing further evidence with regard to the real character of the whole complex of buildings concealed in Mound B, we may well abstain from enumerating them one by one and describing their peculiarities in detail.

What was the original purpose of all these separate walls and crumbling constructions, which at some time apparently constituted an organic whole? Certain pronounced architectural features still to be recognized in the central buildings of the two lowest platforms, and a careful examination of the different antiquities taken from the accumulated rub-

[1] Comp. the *khaṣâru* of the Neo-Babylonian contracts.

[2] For further details as to their construction and use, comp. Hilprecht, "The Babylonian Expedition of the University of Pennsylvania," series A, vol. x (in press).

bish within and around them, will enable us to answer the question and to determine the general character of the vast enclosure with reasonable certainty.

We notice, first of all, that the most prominent structure discovered in the stratum of the period of Ur-Ninâ, about thirty-five feet long and twenty-four wide, shows no trace of a door or any other kind of entrance, though its walls, when excavated, were still standing to the height of nearly four feet. It is therefore evident that access to it must have been had from above by means of a staircase or ladder now destroyed, and that for this reason it could never have been used as a regular dwelling-place for men or beasts. A

French Excavations at Tellô under De Sarzec

Southeast façade of the storehouse of King Ur-Ninâ, about 4000 B. C.

similar result is reached by examining the more archaic but somewhat smaller building below, which presents even greater puzzles from an architectural standpoint.

The inner disposition of the upper edifice is no less remarkable than its external appearance. It consists of two rooms of different size, which, however, do not extend directly to the outer walls, but are disconnected by a passageway or corridor over two feet and a half wide, running parallel with the latter and also separating the two rooms from each other. These inner chambers likewise have no opening. With good reason, therefore, Heuzey regards this curious building as a regular store or provision house similarly constructed to those known in ancient Egypt. This view is strengthened by the fact that the inscriptions of Ur-Ninâ, Enannatum, Urukagina, and especially those of Entemena repeatedly refer[1] to such a magazine or depot of the god Nin-Su(n)gir. The ancient kings and *patesis* of Lagash used to fill it with grain, dates, sesame oil, and other produce of the country required for the maintenance of the temple servants, or needed as supplies for their armies, which fought frequent battles in the name of their tutelary deity. The double walls, which form a characteristic feature also of a number of chambers in the outer wall of the huge Parthian fortress at Nippur, were useful in more than one regard. They excluded the extreme heat of the summer and the humidity of the winter, while, at the same time, they insured the safety of the stored provisions against damage from crevices, thieves, and troublesome insects. A coat of bitumen covering the walls and floors of the rooms and corridor answered the same purpose.

At a distance of thirteen feet from the principal building De Sarzec discovered eight bases made of baked brick, two on each side, which originally supported as many square pillars, clearly indicated by the remains of charred cedar-wood found near them. It is therefore apparent that a large gallery, a kind of portico or peristyle, as we frequently see it attached to the modern houses of Kurdish and Armenian peasants in Asia Minor, surrounded the ancient Babylonian edifice on all four sides, furnishing additional room for the temporary storage of goods, agricultural implements, and

[1] Comp. Thureau-Dangin in *Revue d'Assyriologie*, vol. iii, pp. 119, *seqq.*

large objects which could not be deposited within. On this theory it is easy to explain the existence of so many artificial reservoirs, water-courses, and wells in the immediate neighborhood of this interesting structure. As indicated above, they served various practical purposes in connection with this large rural establishment, such as cleansing and washing, the storing of dates, the preparation of date wine, and the pressing of oil.

Like the storerooms of the temple at Sippara so frequently mentioned in the later cuneiform inscriptions, this sacred magazine of the earliest rulers of Lagash was not exclusively a granary and oil-cellar. According to time and circumstances, it was turned into an armory or into a safe for specially valuable temple property, vessels and votive offerings of every description, as a small lot of copper daggers, fragments of reliefs, and two inscribed door-sockets found on the floor of the rooms sufficiently demonstrate. Many other objects of art gathered from the débris around this building may therefore have formed part of the treasures which, previous to the final destruction of the city, were kept within its walls. Modest and simple as this whole temple annex appears to us from our present standpoint, it was in every way adapted to the needs of the ancient population of *Shir-pur-la*, on its lofty terrace equally protected against the annual inundations of the rivers and the sudden invasion of hostile armies.

Among the portable antiquities which rewarded De Sarzec's labors during the three campaigns conducted from 1893 to 1895, about 30,000 baked cuneiform tablets and fragments constitute his most characteristic discovery. In 1894 and 1895 they were found in a small elevation a little over 650 feet distant from the large hill which contained the buildings of the ancient princes of Lagash just described. The successful explorer informs us[1] that he came upon two

[1] Through Heuzey, in *Revue d'Assyriologie*, vol. iii, pp. 65–68.

distinct groups of rectangular galleries constructed of crude bricks, upon which these first large collections of clay tablets from Tellô were arranged in five or six layers, one above another. Unfortunately, soon after their discovery, these interesting depots, which must be regarded as regular business archives of the temple, similar to others unearthed at Abû Habba and Nuffar, were plundered by the natives. Nearly all the leading museums of Europe and America have profited therefrom. But nevertheless it will always remain a source of deep regret that the French government does not appear to have succeeded in establishing regular guards at Tellô.[1] Even when De Sarzec was in the field, the ruins were not sufficiently protected at night, to say nothing of the frequent and long intervals in his work when no one was left on guard and those precious mounds remained at the mercy of unscrupulous merchants and of the neighboring Arabs, who soon began to realize the financial value of these almost inexhaustible mines.[2] A large number of the stolen tablets are still in the hands of the antiquity dealers. At first greedily bought by the latter in the sure expectation of an extraordinary gain, this archæological contraband began recently to disappoint them, the comparatively uninteresting and monotonous contents of the average clay tablet from Tellô offering too little attraction to most of the Assyriological students.

As a rule they refer to the administration of temple pro-

[1] The ruins of Nuffar, the neighborhood of which is as unsafe as that of Tellô, and the property of the expedition of the University of Pennsylvania (house and gardens, and stores, furniture and utensils locked up in the former) were always entrusted to native guards during our absence from the field, the ʻAfej shaikhs agreeing to guarantee their inviolability for a comparatively small remuneration. They have always kept their promise faithfully, notwithstanding the wars which they frequently waged against the Shammar or against each other in the meanwhile.

[2] Comp. Heuzey, *Catalogue de la Sculpture Chaldéenne au Musée du Louvre*, Paris, 1902, Introduction.

perty, to agriculture and stock-raising, to trade, commerce, and industry. There are lists of offerings, furniture, slaves, and other inventories, bills of entry, expense lists, receipts, accounts, contracts, and letters; there are even land registers, plans of houses, of fortifications, rivers, and canals. Especially numerous are the lists of animals (temple herds, and the like) and statements of the produce of the fields, testifying to the eminently agricultural and pastoral character of the ancient principality of Lagash. Among the more interesting specimens we mention the fragments of a correspondence between Lugal-ushumgal, *patesi* of *Shir-pur-la*, and a contemporaneous king of Agade (Sargon or Narâm-Sin), his suzerain. Or we refer to a number of inscribed seal-impressions in clay, as labels attached to merchandise and addressed to various persons and cities.[1] For we learn from a study of these long-buried archives that northern Babylonia largely exported grain and manufactured goods to the south, while the latter dealt principally in cattle, fowl, wool, cheese, butter, and eggs — precisely the same characteristic products which the two halves of Babylonia exchange with each other to-day.

With regard to their age, these tablets cover a considerable period. Some of them antedate the dynasty of Ur-Ninâ (4000 B. C.); others bear the name of Urukagina, "king of *Shir-pur-la*," whose time has not been fixed definitely;[2] again others belong to the age of Sargon and Narâm-Sin (3800 B. C.) and are of inestimable value for their dates, which contain important historical references;[3]

[1] Comp. Heuzey in *Comptes Rendus des Séances de l'Académie des Inscriptions et Belles-Lettres*, 1896 (4th series, vol. xxiv), session of April 17, and in *Revue d'Assyriologie*, vol. iv, pp. 1–12.

[2] According to Thureau-Dangin, he lived after Entemena. Comp. *Zeitschrift für Assyriologie*, vol. xv, p. 404, note 1.

[3] Babylon, written KA-DINGIR-RA-KI, appears on one of these tablets — according to our present knowledge the first clear reference to the famous city known in history.

a few are the documents from the reign of Gudea (about 2700 B. C.); by far the largest mass of the tablets recovered belongs to the powerful members of the later dynasty of Ur, about 2550 B. C.[1]

Numerous other inscribed antiquities of a more monumental character, such as statuettes with intact heads, truncated cones, stone cylinders, and, above all, the large pebbles of Eannatum, grandson of Ur-Ninâ, with their welcome accounts of the principal historical events occurring during his government, were taken from the clay shelves of the same subterranean galleries. Unique art treasures were found at different parts of the ruins as previously indicated, but they were especially numerous in the neighborhood of the storehouses and temple archives. Among those from Tellô which exhibit the most primitive style of art so far known, the fragments of a circular bas-relief representing the solemn meeting of two great chiefs followed by their retinues of warriors hold a very prominent place. It is contemporaneous with the earliest building discovered in mound B, while three excellent specimens of Old Babylonian metallurgy, two bulls' heads in copper[2] and a peculiarly formed vase in the same metal, belong to the more advanced period of Ur-Ninâ and his successors.

For many years to come the excavations of De Sarzec in and around mound B have furnished rich material for the student of ancient languages, history, and religion. Though

[1] Comp. especially Thureau-Dangin in *Comptes Rendus*, 1896, pp. 355–361, and in *Revue d'Assyriologie*, vol. iii, pp. 118–146; vol. iv, pp. 13–27 (also Oppert, *ibidem*, pp. 28–33), 69–84 (accompanied by 32 plates of representative texts). The latest inscribed cuneiform document so far obtained from Tellô is an inscribed cone of Rîm-Sin of Larsam, according to a statement of Heuzey in *Comptes Rendus*, 1894, p. 42.

[2] Two fine heads of Markhur goats in the same metal and of the same period were obtained by the present writer from the pre-Sargonic mounds of Fâra. Comp. Helm and Hilprecht in *Verhandlungen der Berliner anthropologischen Gesellschaft*, February 16, 1901, pp. 162, *seqq.*

none of the shrines and temples of the different local gods worshipped here has as yet been identified with certainty, the crumbling remains of so many buildings unearthed, the exceptionally large number of fine objects of art, and the mass of clay tablets and monumental inscriptions already recovered, enable us to form a tolerably fair idea of the general character and standard of civilization reached by the early inhabitants of the Euphrates and Tigris valleys at the threshold of the fifth and fourth millenniums before our era. This civilization is of no low degree, and is far from taking us back to the first beginnings of human order and society. Of course art and architecture, which developed in close connection with the religious cults and conceptions of the people, and were strongly influenced in their growth by the peculiarities of climate and the natural conditions of the soil, are simple, and in accordance with the normal development of primitive humanity. The alluvial ground around Lagash furnished the necessary material for making and baking bricks for the houses of the gods. During the first period of Babylonian history rudely formed with the hand, small in size, flat on the lower and slightly rounded on the upper side, which generally also bears one or more thumb marks, these bricks looked more like rubble or quarry stones, in imitation of which they were made, than the artificial products of man. Gradually they became larger in size, and under Ur-Ninâ they frequently have even a short inscription in coarse linear writing on the upper surface. But still they continued to retain their oblong plano-convex form down to the reign of Entemena, the great-grandson of the former, who was the first ruler at Lagash to employ a rectangular mould in the manufacture of his building material. As we learned from the results of the Philadelphia expedition to Nuffar, later confirmed by De Sarzec's own discoveries at Tellô, the principle of the arch was well known in the earliest times and occasionally applied in connection with draining. There is much in favor of Heuzey's view that the origin of the arch may possibly be traced to the peculiar form of the native reed-huts called *sarîfas* by the Arabs of modern Babylonia (comp. the illustration on p. 160). They are the regular dwelling places of the poor Ma'dân tribes which occupy the marshy districts of the interior to-day, and they doubtless represent the earliest kind of habitation in the "country of canals and reeds" at the dawn of civilization. The common mortar found in the buildings of the lowest strata is bitumen (comp. Gen. 11 : 3), which was easily obtained from the naphtha springs of the neighboring regions, while at least three different kinds of cement were employed in later centuries (comp. p. 32, above).

Vessels of different shapes and sizes were made of terra-cotta and stone, sometimes even of shell handsomely decorated. It is a remarkable fact that in material, form, and technique the earliest Babylonian vases often strikingly resemble those found in the tombs of the first dynasties of Egypt. A kind of veined limestone or onyx geologically known as calcite appears as a specially favorite material in both countries. The art of melting, hardening, casting, and chasing metals, especially copper and silver, was well established. The chemical analysis of early metal objects by the late Dr. Helm[1] has recently shown that the ancient Babylonian brass founders who lived about 4000 B. C. used not only tin but also antimony, in order to harden copper and at the same time to render it more fusible. Statues and bas-reliefs are less graceful and accurate in their design and execution than realistic, sober and powerful through their very simplicity. In order to give more life and expression to animals and men carved in stone or cast in metal, the eyes of such statues are frequently formed by

[1] Comp. Helm and Hilprecht in *Verhandlungen der Berliner anthropologischen Gesellschaft*, Feb. 16, 1901, pp. 157 *seqq*.

incrustation, the white of the apple of the eye being represented by shell or mother of pearl and the pupil by bitumen, lapis lazuli, or a reddish-brown stone. Red color is also sometimes used to paint groups of figures, which with an often surprising grace and fidelity to nature are incised in thin plates of shell or mother of pearl, in order to set them off better from the background,[1] somewhat in the same manner as the Phenician artist of the sixth century treated the two inscriptions of Bostân esh-Shaikh (above Sidon) recently excavated by Makridi Bey for the Imperial Ottoman Museum.[2]

We do not know when writing (which, contrary to Delitzsch's untenable theory,[3] began as a picture writing) was first introduced into Babylonia. About 4000 B. C. we find it in regular use everywhere in the country. Moreover, the single linear characters are already so far developed that in many cases the original picture can no longer be recognized. Only a few short inscriptions of the earliest historical period, when writing was still purely pictorial, are at present known to us. The one is in the Archæological Museum of the University of Pennsylvania, another in New York, a third in Paris. Owing to the scarcity of this class of inscribed stones, their precise date cannot yet be ascertained. They probably belong to the beginning of the fifth millennium.

These first few conclusions drawn from the architectural remains, the sculptures, and inscriptions of the period of Ur-Ninâ, incomplete as the picture obtained thereby

[1] A large number of such colored plates of mother of pearl obtained from Fâra and other South-Babylonian ruins is in the possession of the present writer.

[2] Comp. Hilprecht in *Deutsche Litteraturzeitung*, Nov. 30, 1901, pp. 3030, *seq.*; and in "Sunday School Times," Dec. 21, 1901, p. 857.

[3] Comp. Delitzsch, *Die Entstehung des ältesten Schriftsystems*, Leipzig, 1897.

naturally is, will be sufficient for our present purpose to show that the civilization represented by his dynasty must be regarded as a very advanced stage in the gradual development of man, and that thousands of years of serious striving and patient work had to elapse before this standard was reached. The political conditions in the country were by no means always very favorable to the peaceful occupations of its inhabitants, to the tilling of the ground, to the expansion of trade, to the advancement of art and literature. At the time of Ur-Ninâ, Babylonia was divided into a large number of petty states, among which now this one, now that one exercised a passing hegemony over the others. The three Biblical cities Erech, Ur, Ellasar (*i. e.*, Larsam), Nippur (probably identical with Calneh, Gen. 10 : 10), Kîsh, Lagash, and a place written *Gish-Khu*,[1] the exact pronunciation of which is not yet known, are the most frequently mentioned in the inscriptions of this remote antiquity. Every one of these fortified cities had its own sanctuary, which stood under the control of a *patesi* or "prince-priest." The most renowned religious centre of the whole country was Nippur, with the temple of Enlil or Bêl, "the father of the gods," while for many years the greatest political power was exercised by the kings of Kîsh, a city "wicked of heart," until Ur-Ninâ and his successors established a temporary supremacy of Lagash over the whole South.

The last-named place consisted of several quarters or suburbs grouped around the temples of favorite gods and goddesses. Sungir, generally transliterated as Girsu, and possibly the prototype of the Biblical Shinar (שנער Gen. 10 : 10; 11 : 2)[2] and of the Babylonian Shumer, which is only dialectically different from the former, was one of them,

[1] According to Scheil probably represented by the ruins of Jôkha.

[2] Comp. Hilprecht, "The Babylonian Expedition of the University of Pennsylvania," series A, vol. 1, part 2 (1896), pp. 57, *seq.*; and Radau, "Early Babylonian History," New York, 1900, pp. 216, *seqq.*

indeed the most important of all the quarters of the city. It furnished the new dynasty from its nobility and took the leading position in the fierce struggle against the powerful neighbors and oppressors. Nin-Sungir, "the Lord of Sungir," was raised to the rank of the principal god, and his emblem — the lion-headed eagle with its outspread wings victoriously clutching two lions in its powerful talons [1] — became the coat of arms of the united city [2] and characterizes best the spirit of independence and bold self-reliance which was fostered in his sanctuary.

According to all indications the dynasty of Ur-Ninâ was one of the mightiest known in the early history of Babylonia. The founder himself seems to have devoted his best strength and time to the works of peace. The numerous temples and canals received his attention, statues were carved in honor of the gods, and new storehouses constructed to receive "the abundance of the country." Caravans were sent out to obtain the necessary timber from foreign countries, and the walls of the city were repaired or enlarged in anticipation of future complications and troubles. It was, however, reserved to Eannatum, the most illustrious representative of the whole dynasty, to fight those battles for which his grandfather had already taken the necessary precautions. Like his ancestors he continued to develop the natural resources of the country by digging new canals and wisely administering the inner affairs of his city. But, above all, he was great as a warrior, and extended the sphere of his influence far beyond the banks of the Shatt el-Haï and the two great rivers, by defeating the army of Elam, subduing *Gish-khu*, carrying his weapons victoriously against Erech and Ur, destroying the city of Az on the Persian Gulf, and crushing even the power of the kings

[1] Comp. the illustration ("Silver Vase of Entemena") facing p. 241, above, and what has been said on p. 235.

[2] Comp. Heuzey, *Les armoiries Chaldéennes de Sirpourla*, Paris, 1894.

of Kîsh, the old suzerains and hereditary enemies of the princes of Lagash.

More than once in my preceding sketch of De Sarzec's labors and results I have referred to his discovery of new fragments of the so-called "stele of vultures." This famous monument of the past, one of the most interesting art treasures unearthed in Tellô, received its name from a flock of vultures which carry away the hands, arms, and decapitated heads of the enemies vanquished and killed by Eannatum and his soldiers. It was originally rounded at the top, about five feet wide and correspondingly high, and covered with scenes and inscriptions on both its faces. The representations on the front celebrate King Eannatum as a great and successful warrior, while those on the reverse, so far as preserved, are of a mythological character, showing traces of several gods and goddesses in whose names the battles were fought, and who seem to be represented here as assisting their pious servant in the execution of his great and bloody task. The stele of vultures, which indicates a very decided progress in its style of art and writing as over against the more primitive monuments of Ur-Ninâ, was erected by Eannatum to commemorate his victory over the army of *Gish-khu*, and his subsequent treaty concluded with Enakalli, *patesi* of the conquered city, whom he made swear never again to invade the sacred territory of Nin-Sungir nor to trespass the boundary established anew between the two principalities.

During the early months of 1898 and 1900 De Sarzec conducted his last two campaigns at Tellô. Little as yet has been published with regard to their results. Heuzey announced[1] that among the precious monuments obtained through the excavations of the tenth expedition (1898) there are the first inscribed bricks of Ennatuma I., brother and successor of Eannatuma, and two carved oblong plates,

[1] In *Comptes Rendus*, 1898, pp. 344–349.

or slabs, of Narâm-Sin, in slate and diorite, apparently intended as bases for small statues or some other kind of votive objects. Both slabs are provided with square holes in their centres and engraved with inscriptions of considerable interest. We learn from the one legend that the conquests of the last-mentioned powerful king, whose empire extended from the mountains of Elam to the boundary of Egypt, included the country of Armanu.[1] The other makes us acquainted with a son and with a granddaughter of Narâm-Sin, who served as a priestess of Sin, so that practically we now know four generations of the ancient kings of Agade.

According to a personal communication from De Sarzec, his eleventh campaign, which lasted only twelve weeks, yielded no less than 4000 baked cuneiform tablets and fragments of the same general character as those described above, two exquisite new heads of statues in dolerite, and several other monuments of the period of Ur-Ninâ and his successors, the first description of which we must leave to the pen of Heuzey, the eloquent and learned interpreter of his friend's epoch-making discoveries in Southern Babylonia. The tablets have been studied very recently by Thureau-Dangin.[2] According to his information they contain several new governors (*patesis*) of *Shir-pur-la* from that obscure period which lies between the reigns of Narâm-Sin (about 3750 B. C.) and Ur-Gur (at present read Ur-Engur by the French scholar[3]), the probable founder of the later dynasty of Ur (about 2700 B. C.). They also give us an insight into the administrative machinery of the powerful kingdom of Ur, and are of especial importance for the long government of Dungi, son and successor of Ur-Gur, who

[1] Which can scarcely be separated from *Ar-man* mentioned v *R.* 12, No. 6, 47. Comp. Delitzsch, *Wo lag das Paradies?* Leipzig, 1881, p. 205.

[2] Comp. *Comptes Rendus*, 1902, session of Jan. 10, pp. 77-94.

[3] *L. c.* p. 82, note 2.

occupied the throne of his father for about half a century. They instruct us concerning many valuable chronological, historical, and geographical details, among other things furnishing almost definitive new proof for the theory that Dungi, "king of Ur, king of the four quarters of the world," and Dungi, "king of Ur, king of Shumer and Akkad," are one and the same person.

Towards the middle of February, 1900, the French explorer descended the Tigris for the last time, in order to reach Kûd(t) el-'Amâra and the scene of his activity on the eastern bank of the Shatt el-Haï. At the same time the present writer ascended the river, being on his way to Baghdad and to the swamps of the 'Afej. A heavy thunderstorm was raging over the barren plains of 'Irâq, and the muddy waters of the Tigris began suddenly to rise, greatly interfering with my progress, when the two steamers came in sight of each other. I stood on the bridge of the English "Khalîfa," intently looking at the approaching Turkish vessel, which flew the French colors from the top of its mast. A tall figure could be faintly distinguished on the passing boat, leaning against its iron railing and eagerly scanning the horizon with a field-glass. A flash of light separated the thick black clouds which had changed day into twilight, and illuminated the two steamers for a moment. I recognized the features of De Sarzec, the newly (1899) appointed minister plenipotentiary of France, who in an instant had drawn a handkerchief, which he waved lustily on his fast disappearing boat as a greeting of welcome to the representative of the Philadelphia expedition. A month later a cordial and urgent invitation was received from the French camp near Tellô. I still regret that at that moment my own pressing duties at the ruins of Nuffar did not allow of an even short visit to Southern Babylonia, and that consequently I missed my last chance of seeing De Sarzec in the midst of his trenches and directing his famous excavations in person.

Towards the end of May we both were back in Baghdad, and for a whole week we met regularly at the hospitable house of the American vice-consul, communicating to each other the results of our latest expeditions, discussing our new plans and dwelling with especial pleasure on the bright prospect of methodical explorations in the numerous ruins of Shumer and Akkad. Seated on the flat roof of our temporary abode, we used to enjoy the refreshing evening hours of a Babylonian spring, — over us that brilliant sky in the knowledge of which the early inhabitants of the country excelled all other nations, below us the murmuring waters of the Tigris which gradually expose and wash away the tombs of by-gone generations, carrying their dust into the realm of the god Ea, "the creator of the Universe," and far away into the ocean to the island of the blessed. De Sarzec himself looked exceedingly tired and frequently complained of chills and fever. When we finally separated, he took the direct route to the coast of the Mediterranean by way of Dêr and Aleppo, while the present writer rode along the western bank of the Tigris and examined the ruins of Assyria and Cappadocia before he reached Europe at Constantinople. De Sarzec's hope of a speedy return to his Arabs and ruins was not to be realized. On May 30, 1901, at the age of sixty-four years, the great French explorer succumbed suddenly, at Poitiers, to a disease of the liver, which he had contracted during his long sojourn in the East. Only a few weeks later his faithful companion, who so often had dwelt with him in the tents of the desert, assisting and encouraging him in the great task of his life, followed her husband on his last journey to "the land without return."

The French government, fully recognizing the extraordinary importance of De Sarzec's work and the necessity of its continuation, has taken steps at an early date to resume the exploration of Tellô, so gloriously initiated and for nearly a quarter of a century carried on by its own representative. Great results doubtless will again be forthcoming. But significant and surprising as the success of future expeditions to this ancient seat of civilization may be, the name of De Sarzec, to whom science owes the resurrection of ancient Chaldean art and the restoration of a long forgotten leaf in the history of mankind, will always stand out as an illustrious example of rare energy, great intelligence, and indefatigable patience devoted to the cause of archæology in the service and for the honor of his country.

ENGLISH EXCAVATIONS UNDER RASSAM AT BABYLON, EL-BIRS, AND ABÛ HABBA

The exceptional terms and the wide scope of the firmân granted to Sir Henry Layard in 1878, induced Hormuzd Rassam, then in charge of the British excavations in Assyria, to extend his operations at once to as many ruins as possible. In the interest of a strictly scientific exploration of the ancient remains of Asshur and Babel, this decision must be regretted, unless we regard the rapid working of new mines of antiquities and the mere accumulation of inscribed tablets the principal — not to say the only — object of archæological missions to the countries of the Euphrates and Tigris. But whatever may be said against Rassam's strange methods, radically different from those of other recent Babylonian explorers, and largely responsible for the irreparable loss of many important data necessary for a satisfactory reconstruction of the topography and history of the different sites excavated by him, he deserves credit for his extraordinary mobility and devotion to what he regarded his duty,[1] and by which he was enabled to gather an immense number of cuneiform texts and to enrich the collections of the British Museum with many priceless treasures.

[1] Comp. Rassam, "Asshur and the Land of Nimrod," New York, 1897, p. 363.

Towards the middle of February, 1879, he commenced his excavations of Babylonian mounds, which for more than three years [1] were carried on by native overseers under his general supervision. The first ruins to which he directed his attention were Babylon and Borsippa (El-Birs). Arab diggers, forming a secret and strong combination, were then engaged in extracting bricks from the walls and buttresses of Bâbil. As soon as they heard of the foreigner's intentions, they began to watch his movements with jealousy and suspicion. In order to protect himself against their unscrupulous machinations, and at the same time to secure their confidence and assistance for his own operations, Rassam proposed to them to enter his service on the promise that all the plain bricks which might be unearthed should become their property. Naturally they agreed readily to an arrangement which gave them regular wages besides their ordinary share in the excavated building material. During the two or three months which, in the course of his Babylonian excavations, he could spend in the trenches near Hilla, he examined and followed the excavations of the Arab brick-diggers at Bâbil with undivided attention. No sooner had they struck four exquisitely built wells of red granite in the southern centre of the mound, than he hurried to the scene and uncovered them entirely. They still were 140 feet high, and communicated with an aqueduct or canal supplied with water from the Euphrates. From the peculiarity of their material, which must have been brought from a great distance in Northern Mesopotamia; from the fine execution of the enormous circular stones,[2] which had been bored and made to fit each other so exactly that each well appeared as if hewn in one solid block; from the numerous remains of huge walls and battlements built of kiln-

[1] Comp. the summary of Rassam's activity on Assyrian and Babylonian ruins given on p. 203, *seq.*, footnote. He ceased his excavations July, 1882.

[2] Each stone was about three feet high.

burned bricks, so eagerly sought by the Arabs; from the commanding position of the whole lofty mound, — details which agreed most remarkably with characteristic features of the hanging gardens, as described by Diodorus and Pliny, — Rassam came to the conclusion that this great wonder of the ancient world could only be represented by Bâbil, a view first held by Rich, and for various additional reasons also shared by the present writer.

On the assumption that the large basalt lion of the Qasr, so often mentioned by earlier explorers, must have flanked the gate of a palace in the days of the Babylonian monarchs, he searched in vain for "another similar monolith, which stood on the opposite side of the entrance." After cutting a few trial trenches into the centre of the mound, not far from the ruin where Mignan, Layard, and Oppert had left their traces, Rassam abandoned this unpromising site for other less disturbed localities in its neighborhood.

As long as he employed workmen on the ruins of the capital of Amraphel and Nebuchadrezzar, he concentrated his efforts at the two southern groups of the vast complex, known under the names of 'Omrân ibn 'Alî and Jumjuma.[1] Though succeeding as little as those who excavated there before him in finding large sculptured monuments, Rassam was amply repaid for his labors at the last-named place, by discovering a great many of the so-called contract tablets, left by private individuals, or forming part of the archives of business firms, among which the famous house of Egibi played a most prominent rôle. Unfortunately not a few of these documents crumbled to pieces as soon as they were removed, the damp soil in which they had been lying being impregnated with nitre. The first great collection of this class of tablets had come from the same mound in the winter of 1875–76, when Arab brick-diggers unearthed a number of clay jars filled with more than 3000 documents, which, shortly before his death,

[1] Comp. Map No. 2.

George Smith had acquired for the British Museum. They all belonged to the final period of Babylonian history, to the years when for the last time Nabopolassar and his successors restored the glory of the great city on the Euphrates. Their contents revealed to us an entirely new phase of Babylonian civilization. We became acquainted with the every-day life of the different classes of the population, and we became witnesses of their mutual relations and manifold transactions. We obtained an insight into the details of their households, their kinds of property and its administration, their incomes and their taxes, their modes of trading and their various occupations, their methods in irrigating and cultivating fields and in raising stocks, their customs in marrying and adopting children, the position of their slaves, and many other interesting features of the life of the people. Above all, these tablets showed us the highly developed legal institutions of a great nation, thus furnishing an important new source for the history of comparative jurisprudence. There is scarcely a case provided against by the minute regulations of the Roman law which has not its parallel or prototype in ancient Chaldea.

Valuable as all these small and unbaked tablets proved for our knowledge of the private life, the commercial intercourse, and the chronology of the time of the Chaldean and Persian dynasties, they did not constitute the entire harvest which Rassam could gather. There were other important documents of a literary and historical character rescued from the same vicinity. We mention only the broken cylinder of Cyrus containing the official record of the conquest of Babylon (539 B. C.), and in its phraseology sometimes curiously approaching the language of Isaiah.[1]

[1] Comp. chaps. 44 (end) and 45 with my remarks on Pl. 33 of the "New Gallery of Illustrations" in Holman's "Self-pronouncing S. S. Teachers' Bible," Philadelphia, 1897. According to Rassam's own statement (*l. c.*, p. 267), the cylinder of Cyrus was not found in the ruins of

Rassam's excavations, conducted at the foot of El-Birs and in the adjoining mound of Ibrâhîm el-Khalîl, which doubtless conceals some of the most conspicuous buildings of ancient Borsippa, were likewise productive of good results. A fine collection of inscribed tablets came from the latter ruin, while about eighty chambers and galleries of a large building were laid bare on the platform to the east of the stage-tower which in previous years had been partly explored by Rawlinson. This unique complex, mistaken by Rassam for "another palace of Nebuchadrezzar," turned out to be nothing less than the famous temple of Ezida, sacred to Nebo, the tutelar deity of Borsippa. All the rich property of the god and his priests, with the many valuable gifts deposited by powerful kings and pious pilgrims, had been carried away long before. Heaps of rubbish, broken capitals and fallen pillars, interspersed with pieces of enamelled tiles once embellishing its ceilings and walls, were all that was left of the former splendor. A small bas-relief, two boundary stones, an inscribed barrel cylinder, and the fragment of a heavy bronze threshold of Nebuchadrezzar, on the edge of which the first[1] six lines of a cuneiform legend had been wrongly arranged by an uneducated engraver, were the few antiquities of true Babylonian origin which, after infinite labor and pain, could be rescued from this scene of

the Qasr, as asserted, *e. g.* by Hagen, *Beiträge zur Assyriologie*, vol. ii, p. 204, and Delitzsch, *Babylon*, 2d ed., Leipzig, 1901, p. 13, but in the mound of Jumjuma.

[1] There are remains of three cuneiform characters at the end of the broken edge, which is four inches thick, so that the inscription must have had at least nine lines. Properly speaking, the preserved portion of the inscription consists of two columns, three lines each. But by disregarding the separating line between the two columns on the tablet from which he copied, the scribe changed the six short lines into one column with three long lines. A picture of the threshold, which, in its present state, measures a little over five feet by one foot eight inches, was published by Rassam in his first report, "Transactions of the Society of Biblical Archæology," vol. viii, p. 188.

utter devastation. But the well-preserved terra-cotta cylinder proved of exceptional value in giving us the brief history of the final restoration of Nebo's renowned sanctuary, in 270 B. C., by Antiochus Soter, "the first-born son of Seleucus, the Macedonian king." So far as our present knowledge goes, it is the last royal document composed in the Old-Babylonian writing and language.

There are many important finds connected with the name of Rassam as an Assyrian and Babylonian explorer. The discovery of Ashurbânapal's north palace, with its library and art treasures at Qoyunjuk, and the unearthing of Shalmaneser's bronze gates at Balawât, will alone suffice to keep his memory fresh forever in the history of Assyrian excavations. But among all the remarkable results which through his skill and energy he wrested from the soil of Babylonia there is none greater and more far-reaching in its bearings upon the whole science of Assyriology than his identification and partial excavation of the site of Sippara. Every trace of this famous ancient city, in connection with Agade or Akkad (Gen. 10 : 10), so often mentioned in the cuneiform literature, and occasionally referred to even by classical writers, seemed to have vanished completely. Numerous attempts had been made to determine its ruins. Rassam himself had thought for a while of Tell Ibrâhîm, which Rawlinson identified with Cuthah (2 Kings 17 : 24); others had hit upon Tell Shaishabar, about eighteen miles to the south of Baghdad; others again were fully convinced that it was represented by Tell Sifaira, between the Nahr 'Îsâ and the Euphrates; while modern geographers inclined generally to place it at the present Musayyib. This only seemed certain, that the city must have been situated in Northern Babylonia, not far from the banks of the Euphrates. George Smith was the first to propose the ruins of Abû Habba as its probable site. They extend to the south of the Nahr el-Malik (the Naarmalcha of Pliny), to-day more commonly called the Nahr

Yûsufîye, about halfway between "the great river"[1] and the caravan road which leads from Baghdad to Kerbelâ and Hilla. Nobody, however, had apparently taken notice of his stray remark in the "Records of the Past,"[2] and Rassam, unfamiliar as he was with Assyriological publications, had surely never heard about it. He went to search for the site of the city in his own way.

It was in December, 1880. After half a year's absence from the plains of 'Irâq el-'Arabî he had returned from Kurdistân and Mosul to superintend his excavations at Babylon and Borsippa in person, and to examine the districts to the north and south of them with a view of locating other promising ruins for future operations. As soon as he had satisfied himself that in the immediate environments of Hilla and El-Birs there was no ruin to tempt him, he proceeded northward by way of Tell Ibrâhîm and Mahmûdîye, "bent upon visiting every mound in the neighborhood, and seeing if he could not hit upon the exact site [of Sippara] to the north of Babylon." Dissatisfied with the results of various trials to locate it, he finally had arrived and settled temporarily at Mahmûdîye. The number of his workmen from Jumjuma, soon increased from the ranks of passing pilgrims and wayfaring loiterers, were ordered to dig at some of the principal ruins around the village. Meanwhile he himself wandered from mound to mound, searching and hoping, only to be later disappointed.

On previous occasions he had repeatedly heard of three other conspicuous *tells* to the north and northwest of Mahmûdîye, called by the Arabs Ed-Dêr, Abû Habba, and Harqâwi.[3] His way from Baghdad to Hilla had often led

[1] From which they are distant not more than four miles in a direct line. Comp. Rassam, "Asshur and the Land of Nimrod," New York, 1897, p. 403.

[2] 1st ed., vol. v (London, 1875), p. 107, No. 56.

[3] Generally pronounced Hargâwi in the modern dialect of the country, and

him close by them. But as the peculiar topographical and atmospheric conditions of Babylonia render it extremely difficult to judge the height of a mound correctly from a distance, or to distinguish it from the huge embankments of the numerous canals which intersect the alluvial plain everywhere, Rassam had never paid much attention to the stories of the natives. This time, however, his interest was suddenly aroused. We quote from his own account: "One day, on returning to my host's house at Mahmûdîye, his brother, Mohammed, showed me a fragment of kiln-burnt brick with a few arrow-headed characters on it, which he said he had picked up at the ruins of Dêr when he was returning from a wedding to which he had been invited. I no sooner saw the relic than I began to long for a visit to the spot, and I lost no time the next day in riding to it. It happened then that the Euphrates had overflowed its banks, and the Mahmûdîye Canal, which is generally dry nine months in the year, was running and inundating the land between Dêr and the village of Mahmûdîye; the consequence was we had to go a round-about way to reach that place. We had first to pass the Sanctuary of Seyyid 'Abdallah, the reputed saint of that country, situated about six miles to the north-west of Mahmûdîye; and we then veered to the right and proceeded to Dêr in an easterly direction. In about half an hour's ride further, we came to an inclosure of what seemed to me an artificial mound, and on ascending it I asked my guide if that was the ruin in which he had picked up the inscribed brick. He replied in the negative, but said that we were then at Abû Habba, and Dêr was about an hour further on. I could scarcely believe my eyes on looking down and finding everything under my horse's feet

situated to the west of Abû Habba, while Ed-Dêr is found to the northeast of the latter. Here, as well as in passages where I quote literally from Rassam, I have quietly changed his wretched spellings of Arabic and Turkish names in accordance with a more scientific method.

indicating a ruin of an ancient city; and if I had had any workmen at hand I would have then and there placed two or three gangs to try the spot. I was then standing near a small pyramid situated at the westerly limit of the mound, which I was told contained a golden model of the ark in which Noah and his family were saved from the Deluge, and that the second father of mankind had it buried there as a memorial of the event," — apparently a faint and distorted reminiscence of the old Babylonian tradition preserved by Berossos, and according to which before the great flood Xisouthros (*i. e.*, Noah), by order of his god, buried the tablets inscribed with "the beginning, middle, and end of all things," at Sippara.

Though rising scarcely more than thirty to forty feet above the desert, the ruins of Abû Habba are of considerable extent. Except on the western side, where the conical remains of the stage-tower are situated near a dry branch of the Euphrates, they are surrounded by large walls, which on the northwest and northeast are almost perfect. The rectangular parallelogram thus formed encloses an area of more than 1,210,000 square yards,[1] or about 250 acres, its longest side measuring more than 1400 yards. Only the third part of this whole space is occupied by an irregular conglomeration of mounds which conceal what is left of the ancient city. As soon as Rassam had taken a hasty survey of the prominent site, he lost no time in making the neces-

[1] The 3500 square yards given by Rassam ("Asshur and the Land of Nimrod," New York, 1897, p. 399) for the whole area are an evident mistake, the temple mound alone being considerably larger. The measurements quoted above are based upon my own calculations in connection with a personal visit to the ruins. They were recently confirmed by Scheil, who kindly sent me the following statement before the final proof was passed: "The enclosure of Sippar is 1300 meters [1422 yards] long, and 800 m. [875 yards] wide. The temple enclosure is about 400 m. [437 yards] square." In other words the temple area represents about 190,969 square yards, or nearly 39½ acres.

sary preparations for immediate excavations. No Arab encampment being anywhere near the ruins, he established his headquarters at Seyyid 'Abdallah, where the guardian of the sanctuary and his near relatives lived in peaceful seclusion.

Operations were commenced near the pyramid in January, 1881. On the very first day the workmen dug up pieces of a barrel cylinder and fragments of inscribed bricks and bitumen. A little later they came upon the wall of a chamber which presented all the characteristic features of true Babylonian architecture. Soon afterwards they discovered similar rooms in different parts of the same mound. There could be no longer any doubt; Rassam had struck a large ancient building of great interest and importance. Encouraged by this rapid success of the first few days, he prosecuted his researches with redoubled energy. As he proceeded with his work, he entered a chamber which attracted his curiosity at once. Contrary to his previous experience, it was paved with asphalt instead of marble or brick. He ordered his men to break through the pavement and to examine the ground below. They had scarcely begun to remove the earth at the southeast corner, when three feet below the surface they discovered an inscribed terra-cotta trough or box closed with a lid. Inside lay a marble tablet, eleven inches and a half long by seven inches wide, broken into eight pieces, but otherwise complete. It was covered with six columns of the finest writing, and adorned with a beautiful bas-relief on the top of the obverse. The subject represented is the following: A god seated in his shrine is approached by two priests and a worshipper, who is probably the king himself. The three persons stand before the disk of the sun, placed upon an altar and held with ropes by the two divine attendants of Shamash, Malik and Bunene, who, according to Babylonian mythology, as guides direct the course of the fiery orb "covering heaven and earth with lustre."[1] The cuneiform legend in front of the sanctuary is identical with the label inscribed on each side of the box in which the tablet was placed, and serves as an explanation of the pictorial representation: "Image of Shamash [the Sun-god], the great lord, dwelling in Ebabbara, situated in Sippar." The interpretation of the other two small legends written above and below the roof of the shrine has offered considerable difficulty. They are evidently also labels which, in the briefest possible form, indicate important and characteristic details of the golden image mentioned in the long inscription below, and of which the stone relief is a faithful reproduction. Similar to those found by Smith on clay tablets in the royal library of Nineveh,[2] they are to be

Marble Tablet of King Nabû-apal-iddina, about 850 B. C.
From the temple of the Sun god at Sippuru

[1] Comp. iv *R.* 20, No. 2, l. 4, and the beautiful hymn to the Sun-god, first published by Pinches, in the "Transactions of the Society of Biblical Archæology," vol. viii, pp. 167, *seq.*

[2] Comp. p. 198, above, and George Smith, "Assyrian Discoveries," 3d

regarded as instructions and explanations for the artist[1] who in days to come may be called upon to make another image. Two terra-cotta moulds,[2] showing all the details of our bas-relief, were found in the box with the stone tablet. The

ed., New York, 1876, p. 411, *seqq*. Comp., also, Bezold, "Catalogue of the Cuneiform Tablets in the Kouyunjik Collection of the British Museum," vol. v (London, 1899), pp. xix and xxvii, 5.

[1] The upper inscription reads: *Sin, Shamash, Ishtar ina pu-ut apsî ina bi-rit Ṣîri ti-mi innadû* (*-ú*), *i. e., Sin, Shamash, and Ishtar* (whose symbols are engraved below this inscription) *have been placed* (on the golden image, or *are to be placed* on a new image that may be made; the verbal form can be regarded as preterite or present tense) *opposite the ocean* (indicated at the lower end of the bas-relief by wavy lines; comp., also, v *R*. 63, col. ii, 5) *between the snake* (in the year 1887, when at the request of Dr. Hayes Ward I gave him my interpretation of this bas-relief at his house in Newark, I called his attention to the important fact generally overlooked, that the back and top of the shrine represents an immense snake, whose head can be clearly recognized over the column in front of the god) *and the rope* (= *timmi*, by which the altar and disk of the sun are suspended. But it is perhaps better to interpret *ti-mi* as a dialectical or inexact writing for *di-mi*, intended for *dimmi*, "column," which we see immediately before the god supporting the roof of his house).

The lower inscription, which stands as a label near the head-dress of the god, reads: *agû Shamash, mushshi agû Shamash*, which I interpret, *tiara of Shamash, make the tiara of Shamash bright* (*mashû* = *namâru*, ii *R*. 47, 58, and 59 e, f, here imperat. ii.[1] This special order must be interpreted in the light of the difficult passage, v *R*. 63, col. i, 43 to col. ii, 40, especially col. ii, 36–39, "I made the golden tiara [of Shamash] anew and made it bright as the day"). The Sun-god was the bringer of light; rays of light therefore were supposed to go forth from his head and tiara, as they did from the head of Apollo on the coins of Rhodes. Even if *mushshi* be interpreted as a noun, it cannot refer to the wand and rod in the right hand of Shamash, as has been supposed, but it must refer to the tiara, of which then it possibly denotes a part, — a view supported by the fact that the two lines form but one label, and by the circumstance that in v *R*. 63, col. i, 43, *seqq*., Nabonidos gives a detailed description as to how a correct tiara of the Sun-god has to look.

[2] One of them, together with a cylinder of Nabonidos, is in the Ottoman Museum at Constantinople.

golden image, just referred to, was the work of King Nabû-apal-iddina. In connection with the pillaging of the temple by Sutean hordes in a previous war, the old image of the god had been destroyed. All efforts to find a copy of the famous representation had proved in vain. Finally, in 852 B. C., a terra-cotta relief[1] was accidentally discovered on the western bank of the Euphrates, which enabled Nabû-apal-iddina to revive the ancient cult in its former glory. In order to secure its continuity, in case another national calamity should befall his country, the king had an exact copy of the original with explanatory labels carved at the top of his memorial tablet, which was buried in the ground.

In unearthing this stone, Rassam had discovered the famous temple of Shamash and, at the same time, identified one of the earliest Babylonian cities. He stood in the very sanctuary in which Babylonian monarchs once rendered homage to the golden image of their god. In a room adjoining the one just described, the fortunate explorer found two large barrel cylinders of Nabonidos in a fine state of preservation, and "a curiously hewn stone symbol . . . ending on the top in the shape of a cross," and "inscribed with archaic characters." The text of these cylinders proved an historical source of the utmost importance. The royal archæologist, to whom we are indebted for so many precious chronological data, delighted more in excavating ancient temples and reviving half-forgotten cults than in administering the affairs of his crumbling empire. Sippara, situated scarcely thirty miles to the north of Babylon, and renowned equally for its venerable cult and its magnificent library, naturally received his special attention. After a poetical description of the

[1] Col. iii, 19, *seq.*: *uṣurti ṣalmishu ṣirpu sha khaṣbi*, "the relief of his image in terra-cotta." For *ṣirpu sha khaṣbi*, "something in terra-cotta," a terra-cotta relief, figurine, etc., comp. the verb *ṣarâpu*, "to burn, bake (bricks)," quoted by Meissner, *Suppl. zu den Assyr. Wörterbüchern*, p. 82.

principal circumstances and events which led to the destruction and his subsequent restoration of the temple of Sin at Haran, Nabonidos proceeds to inform us how the temple of Shamash, "the judge of heaven and earth," had decayed in Sippar within less than fifty years after its reparation by Nebuchadrezzar. To the mind of the king there was only one reason which could account sufficiently for this alarming fact, — the displeasure of the god himself. His predecessor apparently had not followed the exact outline and dimensions of the oldest sanctuary, which, according to Babylonian conception,[1] must be strictly kept to insure the favor of the god and the preservation of his dwelling place on earth. Nabonidos, therefore, ordered his soldiers to tear down the walls and to search for the original foundation stone. Eighteen cubits deep the workmen descended into the ground. After infinite labor and trouble the last Chaldean ruler of Babylon succeeded in bringing to light the foundation stone of Narâm-Sin, the son of Sargon of Agade, "which for 3200 years no previous king had seen," conveying to us by this statement the startling news that this great ancient monarch lived about 3750 B. C., a date fully corroborated by my own excavations at Nuffar.

No sooner had the rumor of Rassam's extraordinary discovery spread in the neighboring districts than new difficulties were thrown in his way by jealous property owners and intriguing individuals. But with his old pertinacity he held his own and stuck to the newly occupied field, the real value of which he had been the first to disclose. For eighteen months British excavations were carried on at Abû Habba without interruption. Rassam could remain at the ruins only the third part of all this time, — the expiration of the annual grant by the British Museum and his desire to have the old firmân renewed as soon as possible

[1] Comp. Hilprecht, *Assyriaca*, part I, Boston and Halle, 1894, pp. 54, *seq.*

requiring his journey to Europe. But, as usual, during his absences native overseers were entrusted with the continuation of the explorations under the general control of the British Resident at Baghdad.

In the spring of 1882, after many fruitless efforts to obtain again those former privileges, which the awakened Turkish interest in archæological treasures could concede no longer, he returned to Babylonia for the last time. As long as his permit lasted (till Aug. 16, 1882) he worked with all his energy, deepening and extending his trenches at Bâbil and Abû Habba, and despatching whatever was found to England. It was particularly the temple complex at the latter place upon which he concentrated his personal attention. According to his calculation, the chambers and halls buried here must have amounted to nearly three hundred, one hundred and thirty of which he excavated. They were grouped around open courts, and apparently divided into two distinct buildings enclosed by breastworks. The one was the temple proper, and the other contained the rooms for the priests and attendants. That King Nabonidos had not cleared away all the rubbish of the older structure, became very evident from the fact that Rassam found the height of the original chambers and halls to be twenty-five feet, while the asphalt pavement, in the room described above, and the floors of the adjoining chambers rested upon débris which filled half their depth.

The number of inscribed objects and other antiquities rescued from the ruins of Abû Habba within the comparatively short period of a year and a half is enormous. About 60,000 inscribed clay tablets are said to have been taken from different rooms of the temple. Unfortunately they were not baked as those from Qoyunjuk; and though Rassam did his best to save their contents by baking them immediately after their discovery, thousands of them, sticking together or heaped upon one another, crumbled to pieces before they could be removed. For the greater part, these documents are of a business character, referring to the administration of the temple and its property, to the daily sacrifices of Shamash and other gods, to the weaving of their garments, the manufacture of their jewelry and vessels, the building and repairing of their houses, and to the execution of various orders given in connection with the worship of their images and the maintenance of their priesthood. At the same time they make us acquainted with the duties and daily occupations of the different classes of temple officers and their large body of servants, with the ordinary tithes paid by the faithful, and with many other revenues accruing to the sanctuary from all kinds of gifts, from the lease of real estate, slaves, and animals, and from the sale of products from fields and stables. As tithes were frequently paid in kind, it became necessary to establish regular dépôts along the principal canals, where scribes stored and registered everything that came in. Among the goods thus received we notice vegetables, meat, and other perishable objects which the temple alone could not consume, and which, therefore, had to be sold or exchanged before they decayed or decreased in value. No wonder that apart from its distinct religious sphere the great temple of Shamash at Sippara in many respects resembled one of the great business firms of Babel or Nippur.

Apparently the bulk of the temple library proper lies still buried in the ruins of Abû Habba. Yet among the tablets excavated by Rassam there are many of a strictly literary character, such as sign-lists and grammatical exercises, astronomical and mathematical texts, letters, hymns, mythological fragments, and a new bilingual version of the Story of the Creation, which originally formed part of an incantation. The large monuments and artistic votive offerings deposited by famous monarchs and other prominent worshippers in the temple of Shamash had mostly perished or been carried away. But numerous fragments of vases and statues engraved with the names of Manishtusu and Urumush (Alusharshid), two ancient kings of Kîsh, the fine mace-head of Sargon I., the curious monument of Tukulti-Mer, king of Khana, the lion-head of Sennacherib, several well-preserved "boundary stones," including the so-called charter of Nebuchadrezzar I. (about 1130 B. C.), and more than thirty terra-cotta cylinders bearing Sumerian or Semitic records of the building operations of Hammurabi, Nebuchadrezzar II., Nabonidos, and other Babylonian and Assyrian rulers testify sufficiently to the high antiquity of the sanctuary and to the great renown in which it was held by natives and foreigners alike from the range of the Taurus to the shores of the Persian Gulf. The proposed and much repeated identification of Sippara with the Biblical Sepharvaim is, however, a philological and geographical[1] impossibility.

In accordance with his usual custom, followed in Assyria and elsewhere, Rassam cut trial trenches into other conspicuous mounds whenever he was in Babylonia. But from the nature of the ruins and the superficial character of his work, it was to be expected that they would be barren of results unless a fortunate accident should come to his assistance. The principal sites selected by him for such tentative operations were the group of mounds called Dilhîm,[2] about ten miles to the south of Hilla, where he discovered a few inscribed clay tablets; the low but extensive ruins of El-Qrênî,[3]

[1] According to 2 Kings 18 : 34; 19 : 13 (comp. Is. 36 : 19; 37 : 13) Sepharvaim must have been situated not in Babylonia, but in Syria. Comp. Halévy in *Journal Asiatique*, 1889, pp. 18, *seqq.*; *Zeitschrift für Assyriologie*, vol. ii, pp. 401, *seq.*

[2] Called by Rassam Daillum or Tell-Daillam; comp. his "Asshur and the Land of Nimrod," New York, 1897, pp. 265 and 347.

[3] Rassam, *l. c.*, pp. 347, *seq.*, where he spells the name *Algarainee* according to its modern pronunciation.

about four miles to the north of Bâbil, where nothing but bricks indicated their Babylonian origin; the numerous *tells* in the neighborhood of Mahmûdîye mentioned above, especially Dêr,[1] which yielded only the common bricks of Nebuchadrezzar; and above all, the enormous ruins of Tell Ibrâhîm, about fifteen miles to the northeast of Hilla, with the nest of mounds situated to the southeast of it.[2] Under extraordinary deprivations caused by the absence of water and frequent sandstorms, several of his best gangs of workmen remained a month in the desert around Tell Ibrâhîm. But though they showed a rare energy and labored with all their might, opening no less than twenty different tunnels and trenches and penetrating deep into the mass of rubbish, nothing but stray bricks of Nebuchadrezzar, a few cuneiform tablets and terra-cotta bowls covered with Hebrew inscriptions had been brought to light when they finally quitted this inhospitable region.

We cannot close this sketch of Rassam's archæological work in Babylonia without referring briefly to his hasty visit to the southern districts of 'Irâq, which lasted from February 24 to March 13, 1879.[3] The news of De Sarzec's secret proceedings at Tellô had spread rapidly among the Arabs, and naturally reached the ear of Rassam immediately after his arrival at Baghdad, in the beginning of February, 1879. A faithful and jealous guardian of British interests, as he proved to be during his long career in the East, he decided at once to examine those remarkable ruins in person with a view of occupying them, if possible, for his own government somewhat in the same manner as he previously had obtained the palace of Ashurbânapal in the northern part of Qoyunjuk. His task seemed to be facilitated by the circumstance that De Sarzec had made his first

[1] Rassam, *l. c.*, pp. 398, *seqq.*

[2] Rassam, *l. c.*, pp. 396, *seq.*, 409, *seqq.*

[3] Rassam, *l. c.*, pp. 272, *seqq.*

tentative excavations at Tellô "without any firmân from the Porte." No sooner had he therefore established his workmen, under native overseers, upon the ruins of Babylon and Borsippa, than he hurried back to Baghdad, descended the Tigris on a Turkish steamer as far as Kûd(t) el-'Amâra, and sailed through the Shatt el-Haï until he reached the object of his journey. But upon landing he found, to his consternation, that Tellô was not within the sphere of British influence. Shortly before Sir Henry Layard had obtained his far-reaching permit for simultaneous excavations in the vilayets of Baghdad, Aleppo, and Wan, the Ottoman government had reduced the large province of Baghdad in size by creating a new and independent pashalic with Basra as capital,[1] and including all the Turkish territory to the east and south of the Shatt el-Haï.[2] For the time being Rassam had, therefore, no legal right to make any excavations at Tellô. But having gone to the expense of a voyage thither, he did not intend to turn away from the ruins without having convinced himself whether "it would be worth while to ask the British ambassador at Constantinople to use his influence with the Porte, so that his license might be extended to that province." Accordingly he engaged a

[1] According to information obtained through the kindness of Dr. H. Gies, first dragoman of the German embassy in Constantinople, the military administration of the *kölemen* was brought to an end in 'Irâq in 1243 (*Rûmi* = 1827 A. D.). Henceforth Basra was ruled by the Ottoman government directly through *mutesarrifs*, subject to the orders of the wâli of Baghdad, or through independent wâlis. The first wâli of Basra, appointed in 1875, was Nâsir Pasha, the famous shaikh of the Muntefik(j). Comp. p. 218, above. In 1884 the province of Baghdad was again reduced in size by the creation of the vilayet of Mosul. For further details, see *Salname of Basra* of the year 1309 (*Hijra* = 1307 *Rûmi*).

[2] The line of demarcation is at Kûd(t) el-Haï. Only generally speaking the Shatt el-Haï forms the natural boundary between the two vilayets, for certain portions to the west of it, as, *e. g.*, the ruins of Senkere, and other smaller sites as far north as Durrâjî, belong to the southern vilayet of Basra.

guide and some workmen, and walked for a few days every morning the three miles from the embankment of the canal to the site of Tellô. The large statue in dolerite discovered and reburied by the French explorer had been exposed again by the Arabs after De Sarzec's departure in the previous year. It naturally attracted Rassam's attention first. Having cleared it entirely, and taken a squeeze of its inscription for the British Museum, he opened trenches in different parts of the ruins. Antiquities were often found almost directly below the surface. The very first day he came upon the remains of a temple [?] and discovered two inscribed door sockets of Gudea at its entrance. In another place he unearthed a large number of unbaked clay tablets, while still other trenches yielded several inscribed maceheads in red granite, and many of those mushroom-shaped clay objects (*phalli*) with the names of Ur-Bau and Gudea upon them, in which the ruins of Tellô abound. If Rassam had continued his researches one day longer in the highest mound and driven his trenches only two or three feet deeper, he could not have missed those fine statues in dolerite which now adorn the halls of the Louvre. But *kismet* (fate) — to quote an Oriental phrase — was this time decidedly against him. The threatening attitude of the Arabs in the neighborhood, the inclemency of the weather, and his own conscience, which told him that he was "carrying on his work under false pretences," drove him away from the ruins after three days' successful trial. He expected to return later, as soon as he had managed to obtain the necessary permit from the Porte. But De Sarzec was on the alert and quicker of action than Victor Place. While Rassam was meditating and planning in Babylonia, the French representative took decisive steps at Paris and Constantinople which secured for his nation the much-coveted ruins of Tellô, and through them those priceless treasures with which we have occupied ourselves in the previous chapter.

GERMAN EXCAVATIONS AT SURGHUL AND EL-HIBBA, UNDER MORITZ AND KOLDEWEY

Long after English and French pioneers had established and considerably developed the science of Assyriology, German scholars began to remember their obligations towards a discipline the seed of which was sown in the land of Grotefend, and to occupy themselves seriously with those far-reaching researches which later were to find their strongest representation at their own universities. The first Assyrian courses delivered in Germany were given privately [1] at Jena, where Eberhard Schrader, appropriately called the father of German Assyriology, defended its principles and applied its results to the elucidation of the Old Testament Scriptures. His careful and critical examination of all that had been accomplished in the past, and his successful repelling of Alfred von Gutschmid's violent attack upon the very foundations of Assyrian deciphering, were the beginning of a great movement which soon led to the establishment of the Leipzig school of Assyriologists under Friedrich Delitzsch, and to the subsequent consolidation of the whole science by him and his pupils. The old loose and unsatisfactory manner of dealing with philological problems, to a large extent responsible for the discredit in which Assyriological publications were held in Germany, was abandoned, and exact methods and a technical treatment of grammar and lexicography became the order of the day. Theories proclaimed and accepted as facts had to be modified or radically changed, and the interpretation of Assyrian and Sumerian cuneiform inscriptions was placed upon a new basis.

Problems partly or entirely unknown to the older school

[1] According to direct information received from Professor Schrader, of Berlin, by letter, these courses were given in the summer of 1873, when Friedrich Delitzsch attended his lectures on Genesis at the university, while at the same time he was introduced privately by him into the study of Assyrian.

came up for discussion, and representative scholars from other nations began to participate in a thorough ventilation of the interesting subjects. The Sumerian question arose,[1] and with it a multitude of other questions. If one riddle was solved to-day, another more difficult presented itself to-morrow. Our whole conception of the origin and development of Assyrian art and literature, of the beginnings of cuneiform writing, of the historical position and influence of the primitive inhabitants of Babylonia, of the age and character of Semitic civilization in general, and of many important details closely connected therewith seemed to be in need of a thorough revision. The Assyriological camp was soon split into factions, often fighting with bitterness and passion against one another.

The extraordinary results of De Sarzec's epoch-making excavations at Tellô furnished a mass of new material which was eagerly studied at once and essentially helped to extend our horizon. But important as their influence proved to be on the gradual solution of the Sumerian problem, on the clearing of our views on Babylonian art and civilization, and on the many other questions then under consideration, being felt alike in palæography and philology, archæology, history, and ancient geography, their greatest significance lies, perhaps, in the fact that they gave rise to the methodical exploration of the Babylonian ruins and kindled fresh enthusiasm for the organization and despatch of new expeditions. The statues in dolerite and the inscribed bas-reliefs and cylinders from Tellô had clearly shown that the ruins of Southern Babylonia conceal sculptured remains of fundamental value, and, moreover, that the period to which these discoveries lead us is considerably older than that which had been reached by the previous Assyrian ex-

[1] Started in 1874 by Professor J. Halévy of Paris. On the whole subject comp. Weissbach, *Die Sumerische Frage*, Leipzig, 1898, and Halévy, *Le Sumérism et l'histoire Babylonienne*, Paris, 1901.

cavations. Indeed, the marble slabs from the royal palaces of Dûr-Sharrukên, Calah, and Nineveh looked very recent when compared with the much-admired monuments of Lagash. All indications pointed unmistakably to the districts of the lower Euphrates and Tigris as the cradle of the earliest Babylonian civilization.

The first attempt at imitating De Sarzec's example was made in Germany. And though in the end it proved to be unproductive of great tangible results, and barren of those startling discoveries without which an expedition cannot command the general support of the people, it was important, and a sure sign of the growing popularity of cuneiform studies in a land where only ten years previous even university professors kept aloof from the Assyriological science. Through the liberality of one man, L. Simon, who in more than one way became a patron of archæological studies in Germany, the Royal Prussian Museums of Berlin were enabled to carry on brief excavations at two Babylonian ruins during the early part of 1887. These researches were in control of Dr. Bernhard Moritz and Dr. Robert Koldewey, faithfully assisted in the practical execution of their task by Mr. Ludwig Meyer, the third member of their mission. Leaving Berlin in September, 1886, they reached the scene of their activity in the beginning of the following year. The mounds which were selected for operation are called Surghul and El-Hibba, distant from each other a little over six miles, and representing the most extensive ruins in the large triangle formed by the Euphrates, the Tigris, and the Shatt el-Haï. Situated in the general neighborhood of Tellô, and about twenty miles to the northeast of Shatra, Surghul, the more southern of the two sites, rises at its highest point to almost fifty feet above the flat alluvial plain and covers an area of about 192 acres, while the somewhat lower mounds of El-Hibba enclose nearly 1400 acres. The excavations conducted at Surghul lasted from January 4 to

February 26, those at El-Hibba from March 29 to May 11, 1887. But in addition to this principal work in Southern Babylonia, the expedition occupied itself with the purchase of antiquities and the examination of other mounds in 'Irâq el-'Arabî, with a view to determine some of the more promising sites for future exploration.

It soon became evident to the German party that a thorough examination of the enormous ruins was far beyond the time and means at their disposal. Under these circumstances it was decided to confine themselves to ascertaining the general contents of the most conspicuous elevations by means of long trial trenches. When remains of buildings were struck, their walls were followed to discover the ground-plans, while the interior of the chambers was searched for archæological objects. Deep wells constructed of terracotta rings, which abound in both ruins, were, as a rule, exposed on one side in their entire length in order to be photographed before they were opened. The results obtained from the different cuttings in the two sites were on the whole identical. The explorers found a large number of houses irregularly built of unbaked bricks, and intersected by long, narrow streets, which rarely were more than three feet wide. These edifices formed a very respectable settlement at El-Hibba, where the passageways between them extended fully two miles and a half. As to size and arrangement the buildings varied considerably, some containing only a few rooms, others occupying a large space, — in one instance a house covering an area of 72½ feet by nearly 51 feet, and containing 14 chambers and halls. The walls of most of these constructions had crumbled so much that generally their lower parts, often only their foundations, remained, which could be traced without difficulty after an especially heavy dew or an exceptional shower. Characteristic of many of these houses are the wells mentioned above, which, according to Koldewey's erroneous view, doubtless abandoned since, were intended to provide the dead with fresh water. One of the buildings examined had no less than nine such wells, another eight, four of which were in the same room, which was only 25½ feet by about 8 feet.

Wherever the mounds were cut, they seemed to contain nothing but remains of houses, wells, ashes, bones, vases, and other burial remains. Koldewey therefore arrived at the conclusion that both ruins must be regarded as "fire necropoles," dating back to a period "probably older than that of the earliest civilizations;" that the houses were not dwelling-places for the living, but tombs for the dead, and that the whole mass of artificial elevations forms the common resting-place for human bodies more or less consumed by fire.[1]

There were two kinds of burial, "body-graves" and "ash-graves," thus styled by Koldewey in order to indicate the manner in which corpses were treated after their cremation; for the characteristic feature of all these burials was the destruction of the body by fire previous to its final interment, though in later times the complete annihilation of the body by intense heat seems to have given way to a rather superficial burning, which in part degenerated to a mere symbolic act. The process "began with the levelling of the place, remains of previous cremations, if such had occurred, being pushed aside. The body was then wrapped in reed-mats (seldom in bituminous material), laid on the ground, and covered all over with rudely formed bricks, or with a layer of soft clay. The latter was quite thin in the upper parts, but thicker near the ground, so that as little resistance as possible was offered to the heat attacking the body from above, while at the same time the covering retained

[1] Comp. Koldewey, *Die altbabylonischen Gräber in Surghul und El Hibba*, in *Zeitschrift für Assyriologie*, vol. ii, 1887, pp. 403–430. To my knowledge no more complete report on these first German excavations in Babylonia has yet been published.

the solidity necessary to prevent too early a collapse under the weight of the fuel heaped upon it." In order to concentrate the heat, a kind of low oven was sometimes erected, "but, on the whole, it seems as though in the oldest period the complete incineration under an open fire was the rule."

Weapons, utensils, jewelry, seal-cylinders, toys, food, and drink were frequently burned with the body, and similar objects were generally deposited a second time in the tomb itself, where the charred remains found their final resting-place. Which of the two methods of burial referred to above ("body-graves" or "ash-graves") was chosen, depended essentially on the intensity of the cremation. If considerable portions of the body were afterwards found to be untouched or little injured by the fire, the remains were left where they had been exposed to the heat; in other words, the funeral pyre became also the grave of the dead person (so-called "body-grave"). If, on the other hand, the cremation was successful, and the body reduced to ashes or formless fragments, the remains were generally gathered and placed in vases or urns of different sizes and shapes, which, however, were often too small for their intended contents. In many instances the ashes were merely collected in a heap and covered with a kettle-formed clay vessel. Burials of this kind, the so-called "ash-graves," are both the more common and the more ancient at Surghul and El-Hibba. The urns of ordinary persons were deposited anywhere in the gradually increasing mound, while the rich families had special houses erected for them, which were laid out in regular streets. It must be kept in mind, however, that cremation was practically the main part of the burial, the gathering of the ashes being more a non-essential act of piety.

Frequent sandstorms and the heavy rains of the South-Babylonian fall and spring must often have ruined whole sections of these vast cemeteries, and otherwise greatly interfered with the uniform raising of the whole necropolis. From time to time, therefore, it became necessary to construct large walls and buttresses at the edges of the principal elevations in support of the light mass of ashes and dust easily blown away; to level the ground enclosed; to cover it with a thick layer of clay, and to provide the houses of the dead with drains[1] to keep the mound dry and the tombs intact. The rectangular platforms thereby obtained were reached by means of narrow staircases erected at their front sides. Thus while most of these artificial terraces owe their origin to secondary considerations, the large solid brick structure of El-Hibba must be viewed in a somewhat different light, contrary to the theory of Koldewey, who is inclined to regard even this elevation as the mere substructure of an especially important tomb. It represents a circular stage-tower of two stories, resting directly on the natural soil, and in its present ruinous state still twenty-four feet high. The diameter of the lower story, rising 13 feet above the plain, is 410 feet, while that of the second story is only 315 feet. The entire building is constructed with adobes, and the second story, besides, encased with baked bricks laid in bitumen. The upper surfaces of both stories are paved with the same material to protect them against rain. Water was carried off by a canal of baked bricks, which at the same time served as a buttress for the lower story. Remains of a house and many of those uninscribed terra-cotta nails which,

[1] That the "wells" mentioned by Koldewey had this more practical purpose rather than to provide fresh water for the dead, becomes very evident from the fact that they are frequently constructed of jars with broken bottoms joined to each other, that the terra-cotta rings of which they are usually composed, like the top-pieces covering their mouths, are often perforated, and — apart from many other considerations — that in no case the numerous similar wells examined by me at Nuffar descended to the water level. Real wells, intended to hold fresh water, doubtless existed in these two ancient cemeteries, but they are always constructed of baked bricks (arranged in herring-bone fashion in pre-Sargonic times), and have a much larger diameter than any of these terra-cotta pipes described by Koldewey.

in large masses, were found at the base of the stage-tower at Nippur,[1] were observed on the upper platform. With the exception of its circular form, which, however, cannot be regarded as a serious objection to my theory, the solid brick structure of El-Hibba presents all the characteristic features of a *ziggurrat*, with which I regard it as identical,[2] the more so because I have recently found evidence that, like the Egyptian pyramid, the Babylonian stage-tower (or step-pyramid) without doubt was viewed in the light of a sepulchral mound erected in honor of a god,[3] and because it seems impossible to believe that a deeply religious people, as the early inhabitants of Shumer doubtless were, should have cremated and buried their dead without appropriate religious ceremonies, and should have left this vast necropolis without a temple. It is certainly no accident that the only remains of pictorial representations in stone discovered in the course of the German excavations (part of a wing, fragments of a stool, and a pair of clasped hands) were unearthed at the foot of this structure, and near the second large elevation of El-Hibba — the only two places which can be taken into consideration as the probable sites for such a sanctuary.

[1] Evidently they had fallen from a building once crowning its summit.

[2] I am also inclined to see a last reminiscence of the Babylonian *ziggurrat* in the *meftûl*, the characteristic watch-tower and defensive bulwark of the present Ma'dân tribes of Central Babylonia. Notwithstanding the etymology of the Arabic word, a *meftûl* is seldom round (against Sachau, *Am Euphrat und Tigris*, Leipzig, 1900, p. 43, with picture on p. 45), but like the *ziggurrat*, generally rectangular, and from forty to eighty feet high. Almost without exception these towers are built of clay laid up en masse. Throughout my wanderings in Babylonia I met with only one fine (rectangular) specimen constructed entirely of kiln-burnt bricks. It is situated on a branch of the Shatt el-Kâr, a few miles to the west from the ruins of Abû Hatab and Fâra, which I recently recommended for excavations to the German Orient Society.

[3] Comp. my later remarks in connection with the results of the excavations at Nuffar, Fourth Campaign, Temple Mound, section 3.

There can be no doubt that most of these tombs belong to the true Babylonian age. The entire absence of the slipper-shaped coffin, which forms one of the most characteristic features of the Parthian and Sassanian periods, enables us to speak on this point more positively. On the other hand, the thin terra-cotta cups, in form very similar to a female breast, which Koldewey mentions,[1] betray late foreign influence. They cannot be older than about 300 B. C., and are probably somewhat younger, as they occur exclusively in the upper strata of Nuffar. It is more difficult to determine the time when these cemeteries came first into use. However, the scattered fragments of statues and stone vessels of the same type and material as those discovered at Tellô and Nuffar (near the platform of Sargon and Narâm-Sin), the inscribed bricks and cones referred to by various explorers, the characteristic situation of the two mounds in the neighborhood of the first-named ruin, the peculiar form and small height of the *ziggurrat*, the pre-Sargonic existence of which was recently proved by the present writer,[2] certain forms of clay vessels which are regularly found only in the lowest strata of Nuffar, and various other reasons [3] derived also from the study of the inscriptions and bas-reliefs of Tellô go far to show that the pyres of Surghul and El-Hibba already blazed when the Sumerian race was still in the possession of the country.

[1] Koldewey, *l. c.*, p. 418.

[2] Comp. p. 232, above, note 2.

[3] It is to be regretted that Koldewey did not give a description of the forms and sizes of the various bricks, which, as I have pointed out in my "Old Babylonian Inscriptions chiefly from Nippur," part ii, p. 45, are a very important factor in determining pre-Sargonic structures. The rudely formed bricks mentioned by him (comp. p. 284 above) point to the earliest kind of bricks known from Nuffar and Tellô.

AMERICAN EXCAVATIONS AT NUFFAR UNDER THE AUSPICES OF THE UNIVERSITY OF PENNSYLVANIA.

The importance of the study of Semitic languages and literature was early recognized in the United States. Hebrew, as the language of the Old Testament, stood naturally in the centre of general interest, as everywhere in Europe; and the numerous theological seminaries of the country and those colleges which maintained close vital relations with them were its first and principal nurseries. But in the course of time a gradual though very visible change took place with regard to the position of the Semitic languages in the curriculum of all the prominent American colleges. The German idea of a university gained ground in the new world, finding its enthusiastic advocates among the hundreds and thousands of students who had come into personal contact with the great scientific leaders in Europe, and who for a while had felt the powerful spell of the new life which emanated from the class rooms and seminaries of the German universities. Post-graduate departments were organized, independent chairs of Semitic languages were established, and even archæological museums were founded and maintained by private contributions. Salaries in some cases could not be given to the pioneers in this new movement. They stood up for a cause in which they themselves fully believed, but the value of which had to be demonstrated before endowments could be expected from the liberal-minded public. They represented the coming generation, which scarcely now realizes the difficulties and obstacles that had to be overcome by a few self-sacrificing men of science, before the present era was successfully inaugurated.

The study of the cuneiform languages, especially of Assyrian, rapidly became popular at the American universities. The romantic story of the discovery and excavation of Nineveh so graphically told by Layard, and the immediate bearing of his magnificent results upon the interpretation of the Old Testament and upon the history of art and human civilization in general, appealed at once to the religious sentiment and to the general intelligence of the people. The American Oriental Society and the Society of Biblical Literature and Exegesis became the first scientific exponents of the growing interest in the lands of Ashurbânapal and Nebuchadrezzar. The spirit of Edward Robinson, who more than sixty years before had conducted his fundamental researches of the physical, historical, and topographical geography of Syria and Palestine, was awakened anew, and the question of participating in the methodical exploration of the Babylonian ruins, to which De Sarzec's extraordinary achievements at Tellô had forcibly directed the public attention, began seriously to occupy the minds of American scholars. "England and France have done a noble work in Assyria and Babylonia. It is time for America to do her part. Let us send out an American expedition," — was the key-note struck at a meeting of the Oriental Society which was held at New Haven in the spring of 1884. This suggestion was taken up at once, and a committee was constituted to raise the necessary funds for a preliminary expedition of exploration, with Dr. W. H. Ward of "The Independent" as director. The plan was sooner realized than could have been anticipated. A single individual, Miss Catherine Lorillard Wolfe of New York, gave the $5000 required for this purpose, the Archæological Institute of America took control of the undertaking, and on September 6 of the same year Dr. Ward was on his way to the East. His party consisted of Dr. J. R. S. Sterrett, now professor of Greek in Amherst College, Mr. J. H. Haynes, then an instructor in Robert College, Constantinople, who had served as photographer on the Assos expedition, and Daniel Z. Noorian, an intelligent Armenian, as interpreter.

Before the four men could enter upon their proper task,

Dr. Sterrett fell seriously ill on the way, so that he was obliged to remain at Baghdad. The others left the city of Hârûn ar-Rashîd on January 12, and devoted nearly eight weeks to the exploration of the Babylonian ruins to the south of it. After a hurried visit to Abû Habba, Babylon, and El-Birs, they struck for the interior, and on the whole followed in the wake of Frazer and Loftus. Though, like the former, at times suffering severely from lack of proper food and water and from exposure to cold and rain, they executed their commission of a general survey of the country in a satisfactory manner, as far as this was possible within the brief period which they had set for themselves. They examined most of the principal sites of 'Irâq el-'Arabî down to El-Hibba and Surghul, Tellô, and Muqayyar, recorded numerous angular bearings from the various mounds, took photographs and impressions of antiquities whenever an opportunity presented itself,[1] and worked diligently to gather all such information as might prove useful in connection with future American excavations in the plains of Shumer and Akkad. Upon his return, in June, 1885, Dr. Ward submitted a concise "Report on the Wolfe Expedition to Babylonia" to the Institute which had sent him, and continued in many other ways to promote the archæological interests of his country.[2] But it seemed as if the

[1] We thus owe our only knowledge of one of the earliest Babylonian inscriptions to a photograph taken by Dr. Ward at Samâwa on February 17, 1885, and soon afterwards published by him in the "Proceedings of the American Oriental Society," October, 1885. This legend was engraved upon a stone, in the possession of Dr. A. Blau, a German, who had formerly served as a surgeon in the Turkish army, but was then engaged in trade at Samâwa. All traces of the important monument have since been lost.

[2] His "Report" appeared in the "Papers of the Archæological Institute of America," Boston, 1886. Comp. "The Wolfe Expedition," by the same author, in "Journal of the Society of Biblical Literature and Exegesis," June to December, 1885, pp. 56–60, and his article "On Recent Explo-

public at large was not yet prepared to contribute money for excavations in an unsafe foreign country, however closely connected with the Bible. Moreover, with the despatch of this preliminary expedition, the original committee of the Oriental Society very evidently regarded the work for which it was called together as finished, and accordingly passed out of existence.

Among the Semitic scholars who in 1884 had met at New Haven to discuss the feasibility of independent American explorations in different sections of Western Asia, Rev. Dr. John P. Peters, Professor of Hebrew in the Episcopal Divinity School of Philadelphia, had been especially active in promoting that first expedition and in raising the funds required for it. He and others had quietly cherished the hope that the lady who so generously defrayed all the expenses of Dr. Ward's exploring tour would also take a leading part in future archæological enterprises of the country. But for some reason or other their well-founded expectations were doomed to disappointment.[1] If, therefore, the former comprehensive scheme of starting American excavations in one or more of the recommended Babylonian sites was ever to be realized, it became necessary above all things to arouse greater interest among the religious and educated classes of the people by public lectures on Semitic and archæological topics, and to make especial efforts to win the confidence and coöperation of public-spirited men of influence and wealth, on whose moral and financial support the

rations in Babylon" in "Johns Hopkins University Circulars," No. 49, May, 1886. A large portion of Dr. Ward's abridged diary was published by Dr. Peters in "Nippur," vol. I, appendix F, pp. 318–375.

[1] This circumstance is mentioned especially, because as late as 1900 Mr. Heuzey, director of the Oriental Department of the Louvre and editor of the monuments from Tellô, assigns the origin of the Nuffar expedition of the University of Pennsylvania to a legacy left by Miss Wolfe to that institution for excavations in Babylonia. Comp. De Sarzec and Heuzey, *Une Ville Royale Chaldéenne*, Paris, 1900, pp. 31 *seq.*

practicability of the intended undertaking chiefly depended; for direct assistance from the United States government was entirely out of the question. Such courses were given in the University of Pennsylvania in the winter of 1886–1887.

But where could a sufficient number of enlightened men and women be found who had the desire and courage to engage in such a costly and somewhat adventurous enterprise as a Babylonian expedition at first naturally must be, as long as there were more urgent appeals from churches and schools, universities and museums, hospitals and other charitable institutions, which needed the constant support of their patrons, and while there were plenty of scientific enterprises and experiments of a more general interest and of more practical value with regard to their ultimate outcome constantly carried on immediately before the eyes of the public at home? Indeed, the prospect for excavations in the remote and lawless districts of the Euphrates and the Tigris looked anything but bright and encouraging.. It was finally Dr. Peters' patient work and energy which secured the necessary funds for the first ambitious expedition to Babylonia through liberal friends of the University of Pennsylvania, where a short while before (1886) he had been appointed Professor of Hebrew, while the present writer was called to the chair of Assyrian.

The university was then ably managed by the late provost, Dr. William Pepper, a man of rare talents, exceptional working power, and great personal magnetism, under whom it entered upon that new policy of rapid expansion and scientific consolidation which under his no less energetic and self-sacrificing successor, Dr. C. C. Harrison, brought it soon to the front of the great American institutions of learning. The remarkable external growth of which it could boast, and the spirit of progress fostered in its lecture halls were, to a certain degree, indicative also of the high appreciation of scholarship and original investigation on the part of the educated classes of the city in which it is situated. It will therefore always remain a credit to Philadelphia that within its confines a small but representative group of gentlemen was ready to listen to Dr. Peters' propositions, and enthusiastically responded to a call from Mr. E. W. Clark, a prominent banker and the first active supporter of the new scheme, to start a movement in exploring ancient sites under the auspices of the University of Pennsylvania which is almost without a parallel in the history of archæological research. The immediate fruit of this unique demonstration of private citizens was the equipment and maintenance of a great Babylonian expedition, which has continued to the present day at a cost of more than $100,000, and which was soon followed by the organization or subvention of similar enterprises in Egypt, Asia Minor, North and Central America, Italy and Greece. It has well been stated that no city in the United States has shown an interest in archæology at all comparable with that displayed by Philadelphia within the last fifteen years.

The history and results of this Babylonian expedition of the University of Pennsylvania will be set forth in the following pages. Its work, which centred in the methodical exploration of one of the earliest Babylonian cities, the ruins of Nuffar, the Biblical Calneh (Gen. 10 : 10), was no continuous one. Certain intervals were required for the general welfare and temporary rest of its members, for replenishing the exhausted stores of the camp, and, above all, for preparing, studying, and, in a general way, digesting the enormous mass of excavated material, in order to secure by preliminary reports the necessary means for an early resumption of the labors in the field. For as to the wealth of its scientific results, this Philadelphia expedition takes equal rank with the best sent out from England and France, while it eclipses them all with regard to the number and character of the inscribed tablets recovered. Four distinct campaigns were conducted before those priceless treasures of literature and art which are now deposited in the two great museums on the Bosphorus and the Schuylkill could be extracted from their ancient hiding places.

Each had its own problem and history, its special difficulties and disappointments, but also its characteristic and conspicuous results. The work of *the first expedition* (*1888–89*) was on the whole tentative, and gave us a clear conception of the grandeur of the task to be accomplished. It included an accurate survey of the whole ruins, the beginning of systematic excavations at the temple of Bêl, the discovery of a Parthian palace, and the unearthing of more than two thousand cuneiform inscriptions representing the principal periods of Babylonian history, and including numerous tablets of the ancient temple library. *The second* (*1889–90*) continued in the line of research mapped out by the first, explored the upper strata of the temple, and by means of a few deep trial trenches produced evidence that a considerable number of very ancient monuments still existed in the lower parts of the sacred enclosure. It resumed the excavation of the Parthian palace, discovered important Cassite archives, and acquired about eight thousand tablets of the second and third pre-Christian millenniums. *The third* (*1893–96*) also directed its chief attention to the temple mound, but at the same time made a successful search for inscribed monuments in other sections of the ruins, gathering no less than twenty one thousand cuneiform inscriptions largely fragmentary. It removed the later additions to the stage-tower; revealed the existence of several platforms and other important architectural remains in the centre of the large mound, thereby enabling us to fix the age of its different strata with great accuracy; it excavated three sections of the temple court down to the water level, and discovered the first well-preserved brick arch of pre-Sargonic times (about 4000 B. C.), with numerous other antiquities, including the large torso of an inscribed statue in dolerite of the period of Gudea, and over five hundred vase fragments of the earliest rulers of the country. The *fourth expedition* (*1898–1900*) was the most successful of all. It explored the Parthian palace completely, and examined more than one thousand burials in various parts of the ruins. It proved that, contrary to former assertions, the upper strata of the temple complex did not belong to the Babylonian period proper, but represented a huge Parthian fortress lying on the top of it. It definitely located the famous temple library of Nippur, from which thousands of tablets had been previously obtained, and in addition to many other inscribed objects, like the votive table of Narâm-Sin, a large dolerite vase of Gudea, etc., it excavated about twenty-three thousand tablets and fragments, mostly of a literary character. Above all it endeavored to determine the extent of the pre-Sargonic settlement, discovered a very large ancient wall below the level of the desert in the southwestern half of the ruins, exposed nearly the whole eastern city wall, ascertaining the different periods of its construction and uncovering the earliest remains of its principal gate deeply hidden in the soil of the desert. It traced the ancient southeast wall of the inner temple enclosure, found its original chief entrance in a tolerably good state of preservation, ascertained the precise character of Bêl's famous sanctuary, and demonstrated by indisputable facts that the *ziggurrat*, the characteristic part of every prominent Babylonian temple, does not go back to Ur-Gur of Ur, about 2700 B. C., but was a creation of the earliest Sumerian population.

It is evident from a mere glance at this summary of the total results obtained that they cannot be fully comprehended if treated exclusively under the head of each single campaign. On the other hand, it cannot be denied that a certain feeling of justice towards the various members of the expedition, who worked under different conditions and served at different times, render a separate treatment of the origin and history of every campaign almost imperative. We therefore propose first to relate the history and progress of the four campaigns in their natural order, and afterwards to sketch their principal results — due as much to the extraordinary efforts of the subscribers and the careful watchfulness and directions of the committee at home as to the faithful services and self-denying spirit of those in the field — in their mutual relation to each other, and chiefly from a topographical point of view.

A. ORIGIN AND HISTORY OF THE EXPEDITION.

First Campaign, 1888–89. The meeting at which Dr. Peters submitted his plans to the public was held at the house of Provost Pepper on November 30, 1887. About thirty persons were present, including Dr. Ward, the previous leader of the Wolfe Expedition, and Professor Hilprecht, as the official representative of Assyriology in the University of Pennsylvania. Both had been invited by the chairman to express their respective views with regard to the contemplated undertaking. In the course of the discussion it became more and more apparent that the enthusiastic originator of the new scheme and the present writer differed essentially from each other on fundamental questions. On the basis of Dr. Ward's recommendation, the former declared in favor of a large promising site, like Anbâr, Nuffar, El Birs, etc., as most suitable for the Philadelphia excavations. He proposed that the staff of the expedition should consist of four persons, a director, a well-known Assyriologist, formerly connected with the British Museum, and the photographer and the interpreter of the Wolfe Expedition; and he estimated the total expense for a campaign of three consecutive years, as previously stated by him, at $15,000. The present writer, on the other side, pointed out that while he fully agreed with Dr. Peters as to the importance of either of the proposed mounds[1] for archæological research, especially of Nuffar, so frequently and prominently mentioned in the earliest cuneiform inscriptions, he nevertheless felt it his duty to affirm that none of these extensive mounds could be excavated in the least adequately within the period stated, and that, moreover, according to his own calculations, even a small expedition of only four members and a corresponding number of servants and workmen would necessarily cost more in the first year than the whole sum required for three years.[2] He furthermore called attention to the fact that the national honor and the scientific character of this first great American enterprise in Babylonia would seem to require the addition of an American Assyriologist and architect, and, if possible, even of a surveyor and a naturalist, to the proposed staff of the

[1] Notwithstanding all that has been said against Anbâr (Persian, "magazine, granary") as a Babylonian site, I still hold with Dr. Ward, on the ground of my own personal examination of the immense ruins and of the topography of that whole neighborhood, that long before the foundation of Pêrôz Shâpûr a Babylonian city of considerable importance must have existed there. Traces of it would doubtless be revealed in the lower strata of its principal mounds. The mere facts that here the Euphrates entered Babylonia proper, that here the first great canal — on the protection of which the fertility and prosperity of an important section of the country depended — branches off, and that here a military station is required to complete the northern fortification line of the empire, — indicated by Tell Mohammed between the Tigris and the Diyâlâ (covering the remains of a palace of Hammurabi, comp. p. 158, above), and 'Aqarqûf between the Tigris and the Euphrates (the ancient Dûr-Kurigalzu, comp. pp. 38, *seq.*, above), — forces us to look for the ruins of a Babylonian city on the site of Anbâr, which represents the most important point on the whole northern boundary.

[2] At Dr. Pepper's request, I handed my own views to him in writing as to the composition, task, expenses, etc., of a Babylonian expedition on the morning following this meeting. This paper was returned to the writer shortly before Dr. Pepper's untimely death. The probable expenses of such an expedition with a staff of five or six persons was estimated for the first year at $19,200.

expedition. If, however, in view of a very natural desire on the part of the director and his financial supporters, the principal stress was to be laid on the rapid acquisition of important museum objects and inscribed tablets rather than on the methodical and complete examination of an entire large ruin, it would be by far wiser to select from among the different sites visited by Dr. Ward one which was somewhat smaller in size and considerably less superimposed with the remains and rubbish of the post-Babylonian period than any of the ruins submitted for consideration.[1] The results showed only too plainly that the view maintained by the present writer was correct, and that his objections, raised for the sole purpose of preventing unpleasant complications and later disappointments with regard to "the white elephant," as the expedition was soon to be styled, were based upon a careful discrimination between uncertain hopes and sober facts.

The same evening "The Babylonian Exploration Fund" was called into existence, about half of the sum requested ($15,000) subscribed, and an expedition with Dr. Peters as director recommended. On March 17, 1888, the organization of the new corporation was completed by the election of Provost Pepper as president, Mr. E. W. Clark as treasurer, and Professor Hilprecht as secretary.[2] Dr.

[1] I had in mind a ruin of the type of Fâra (recently recommended by me to the German Orient Society for similar consideration, comp. *Mittheilungen*, no. 10, p. 2), where the pre-Sargonic stratum reaches to the very surface of the mound.

[2] The whole Executive Committee consisted of fifteen members, including the three officers mentioned and the director of the expedition. The other members were Messrs. C. H. Clark (chairman of the Publication Committee), W. W. Frazier, C. C. Harrison (the present provost), Joseph D. Potts (†), Maxwell Sommerville, H. Clay Trumbull, Talcott Williams, Richard Wood, Stuart Wood, of Philadelphia; Professor Langley, of the Smithsonian Institute, Washington; and Professor Marquand, of Princeton University.

Peters was confirmed as director, but the general plan previously outlined by him was somewhat modified in accordance with the writer's suggestions. Upon the director's recommendation, Dr. Robert Francis Harper, then instructor in Yale University, was appointed Assyriologist,[1] Mr. Perez Hastings Field, of New York, architect and surveyor, Mr. Haynes photographer and business manager, and Mr. Noorian interpreter and director of the workmen, while Mr. J. D. Prince, just graduating from Columbia College and offering to accompany the expedition at his own expense, was attached as the director's secretary. But having fallen seriously ill on the way down the Euphrates valley, he left the expedition at Baghdad, and returned to America by way of India and China.

On April 4, I received an urgent note from Provost Pepper requesting me to see him at once and stating that it was his especial desire that I should serve on this expedi-

[1] Peters, *l. c.*, p. 9, adds: "At the time it was understood that Professor Hilprecht's health was too delicate to permit him to serve in the field. Later the physicians decided that he could go." Where and how this "it was understood" originated, I do not know. There is an apparent misunderstanding on the part of Dr. Peters concerning the whole matter which I do not care to discuss within the pages of this book. Yet nevertheless I desire to state briefly as a matter of fact, 1. That I never had been asked to go to Babylonia before April 4, 1888. 2. That I never consulted any physician with regard to my accompanying that first Babylonian expedition. 3. That consequently I never received medical advice or "decision" from any physician in reply to such a question. Dr. Peters's two volumes ("Nippur," New York, 1897) unfortunately contain many other erroneous statements (comp. Ward's review in "The Independent," July 29, 1897, p. 18, and Harper's in "The Biblical World," October, 1897). In order not to appear through my silence to approve of them in this first coherent sketch of the history of the whole expedition, I am unfortunately frequently obliged to take notice of them. Personal attacks, however, have been ignored entirely; other misstatements, as a rule, have been changed quietly; only fundamental differences with regard to important technical and scientific questions have been stated expressly in the interest of the cause itself.

tion as the University of Pennsylvania's Assyriologist, all the necessary expenses to be paid by himself and Rev. Dr. H. Clay Trumbull, editor of "The Sunday School Times." I consented to go without a salary, as Harper and Field had done before. In the course of the summer the members of the expedition left at intervals for the East, finally meeting at Aleppo on December 10. Peters and Prince had spent three months in Constantinople to obtain a firmân for successive excavations at El-Birs and Nuffar; Harper, Field, and Haynes had visited the Hittite districts of Senjirli, Mar'ash and Jerâbîs (Carchemish);[1] while the present writer had worked on the cuneiform inscriptions of the Nahr el-Kelb and Wâdi Berîsa,[2] at the same time searching the whole Lebanon region for new material. After an uneventful trip down "the great river"[3] and a fortnight's stay at Baghdad, largely devoted to the examination and purchase of antiquities,[4] the party proceeded by way of

[1] Comp. Harper in "The Old and New Testament Student," vol. viii (1889), pp. 183, *seq.* ("A Visit to Zinjirli") and vol. ix (1889), pp. 308, *seq.* ("A Visit to Carchemish").

[2] Comp. Hilprecht in "The Sunday School Times," vol. xxxi. (1889), p. 163 ("The Mouth of the Nahr el-Kelb"), pp. 547, *seq.* ("The Inscriptions of Nebuchadrezzar in Wadi Brissa"), and vol. xxxii (1890), pp. 147, *seq.* ("The Shaykh of Zeta"); also *Die Inschriften Nebukadnezar's im Wadi Brissa*, in Luthardt's *Zeitschrift für kirchliche Wissenschaft und kirchliches Leben*, vol. ix (1889), pp. 491, *seqq.*

[3] Comp. Harper in "The Old and New Testament Student," vol. x (1890), pp. 55, *seqq.*, 118, *seq.*, 367, *seq.* ("Down the Euphrates Valley," i–iii); and *l. c.*, vol. xiv (1892), pp. 160, *seqq.*, 213, *seqq.*, and vol. xv (1892), pp. 12, *seqq.* ("The Expedition of the Babylonian Exploration Fund," A–C).

[4] In the course of the first expedition there were purchased through different members of the staff five distinct collections of Babylonian antiquities, containing about 1800 specimens (tablets, seals, jewelry), namely, Colls. Kh(abaza)[1], Kh[2], Sh(emtob), Mrs. H. V. H(ilprecht), D. J. P(rince), besides a collection of Cappadocian tablets and other antiquities, and a set of plaster casts of Assyrian and Babylonian monuments from the British Museum. Apart

Hilla to Nuffar, the scene of its future activity. For after a visit to the high-towering mound of El-Birs and the adjoining site of Tell Ibrâhîm el-Khalîl, which together constitute the remains of ancient Borsippa, it had been decided unanimously not to commence operations here, but to move further on to the second place granted by the firmân, which practically represented an entirely fresh site only superficially scratched before by Layard.[1]

The next military station from Nuffar is Dîwânîye, situated on both sides of the Euphrates and (according to the season and the extent of the inundations) about six to nine hours to the southwest of it. At the time of our first campaign it was a miserable and fast decreasing town consisting chiefly of mud houses, and governed by a *qâimmaqâm*, under whose immediate jurisdiction we were to be. But since the water supply of the lower Euphrates has been regulated through the construction of the Hindîye dam above Babylon, it has rapidly changed its aspect and become a neat and flourishing town. At the expense of Hilla it has been raised to the seat of a *mutesarrif* and received a considerable increase of soldiers, including even artillery, in order to check the predatory incursions of the roaming Bedouins of the desert, and to control the refractory 'Afej tribes around Nuffar, which until recently acknowledged only a nominal allegiance to the Ottoman government,

from Mrs. Hilprecht's and Mr. Prince's contributions, which did not pass through the treasurer's hands, Messrs. C. H. and E. W. Clark, W. W. Frazier, C. C. Harrison, Wm. Pepper, and Stuart Wood spent $6500 extra for the purchase of these collections, including a number of Palmyrene busts obtained by Dr. Peters in the following year, and the valuable plaster reproductions of the ruins of Nuffar, which were afterwards prepared under Field's supervision in Paris. As to the Khabaza and Shemtob collections, comp. Harper in *Hebraica*, vol. v, pp. 74, *seqq.*; vol. vi, pp. 225, *seq.* (vol. viii, pp. 103, *seq.*).

[1] Comp. pp. 159, *seqq.*, above.

The Shammar Bedouins appearing at the Mounds of Nuffar

regarding themselves as perfectly safe in the midst of their swamps and mud castles, the so-called *meftûls*.[1] Peters, Harper, and Bedry Bey, our Turkish commissioner, took this circuitous route by way of Dîwânîye, to pay their respects to the local governor there and to make the necessary arrangements for the prompt despatch and receipt of our mail.

The rest of us, accompanied by thirty-two trained workmen from Jumjuma and another village near El-Birs, a crowd of women and children attached to them, and a large number of animals carrying our whole outfit, provisions, and the implements for excavations, struck directly for Nuffar. The frequent rumors which we had heard at Baghdad and Hilla concerning the unsettled and unsafe condition of this section of the country, inhabited as it was said to be by the most unruly and turbulent tribes of the whole vilayet, were in an entire accord with Layard's reports,[2] and only too soon to be confirmed by our own experience. The 'Afej and the powerful Shammar, who sometimes descend as far down as the Shatt el-Haï, were fighting for the pasture lands, driving each other's camels and sheep away, and two of the principal subdivisions of the 'Afej had a blood-feud with each other. On the second day of our march, while temporarily separated from our caravan, we were suddenly surprised by a *ghazu* (razzia) and with difficulty escaped the hands of the marauding Arabs. The nearer we came to the goal of our journey, the more disturbed was the population. Finally on the third morning Bint el Amîr, majestically towering above the wide stretched mounds of Nuffar, rose clear on the horizon. More than 2000 years ago the huge terraces and walls of the most renowned Baby-

[1] Comp. p. 287, note 2, above, and the illust. facing p. 349, below.

[2] Comp. Layard, "Nineveh and Babylon," London, 1853, p. 565: "The most wild and ignorant Arabs that can be found in this part of Asia."

lonian sanctuary had crumbled to a formless mass. But even in their utter desolation they still seemed to testify to the lofty aspirations of a bygone race, and to reëcho the ancient hymn[1] once chanted in their shadow: —

> "O great mountain of Bêl, Imǵarsag,
> Whose summit rivals the heavens,
> Whose foundations are laid in the bright abysmal sea,
> Resting in the land as a mighty steer,
> Whose horns are gleaming like the radiant sun,
> As the stars of heaven are filled with lustre."

Even at a distance I began to realize that not twenty, not fifty years would suffice to excavate this important site thoroughly. What would our committee at home have said at the sight of this enormous ruin, resembling more a picturesque mountain range than the last impressive remains of human constructions! But there was not much time for these and similar reflections; our attention was fully absorbed by the exciting scenes around us. The progress of the motley crowd along the edge of the cheerless swamps was slow enough. The marshy ground which we had to traverse was cut up by numerous old canals, and offered endless difficulties to the advance of our stumbling beasts. Besides, the whole neighborhood was inflamed by war. Gesticulating groups of armed men watched our approach with fear and suspicion. Whenever we passed a village, the signal of alarm was given. A piece of black cloth fluttered in an instant from the *meftûl*, dogs began to bark savagely, shepherds ran their flocks into shelter, and the cries of terrified women and children sounded shrill over the flat and treeless plain. Greeted by the wild dance and the rhythmical yells of some fifty ʻAfej warriors, who had followed our movements from a peak of the weather-torn ruins, we took possession of the inheritance of Bêl.

Immediately after our arrival we began to pitch our tents

[1] Comp. iv *R.*, 27, no. 2, 15–24.

on the highest point of the southwestern half of the ruins, where we could enjoy an unlimited view over the swamps and the desert, and which at the same time seemed best protected against malaria and possible attacks from the

Plan of the Ruins of Nuffar

I. Ziggurrat and Temple of Bêl, buried under a huge Parthian fortress. II. North-east city wall. III. Great north-east (pre-Sargonic) city gate. IV. Temple library, covered by extensive ruins of a later period. V. Dry bed of an ancient canal (Shatt en-Nîl). VI. Pre-Sargonic wall, buried under sixty feet of rubbish with archives of later periods. VII. Small Parthian palace, resting on Cassite archives. VIII. Business house of Murashû Sons, with more ancient ruins below.

Arabs. With the aid of Berdi, shaikh of the Warish (a subdivision of the Hamza), who was ready to assist us, a number of native huts, so-called *sarîfas*, made of bunches of reed arched together and covered with palm-leaf mats, were placed in a square around us. They served for stables, store-rooms, servants' quarters, workshop, dining-room, kitchen and other purposes, and also protected us against the sand storms and the thievish inclinations of the children of the desert. Before this primitive camp was established, Field began surveying the mounds, as a preliminary map had to be submitted to the wâli of Baghdad, in order to secure his formal approval of our excavations. In the mean while the director and the two Assyriologists used every spare moment to acquaint themselves with the topography of the ruins and to search for indications on the surface which might enable them to ascertain the probable character and contents of the more prominent single mounds.[1]

In connection with repeated walks over the whole field I prepared a rough sketch of the principal ruins for my own use, gathered numerous pieces of bricks, stone and pottery, and immediately reached the following general conclusions: 1. Certain portions of the ruins are remarkably free from blue and green enamelled pottery, always characteristic of late settlements on Babylonian sites, and show no trace of an extensive use of glass on the part of its inhabitants. As the latter is never mentioned with certainty in the cuneiform inscriptions (then at our disposal), and as the Assyrian excavations at Khorsabâd, Nebî Yûnus, and Nimrûd had yielded but a few glass vessels, these parts of ancient Nippur must have been destroyed and abandoned at a comparatively early date. 2. In accordance with such personal observations and inferences and in view of Layard's discoveries in the upper strata of Nuffar,[2] it became evident that the southwest half of the ruins, which on an average is also considerably higher than the corresponding other one, was much longer inhabited and to a larger extent used as a graveyard in the post-Christian period than the northeast section. 3. As Bint el-Amîr, the most conspicuous mound of the whole ruins, no doubt represents

[1] Comp. the brief description of the ruins on pp. 160, *seq.*, above, under Layard.

[2] Comp. pp. 161, *seqq.*, above.

the ancient *ziggurrat* or stage-tower, as generally asserted, it follows as a matter of course, that the temple of Bêl, of which it formed part, must also have been situated in the northeast section, and therefore is hidden under the mounds immediately adjoining it towards the east. 4. The question arose, what buildings are covered by the two remaining groups of mounds to the northwest and southeast of the temple complex. The important rôle which from the earliest times the cult of Bêl must have played in the life and history of the Babylonian people, as testified by the enormous mass of ruins and numerous passages in the cuneiform literature, pointed unmistakably to the employment of a large number of priests and temple officers, and to the existence of a flourishing school and a well equipped temple library in the ancient city of Nippur. Which of the two mounds under consideration most probably represented the residences of the priests with their administrative offices and educational quarters? 5. The large open court to the northwest of the temple, enclosed as it was on two sides by the visible remains of ancient walls, on the third by the *ziggurrat*, and on the fourth by the Shatt en-Nîl, suggested at once that the undetermined northwest group flanking this court served more practical purposes and contained out-houses, stables, store-rooms, magazines, sheds, servants' quarters, etc., which were not required in the immediate neighborhood and in front of the temple. 6. It was therefore extremely probable that the houses of the priests, their offices, school, and library must be looked for in the large triangular southeast mound (IV), separated by a branch of the Shatt en-Nîl from the temple proper. Situated on the bank of two canals, in close proximity to the sanctuary of Bêl, open on all sides to the fresh breezes in the summer, and yet well protected against the rough north winds, which swept down from the snow-capped mountains of Persia during the winter, this section of the ruins seemed to fulfil all the conditions required, and from the very beginning was therefore pointed out by the present writer as the most important mound for our work next to the temple ruin proper.

It will always remain a source of deep regret that Dr. Peters did not rely more upon the judgment and scientific advice of his Assyriologists in deciding strictly technical questions, but that in his anxious but useless efforts to arrange all the essential details of this first expedition in person, he allowed himself frequently to be led by accidents and secondary considerations rather than by a clearly definite plan of methodical operations. The first trenches were opened on February 6 by the thirty-two workmen hired in Hilla. The circumstance that some of the Arabs, while gathering bricks for certain constructions in our camp, had accidentally struck a large tomb in a small gully near us influenced the director to begin the excavations at this point (VII), which soon led to the discovery of a construction of columns made of baked bricks and of such a mass of slipper-shaped coffins, funeral urns, bones, ashes, and other remains of the dead, that at first we were inclined to regard the whole southwestern half of Nuffar as a vast graveyard or a regular "city of the dead," similar to those explored by Moritz and Koldewey at Surghul and El-Hibba. The next point attacked by him was an extremely insignificant out-of-the-way mound at the northwestern end of the Shatt en-Nîl, selected chiefly because it was small enough to be excavated completely within a few weeks. Several days later, when a sufficient number of workmen had been obtained from the neighboring tribes, the systematic exploration of Bint el-Amîr was undertaken in accordance with a plan prepared by the Assyriologists and the architect. The first task which we had set for ourselves was to determine the corners and walls of the stage-tower, and to search for barrel cylinders and other documents which might have been deposited in

Slipper-Shaped Coffins in their Original Position. About 100 A. D.

this ancient structure by the different monarchs who restored it. If ever they existed, — and certain discoveries made later in the rubbish around its base proved that they actually did, — these building records must have been destroyed at the time of the Parthian invasion, when the whole temple complex was remodelled for military purposes.

Apart from a stray cuneiform tablet of the period of Sargon I. — the first of its kind ever discovered, — three small fragments of inscribed stone picked up by the Arabs, a few Hebrew bowls, and a number of bricks bearing short legends of the kings Ur-Gur, Bur-Sin I., Ur-Ninib, and Ishme-Dagan, all of the third pre-Christian millennium, no inscribed documents had been unearthed during the first ten days of our stay at Nuffar. No wonder that Dr. Peters, who began to realize that his funds of $15,000 were nearly exhausted, grew uneasy as to the tangible results of the expedition, the future of which depended largely upon quick and important discoveries. I seized this opportunity to submit once more for his consideration my views, given above, concerning the topography of the northeast half of the ruins, pointing out that in all probability tablets would be found in that large isolated hill, which I believed to contain the residences of the priests and the temple library (IV), and requested him to let me have about twenty men for a few days to furnish the inscribed material so eagerly sought after. This was a somewhat daring proposition, which scarcely would have been made with this self-imposed restriction of time had I not been convinced of the general correctness of my theory. After some hesitation the director was generous enough to place two gangs of workmen at my disposal for a whole week in order to enable me to furnish the necessary proof for my subjective conviction. On February 11 two trenches were opened at the western edge of IV on a level with the present bed of the ancient canal. Before noon the first six cuneiform tablets were in our possession, and at the close of the same day more than twenty tablets and fragments had been recovered. Thus far the beginning was very encouraging, and far surpassed my boldest expectations. But it remained to be seen whether we had struck only one of those small nests of clay tablets as they occasionally occur in all Babylonian ruins, or whether they would continue to come forth in the same manner during the following weeks and even increase gradually in number. At the end of February several hundred tablets and fragments had been obtained from the same source, and six weeks later, when our first campaign was brought to a sudden end, mound IV had yielded more than two thousand cuneiform inscriptions from its seemingly inexhaustible mines. For the greater part they were unbaked, broken, and otherwise damaged. With regard to their age, two periods could be clearly distinguished. The large mass was written in old Babylonian characters not later than the first dynasty of Babylon (about 2000 B. C.), but less than one hundred tablets gathered in the upper strata were so-called neo-Babylonian contracts generally well preserved and dated in the reigns of Ashurbânapal, Nabopolassar, Nebuchadrezzar, Evil-Merodach (2 Kgs. 25 : 27; Jer. 52 : 31), Nabonidos, Cyrus, Cambyses, Darius, and Xerxes. Three of them were of unusual historical interest. Being dated in the second and fourth year of Ashuretililâni, "king of Assyria," they proved conclusively that Nabopolassar's rebellion against the Assyrian supremacy (626 B. C.) was originally confined to the capital and its immediate environment, and that, contrary to the prevalent view, long after Babylon itself had regained and maintained its independence, important cities and whole districts of the Southern empire still paid homage to Ashurbânapal's successor on the throne of Assyria.[1]

But the earlier inscriptions, though as a rule very fragmentary, were of even greater significance. None of them

[1] Comp. Hilprecht, in *Zeitschrift für Assyriologie*, vol. iv, pp. 164, *seqq.*

was evidently found *in situ*, except ten large tablets in a most excellent state of preservation taken from a kiln, where they had been in the process of baking when one of the terrible catastrophes by which the city was repeatedly visited overtook ancient Nippur. They consisted of business documents referring to the registry of tithes and to the administration of the temple property, and of tablets of a decided literary character, comprising some very fine syllabaries and lists of synonyms, letters, mathematical, astronomical, medical and religious texts, besides a few specimens of drawing and a considerable number of mostly round tablets which must be classified as school exercises. Those which were dated bore the names of Hammurabi, Samsu-iluna, Abeshum, Ammisatana, and Ammisadugga. As about four fifths of all the tablets were literary, there could no longer be any doubt that we were not far from the famous temple library, unless indeed we already were working in its very ruins. In order to arrive at more definite results, it would have been necessary to continue the two large trenches which I had started, through the centre to the eastern edge of the mound. In the course of the second half of March five extra gangs were put on "the tablet hill," as it was henceforth styled, to carry out this plan. But time and money were soon lacking, and circumstances arose which forced us to evacuate Nuffar before many weeks were over. Otherwise we could not have failed to discover, in 1889, those tablet-filled rooms which were unearthed eleven years later, when the present writer personally was held responsible for the preparation of the plans and the scientific management of the expedition.

The work at the temple complex, where finally more than one hundred men were employed, proceeded but slowly, owing to the enormous amount of rubbish accumulated here and to the tenacity of the unbaked bricks which had to be cut through. Small and graceful terra-cotta cones similar to those discovered by Loftus at Warkâ,[1] but generally broken, were excavated in large number along the base of the northwest wall of the *ziggurrat*. Evidently they had fallen from the top of the tower, and once belonged to a shrine contemporaneous with the inscribed bricks of Ashurbânapal, the last known restorer of the temple of Bêl, near whose material they were lying. The remains of the lowest story of the huge building began to rise gradually out of the midst of the encumbering ruins. But they offered problems so complicated in themselves and with regard to other constructions discovered all around the *ziggurrat* at a much higher level, that it was well-nigh impossible to form a satisfactory idea of the character and extent of the temple, before the whole neighborhood had been subjected to a critical examination. For very apparent reasons there were only a few and very late tombs unearthed in this part of the city, while again they occurred more frequently in the lower mounds to the southwest of the temple. Among the various antiquities which came from the trenches of the sanctuary itself may be mentioned especially about a dozen vase fragments inscribed with very archaic characters, two of them exhibiting the name of Lugalzaggisi, an otherwise unknown king of Erech whose precise period could then not be determined; a well preserved brick stamp of Narâm-Sin (about 3750 B. C.), the first document of this half-mythical monarch which reached the shores of Europe; a fine marble tablet containing a list of garments presented to the temple; and a door-socket of the Cassite ruler Kurigalzu.

In the course of time our workmen had been gradually increased to about 250, so that experimental trenches could also be cut in the extreme western and southern wings of the ruins. A number of contract tablets of the time of the Chaldean and Persian dynasties were excavated in the upper strata of the last mentioned section. The fragment of a

[1] Comp. pp. 148, *seq.*, above.

Rooms and Towers excavated in the Upper Strata of the Southeastern Temple Enclosure

barrel cylinder of Sargon, king of Assyria, which came from the same neighborhood, indicated that a large public building must have occupied this site previously, a supposition subsequently strengthened by the discovery of two more fragments which belonged to duplicates of the same cylinder. Stray cuneiform tablets and seal cylinders; a considerable number of terra-cotta figurines, mostly bearded gods with weapons and other instruments in their hands, or naked goddesses holding their breasts or suckling a babe; and a few clay reliefs, among which an exquisitely modelled lioness excited our admiration, were discovered in various other parts of the ruins. They belonged to the Babylonian period, in which naturally our interest centred. But, as was to be expected, most of the trenches yielded antiquities which illustrated the life and customs of the early post-Christian inhabitants of the country rather than those of the ancient Babylonians. Especially in the ruins of the Parthian building, with its interesting brick columns, which in the first week the Arabs had disclosed to the east of our camp, we uncovered hundreds of slipper-shaped coffins and funeral urns, numerous vases and dishes, and small peculiar tripods, so-called stilts, which were used in connection with the burning of pottery in exactly the same way as they are employed in china-manufactories to-day. Terra-cotta toys, such as horses, riders, elephants, rams, monkeys, dogs, birds, eggs, marbles, and baby rattles in the shape of chickens, dolls and drums, spear-heads and daggers, metal instruments and polishing stones, Parthian coins, weights and whorls, jewelry in gold, silver, copper, bone, and stone, especially necklaces, bracelets, ear and finger rings, fibulae and hair-pins, together with about thirty bowls inscribed with Hebrew, Mandean and Arabic legends, and frequently also covered with horrible demons supposed to molest the human habitations and to disturb the peace of the dead, completed our collections.

Soon after we had reached Nuffar, Dr. Peters had made

us acquainted with the low ebb in the finances of the expedition. It was, therefore, decided to close the excavations of the first campaign at the beginning of May. But the working season was brought to a conclusion more quickly than could have been anticipated. The trouble started with the Arabs. The methodical exploration of the ruins had proceeded satisfactorily for about nine weeks till the middle of April, tablets being found abundantly, and the topography of ancient Nippur becoming more lucid every day. Notwithstanding those countless difficulties which, more or less, every expedition working in the interior of Babylonia far away from civilization has to meet at nearly every turn, we began to enjoy the life in the desert and to get accustomed to the manners of the fickle Arabs, whose principal "virtues" seemed to consist in lying, stealing, murdering, and lasciviousness. And the ʻAfej, on the other hand, had gradually abandoned their original distrust, after they had satisfied themselves that the Americans had no intention of erecting a new military station out of the bricks of the old walls for the purpose of collecting arrears of government taxes. But there existed certain conditions in our camp and around us which, sooner or later, had to lead to serious complications. Hajji Tarfâ, the supreme shaikh of all the ʻAfej tribes, a man of great diplomatic skill, liberal views and far-reaching influence, was unfortunately absent in the Shamîye when we commenced operations at Nuffar. His eldest son, Mukota, who meanwhile took the place of his father, was a sneaking Arab of the lowest type, little respected by his followers, begging for everything that came under his eyes, turbulent, treacherous, and a coward, and brooding mischief all the while. Two of the principal ʻAfej tribes, the Hamza and the Behahtha, both of which laid claim to the mounds we had occupied, and insisted on furnishing workmen for our excavations, were at war with each other. At the slightest provocation and frequently without any apparent reason they

Arab Workmen at Nuffar dancing, chanting, and brandishing their Guns (executing a so-called *hausa*)

threw their scrapers and baskets away and commenced the war-dance, brandishing their spears or guns in the air and chanting some defiant sentence especially made up for the occasion, as, *e. g.*, "We are the slaves of Berdi," "The last day has come," "Down with the Christians," "Matches in his beard who contradicts us," etc. The Turkish commissioner and the *zabtîye* (irregular soldiers), — whose number had been considerably increased by the *qâimmaqâm* of Dîwânîye, much against our own will, — picked frequent quarrels with the natives and irritated them by their overbearing manners. The Arabs, on the other hand, were not slow in showing their absolute independence by wandering unmolested around the camp, entering our private tents and examining our goods, like a crowd of naughty boys; or by squatting with their guns and clubs near the trenches and hurling taunting and offensive expressions at the Ottoman government.

It was also a mistake that we had pitched our tents on the top of the ruins. For as the mounds of Nuffar had no recognized owner and yet were claimed by the Turks, the Bedouins, and the Ma'dân tribes at the same time, we were practically under nobody's protection, while by our very conspicuous position we not only suffered exceedingly from hot winds and suffocating sand storms, but invited plundering by every loiterer and marauder in the neighborhood. Moreover, unacquainted as we all were then with the peculiar customs of Central Babylonia, we had not provided a *mudhîf* or lodging house, a spacious and airy *sarîfa*, which in every large village of the country is set apart for the reception of travellers and guests. What wonder that the simple-minded children of the desert and the half-naked peasants of the marshes, who noticed our strange mode of living and saw so many unknown things with us for which they had no need themselves, shook their heads in amazement. On the one hand they observed how we spent large sums of money for uncovering old walls and gathering broken pottery, and on the other they found us eating the wild boar of the jungles, ignoring Arab etiquette, and violating the sacred and universal law of hospitality in the most flagrant way,—reasons enough to regard us either as pitiable idiots whom they could easily fleece or as unclean and uncouth barbarians to whom a pious Shiite was infinitely the superior.

Repeated threats to burn us out had been heard, and various attempts had been made to get at our rifles and guns. One night our bread-oven was destroyed, and a hole was cut in the reed-hut which served as our stable. Soon afterwards four sheep belonging to some of our workmen were stolen. The thief, a young lad from the Sa'îd, a small tribe of bad repute, half Bedouin and half Ma'dân, encouraged by his previous success, began to boast, as Berdi told me later, that he would steal even the horses of the Franks without being detected. Though he might have suspected us to be on the alert, he and a few comrades undertook to execute the long-cherished plan in the night of the fourteenth of April. Our sentinels, who had previously been ordered to occupy the approaches to the camp night and day, frustrated the attempt and opened fire at the intruders. In an instant the whole camp was aroused, and one of the thieves was shot through the heart. This was a most unfortunate occurrence, and sure to result in further trouble. No time was therefore lost to inform the 'Afej chiefs, to despatch a messenger to the next military station, and to prepare ourselves for any case of emergency. "Then followed a period of anxious suspense. Soon the death wail sounded from a village close beneath us," indicating that the body of the dead Arab had been carried off to the nearest encampment. "Then a signal fire was kindled. This was answered by another and another, until the whole plain was clothed with little lights, while through the still night came the sounds of bustle and preparation for the attack." On the next morning we decided to avoid the consequences of the severe laws of Arab blood revenge by paying an adequate indemnity to the family of the fallen man. But our offer was proudly rejected by the hostile tribe, and an old Sa'îd workman, employed as a go-between, returned with torn garments and other evidences of a beating. The American party was equally prompt in refusing to give up the "murderer." The days and nights which followed were full of exciting scenes. Mukota, Berdi, and other 'Afej shaikhs, who professed to come to our assistance, had occupied the spurs around us. Thirty irregular soldiers, with six hundred rounds of cartridges, were sent from Dîwânîye and Hilla, and others were expected to arrive in the near future. There were constant alarms of an attack by the Sa'îd. The 'Afej, not concealing their displeasure at seeing so large a number of *zabtîye* in their territory, were evidently at heart in sympathy with the enemy. Besieged as we practically were, we were finally forced to withdraw our laborers from the trenches and make arrangements for quitting Nuffar altogether. On Thursday, April 18, long before the sun rose, the whole expedition was in readiness to vacate the mounds and to force their way to Hilla, when upon the treacherous order of Mukota, an Arab secretly set fire to our huts of reeds and mats and laid the whole camp in ashes in the short space of five minutes. For a while the utmost confusion prevailed, the *zabtîye* got demoralized, and occupied a neighboring hill; and while we were trying to save our effects, many of the Arabs commenced plundering. Half the horses perished in the flames, firearms and saddle-bags and $1000 in gold fell into the hands of the marauders, but all the antiquities were saved. Under the war-dance and yells of the frantic Arabs the expedition finally withdrew in two divisions, one on horseback, past Sûq el-'Afej and Dîwânîye, the other on two boats across the swamps to Daghâra, and back to Hilla, where soon afterwards the governor-general of the province arrived, anxious about our welfare and determined, if necessary, to come to our rescue with a military force.

On the way to Baghdad Harper handed in his resignation, Field gave his own a day later, Haynes, who, on the recommendation of the Philadelphia Committee, had been appointed United States Consul at Baghdad, prepared to settle in the city of Hârûn ar-Rashîd, and with Noorian to await further developments, Peters was recalled by cable to America, and the present writer was requested to remain in charge of the expedition in Mesopotamia. But circumstances beyond his control made it impossible for him to accept this trust at once, and necessitated his immediate return to Europe.[1] Our first year at Babylonia had ended in a serious disaster. Dr. Peters, to quote his own words, "had failed to win the confidence of his comrades,"[2] and more than $20,000 had been expended merely to scratch the surface of one of the most enormous ancient sites in all Western Asia. How would the Ottoman government view the unexpected turn in our work among the turbulent Arabs? Would they allow the expedition to return

[1] In the fall of 1888, when I departed from Germany for the East, my wife was so ill that her recovery was doubtful. Upon her own special request, however, I left her to meet my obligations in Asia. Soon after my return from Nuffar to Baghdad, April, 1889, I was informed that meanwhile she had been operated upon unsuccessfully, and that a second operation, for which my immediate return was required, was necessary. Twelve years later, when I was in the Orient again upon an important mission in connection with this expedition, she actually sacrificed herself for the cause of science, by concealing her serious illness in order not to interfere with my work, and by writing cheerful and encouraging letters to me, while she was sinking fast, and knew that she would not recover. When I finally returned to Germany in perfect ignorance of her condition, she was already beyond human aid and died soon afterwards (March, 1902), using the last hours of her unselfish life to execute a noble deed in the interest of Assyriology.

[2] Comp. Peters, "Nippur," New York, 1897, vol. i, p. 288. Besides this volume, which gives a subjectively colored and not always very reliable account of the origin and history of the first campaign, comp. Hilprecht in *Kölnische Zeitung*, June 30, 1889, Sunday edition, second paper, and Harper in "The Biblical World," vol. i, pp. 57–62.

in the fall? And if no obstacle was raised in Constantinople, would the Philadelphia Committee, after so many disappointments, be willing to resume the exploration of Nuffar, which had proved to be a task by far more expensive and wearisome than most of the contributors could have expected?

Second Campaign, 1889–1890. It is to the great credit of the small number of enthusiastic gentlemen who had previously furnished the funds, that far from being discouraged by what had occurred, they were rather "favorably impressed with the results accomplished by the first year's campaign," and decided to continue the excavations at Nuffar for another year under Dr. Peters, provided that the Turkish authorities at Constantinople would approve of their plan. The wâli of Baghdad, who was principally held responsible for the safety of the party in a section of his province over which he had little control, most naturally opposed the return of the expedition with all his power. But thanks to the lively interest and the energetic support of Hamdy Bey, the Grand Vizier viewed the whole matter very calmly and in a different light from what it had been represented to him by the local officials. Accordingly he authorized the University of Pennsylvania's expedition to resume its interrupted labors in Babylonia in the same year. On October 10, Dr. Peters was able to leave the Turkish capital for Beirût, and from there, by way of Damascus and Palmyra, to travel to Baghdad, which he reached about the middle of December.

Important changes had meanwhile taken place in 'Irâq el-'Arabî. Soon after our departure, in May, 1889, a fearful cholera epidemic had broken out in lower Babylonia, and, following the courses of the two rivers, had spread rapidly to the northern districts. With the exception of Hît, Nejef, and some other remarkably favored places, it had devastated the entire country, with special fury raging in the marshy districts between Nuffar and the Shatt el-Haï, where our old enemy, Mukota, was carried off as one of its first victims, and in certain notoriously unclean and densely populated quarters of Baghdad, which for several weeks in the summer were almost completely deserted by the frightened population. In view of the lingering presence of the dreaded scourge in the valleys of the Euphrates and the Tigris, and the possibility of a renewed outbreak of the same plague in the spring, the director deemed it necessary to engage the services of a native physician of Syria, Dr. Selîm Aftimus, who at the same time was expected to make those botanical and zoölogical collections for which the present writer had earnestly pleaded, before the first expedition was organized. Haynes and Noorian were again induced to associate themselves with the practical management of the undertaking on the road and in the field, and to serve in the same capacities in which they had been employed the previous year. But, at the special desire of Dr. Peters, this time an American scientific staff was entirely dispensed with, though Field and Hilprecht would have been willing to accompany the expedition again, without a salary but with increased responsibility. This was a most unfortunate decision on the part of the director. It is true, a solid scientific basis of operations had been established in the first campaign, and consequently there was no immediate need of an architect and Assyriologist at the beginning of the new excavations; and yet it was impossible to excavate properly for any length of time without the constant advice of either of them. If, nevertheless, this expedition, sent out to investigate the history of one of the largest, most ancient, and, at the same time, most ruined and complicated sites in the country, attempted to solve its difficult problem without the trained eyes and scientific knowledge of technically prepared men, it necessarily had to be at the expense of a strictly methodical exploration and at the sacrifice of half of the possible results, of which it deprived itself in consequence of its inability to follow up every indication on the ground, and to determine most of the perplexing archæological questions in the trenches.

But while in the interest of scientific research we cannot approve of Dr. Peters' fatal course, to a certain degree we can explain it. He was anxious to save expenses in connection with an undertaking the original estimate of which he had considerably underrated; and not fully aware of the fact that he damaged his own cause, for which he was working with such an admirable patience, energy, and courage, he desired a greater freedom in his movements and decisions from the influence of specialists, who formerly had caused him great trouble, as they frequently differed with him in regard to the most fundamental questions. His mind being firmly fixed upon tangible results which by their mere number and character would appeal to the public, he naturally took great pains to obtain them at the least possible outlay of time and money, according to the manner of Rassam and other earlier explorers, rather than to examine these immense ruins systematically according to the principles laid down by the modern school of archæologists. We must bear this circumstance in mind, in order to understand and judge his work leniently and to appreciate his results, which, though one-sided and largely misunderstood by him, proved ultimately to be of great importance for our knowledge of the Cassite and Parthian periods of Babylonian history, and furnished welcome material for our restoration of the chronology of the second millennium.

On the last day of 1889 the caravan left Baghdad. After repeated unsuccessful attempts by the local governors of Hilla and Dîwânîye at preventing the expedition's return to the ruins, the excavations were resumed on January 14, with about two hundred workmen from Hilla, who, in consequence of the ravages of cholera, lack of rain, and failing crops, had been reduced to the utmost poverty, and now looked eagerly for employment in the trenches of Nuffar. They continued this time for nearly four months, and terminated peacefully on May 3, 1890. In accordance with the advice of the natives, and profiting from our last year's experience, Dr. Peters and his comrades pitched their somewhat improved camp in the plain to the south of the western half of the ruins, and placed themselves under the protection of but a single chief, Hamid el-Birjûd, shaikh of the Nozair, one of the six tribes which constitute the Hamza, a subdivision of the 'Afej.

There could be little doubt that the Arabs of the whole neighborhood were glad to see the expedition once more established among them. All the preceding troubles seemed to be forgotten entirely. The Sa'îd themselves had conducted Haynes and his workmen to the mounds in the natural expectation of receiving some kind of recognition for their friendly attitude, doubly remarkable, as the old blood-feud existing between them and the expedition had not yet been settled. An excellent opportunity was thus given to remove the only cause for much annoyance and anxiety on the part of the Americans, and to make friends and valuable supporters out of deadly enemies, by recognizing the general law of the desert and paying a small sum of money to the family of the man who had been killed in the act of robbery. Only ten Turkish liras (=$44) were demanded. But unfortunately, Dr. Peters, who otherwise entered into the life and feelings of the people most successfully, mistook the acknowledgment and prompt arrangement of the whole affair for a sign of weakness, and refused to listen to any proposal, thereby creating a feeling of constant uneasiness and unsafety on the part of Haynes, which was not at all unreasonable, and as a matter of course at times interfered seriously with the work of the expedition.

Like the Sa'îd, who vainly endeavored to obtain a certain

The Camp of the Second Babylonian Expedition of the University of Pennsylvania at Nuffar

share in our work, the 'Afej could not always be trusted. They all wanted to guard the rare "goose that laid the golden egg," and soon became jealous of the Nozair chief, who had pledged himself for the security of the party. "Fabulous stories of our immense wealth were in circulation. Everything was supposed to contain money, even our boxes of provisions." "The Arabs believed that we were digging out great treasures, and it was confidently asserted that we had secured the golden boat, or *turrâda*,[1] which from time immemorial had been supposed to be contained in these mounds." The mere sight of a gold crown on one of Peters' teeth, which was eagerly pointed out by those who had discovered it to every friend and newcomer, seemed to strengthen their conviction and excite their lust. The comparative ease with which in the previous year so much spoil had been carried off through Mukota's treacherous behavior, aroused the cupidity of all the Arabs and their ardent desire to repeat his example. The presence of two hundred workmen from Hilla and Jumjuma, who could not always be managed to keep peace with one another, was regarded by the 'Afej shaikhs as an affront intended to diminish their personal income, since they were entitled to one sixth of the wages received by their own tribesmen. Besides, murderers and other desperadoes, who had fled from various parts of the country to the safer districts of the Khôr el-'Afej, were never lacking, and were always ready to join in a conspiracy which would lead to stealing and burning, and thus raise their importance in the eyes of the people. In spite of the friendly assurances from the Arabs, there prevailed a general sense of insecurity all the while around Nuffar, which, indeed, is the atmosphere more or less characteristic of all modern Babylonia.

Fortunately, however, there was one circumstance which proved of priceless value to the members of the expedition.

[1] Comp. Layard, "Nineveh and Babylon," London, 1853, p. 557.

The notion was spread among the 'Afej and their neighboring tribes that the foreigners were armed with great magical power, and that, in punishment of the firing and plundering of their camp, they had brought upon their enemies the cholera, which was not quite extinct even in the year following. Several successful treatments of light ailments, and exceedingly bitter concoctions wisely administered to various healthy chiefs, who were curious to see and to taste the truth of all that was constantly reported, served only to assure and confirm this belief; and Peters, on his part, seized every opportunity to encourage and to develop such sentiment among the credulous 'Afej. He intimated to them that nothing was hidden from his knowledge, and that the accursed money which had been stolen would find its way back to him; he made mysterious threats of sore affliction and loss by death which would cause consternation among them; and to demonstrate his superior power and to indicate some of the terrible things which might happen at any moment, he finally gave them a drastic exhibition of his cunning art, which had a tremendous effect upon all who saw it. We will quote the story in his own language: "Just before sunset, when the men were all in camp and at leisure, so that I was sure they would notice what we did, Noorian and I ascended a high point of the mound near by, he solemnly bearing a compass before me on an improvised black cushion. There, by the side of an old trench, we went through a complicated hocus-pocus with the compass, a Turkish dictionary, a spring tape-measure, and a pair of field glasses, the whole camp watching us in puzzled wonder. Immediately after our dinner, while most of the men were still busy eating, we stole up the hill, having left to Haynes the duty of preventing any one from leaving the camp. Our fireworks were somewhat primitive and slightly dangerous, so that the trench which we had chosen for our operations proved rather close quarters. The first rocket had scarcely gone off when we could hear a buzz of excited voices below us. When the second and third followed, the cry arose that we were making the stars fall from heaven. The women screamed and hid themselves in the huts, and the more timid among the men followed suit. As Roman candles and Bengal lights followed, the excitement grew more intense. At last we came to our *pièce de résistance*, the tomato-can firework. At first this fizzled and bade fair to ruin our whole performance. Then, just as we despaired of success, it exploded with a great noise, knocking us over backward in the trench, behind a wall in which we were hidden, and filling the air with fiery serpents hissing and sputtering in every direction. The effect was indescribably diabolical, and every man, woman, and child, guards included, fled screaming, to seek for hiding-places, overcome with terror."

Great as the immediate impression of the fearful spectacle was upon the minds of the naïve children of the desert, who firmly believed in the uncanny powers of demons or *jinna*, this successful coup did not stop future quarrels, pilfering, and murderous attempts altogether, nor did it secure for the camp a much needed immunity from illness and the embarrassing consequences of the great drought which at the outset was upon the waters of Babylon, or of the subsequent deluge, which turned the whole country into one huge puddle and the semi-subterranean storehouses, kitchens, and stables of the camp into as many cisterns. Poor Dr. Aftimus, on whose technical knowledge the fondest hopes had been built, was himself taken down with typhoid fever the very day the party arrived at Nuffar. Without having treated a single Arab he had to be sent back to Baghdad while in a state of delirium, but fortunately he recovered slowly in the course of the winter. After this rather discouraging first experience of medical assistance in connection with our archæological explorations, we have never had courage to repeat the experiment. With a simple diet, some personal care, and a strict observation of the ordinary sanitary laws, the expedition as a whole escaped or overcame the peculiar dangers of the Babylonian climate during the following campaigns.

In spite of all the disappointments and hardships, which were scarcely less in the second year than they had been in the first, the great purpose of the expedition was not for a moment lost sight of. Our past excavations had been scattered over the entire surface of the mounds. Trial trenches had been cut in many places, to ascertain the general character and contents of the ruins, until work finally concentrated at three conspicuous points, — the temple (I), the so-called tablet hill (IV), and the more recent building with its fine court of columns near our old camp (VII) and the long ridge to the southeast of it. By means of written documents, the first expedition had adduced conclusive evidence that the ruins of Nuffar contained monuments of the time of Narâm-Sin (about 3750 B.C.) and even of a period considerably antedating it. It had discovered numerous remains of the third pre-Christian millennium, and clearly demonstrated that thousands of tablets and fragments of the ancient temple library still existed in the large triangular mound to the south of the temple complex, thereby almost determining the very site of this famous library. It furthermore had traced the history of Nippur by a few inscriptions through the second millennium down to the time of the Persian kings, and lastly shown, in connection with Parthian coins and constructions, Sassanian seals, Hebrew and Mandean bowls, Kûfic coins of the ʻAbbâside caliphs, and other antiquities, that parts of the ruined city were inhabited as late as the ninth century of our own era. In other words, it had submitted material enough to prove that at least five thousand years of ancient history were represented by this enormous site. It remained for the second and the following expeditions to fill this vast period with the necessary details, and, if possible, even to extend its limits by concentrated methodical excavations at the principal elevations.

Babylonian Pottery of the Parthian Period. About 250 B. C. to A. D. 200.

Among the various mounds and ridges which constitute the ruins of Nuffar, there was none more important than the conical hill of Bint el-Amîr with its irregular plateau of *débris* (I), containing the stage-tower and temple of Bêl. "This great mass of earth covered a surface of more than eight acres," the careful examination of which was an ambitious problem in itself, especially as none of the large Babylonian temples had yet been excavated completely. At the outset the expedition had therefore decided to investigate this complex methodically, to determine its characteristic architectural features, and to trace its development through all the periods of Babylonian history down to its final decay. But owing to the large accumulations of rubbish and the very limited time in the first year at our disposal, we had not been able to do much more than to fix the corners of the ancient *ziggurrat* and to run trenches along its peculiar lateral additions. As the latter were constructed of large crude bricks and surrounded by extensive remains of rooms built of the same material, and as numerous antiquities of the Hellenistic period and coins of the Arsacide kings (about 250 B. C.–226 A. D.) were unearthed in connection with them, I had "reached the conclusion that the ruins we had found were those of a Parthian fortress built on the site of the ancient temple; and the majority of the members of the expedition inclined to this opinion."[1] But soon afterwards Peters changed his conviction and put forth his own theory, according to which we "had found the ancient temple of Bêl" itself. For the following years it was impossible for me to test his statements by a personal examination of the trenches; and as Haynes simply adopted his predecessor's theory and failed to throw any new light on this funda-

[1] Comp. Peters, "Nippur," vol. ii, p. 118, where he reproduces my view correctly, except that he substitutes Sassanian for Parthian, owing to his frequently indiscriminate use of these two words (comp. p. 129 of the same work).

mental question, there remained nothing but either to acquiesce in Peters' view, which, however, ignored essential facts brought to light by the previous excavations, and was contrary to certain established laws of Babylonian architecture, or to regard the famous sanctuary of Bêl as a hopeless mass of crumbling walls, fragmentary platforms, broken drains, and numerous wells, reported by Haynes to exist at widely separated levels, often in very strange places and without any apparent connection with each other.

What were the new features developed at this "perplexing mound" in the course of the second campaign? By engaging a maximum force of four hundred Arab laborers, half from Hilla and Jumjuma, half from the 'Afej tribes around Nuffar, and by placing the greater part of his men at the temple mounds, the director was able to attack the problem more vigorously and to remove such an enormous mass of rubbish that at the end of his work he could boast "that in cubic feet of earth excavated, and size and depth of trenches," his excavations "far surpassed any others ever undertaken in Babylonia," and that De Sarzec's work of several seasons at Tellô "was probably not even the tenth part as large as our work of as many months." But this difference was due to various causes, and not the least to the difference of methods pursued by the two explorers, quite aside from the fact that the amount of rubbish extracted from a ruin can never be used as a standard by which the success or failure of an archæological mission is to be judged. Peters himself characterizes his manner of excavating as follows: "We sank small well-shafts or deep narrow trenches, in many cases to the depth of fifty feet or more, and pierced innumerable small tunnels (one of them 120 feet in length) after the native method."[1] In other words, he examined the mounds pretty much as the Arab peasants did at Babylon, El-Birs, and other places, only on

[1] Comp. Peters, *l. c.*, vol. ii, pp. 111, *seq.*

a larger scale, — either by deep perpendicular holes or by "innumerable" horizontal mines, instead of peeling off the single layers successively and carefully. Was this scientific research? The results, as indicated above, were naturally commensurate with the method employed. Peters did not procure a satisfactory plan nor the necessary details of the originally well-preserved vast complex of buildings which occupied the site of the temple of Bêl "at the time of its last great construction;" he failed to ascertain its character and purpose, and to define its precise relation to the *ziggurrat;* he was unable to determine its age, or even to fix the two extreme limits of the three successive periods of its occupation; and he did not recognize that the line of booths situated outside of the southeast fortified enclosure and yielding him a fine collection of inscribed Cassite monuments belonged to the same general epoch as the mass of crude brickwork covering the temple. As far as possible, his assertions have either been verified or corrected by the present writer's later investigations on the ruins. But, unfortunately, much of the precious material had been removed in the course of the second and third campaigns, or was subsequently destroyed by rain and other causes, so that it could no longer be used for the study and reconstruction of the history of the venerable sanctuary of Nippur.

The following is Peters' own view in a nutshell: There are about sixteen feet of ruins below a surface layer of three feet, which represent the last important restoration of the ancient temple by a monarch "not far removed from Nebuchadrezzar in time," and living about 500 B. C. This ruler consequently can have been only one of the Persian kings, notably Darius I, or perhaps Xerxes. The sacred precincts were no longer "consecrated to the worship of Bêl," but stood in the service of "a new religion." The old form of the *ziggurrat* was changed by "huge buttress-like wings added on each of the four sides," which gave the structure "a cruciform shape unlike that of any other *ziggurrat* yet discovered." The sanctuary continued to exist in the new form for about three hundred to three hundred and fifty years, until after the Seleucidan period, somewhere about or before 150 B. C., when men ceased to make additions or repairs, and the ancient temple of Bêl fell gradually into ruins.

It is unnecessary to disprove this fantastic theory in detail. Peters' own excavations and our previous and later discoveries make it entirely impossible. But while we cannot accept his inferences, which are contrary to all the evidence produced, we recognize that he brought to light a number of facts and antiquities, which enable us to establish at least some of the more general features of this latest reconstruction. He showed that a considerable area around the *ziggurrat* was enclosed by two gigantic walls protected by towers. He ascertained their dimensions, followed their courses, and described the extraordinary size of their bricks. He excavated fourteen chambers on the top of one of the outer walls, and found the entire space between the inner wall and the *ziggurrat* occupied completely by similar rooms. He arrived at the conclusion that the various constructions belonged together and formed an organic whole. A long, narrow street, however, which ran parallel with the southeastern line of fortifications, divided the houses in the interior into two distinct sections. Several of the chambers in the southern part were filled with "great masses of water-jars piled together." They doubtless had served as storerooms; others were kitchens, as indicated "by the fireplaces and other arrangements;" while in some of the rooms "were curious closets with thin clay partitions." The rubbish of most of the chambers yielded numerous fragments of pottery of the Hellenistic and Roman periods, remarkable among them a fine brown enamelled lamp (head of Medusa), and many terra-cotta figurines, especially heads of women frequently wearing a peculiar high head-dress, children, and groups of lovers. It is a characteristic feature of these late Babylonian terra-cottas that they are generally hollow in the interior, while their outside is often covered with a chalk paste by which the artist endeavored to work out the delicate facial lines, the curled hair, the graceful foldings of the garments, and other details, with greater accuracy,[1] and thus to produce a better effect of the whole figure, which sometimes also was colored. Teeth of wild boars repeatedly found in this stratum indicate that the occupants of those later constructions were fond of hunting the characteristic animal of the swamps around Nippur.

Lamp in Brown Enamelled Terra cotta

From a room of the latest temple construction

From the extraordinary amount of dirt and débris accumulated during the period of occupancy of the rooms, and from the different styles of art exhibited by the antiquities discovered in them, it became evident that these latest constructions must have been inhabited for several

[1] Comp. *e. g.*, the central head of the illustration facing p. 128 of Peters' second volume, and Nos. 31 and 32 of Hilprecht, "The Babylonian Expedition of the University of Pennsylvania," series A, vol. ix, plates xiv and xv, Nos. 31 and 32.

hundred years. A similar result was obtained by an examination of the stage-tower. It was observed that the *ziggurrat* of the cruciform shape above referred to, which consisted only of two stages, had two or three distinct additions, and that the unbaked material employed in them was identical with that found in the rooms around it.

In his endeavor to reach the older remains before the more recent strata had been investigated in the least adequately, Peters broke through the outer casing of the *ziggurrat* built of "immense blocks of adobe," in a cavity of which he discovered a well-preserved goose egg, and perceived that there was an older stage-tower of quite a different form and much smaller dimensions enclosed within the other. By means of a diagonal trench cut through its centre, he ascertained its height and characteristic features down to the level of Ur-Gur, and came to the conclusion (which, however, did not prove correct) that the *ziggurrat* of this ancient monarch was the earliest erected at Nippur. "Wells and similar shafts were sunk at other points of the temple," especially at the northern and western corners, where he reached original constructions of Ashurbânapal (668–626 B. C.) and Ur-Gur (about 2700 B. C), and discovered scattered bricks with the names of Esarhaddon (681–668 B. C.), Rammanshumusur (about 1100 B. C.), Kadashman-Turgu (about 1250 B. C.), Kurigalzu (about 1300 B. C.), Bur-Sin of Nisin (about 2500 B. C.), in addition to those previously found, "showing that many kings of many ages had honored the temple of Bêl at Nippur." At a place near the western corner of the *ziggurrat*, on the northwestern side, he descended through a tunnel some six feet below the plain level, striking a terra-cotta drain with a platform at its mouth and a wall of plano-convex bricks similar to those preceding the time of Ur-Ninâ at Tellô, in which he unearthed also a beautiful, highly polished jade axe-head and an inscribed pre-Sargonic clay tablet.

Immediately in front of the southeastern face of the stage-tower, Peters conducted a larger trench with a view of ascertaining the successive strata of the whole temple plateau. Below the level of the Parthian castle he disclosed "a mass of rubble and débris containing no walls, but great quantities of bricks, some of them with green glazed surfaces, and many bearing inscriptions of Ashurbânapal." In penetrating a few feet farther, he came upon fragments of pavements and soon afterwards upon the crude brick terrace of Ur-Gur. As he saw that the walls and towers of the Parthian fortress, which required a more solid foundation, descended to this deep level, he unhesitatingly pronounced them to have been in existence 2500 years before they were built, and "thought it not impossible" that at that ancient time two of these formidable fortification towers "were columns of the same general significance as the Jachin and Boaz which stood before the Temple of Yahweh [Jehovah] at Jerusalem"! While excavating in the stratum immediately above Ur-Gur's platform, he came accidentally upon the first three door-sockets and a brick stamp of Shargâni-shar-âli, soon afterwards identified by me as Sargon I, the famous king of Agade, who according to Nabonidos lived about 3800 B. C., but who until then had been regarded generally as a half-mythical person. In the same layer there were found about eighty fragments of stone vases and other antiquities inscribed with the names of Manishtusu and Urumush (Âlusharshid), two kings of Kîsh little known, who lived about the same time; Lugalzaggisi and Lugalkigubnidudu, two even earlier rulers of Erech, and Entemena, *patesi* of Lagash, familiar to us from De Sarzec's excavations. In spite of Haynes' very emphatic statement to the contrary, Peters claims to have reached the real level of Sargon and his predecessors at two points within the court of the *ziggurrat*, in one case descending almost sixteen feet below the present plain. Be this as it may, the building remains, which he had hitherto disclosed, were examined by him far too poorly and unsystematically to convey to us even a tolerably clear idea of the revered sanctuary of Bêl; and the inscriptions gathered were so small or fragmentary that they furnished us little more than the names and titles of ancient kings and *patesis*. But the material obtained sufficed to show that there were considerable ancient Babylonian ruins, and numerous though generally broken cuneiform inscriptions, including even antiquities contemporaneous with the earliest monuments of Tellô, contained in the temple hill of Nuffar.

It is characteristic of Peters' work in the second year that it was not carried on with the purpose of excavating one or two layers at one or more of the principal mounds of the enormous site methodically, but with the intention of "sounding" as many places as possible, and of discovering inscribed objects. Consequently he dug a little here and a little there and disturbed many strata at the same time. No wonder that he opened trenches also in the southern and southeastern ridges of the *ziggurrat*. Nothing of importance came to light in the former, but his labors were crowned with a remarkable success in the latter. Examining the plan of the ruins of Nuffar on p. 305, it will be observed that the temple mound (I) is separated from mound IV, which I regarded as the probable site of the library, by a deep depression doubtless representing an old branch of the Shatt en-Nîl. On the northeastern edge of this gully there is a low wall-like elevation, which rises only about thirteen feet above the plain. It was in this narrow ridge that Peters excavated more than twenty rooms resting on a terrace of earth and built of precisely the same material — "unbaked bricks of large, almost square blocks," as characterizes the late construction on the top of the temple of Bêl. Under ordinary circumstances he probably would have drawn the obvious inference that both belong to the same period. But the discovery in one of these rooms of a large number of Cassite votive objects — the first great collection of antiquities of this dynasty ever found — induced him to ascribe this whole row of booths to a time a thousand years earlier than it actually was. He formulated a new fantastic theory, according to which these cameos of agate and thin round tablets of lapis lazuli, with their brief votive inscriptions, were sold as charms to pilgrims, some of them being "a sort of masses said for the repose of the soul of such and such a king." The true facts are the following. All these interesting Cassite relics in agate, magnesite, feldspar, ivory, turquoise, malachite, lapis lazuli, and an imitation of the last-mentioned three stones in glass, "together with gold, amethyst, porphyry and other material not yet worked," were originally contained in a wooden box, traces of which (carbonized fragments and copper nails) were lying around them. Most, if not indeed the whole, of this unique collection had been presented by a number of Cassite kings to various shrines of the temple of Bêl somewhere between 1400 and 1200 B. C. A thousand years later, when the temple was in ruins, an inhabitant of Nippur, and himself a dealer in precious stones, searched in the neighborhood of his booth for raw material, and discovered them, or purchased them from other diggers. He was about to manufacture beads for necklaces and bracelets, rings, charms, and the like out of them,[1]

[1] A votive cylinder of Kurigalzu in agate had been cut into three beads without regard to its legend; a votive inscription had been erased insufficiently from an axe-head in lapis lazuli; a small block of the same material showed a deep incision beneath the inscribed portion, just about to be cut off, while several other blocks in lapis lazuli and magnesite had been reduced considerably from their original weight, as could easily be established. Comp. Hilprecht, "The Babylonian Expedition of the University of Pennsylvania," series A, vol. i, part 1, nos. 28, 50, 74, and plate xi, nos. 25 and 28; part 2, no. 140, and *Zeitschrift fur Assyriologie*, pp. 190, *seqq.*, where, misled by Peters' reports, I gave an erroneous interpretation of the facts treated above.

when another catastrophe befel Nippur. Several other "jeweller's shops" of the Parthian period excavated by our expedition at different sections of the ruins established the correctness of this interpretation beyond any doubt. And when in May, 1900, I spent a few days with the expedition at Babylon, Koldewey had found a similar shop in the mound of 'O(A)mrân ibn 'Alî, which, besides purely Parthian antiquities, contained several more ancient objects from various Babylonian ruins, and for this reason proved particularly instructive. No sooner had the German explorer submitted the inscribed objects of this shop to me for examination, than I recognized and pointed out to him a number of Cassite objects, which, according to their material, forms, and inscriptions belonged originally to the temple at Nippur, illustrating in an excellent way how the trade in "useful" antiquities flourished in Babylonia even two thousand years before our own time.

An even more far-reaching discovery, the real significance of which lies in its bearing upon the topography of ancient Nippur, but again unfortunately not recognized by Peters, was made a little to the northwest of these booths. This was a shrine of Bur-Sin I,[1] the walls of which were built of baked brick laid in bitumen, and were still seven to fourteen courses high. Consisting of two rooms, it stood upon a platform of the same material and faced inward toward the entrance to the court of the *ziggurrat*. According to the legends inscribed on the bricks and on two door-sockets found *in situ*, it had been dedicated to Bêl himself about 2600 B. C. A pair of clasped hands from a dolerite statue similar to those excavated at Tellô, a number of inscribed fragments of bas-reliefs, and an archaic mortar dec-

[1] As Thureau-Dangin has recently shown that there was only one dynasty of Ur in the third pre-Christian millennium, Bur-Sin of Nisin, hitherto classified as Bur-Sin I, must henceforth be called Bur-Sin II, while Bur-Sin of Ur takes the first place.

Bath-Tub-Shaped Coffin and Large Burial Urn in their Original Position

orated with an eagle and a snake evidently fighting with each other were taken from the débris around it, bearing witness to the elaborate manner in which the ancient Babylonians embellished their temples. As we shall have to say a few words about the relation of this shrine to the *ziggurrat* later, when we give a summary of the principal results of the Philadelphia expedition, we continue at present to sketch Dr. Peters' explorations on the other mounds of Nuffar.

To the east of our first camp we had previously discovered the remains of tapering brick columns, symmetrically arranged around an open square court (VII). It was natural to suppose that this peculiar structure belonged to a more pretentious building with interesting architectural features, as the mere presence of columns indicated sufficiently. Though the present writer had assigned it without hesitation to the Seleucido-Parthian period (about 250 B. C.), it was desirable and necessary to excavate it completely, before the more important Babylonian strata beneath it should be examined. In order to execute this task, Peters began to remove the Jewish and early Arabic houses representing the latest traces of human settlements everywhere in the precincts of ancient Nippur, and the numerous Parthian and Sassanian coffins, sepulchral urns, and pottery drains immediately below them. The former were characterized by Kûfic coins, Hebrew, Arabic, and Mandean incantation bowls, and other articles of domestic use, which were generally found in low and narrow rooms made of mud-bricks. We had frequently noticed the outlines of their walls in the preceding year, as we walked over the hills in the early morning, when the rapidly evaporating humidity of the ground drew the saltpetre contained in the clay to the surface.[1] The tombs, on the other hand, occurred in an indescribable confusion in all possible positions and at nearly

[1] Comp. p. 283, above.

every depth in the layer of rubbish which filled the space between the uppermost settlement and the floor of the building just mentioned to the height of six to ten feet. In no instance, however, were they discovered below the level of the court of columns, while repeatedly the burial-shafts were cut through the walls of the rooms grouped around it. Hence it follows that these interments must have taken place at a time when the imposing building was already in ruins,—in other words, at a period commencing shortly before our own era, and terminating about the sixth or seventh century A. D., if the palace in question was really of Seleucido-Parthian origin. This, however, was contested by Peters, who believed to have found evidence that the structure was a thousand years earlier. His work in and around this building may be sketched briefly as follows:—

The open court flanked by columns having been excavated completely in 1889, Peters undertook next to search for the rooms to which it probably gave light and access. As, in consequence of the slope of the hill, a considerable part of the ancient building had been washed away in the northeast and southeast directions, he concentrated his efforts upon an examination of the highest section of the mound, exploring especially the ruined mass southwest of the colonnade. He was soon able to show that, contrary to our previous theory, certain pieces of charred wood and small heaps of ashes discovered along the edge of the court did not belong to subsequent burials, but were remains of palm beams which originally rested on the columns and stretched across a narrow space to the walls of chambers surrounding the former on all four sides. We should expect that Peters, once having established this interesting fact, would have spared no pains to examine a building systematically, which, as late as 1897, he described as "the most interesting and ambitious structure excavated at Nippur next to the temple." But judging, as he did, the success of his expedition mainly "by the discovery of inscribed objects or failure to discover them,"[1] and nervously endeavoring to secure them at all hazards, he unfortunately adopted the injurious and antiquated methods of Layard and Rassam, which I have characterized above,[2] also for the exploration of the west section of the ruins. Instead of removing layer after layer of all the superincumbent rubbish, he excavated only portions of seven rooms with their adjoining corridors by digging along their walls and leaving the central mass untouched. And when even this process proved too slow and tedious, he drove tunnels into the mound above and below the floor of the building, which afterwards caved in, ruined part of the construction, and caused infinite trouble to himself and his successors.[3] At the same time the excavated earth was not carried to a previously explored place at a safe distance, but was dumped on the same mound, and in part on an unexplored section of the very ruins which he was desirous to examine, and whence the present writer had to remove it ten years later.

We cannot, therefore, be surprised that the results finally obtained were correspondingly meagre and unsatisfactory. Peters ascertained that a building of considerable extent and importance, constructed "of unbaked brick in large blocks," was buried there; he determined its west corner,

[1] On p. 202 of his "Nippur," vol. ii, Peters makes the committee in Philadelphia responsible for his methods of exploration. As I was secretary of that committee, I should know of "the constant demand of the home committee" for inscribed objects. But there is no such "demand" contained anywhere in our minutes, nor do I remember any such order ever having been sent through me to Dr. Peters. The true attitude of the committee is illustrated by the fact that it was "favorably impressed with the results accomplished by the first year's campaign" (comp. Peters, *l. c.*, vol. ii, p. 5), and that ten years later it supported me energetically in my efforts to change the obnoxious methods of excavation inaugurated by Peters and adopted by Haynes.

[2] Comp. pp. 103, *seq.*, 194, *seq.*, 321, *seq.*, 328, *seq.*

[3] Comp. Peters, *l. c.*, vol. ii, pp. 179, *seq.*, and the plan facing p. 178.

traced its southwestern boundary wall for 164 feet, found several uninscribed door-sockets *in situ*, and inferred from the numerous remains of charred wood, burned barley, and large red spots seen everywhere on the walls, doubtless due to the effects of intense heat, that the whole complex must have been destroyed by fire. Thus far we can follow him without difficulty. But though nothing but late antiquities [1] had been discovered within this enclosure, he arrived at the startling conclusion that the large structure was a Cassite palace, "erected somewhere between 1450 and 1250 B. C." How was this possible? These are his arguments: On the one hand, he unearthed a nest of about three hundred fine clay tablets and many fragments dated in the reigns of Kurigalzu, Kadashman-Turgu and Nazi-Maruttash, lying in the loose earth outside the southwest wall of the building in question, several yards away from it, and slightly below its level. On the other hand, he saw a building with similar columns on the top of a mound otherwise unknown, called Abû Adhem, a little to the south of Jôkha. As antiquities of a period preceding 2000 B. C. had been picked up by various travellers at Jôkha and other neighboring hills, which are situated "in the sphere of influence of Tellô," [2] he concluded — strange to say — that the building at Abû Adhem "belonged to the middle of the third millennium B. C." [3] I confess my inability to follow this kind of reasoning or to appreciate his "evidence of the surrounding mounds." If, indeed, the colonnade of Abû Adhem were as ancient as Dr. Peters supposes it to be, and

[1] Except the fragment of a statue in dolerite (a woman holding a lamb, comp. Peters, *l. c.*, vol. ii, p. 184), which belonged to the third pre-Christian millennium. Being out of its original place, it was discovered in a Jewish house on the top of the hill.

[2] A ruin which, by the way, also has its Seleucido-Parthian palace lying on the top of the temple mound.

[3] As to Peters's naïve arguments, comp. his "Nippur," vol. ii, pp. 186, *seqq.*

Co ırt of Columns of a Parthian Palace on the Western Bank of the Chebar. About 250–150 B. C.

not, rather, Parthian, as everything indicates, why did he not make the columns of Nippur, which are "precisely like them," precisely as old? Apparently because the discovery of Cassite tablets outside the large complex did not allow this. But are we on their account justified in claiming the structure as Cassite? Certainly not. On the contrary, they prove that the Cassite houses once occupying this site must have been in ruins at the time when the palace was erected, and that consequently the latter and its brick terrace, for the construction of which the older stratum had to be disturbed and levelled, cannot be contemporaneous with the Cassite rulers mentioned above, but must be of a considerably more recent date.

The exploration of the large and important building remains grouped around the *ziggurrat* and "the court of columns" had formed one of Peters' principal tasks during his second campaign. But his hope of discovering many inscribed Babylonian tablets while excavating these ruins was not to be realized. To find these eagerly-sought treasures somewhere in the vast mounds he had conducted extensive excavations from the beginning in several other parts of the ruins. Above all, he most naturally had directed his attention to the triangular mound (IV)[1] to the south of the temple, which had yielded almost all the tablets obtained by the first expedition. He now "riddled it with trenches everywhere"[2] and without difficulty secured about 2000 tablets more of the same general type as those discovered previously — business documents, school exercises, and numerous tablets of a strictly scientific or literary character, especially astronomical, mathematical, and medical. As, however, Peters did not possess the necessary Assyriological knowledge to determine their age and contents, and as, moreover, these tablets were never deposited in any large

[1] Comp. the plan of the ruins on p. 305, above.

[2] Comp. Peters, *l.c.*, vol. ii, p. 199.

number together, but "seemed to lie loose in the earth" or "confused among buildings with which they did not belong,"[1] he came to the conclusion that this hill with its two principal strata, which I had declared to be the probable site of the temple library, was "the home of well-to-do citizens, rather than the site of the great public building of the city," and abandoned it towards the middle of March, "because he had ceased to find tablets in paying quantities."

It was about the same time that the southeastern wing of the mounds on the other side of the canal (VI, and the ridge immediately to the northwest of it) began to yield tablets "in an extraordinary manner." The prospect of a more rapid increase of the coveted inscriptions being thus given, all the "tablet diggers" were transferred at once to this new promising locality. Before many weeks had elapsed, more than 5,000 tablets and fragments had been gathered, so that with regard to the mere number of clay documents recovered, Peters might well be pleased with the success which he had scored. Without troubling himself about the methodical examination and removal of the highest strata, which in the previous year had yielded contracts of the late Babylonian and Persian periods, he cut "sounding-trenches at various points in the interior, where the water had washed out deep gullies." In every instance he came upon rooms of mud brick containing "quantities of tablets," mixed with earth and grotesque clay figures of Bêl and his consort. There was in particular one chamber, thirty-two feet long by sixteen feet wide, which was literally filled with them. So numerous were the tablets there "that it took thirty or forty men four days to dig them out and bring them into camp." For the most part they were unbaked, and lay in fragments on the floor. But as the ashes observed in connection with them clearly indicated, they originally "had been placed around the walls of the

[1] Comp. *ibidem*, pp. 200–203.

Bêl, "the Father of the Gods"

Bêltis, his Consort

Terra-Cotta Images of Bêl and his Consort
About 2500 B. C.

room on wooden shelves," which broke or were burned, when the house was destroyed and the roof fell in. All the tablets discovered in these rooms and in this ridge in general are so-called private contracts and official records, such as receipts, tax-lists, statements of income and expense written in behalf of the government and of the temple,[1] and, as a rule,[2] are dated according to the reigns of the last kings of Ur (about 2600 B. C.), the first dynasty of Babylon (about 2300–2000 B. C.), Rîm-Sin of Larsa (a contemporary of Hammurabi), and especially several kings of the Cassite dynasty (about 1400–1200 B. C.). The older documents are valuable chiefly for their closing lines containing brief references to the principal historical events, after which the single years of the monarchs were called and counted. The tax-lists from the latter half of the second millennium are of importance because of their bearing upon the chronology of the Cassite kings, and because they give us a first insight into the civil administration of Central Babylonia under those foreign conquerors of whom previously we knew little more than their names, and these often enough only very imperfectly.

Peters confesses frankly: "My trenches here were dug principally for tablets."[3] Little attention, therefore, could be paid to the fundamental question, whether at the different periods of its occupation this ridge was covered with "ordinary houses" only,[4] or whether the single rooms formed an organic whole, an annex of the temple, a large government

[1] Peters' statement, *l. c.*, vol. ii, p. 212, is one sided and incorrect.

[2] There are only about fifty to one hundred tablets among them which are dated in the reigns of Assyrian, neo-Babylonian, and Persian kings. They were taken from the upper stratum.

[3] *L. c.*, vol. ii, p. 212.

[4] Peters' statement "In no case did we find structures of any importance" (p. 211) is of little value. His comparison of the "ordinary houses" discovered in this ridge with those unearthed in mound IV illustrates his curious conception of the character of Babylonian public buildings.

building with registering offices, a kind of bazaar, or both, as seems to result with great probability from a study of the tablets and from later discoveries made in this neighborhood by the present writer. Indeed, it was a dark day when Peters decided to excavate the ruins of Nuffar without the aid of a specialist, whether Assyriologist or architect. Fortunately Pognon, then French consul at Baghdad, occasionally lent a helping hand in determining the age and contents of some of the better preserved inscriptions from squeezes and photographs submitted to him,[1] and Peters could congratulate himself that at the time of his greatest need a Hungarian engineer, in the employ of the Ottoman government, Coleman d'Emey, appeared suddenly in the camp to hunt in the Babylonian swamps. He was easily induced to devote part of his time to a renewed survey of the principal ruins and to the preparation of plans of the excavated walls and rooms of the two Parthian palaces. It is true, according to the director's own statement, the real merits of his drawings are to be judged leniently,[2] but in connection with Peters' scanty notes they enabled us at least to form a general idea of the character and disposition of the latest constructions on the temple mound.

On the third day of May the excavations of the second campaign came to a more peaceful ending than those in the previous year. Before the trenches were abandoned, Peters very wisely decided to send part of his material out of the country, "to insure the preservation of something in case of disaster." For in consequence of his stubborn refusal to pay the often demanded blood-money to the Sa'îd, the disappointed tribe very naturally sought to indemnify itself in another way. A first boat-load of antiquities had left Nuffar safely towards the end of April. At the same time Haynes, who not without reason feared being waylaid and

[1] Comp. Peters, *l. c.*, vol. ii, pp. 51 and 280.

[2] Comp. Peters, *l. c.*, vol. ii, pp. 90, *seqq.*

plundered by a *ghazu*, "stole away in the night," and "pressed through to Hilla in hot haste." To prevent an attack planned by the enemy upon his camp for the night preceding the final departure of the expedition, Peters "resorted once more to stratagem, and gave a second exhibition of fireworks," which again had the desired effect. The Sa'îd then hoped to intercept him as he left the territory of the 'Afej, and try to extort blackmail. But the American slipped out of their hands before they realized that he had gone. As soon as all the workmen from Jumjuma had been sent in detachments through the marshes and everything was packed upon the last boats, including the Turkish commissioner and the *zabtîye*, Peters and Noorian, accompanied by some trusted Arab laborers and a personal servant, turned to the village of Hajji Tarfâ to examine the more prominent mounds in the south. With a door-socket of Gimil-Sin of Ur (about 2550 B. C.) picked up at Muqayyar, and with another of the same monarch and a whole box of fine tablets, through a fortunate accident discovered at Jôkha after a little scratching of the surface, they returned to the north by way of Samâwa, Nejef, and Kerbelâ, reaching Baghdad on the 7th of June, 1890. About a week later Peters was on his way to the Mediterranean coast, returning to America in November, while Haynes and Noorian left the country separately by different routes and at different times in the course of the same year.

Third Campaign, 1893–1896. In view of the large number of inscribed objects unearthed by him, Peters felt greatly encouraged as to future explorations at Nuffar, and looked upon his method of excavating in a somewhat different light from that in which it has been viewed by others. He was so much pleased with the tangible results which he had to show that before leaving the ruins he wrote to the committee urging early resumption of the work under Haynes alone according to the principles laid down by him. As the two men were in entire accord as to the feasibility of such a plan,[1] and as two members of the committee "warmly advocated it,"[2] promising to work towards its realization if the Ottoman government should apportion a sufficient number of antiquities to the University of Pennsylvania, Dr. Peters' methods of exploring soon had another chance of being tested with regard to their actual merits. For upon the recommendation of Hamdy Bey, who had not forgotten the extraordinary difficulties and losses of our first expedition and the praiseworthy energy and perseverance displayed by the second, the Sultan presented to the American university all those tablets and archæological objects not required to complete the collections of the Imperial Museum.

As soon as the present writer had sufficiently recovered from a long and severe illness contracted at Nuffar, which had made him an invalid for almost a year, he commenced the study of the newly acquired cuneiform material and reported on its great interest and value. In the spring of 1892 the committee decided upon another expedition, the details of which were arranged "at a meeting in Newport between Dr. Pepper, Mr. E. W. Clark, Mr. Haynes, and Dr. Peters."[3]

The last-mentioned gentleman "drew up with Haynes the plan of work, and drafted general instructions for the conduct of the excavations,"[2] while it was left to Professor Hilprecht to prepare a list of all the known Babylonian kings and *patesis* in cuneiform writing with an accurate reproduction of the palæographical peculiarities of the Nuffar inscriptions, and to write down such additional hints as might enable Haynes to find and to identify the names of the principal rulers on the different monuments.

About the same time a committee on publications was

[1] Comp. Peters' own story, *l. c.*, vol. ii, pp. 342, *seq.*
[2] Comp. Peters, *l. c.*, vol. ii, pp. 369, *seqq.*
[3] Comp. Peters, *l. c.*, vol. ii, p. 371.

formed with Mr. C. H. Clark as chairman, and H. V. Hilprecht as secretary and editor-in-chief. On the basis of a detailed plan submitted by the latter, the results of the expeditions were authorized to be published in four distinct series. With the aid of the American Philosophical Society the first volume of Series A appeared in 1893, and a second part in 1896, while two years later (1898), through the deep interest of a public-spirited citizen of Philadelphia, Mr. Eckley Coxe, Jr., the University of Pennsylvania was enabled to issue a third volume under its own name.[1] As the most important antiquities had remained in Constantinople, it soon became necessary for the committee to despatch its editor to the Turkish capital for the examination of those antiquities. While engaged in this work, in 1893, he was approached by the administration of the Imperial Ottoman Museum with the proposition to reorganize its Babylonian section during his summer vacations in the course of the following years. He accepted the honorable task,[2] but in

[1] "The Babylonian Expedition of the University of Pennsylvania, edited by H. V. Hilprecht, Series A: Cuneiform Texts." The volumes thus far published are vol. i, "Old Babylonian Inscriptions, chiefly from Nippur," by the editor, part 1, 1893, part 2, 1896; and vol. ix, "Business Documents of Murashû Sons of Nippur," by H. V. Hilprecht and A. T. Clay, 1898. Several other volumes are in the course of preparation. A more rapid publication was hitherto impossible, owing to the extraordinary difficulties connected with the deciphering and restoration of the fragmentary inscriptions (comp. vol. i, part 2, plates 36–49) and the faithful reproduction of all their palæographical peculiarities by hand, and no less to the unusually heavy duties of the editor, who until 1899 was without an assistant in his manifold labors as academical teacher and curator of two museums, not to mention the fact that since 1893 he had to work almost every year in three different parts of the world, spending part of his time in America, part in Constantinople, and part in the interior of Asia Minor. In 1899 Dr. Clay was called as his assistant, and at the end of 1901 further steps were taken by the Board of Trustees and the Committee of the Expedition to relieve him and to secure his principal time for the scientific study and publication of the results obtained at Nuffar.

[2] Comp. pp. 69 and below, under "Turkish Gleanings at Abû Habba."

declining the liberal remuneration offered, asked for the favor of this opportunity to show his personal appreciation of the energetic support which the Ottoman government had granted to the Philadelphia expeditions. With especial gratitude I testify here also to the extraordinary help which our subsequent scientific missions have received from the same government. Thanks to the gracious personal protection which His Majesty the Sultan henceforth extended to our various labors in his domain, and to the lively and cordial interest with which his ministers and the two directors of the Imperial Museum accompanied the progress of the work in Constantinople and at Nuffar, our ways were smoothed everywhere in the Ottoman empire. As often as I needed a firmân, it was readily granted, while besides, His Majesty, desiring to give special proof of his personal satisfaction with the confidence thus established and with the services rendered, most generously and repeatedly bestowed magnificent gifts of antiquities upon the present writer, which subsequently were presented to the University of Pennsylvania, making the scientific value of its Babylonian collections not only equal but in many respects superior to those of the British Museum.

On August 28, 1892, Haynes left America, spending the rest of the year in Europe. In the first week of January, 1893, he landed at Alexandretta and travelled the ordinary route down the Euphrates valley to Baghdad. Towards the middle of March we find him at Hilla. In order to avoid the territory of the Sa'îd and to pay a brief visit to the *qâimmaqâm* of Dîwânîye, he hired three large native boats (*meshhûfs*) and sailed, accompanied by thirty-five skilled laborers and six *zabtîye*, who were to remain with him, through the Daghâra canal to Sûq el-'Afej. Cordially received by Hajji Tarfâ, to whom he presented a gold watch from the committee in recognition of his past services, he appealed again to him for protection during his subsequent

Mud Castle (*Meftûl*) of ‘Abud el-Hamid, Supreme Shaikh of the Six Hamza Tribes

stay at the ruins. The two principal shaikhs of the Hamza, 'Abud el-Hamid and Hamid el-Birjûd, in whose territory the mounds of Nuffar are situated, were summoned to the guest-chamber (*mudhîf*) of the ruler of all the 'Afej. But having carefully laid their own scheme, through which they hoped to squeeze the largest possible revenues out of the pockets of their old friends from beyond "the great upper sea in the West," they did not respond very eagerly to the call of the messenger. When finally they appeared in the course of the following day, both declared that it was utterly impossible to guarantee the safety of the expedition without a permanent guard of forty men from their own tribes. After much haggling the two interested parties agreed upon ten Arabs as a sufficient number to insure the welfare of Haynes and his party. Two hours later the explorer arrived with his boats at Berdi's old village, then governed temporarily by the latter's younger brother, 'Âṣî, with whom he pitched his tents for a few days until he had selected a suitable site for his own camp at Nuffar.

After an absence of nearly three years he walked, on March 20, for the first time again to the ruins, a mile and a half from 'Âṣî's tower and reed huts. As the third expedition was expected to remain considerably longer in the field than either of the two previous ones, it became necessary to erect a more solid structure than mere tents and *ṣarîfas*, a building which should afford coolness in the summer, shelter during the rainstorms, and protection against fire and the thievish inclinations of the Arabs. In the plain to the south of the ruins, not very far from Peters' last enclosure, Haynes marked out a spot, seventy feet long and fifty feet wide, on which, with the aid of his men from Hilla, he constructed a *meftûl* or mud house with sloping walls and without external windows. By the middle of April the primitive but comfortable quarters were finished, combining "the features of a castle, a store-house and a dwelling for the members of the party." And it was "with a perfect delight" that they all spent the first night within real walls, "free from the prying crowds of curious and covetous idlers" who looked upon every box of provisions as being filled with marvellous treasures of gold and silver.

About the same time (April 11) the excavations were started in the enormous ridge which stretches along the southwest bank of the Shatt en-Nîl (VI–VIII on the plan of the ruins, p. 305), not only because it was nearest to the house, but because a large number of tablets had been discovered there by the second expedition. In accordance with instructions received from Philadelphia, this time Haynes employed only a maximum force of fifty to sixty laborers whom he could control without difficulty. Under these circumstances the work proceeded naturally much more slowly than under Peters. Nevertheless before fifteen weeks were over he had collected nearly eight thousand tablets and fragments from his various shafts, tunnels, and trenches. But toward the end of August the inscribed documents began to flow less abundantly, so that he regarded it best to transfer all his men to the temple mound, which he explored till April 4, 1894, without any serious interruption. As we prefer to consider later and coherently the whole archæological work of the three consecutive years which Haynes spent in Babylonia, we confine ourselves at present to a brief statement of the general course of the expedition and of the principal events which affected the life and efficiency of the party during its long sojourn among the 'Afej.

At the beginning of 1894 it seemed for a while uncertain whether the home committee could secure the necessary financial support to authorize the continuation of the Babylonian mission for another year. A special effort was therefore made by several of its members, including the present writer, to raise new funds which should enable the expedition to remain in the field until a certain task had been accomplished. But the telegraph wires between Constantinople and Mosul being broken for almost two weeks, Haynes had left the mounds with about fifty large cases of antiquities (half of them containing slipper-shaped coffins and bricks), before the news of the fortunate turn which things had taken in Philadelphia could reach him. On June 4 he was back again in his trenches at Nuffar. During the few intervening weeks which he spent at Baghdad he had met a young American, Joseph A. Meyer, a graduate student in the department of architecture at the Massachusetts Institute of Technology, Boston, who held a travelling fellowship for two years and was on his way from India to the Mediterranean coast. Beginning to realize by this time that it would be impossible for him to excavate the temple complex, with its many complicated problems, without the constant assistance of a trained architect, Haynes readily induced Meyer to change his plans and to accompany him without a salary for a year to the ruins of Nuffar.

A second time Providence itself, unwilling to see the most renowned sanctuary of all Babylonia cut up and gradually ruined by tunnels and perpendicular shafts, provided the much needed specialist, who through Peters' unfortunate recommendation had been withheld so long from the expedition. Indeed, the young architect seemed eminently qualified for the peculiar duties required of him. He was deeply interested in the historical branch of his science; he had gathered considerable practical experience through his study of the ancient monuments in Europe, Egypt, Turkey and India; he was an accurate draughtsman and enthusiastically devoted to his subject; and, further than this, he proved a genial and faithful companion to Haynes, who after his last year's isolation from all educated men naturally longed for a personal exchange of thoughts and the uplifting association with a sympathetic countryman, to whom he could speak in his own language. The influence of Meyer's active mind and technical knowledge upon the work at Nuffar was felt immediately. Haynes' reports, previously and afterwards often lacking in clearness and conciseness and devoted more to the description of threatening dangers, illness of the servants, and other interesting though secondary questions than to the exposition of archæological facts, aimed now at setting forth the characteristic features of the work in which he was engaged and at illustrating the weekly progress of the excavations by accompanying measurements, diagrams, and drawings. In order to derive the greatest benefit for the expedition from Meyer's presence, the exploration of the temple mound was made the principal object of their united efforts, and with the exception of a few weeks in September, all the laborers were concentrated around the *ziggurrat*. The trenches grew deeper every day, and Ashurbânapal's lofty terraces rose gradually out of the encumbering mass of later additions. The hot and trying Babylonian summer, more uncomfortable and inconvenient than dangerous to health, passed by without any noteworthy incident. But when the cooler nights indicated the approaching fall and brought with them the usual colds and chills frequently complicated by dysentery and malarial poisoning of the human system, Meyer's weakened body proved unequal to the demands made upon it.

At the end of September his physical powers of endurance gradually gave way. For seven weeks more he endeavored hard to overcome the effects of the malignant disease and remained faithfully at his post. By the end of November his condition had become so critical that notwithstanding the extraordinary hardships of the journey, it became necessary to convey him by boat to Hilla and from there in a covered litter to Baghdad. But his case was beyond human aid long before he left Nuffar. On December 20, 1894, he died in the house of Dr. Sundberg, Haynes' successor as United States consul at Baghdad, like

George Smith having fallen a brave soldier in the cause of science. He was buried in the little European cemetery of the city on the banks of the Tigris. In the course of time the sandstorms of 'Irâq may efface his solitary grave. But what matters it? His bones rest in classic soil, where the cradle of the race once stood, and the history of the resurrection of ancient Babylonia will not omit his name from its pages.

The reaction of this sudden and serious loss upon the mind and activity of Haynes was soon apparent. He was alone once more on the vast ruins of an inhospitable region, directing his workmen in the trenches by day and developing negatives or packing antiquities at his " castle " in the evening. Feeling his inability to continue the exploration of the temple mound without technical advice and assistance, he wisely transferred his entire force to the southeastern extremity of the previously mentioned ridge on the other side of the canal (VI) and undertook to unearth a sufficient quantity of tablets to meet Peters' growing demands for inscribed material. He was successful again beyond expectation. At the beginning of January, 1895, he had gathered several thousand tablets and fragments and had obtained a fair collection of pottery, seal cylinders, domestic implements, and personal ornaments mostly found in the loose earth or taken from graves in which the upper twenty feet of rubbish abound everywhere at Nuffar. But unfortunately his methods of excavating and his weekly reports began to show the same deficiencies which characterized them before Meyer's timely arrival. We learn from them little beyond the fact that a larger or smaller " lot of tablets," enough to fill so and so many " cases of the usual size," had been discovered. Here and there an especially interesting antiquity or the number of tombs opened and the coffins prepared for transport are mentioned. Occasionally we even meet with some such statement as: " In nearly all of the trenches crude bricks, eleven inches square and four inches thick, occur. They are finely modelled bricks, and are firm and solid, as they are taken from their walls. They are the prettiest crude bricks I have anywhere seen." But we look in vain for an attempt to describe these remarkable walls, to trace their course, to measure their dimensions, to draw their ground plan, or to ascertain the prominent features and original purpose of the rooms and houses which he was clearing all the while of their contents.

It was the depressive and enervating effect of the solitude of the Babylonian desert and marshes which began seriously to tell upon Haynes. The rapidly growing fear of constant danger from "greedy" and revengeful Arabs, which was the natural outcome of the former, took hold of him in an alarming manner. "The great strain of maintaining security of life and property is a weariness to the flesh." "The atmosphere is thickening with danger, and I have been compelled to appeal to the governor general of Baghdad for protection." "I am getting worn out with the very intensity of the increasing strain and struggle." "I have never seen the time at Nuffar when the danger was so great as it is in these wearisome days of intrigue and fanaticism, of murder and robbing." These are only a few of the sentences which I quote from as many different letters written in February and March, 1895. Three years later Haynes viewed the conditions around Nuffar more calmly and in a more objective light, for he did not hesitate for a moment to take his wife among the same Arabs. And it is a remarkable fact, deserving special notice, that in all the ten years during which the expedition has owned its house (*meftûl*) at the edge of the Babylonian swamps, no attempt has ever been made to open its door, to cut a hole into its walls, or to steal its furniture and stores, whether the building was occupied or left to the care of the neighboring tribes.

There can be no doubt that excavations carried on in the

territory of the warlike ʻAfej or in other remote districts of ʻIrâq el-ʻArabî are even to-day beset with certain dangers, for the greater part unknown to explorers of ruins like Babylon, Abû Habba, Tellô, and others which are situated near the caravan road or larger towns protected by a strong garrison. The experience gathered by the first two Philadelphia expeditions, and the stories told by different travellers who visited Nuffar prove it sufficiently. But conditions have considerably changed from what they previously were, and every year the feeling of the Arabs has grown more friendly towards us. In 1894 Haynes could state with great satisfaction that the entire community from shaikh to the humblest individual openly rejoiced over his speedy return, ascribing the copious rains, the abundant crops, and all other blessings to his presence among them. Besides Hajji Tarfâ himself, the powerful and renowned chief of all the ʻAfej, had guaranteed the safety of the new expedition. And further than this, the two principal shaikhs of the Hamza had furnished the necessary guards, while the Ottoman government had stationed six *zabtîye* at the mounds, ready to increase their number at any time. The only real cause for anxiety was our blood-feud with the Saʻîd, but a pair of boots and a bright-colored garment which soon after his arrival in 1893 Haynes had sent as a present to their shaikh Ṣigab (generally pronounced Ṣugub), had been favorably received by him, and seem to have reconciled his tribesmen temporarily, for the explorer was never molested by them during his long stay at Nuffar.

And yet in further explanation of Haynes' extraordinary state of nervousness, it must not be forgotten that the peculiar climate and the frequent unforeseen disturbances of the country where conditions and persons sometimes change kaleidoscopically, require the full attention of every foreigner at all times, especially when he is alone, as Haynes generally was during the third campaign. In the first summer of his long stay he was greatly hampered in his movements through the repeated illness of his servants, while at the same time cholera was reported to be advancing from Nasrîye and Hilla. It really never reached the camp, but the mere anticipation of a possible outbreak of the dreaded disease weighed heavily upon him. Moreover, the Arabs were frequently on the war path. Sometimes the whole region around Daghâra and Sûq el-'Afej was in a state of great unrest and excitement, no less than fifteen or sixteen petty wars being carried on between the various tribes within one year. One day the 'Afej quarrelled with the Elbûdêr, who lived to the south of the swamps, about disputed lands. Another time the Hamza were at loggerheads with Hajji Tarfâ over revenues from certain rice fields. Then again the former fought with the Behahtha on some other matter. And at the beginning of December, 1893, when the capital of the *sanjak* was transferred from Hilla to Dîwânîye, to protect the newly acquired crown property of the Sultan near Daghâra and Sûq el-'Afej, and to reduce the rebellious 'Afej to submission, an unusually hot battle took place between the latter and the Behahtha, in which seventy-one warriors were slain. Though the sound of firing could often be heard in the trenches of Nuffar, these turmoils never threatened the safety of the expedition in a serious way, and they affected its efficiency directly only in so far as it became sometimes difficult to find a neutral messenger to carry the weekly mail through the infested territory, or to obtain suitable substitutes for native basket men, who in obedience to the summons of their shaikhs would suddenly throw down their peaceful implements, seize their clubs and antiquated matchlocks, improvise a war-song, and with loud yells run away to the assistance of their fighting comrades.

It unfortunately happened also that in the years 1894 and 1895 the 'Afej swamps, always a favorite place of refuge, a regular land of Nod (Gen. 4 : 16), for dissatisfied elements and the doubtful characters of modern Babylonia, harbored a famous Kurdish outlaw and bold robber, Captain (*yüs-bashi*) Ahmed Bey, a deserter from the Turkish army, who during eighteen months terrorized all travellers between Hilla and Baghdad and extended his unlawful excursions even to the districts of Kûd(t) el-'Amâra on the banks of the Tigris, until after many futile efforts on the part of the government he was finally captured and killed by an Arab. In order to prevent any combined action against himself by the consuls, he had been very careful never to attack any foreigner. It is therefore reasonably certain to assume that he would not have dared to molest an American who, moreover, was the especial *protégé* and guest of the same tribes with whom he generally hid himself and his plunder. But troubled in mind as Haynes was in those days by the weight of responsibility and by numerous other causes, the temporary presence of the Kurd in the neighborhood of Nuffar increased his nervous condition and sleeplessness to such a degree that he smelled danger and complots against his life everywhere, and, to quote his own words, looked upon "every bush as concealing a waiting robber." What wonder that under these circumstances the daily petty annoyances from the good-natured and hard-working but undisplined laborers, who frequently behaved more like a crowd of frolicsome and naughty children than like real men, began to worry him beyond measure; that their occasional small pilferings of seal cylinders; a short-lived and almost ridiculous strike of the native basketmen misled by a disloyal overseer from Jumjuma; the broken leg of a foreman injured by falling bricks, or the more serious sudden cave-in of a deep undermined trench and the subsequent death of another workman — occurrences familiar to him from the previous expeditions — should in his mind assume an importance entirely out of proportion to their real significance.

The committee at home was not slow in recognizing the real cause of this growing melancholy on the part of its delegate at Nuffar, and the detrimental influence which it began to exercise upon the work of the archæological mission entrusted to him. At first favorably impressed with the contents of the reports and the character of the drawings received during the six months of Haynes' and Meyer's common activity on the ruins, it had authorized the two explorers to continue their excavations till February, 1896, a decision which was in entire accord with the former's frequently expressed personal desire. But at the end of March, 1895, when it became fully aware of all the details which threatened to undermine the health of its representative, it advised him by cable to return at once to America for rest, and to resume his work later. However, the encouragement drawn from the committee's sympathetic letters, the brief visit of an Englishman returning from India to London by way of Nuffar, and the approaching spring with its new life and tonic air seem to have revived Haynes' depressed spirits so completely that he now viewed the danger as practically over, and immediately asked permission to remain a year longer among the 'Afej, at the same time earnestly pleading for a postponement of the announced despatch of an architect until another expedition should be organized. This last-mentioned recommendation, well meant as it doubtless was, could not be received favorably in Philadelphia, where every member of the board of the expedition by that time understood the need of having specialists in the field to assist Haynes. Mr. E. W. Clark began to take matters into his own hands, and a sub-committee consisting of himself and the present writer, later increased by the addition of the treasurer, Mr. John Sparhawk, Jr., was appointed to engage the services of an experienced architect, and to devise such other means as should lead to more efficient and scientific exploration of the ruins and to the complete success of the expedition. This committee has been in session at stated times until the present day.

In the meanwhile Haynes continued to deepen his trenches and to extend his tunnels in the long ridge on the west side of the ancient canal as fast as he could, endeavoring to exhaust the supply of tablets in this section sufficiently to create the general impression at the time of his departure that no more tablets were to be found at Nuffar. For the constant rumors of whole donkey loads of tablets passing through Sûq el-'Afej[1] on their way from Tellô, and the great eagerness with which, in many places, Arabs had abandoned their flocks and cultivation for the more profitable secret diggings at De Sarzec's inexhaustible ruin, where the business archives of the temple had been found almost intact, foreshadowed the fate of every other Babylonian ruin upon which the antiquity dealers of Hilla and Baghdad might cast their covetous eyes. By the middle of July the proper moment seemed to have come to withdraw all the workmen from those attractive mounds which had been Haynes' great tablet mine in the past, yielding him nearly nineteen thousand inscriptions in the course of the third expedition. About the sixth part of these documents represents complete tablets, while the other fifteen thousand are more or less damaged and mutilated, including many fragments of very small size.

The last half year of the period set apart for the exploration of Nuffar commenced. It was devoted almost exclu-

[1] Before the Arabs understood the full value of these treasures, they sold them at ridiculously low prices to the dealers, who sometimes made 5,000 per cent., and even considerably more, on them. According to exaggerated rumors, a woman was doing the marketing for her tribesmen, selling the tablets at the uniform rate of a *qûfa* (a round boat) full for one Persian *krân*, then worth about two and a half Turkish piastres, or eleven cents in United States currency. This clandestine business continued at Tellô, until at Hamdy Bey's representation the government ordered the "tablet mine" to be closed, and even placed a temporary guard over it.

sively to an examination of the southeastern part of Bint el-Amîr (I). Only for a fortnight in the middle of the summer Haynes transferred his entire force in the morning hours regularly to the narrow ridge of mounds (II–III) which confine the large open space to the northwest of the *ziggurrat*, in order to determine the foundations of the great wall wherein he and' Meyer in the previous year had discovered crude bricks with the name of Narâm-Sin. Owing to the relative height of the stage-tower and the enormous mass of Parthian ruins grouped around it, and no less owing to Haynes' peculiar method of excavating the lowest strata of the open court beneath them, it became more and more wearisome for the basketmen to climb the rude steps and steep roads leading from the interior of the hollowed mound to the dumping places on the top of the neighboring ruins. The photographs of the indefatigable explorer illustrated his remarkable progress in clearing the lower temple court of more than sixty thousand cubic feet of earth, but they also revealed the alarming growth of important unexplored sections of the adjoining mounds. These were high enough in themselves, but they were raised fifty to eighty feet higher by the rubbish deposited on them, so that their future excavation threatened to become a serious problem (comp. the frontispiece).

After many fruitless endeavors the committee had succeeded in despatching two young Englishmen to Babylonia at the beginning of October. They had served for a little while under Flinders Petrie in Egypt, and seemed to be fairly well prepared for the more difficult labors awaiting them at Nuffar. They had received instructions to work several weeks under Haynes, until they were generally acquainted with the mounds, the history of our past excavations, the country and the manners of the Arabs, upon whose good will the success of the expedition largely depended. At the same time our representative at the ruins was requested to initiate his assistants properly into their various duties, and then to leave them in charge of the field, and to return for a vacation to America, until the time should have come for his resumption of the work in company with the two Englishmen and such other assistants as the committee might deem necessary to send out with him. In consequence of quarantine and other delays, the two substitutes unfortunately did not arrive at Nuffar before February, 1896, about the same time when he whom they were expected to relieve had planned to depart from the country. Much to our astonishment and regret, Haynes did not find it advisable to execute the instructions of his committee, but induced the two young men, after they had spent a few days at the ruins, to return with him to Europe, as he regarded it "both unwise and emphatically unsafe to commit the property and work to the care of any young man who has not had a long experience in this place, and with this self-same defiant, covetous, treacherous, and bloody throng about us."

In examining Haynes' three years' labors with regard to his methods, discoveries and views on the latter, as they are laid down in his weekly reports to the committee and illustrated by numerous photographs and Meyer's drawings, we must not forget that, like Peters, he was no expert in architecture, Assyriology, or archæology, and, therefore, could furnish only raw material for the use of the specialist. He will always deserve great credit for having demonstrated for the first time, by his own example, that it is possible to excavate a Babylonian ruin even during the hottest part of the year without any serious danger to the life of the explorer. With an interruption of but two months, and most of the time alone, he spent three consecutive years "near the insect-breeding and pestiferous 'Afej swamps, where the temperature in perfect shade rises to the enormous height of 120° Fahrenheit, and the stifling sand-storms from the desert often parch the human skin with the heat of a furnace, while the ever-present insects bite and sting and buzz through day and night." Surrounded by turbulent tribes and fugitive criminals, he worked steadfastly and patiently towards a noble aim; he even clung to his post with remarkable tenacity and great self-denial when his lonely life and a morbid fear of real and imagined dangers threatened to impair his health and obscured his judgment. But on the other hand, he also illustrated anew by his example that even the most enthusiastic explorer, cautious in his course of proceeding, accustomed to climate, and familiar with the life and manners of the natives, as he may be, is plainly unable to excavate a Babylonian ruin satisfactorily without the necessary technical knowledge and the constant advice of an architect and Assyriologist. Haynes' principal mistake lies in the fact that, in accordance with Peters' unfortunate proposition, he consented to imitate the latter's example with regard to the methods of excavation, and to dwell and to dig at Nuffar alone without educated technical assistance; and furthermore that when the committee as a whole, realizing the impossibility of such an undertaking, called him home or proposed to send him assistance, he preferred to remain in the field and declined the latter.

According to the manner of Rassam and Peters, Haynes gathered an exceedingly large number of valuable antiquities, he removed an enormous mass of rubbish, he made us acquainted with a great many details of the interior of the mounds, he worked diligently in exposing walls, following drains and uncovering platforms. But these discoveries remained isolated and incoherent. It was frequently impossible to combine them and to obtain even a moderately accurate picture of the temple of Bêl by means of his reports in the form in which they were written.[1] Often unable to

[1] At the time these reports were received, it was naturally understood that they were only preliminary letters written under peculiarly trying circum-

Well built of Bricks and Two Terra-Cotta Drains

Descending from the floor of a Parthian tomb

distinguish between essentials and secondary matters, or failing to recognize the significance of certain small traces occurring in the loose débris or represented by fragmentary walls which are of paramount importance to the archæologist, he would remove them without attempting to give their accurate location and description, and occasionally allow his imagination to become an inadequate substitute for sober facts and simple measurements by feet and inches. In consequence of these peculiarities his reports frequently enough present almost as many puzzles as Nuffar itself, and require their own excavation, through which the original details furnished by the trenches scarcely improve. What with Meyer's aid he submitted concerning the *ziggurrat* of Ashurbânapal,[1] its dimensions, conduits, etc., was on the whole correct and in many ways excellent. It showed what Haynes might have accomplished in addition to the unearthing of the numerous tablets, sarcophagi, drains, and walls which we owe to his untiring efforts, had he been assisted properly. We must keep this in mind in order to explain, and to a certain degree excuse his methods and subsequent one-sided results, but also to understand, in part at least, why the picture of the temple of Bêl, which I drew in 1896 on the basis

stances, and that all the scientific details required to complete them would be found in the books of entry, exhaustive diaries and many other note-books, as they are usually kept by every expedition. It became apparent, however, in 1900, that no such books existed, and that these weekly or fortnightly letters represented all the written information which Haynes had to give on his long work of three years. I am still inclined to explain this strange fact to a certain degree by his mental depression referred to above, though, to my sincere regret, the words of praise as to the character of his work, so liberally expressed in my introduction to "The Bab. Exp. of the Univ. of Pa.," series A, vol. i, part 2 (Philadelphia, 1896), pp. 16, *seqq.*, will have to be modified considerably.

[1] Not of Ur-Gur, as on the basis of Haynes' reports was stated in my first tentative sketch of the *ziggurrat*, "The Bab. Exp. of the Univ. of Pa.," series A, vol. i, part 2, pp. 16, *seqq.*

of his reports, is inaccurate and differs considerably from what I have to present below after my personal visit to the ruins in 1900, when I had an opportunity to study the architectural remains as far as they were still preserved, and to submit all the tunnels and trenches of my predecessors to a critical examination.

As indicated above, Haynes excavated chiefly at two places during his long stay at Nuffar, devoting about eighteen months to Bint el-Amîr (I), which represents the ancient *ziggurrat*, and twelve to the long furrowed ridge situated on the southwest side of the canal and defined by the numbers VI and VIII respectively on the plan of the ruins (comp. p. 305), while two to three months were allowed for the exploration of several other sections, including a search for the original bed of the Shatt en-Nîl. In order to enable the reader to follow his work on the stage-tower with greater facility, I shall classify and consider it in the following order: *a*, His examination of a part of the latest constructions; *b*, his clearing of the stage-tower of Ashurbânapal; *c*, his excavation of three sections on the southeast court of the *ziggurrat* down to the water level.

a. In continuing Peters' work on the temple mound, Haynes committed the same grave error, to start with, as the first director of the expedition. He descended to the successive Babylonian strata by means of deep shafts, and cleared important sections even down to the virgin soil, before the uppermost imposing structure had been excavated completely and methodically. This is the more remarkable as Haynes, like his predecessor, regarded this gigantic settlement around the remodelled *ziggurrat* not as an entirely new Parthian creation, as the present writer did, but as the latest historical development of the famous sanctuary of Bêl at the time of "the second Babylonian empire," or about the period 600–550 B. C., — reason

Perpendicular Drain composed of Jars. About 200 B. C.

enough to treat it with special reverence and to examine it with the greatest care. In consequence of his strange procedure he could not help destroying essential details of all the different strata which later were missing, and at the same time to report other discoveries inaccurately and incoherently. It became, therefore, exceedingly difficult, and in many cases impossible, for me to determine and to arrange the defective results of all these perpendicular cuttings, with their eight to ten different strata, in a satisfactory manner, the more so as they often had been obtained at long intervals, and as a rule were unaccompanied by even the poorest kind of sketch or ground plan, while the portable antiquities had never been numbered to allow of their identification with certainty afterwards.

In spite of the plainly un-Babylonian character of the large crude bricks which constitute the bulk of the latest fortified walls around the *ziggurrat*, Haynes regarded them with Peters as the work of Ur-Gur, differing, however, from him in one important point, by declaring at least a large part of the southeast enclosing wall as the work "of the first rebuilder of the *ziggurrat* in cruciform style [about 600 B. C.]." He removed a number of rooms in the east corner of this settlement, and as Meyer fortunately was on the ground a few months later, we have a well executed plan of these chambers in addition to a few sketches and a general description of their principal features and contents by Haynes. The two explorers came to the interesting conclusion, confirmed later by my inspection of the few remains of their trenches, that three different periods are clearly to be distinguished with regard to their occupancy. They also make us acquainted with the exact dimensions of these rooms and their mutual relation to each other, with the average thickness and height of their ruined walls, with certain important details of their doors, with their drainage and ventilation and several fireplaces discovered in them. Apart from a few stray Babylonian antiquities which later may have been used again, all the typical objects gathered in these rooms are decidedly later than 300 B. C., as I convinced myself by a careful investigation. Among the objects betraying an undoubtedly Greek influence I only mention several fragments of a cornice in limestone representing the vine-branch, well known from the so-called sarcophagus of Alexander the Great, and the stamped handle of a Rhodian amphora bearing the inscription ΕΠΙ ΘΕΑΙΔΗΤΟΥ ΒΑΤΡΟΜΙΟΥ, *i. e.*, "[this amphora was made or gauged] under [the eponymous magistrate] Theaidetos in [the month of] Badromios."[1] According to Professor Furtwängler of Munich, to whom I submitted a photograph of the last mentioned antiquity, this magistrate is known from other similar handles found on the isle of Rhodes itself,[2] and must have lived in the second or first century preceding our era. The same scholar confirmed my conclusions with regard to the age of the characteristic terra-cotta figurines previously described (comp. pp. 330, *seq.*), which I had unhesitatingly assigned to the Parthian, *i. e.*, the Hellenistic and Roman periods.

The removal of the enormous mass of crude bricks with which the builders of this latest settlement had covered, changed, and enlarged the old stage-tower of Bêl was a slow and tedious task. But it was not without interesting results. Babylonian antiquities of the Cassite, and even much earlier times, were repeatedly discovered inside these bricks. Their comparatively fine state of preservation, their frequent occurrence, and, in a few cases, their large size, proved sufficiently that they had not gotten accidentally into these walls, while the long period of about two thousand

[1] The T in the name of the month as offered by the inscription is a mistake of the scribe, as Furtwängler informs me.

[2] Comp. Hiller de Gaertringen, *Inscriptiones Græcæ insularum Rhodi*, etc., 1895, No. 1135.

years represented by them, their character and their inscriptions, indicated in some manner how and where they had been obtained. Most of them came from the temple complex, where they had been found when the ground was levelled and important early structures destroyed to furnish welcome building material for the later descendants of the ancient population. All the objects unearthed had been gathered scrupulously, for they were no less valued in those days than they are to-day by the modern inhabitants of the country. They were either sold as raw material to engravers and jewellers (comp. p. 335), or worn as personal ornaments, or converted into useful household implements, or used as talismans which protected the living and the dead alike against the evil influence of demons. We found inscribed tablets, seal cylinders, and other Babylonian antiquities of the most different periods very commonly in and around the Parthian and Sassanian urns, coffins and tombs of Nuffar. These discoveries ofttimes led Peters and Haynes astray in their efforts to prove the Babylonian character of these burials and to support their startling theories concerning the age and the different types of ancient pottery. But they also occur in platforms, under thresholds, in the foundations of houses, inside numerous bricks, as stated above, and for very simple reasons, especially frequently in the mortar uniting the latter. No wonder that Haynes discovered them in considerable quantities in the clay mortar of the fortified palace which rests on the ruins of the ancient temple, thereby unconsciously establishing an exact parallel to De Sarzec's results in the upper strata of the temple mound at Tellô (comp. pp. 226, *seqq.*, particularly pp. 232, *seq.*), and at the same time providing further evidence against his own personal view of the signification of these antiquities.

In addition to their talismanic character many of the objects deposited seem to have carried with them the idea of a sacrifice or an act of devotion on the part of their donors to secure greater stability for this public building, to express gratitude for an unknown successful transaction, or to obtain the favor of the gods for the fulfilment of a certain desire. In the light of such votive offerings I view a collection of antiquities discovered together in the foundation of the latest southeast enclosing wall and comprising a Persian seal, a Babylonian seal cylinder, a pair of silver earrings, eleven pieces of corroded silver, about forty silver beads and three hundred odd stone beads, which apparently represent the gift of a woman; or the goose-egg with its undeveloped germ of life to be sacrificed (comp. p. 332),[1] and, above all, a surprising find which was made on the northwestern side of the *ziggurrat*. Imbedded in the mortar of clay and straw that filled a large space between Ashurbânapal's stage-tower and its later addition Haynes uncovered three human skulls placed on the same level at nearly equal distances from each other. There can be no doubt that we here have an authentic example of the practice of bloody sacrifices offered in connection with the construction of important new buildings, — a practice widely existing in the ancient world and prevailing even to-day in several parts of the Orient.[2]

b. The labor that would have been required to clear the original Babylonian stage-tower entirely of the later additions will be easily understood by considering that more than one hundred thousand cubic feet of tenacious *lib*(*e*)*n*, or mud bricks, and other accumulated rubbish had to be removed before only one of the four huge arms which proceeded from the centres of the four sides of the ancient *ziggurrat* far into the court had disappeared, — a fact sufficiently illustrating the remarkable power and energy of these

[1] Peters, failing to recognize the meaning of this class of antiquities, comes to the remarkable conclusion (*l. c.*, vol. ii., p. 123), that "some humorous or mischievous workman had walled it in two thousand years or so ago."

[2] Comp. H. Clay Trumbull, "The Blood Covenant," 2d edition, Philadelphia, 1893, and "The Threshold Covenant," New York, 1896.

Northwestern Façade of the Ziggurrat as restored by Ashurbânapal about 650 B. C.

Parthian rulers, who were able to erect similar castles on the top of most of the large temple ruins in the country. In view of the great difficulties in his way, Haynes confined himself to a complete removal of the southeastern wing, cutting away only so much of the other three arms as was absolutely necessary to disengage the earlier building from its surrounding brickwork by means of narrow perpendicular trenches. Applied to the huge massive lateral arms alone, this method was doubtless correct, as it saved considerable time and expense, and did not deprive us of any essential knowledge for the time being. But as soon as it was carried further than this it became incompatible with a systematic investigation of the entire mound. These dimly lighted narrow corridors prevented the photographing of important details of the lowest story of the stage-tower, while at the same time they gave cause for Haynes' further descent into the depth, before the rest of the sacred enclosure had received proper attention. Consequently it was impossible until very recently to determine the precise relation of the *ziggurrat* to the temple with which it formed an organic whole, or even to find out what the entire court around the former looked like at any given period of its long and varied history. As a matter of fact, the following picture presented itself to me upon my arrival at Nuffar in 1900. The crumbling remains of the *ziggurrat* had been exposed to the level of the period of Kadashman-Turgu, large sections in its neighborhood were explored only to the level of the Parthian fortress, others had not been touched at all, again others were cleared to the platform of Ur-Gur, still others down to the upper Pre-Sargonic remains, while by far the greater part of the large place in front of the stage-tower, which contained a number of brick pavements, serving as an excellent means for dating the different strata of the whole enclosure, had been excavated down to the virgin soil (comp. frontispiece). At one time

Haynes himself very keenly felt the unsatisfactory manner in which he was proceeding. For in one of his reports of 1894, written during Meyer's presence at the ruins, we read the significant passage: "I should like to see systematic excavations undertaken on this temple enclosure, not to be excavated section by section, but carried down as a whole, to distinguish the different epochs of its history, each well defined level to be thoroughly explored, sketched, photographed, and described, before the excavation of any part should be carried to a lower level. This method would be more satisfactory and less likely to lead to confusion of strata and levels." We naturally ask in amazement: Though knowing the better method, why did he never adopt it at a time when he was in complete charge of the expedition in the field, and the committee at home ready to support him with all the necessary technical assistance?

In tracing the upper stages of the *ziggurrat*, Haynes discovered the fragment of a barrel cylinder inscribed with the cuneiform signs characteristic of the period of the last great Assyrian kings (722–626 B. C.). It belonged to Sargon or Ashurbânapal, both of whom took part in restoring the temple of Bêl. Small as it was, it proved that documents of this kind once existed at Nuffar, as they did in other Babylonian stage-towers. But in order to determine the number and size of the upper stories, which no longer had facing walls of baked brick, the explorer had to proceed from the better-preserved lowest one. For the later occupants of the temple mound, while utilizing all the other baked material of the older building for their own purposes, had evidently been obliged to leave the panelled walls of baked bricks in the lowest story standing in order to prevent the gradual collapse of the heavy mass above it. More than this, they had trimmed its corners and repaired other defective places, as could easily be recognized from the bricks there employed and their use of clay mortar instead of bitumen, the common binding material of all the baked bricks of the *ziggurrat* found still *in situ*. This circumstance explains why even the lowest stage of the tower yielded us no building records, though Haynes continued to search for them.

Most of the stamped bricks taken from this story bore the Old Babylonian inscription: "To Bêl, the king of the lands, his king, Ashurbânapal, his favorite shepherd, the powerful king, king of the four quarters of the earth, built Ekur, his beloved temple, with baked bricks." Intermingled with them were bricks of Kadashman-Turgu (about 1300 B. C.) and Ur-Gur (about 2700 B. C.), the latter's name occurring in the lowest courses frequently to the exclusion of all others. It was therefore clear that each subsequent restorer of the tower had made extensive use of the material of his predecessors, thereby enabling us to fix at least the principal periods of this monumental structure. But some of the royal builders had not been satisfied with a mere repairing of cracks and replacing of walls; they at the same time had enlarged the original size of the tower. This fact was disclosed by a trench cut into the northeast face of the *ziggurrat*, where Haynes discovered the fragmentary remains of Ur-Gur's casing wall six feet behind the outside of Ashurbânapal's. The southeast façade alone seems to have remained unchanged for more than two thousand years; for all the inscribed bricks removed from this neighborhood exhibited the name of the ancient king of Ur on their lower faces, a sure indication that they were still in their original position. What is the reason for the unique preservation of this particular side during such a long period? Two almost parallel walls, constructed by the same monarch and running at right angles from the southeast face of the *ziggurrat* into the large open court, acted as a kind of buttress and prevented an uneven settling of the ponderous mass behind and above it. But this was not their original and chief purpose. Certain projections of the second stage over this so-called causeway,[1] which are absent from the other three sides of the pyramid, prove conclusively that here we have the last remains of the ancient approach to the top of the *ziggurrat*. A door-socket in dolerite inscribed with the ordinary votive legend of Ur-Gur was found at the foot of this stairway, while a stray soapstone tablet of the same king came from a room of the Parthian fortress considerably above it.

The excavation of the southwest and northeast façades were no less important for our knowledge of the architectural details of the *ziggurrat*. Both contained deep and well-built conduits in their centres, designed to carry the profuse water of the Babylonian autumn and winter rains from the higher stories over the foundations of the lowest encasement walls into a gutter which surrounded all but the front sides of the high-towering building. Loftus' so-called "buttresses" of the Buwêrîye at Warkâ, "erected on the centre of each side for the purpose of supporting the main edifice" (comp. p. 146, above), are evidently nothing but such water conduits, misunderstood by him, and the remains of an entrance to the top of the tower. If we can rely upon Haynes' examination, the southwest conduit was the exclusive work of Ur-Gur, except at the bottom, where it had repeatedly been filled and paved to discharge the water at a higher level in accordance with the gradual rising of the court below. The northeast conduit, on the other hand, goes back only to Ashurbânapal, who repaired the conduit of Kadashman-Turgu, placed over the older one of Ur-Gur.

[1] Haynes did not recognize the significance of these projections for the whole question of the original ascent, but, substituting his lively fantasy again for an accurate description, imagines that "a sacred shrine or altar may have stood at the far end of the causeway," or "that the officiating priest may at times have harangued the people in the great court below him from that height." What a conception of a Babylonian temple!

Water Conduit built by King Ur-Gur, 2700 B. C.

In the southwestern façade of the ziggurat

It is Haynes' view, as reproduced by me in 1896, that, with the exception of the lowest front face and the two conduits, Ur-Gur's *ziggurrat* was built entirely of crude bricks, and that even at the time of the Cassite and Assyrian occupations the upper stories had no casing walls of baked bricks. This theory seems to me untenable. For there are many indications which necessarily lead to the conclusion that the whole pyramid, from the time of Ur-Gur down to Ashurbânapal, was properly protected. I cannot go into details here. To mention only one circumstance, it would be impossible to explain the presence of so many stamped bricks of Ur-Gur, found out of their original position everywhere in the ruins of Nuffar, except on the assumption of a casing wall for every stage of the *ziggurrat*. It was only natural that the bricks of the earlier builders should be removed by the later monarchs before they repaired and enlarged the temple. But the very fact that the material of Ashurbânapal's casing walls of the lowest story consists largely of bricks of Ur-Gur and Kadashman-Turgu, and that the construction of the Seleucido-Parthian rulers contained a great number of stamped and unstamped bricks of all the three Babylonian kings mentioned, is alone sufficient evidence to demonstrate that the entire outside of the *ziggurrat* must have been built of baked bricks.

While working towards the second stage from the upper edge of the lowest story, Haynes discovered the opening of a large well in the centre of its northeast façade and partly overlapping the ancient conduit. It was built of baked bricks, and descended through the crude mass of the stage-tower down to the water level. Though unable to determine its age and special purpose at this remarkable place, Haynes was inclined to ascribe it to Ashurbânapal. But this is impossible. In connection with my subsequent visit to the ruins, I could prove conclusively that this well did not belong to the *ziggurrat* proper, but was constructed of Kadashman-Turgu's and Ashurbânapal's material by the Seleucido-Parthian princes, who selected this peculiar place in order to obtain the coolest water possible and to secure its supply for the highest part of their castle, even in case the lower palace should have been taken by an enemy.

A word remains to be said about the interior and the upper stages of the *ziggurrat*. The large body of the high-towering building consisted of crude bricks nine by six by three inches in size. They represent the standard dimension of Ur-Gur's material, but they were already in use before his time. For bricks of the same size and form, but different in color (the latter being yellowish, the former gray), were discovered in the lower courses of the interior of the *ziggurrat*.[1]

Apart from the unusually large adobes employed by the Parthian builders and completely covering and embedding the ancient stage-tower, there is only one other kind of crude bricks traceable in its upper part, which may belong to one of the Cassite rulers or to Ashurbânapal. This fact will scarcely surprise us, since little is left of the higher stages of the *ziggurrat*. We can state with certainty only that Haynes found considerable remains of a sloping second terrace, largely ruined in the centre of its southwest and northeast façades, where apparently water conduits, similar to those of the first story, previously existed, and that he believes himself to have discovered faint traces of a third story. The amount of rubbish accumulated on the top of the second stage is comparatively small. But this circumstance does not constitute an argument against the assumption of more than three stages. It only testifies to the rapid disintegration of crude bricks after they had been exposed to the combined action of heavy rains and extraordinary heat, and to the remarkable changes which the *ziggurrat* under-

[1] Comp. what is said below, p. 390, in connection with the two treasury vaults opening into the pavements of Ur-Gur and Narâm-Sin.

Parthian Well in the Centre of the Northeast Façade of Ashurbânapal's Stage-Tower

The opening of the well was originally at a much higher level

went at the hands of the occupants of the latest castle, who practically turned the Babylonian ruin into a huge cruciform terrace with an additional central elevation or watch-tower.

c. The excavation of the southeast court of the *ziggurrat* forms the most interesting though the most pernicious part of Haynes' work on the temple of Bêl. He accomplished it in his own manner during the last half year of his stay at the ruins by dividing the whole space into four sections and clearing three of them by as many large perpendicular shafts from the walls of the Parthian rooms down to the virgin soil. The fourth had been excavated only to the brick pavement of Ashurbânapal, when he departed from Nuffar on February 19, 1896. Whatever seemed important enough at the different altitudes, he left standing, supporting the uncovered remains of the past by solid pillars of earth, or by artificial arches cut out of the rubbish below them. In consequence of this unique method of operation, the southeast section of the temple court, as seen in the frontispiece, looks as picturesque and attractive as possible, while in reality it presents a picture of utter confusion and devastation to the archæologist. In sketching Haynes' work, therefore, I can only attempt to set forth certain striking features of the different strata which I have been able to develop out of his incoherent and frequently contradictory reports, and to give a brief description of some of the more important antiquities discovered by him. For the sake of greater clearness we take a pavement of Sargon and Narâm-Sin, which extends through a considerable part of the mound, as a dividing line, and examine the ruins which lie above it first, and afterwards those which were hidden below it.

1. *Post-Sargonic Ruins.* The rubbish which filled the court between the platform just mentioned and the bottom of the stratum of well-packed earth, prepared by the Seleucido-Parthian princes as a foundation for their fortified

palace, was about sixteen to seventeen feet high, or a little less than the remains of buildings above the latter, which represent the post-Babylonian history of Nippur. This mass of débris accumulated within a period of more than three thousand years (3800–350 B. C.), was graduated to a certain degree, if I may use this graphic expression. For a number of pavements, running almost parallel with that of Narâm-Sin, divided it into as many horizontal layers of different depth and importance. At the time of excavation none of these pavements were complete, for the very simple reason that every king who levelled the court with its ruined constructions and laid a new pavement, saved as many of his predecessor's bricks as he could extract from the rubbish without difficulty. The fact that from the time of Ur-Gur practically the same mould (eleven to twelve inches square), was adopted for the ordinary baked bricks by all the Babylonian monarchs who repaired the renowned sanctuary at Nippur, encouraged their liberal employment of the old material, the more so as proper fuel was always scarce and expensive in the valleys of the lower Euphrates and Tigris.

The topmost of these pavements extended from the "causeway" of the *ziggurrat*, a distance of sixty-three feet towards the southeast, and was covered with débris one foot to one and a half high. Though none of its bricks was stamped, I have no doubt that it goes back to Ashurbânapal, whose inscribed bricks, sometimes green (originally blue) enamelled on the edges, were repeatedly found near its upper surface. As Haynes reports to have seen no trace of buildings of any sort resting upon the pavement, this section of the court seems to have been a large open place at the time of the last great Assyrian king (seventh century B. C.).

Several photographs clearly show that originally there was another pavement about two feet to two and a half below

Excavated Section of the Southeastern Court of the Ziggurrat in Nippur

Showing the different brick pavements laid by Babylonian kings. 1. The pavement of Sargon I. and Narâm-Sin. 2. The crude brick pavement of Ur-Gur. 3. The constructions resting upon it, and probably first erected by the same monarch. 4. The pavement of Ur-Ninib. 5. The pavement of Ashurbânapal.

the first. If ever it covered the entire court,[1] only fractional parts of it had been preserved, so that the illustration facing this page does not even indicate its former existence. The layer of earth enclosed between the upper and the lower pavements was "so firmly stratified that it seemed to have been formed gradually by the agency of water," which was incessantly washing away the unprotected parts of the *ziggurrat*. But Haynes' observation is not quite accurate; for a band of "mingled bitumen, charcoal, and wood ashes, varying in thickness from two to four inches," and running nearly through the middle of this stratum, indicates sufficiently that some kind of light structures must have existed on this part of the court at some time during the second millennium, to which I ascribe the second pavement. In all probability it was laid by a Cassite ruler, presumably Kadashman-Turgu, who not only restored but enlarged the *ziggurrat* and provided it with new casing walls. If I interpret correctly Haynes' somewhat confused reports of the different sections of the court excavated by him, and adjust his results properly with one another, this pavement must be regarded as a continuation of the lower course of a border pavement, which surrounded the four sides of Kadashman-Turgu's stage-tower, being ten feet wide in front of the latter and somewhat narrower on its other three sides, where it terminated in a gutter. This border pavement consisted of two courses of bricks laid in bitumen, and served as a basis for a sloping bed of bitumen designed to protect the foundations of the pyramid from falling rain. None of the bricks were inscribed except one, which contained the name of Ur-Ninib on its upper face, thereby indicating that it was out of its original position and belonged

[1] It seems as if the pavement of baked bricks was confined to the immediate environments of the *ziggurrat* and continued by a pavement of crude bricks (11½ by 11½ by 4½ inches), repeatedly referred to by Haynes at about the same level.

to much older material used again. An interesting discovery made at the same level, on the back side of the *ziggurrat* near its west corner, confirms my theory expressed above that the whole court around it was studded with smaller buildings at the time of the Cassite dominion. For while clearing the northwest face of the stage-tower Haynes came upon a room resting on the brick pavement now under consideration, and containing six whole cuneiform tablets, a little over a hundred small fragments of others, and an unpolished marble weight in the shape of a duck, which was nearly a foot long.

At an average depth of a foot and a half below the second pavement was a third, much better preserved. It was laid by Ur-Ninib, one of the kings of the dynasty of (N)isin, which occupied the throne of Babylonia about the middle of the third pre-Christian millenium. Out of a section of 143 bricks, taken up by Haynes, 135 bore the inscription: "Ur-Ninib, the glorious shepherd of Nippur, the shepherd of Ur, he who delivers the commands of Eridu, the gracious lord of Erech, king of (N)isin, king of Shumer and Akkad, the beloved consort of Ishtar." One was stamped with Ur-Gur's well-known legend, and six were uninscribed. From the reports before us we receive no information as to any walls or noteworthy antiquities having been discovered in the layer of rubbish once covering the pavement.

The most important of all the strata above the level of Narâm-Sin is that which lies between the pavement of Ur-Ninib and the next one below. As the former was not always exactly parallel to the latter, it is in some places almost three feet deep, though its average thickness is scarcely more than two. It rests upon a "platform" of clay and unbaked bricks, which, in size, color, and texture are identical with the mass of crude bricks forming the body of the *ziggurrats* of Nuffar and Warkâ, and therefore may be safely ascribed to Ur-Gur, king of Ur (about

2700 B. C.). The layer of rubbish and earth which covered the pavement deserves our special attention, as it yielded more inscribed antiquities than any other part of the temple enclosure hitherto examined. Over six hundred fragments of vases, statues, slabs, brick-stamps, and a number of doorsockets were gathered by the different expeditions in this remarkable stratum, doubly remarkable as most of the objects obtained from it did not belong to Ur-Gur and his successors, as at first might be expected, but to kings and high officials whom, on the basis of strong palæographic evidence and for various other reasons, I was forced to ascribe to the earliest phase of Babylonian history antedating Sargon I (about 3800 B. C.) by several centuries. As practically nothing but heavy door-sockets in dolerite and some shapeless blocks of veined marble (technically known as calcite stalagmite) were found whole; as most of the fragments were extraordinarily small in size, and as, moreover, portions of the same vases repeatedly were discovered at places widely distant from each other, we cannot avoid the conclusion that these precious antiquities had been broken and scattered on purpose; in other words, that these numerous inscribed vases and more than fifty brick-stamps with the names of Sargon and Narâm-Sin upon them, which had been scrupulously preserved and handed down from generation to generation, must have been stored somewhere within the precincts of the court of the *ziggurrat*, until they were rudely destroyed by somebody who lived between the reigns of Ur-Gur of Ur, and Ur-Ninib of (N)isin. Apart from a brick of Ur-Ninib, the latest inscribed monument recovered from this well-defined stratum is a door-socket of Bur-Sin of Ur, or rather an inscribed block of dolerite, presented to Bêl by Lugalkigubnidudu, a very ancient king of Ur and Erech, and afterwards turned into a door-socket and rededicated to the temple of Nippur by Bur-Sin. Hence it follows that the last-mentioned monarch must have lived before Ur-Ninib, and is more closely connected with Ur-Gur than has generally been asserted, a fact fully corroborated by the recent investigations of Thureau-Dangin, who has shown that there was only one dynasty of Ur in the third pre-Christian millennium. But we draw another important conclusion. It is entirely impossible to assume that a native Babylonian usurper of the throne, however ill-disposed toward an ancient cult and however unscrupulous in the means taken to suppress it, should have committed such an outrage against the sacred property of the great national sanctuary of the country. The breaking and scattering of the vases not only indicates a period of great political disturbance in Babylonia, but points unmistakably to a foreign invasion. Whence did it come?

We know on the one hand, from the chronological lists of dates and the last lines of thousands of business tablets of the third millennium, that the powerful kings of Ur had led their armies victoriously to Elam, conquered even Susa, and established a Babylonian hegemony over the subdued cities and districts of their ancient enemies. And we know on the other hand, from numerous references in Babylonian and Assyrian inscriptions, remarkably confirmed by De Morgan's excavations in Susa, that towards 2300 B. C. the Elamites were for a while in the complete possession of the lower country of the Euphrates and Tigris, even establishing an Elamitic dynasty at Larsa after they had devastated and ransacked all the renowned temples of Shumer and Akkad. Between these two historical events, which reversed the political relations between Babylonia and Elam completely, we must place the native dynasties of (N)isin and Larsa, preceded by a first Elamitic invasion, which occurred about two hundred years before the second one. It was this first Elamitic invasion which caused the destruction of the temple property at Nippur, brought about the downfall of the dynasty of Ur, and apparently led to the rise of the dynasty of (N)isin, to which Ur-Ninib belongs, whose pavement covered the layer of débris with the numerous broken vases. If the text of a votive inscription of Enannatuma, son of Ishme-Dagân, king of (N)isin, king of Shumer and Akkad, published many years ago by Rawlinson,[1] is entirely correct, the last representative of the dynasty of Ur would have been Gungunu, since he no longer has the proud title of his immediate predecessors,[2] "king of the four quarters of the earth," nor the less significant one borne by his first two ancestors,[3] but is styled only "king of Ur." In this case Ishme-Dagân should have been the founder of the new dynasty, who allowed Gungunu to lead the life of the shadow of a king until his death,[4] under the control of one of his own sons, whom he invested with the highest religious office in the temple of Sin at Ur. If, however, Gungunu, "king

[1] Comp. i *R.* 2, no. vi, 1, and 36, no. 2.

[2] Bur-Sin I, Gimil-Sin, Ine-Sin.

[3] Ur-Gur and Dungi. The latter was the first to adopt the more comprehensive title in connection with his successful wars some time between the x + 21st and x + 29th years of his long government. Comp. Thureau-Dangin in *Comptes Rendus*, 1902, pp. 84, *seqq.*

[4] Comp. the date of a tablet mentioned by Scheil in Maspéro's *Recueil*, vol. xxi (1899), p. 125: *mu Gu-un-gu-nu ba-til*, "the year when G. died." If the former view, set forth above, be correct, this tablet would belong to the government of Ishme-Dagân or his successor, and its peculiar date would thus find an easy explanation. In the other case the date would appear somewhat strange, as it was not customary to call a year after the death of an actual ruler, but rather after his successor's accession to the throne. There exist a few other tablets which are dated according to the reigns of kings of the dynasty of (N)isin. Among the results of the third Philadelphia expedition I remember distinctly to have seen one dated in the reign of Ur-Ninib, and Scheil (in *Recueil*, vol. xxiii, 1901, pp. 93, *seq.*) mentions another from Sippara which bears the name of King Damiq-ilishu, a second member of the same dynasty (comp. next page below), whom Scheil, however, wrongly identified with his namesake of the second dynasty of Babylon.

of Ur," mentioned in Enannatuma's inscription should prove to be a mistake for Gungunu, " king of Larsa," a ruler whose existence was recently[1] communicated to me by Thureau-Dangin, Ishme-Dagân would be the last and Ishbigirra (succeeded by Ur-Ninib?) probably the first representative of the dynasty of (N)isin. In this case Gungunu must have been the founder of the native dynasty of Larsa, which would have followed immediately upon that of (N)isin, continuing to reign (Nûr-Rammân and Sin-idinnam), until it was overthrown in connection with the second Elamitic invasion, about 2300 B. C. However this may be, whether we have to distinguish two kings by the name of Gungunu — the one king of Ur, the other king of Larsa (as we have two rulers, Bur-Sin, the one king of Ur, the other king of (N)isin), — or whether there was only one Gungunu, namely, the king of Larsa, this much can be regarded as certain, that the dynasties of Ur, (N)isin and Larsa succeeded each other in the order just quoted, and that for at least one hundred and fifty to two hundred years[2] the city of (N)isin appeared as the champion of Babylonian inde-

[1] In a personal letter of July 29, 1902, in which, on the basis of a new brick fragment recently acquired by the Louvre, Thureau-Dangin is inclined to doubt the existence of a Gungunu, king of Ur. The fact that in both of his inscriptions Enannatuma has the title *shag Uruma*, which (along with *u-a Uruma*) the Babylonian kings of Larsa place at the head of their titles, speaks decidedly in favor of an identity of Gungunu of Ur with Gungunu of Larsa. For evidently the rise of the dynasty of Larsa was connected as closely with the possession of the sanctuary of Sin at Ur as the rise of the dynasty of (N)isin with that of the temple of Bêl at Nippur (comp. the fact that all the members of this dynasty place *sib* (*ú-a* or *sag-ush*) *Nippur* before all their other titles).

[2] It comprised at least seven kings, Ishbigirra, Ur-Ninib, Libit-Ishtar, Bur-Sin II, Damiq-ilishu, Idîn-Dagân, and Ishme-Dagân, all but the first and the sixth kings being represented by inscriptions from Nippur. The question arises now, whether kings like Bêl-bâni, Rîm-Anum, etc., generally classified with the kings of the first dynasty of Babylon, must not be regarded rather as members of the dynasty of (N)isin.

pendence, until its leading position was contested by Babylon under Sin-muballit in the North. But how important a rôle to the very last (N)isin must have played in resisting the imperialistic ideas of the Elamitic invaders, whose ultimate aim was the establishing of a kingdom of Shumer and Akkad under the sceptre of an Elamitic prince, becomes evident from the mere fact, that Rîm-Sin, son of Kudur-Mabuk, who supplanted the native kings of Larsa and realized the Elamitic dream for about twenty-five to thirty years, introduced a new era by dating the single years of his government after the fall of (N)isin.

As remarked above, with but few exceptions all the objects rescued by Haynes from the stratum beneath Ur-Ninib's platform were in a most lamentable condition. Yet, after infinite toil, I succeeded in dividing them in groups according to certain palæographic peculiarities exhibited by them, and ultimately restored a number of inscriptions almost completely, notably the famous text of Lugalzaggisi, "king of Erech, king of the world," with its 132 lines of writing obtained from eighty-eight often exasperatingly small fragments of sixty-four different vases. The new material proved of fundamental importance for our knowledge of the early history of Babylonia in the fifth and fourth pre-Christian millenniums. In connection with the inscriptions from Tellô these texts enabled us to follow the general trend of the political and religious development of the country. We see how a number of petty states, sometimes consisting of nothing more than a walled city grouped around a well-known sanctuary, are constantly quarrelling with one another about the hegemony, victorious to-day, defeated to-morrow. The more prominent princes present votive offerings to Bêl of Nippur, which stands out as the great religious centre of Babylonia at the earliest period of its history. For the first time we meet with the names of Utug, *patesi*, and Urzag(?)uddu[1] and En-Bildar,[2] kings of Kîsh, En-shagkushanna, "lord of Kengi, king of the world," Lugal-kigubnidudu and Lugalkisalsi, kings of Erech and Ur, Urumush, "king of Kîsh," and others, or we gather further details concerning monarchs previously known, as, *e. g.*, Entemena of Lagash, Manishtusu of Kîsh, Sargon and Narâm-Sin of Agade. Above all, we get acquainted with the great "hero," Lugalzaggisi, "who was favorably looked upon by the faithful eye of Bèl, . . . to whom intelligence was given by Ea . . ., and who was nourished with the milk of life by the goddess Ningarsag." Indeed a great conqueror he must have been, one of the mightiest monarchs of the ancient East thus far known, a king who, long before Sargon I was born, could boast of an empire extending from the Persian Gulf to the shores of the Mediterranean Sea.

In addition to the many broken vases with their interesting forms and inscriptions equally important for archæology, history, and palæography, this unique stratum also yielded a few fragments of statues, reliefs, and other antiquities similar to those of Tellô. They illustrate again that the Babylonian artist was as ready to glorify Bêl of Nippur as he was to place his talents in the service of Ningirsu and Bau of Lagash. And they indicate at the same time that in all probability great surprises will await the future explorer of Nuffar who will turn his attention from the *ziggurrat* to the temple proper, which to the present day has scarcely been touched, as both Peters and Haynes regarded the temple of Bêl and its stage-tower practically as the same thing, and, unconscious of what they were doing, covered the

[1] The second sign is doubtful. Possibly my former reading Ur-Dun (Shul) pauddu is correct.

[2] The name means "Bildar (a well-known star-god) is lord." This reading of Hommel is preferable to Thureau-Dangin's *Enbi-Ishtar* or my former provisional reading *Enne-Ugun*.

neighboring ruins with fifty to seventy feet of rubbish, excavated by them in the court of the *ziggurrat*. Among the objects of art from beneath the pavement of Ur-Ninib which claim our special attention, I only mention a straight nose in basalt originally belonging to a statue in life size; the tolerably well-preserved shaved head of a small white marble statue of the period of Ur-Ninâ; and the torso of a large

Torso of an Inscribed Statue in Dolerite, about 2700 B. C.

Original two-thirds of life size

statue in polished dolerite, about two-thirds of life size. The material and certain details of the statue remind us of the famous sculptures of Gudea (comp. p. 237, above). The attitude of the whole body, the peculiar position of the arms with the clasped hands, the swelling of the muscles of the right arm, the delicately carved nails of the fingers, and the fine shawl with its graceful folds passing over the right breast and loosely thrown over the left arm are equally characteristic of the statue of Nippur and of those from Tellô. But on the other hand the torso under consideration presents distinctive features of its own. It has a long and flowing beard already curled and twisted in that conventional style with which we are familiar from the Assyrian monuments of Nineveh and Khorsabâd.[1] A richly embroidered band, one inch and a third wide, passes over the left shoulder, and seems to be fastened to the shawl, which it holds in place. Each wrist is encircled with a bracelet of precious stones, and the neck is adorned with a necklace of large beads strung on a skein of finely spun wool, and in its whole appearance not unlike the *'ugâl* with which the modern Arab shaikhs of Babylonia fasten their silken head-dress (*keffîye*). A short legend with the names of Bêl and the donor of the monument was originally engraved on the back of the statue between its two shoulders. But the barbarous and revengeful Elamites who broke so many fine votive gifts of the temple at Nippur cut the inscription away with the exception of the last line, "he made it." In all probability the statue was erected by one of the kings of the dynasty of Ur (between 2700 and 2600 B. C.).

The storage room where all the antiquities referred to had originally been kept was discovered by Haynes in his excavations along the southeast wall of the fortified enclosure. It was a well-planned cellar, 36 feet long, 11½ feet wide, and 8½ feet deep, built entirely into this wall, evidently by Ur-Gur himself.[2] Descending as far down as the level of the pavement of Narâm-Sin, it had, some two and a half feet above the floor of stamped earth, a ledge of crude bricks 1½ feet wide, which was capped by a layer of baked bricks

[1] Comp. the terra-cotta head from Nippur published by me in "The Bab. Exp. of the U. of Pa.," series A, vol. ix, pl. xii, no. 22.

[2] Comp. my treatment of the whole question in "The Bab. Exp. of the U. of Pa.," vol. i, series A, part 1, pp. 28, *seqq.*

and extended completely around the four walls of the room. A discovery made in connection with the next pavement below proved that it had served as a shelf for the safe keeping of treasures, sacrificial gifts, and documents.[1] A construction of baked bricks, which we notice in the illustration facing p. 377 (No. 3), seems also to have been built first by one of the kings of the dynasty of Ur, possibly by Ur-Gur himself. But as Haynes did not extend his excavations of the third campaign to the northeast section of the court, we leave it for the present out of consideration.

A word must be said about Peters' and Haynes' so-called "platform of Ur-Gur," which was covered with the layer of débris containing the precious vase fragments and the door-sockets of Sargon I. Some portions were made of crude bricks, but by far the greater part of it consisted of large lumps of kneaded clay, which "in a moist condition, had been laid up *en masse* in two thick layers," each one about four feet thick. This "platform," however, did not constitute a large terrace, raised to support the *ziggurrat* itself, and consequently did not run through the whole mound, as I formerly assumed in accordance with the erroneous views of my predecessors; but, like all the pavements lying above it, it was only an especially thick pavement laid by Ur-Gur as a solid floor for his open court around the stage-tower, and naturally also bore the weight of his additions to the latter. As soon as Haynes commenced to remove it, he made an interesting discovery, which illustrates the great antiquity of a custom previously observed in connection with the Parthian fortress (comp. pp. 366, *seqq.*). At different places between its layers of clay he found a number of valuable antiquities. These evidently had been taken from the rubbish below at the time when Ur-Gur levelled the court, to be placed as talismans in the new foundation. Among the objects thus obtained, we

[1] Comp. pp. 247, *seqq.*, above.

mention several well-formed copper nails and fragments of copper vessels, a fine brick stamp of Sargon I., the fragment of a pre-Sargonic mace-head, two slightly concave seal cylinders in white shell and stone, about twenty well-preserved unbaked clay tablets antedating the period of Sargon, a great quantity of large but badly broken fragments of similar tablets, and, above all, an important stone tablet 7 inches long, 5½ inches wide, and a little over 2 inches thick, completely covered on all its six faces with the most archaic cuneiform writing known from the monuments of Nuffar and Tellô.

Ur-Gur's clay pavement was separated from the next one below, *i. e.*, the fifth one from the top, by a layer of earth generally only a few inches deep, — a circumstance that cannot surprise us, as that ruler very evidently removed a considerable mass of débris in order to secure a solid basis for his own unusually thick pavement. Having cut through this thin layer, Haynes, in truth, could exclaim with King Nabonidos: What for ages no king among the kings had seen, the old foundation of Narâm-Sin, son of Sargon, that saw I. More than this, he saw the inscribed bricks of both of these ancient rulers, whose very existence until then had been seriously doubted by different scholars. The extraordinary value of this pavement for Babylonian archæology lies in the fact that it supplied the first irrefutable proof of the historical character of this ancient Semitic kingdom, that it enabled us more clearly to comprehend the chronological order of the rulers of Tellô and Sargon I, and that it enabled us to establish new and indubitable criteria to distinguish between pre-Sargonic and post-Sargonic constructions and antiquities. It is, therefore, a matter of the utmost regret that Haynes, not fully realizing the unique importance of what he had been so fortunate to discover, removed this precious pavement almost completely. It consisted of two courses of baked bricks. The upper one was composed of enormous bricks of uniform size and mould, 15½ to 16½ inches square and 3½ inches thick. Several of them were stamped with the brief legend: "Shargâni-shar-âli (the original fuller name of Sargon[1]), king of Agade, builder of (at) the temple of Bêl;" others bore the words: "Narâm-Sin, builder of (at) the temple of Bêl," while still others were without any inscription. The bricks of Narâm-Sin were more numerous than those of his father, the ratio between them being about three to one. Haynes adds the interesting observation that some of these bricks were colored red when he found them, but that their color faded slowly whenever they were exposed to the air and the sunlight. The lower course contained only imperfect bricks of both Sargon and his son and many plano-convex bricks with a thumb-mark on their upper (convex) side. It became evident at once that these peculiar plano-convex bricks, 11 by 7 by 2 inches in size, represent an earlier (pre-Sargonic) period, and that the pavement itself was originally laid by Sargon and relaid by Narâm-Sin, both of them utilizing older material in connection with their own bricks.

The same intermingling of earlier bricks with those of the Sargon dynasty was noticed in connection with several fragments of narrow watercourses, which Haynes found at the level of Narâm-Sin's pavement, but, as it seems, disconnected with it. His notes at our disposal are very meagre, and refer only to one of these conduits, which came from the middle of the open court and very perceptibly sloped down towards the angle formed by the front face of the *ziggurrat* and the two parallel walls representing part of its entrance. This meandering section, which was traced for twenty-five feet, consisted of nine joints of trough-

[1] Comp. my discussion on this question in "The Bab. Exp. of the U. of Pa.," series A, vol. i, part 1 (1893), pp. 16, *seqq.*, and part 2 (1896), pp. 19, *seq.*

shaped tiles, 15¾ feet in aggregate length, with an average depth of 2 inches and an average breadth of 3½ inches, and continued on either side by peculiarly arranged bricks laid in a clay cement (comp. frontispiece).

As Ur-Gur's pavement rested in some places almost directly upon that of his predecessor, no remains of other buildings were noticed by Haynes in the thin layer between them. However, beneath the storeroom referred to above, but separated from its floor by two feet of rubbish, was found an earlier cellar of the same form, yet slightly smaller in its dimensions.[1] It was also provided with a ledge, upon which a circular tablet, two small rectangular ones, and the fragments of five others were still lying. Four brick stamps of Sargon, with broken handles, which, together with the tablets just mentioned, seem to have been left intentionally or by mistake when Ur-Gur removed the contents of this earlier vault into his own cellar, were recovered from the débris which filled it, while a fifth one was found immediately underneath its eastern corner. The partly ruined walls of this lower structure were only 3 feet high, but originally they must have measured between 5 and 6 feet. About one foot below their top was a deep bowl of yellow pottery, decorated with a rope-pattern ornament on its outside, and set in a rim of thumb-marked bricks. Its use could no longer be determined. The building material of both storerooms was identical in form and size, though somewhat different in color and texture. It follows, therefore, that the small mould employed by Ur-Gur for his crude flat bricks originated at a much earlier period, a result which is in entire accord with what we learned from our study of the interior mass of the *ziggurrat* (p. 374, above). The important new fact derived from an examination of this lower cellar is that these small crude bricks (9 by 6 by 3 inches) can be traced to about the

[1] It was 32 feet long by 7 feet wide.

Treasury Vault and Temple Archive of the Time of Sargon I. About 3800 B. C.

time of Sargon and Narâm-Sin, who in all probability were the original builders of the southeast enclosing wall.

2. *Pre-Sargonic Ruins.* According to the date furnished by Nabonidos (comp. p. 273), from which we have no reason to deviate, the pavement of Sargon and Narâm-Sin marks the period of about 3800–3750 B. C. in the history of Bêl's sanctuary at Nippur. As we saw previously, the accumulation of débris above this pavement during the subsequent 3500 years amounted to 16 or 17 feet, including the clay pavement of Ur-Gur — which alone was 8 feet thick — or 8 to 9 feet, disregarding the latter. This is comparatively little for such a long period, considering the rapidity with which ordinary mud buildings, such as doubtless occupied the temple court at different times, generally crumble and collapse. However, we must not forget that every ruler who laid a new pavement razed the ruined buildings of his predecessors and levelled the ground for his own constructions. But a real surprise was to await us in the lowest strata. In descending into the pre-Sargonic period below Narâm-Sin's pavement, which itself lies six to eight feet above the present level of the desert, Haynes penetrated through more than thirty feet of ruins before he reached the virgin soil, or thirty-five feet before he was at the water level.[1]

What do these ruins contain? To what period of human history do they lead us? How was this great accumulation beneath the level of the desert possible? What geological changes have taken place since to explain this remarkable phenomenon? Such and other similar questions may have come to many thoughtful students when they first read these extraordinary facts. Naturally enough, they also occupied the mind of the present writer seriously for the last six

[1] These measurements are quoted from the results of an accurate survey of the remains at the southeast court of the *ziggurrat* by Geere and Fisher in 1900, when I was personally in charge of the excavations.

or seven years. I will try to give an answer later in connection with our fourth campaign, when I had the much desired opportunity to study personally the few remains left by my predecessors in the southeast court of the *ziggurrat*, and to compare them with the results of my own excavations in the same temple complex. With the mere reports of Peters and Haynes to guide us, I am afraid we would never have suspected the real nature of these pre-Sargonic ruins. For though the numerous brick and pipe constructions laid bare in the lower strata belonged to the most characteristic and best preserved antiquities unearthed by the Philadelphia expeditions, the work of the two explorers in the débris around them is, perhaps, the least satisfactory part of all their excavations at Nuffar. In consequence of their destructive methods and their superficial work in the upper strata, not being sufficiently prepared for the much more difficult task in the lower ones, they found themselves, with their untrained eyes, suddenly surrounded by the little known remains of Babylonia's earliest civilization,—small bits of mud walls crushed and half dissolved, indistinct beds of ashes, and thousands and thousands of fragments of terra-cotta vases generally not only broken, but forced out of their original shape and position by the enormous weight of earth lying above them. What wonder that they were unable to recognize the essential features of this *tôhû wābôhû* themselves, or to communicate what they saw in such a manner as to make it intelligible to others who might feel inclined to try to untangle the problem for them.[1]

Haynes' task in the lower strata of the temple court was

[1] What after hard work and with an unbiassed mind I could put together from Haynes' reports was published in "The Bab. Exp. of the Univ. of Pa.," series A, vol. i, part 2, pp. 23, *seqq.* It is natural that the picture had to be defective, as the premises communicated on which it was drawn turned out to be largely incorrect.

as clearly defined as that in the upper strata. He had to determine (*A*) the earliest form of Bêl's sanctuary beneath the *ziggurrat*, as far as this could safely be done by means of tunnels and without a complete removal of the whole ponderous mass above it; (*B*) the character and contents of the court adjoining the latter on the southeast. The proper way to proceed would have been to descend gradually and equally on the whole section to be excavated. But Haynes, repeating his former mistake, attempted to carry out the two parts of his task consecutively, thereby lessening our chances of comprehending the sanctuary as a whole and depriving us of an opportunity of controlling and checking his results at every step. He accordingly descended first by two shafts along the southeast face of the *ziggurrat*, and excavated what was left of the court afterwards.[1] Much against my will, I am obliged to observe his arrangement and to present his work in the manner in which he executed it. He again made several interesting and important discoveries, but he totally failed to ascertain the character of the sanctuary and the real contents of its surroundings, and was often unsuccessful in understanding the single antiquities excavated and their mutual relation to each other.

A. Haynes was doubtless most eager to find out what was lying beneath the *ziggurrat*. In the course of his excavations he disclosed four constructions either beneath the tower or in its immediate neighborhood, which deserve our special attention. They stood apparently in direct connection with the earliest sanctuary, or even formed part of it.

1. About three and a half feet below Narâm-Sin's pavement he came upon the top of a narrow strip of burned brickwork (No. 6). It was about twelve feet distant from the front face of the stage-tower, with which it ran roughly parallel, continuing its course equally to the southwest

[1] Comp. the illustration facing p. 453, which enables the reader to understand the method by which Haynes proceeded.

under the entrance walls of Ur-Gur and to the northeast of the court-yard, in the rubbish of which it disappeared. This peculiar curb seemed to define an earlier sanctuary towards the southeast. It was 18 inches high, and consisted of seven courses of plano-convex bricks (8¾ by 5¾ by 2¼

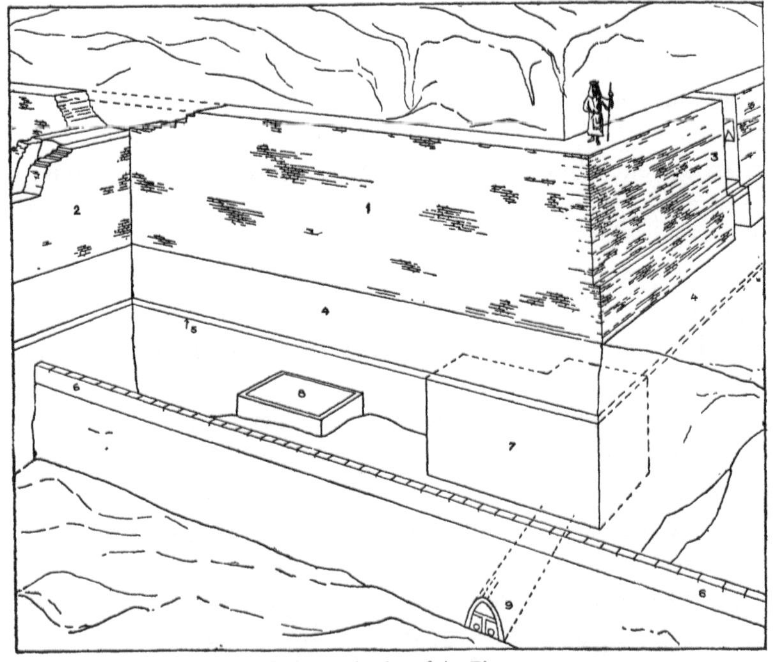

South-Eastern Section of the Ziggurrat.
Designed by H. V. Hilprecht, drawn by C. S. Fisher.

1. Southeast façade built by Ur-Gur. 2. Remains of the entrance walls built by the same. 3. Northeast conduit built by Ur-Gur, repaired by Kadashman-Turgu and Ashurbânapal. 4. Pavement of Ur-Gur. 5. Pavement of Narâm-Sin. 6. Pre-Sargonic curb. 7. The L-shaped structure. 8. The so-called altar. 9. Drain with arch.

inches and evidently forming the basis for Ur-Gur's standard size of flat bricks). They were curiously creased lengthwise, and their convex surface, without exception, was placed upward in the wall.

2. Inside this enclosure, directly below the pavement (No. 4) of Ur-Gur's *ziggurrat* (No. 1) and practically leaning

against the latter, if we imagine its front face continued farther down, stood another interesting structure (No. 8). Its top was three feet below Narâm-Sin's pavement, and accordingly two feet higher than the base of the curb, from which it was distant about four feet. It was 13 feet long, 8 feet wide, and constructed of unbaked bricks laid in bitumen. The upper hollowed surface of this massive concern was surrounded by a rim of bitumen, 7 inches high, and was covered with a layer of white ashes 2½ inches in depth, which contained evident remains of bones. To the southwest of it Haynes discovered a kind of bin also built of crude bricks and likewise filled with (black and white) ashes about a foot deep. He arrived at the conclusion, therefore, that this was an altar, "the ancient place where the sacrificial victims were burned." This explanation is possible, but not probable. In fact, the enormous size of the structure and the rim of bitumen, which necessarily would have been consumed at every large sacrifice, speak decidedly against his theory. Besides, an Old-Babylonian altar has an entirely different form on the numerous seal cylinders where it is depicted. My own explanation of this structure will be found in connection with the results of the fourth expedition.

3. Directly below the east corner of Ur-Gur's *ziggurrat*, and parallel with its northeast and southeast faces, was another building, exhibiting the peculiar ground-plot of an L (No. 7), but with regard to its original purpose even more puzzling than either of the two structures just described. Its top was on a level with Narâm-Sin's pavement, while its foundation was laid eleven feet below it. This solid tower-like edifice, disconnected with any other structure in its neighborhood, "had an equal outside length and breadth of 23 feet" (northeast and southeast sides), and was about 12 feet thick. "Its splendid walls, which show no trace of a door or opening of any kind, were built of large

crude bricks" (on an average 16 inches square and 3½ inches thick), made of "tenacious clay thoroughly mixed with finely cut straw and well kneaded." They are "of good mould, and in proportions, size, and texture closely resemble the stamped crude bricks of Narâm-Sin." Though Haynes devoted much time to their identification, he could determine neither the design of the building nor "the era of its construction." Yet he felt sure that it was "the lowest and most ancient edifice" thus far discovered in the temple enclosure of Nippur, and that its bricks are "the prototype of those of Narâm-Sin, which they doubtless preceded by at least several centuries." To my regret, I must differ again with these conclusions after having studied the history of the *ziggurrat* in connection with a second personal visit to the ruins in 1900.

While examining the surroundings of this interesting edifice, Haynes came first upon the same gray or black ashes as are found everywhere in the court of the *ziggurrat* immediately below Narâm-Sin's pavement, next upon "lumps of kneaded clay," then upon several stray bits of lime mortar. All these traces of human activity were imbedded in the débris characteristic of the lower strata, which largely consist of earth, ashes, and innumerable potsherds. When he had reached a depth of nine feet from the top of the solid structure, — in other words, had descended about four feet below the bottom of the ancient curb on the southeast side of the stage-tower, — he found a large quantity[1] of fragments of terra-cotta water pipes of the form here shown. Though the reports before me offer no satisfactory clue as to their precise use, there can be little doubt that they belong to the real pre-Sargonic period. I will try to

T-Pipe Joint

[1] "Several hundred of these objects were found within a radius of five feet."

explain their purpose later, Haynes' interpretation being better passed over in silence.

4. The explorer's curiosity was aroused at once, and having sunk his shaft a few feet deeper at the spot where the greatest number of these terra-cotta pipes were lying, he made one of the most far-reaching single discoveries in the lower strata of Nippur. After a brief search he came upon a very remarkable drain (No. 9), reminding us of the advanced system of canalization, as *e. g.* we find it in Paris at the present time. It ran obliquely under the rectangular building described above, starting, as I believe, at a corner of the early sanctuary, but evidently having fallen into disuse long before the L-shaped building was erected. It could still be traced for about six feet into the interior of the ruins underlying the *ziggurrat*. But its principal remains were disclosed in the open court, into which it extended double that length, so that its tolerably preserved mouth lay directly below the ancient curb, — a fact of the utmost importance. For it constitutes a new argument in favor of the theory previously expressed that this curb marked the line of the earliest southeast enclosure of the *ziggurrat*, or whatever formerly may have taken the place of the latter. But it also follows that a gutter of some kind, which carried the water to a safe distance, must have existed in this neighborhood outside the curb.

No sooner had Haynes commenced removing the débris from the ruined aqueduct than he found, to his great astonishment, that it terminated in a vaulted section 3 feet long and was built in the form of a true elliptical arch, — the oldest one thus far discovered. The often ventilated question as to the place and time of origin of the arch was thereby decided in favor of ancient Babylonia.[1] The bottom of this reliable witness of pre-Sargonic civilization lies

[1] A similar arch, though not quite as old, was soon afterwards unearthed in Tellô. Comp. pp. 251, *seq.*, above.

fifteen feet below Narâm-Sin's pavement, or ten feet below the base of the curb, which it probably antedates by a century or two. We may safely assign it, therefore, to the end of the fifth pre-Christian millennium. It presented a number of interesting peculiarities. Being 2 feet 1 inch high (inside measurement), and having a span of 1 foot 8 inches and a rise of 1 foot 1 inch, it was constructed of well baked plano-convex bricks laid on the principle of radiating *voussoirs*. These bricks measured 12 by 6 by 2½ inches, were light yellow in color, and bore certain marks on their upper or convex surface, which had been made either by pressing the thumb and index finger deeply into the clay in the middle of the brick, or by drawing one or more fingers lengthwise over it. Primitive as they doubtless are, they do not (as Haynes inferred) "represent the earliest type of bricks found at Nippur or elsewhere in Babylonia," — which are rather smaller and sometimes a little thicker,— though for a considerable while both kinds were used alongside each other and often in the same building.[1] The curve of the arch was effected "by wedge-shaped joints of the simple clay mortar used to cement the bricks." "On the top of its crown was a crushed terra-cotta pipe about 3 or 3½ inches in diameter," the meaning of which Haynes declares unknown. I cannot help thinking that it served a purpose similar to the holes provided at regular intervals in our modern casing walls of terraces, etc.; in other words, that the pipe was intended to give exit to the rain water

[1] Thus, *e. g.*, in a drain discovered by the fourth expedition in the east section of the temple court at the lowest level of any of the baked brick constructions hitherto excavated at Nuffar. It contained bricks of the size 12 by 5⅞ by 2¼ inches, and others measuring only 8⅝ by 4⅞ by 2 inches, while at the foundation of the northeast city gate of Nippur the two kinds of bricks marked two pre-Sargonic periods succeeding each other precisely as in the two lowest buildings of Mound B at Tellô (comp. p. 241, above). Comp. also p. 251, above. He who built the drain in part doubtless used older material.

The Earliest Babylonian Arch known. About 4000 B. C.

Seen from the inside of a vaulted tunnel. Observe the T-shaped brick construction at its opening, and a portion of the two clay pipes imbedded in its bottom.

percolating the soil behind and above it, and in this way to prevent the softening of the clay cement between the bricks of the arch, and the caving-in of the whole vault which would result from it. This explanation being accepted, it necessarily follows that the floor of the court surrounding the earliest sanctuary was not paved with burned bricks, an inference entirely confirmed by the excavations.

There is much to be said in favor of the theory that this skilfully planned tunnel was arched over originally along its entire length. Like its vault, the lower part of the aqueduct presented several most surprising features. "Just beneath the level of the pavement and in the middle of the water channel were two parallel terra-cotta tiles, 8 inches in diameter, with a 6-inch flanged mouth." Haynes, regarding this tunnel as a drain rather than the protecting structure for a drain, was at a loss to explain their presence and significance. They were laid in clay mortar and consisted of single joints or sections, each 2 feet long, cemented together by the same material. We may raise the question: Why are there two small pipes instead of one large one? Evidently because they carried the water from two different directions to a point inside the sacred enclosure, where they met and passed through the arched tunnel together. They surely testify to a most highly developed system of drainage in the very earliest period of Babylonian history. I have, therefore, no doubt that the so-called "water-cocks" previously mentioned served some purpose in connection with this complicated system of canalization, and that in all probability they are to be regarded as specially prepared joints intended to unite terra-cotta pipes meeting each other at a right angle.

The mouth of the tunnel was provided with a T-shaped construction of plano-convex bricks, which Haynes is inclined to consider as "the means employed for centring the arch," or as "a device to exclude domestic animals, like sheep, from seeking shelter within it against the pitiless sun's rays in midsummer," while the present writer rather sees in it a strengthening pillar erected to protect the most exposed part of the tunnel at the point where the arching proper begins and the side walls are most liable to yield to the unequal pressure from the surrounding mass of earth. That the last-mentioned view is the more plausible and the explanation of the single pipe placed over the arch as given above is reasonable, follows from what happened in the course of the excavations. A few months after Haynes had removed the brick structure with its two arms, he reported suddenly that the arch had been "forced out of its shape, probably from the unequal pressure of the settling mass above it, which had been drenched with rain water." Truly the original purpose of these simple means, which had secured the preservation of the arch for six thousand years, could not have been demonstrated more forcibly. At the same time, Haynes, who never thought of this occurrence as having any bearing upon the whole question, could not have paid a higher compliment to the inventive genius and the extraordinary forethought of the ancient Babylonian architects.

Like all other parts, the long side walls of this unique tunnel were built with remarkable care. They consisted of eleven courses of bricks laid in clay mortar — a sure indication that the tunnel itself was not intended to carry water.[1] The six lowest courses, the eighth, the tenth, and eleventh, were placed flatwise with their long edge presented to view, while the seventh and ninth courses were arranged on their long edges like books on a shelf with their small edge visible. Considering all the details of this

[1] In the earliest days of Babylonian architecture, bitumen is the regular cement used for important baked brick walls constantly washed by water. Comp. p. 252, above. Small gutters and similar conduits carrying water over open places, etc., show clay mortar occasionally.

excellent system of canalization in the fifth pre-Christian millennium, which not long ago was regarded as a prehistoric period, we may be pardoned for asking the question: Wherein lies the often proclaimed progress in draining the capitals of Europe and America in the twentieth century of our own era? It would rather seem as if the methods of to-day are little different from what they were in ancient Nippur or Calneh, one of the four cities of the kingdom of "Nimrod, the mighty hunter before the Lord" (Gen. 10: 9, *seq.*), at the so-called "dawn of civilization," — a somewhat humiliating discovery for the fast advancing spirit of the modern age! How many uncounted centuries of human development may lie beyond that marvellous age represented by the vaulted tunnel with the two terra-cotta pipes imbedded in cement at its bottom, four feet below the former plain level of "the land of Shinar"!

Pre-Sargonic Drain in Terra-Cotta
About 4500 B. C.

B. The results obtained by Haynes in excavating the space between the ancient curb and the later enclosing wall of the *ziggurrat* cannot be considered separately, as they are not only less conspicuous than those just described, but have been reported in such a manner as to defy all efforts to comprehend them from any point of view. At different levels and apparently belonging to different epochs, he found perpendicular drains almost everywhere in the court. They were constructed of single terra-cotta rings, sometimes with perforations in their sides, placed above each other, and occasionally provided with a bell-shaped top-piece, in one case[1] even bounded by a terra-cotta floor, with a rim around it and made in four sections. The level at which the opening of the lowest perpendicular drain seems to occur lies ten and a quarter to eleven feet below Narâm-Sin's pavement, according to my own measurements of the remains of Haynes' excavated antiquities. It is about identical with that which I ascertained from later researches at the ruins as the original plain level. Here and there Haynes struck a small piece of pavement, which he explained as a fire-place, because of the ashes seen near and upon it. At some places he unearthed fragments of gently sloping water conduits, at others wells built of plano-convex bricks laid in herring-bone fashion,[2] at still others low walls, remains of rooms, too nearly ruined, according to his statements, to allow of a restoration of their ground plan. But above all, he discovered many large terra-cotta jars in various forms and sizes, and without any order, standing in the rubbish around and below them. Wherever he dug he came upon "a multitude of potsherds scattered profusely through the vast accumulation of débris, earth, decomposed refuse matter and ashes." The lowest vase of this large type found whole by him stood about twenty feet below Narâm-Sin's

[1] This special drain, shown in the illustration on p. 401, descended six and a half feet and had an average diameter of 2¾ feet.

[2] Comp. the illustration below ("Section of a Pre-Sargonic Well, Bricks laid in Herring-bone Fashion") in the chapter "On the Topography of Ancient Nippur."

pavement. Haynes' idea is that all these vases — and he excavated no less than fifteen at one place within a comparatively small radius — served "for the ablutions of the pilgrims," while some of the drains he regards as urinals and the like. To what inferences are we driven by his reports! The entire sacred precinct of the earliest *ziggurrat* of Bêl one huge lavatory and water-closet situated from nine to twenty feet below the ancient level of the plain!

A few additional facts which I have been able to gather after much toil from his reports and descriptions of photographs may follow as an attempt on my part to complete the strange picture of these lowest excavations. They have been arranged according to the levels given by Haynes. Yet be it understood expressly that the present writer cannot always be held responsible for the correctness of the recorded observations. A little below the pavement of Narâm-Sin there seems to have been "a very large bed of black [and gray] ashes of unknown extent, varying in depth from 1 to 1½ feet." The next objects below this which attracted Haynes' attention are "a fragment of unbaked clay bearing the impression of a large seal cylinder, and a large vase, 2 feet 8 inches in height, which contained the skeleton of a child, several animal bones, and small vases." The importance of this unique find as the first sure example of a pre-Sargonic burial is

Pre-Sargonic Clay Tablet

apparent. We therefore look naturally for further details. But our search is unsuccessful. The notes before us contain nothing beyond what I have stated and the remark that "the skeleton is by no means complete; even parts of the skull have decayed."

At about the same level ("two feet below the pavement" mentioned), but evidently at another locality, Haynes reached another "bed of mingled light gray ashes and earth not less than 9 feet in diameter and perhaps 8 inches in extreme depth." It contained two seal cylinders,[1] one gold bead, one badly corroded silver bead, two hundred stone beads, "chiefly of a dull gray slate color, quite in contrast to the more highly colored beads of agate, jasper, etc., generally found in these mounds," and six finger-rings made of several silver wires each about 3/8 of an inch in diameter.

Our interest is roused again by a label accompanying a photograph. It reads: "A large covered jar set in a dais of brick-work. Its top is four feet below the level of Narâm-Sin's pavement." We ask at once: Was there anything in it to show its purpose — ashes, earth, deposits of some kind? The veil drops; we hear nothing more about it. From the same stratum we have "a perfect and well wrought copper nail, 1 3/4 inches long," and the fragment of a copper knife [or sword?], 4 3/8 inches long and 1 5/16 inches wide. "Five archaic tablets" are also reported to have been found "not less than four feet below the level of the same pavement." They are "rudely fashioned, and appear to be inscribed with numbers only represented by straight and curved lines in groups of two, three, nine, and ten. In one instance a column of nine curved marks made by the thumb nail is flanked on either side by a

[1] One in bone. "It is deeply and rather rudely engraved with two large birds standing upright with outstretched wings." "Between the birds is an unknown animal form."

column of ten straight lines, made by the use of some other instrument than the stylus. One tablet has a single group of nine marks on one side of the tablet, and on the opposite side are two groups of two lines or marks each." This description of the first pre-Sargonic cuneiform tablets found *in situ* at Nippur is brief and lacks essential details, but for the time being it sufficed, as the present writer was expected to examine the originals later in Constantinople, and therefore had an opportunity to verify and supplement the reports sent from the field. He found them to be the school exercises of a Babylonian child living in the fifth pre-Christian millennium. But the case unfortunately was different with regard to the many large pre-Sargonic vases unearthed in the lower strata of the court of the *ziggurrat*. Precious as these witnesses of a hoary antiquity appear to us as welcome links in the history of archæology, they do not seem to have been viewed by Haynes in the same light. He took photographs of a few of the jars and caldrons, but he saved none of the originals, though quite a number of them were discovered whole or only slightly broken, and others, which were dug out in fragments, could have been restored without difficulty. If, indeed, any was packed and forwarded with the other excavated antiquities, it surely was not accompanied by a label, and consequently has not been identified.

Exercise Tablet of a Child
From the pre-Sargonic Fire Necropolis

The lack of accurate information is especially felt in connection with the following two specimens of early Babylonian pottery which are reported to have been found in a room the walls of which were 11 feet high and lay entirely below Narâm-Sin's pavement. How large this room was, whether it had any door, and other necessary details are not stated. It contained two open vases about fourteen feet distant from each other.[1] They stood in their original positions at two different levels, the one being placed about two and a half feet higher than the other. We notice remarkable differences also with regard to their forms and sizes. One was bell-shaped, and had a flat bottom about twice as large in diameter as its mouth. The other was a little over two feet high, measured one foot nine inches across the top, and was decorated with a rope pattern.[2]

In descending a little farther and reaching a level of fifteen feet below the often mentioned pavement, Haynes picked up "a fragment of red lacquered pottery" so much superior in quality to "anything unearthed in the strata subsequent to the time of Ur-Gur," that he at first doubted whether it really belonged to that ancient period. But soon afterwards he obtained another red piece twenty-three feet below the line of demarcation given above, and a small fragment of a black cup of the same high degree of workmanship three feet below that. It is a well known fact today that similar vases occur also in the lowest strata of Susa in Persia and in the earliest Egyptian ruins.

We cannot close this brief résumé of Haynes' activity in the lowest strata of the temple mound without mentioning briefly that he found "a fragment of black[3] clay bearing several human forms in relief upon its curved surface," also twenty-three feet below Narâm-Sin's pavement, and another

[1] According to my estimate, the accuracy of which I cannot guarantee.

[2] Comp., also, the illustration published in Hilprecht, "The Bab. Exp. of the U. of Pa.," series A, vol. i, part 2, plate xxvii. It appears to have been found in a fine state of preservation according to the photograph, but according to Haynes' report it was "too much broken to be removed."

[3] This seems to have been blackened by fire.

Pre-Sargonic Chamber with Two Large Vases. About 4500 B. C.

Immediately adjoining the sacred enclosure of the earliest temple at Nippur

larger piece two feet deeper; and furthermore, that he took a small gray terra-cotta vase, which he fortunately saved, from the layer between these two objects and described by him as being "literally filled with potsherds of small size, and generally brick red in color." He concludes his observations by stating that "the lowest strata show a large proportion of black ashes and fine charcoal mingled with the earth," but contain "potsherds in only moderate quantities;" and that "the very earliest traces of civilization at Nippur" — thirty feet below Narâm-Sin's pavement! — "are ashes where fires were built on the level plain." But Haynes' "level plain" lies rather eighteen to nineteen feet below where it actually was. He will, therefore, pardon us for looking for a more reasonable explanation of these remarkable ashes and potsherds discovered — as the Babylonian scribes would say — in "the breast of the earth," around the sanctuary of Bêl, instead of accepting his own, according to which "they mark the level of the alluvial plain where the first inhabitants grazed their flocks and made their primitive abodes."

Earliest Vase from Nippur

Pre-Sargonic Cup

In view of the prominent position which the temple of Bêl, as the oldest and most renowned sanctuary of all Babylonia, occupied in the political and civil life of its population, it has been necessary to lay before the reader all the principal facts which I could extricate from the often obscure reports at my disposal, in order to enable him to comprehend the condition and characteristic features of the ruins and to acquaint himself with the history and methods of their exploration. My review of Haynes' work on the western side of the Shatt en-Nîl will have to be briefer, as he, like Peters, never attempted to explore those mounds systematically, but, on the whole, was satisfied with recovering all the tablets and other antiquities from the numerous unbaked brick buildings which they contained. Most of the twenty thousand cuneiform records and fragments excavated between 1893 and 1896 in the long ridge limited by the numbers VI and VIII on the plan of the ruins (p. 305) are lists (and a few contracts) dated in the reigns of Cassite rulers (about 1500–1250 B. C.), several of which show exceedingly interesting and peculiar seal impressions. Some two or three thousand belong to the third pre-Christian millennium. They include many so-called contracts (and receipts) from the time of the kings of the dynasties of Ur, (N)isin, Larsa, and Babylon.[1] There are a few letters and literary tablets among them, which may originally have formed part of the temple library situated on the opposite bank (IV) of the canal. The neo-Assyrian, Chaldean and Persian dynasties are represented by about twelve hundred contract tablets.

More than seven hundred of these are of especial importance. At the end of May, 1893, they were discovered in one of the rooms of a ruined building at a depth of twenty feet below the surface (VIII on the plan of the

[1] I remember, *e. g.*, a tablet dated in the government of Ur-Ninib of (N)isin, about five hundred to eight hundred dated according to Rîm-Sin's new era (fall of (N)isin), several dated in the reign of a king Bêl-bâni, and a few dated in the reigns of other kings previously not known. Comp. p. 382.

ruins, p. 305). The great care with which they had been made, the exceptionally pure and soft clay chosen, and the large number of fine seal impressions exhibited by many of them attracted my attention at once. Upon closer examination they proved to belong to the business archives of a great Babylonian firm, Murashû Sons, bankers and brokers at Nippur, who lived in the time of Artaxerxes I. (464–424 B. C.) and Darius II. (423–405 B. C.), in whose reigns the documents are dated. According to a system better known

Clay Tablet with Seal Impressions from the Archives of Murashû Sons

from the later Roman Empire, this banking-house acted also as an agent for the Persian kings, from whom it had rented the taxes levied upon their Babylonian subjects at Nippur and neighboring districts. The contents of these 730 tablets accordingly had an unusual interest. The active life and motion which pulsated in the streets of the famous "city of Bêl," in the fore-courts of its temple, and in the fields on the palm and corn-laden banks of "the great canal" at the time when Ezra and Nehemiah led the descendants of Nebuchadrezzar's exiled Jews from these very plains to Palestine, were unfolded vividly before our eyes. We were enabled to confirm and supplement what the Greeks tell us about the large number of Persians settled in the various provinces of the vast empire. We became acquainted with the names and titles of the different officers — among them the *dâtabâri*, known from Daniel 3 : 2, *seq.* — who were stationed all over the fertile country between the lower Euphrates and Tigris, to look after the interests of their government.

From early days Babylonia was a land of many tongues, but at no other period of its varied history are we so impressed with the great proportion of the foreign element in this rich alluvial plain as during the centuries following the fall of Babylon, 538 B. C. The population of Babylonia at the time of Artaxerxes I and Darius II appears about as thoroughly mixed as that of the United States in our own time. And as the emigrants from Europe and Asia brought their customs and religions, their languages and the local and personal names of their native lands to their new settlements in the New World, so Persians and Medians, Arameans and Sabeans, Judeans and Edomites, etc., transplanted those of their former abodes, from which they often had been carried away by the vicissitudes of war, to ancient Babylonia. Very numerous are Persian and Aramean personal proper names in these documents. Unusually large is the number of Jewish names known from the Old Testament, especially from the books of Ezra and Nehemiah. There can be no doubt that a considerable number of the Jewish prisoners carried away by Nebuchadrezzar were settled in Nippur and its neighborhood, where many of their descendants continued to live as long as the city existed (about 900 A. D.), to judge from the many inscribed Hebrew bowls excavated everywhere in the upper strata of its ruins. The Talmudic tradition which identifies Nippur with the Biblical Calneh gains new force in the light of these facts, strengthened by the argument that the earliest and most important Babylonian city, which occupies the first place in the Sumerian story of the creation, could not well have been omitted by the writer of Genesis 10: 10. And we feel we tread on sacred ground, considering that even Ezekiel himself, while among the captives of his people at Tel-Abib,[1] while admonishing and comforting the scattered inhabitants of Judah's depopulated cities, and while seeing his famous visions of the cherubims on the banks of "the river Chebar in the land of the Chaldeans" (Ezek. 1 : 1, 3;

[1] Since the publication of Tiele, *Babyl.-Assyr. Geschichte*, p. 427, the modern commentators have begun to change the Hebrew תל אביב (*Tel-Abîb*, "Mound of the ear of corn") with good reason into the Babylonian תל אבוב, *Til-Abûb*, "Mound of the storm-flood," a name by which the Babylonians used to denote the large sand-hills scattered over their plain even in those early days. Comp. especially the late Richard Kraetzschmar's *Das Buch Ezechiel*, Göttingen, 1900, pp. 5, *seq.*, 34. To-day such enormous sand-hills are found in several districts of 'Irâq, notably in the neighborhood of Jôkha, Warkâ (comp. pp. 144 and 152, above), Tell-Ibrâhîm (= Cuthah, comp. p. 277, above), and Nuffar. Those of Nuffar are very extensive, but not very high. They rise about ten to thirty feet above the desert, three to four miles to the north of the ruins. I regard them as identical with the *Til-Abî(û)b* of Ezekiel chiefly for the following four considerations: 1. The archives of Murashû Sons proved that many Jewish exiles actually must have been settled in the districts around Nippur. 2. All these Babylonian sand-hills, while constantly changing their aspect within the area covered by them owing to certain whirlwinds, and gradually extending even farther into the fertile plain, on the whole have remained stationary, as we can infer from a comparison of the reports of early travellers with our own observations. 3. The remarkably large number of Hebrew bowls found everywhere in the smaller mounds within a radius of five to ten miles to the east and north of Nuffar testify to a great Jewish settlement in these regions as late as the seventh century of our own era. 4. The extensive sand-hill, or *til-abûb*, of Nuffar lies about a mile or more to the east of the ancient bed of the Shatt en-Nîl, a fact which agrees most remarkably with a statement in Ezek. 3 : 15, according to which the prophet went from the Chebar to Tel-abî(û)b, so that this Jewish colony cannot have been situated in the immediate fertile neighborhood of "the great canal."

3 : 15 ; 10 : 15), stood in the very shadow of Babylonia's national sanctuary, the crumbling walls of the great temple of Bêl. For soon after the business archives of Murashû Sons had been cleaned and catalogued by the present writer, he was fortunate enough to discover the river Chebar, for which hitherto we had searched the cuneiform literature in vain, in the *nâr Kabari*, one of the three or four large navigable canals of ancient Nippur.

The question arose at once, which one of these canals still to be traced without difficulty by their lofty embankment walls represents "the river" under consideration. It seemed natural to identify "the Chebar," or *nâr Kabari*, meaning literally "the great canal," with the now dry bed of the Shatt en-Nîl, which passes through the ruined city. But while having even so expressed myself in my lectures, I preferred to withhold this theory from my introduction to vol. ix of our official publication until I could examine the topography of the entire region once more personally and search the inscriptions for additional material. I am now prepared to furnish the required proof and to state the results of my later investigations briefly as follows: 1. The largest of all the canals once watering the fields of Nippur is often written ideographically as "the Euphrates of Nippur," a name occurring even in the old-Babylonian inscriptions of the third millennium.[1] It is evident that only the canal on which Nippur itself was situated, *i. e.*, the Shatt en-Nîl of the Arabs, which divides the mounds into two approximately even halves, could have been designated in this manner. 2. An examination of all the inscriptions at my disposal revealed the fact that *nâr Kabari* is the phonetic pronunciation of the ideographic writing "The Euphrates of Nippur," and therefore also the former Babylonian name

[1] For the present comp. the passages quoted by me in "The Bab. Exp. of the U. of Pa.," series A, vol. ix, p. 76, and the cone inscription of Samsu-iluna translated below (Fourth Campaign).

of the Shatt en-Nîl. Hence it follows that "the river Chebar in the land of the Chaldeans" was the greatest canal of Babylonia proper, "the great canal" *par excellence*, which branched off from the Euphrates somewhere above Babylon and ran through almost the whole interior of the country from north to south. It was the great artery which brought life and fertility to the otherwise barren alluvial plain enclosed by the Euphrates and the Tigris and turned the whole interior into one luxuriant garden. The *nâr Kabari* had the same significance for Nippur, the most ancient and renowned city of the country, as the Euphrates for Sippara and Babylon, or the Nile for Egypt, and therefore was called most appropriately "the Euphrates of Nippur" by the Sumerians, "the great canal" by the Semitic Babylonians, and the "river Nile" by the Arabic population of later times. In some parts of Southern Babylonia the bed of the canal was wider than that of the present Euphrates below Hilla, while its average depth at Nippur measured from fifteen to twenty feet.

Wherever Haynes drove his tunnels into the real Babylonian strata of the long ridge on the west bank of the Shatt en-Nîl, he came upon extensive remains of mud buildings, broken tablets, scattered weights and seal cylinders. My

Oblong Weight in Hematite
Fifteen (shekels)

examination of all the portable antiquities excavated there led in every case to the same result, that this long-stretched mound represents the business quarter of ancient Nippur, and conceals the large mercantile houses, the shops of handicraftsmen, — the bazaars of the city, which occupied this site at least from the time of Ur-Gur, and probably even from the days of Sargon I. The contents of the archives of the firm of Murashû Sons; the strictly businesslike character of all the neo-Babylonian tablets obtained from there; the eighteen thousand administrative lists and books of entry of the Cassite period; the thousands of case tablets of the third pre-Christian millennium; the large number of triangular clay labels — and more especially fifty-six of ellipsoidal form found together in one room — all of which bear a short legend or a seal impression, or both at the same time, and without exception are provided with holes for the thread by which they were tied to sacks, baskets, boxes, merchandise of every description;[1] the many oblong[2] and duck-shaped weights in stone, one (fragmentary) even sculptured in the form of a resting lamb inscribed with seven lines of early Babylonian writing, and the much more numerous ones in clay, sometimes evidently belonging to a series; the exceptionally large number of seal cylinders, as a rule cracked, broken, badly effaced or otherwise damaged by fire, which for the greater part were gathered in the accumulated débris of the ravines or in the loose earth

Triangular Label ("One Lamb, the Shepherd Uzi-ilu")

Label with Seal Impression
About 2200 B. C.

[1] Haynes regarded them as amulets or charms, a pardonable mistake, as he could not read their inscriptions.

[2] Among them the fine inscribed hematite weight with the inscription, "ten shekels, gold standard, the *damkar*," published in Hilprecht, "The Bab. Exp. of the U. of Pa.," series A, vol. i, part 2, no. 132.

on the slopes of the mounds, — these and many other facts and considerations which cannot be set forth here in detail afford positive proof for the correctness of my theory.

Some of the houses seem to have covered a considerable area. Haynes calls them palace-like buildings. It is, therefore, the more to be regretted that the unscientific method of excavating introduced by Peters and continued by Haynes especially in this section, where confessedly they endeavored to secure the largest possible amount of inscribed material at the least possible outlay of time and money, has thus far deprived me of the possibility of restoring the ground plan and describing the inner arrangement of even a single real Babylonian business house. In several instances "the archives were found in the very position in which they had been left when the building was destroyed." The tablets were "placed on their edges reclining against each other like a shelf of leaning books in an ill-kept library of to-day." As a rule, however, they lay broken and in great confusion on the ground, or they were buried between the layers of rubbish which covered the floor. Some of the tablets, particularly those of the Cassite period, must have been of an enormous size. Restored on the basis of excavated fragments, the largest unbaked tablet was 10 by 14 by 3 inches and the largest baked, 16 by 12 by 3½ inches. As most of the tablets discovered were unbaked or baked insufficiently, they not only are badly broken and chipped off everywhere, but they have suffered exceedingly from the humidity of the soil in which they lay. In many cases the salts of nitre contained in the clay had crystallized and caused the gradual disintegration of complete documents, or at least, the flaking off of the

Ellipsoidal Label. Dated in the Reign of King Ammisadugga

inscribed surfaces. Frequently they crumbled to dust immediately after their discovery or soon afterwards, on their way from Nuffar to Constantinople. The often advised baking of such tablets was not only useless, but proved repeatedly even most damaging, as it accelerated the process of dissolution and hardened the dirt, filling the cuneiform characters to such a degree that it could not be removed later. Thus far, none of the means generally recommended has proved an effective preservative for tablets doomed to destruction long before they are discovered.

While the large mass of documents obtained from this ridge (VII–VIII) has to do with transactions of private individuals, there are others which evidently have reference to government affairs and to the business administration of the temple. This is especially the case with a number of tablets excavated in the southeast section (VI), situated opposite the priests' quarters and the temple library (IV). It seems, therefore, not unlikely that the temple owned some property on the west side of the canal also, and that a large government building once occupied part of this mound. The fragments of several barrel cylinders of Sargon of Assyria (722–705 B. C.) discovered at VI by the first (comp. pp. 312, *seq.*, above) and third expeditions point in this direction. It cannot be denied, on the other hand, that a number of the objects coming from these hills most assuredly were out of their original places, and very

Cassite Account Tablet. About 1400 B. C.

probably were carried at different times from the temple quarters to the west part of the city. I count among these antiquities a terra-cotta dog with a brief neo-Babylonian legend; several stray lapis lazuli discs from the upper strata with votive inscriptions of Kurigalzu, Nazi-Maruttash and

Votive Tablet of Ur-Enlil. About 4000 B. C.

Upper Section: Ur-Enlil offering a libation to Enlil (Bêl).
Lower Section: A pastoral scene (goat, sheep, herdsmen).

Kadashman-Turgu (about 1400 B. C.); a fine inscribed terra-cotta vase, about 3 inches high, of the third pre-Christian millennium, originally filled "with the choicest oil" and presented as "a bridal gift" to some deity; the flat round ends of two inscribed terra-cotta cones found in

1893 and 1895 respectively, at places and levels widely apart from each other, and containing identical inscriptions of Damiqilishu, a little-known "powerful king, king of (N)isin, King of Shumer and Akkad,"[1] who "restored the great wall of (N)isin and called its name *Damiqilishu-migir-Ninib*" ("D. is the favorite of the god Ninib"); three inscribed unbaked clay prisms of the same period; a soapstone tablet of Dungi of Ur recording his constructing a temple to the goddess Damgalnunna in Nippur;[2] the very ancient exquisite stele of Ur-Enlil, a high officer in the service of Bêl,[3] and several other valuable votive objects, sculptured and inscribed. Most of them were gathered in the loose earth, or in the rubbish which had accumulated at the foot of the mounds and along the ancient bed of the Shatt en-Nîl. Haynes discovered even a brick stamp of Narâm-Sin and fragments of others, and one red-colored stamped brick of the same great ruler, of which he speaks himself as not having been found *in situ*.

From the material before us it becomes certain that this whole ridge must have been occupied from the earliest times to the Christian period. The numerous slipper-shaped coffins with their ordinary contents, a good many Kûfic and Arsacide coins, Hebrew bowls, the fragments of an egg-shell inscribed with Hebrew letters in black ink, and other antiquities taken by Haynes from rooms just beneath the crest of the long-stretched hill belonged to the latest inhabitants of Nippur in the first millennium of our era. The last three thousand years of Babylonian history are represented by dated business documents found in crude brick structures lying one above another. The age of these houses can frequently be determined also from the different sizes of bricks employed in them, which are familiar to us

[1] Comp. p. 382, note 2.

[2] Comp. Hilprecht, *l. c.*, vol. i, part 2, no. 123.

[3] Comp. the illustration on the previous page (417).

from the study of the successive strata in the southeast court of the *ziggurrat*. The deepest trenches and tunnels cut by Haynes into different parts of this ridge revealed abundant plano-convex bricks, crude and baked, with the well-known finger impressions which characterize the pre-Sargonic settlements everywhere in Babylonian ruins.

In connection with the last statement it is interesting and important to know that not far from the place which indicates the business house of Murashû Sons on our plan of the ruins (p. 305, above), Haynes sank a shaft, 4 [?] feet square, through nearly ninety-eight feet of débris, the last eighteen or nineteen feet of which lie below the present level of the desert. Only the lowest thirty feet of these ancient remains of human civilization thus examined deserve our attention, as the shaft was by far too narrow to determine details and differences in the higher strata which could claim a scientific value. Here, as at the temple mound, the lowest thirty feet consist principally of ashes, potsherds, and lumps of clay worked by the hand. "Numerous traces of fire abound everywhere." . . . "The fire or ash-pits are still clearly shown." . . . "The ashes are often three or more inches in depth." . . . "Occasionally a decayed bone is met with." . . . "Bits of charcoal and unconsumed brands charred" are mixed with ashes and earth. In view of Haynes' theory concerning the lowest strata of the court of the *ziggurrat*, it cannot surprise us to find that he connects all these traces with the daily life of the earliest inhabitants, and interprets them as "marking the places where the evening camp-fires were built by the first semi-migratory dwellers on this spot."

The lowest real brick structure observed by the excavator was about thirty feet above the undisturbed soil; in other words, at about the level of Narâm-Sin's pavement in the temple mound. We are led to this period also by an examination of the crude bricks, which measured 17 inches square and about 4 inches thick. What was the nature of this ancient structure? "It was a long, narrow cell, 5 feet 9 inches long, 1 foot 7 inches wide, and 1 foot 1 inch high, — a grave covered by a gable roof made of similar bricks, which rested on the sides of the low wall and met in an imaginary ridge-pole like the letter A." The tomb contained nothing but the crumbling remains "of a medium-sized adult and a broken vessel of coarse pottery."

Corbelled Arch of Crude Bricks
About 2500 B. C.

A corbelled arch of crude bricks and "a vaulted cellar of burned bricks," the latter about 12 by 8 feet in length and breadth, were discovered somewhere at "a low level" in the same mounds. From general indications, I should ascribe them to about 2500 B. C. They give evidence to the fact that arches and vaults were by no means uncommon in ancient Nippur, but as accurate details have not been given by the excavator, we must be satisfied with this simple statement.

In August, 1893, Haynes began a search for the original bed and embankment of the Chebar. He accordingly cut a long trench into the narrowest part of the depression marked V on the plan of the ruins (p. 305), and directed it from the middle of this open area to its northeast boundary and along the latter. At a depth of twenty and a half feet below the surface, which is somewhat higher than the present level of the desert, he reports to have found the ancient bed "in the middle of the stream." The north-eastern embankment of the canal proved to be "a sloping bank of reddish clay," so that the natural inference would be "that there was no well-built quay at this point" of the watercourse. While excavating the rubbish accumulated in the bed of the canal, Haynes unearthed three large fragments of a round terra-cotta fountain originally from 1½ to 2 feet in diameter, and on its outer face showing a group of birds in high relief coarsely executed.

Early Babylonian Terra-Cotta Fountain from the Bed of the Chebar

One of the fragments exhibits a richly dressed person standing on the backs of two of these creatures, through the open mouths of which the water passed. The antiquity belongs to a period prior to 2000 B. C.

It is unnecessary to follow Haynes through all the trial

trenches which at various times he opened in the mounds around the temple complex. Among the Parthian and Sassanian graves in which the upper strata abound everywhere, I mention particularly one containing "a very

Three Jars found at the Head of a Parthian Coffin. About 200 B. C.

high bath-tub coffin" and three jars placed around the head. The latter were filled with as many beautiful small alabaster bottles, a large number of decayed pearls, precious stones, necklaces, earrings, nose-rings, finger-rings, one inscribed seal cylinder in red jasper still retaining its bronze mounting, and sixteen uninscribed ones, several scarabæi, a pair of iron tweezers, and remains of linen and woolen stuffs showing the structure and fibre of the fabrics, and the white and dark-brown colors of the threads. Haynes opened altogether six hundred graves in the different parts of Nuffar, some of them very elaborate, most of them, however, being slipper- and bath-tub-shaped coffins in terra-cotta. Others were crude brick boxes; many consisted only of one or two urns greatly varying in size and form; a few were made of wood, which generally had crumbled to dust. Nearly fifty representative urns and coffins were saved and sent to Constantinople. One gray slipper-shaped coffin was decorated with "a male figure with sword and short tunic over a long shirt, four times repeated in as many panels." Another richly ornamented and blue enamelled but fragmentary sarcophagus of the same type showed "six human-headed bulls in two long, narrow panels." By far the greatest number of the enamelled slipper-shaped

Blue Enamelled Slipper-Shaped Coffin with Conventional Female Figures

coffins were decorated with a conventional female figure, a pattern seemingly reserved for the burial of women.

The northwest mound of the eastern half of the ruins yielded a few unbaked tablets of the neo-Babylonian and Assyrian periods, a stray stamped brick of Dungi, and the largest uninscribed baked brick hitherto discovered at Nuffar, measuring no less than 20 inches square. In the upper strata of the low mounds which lie about midway between the temple of Bêl and the Shatt en-Nîl, Haynes unearthed a peculiar building originally covered with a dome, "in the style of the ziarets or holy tombs of India, Persia, and Turkey." Its ruined walls, which formed a square 32 feet long, were constructed of specially made soft yellow baked bricks (12½ inches square by 3 inches thick) laid in lime mortar. They were 6 feet 9 inches thick, and still stood 7 feet 8 inches high. In the sides, which run parallel with the four faces of the *ziggurrat*, were openings 7 feet 10 inches wide. The one towards the southeast was partly occupied by an altar, which stood upon a raised platform and consisted of three receding stages. Within the building and exactly in front of the altar was a raised block of crude bricks "smoothly plastered with lime mortar," like the sides of the latter and the walls of the edifice. "Upon and around the altar to a considerable distance from it were wood ashes 6 inches in depth, an accumulation that could not have been accounted for by an occasional fire." It doubtless represents a sanctuary of the late Parthian period.

The most important discovery reported from the trenches in the western section of the same mounds, where they slope gradually towards the Shatt en-Nîl, is the quadrangular terracotta lid of a coffin ornamented with the rude bas-relief of a lion. It belongs to the same age as the building just mentioned.. For a few days excavations were carried on also in the great elevation to the east of the temple. They revealed the existence of unbaked cuneiform tablets of a very large size in a part of the ruins scarcely yet touched by the expedition. The large triangular mound to the south of the temple (in 1889 designated by the present writer as the probable site of the temple library) was not examined by the explorer during the three years which he passed almost without interruption at Nuffar.

It was stated above (p. 360) that in the summer of 1895 Haynes spent the morning hours of two weeks at the long, narrow ridge (II–III) to the north of the temple, in order to ascertain the foundations and dimensions of the ancient city wall, where in 1894 he and Meyer had discovered stamped crude bricks of Narâm-Sin immediately below

Ruins of a Parthian Temple. Altar in front. About A. D. 100.

Ur-Gur's material. He unearthed great numbers of terra-cotta cones, sometimes colored red or black at their round bases, and fragments of water spouts "in the débris that had gathered at the bottom of the wall." The former were either small and solid or large and hollow, and evidently had been used for decorating[1] its parapet; the latter had served for draining the upper surface of the structure. As Haynes accidentally had laid his trench diagonally through a bastion of the wall,[2] as was determined by the architects of the fourth expedition, his measurements obtained at that time[3] proved by far too great, and consequently may be disregarded at present, while his theory connected with the occupation of "the spacious and airy summit" of the wall by rooms for the pilgrims is based upon the plan of modern *khâns* or caravansaries rather than upon a correct conception of an early Babylonian temple, and therefore has no real merit. We close this sketch of his work at the city wall by mentioning that he reports to have discovered "a bubbling spring" — he probably means an open well — on the northeastern side of the great open court confined by this rampart, and "the brick platforms and curbs where the water-pots rested" on either side of the "spring." The bricks were those in use at the time of Narâm-Sin and his immediate successors.

Fourth Campaign, 1898–1900. The first three American expeditions to Nuffar had been sent out by the trustees of the Babylonian Exploration Fund of Philadelphia in affiliation with the University of Pennsylvania; the fourth stood under the direct control of the University of Pennsylvania. A large new museum building had been erected principally

[1] Comp. p. 148, above.

[2] Comp. the zinctype of a section of this wall below (Fourth Campaign, Temple Mound, Section 6).

[3] As reproduced in Hilprecht, "The Bab. Exp. of the U. of Pa.," series A, vol. i, part 2, pp. 20, *seq.*

by private subscriptions,[1] and a reorganization of the Archæological Department of the University had taken place under Provost Harrison. The late Dr. Pepper, who had worked so energetically for the development of archæological interests in his city, became its first president. The property of the Exploration Fund was transferred to the university, and the expedition committee henceforth discharged its duties in immediate connection with and as one of the most effective bodies of the new department. The beginning of actual American excavations in Babylonia will forever remain connected inseparably with the name of E. W. Clark, of Philadelphia, who was faithfully assisted by Mr. W. W. Frazier. It was at the initiative of the former's brother, Mr. C. H. Clark, the well-deserving chairman of the Babylonian Publication Committee, that the fourth expedition was called into existence. A small but distinguished group of generous Philadelphia citizens, whose names have become regular household words in the archæological circles of the United States, was ready again to support the scientific undertaking. In May, 1898, the present writer left New York, in order to secure the necessary firmân for the new expedition. As His Majesty the Sultan continued his gracious attitude towards the University's representative, and as the Ottoman government and the directors of the Imperial Museum facilitated his work in every way, the important document was granted so speedily that a fortnight after his arrival in Constantinople he was enabled to cable the welcome news to Philadelphia and to advise the formal appointment of the new expedition staff, the details of which had been arranged previously. Soon afterwards Dr. Pepper died suddenly in California, from heart-failure. His loss was seriously felt; but Mr. E. W. Clark, as chairman of the

[1] The fine large pavilion erected for an exhibit of antiquities obtained chiefly from the temple of Bêl was the magnificent gift of Mr. Daniel Baugh, of Philadelphia, whose name it very appropriately bears.

Expedition Committee, assisted by Mr. John Sparhawk, Jr., as treasurer, carried on the great work with unabated energy.

The Babylonian Committee of the Department of Archæology, considering the serious disadvantages which had accrued to science from the unsatisfactory equipment and the one-sided methods of exploration pursued by the second and third expeditions at Nuffar, was determined to profit from its past experience, and to relieve Haynes, who had offered his services again to the University of Pennsylvania, of that extraordinary nervous stress under which he had been laboring most of the time during the previous years. It was decided to imitate the example set by the British Museum at the first period of Assyrian exploration, when the responsibility of the work in the field was divided successfully between Sir Henry Rawlinson, as scientific director of all the English excavations carried on in Assyria, Babylonia, and Susiana, and Hormuzd Rassam, as chief practical excavator (comp. pp. 128, *seq.*). The present writer accordingly was appointed Scientific Director, and Haynes, as Field Director, was entrusted with the practical management of the work at the ruins. H. Valentine Geere, of Southampton, England, one of the two gentlemen who had been sent in 1895 to the assistance of Haynes (comp. pp. 360, *seq.*), and Clarence S. Fisher of the Department of Architecture at the University of Pennsylvania — the latter going without a salary — were chosen as the two architects of the new expedition. At Haynes' special request his wife was allowed to accompany the party as a guest of the committee, which most generously defrayed all her travelling and living expenses. It should be stated at the very outset that the remarkable comfort which the members of the fourth expedition enjoyed, in comparison with the numerous deprivations experienced by the previous ones, was in no small measure due to Mrs. Haynes' active interest in their personal welfare. She not only assisted her husband as his private secretary in his manifold duties, but she took complete charge of the household of the expedition in such an admirable manner that the members of our camp at Nuffar breathed a true homelike atmosphere thoroughly appreciated by our several visitors from Susa, Babylon, Baghdad, and Basra. This changed condition appeared so strange to the present writer, who had retained such a vivid recollection of the primitive style in which we lived in 1889, that, though our windows consisted only of spoiled photographic negatives, he at times could almost imagine himself transplanted to one of the watering-places of the Arab caliphs in the desert.[1]

On September 22, 1898, the formal contract was executed with Haynes, and the resumption of the excavations at Nuffar authorized for a period of two years, including the time consumed by travel, at an expense of $30,000, the work in the field to be carried on with an average force of 180 Arab laborers. Two days later Haynes left New York for England, where he was to meet his architects and to complete the necessary outfit, to which a number of prominent American firms most liberally had contributed general supplies, foods, and medicine.[2] Soon afterwards a final meeting was held by the present writer with the members of the expedition at the harbor of Southampton, in which the plans of operation and other details were discussed once more,

[1] Comp. Alois Musil, *Quseir 'Amra und andere Schlösser östlich von Moab*, part i, in *Sitzungsberichte der Wiener Akademie der Wissenschaften, phil.-hist. Cl.*, cxliv, vol. 7, pp. 1–51 (1902).

[2] In behalf of the committee and the members of the expedition, I take this opportunity to express the University's warm appreciation of the public spirit displayed by the representatives of these firms in the interest of science, and append their names in alphabetical order: The Adams & Westlake Co., Chicago, Ill.; Z. & W. M. Crane, Dalton, Mass.; Erie Preserving Co., Buffalo, N. Y.; Genesee Pure Food Co., Leroy, N. Y.; H. J. Heinz & Co., Pittsburg, Pa.; C. I. Hood, Lowell, Mass.; Horlick Food Co., Racine, Wis.; Libby, McNeill & Libby, Chicago, Ill.; Richardson & Robbins, Dover, Del.; Rumford Chemical Works, Providence, R. I.; Edward G. Stevens, New York; Trommer Extract of Malt Co., Fremont, Ohio.

whereupon the former returned to Philadelphia in the hope of joining the party at Nuffar in the course of the following year, as soon as the organization of the University Museum should have been completed. Mr. Haynes, with his wife and the two architects, proceeded to Marseilles, whence they sailed to Baghdad by way of Port Saïd, Aden, and Basra, arriving in the city of Hârûn ar-Raschîd on December 18 in the same year.

The sub-committee created in 1895 (comp. pp. 358, *seq.*), and consisting of Messrs. E. W. Clark, John Sparhawk, Jr., and the Scientific Director, acted again as an advisory board to those in the field. The plan which I had outlined as a basis for the work of the fourth campaign was, if possible, to determine the following points: 1. The precise character of the temple of Bêl at the principal periods of its long history, and especially before the time of King Ur-Gur (about 2700 B. C.), whom Haynes regarded as the probable monarch who at Nippur had introduced the stage-tower, the most important part of all the large Babylonian temples.[1] 2. The general dimensions of pre-Sargonic Nippur; that is, to ascertain whether outside of the temple of Bêl and the ashes and potsherds, etc., previously disclosed by Haynes' tunnels and shafts in the ridge to the west of the Shatt en-Nîl, trails could be found which would allow us to draw more positive conclusions with regard to the size and nature of the earliest settlements. 3. The length and the course of the city walls, so far as they were not discernible above ground, and the location of one or more of the three or four large city gates of Nippur, so frequently mentioned in the later Babylonian inscriptions which had been unearthed by the first three expeditions. 4. The exact position, extent, and character of the temple library, which, since my first ride over the mounds of Nuffar, I had consistently declared was buried in

Comp. Hilprecht, "The Bab. Exp. of the U. of Pa.," series A, vol. i, part 2, p. 17.

the most southern group of mounds on the eastern side of the Shatt en-Nîl (IV). 5. The distinguishing features in the modes of burials practised at ancient Nippur, and the various types and forms of pottery once used, by means of well-defined strata, dated documents, and accurate labels, in order to obtain satisfactory rules for dating the numerous vases which, so far, we had been unable to assign to any period of Babylonian history with a reasonable degree of certainty. 6. To these important problems, at Mr. E. W. Clark's special request, was added the task of excavating completely the large building with its colonnade on the west side of the Shatt en-Nîl (VII), which had been discovered and partly explored by the first expedition (comp. pp. 308, 313), and which received some attention also during the second campaign by Dr. Peters (comp. pp. 337, *seqq.*), who assigned it to the Cassite period (about 1300 B. C.), while the present writer had declared it to be Parthian (about 250 B. C.).

In order not to influence Haynes unduly in his own judgment, and to secure for him a necessary amount of liberty of action in the field within the bounds of a clearly defined course, it was decided not to communicate to him the reasons for our plans nor the hopes we expected to realize by their proper execution. Accordingly we confined ourselves to positive instructions with regard to the use of photography, the manner in which his note-books were to be kept, the preserving and packing of the antiquities desired for transport, and impressed upon him the following rules as a basis for his operations: 1. To devote only one third to one fourth of his force to the methodical exploration of the temple mound; to select the east section of the court of the *ziggurrat* and the enclosing wall of the latter as the object of his mission; and to pay greater attention to the peculiarities of the different layers than had been the case in the past. 2. While recommending "the whole of the mounds" to his care, to concentrate his efforts principally upon two of the other mounds, namely, the so-called "Tablet Hill" (IV, the probable site of the temple library), which he had not touched at all during the third campaign, and which, above all, needed a methodical exploration; and the mound represented by the so-called "Court of Columns" (VII) at the north end of the ridge to the west of the Shatt en-Nîl. 3. To make the settling of the numerous topographical questions one of the most essential tasks of this expedition, and to regard the location of one or more of the ancient city gates, particularly of the eastern and southern gates, in all probability represented by the *abullû rabû* ("the large gate"), and the *abullu Shibi*

The Daghâra Canal and a Freight-Boat (*Meshhûf*) of the Expedition

Uruku of the inscriptions, as "one of the necessary points to be determined during this campaign." The critical examination of the exposed structures and antiquities, the determination of their age, character, or contents, and their topographical and historical bearing upon our knowledge of ancient Nippur, and the acquiring of all such other details as should enable us to carry the plan, as outlined above, to a successful issue, had naturally to constitute the Scientific Director's principal share in the work of the fourth expedition.

How far did the proceedings of the party in the field justify the committee's hopes and expectations? Towards the end of January, 1899, the expedition left Baghdad, accompanied by a caravan of sixty-two camels and several mules, which carried its equipment and stores to Hilla. Here they were transferred to six large native sailing-boats, used also for conveying the staff and the Ottoman commissioner, half-a-dozen servants, about 150 of our former workmen from the vicinity of Babylon with their families and supplies, and six *zabtîye* furnished by the government as a guard, down the Euphrates, through the Daghâra canal and the Khôr el-'Afej to Nuffar. Unfortunately by that time the active staff had been reduced temporarily to Haynes alone. A few weeks after the expedition's arrival at Baghdad, Geere fell violently ill with pneumonia and dysentery, which gradually developed into typhoid fever and excluded him for a long while from the field. And scarcely had he recovered sufficiently from the two maladies when he was attacked by six date-boils at the same time. Truly this beginning was anything but encouraging; and to make matters worse, the English physician was then absent from the city, and an "intelligent English-speaking trained nurse" could not be had, so that Fisher's very natural proposal, to remain with his sick comrade until together they could join the party in the field, was accepted by Haynes.

On February 4, the six boats reached Nuffar. Welcomed by a special messenger from Hajji Tarfâ and by a large crowd of the Hamza, who did not conceal their pleasure at seeing the expedition again among them, well knowing that the presence of the foreigners "meant to them a season of prosperity," the party established itself at once in its old quarters. The seals attached to the *meftûl* were found unbroken, and the three Arab guards, to whom the property

Headquarters of the University of Pennsylvania's Fourth Expedition at Nuffar
Meftûl surrounded by gardens and reed-huts at the south foot of the ruins. The 'Afej swamps in the background.

had been entrusted, had remained "faithful to their charge under very great discouragement," waiting year after year patiently for Haynes' return and for the expected reward of their doubtless conspicuous services. They had lived near the house, and also watered the garden regularly, so that many date trees had sprung up spontaneously from the stones which our former workmen had thrown away thoughtlessly. The little plants, scarcely visible when Haynes departed from the ruins in 1896, had become waving palm trees. Some of them even bore fruit after a growth of only three and four years,[1] thus vividly illus-

[1] The ordinary time required for a date-palm to bear fruit is five years at Basra, and eight years in the less tropical gardens of Baghdad, according to

trating the proverbial fertility of ancient Babylonia, and through their flourishing state demonstrating more forcibly than many arguments could do, what might be made again of the treeless desert and pasture grounds of modern 'Irâq through well-directed human labor and proper irrigation.

The first task for Haynes was to put the wells in order, as the procuring of suitable drinking-water had gradually become a vital question for the expedition. During the first and second campaigns, which lasted only a few months, we had troubled ourselves very little about the quality of the water. We drank it as the Arab women brought it from the marshes, without boiling it and with an occasional joke as to the animal life which we observed in our jars and cups. But in 1893, when Haynes went to Nuffar with the understanding that he was to remain there through summer and winter for several years, he had to take greater care of his health and to face the problem, how to obtain the necessary supply of water during the hottest months of the year, when the marshes usually recede from the ruins. At first he had adopted the Arab method, and conducted the water to his "castle" by digging a small but sufficiently deep canal to one of the principal streams in the midst of the *Khôr*. But after the neighboring tribes, for the sake of gain, repeatedly had closed his canal, he decided in 1894 to make his camp independent of the interferences of the Arabs by digging wells around his house. This experiment led to a very unique result. The water obtained from three of them, dug at a distance of only forty to forty-five feet from each other, was as different as it possibly could be. That of the first well was "very bitter," that of the second "absolutely undrinkable for men and animals," that of the third, which subsequently was lined with bricks and provided with a pump, was "drinkable, slightly impreg-

the information which I received directly from the Arab gardeners at both places.

nated with various salts, and yet scarcely rendered unpalatable thereby." In the latter part of the fourth campaign a still purer and, in fact, most excellent water, was procured from a new fourth well, which afterwards was vaulted over entirely to prevent its pollution by the Arabs, while the precious liquid was conducted by subterranean pipes into the court of the *meftûl*, so that in case of a siege we should never suffer from lack of water.

For almost three years the building of the expedition had remained unoccupied and had been exposed to the heavy rains of the winter and the equally damaging effect of the hot rays of the sun. But though consisting only of clay laid up *en masse*, it was found in better condition than could reasonably have been anticipated. As the fast days of Ramadhân were drawing to their close, Haynes, in true Arab style, had it announced by heralds in the camps and villages of the 'Afej that no native workman would be engaged before the approaching festival of Bairâm was over. At the same time he divided his large body of Hilla men into three groups, ordering the one section to prepare the tools for work in the trenches and to re-open the excavations; the second to dig roots and gather thorn bushes as fuel for the kitchen; the third to build reed huts for the families of the laborers and to repair the "castle." In consequence of the increased staff of the expedition, the *meftûl* proved by far too small. Arrangements had, therefore, to be made at once to accommodate the larger party by adding another story to the old structure. As a number of Arabs, well versed in the art of primitive house-building, were at Haynes' disposal, the difficulty was soon removed, and all his time could be devoted to the principal task of the expedition.

A word remains to be said about the attitude of the 'Afej, Hamza, Sa'îd and other neighboring tribes. Without exception, they remained friendly towards us during the whole campaign. Hajji Tarfâ proved the same staunch supporter of our plans as he always had been. Though less elastic in his movements than when we met him the first time, and slightly bent by the burden of years, the "Moltke of the 'Afej," as he was styled very appropriately by the wâli of Baghdad, had understood how to retain and even to increase his influence among his shiftless but refractory subjects, and hold the younger shaikhs in discipline, who often were eager to win their own laurels and to strengthen their position at the expense of the venerable patriarch. The Turkish government, realizing how valuable his services were in controlling the most troublesome province of the whole vilayet, was ready to assist him in his efforts to keep peace, and repeatedly gave him visible proofs of the high esteem in which he was held throughout the country. At

Hajji Tarfâ's Garden and Reception Room (*Mudhîf*)

his earliest opportunity Haynes hurried over to the great chieftain's *meftûl*, about six miles distant, to pay him an official visit. In the presence of his warriors he put around his neck a long chain of gold (for the watch previously given to him), and threw over his shoulder a fine cloak (*'abâ*), woven with silver thread, presents from the committee, to which, a year later, the present writer added a Whitman saddle, for which Hajji Tarfâ had expressed a genuine admiration.

The care for the safety of the expedition through proper guards was entrusted by the shaikh of all the 'Afej to the same two Hamza leaders who in former years had been responsible to him. They kept their pledges honorably to the end of the campaign. All the tribes inhabiting the borders of the marshes intermingled freely with our men and looked upon us with a certain feeling of pride, almost as upon members of their own clans, who from time to time appeared on their territory, for a while sharing their pasture grounds and leaving behind them untold blessings when they departed. A great change had taken place on these barren plains since I had seen them last. It was the natural result of the transfer of the capital to Dîwânîye, and in no small measure due to the tactful but energetic treatment of the 'Afej tribes on the part of the Ottoman government. A sacred calm lay in the air, — not the calm preceding a disastrous storm, but that divine calm which announces a new era of happiness to the people. Every flower and reed, every shepherd and bird seemed to be conscious of it and to realize that Isaiah's and Jeremiah's curse of two thousand years was about to lift from the country. The dry bones of Babylonia's vast graveyard began to rise and to be clad again with sinews and flesh under Jehovah's life-breathing spirit that blew softly through the land of Bêl (Ezek. 37). There can be no doubt that Babylonia stands at the dawn of a general resurrection. Unmistakable signs of a new and more peaceful development of the many natural resources of Shumer and Akkad are visible everywhere. A great movement and expectation has taken possession of the tribes of the interior, partly brought about in consequence of the acquisition and cultivation of large tracts of land along the canals for the Sultan, and partly inspired by the various scientific missions from Europe and America. Through their continued exploration of the ruins these foreign excavators have introduced new ideas into the country, made the people acquainted with important inventions, and, above all, taught them the value of time and work, thus preparing the way for the planned German railroad, of which even the 'Afej speak with great anticipation, and which surely will play the chief missionary rôle throughout the country.

When, after a long absence, I stood again on the airy top of Bint el-Amîr, as far as my eye could scan the horizon I saw nothing but immense flocks of sheep and goats, donkeys and cows and buffaloes pastured by cheerful boys and men, Arab villages and encampments scattered over the plain, and small green patches of cultivated ground on the edges of the inundated districts; the camel herds and black tents of the Sa'îd in the distance, and far away beyond the Tigris towards the east, only now and then visible, the snow-capped mountains[1] of Lûristân. At my first meeting with the Hamza shaikhs and their retinues, they were somewhat disappointed because they did not recognize me. In order to establish my identity, they submitted me to a cross-examination, inquiring whether I remembered the burning of our camp. But scarcely had I begun to recount the details of the disaster, the destruction of my fine horse, Marduk, and the fortunate escape of another, *Abû khams* ("father of five," namely, Turkish liras), as I had named it, with due regard to its low price — a joke thoroughly appreciated by the Arabs, — and to refer to the principal persons connected with the catastrophe, asking on my part for the ill-fated

[1] The Assyrian word for "east" is *shadû*, "mountain," as the Hebrew one for "west" is *yâm*, "ocean."

Camel Herds of the Shammar browsing among the Thorn-Bushes around Nuffar

Mukota's little son and Berdi's tall brother, who restored my saddle-bags, when their eyes sparkled with excitement. They exclaimed, "*Wallah* [by God], he is *Abû dhaq(a)n* [father (*i. e.*, owner) of a beard]," the name by which I used to be known among them; and drawing closer upon me, they lighted their cigarettes, drank their coffee, rehearsed old jokes, chatted like children, and asked hundreds of questions about Harper and Field, the new railroad, the speed of its trains, their prospect of exporting sheep and butter and rice, etc. "Oh, *Abû dhaq(a)n*, how times have changed. Once we wanted to rob you, and now you are our brother, whom may Allah bless." Of course the petty quarrels did not cease altogether among the various tribes; and murderers and other desperadoes took refuge in the Khôr el-'Afej then, as they did before, but they never molested us. The most exciting scene that occurred while we were at Nuffar, was the settling of a very old case of blood-feud, under the very walls of our *meftûl*, and the cowardly and atrocious manner in which, on this occasion, the life of a perfectly innocent Arab was taken.

Excavations were commenced at the extreme southeastern end of the west ridge (VI) on February 6, 1899, with all the available workmen from Hilla. In order to strike any possible remains of the ancient city wall, if ever it should have existed in this section of Nippur, Haynes opened a trench at a little distance from the ruins and descended gradually below the level of the plain in the direction of the mounds. But, strange to say, still convinced that his chief task consisted in a "successful tablet-hunting" rather than in a strictly scientific exploration of Nuffar, as had been impressed so emphatically upon him, he also set to work at once to clean a large old trench abandoned three years before, and endeavored "to push the excavations forward into the mounds towards the points where great quantities of tablets had been found" previously.

Three days after the resumption of the work he came upon "a wall of burned bricks crossing the line of the [first mentioned] trench transversely, but lying at a lower level." Our expectations were raised exceedingly when this report reached Philadelphia. But three weeks later, long before the first weekly letter was in our hands, Haynes abandoned it on his own responsibility, having followed its course for 489 feet "without finding either end of it" or discovering "any trace of door or window" in it. We were disappointed. Spring and summer were spent in a well-meant, nervous search for tablets and other portable antiquities by carrying a trench 155 feet wide with an extreme depth of 36 feet a distance of 75 feet into the mound, and by opening smaller trenches and tunnels at other points in the same general locality. In this manner about five thousand cuneiform tablets, mostly fragmentary contracts and lists of the third pre-Christian millennium, about thirty seal cylinders, as a rule much worn off or otherwise damaged, about a dozen interesting clay reliefs, and a few other antiquities were gathered from the lower levels of the ridge in the course of the first six months. An arch of baked bricks and the fragment of a watercourse similar to those discovered in the lower section of the temple mound were also briefly referred to. The upper strata and the slopes of the mounds yielded about 450 late coffins of various types with their usual contents, a number of bronze bowls, several thin blue glass bottles of the post-Christian period, a jar containing miscellaneous coins, articles of jewelry and junk, — the store of a Parthian jeweller! — about thirty Hebrew and Mandean bowls, among them two containing an inscribed skull in pieces, besides other minor antiquities.

The reports became more meagre every day, furnishing practically no information about the excavations beyond a simple statement as to how many tablets, seal cylinders and other more striking objects had been discovered during the week, and how many coffins had been opened. Neither photograph nor sketch accompanied the letters. Haynes doubtless worked very seriously with his 208 Arabs. But notwithstanding his honest efforts, it was naturally impossible for him to control such a large body of men. The results would have been more satisfactory to himself and to the committee, if he had retained only fifty workmen in the trenches as long as he was alone, and devoted a part of his time to a technical description of his excavations, to photographing and other necessary details upon which the success of an expedition largely depends. As matters stood, it became next to impossible for the committee to form any adequate idea as to what actually was going on at Nuffar. Besides, letters required five to seven weeks before they reached Philadelphia. Something had to be done quickly, if the plans we had formulated were ever to be realized. To complicate matters even more, misunderstandings arose between the two architects at Baghdad on the one hand and the managing director in the field on the other. This led to Fisher's resignation in April and his immediate return to England, and for a second time threatened to bring about Geere's separation from the work of the Philadelphia expedition.[1] At the beginning of June we were in the possession of all the facts necessary to meet, to act, and to decide as to the future course of the expedition. The results of this important meeting became soon apparent. Fisher returned to Baghdad in the early fall, and soon afterwards, together with Geere, who by that time had fully recovered his usual health, departed for Nuffar, arriving there on October 20, 1899. Upon the unanimous decision of the committee the scientific director was to follow and to take charge of the excavations at the ruins in person as soon as the organization of the University Museum should have been completed. Haynes at the same

[1] Comp. pp. 360, *seq.*, above.

time received more positive instructions as to the manner in which he was to proceed to carry the work of the expedition to a satisfactory issue. In accordance with the desires of the committee he henceforth directed his attention principally to the exploration of the eastern half of the court of the temple, to the search for the northeast city gate, and to the excavation of the probable site of the temple library, the so-called "Tablet Hill" (IV), so that his Arabs were not scattered over too large a surface, and with the subsequent assistance of the two architects could be controlled without difficulty.

Owing to Haynes' praiseworthy energy and characteristic devotion to his duties, he soon could report conspicuous tangible results, and illustrate them by his own photographs and by sketches drawn by his assistants. He evidently worked hard according to the best of his ability. But unfortunately our positive knowledge as to the topography of the ruins was advanced but little thereby. The statements were too vague to enable us to draw any conclusions. On October 28 he wrote with regard to the northeast city gate: "Up to the present moment, we have found no certain clue beyond a mere fragment of very archaic wall, to indicate the existence at that point of a gate or other structure." The whole important subject was never mentioned afterwards except in the brief title of a photograph despatched three months later, which, however, reached Philadelphia only after my arrival at Nuffar. By the middle of December tablets began to be found in such large quantities in the northeastern part of the "Tablet Hill," that even Haynes was forced to admit that this collection of tablets looked very much as if "constituting a distinct library by itself." But whether it was merely another of these collections of contract tablets so frequently found in the west half of the ruins and always styled by him "libraries," or whether it was *the* library for which I was looking so eagerly, the temple library, could not be determined, as proper descriptions were lacking and no attempt was made to reproduce a few lines of some of the better-preserved documents.

It was very evident that, above all, the assistance of an experienced archæologist and Assyriologist was required at Nuffar to decipher tablets, to determine the characteristic features of strata, to fix the approximate age of walls and other antiquities, to ascertain their probable purpose and use, to lay trenches for other reasons than to find tablets, and to gather all the loose threads together and to endeavor to reconstruct some kind of a picture of the ancient city on the basis of his examination and studies. The architects did their very best to assist Haynes and to promote the cause of the expedition. But entirely unfamiliar with Babylonian archæology as they then were, and for the first time confronted with the complicated problems of a Babylonian ruin, they needed technical advice as to how to overcome the difficulties. Being left entirely to their own resources, they decided to undertake what they were able to do under the circumstances. They sketched drains, tombs, vases and various other antiquities to illustrate Haynes' weekly reports; they tried to make themselves acquainted with the remains of the *ziggurrat* previously drawn by Meyer, and to survey and plot the constructions occupying the eastern corner of the temple court prior to their removal. But they also facilitated my later work on the ruins in one essential point. As we saw above (pp. 371, *seq.*), in the course of the third campaign, Haynes had discovered the remains of the original approach to the *ziggurrat*, indicated by two almost parallel walls, extending nearly at a right angle far into the court from the southeastern face of the stage-tower. It had appeared, therefore, most natural to the present writer to assume that the principal gate or entrance to the temple court must lie in the enclosing wall somewhere opposite that approach. In 1897, when I first had occasion to examine all of Haynes' negatives thoroughly, I was surprised to find that he had exposed a number of stepped recesses precisely at the place where the gate should have existed, and that he had actually discovered the entrance without knowing and reporting it, as unfortunately he had cut one half of the gate completely away by one of his wretched perpendicular shafts which proved so disastrous to the temple court. The architects were not slow in recognizing the importance of these stepped recesses, and asked at once for permission to remove the large round tower of the latest fortification, lying directly on the top of them — the same which Peters had compared with the pillar of Jachin or Boaz at the temple of Jerusalem (comp. p. 333, above).

Haynes gave it reluctantly, as he thought the expense of time and labor involved in this work too great in comparison with the probable results expected by him, and left the architects in complete charge of this excavation. They solved their first independent task very satisfactorily, uncovered the remaining part of the gate, found a door-socket *in situ*, and disclosed the existence of an important tomb near the south corner of the latest enclosing wall, on which we shall have to say a few words later.

By the middle of November, 1899, the scientific director had finished the organization of the Semitic section of the University Museum, so that he could leave for the East to join the other members of the expedition. But in consequence of considerable delays caused to the boats by storms in the Atlantic, by the discharge of a heavy cargo at the Somali coast, by quarantine in the Shatt el-'Arab for having touched at the plague-, cholera-, and small-pox-stricken harbor of Maskat, and finally by the sudden rise of the Tigris, he did not reach Nuffar before March 1, 1900. Having gone out "as the representative of the committee and with the full powers of the committee," he naturally was held responsible for the proper execution of the plans as outlined

The Removal of a Tower of the Seleucido-Parthian Fortress and the Clearing of the Ancient Temple Gate beneath it

above. After a careful examination of all the trenches and a full discussion of the whole situation with Haynes, I found it necessary to change entirely the methods hitherto employed. Accordingly all the excavations carried on for the mere purpose of finding tablets and other antiquities were suspended, especially as I had ascertained through a study of representative tablets, an inspection of the rooms in which they had been discovered, and a brief continuation of the work in the trenches, that the "Tablet Hill" actually represented the site of the temple library, as I had maintained for so many years. I regarded the further exploration of this library as by far less important than the solving of some of the many other complicated topographical problems which in the past had received so little attention, before the exposed building remains should have crumbled beyond recognition. Originally it had been my intention also to excavate the largely untouched southwest section of the temple court methodically, in order to supplement and to correct the one-sided information received previously and to study personally layer after layer, pavement after pavement, with a view of providing new material for settling the question as to whether important buildings had occupied the temple court at the different periods of its history. But when I found that enormous dump-heaps had been raised there by my predecessors I had to give up this plan, as the examination could not begin properly before the latter had been removed to a safe distance — a task alone requiring more time and labor than was at my disposal for the various tasks together.

Considering all the circumstances, there was nothing to be done but to accept the situation as it presented itself, and to make the best of it. In the interest of science I therefore decided to leave the unexplored sections of the court of the *ziggurrat* and the temple library to a subsequent fifth expedition, as both doubtless were safer when covered with earth than if inadequately examined and exposed to the fury of the elements. This expedition was sent out to endeavor to understand Nuffar as a whole, not to remove large mounds of débris merely for the sake of finding portable antiquities and tablets by the bushel and to count their market value in dollars and cents. I was personally despatched to solve scientific problems and to interpret the ruins. The more essential topographical questions once having been settled, it would be a comparatively easy task for the committee to have the single mounds excavated one after another by somebody else, if necessity arose, who was less familiar with the ruins and the history of their exploration than the present writer, who had been connected with this undertaking from its very beginning. Every trench cut henceforth — and there were a great many — was cut for the sole purpose of excavating structures systematically and of gathering necessary *data* for the history and topography of ancient Nippur. If these trenches yielded tangible museum results at the same time, so much the better ; if they did not, I was not troubled by their absence and felt just as well satisfied as if I had packed several thousand tablets, or perhaps even more so. But in order to state this expressly here, antiquities were found so abundantly in the pursuit of the plan described, that the principle was established anew that a strictly scientific method of excavating is at the same time the most profitable.

The number of workmen was increased and maintained until the middle of April, when many of the native Arabs began to quit the trenches to harvest their barley and to look after their agricultural interests. Haynes retained full charge of the men in the field under my general supervision. Fisher and Geere were instructed to make a complete survey of all the remaining walls, buildings, drains, pavements, etc., excavated by the second, third, and fourth expeditions, and

Incantation Bowls inscribed in Hebrew Characters. About 750–850 A. D.

to prepare special plans of all those structures which I was able to assign to certain periods and to bring into closer relation with each other. As far as it served to facilitate their task and to introduce them into the archæological work proper, both were placed in charge of their own gangs under Haynes' immediate control, while I reserved to myself the right of advising them and of modifying or changing the courses of all the trenches whenever new developments in them should require it. The entire length of the northeast city wall was traced and studied, and a number of interesting structures and antiquities found in connection with them. All the explored rooms of the temple library and of the later buildings lying over them were surveyed and drawn. The long brick wall reported to have been found and abandoned by Haynes at the southeast edge of the west half of the ruins (p. 440, above), was explored successfully and its real nature and purpose determined. In accordance with Mr. E. W. Clark's request, the so-called "Court of Columns" (VII on the plan of the ruins) received very considerable attention. After its complete excavation I could only confirm my view formulated in 1889, that this fine little palace belongs to the Hellenistic period, in other words, is of Parthian, not of Cassite origin.[1] The upper strata covering this building afforded me an excellent opportunity to examine into the manner in which the inscribed incantation bowls had been used by the Jewish inhabitants of Calneh in the eighth and ninth centuries of our era. For the present it may suffice to state that most of the one hundred bowls excavated while I was on the scene were found upside down in the ground, as will be seen from the illustration on page 448. It is very evident that they had been placed thus intentionally, in order to prevent the demons adjured by the spiral inscription on the inner face of most of the vases, from doing any harm to the

[1] Comp. p. 337 with p. 340.

people living in that neighborhood. Sometimes two bowls facing one another had been cemented together with bitumen. In one case an inscribed hen's egg was concealed

Hebrew Incantation Bowls in their Original Position
Seven placed upside down, one with the inscribed face upward

under the bowl. This egg, like the inscribed skulls previously reported (comp. p. 440), is probably to be regarded as a sacrifice to those demons to appease their wrath and check their evil influence.[1]

The excavation of those upper strata also enabled me to study the numerous late burials contained therein, which almost exclusively belonged to the post-Christian period. In order to obtain more definite results concerning the dates of other tombs, not so favorably situated, we examined a section of the ruins to the north-

[1] Comp. the skulls and egg discovered in the mortar of the Parthian palace lying on the top of the ruins of Bêl's sanctuary, p. 368, above, and Pognon, *Inscriptions Mandaïtes des Coups de Khouabir*, Paris, 1898, pp. 2, *seq*.

west of the temple, which was literally filled with graves, and compared their forms and contents with the other ones. As it is impossible to present here the results of a study of more than 2,500 tombs excavated by all the four expeditions at Nuffar, including over 1,100 examined during the fourth campaign, I confine myself to stating in this connection that with but few exceptions all those excavated tombs belong to the post-Babylonian period. But it was also ascertained that prior to the time of Sargon I (about 3800 B. C.), as we shall see presently, Nippur was one of the sacred burial-grounds of the earliest inhabitants of the country, who cremated their dead there, as they did at Surghul and El-Hibba.[1]

The most difficult problem confronting me was the explanation of the ruins at Bint el-Amîr and its environments, owing to the previous removal and frequent involuntary destruction of much valuable material on the part of my predecessors. Some of the results which I obtained this time were incorporated in my above sketch of the second and third campaigns. The other more important ones will be treated briefly below. They may be summarized as follows: 1. A stage-tower of smaller dimensions existed at Nippur before Sargon I (about 3800 B. C.). 2. In pre-Sargonic times the ground around the sacred enclosure was a vast graveyard, a regular fire necropolis. 3. One of the names of the stage-tower of Nippur suggested the idea of tomb to the early inhabitants of the country. In the course of time certain *ziggurrats* were directly designated by the Babylonians as tombs of the gods. 4. The stage-tower of Bêl did not occupy the centre of the enclosed platform, but the southwest section of it, while the northeast part was reserved for "the house of Bêl," his principal sanctuary, which stood at the side of the stage-tower. 5. The temple of Bêl consisted of two large

[1] Comp. pp. 283, *seqq.*, above.

courts adjoining each other, the northwest court with the *ziggurrat* and "the house of Bêl" representing the most holy place or the inner court, while the southeast (outer) court seems to have been studded with the shrines of all the different gods and goddesses worshipped at Nippur, including one for Bêl himself. 6. *Imgur-Marduk* and *Nîmit-Marduk*, mentioned in the cuneiform inscriptions as the two walls of Nippur (*dûru* and *shalkhû*), cannot have surrounded the whole city. According to the results of the excavations conducted under my own supervision, only the temple was enclosed by a double wall, while in all probability the city itself remained unprotected. 7. The large complex of buildings covering the top of Bint el-Amîr has nothing to do with the ancient temple below, but represents a huge fortified Parthian palace grouped around and upon the remains of the stage-tower then visible. In order to understand the temple correctly, this fortress has to be eliminated completely from the ruins, as was demanded by the present writer as early as 1889.[1]

A thorough treatment of the whole important question will be found in a special work entitled "Ekur, the Temple of Bêl at Nippur," which will be fully illustrated and accompanied by large plans and diagrams prepared by the architects of the expedition according to my reconstructions and their own survey of the actual remains still existing. For the present I must confine myself to a brief sketch of the principal results as obtained by the combined efforts of all the members of the staff during the latter part of the fourth campaign and interpreted by the present writer.

1. An examination of the inscriptions from Tellô,[2] the fact

[1] Comp. p. 327, above, and Peters' "Nippur," vol. ii, p. 118: "One of our Assyriologists reached the conclusion that the ruins we had found were those of a fortress . . . built on the site of the ancient temple."

[2] Comp. p. 232, note 2, above, and Hommel, *Aufsätze und Abhandlungen*, part iii, 1 (Munich, 1901), pp. 389, *seqq.*

that all the Babylonian temples and stage-towers have Sumerian names, and other considerations had convinced me that the origin of the *ziggurrat* at Nippur must lie far beyond the time of Ur-Gur. The mere circumstances that the pavement of Sargon and Narâm-Sin covered about the same space between the inner wall and the later *ziggurrat* as those of the following rulers; that nowhere in the excavated large section of the temple court it extended beneath the tower; that the store-room or cellar found within the southeast enclosing wall by the third expedition (pp. 386, 390, above), occupied exactly the same place at the time of Sargon as in the days of Ur-Gur, — indicated sufficiently that the temple enclosure showed practically the same characteristic features at 3800 B. C. as at 2800 B. C.

The massive L-shaped structure (p. 395, above) underlying the east corner of Ur-Gur's *ziggurrat*, and constructed of the same unusually large bricks as those which thus far at Nippur have been connected exclusively with the names of Sargon and Narâm-Sin, evidently was the work of a member of that powerful ancient dynasty. As it descended eleven feet below Narâm-Sin's pavement, it is also clear that this structure, which puzzled Haynes so much, must have served a similar purpose as Ur-Gur's crude brick pavement, which was eight feet deep and extended all around and beneath the edges of the stage-tower in support of the latter. In other words, it was the foundation for the east corner of Narâm-Sin's *ziggurrat*. Similar foundations may be found at the three other corners, but it is more probable to assume that it occurs only at this particular point, where the necessity of an extraordinary foundation can be explained without difficulty. We saw above (p. 397), that Haynes discovered a ruined vaulted aqueduct, about 3 feet high, beneath it. With the exception of a small section near the orifice (directly below the ancient curb and supported by the T-shaped structure) the whole upper part of the vault had collapsed without leaving extensive traces of the baked material of which it originally consisted. On the other hand, large numbers of pre-Sargonic bricks were found in the lower row of Narâm-Sin's pavement. It seems therefore reasonable to connect the two facts and to explain the situation as follows. About the time of Narâm-Sin, perhaps even in consequence of his enlarging the heavy mass of the *ziggurrat*, the ancient aqueduct below had caved in. In order to secure a more solid foundation for the east corner, it became necessary to ascertain the cause of the subsequent depression of the surface. Narâm-Sin therefore descended about twelve feet, removed the rubbish, saved all the good bricks for his pavement, and built the peculiarly shaped massive structure eleven feet high directly over it, in order to prevent the formation of crevices in his structure by the uneven settling of the disturbed ground below it.

This much is sure, that the mere existence of this solid foundation at the eastern corner of the *ziggurrat* at the time of Narâm-Sin necessarily leads us to the conclusion that also a large building which it was intended to support, a stage-tower, must have existed at that ancient period in Nippur. This conclusion is fully corroborated by the fact that below Ur-Gur's gray-colored bricks in the centre of the *ziggurrat*, other similar bricks were found, which in texture, color and size are identical with those of Narâm-Sin's store-room or cellar, in the southeast enclosing wall. The southeast face of this early *ziggurrat* was actually discovered by means of a tunnel following a pre-Sargonic water-course which ran into the strata below Ur-Gur's stage-tower. It lay four feet behind Ur-Gur's facing wall, and was carefully built of the same crude bricks just mentioned, which form the kernel of the *ziggurrat*.[1]

Since the water-course thus traced continued its way under

1 Comp. the zinctype "Section of the Stage-Tower and the Adjoining Southeast Court," in the chapter on the topography of Nippur, below.

Southeast View of the Ziggurrat of Nippur. Excavated to the Water Level

Three stages visible. 1. Pre-Sargonic drains. 1a. Pre-Sargonic curb. 2. Ascent to the ziggurrat of Ur-Gur and successors. 3. Pillar of earth left standing to show different strata and original height of mound. 4. Remains of Parthian fortress, formerly covering the entire temple ruins. 5. Temporary building erected by Haynes.

Narâm-Sin's tower, and sloped gently from a point near and within the pre-Sargonic curb towards the former, it was evident that if a pre-Sargonic *ziggurrat* existed at Nippur it must have been considerably smaller than that of Narâm-Sin and lay entirely within and largely below it. In order to ascertain all the desirable details both of Narâm-Sin's and of this possibly earlier structure, it would have been necessary to remove Bêl's *ziggurrat* completely by peeling off layer after layer. This method is the only one by which the precise nature and history of this important part of the venerable sanctuary can be determined satisfactorily, but it involves much time, labor and expense, and the destruction of one of the earliest landmarks of the country.

All that the Philadelphia expedition could do under the circumstances was to operate with a few carefully made tunnels — a somewhat dangerous proceeding in view of the ponderous mass of crude bricks above, but one already successfully begun by Haynes in previous years, and without any serious accident also continued by our ablest workmen during the fourth campaign. It seems, however, absolutely essential, in view of the important problem before us, that a complete vertical section, about a fourth of the whole mass, should be cut out of the *ziggurrat* at one of its four corners by a future fifth expedition. The smooth and plastered surface of the southeast side of a pre-Sargonic *ziggurrat* built of crude bricks was discovered at two places about forty feet distant from each other. It lay nearly fourteen feet within the outer edge of Ur-Gur's facing wall, and was traced for about six to ten feet in its descent to the ancient level of the plain. Whether and how far it went below that point could not be ascertained without exposing the workmen and the explorers to the risk of being entombed and suffocated suddenly within the sacred precinct of Bêl.

Two similar but sloping tunnels were carried into the mass beneath the northeast side of the *ziggurrat*. But as the clay was too wet, the light too poor and the trenches perhaps too short, they did not reveal positive traces of the earlier building. We were, however, rewarded by another discovery made in the most northern trench. At a point several feet below the level of Narâm-Sin's pavement and still outside of the *ziggurrat*, we came upon a well-defined small bed of black and gray ashes 3 to 4 inches high. Several rude blocks of stone lay around it, and the fragments of a bronze[1] sword or dagger were found among the ashes. What did these few ancient remains from below the Sargon level in the neighborhood of the *ziggurrat* indicate? Haynes had found such beds of ashes mixed with fragments of pottery and occasionally accompanied by objects in copper and bronze (nails, knives, battle axes, portions of vessels) or beads in stone, silver, and even gold, rings and other jewelry, seal cylinders, etc., everywhere in the lower strata to the southeast of the stage-tower (comp. pp. 401, *seqq.*). My curiosity was aroused, and I was determined to make an effort to ascertain the meaning of these remarkable relics.

2. Unfortunately the greater part of the southeast section of the temple enclosure had been removed before my arrival. But Haynes' perpendicular cuts enabled me at least to obtain an excellent side view of all the single strata of the remaining unexplored portions from the Sargon level down to the virgin soil. As soon as I began to examine them one after another, I was struck with the enormous mass of larger and smaller fragments of pottery intermingled with ashes which peeped out of the ground wherever my eye glanced. I set to work to extricate these pieces carefully with a

[1] In which antimony took the place of tin. The analysis of one of the fragments by the late Dr. Helm of Danzig showed 96.38 parts of copper, 1.73 parts of antimony, 0.24 part of iron, 0.22 part of nickel, 1.43 parts of oxygen and loss, traces of lead. Comp. Helm and Hilprecht in the proceedings of the *Berliner anthropologischen Gesellschaft*, session of February 16, 1901, p. 159.

large knife, in order to secure the necessary information with regard to the original sizes, forms and structures of these broken terra-cotta vessels. Without exception they belonged to large, thick urns of various shapes, or small pointed vases, peculiarly formed cups, dishes and similar household vessels. In descending gradually from the pavement of Narâm-Sin, I suddenly came, three feet below it, upon a group of potsherds lying in such a manner as to suggest at once to the observer the original form of a large vase, to which they belonged.

It was a large oblong-ovate jar over 2 feet long and nearly 1½ feet at its largest diameter. The heavy weight of the débris of six thousand years lying on the top of it had crushed the vessel, which was placed almost horizontally in the ground, into hundreds of small pieces. It contained gray ashes mixed with small bits of charred wood and earth, and two long but thin streaks of yellowish ashes. Without difficulty I could determine that the gray ashes represented the remains of bones and wood consumed by fire, and the yellowish ashes those of two large bones which had decayed gradually, but apparently had belonged to the same human body. There were four or five fragmentary small cups and dishes in the urn. They were in a much better condition than the large jar which enclosed them. Two of them, which accidentally had stood almost upright and consequently offered much less resistance to the pressure from above than those which lay on their sides, were nearly whole, and had retained even the forms of decayed dates and fish-bones in the fine earth that filled them. Without knowing it, Haynes had cut through the remains of this jar lengthwise, leaving only half of it for my examination. There could be no doubt, we had here a true pre-Sargonic burial. The human body contained in it had been subjected to cremation without, however, being destroyed completely by this process. Both the ashes and the bones had afterwards been gathered, and with food and drink placed in this jar were buried in the sacred ground around the *ziggurrat*. The ash-bed unearthed at the northeast side of the stage-tower represented the place where another body had been cremated, apparently that of a man, perhaps a warrior, as the fragments of a sword found in the ashes suggested.

In the light of this discovery and Haynes' previously reported pre-Sargonic burial (pp. 403 *seq.*), of all the ash-beds and their characteristic objects, so often mentioned but completely misunderstood by him,[1] it was a comparatively easy task for me to trace the outlines of a number of other urns, though even more injured. I also secured a good many tolerably well-preserved cups and dishes, or large fragments of the same, from the débris that filled the whole ground from the undisturbed soil deep below the ancient plain level to the pavement of Narâm-Sin, far above the latter. In short, I gathered sufficient evidence to show that all these ash-beds occurring in a stratum twenty-five to thirty feet deep on all the four sides of the *ziggurrat* are to be regarded as places where human bodies had been cremated. The thousands of urns discovered above and below them, and as a rule badly crushed, but in some cases well preserved, are funeral vases, in which the ashes and bones left by the cremation, together with objects once dear to the person, besides food and drink, were placed and buried. The fragments of unbaked walls and rooms repeatedly met with in these lowest strata,[2] and always containing whole or broken urns, are remains of tombs, so-called funeral chambers. The large number of terra-cotta pipes composed of several (often perforated) rings, and descending eight, ten, and even more feet from the surface of the ancient plain and from higher

[1] Comp. pp. 402, *seqq.*, 419 above.

[2] In two instances the rooms had been vaulted, and were constructed of baked plano-convex bricks.

levels, without, however, reaching the water level, are drains which protected the single tombs and the gradually rising mound as a whole. The less frequent wells, always constructed of plano-convex bricks, were to provide the dead with that "clear [but I fear in this case often brackish !] water," which the departed pious souls were believed to drink in the lower regions.[1]

Koldewey has described the fire necropoles of Surghul and El-Hibba (comp. pp. 283, *seqq.*, above), so intelligently that it is unnecessary to repeat all the details of my own investigations in the pre-Sargonic cemetery of ancient Nippur, which confirm the German scholar's results in all essential details and at the same time prove conclusively that his view concerning the great age of these two South Babylonian ruins is perfectly correct. Suffice it to state, that here as there "ash-graves" and "body-graves" occur alongside each other in the upper layers, while the former, as the older burials, appear exclusively in the lower strata. In all the three ruins we observe the same peculiar forms and positions of urns and vases, the same kinds of sacrifices offered in connection with the cremation and the final burial, the same customs of depositing weapons, instruments, seals, jewelry, toys, etc., both with the body to be cremated and with the remains interred, the same praxis of building drains, wells and houses for the dead, the same characteristic deep red color of so many potsherds (pointing to their long exposure to an open fire), and, above all, the same scattering of ashes, charred pieces of wood, fragments of vases and other remains of human burials which is so appalling to the

[1] Apart from other cuneiform passages, comp. the closing words of several recently published terra-cotta cones from Babylonian tombs: If a person finds a coffin and treats it with due respect, "his manes may drink clear water below!" Comp. Thureau-Dangin in *Orient. Litteratur-Zeitung*, Jan. 15, 1901, pp. 5, *seqq.*, and Delitzsch in *Mitteilungen der Deutschen Orient-Gesellschaft*, no. 11, pp. 5, *seq.*

senses and yet was the natural result of the combined action of man and the elements.

It will now be clear why I was unable to accept Haynes' view as stated above (p. 395), with regard to the large solid structure within the ancient curb, which he interpreted as an immense altar. The white ash-bed found on its hollowed surface, its rim of bitumen, *i. e.*, a material liberally used in connection with the cremations, its extraordinary size (14 feet long and 8 feet wide), the ash-bin discovered near its base, and the peculiar surroundings suggest the idea that it rather represents one of the crematoriums on which the bodies of the dead were reduced to ashes. As it stood within the sacred enclosure we involuntarily connect the cremation and burying of the bodies of all these thousands of ancient Babylonians, who found their last resting-place around the sanctuary of their god, with the *ziggurrat* of Bêl itself, remembering that at El-Hibba Koldewey also excavated a two-staged *ziggurrat*, or, according to his theory, "the substructure of an especially important tomb,"[1] around the base of which, exactly as at Nippur, nothing but "ash-graves" occurred. But we then naturally ask: What was

[1] The stage-tower of El-Hibba was round, consisted of two stages, and was provided with a water-conduit like that of Nippur. Comp. pp. 286, *seq.*, above, and *Zeitschrift für Assyriologie*, vol. ii, pp. 422, *seq.* It appears almost strange at present, that the German explorer discovered and excavated one of the earliest Babylonian *ziggurrats* thus so far known, without realizing it. In view of the existence of a stage-tower at El-Hibba, I am convinced that both Surghul and El-Hibba cannot have been cemeteries exclusively. The German excavations carried on at the two places were by far too brief and limited compared with the enormous extent of those ruins to settle this question. All the pre-Sargonic ruins of Babylonia, as far as I have had an opportunity to examine them, consist largely of tombs. They occur in great numbers also at Nuffar, Fâra, Abû Hatab, and other mounds, but it would be utterly wrong to pronounce them for this reason nothing but "fire-necropoles." The pre-Sargonic monuments of art and the very ancient cuneiform tablets coming from all those mounds enable us to speak more positively on this question.

the original significance of a Babylonian *ziggurrat?* Were these stage-towers, like the step pyramids of Mêdûm and Saqqâra in Egypt,[1] in certain cases at least, only "especially important tombs"? Did the Sumerian population of the country after all somehow connect the idea of death or tomb with Bêl's high-towering terrace at Nippur?

3. It is generally known that Strabo (16 : 5), in speaking of Babylon, mentions "the sepulchre of Bêl" (ὁ τοῦ Βήλου τάφος), evidently referring to *Etemenanki*, the famous stage-tower of the metropolis on the Euphrates, which he seems to regard as a sepulchral monument[2] erected in honor of Marduk or Merodach, "the Bêl of Babel" or "the Bêl of the gods."[3] In a similar manner Diodorus (ii, 7) informs us, that Semiramis built a tower in Nineveh as a tomb for her husband Ninos,[4] a story apparently based upon the conception that the *ziggurrat* of Nineveh likewise was a tomb. This view of classical writers concerning two of the most prominent stage-towers of Babylonia and Assyria has never been taken very seriously by scholars, as nothing in the cuneiform inscriptions seemed to justify it. But we may well ask: Are there really no passages in the Babylonian literature which would indicate that the early inhabitants of Shumer and Akkad themselves associated the idea of "tomb" with their stage-towers?

[1] Comp. the illustrations of the two pyramids, under "Excavations in Egypt," below.

[2] Comp. Ktesias, 29, 21, *seq.*, Aelian, *Var. hist.*, xiii, 3.

[3] Merodach of Babylon is thus styled as the city's supreme god who became heir to the rank and titles of Bêl of Nippur, the "father" and "king of the gods." While reading the last proofs of this book, I received Professor Zimmern's important contribution to the history of Babylonian religion incorporated with Schrader's *Die Keilinschriften und das Alte Testament*, 3d edition, Berlin, 1902, part 2. Comp. pp. 355, *seq.*, 373, *seq.*, of this work.

[4] Interpreted by Hommel as *Nin-ib*, by the present writer as the Sumerian *Nin* (meaning "lord" and "lady") + the Greek ending ος.

Apart from Rawlinson and other earlier explorers, who actually searched for the two above-mentioned tombs, it was Hommel who first expressed it as his conviction that "the Babylonian stage-towers originally were sepulchral monuments,"[1] and that Ningirsu's temple at Tellô was a combination of a sanctuary for the god and of a mausoleum for Gudea, his *patesi.* Though the former statement is too general and comprehensive according to the scanty material at our disposal, and the latter incorrect, since, according to the context, Gudea clearly erected not his own, but his god's "sepulchral chapel" in the temple of Ningirsu, Hommel deserves credit for having recognized an important fact in connection with Babylonian stage-towers and for having endeavored to find proofs for his theory in the inscriptions, before he could have known of the results of a series of investigations carried on by the present writer at Nuffar in March and April, 1900.

It does not lie within the scope of this book to treat all the cuneiform passages which directly or indirectly bear upon the important question under consideration. I shall therefore confine myself to a single text from the latest excavations at Nuffar which will throw some light on the way in which the Babylonians viewed the *ziggurrat* of Bêl at Nippur, and to a few passages of published inscriptions referring to other *ziggurrats.*

Among the antiquities found in the débris that covered the pavement of Ashurbânapal near the east corner of the court of the stage-tower at Nippur, there were three inscribed fragments of baked clay which seemed to belong to a barrel cylinder. When trying to fit them together, I found that they constituted the greater part of a truncated cone of an interesting shape[2] similar to that of the recently published

1 Comp. Hommel, *Aufsätze und Abhandlungen,* part iii, 1 (Munich, 1901), pp. 389, *seqq.,* especially p. 393.

2 Comp. p. 457, above, note. The same peculiar form is known from

cones from Babylonian tombs. The curious form of the document attracted my immediate attention. On closer examination, it proved to be a building record of twenty-five lines of neo-Babylonian cuneiform characters inscribed

Truncated Cone containing Ashurbânapal's Account of his Restoration of the Stage-Tower of Nippur.

lengthwise by " Ashurbânapal, king of Assyria." Only lines 15–19 of the mutilated legend are of importance for the sub-

Nabopolassar's fine cylinder, now in Philadelphia, and containing his building record of *Etemenanki*, "the tower of Babel" (comp. Hilprecht, "The Bab. Exp. of the U. of Pa.," series A, vol. i, part 1, pl. xiii). A "cylinder" from Nuffar containing Samsu-iluna's account of his restoration of the *dûru* (inner wall) of the temple of Bêl, and a cone in the Louvre of Paris, containing Hammurabi's record of his construction "of the wall and canal of Sippara" (according to information received by letter from Thureau-Dangin), also show the same form. It doubtless represents the prototype of the later barrel-cylinder. Nevertheless, it remains a most remarkable fact that cylinders of this peculiar form were deposited both in the *ziggurrats* and their enclosing walls, and also in the ancient tombs which, as we now know, originally surrounded the former.

ject under consideration. I quote them in the king's own language: "*E-gigunû*, the *ziggurrat* of Nippur, the foundation of which is placed in the breast of the ocean, the walls of which had grown old, and which had fallen into decay — I built that house with baked bricks and bitumen, and completed its construction. With the art of the god of the bricks I restored it and made it bright as the day. I raised its head like a mountain and caused its splendor to shine."

This inscription furnishes us a new name of the *ziggurrat* of Nippur, *E-gigunû*,[1] "House of the tomb," the other two names of the same building, with which we were familiar before, being *Imǵarsag*, "Mountain of the wind" or "Mt. Airy," and *E-sagash*, "House of the decision." *E-gigunû*, however, was not altogether unknown to us. There are several cuneiform passages in which it appears in parallelism with *Ekur*, "House of the mountain," the well-known temple of Bêl and Bêltis at Nippur.[2] A fourth name, to state this distinctly here, occurs in another unpublished text inscribed on a large vase of Gudea also belonging to the results of our latest excavations at Nuffar, namely, *Dur-anki*, "Link of heaven and earth." How was it possible that the *ziggurrat* of Nippur, which constitutes the most prominent part of the whole temple complex, this high towering terrace, which "connects heaven and earth," could appear to the Babylonians as "the house of the tomb" at the same time?

Most of the names of Babylonian temples express a cosmic idea. According to the old Babylonian conception of the gods and their relation to the world's edifice, En-lil or Bêl of Nippur is "the king of heaven and earth," or "the father" and "king of the gods" and "the king of the lands," *i. e.*, the earth. Bêl's sphere of influence, therefore, is what we

[1] A fifth (unknown) name seems to have stood in the mutilated passage, ii *R.* 50, if the present sign of line 4, a, was copied correctly from the original.

[2] Comp. Jensen, *Die Kosmologie der Babylonier*, Strasburg, 1890, pp. 186, *seq.*

generally style "the world." It extends from the upper or heavenly ocean (the seat of Anu) to the lower or terrestrial ocean (the seat of Ea), which was regarded as the continuation of the former around and below the earth. In other words, Bêl rules an empire which includes the whole world with the exclusion of the upper and lower oceans, or an empire confined on the one hand by the starry firmament which keeps back the waters of the upper ocean (Gen. 1 : 6–8) and is called heaven (*an*), and on the other hand by that lower "firmament" which keeps the waters of the lower ocean in their place (Gen. 1 : 9, 10) and is called earth (*ki*).[1] But his empire not only lies between these two boundaries, it practically includes them. The *ziggurrat* of Bêl is "the link of heaven and earth" which connects the two extreme parts of his empire; that is, it is the local representation of the great mythological "mountain of the world," '*Kharsag-kurkura*, a structure "the summit of which reaches unto heaven, and the foundation of which is laid in the clear *apsû*,"[2] *i. e.*, in the clear waters of the subterranean ocean, — epithets afterwards applied to other Babylonian *ziggurrats*, some of which bear even the same, or at least a similar,

[1] On the Babylonian conception of the world's edifice, comp. especially Jensen, *Die Kosmologie der Babylonier*, Strasburg, 1890; Hommel, *Das babylonische Weltbild* in *Aufsätze und Abhandlungen*, part iii, 1, Munich, 1901, pp. 344–349; and a monograph received immediately before the issue of this book. It is written by one of my pupils, Dr. Hugo Radau, and bears the title, "The Creation-Story of Genesis 1, a Sumerian Theogony and Cosmogony" (Chicago, London, 1902), — a very useful and commendable treatise, which, however, might have been improved considerably, if the author had written in a more becoming manner about one of his teachers, Professor Hommel, to whose lectures and extraordinary personal efforts in his behalf at Munich he owes some of his best knowledge. Much valuable material is also found in several writings of A. Jeremias, Winckler, and Zimmern.

[2] Comp. the poetical passage quoted above, p. 304, from a hymn addressed to Bêl and his consort. Bêl therefore is designated (ii *R.* 54, 4, a) ideographically also as the god of *Dur-an* (abbreviation for *Dur-an-ki*) or even "the great mountain" itself (*shadû rabû*).

name. Thus, *e. g.*, the *ziggurrat* of Shamash, both at Sippara[1] and at Larsa, was called *E-Duranki*, "House of the link of heaven and earth,"[2] or abbreviated *E-Duranna*, "House of the link of heaven," and the *ziggurrat* of Marduk at Babylon, *Etemenanki*, "House of the foundation of heaven and earth."

Bêl, "the lord" par excellence, who took the place of the Sumerian *En-lil* in the Semitic pantheon, is, as we have seen, the king of this "middle empire." His manifestation is "the wind" (*lil*), and his name designates him therefore as "the lord (*en*) of the wind (*lil*)" or "storm," and of all those other phenomena which frequently accompany it, "thunder," "lightning," etc. The hundreds of terra-cotta images of Bêl or En-lil discovered at Nippur accordingly represent him generally as an old man (a real "father of the gods") with a long flowing beard, and a thunderbolt or some other weapon in his hand.[3] He and his consort Bêltis reside in a house on the top of the great "mountain of the world," which reaches unto heaven (Gen. 11 : 4). There the gods were born,[4] and from thence "the king of heaven and earth" hurls down his thunderbolts. This house is localized in *Ekur* ("House of the mountain"), Bêl's famous temple at Nippur. Though this name generally designates the whole temple complex in the inscriptions, originally, as the etymology of the word indicates, it can have been applied only to the most important part of it,

[1] I infer this from the fact that an ancient king of Sippara, known from a text of the library of Ashurbânapal, has the name *Enme-Duranki*, concerning whom comp. Zimmern, in the third edition of Schrader's *Keilinschriften und das Alte Testament*, vol. i, part 2 (Leipzig, 1902), pp. 532, *seqq.*

[2] Comp. also Jensen, *l. c.*, p. 485.

[3] For the present comp. the illustration facing p. 342, above.

[4] Sargon, "Khorsabâd," 155, *seq.*: "The gods Ea, Sin, Shamash, Nebo, Adad, Ninib, and their sublime consorts, who are born legitimately in the house of [situated on the top of] the great mountain of the world, the mountain of 'the nether world.'"

i. e., the shrine which stood on the top of the *ziggurrat*. This high-towering terrace being regarded as the "link which connects heaven and earth," that divine palace resting on it was a heavenly and terrestrial residence at the same time.

This stage-tower, however, also penetrates far into the earth, its foundation being laid in the waters of the lower ocean. On the one hand it rises from the earth, inhabited by man, unto heaven, the realm of the gods; on the other, it descends to "the great city" (*urugal*) of the dead, the realm of the departed souls. For, according to Babylonian conception, "the nether world" (*Arâlû*), the abode of the dead, lies directly below and within the earth, or, more exactly, in the hollow space formed by the lower part (*kigal*) of the earth (which resembles an upset round boat, a so-called *qûfa*), and by the lower ocean, which at the same time encircles this "land without return." The mountain of the world, therefore, is also called "the mountain of the nether world" (*shad Arâlû*) in the cuneiform inscriptions.[1] As *gigunû*, "grave," "tomb," is used metonymically as a synonym of *Arâlû*, "the nether world,"[2] it follows that the *ziggurrat* of Nippur, which is the local representation of the great mountain of the world, also could be called "the house of the tomb" (*E-gigunû*) or "the house of 'the nether world.'" It is the edifice that rises over the Hades, *quasi* forming the roof beneath which the departed souls reside. It was therefore only natural that the earliest inhabitants should bury their dead around the base of the *ziggurrat* of Nippur to a depth of thirty to forty feet, so that the latter appears to us almost like a huge sepulchral monument erected over the tombs of the ancient Sumerians who rest in its shadow. Rising out of the midst of tombs, as it did, the stage-tower of Bêl even literally may be called

[1] Sargon, Khorsabâd, 155, *seq.* Comp. Jensen, *l. c.*, pp. 203, 231, *seqq.*

[2] Comp. A. Jeremias, *Die Babylonisch-Assyrischen Vorstellungen vom Leben nach dem Tode*, Leipzig, 1887, pp. 61, *seqq.*

a "house of the tomb (s)." In view of what has just been stated in the briefest way possible, it will not surprise us that in the cuneiform literature *Ekur* sometimes is used as a synonym of "heaven," [1] and sometimes stands in parallelism with *Gigunû* and *Arâlû*.[2]

The tower of Bêl at Nippur appears to us as a place of residence for the gods, as a place of worship for man, and as a place of rest for the dead — a grand conception for a sanctuary in the earliest historical period of Babylonia, which has continued even to the present time. For the hundreds and thousands of Christian churches, which contain tombs within their confines or are surrounded by a graveyard, practically express the same idea. As to a certain degree most of the other Babylonian temples were modelled more or less after the great national sanctuary of Bêl at Nippur, we must expect, *a priori*, that excavations at El-Hibba, Fâra, Larsa, Muqayyar, and other pre-Sargonic ruins, will likewise disclose extensive cemeteries around their *ziggurrats*. But it is interesting to observe how certain religious ideas of the Semitic conquerors, possibly in connection with considerations similar to those which led to a transfer of the cemeteries from the environments of the churches to districts outside the cities in our own days, seem finally to have brought about a radical change of the ancient burial customs in Babylonia. With regard to Nippur, this change can be traced to about the period of Sargon I, after whose government no more burials occur in the sacred precinct of *Ekur*. As remarked above, there are comparatively few among the 2500 post-Sargonic tombs thus far examined at Nuffar that can be with certainty assigned to the long interval between Sargon I and the Seleucidan occupation. Nearly all those reported by Peters and Haynes as being true Babylonian are Parthian, Sassanian, and Arabic.[3] In fact we do not

[1] Comp. ii *R.* 54, no. 4. [2] Comp. iv *R.* 24, 3–8; 27, 26, 27 a.
[3] Comp. pp. 154, *seq.*, 233, note 3, above.

know yet how the Semitic inhabitants of ancient Nippur generally disposed of their dead.

From the difficult passage[1] preceding Gudea's account of his restoration of Ningirsu's temple at Lagash, I am inclined to infer that originally a vast fire-necropolis surrounded the sanctuary of Tellô also, and that Gudea did the same for *Shir-pur-la* as Sargon I (or some other monarch of that general period) had done for Nippur. He stopped cremating and burying the dead in the environments of the temple of Ningirsu, and levelled the ground of the ancient cemetery around it, with due regard to the numerous burial urns and coffins previously deposited there. In other words, "he cleaned the city" and "made the temple of Ningirsu a pure place like Eridu," the sacred city of Ea, where, apparently, in the earliest days, burials were not allowed. From the same inscription we learn another important fact. Gudea states expressly, that "he restored *Eninnû-imgig(ǵu)barbara* [Ningirsu's temple] and constructed his [*i. e.* the god's] beloved tomb (*gigunû*) of cedar wood in it."[2] It cannot be ascertained precisely where the god's funeral chapel was, in the extensive household[3] provided for him by Gudea. From another passage (Gudea, Statue D, ii, 7–iii, 1), however, it would seem that it formed part of the temple proper, which stood at the side[4] of the *ziggurrat*, while the room on the summit of the stage-tower (called Epa) was the one chamber above all others in which Ningirsu and his consort, Bau, were supposed to reside, and where, accordingly,

[1] Statue B, iii, 12–v, 11.

[2] Comp. Gudea, Statue B, v, 15–19; Statue D, ii, 7–iii, 1.

[3] Comp. Thureau-Dangin's translation and brief treatment of Gudea's two large cylinders (A and B) in *Comptes Rendus*, 1901, pp. 112 *seqq.* (*Le songe ae Gudéa*, Cyl. A), *Revue d'histoire et de littérature religieuses*, vol. vi (1901), no. 6, pp. 481, *seqq.* (*La famille et la cour d'un dieu chaldéen*, Cyl. B.), and *Zeitschrift für Assyriologie*, vol. xvi (1902), pp. 344, *seqq.* (*Le cylindre A de Gudéa*).

[4] Comp. pp. 469, *seqq.*, below.

"the wedding presents of Bau" were deposited. Here, then, for the first time, we meet with the idea that a Babylonian god has his tomb. Startling as this statement may seem at first, it is in entire accord with the character of the principal god of Lagash, as a god of vegetation and as a sun-god. For Ningirsu, "the powerful champion" and "the beloved son" of En-lil of Nippur,[1] originally the god of agriculture, was later identified with Ninib, "the son of *Ekur*," the god of the rising sun, "who holds the link of heaven and earth[2] and governs everything."[3] According to the Babylonian conception, he suffers death in the same way as Tammûz[4] (Ez. 8 : 14), the god of the spring vegetation and of the lower regions, with whom Ningirsu is practically identical;[5] or as Shamash, the sun-god himself, who descends into the *apsû*, the terrestrial and subterranean ocean, every evening, and rises out of it again in the morning; who in the spring of every year commences his course with youthful vigor, but gradually grows weaker and weaker until he dies during the winter. The sun dwelling in "the nether world" for half a year, the sun-god himself naturally is considered as dead during this period,[6] and Shamash consequently has his tomb in Larsa, and Ai, his wife, at Sippara,[7] as Ningirsu in Lagash. More than this, the *ziggurrat*

[1] Comp. Gudea, Cyl. A, ii, 12, where it is even said that "Ningirsu is lord or prince (*nirgal*) at Nippur."

[2] See i *R*. 29, 3, *seq.*, *markas shamê u irṣiti*, the Assyrian translation of the Sumerian *Duranki*, which, as we saw above, was the name of the *ziggurrat* of *Ekur*.

[3] Comp. Jensen, *Kosmologie*, Index.

[4] Who dies in the month sacred to him.

[5] Comp. Jensen, *l. c.*, pp. 197, *seqq.*

[6] Comp. Winckler, *Arabisch-Semitisch-Orientalisch* in *Mitteilungen der Vorderasiatischen Gesellschaft*, Berlin, 1901, no. 5, pp. 93, *seqq.*

[7] Comp. Scheil, *Code des Lois de Hammurabi* (D. Morgan's *Mémoires*, vol. iv) Paris, 1902, col. ii, 26–28, — a passage which I owe to Hommel, I not yet having seen the book recently published.

of Larsa itself is Shamash's tomb. For on a barrel cylinder from the temple of Shamash and Ai at Larsa, Nabonidos unmistakably calls the god's stage-tower " his lofty tomb."[1]

From what has been said, it follows (1) that the Babylonians themselves associated the idea of " tomb " closely with their *ziggurrats*, and (2) that the inscriptions not only know of tombs of certain deities (of light) in general, but in one case at least directly call the *ziggurrat* of a god " his sepulchre." As Marduk, the supreme god of Babylon, likewise is a sun-god, namely, the god of the early sun of the day (morning) and of the year (spring),[2] we have no reason to doubt any longer that the conception of the classical writers concerning *Etemenanki*, the stage-tower of Marduk, as " the sepulchre of Bêl," is correct, and goes back to trustworthy original sources.[3]

4. The excavations conducted along the southeast enclosing wall of the *ziggurrat* established the important fact that the stage-tower did not occupy the central part of the temple court, and that the ascent to the high-towering terrace and the entrance gate of the enclosing wall did not lie opposite each other. Upon entering the sacred precincts one was compelled to turn westward in order to reach the former. It became, therefore, very probable that the remains of a second important structure were hidden below the rubbish accumulated at the northeast side of the *ziggurrat*. In order to ascertain this, we proceeded with our excavations from the east corner of the temple court

[1] A passage generally misunderstood by the translators. The text was published and first translated by Bezold in the " Proceedings of the Society of Biblical Archæology," 1889. Comp. col. ii, 16 : *zi-ku-ra-ti gi-gu-na-a-shu ṣi-i-ri*.

[2] Comp. Jensen, *Kosmologie*, pp. 87, *seqq*. A somewhat different view of the same scholar is found in Schrader's *K. B.*, vol. vi, p. 562.

[3] Comp. Lehmann in *Wochenschrift für klassische Philologie*, 1900, p. 962, note 1, and *Beiträge zur alten Geschichte*, vol. i, p. 276, note 1. Also Zimmern, *K. A. T.*^{3}, p. 371.

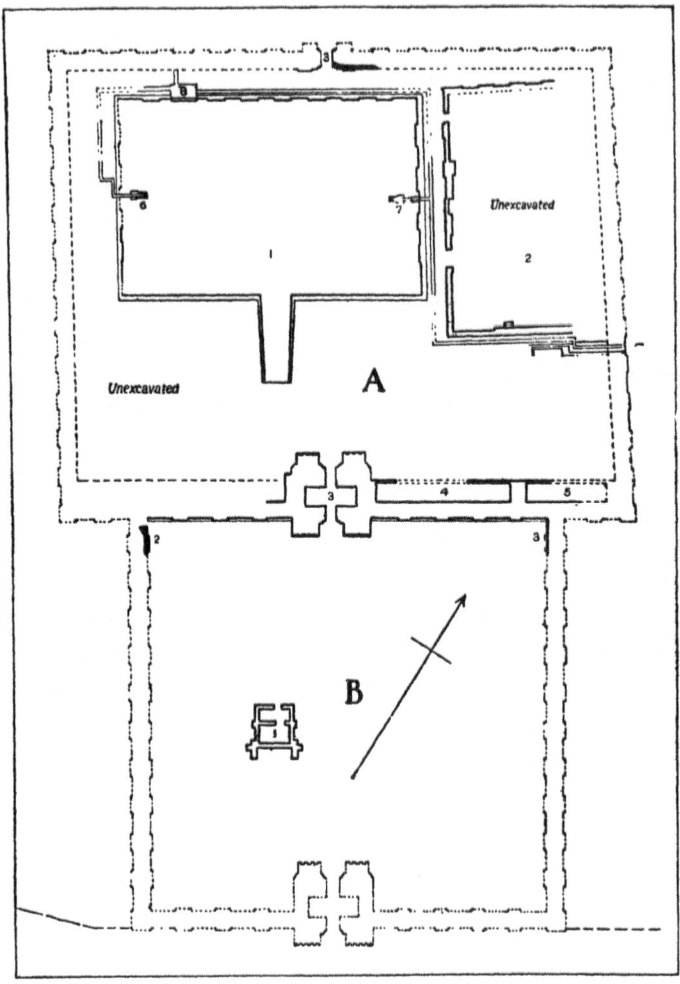

Ground plan of Ekur, Temple of Bêl at Nippur

Restored and designed by Hilprecht, drawn by Fisher

A. Inner Court: 1. Ziggurrat. 2. House of Bêl. 3. Front and rear gates. 4 and 5. Storage vaults. 6 and 7. Water conduits draining the ziggurrat. 8. Shallow basin forming the junction of the watercourses at the rear.

B. Outer Court: 1. Small Temple of Bêl. 2 and 3. Excavated portions of the enclosing walls.

—— *excavated,* - - - *restored walls.*

northward, until we came upon a wall of baked bricks which ran parallel to the southeast enclosing wall. We followed it for a considerable distance towards the southwest, when suddenly it turned off at a right angle in a northwest direction, continuing its course for 157½ feet, nearly parallel with the northeast façade of the *ziggurrat*, and at a distance of nearly sixteen feet from it. When we had reached a point a little beyond the north corner of the stage-tower, it again turned off at a right angle to the east. We traced it for seventy-one feet in this direction by means of a tunnel, without, however, being able to follow it to the end.

The excavated portions sufficed to determine that the wall enclosed a space 152 feet long and about 115 feet wide, *i. e.*, an area of 17,480 square feet. The prominent position which the structure occupied at the side of the stage-tower, the fact that it was built of burned bricks (laid in clay mortar), and the circumstance that, with the exception of the entire southeast side and the adjoining part of the southwest face, the wall was panelled in the same way as the corresponding sides of the *ziggurrat*, indicated clearly that it was not a mere enclosing wall, but the facing of a large house. As it had served as a quarry for later generations, it was unfortunately reduced considerably in height. At some places not more than one or two courses of bricks had been left, while at others there were as many as a score. With the limited time then at my disposal it was impossible to examine and to remove the mass of débris covering the building as carefully as it ought to be done. I therefore decided not to ruin this important section of the temple area by adopting the methods of my predecessors, but to leave its interior as far as possible untouched, and to confine myself to an exploration of its exposed edges. We were thus enabled to gather the following details. *a.* The facing wall varied in thickness from a little over 3 to about 5½ feet. *b.* A number of unbaked brick walls ran at right angles to the facing wall, and with it constituted a number of larger and smaller rooms. *c.* The building had two entrances in its longer southwest side. The one near the south corner, being the principal one, was 10½ feet wide, while that near the north corner measured only about half that width. *d.* As the visible part of this large house seemed to rest on the same level as the pavement of Kadashman-Turgu and was completely covered by the pavement of Ashurbânapal, naturally I assumed that it had been restored for the last time by a member of the Cassite dynasty. The correctness of this theory was proved by an inscription taken from its walls. Among the various bricks examined, one of them (discovered *in situ*) bore a brief legend on one of its edges, from which we learned that "Shagarakti-Shuriash (about 1350 B. C.), king of Babylon, prefect (*sag-ush*) of the house of Bêl," was one of the rulers who devoted his time and interest to this remarkable building. *e.* Immediately beneath the southwest wall of the Cassite edifice are fragments of an earlier wall which ran somewhat nearer to the northeast face of the *ziggurrat*.

What was the original purpose of this extensive structure? To judge from its mere size and conspicuous position in connection with the characteristic inscription just mentioned, there can be no doubt that it represents the "house of Bêl" itself, the palace in which the household of the god and his consort was established, where sacrifices were offered and the most valuable votive offerings of the greatest Babylonian monarchs deposited. In other words, it was the famous temple of Bêl, which, together with the stage-tower, formed an organic whole enclosed by a common wall, and was generally known under the name of *Ekur*, "House of the Mountain." This divine palace stood "at the side of the *ziggurrat*" of Nippur, precisely where, on the basis of Rassam's excavations at Borsippa and Sippara, and according to numerous indications in the building inscriptions of Babylonian temples,[1] I had expected to find it.

My conclusions with regard to the importance and nature of this structure were fully confirmed by the discoveries made in its immediate neighborhood. Apart from numerous fragments of stone vases, as a rule inscribed with the names of pre-Sargonic kings familiar to us from the results of the former campaigns, we unearthed several interesting antiquities in a far better state of preservation than the average relic previously excavated in the court of the temple. Their number increased as we began to approach the large edifice described. Among the objects of art thus obtained I mention the leg of a large black statue from the level of Ur-Gur, the head of a small marble statue covered with a turban, like those of the time of Gudea found at Tellô, and two small headless statues of the same material but considerably older. Each of the latter bore a brief votive inscription of four lines. They came from the same stratum that produced the large mass of broken antiquities gathered by the second and third expeditions. Immediately below it was the section of a pavement which consisted of stones and pieces of baked brick mixed and laid in bitumen. When examined more closely it was found to contain three fragments of a large inscribed slab in limestone once presented to the temple of Bêl by a "king of Shumer and Akkad." Not far from this pavement there was a large heavy vase in dolerite. It stood upright, was over 2 feet high, had a diameter of nearly 1½ feet, and bore the following inscription: "To Bêl, the king of the

1 For the present comp. Nabonidos' barrel cylinder from Larsa (published by Bezold in the "Proceedings of the Society of Biblical Archæology," London, 1889), vol. iii, 13, *seq.*: *pa-pa-khi shu-ba-at i-lu-ti-shu-un sir-tim sha i-te-e zi-qu-ra-tim ri-tu-u te-me-en-shu.*

gods, for the house (*esh*) of Nippur [and, or namely] *Dur-anki*, Gudea, *patesi* of Lagash, has presented the long boat (*i. e.*, a *turrâda*) of *Ekur* for [the preservation of] his life."

It soon became evident that the house of Bêl at the side of the *ziggurrat* must have existed as early as the time of Sargon I and Narâm-Sin. A few brick stamps of the latter, and a door-socket and many brick stamps of the former were discovered slightly above their well-known pavement. Soon afterwards the workmen unearthed a small piece of spirited sculpture (exhibiting the larger part of an incised quadruped), which doubtless belongs to the fourth millennium, and a round marble slab over 2 feet in diameter and nearly 3 inches thick, which contained the name of "Narâm-Sin, king of Agade, king of the four regions of the world," accompanied by the somewhat effaced name of a contemporaneous "priest of Bêl, thy servant."

Even the pre-Sargonic period was represented by several fairly well preserved objects. We refer briefly to the fragment of a perforated votive tablet in limestone showing a sacrificial scene with Nin-lil, or Bêltis,[1] in the centre. The goddess, accompanied by a bird, apparently sacred to her,[2] is seated on a low chair and holds a pointed cup in her right hand. A burning altar (which became the regular ideogram for "fire" in Assyrian) and a lighted candlestick stand in front of Bêltis, while behind her a priest, remarkable for the long hair of his beard and the back of his head, leads a shaved worshipper, carrying a young goat on his right arm, before the goddess. Among the other antiquities found in the immediate neighborhood of Bêl's house, I mention a small carving in mother-of-pearl (a warrior

[1] If it were Bêl, he would be represented with a beard, according to the general custom observed. The garment and the peculiar hair-dress of the deity likewise favor my interpretation.

[2] Comp. the raven of Ningirsu (p. 230, note 1, above), the raven of Woden, the eagle of Jupiter, the peacock of Juno, the owl of Athene, etc.

with drawn bow); a piece of lapis lazuli with a human head in low relief; another round stone slab dedicated to En-lil by King Lugalkigubnidudu; a model in limestone for making plano-convex bricks; about forty fragments of clay bearing impressions of archaic seal cylinders; and more than one hundred inscribed clay tablets taken from below the level of Narâm-Sin. With regard to several other antiquities found in the strata immediately beneath

Pre-Sargonic Votive Tablet in Limestone, Sacrificial Scene

it — as, *e. g.*, a quantity of large beads in crystal (quartz), a hollow cone of silver, a vase of jewelry containing rings and a well preserved chain in the same metal, several excellently fashioned nails, scrapers, knives, a saw, and many fragments of vessels, all in copper — it must remain doubtful whether they belonged to "the house of Bêl" or, as seems more probable to the present writer, in part at least were originally deposited in the numerous ash-graves which begin to appear directly below the pavement of the Sargon dynasty.

Several fragments of small pavements were discovered slightly above that of Narâm-Sin in the east section of the temple court immediately before the sanctuary of Bêl.

They had been laid by unknown persons prior to the time of Ur-Gur. One of these sections contained many inscribed bricks with the short legend: "Lugalsurzu, *patesi* of Nippur, priest of Bêl." A shallow rectangular basin built of burned bricks and coated with bitumen on its floor and sides, an open conduit leading from it to a neighboring vertical drain, and the above-mentioned stone vase of Gudea indicate that it was probably reserved for the ablutions of the priests, for cleansing the sacred vessels, and other functions of the temple service for which water was required. It is possible also that the sheep, goats and other sacrifices to be offered were killed there. From an inscribed door-socket of Bur-Sin of Ur previously unearthed in the eastern half of the temple court,[1] it can also be inferred that a store-room called "the house for honey, cream and wine, a place for his [Bêl's] sacrifices,"[2] must have existed somewhere within the temple enclosure not very far from "the house of Bêl."

The large number of inscribed and sculptured objects gathered in the lower strata of the court of the *ziggurrat* by the American explorers and in its upper ruins centuries ago by the later inhabitants of ancient Nippur,[3] to a certain degree enable us to form an idea of the elaborate manner in which the temple of Bêl was equipped and embellished in early days. But the ruinous state of its walls and the very fragmentary condition in which all the statues and most of the reliefs and vases thus far have been discovered, indicate what in all probability will await us in the interior

[1] Comp. Hilprecht, "The Bab. Exp. of the U. of Pa.," series A, vol. i, part 1, no. 21.

[2] On the use and significance of wine, cream and honey in the Babylonian cults, comp. Zimmern, *K. A. T.*[3], p. 526.

[3] *E. g.*, all the fine votive objects originally deposited by the Cassite kings in the temple of Bêl, but found by Peters in the box of a jeweller of the Parthian period (pp. 335, *seq.*, above), outside of the temple proper.

of the sanctuary itself. A methodical exploration of the large building at the side of the *ziggurrat* will doubtless result in the unearthing of other fragmentary inscriptions and important objects of art, but its principal object will have to be the restoration of the ground-plan of Babylonia's great national sanctuary at the middle of the second pre-Christian millennium.

5. Much has been written on the analogies existing between Babylonian and Hebrew temples, and, strange to say, even an attempt has been made to trace the architectural features of the temple of Solomon to Babylonian sources, though as a matter of fact not one of the large Babylonian temples has as yet been excavated thoroughly enough to enable us to recognize its disposition and necessary details. The little Parthian palace of Nippur on the west side of the Chebar, plainly betraying Greek influence, was quoted as a pattern "of the architecture of Babylonia," and the Parthian fortress lying on the top of the ruined temple of Bêl was interpreted as "affording us for the first time a general view of a sacred quarter in an ancient Babylonian city." There remains little of Peters' theories concerning the topography of ancient Nippur and the age of its excavated ruins that will stand criticism. We can therefore readily imagine to what incongruities any comparison resting on his so-called interpretations of the ruins must lead us. It will be wise to refrain for the present entirely from such untimely speculations until the characteristic features of at least one of Babylonia's most prominent sanctuaries have been established satisfactorily by pick and spade.

In my previous sketch I have endeavored to show, on the basis of my own excavations and researches at Nuffar, that *Ekur*, the temple of Bêl, consisted of two principal buildings, the *ziggurrat*, and "the house of Bêl" at the side of it. Both were surrounded by a common wall called *Imgur-Marduk* in the cuneiform inscriptions. It may reasonably be doubted whether the average pilgrim visiting Nippur was ever allowed to enter this most holy enclosure. The question then arises: Was there no other place of worship, a kind of outer court, to which every pious Babylonian who desired to pay homage to "the father of the gods," had free access?

In 1890 Peters fortunately came upon the remains of a building in the lower mounds situated to the southeast of Bint el-Amîr. He found that most of its bricks were stamped upon their edges, one to three times, with a brief legend, and discovered two door-sockets *in situ*, from which we learned that the little edifice of two rooms was a temple called *Kishaggulla-Bur-Sin*, "House of the delight of Bur-Sin,"[1] erected in honor of Bêl by Bur-Sin of Ur, who reigned about 2550 B. C. (comp. pp. 336, *seq.*, above). Fragments of sculptures scattered in the débris around it testified to the great esteem in which the chapel had been held by the ancient worshippers. From the mere fact that it stood in the shadow of *Ekur*, directly opposite the ascent of the stage-tower, towards which it faced, I arrived at the conclusion that it must have been included in the precincts of the temple, and that future excavations carried on in its neighborhood would show that the complex of the great national sanctuary in all probability extended much farther to the south than, on the basis of Peters' statements, we were entitled to assume. When therefore, in 1899, I went a second time to the ruins, I was in hope of finding some clue as to the precise relation in which this shrine stood to the principal enclosure. As the enormous dump-heaps raised on that important mound by my predecessors again interfered seriously with the work of the expedition, there

[1] Comp. Hilprecht, "The Bab. Exp. of the U. of Pa.," series A, vol. i, part i, no. 20, ll. 15, *seq.* The two signs *shag-gul* (heart + joy, *Herzensfreude*), must be an ideogram with a meaning like "delight, cheerfulness."

remained nothing else to be done but to try to solve the problem in connection with our excavations along the southeast enclosing wall of the court of the *ziggurrat* as far as this was possible. The attempt was crowned with a fair amount of success beyond that which could have been anticipated (comp. the zinctype, p. 470).

While tracing the panelled outer face of the last-mentioned wall, our workmen were suddenly stopped in their progress both at the eastern and southern ends of the long and deep trench by a cross-wall joining the former at a right angle. In order to ascertain the course and nature of these two walls they were ordered to follow them for a certain distance by means of tunnels cut along their inner faces at about the level of Narâm-Sin's pavement. These tunnels revealed the existence of numerous ash-graves in the lower strata, and enabled us to determine that the two walls were constructed of the same unbaked material and adorned with the same kind of panels as the southeast wall of the temple enclosure. The northeast wall was traced forty-eight feet without reaching its end, when the excavations were suspended in order not to destroy valuable remains of constructions which might have been built against it. For the same reason the southwest tunnel was cut less deep, especially as the evidence gained from it sufficed to confirm the results obtained from the other tunnel. It could no longer be doubted that a second, somewhat smaller court, in which Bur-Sin's sanctuary stood, adjoined the court of the *ziggurrat* on the side of its principal entrance. This outer court seems to have extended to the edge of the depression which represents the ancient bed of a branch of the Shatt en-Nîl. An opening in the low narrow ridge running along its northern embankment, and evidently marking the remains of an ancient wall later occupied by Parthian houses, indicates the site of the gate which once gave access to it.

These are all the positive facts that could be gathered. At least two years will be required to remove the dump-heaps completely and to excavate the whole mound systematically. From a tablet found in the upper strata of the temple library, I learned that besides Bêl, at least twenty-four other deities had their own "houses" in the sacred precincts of Nippur. Where have we to look for them? The absence of any considerable building remains in the inner court, apart from those described above, the existence of a small temple of Bêl in the outer court, and several other considerations, lead me to the assumption that in all probability they were grouped around Bêl's chapel in the enclosed space between the southeast wall of the *ziggurrat* and the eastern branch of the Shatt en-Nîl, — in other words, are to be sought for in the outer court of *Ekur*.

6. One of the principal tasks of the latest Philadelphia expedition was to search for the gates and to determine the probable course and extent of the walls of the ancient city. According to the inscriptions, Nippur had two walls, called *Imgur-Marduk* ("Merodach was favorable") and *Nîmit-Marduk* ("Stronghold[1] of Merodach"). The former was the inner wall (*dûru*), the latter the outer wall or rampart (*shalkhû*). The mere fact that both names contain as an element Marduk, the supreme god of Babylon, who, in connection with the rise of the first dynasty of Babylon (about 2300 B. C.) gradually took the place of Bêl of Nippur, indicates that they cannot represent the earliest designations of the two walls. This inference is fully confirmed by a discovery made in the débris near the eastern corner of the court of the *ziggurrat*. In clearing that section the workmen found a small and much-effaced terra-cotta cone of the same form as that of Ashurbânapal described above (p. 461), which originally must have been deposited in the upper part of the temple wall. The docu-

[1] Literally "Foundation, establishment of Merodach."

ment, inscribed with two columns of old-Babylonian writing (twenty-five lines each), and in the Semitic dialect of the country, conveys to us the information that Samsu-iluna, son and successor of Hammurabi, restored the inner wall of Nippur (*dûru*). We thereby obtain new evidence that the kings of the first dynasty did not entirely neglect Bêl's sanctuary, though their apparent reason for fortifying the temple was less religious than political. Their interest in the wall of Nippur seems to be closely connected with their operations against the city of (N)isin, which was situated not far from the latter,[1] and which subsequently became the stronghold of Rîm-Sin of Larsa.

As the greater part of the inscription is intelligible and of importance for our question, I give it in an English translation. "Samsu-iluna, the powerful king, king of Babylon, king of the four quarters of the world. When Bêl had granted him to rule the four quarters of the world and placed their reins into his hand, Samsu-iluna, the shepherd who gladdens the heart of Marduk, in the sublime power which the great gods had given him, in the wisdom of Ea . . . he raised the wall (*dûru*) of Bêl, which structure his grandfather [Sinmuballit] had made higher than before, like a great mountain, surrounded it with marshy ground (*apparam*), dug 'the Euphrates of Nippur' [*i. e.*, cleaned and deepened the river Chebar; comp. pp. 412 *seq.*], and erected the dam of 'the Euphrates of Nippur' along it. He called the name of that wall 'Link of the lands' (*Markas-mâtâtim*),[2] caused the

[1] Sinmuballit's repairing of the wall of Nippur, which we also learn from Samsu-iluna's cone, was probably mentioned in the mutilated passage of the list of dates ("Bu. 91, 5–9, 284"), following his conquest of (N)isin. Accordingly it would have taken place in one of his last three years, immediately before he lost (N)isin and Nippur again to Rîm-Sin of Larsa. Comp. Scheil, *Code des Lois de Hammurabi:* Nippur, *Dur-an* (p. 463, above), *Ekur*.

[2] *I. e.*, the wall which unites all the lands (the whole world). It was thus called, because the title *shar kibrat arba'im*, "king of the four quarters

population of Shumer and Akkad to dwell in a peaceful habitation . . . [and] made the name of Sinmuballit, his grandfather, famous in the world."

From the place where the cone was discovered, from the designation of the wall as *dûr Bêl*, and from the description of the king's work following, it may be inferred with certainty that Samsu-iluna has reference to the temple wall. This result agrees with the fact that our excavations have furnished evidence to the effect that the city proper on the west side of the Shatt en-Nil was never fortified by a wall, to say nothing of two walls. On the other hand, the double wall which surrounded and protected the sanctuary from the earliest days can still be traced without difficulty, notwithstanding the radical changes which took place at the temple complex in post-Babylonian times. The *Markas-mâtâti* of Samsu-iluna and the *Imgur-Marduk* of the later period must therefore designate the same inner wall enclosing the two courts of the sanctuary and separating them from the other buildings of the vast complex which constituted the sacred precincts of Nippur. The general course of this wall was indicated through the boundary line of the Parthian fortress lying directly over it, and besides has been fixed definitely at several points by our excavations. We exposed nearly the whole southeast wall of the inner court, disclosed part of its northwest wall, and traced the two side-walls of the outer court far enough to enable us to reconstruct the general outlines of the temple enclosure.

Aside from the depression in the unexcavated southeast ridge[1] marking the boundary of the outer court, which

of the world," was closely connected with the sanctuary of Nippur, in which Bêl, as "the king of the world," appointed his human representative on earth and bestowed the significant title upon him. Comp. Hilprecht, "The Bab. Exp. of the U. of Pa.," series A, vol. i, part 2, pp. 56, *seq.* (and part 1, pp. 24, *seq.*).

[1] Comp. the plan of the ruins on p. 305.

doubtless represents the principal entrance of the latter, two gates have been found in connection with our explorations around the stage-tower, the large southeast one, which connects the two courts, and another smaller one, which leads from the rear of the *ziggurrat* into the large open space to the northwest of the temple. The axis of the rear gate, which is nearly seventeen feet distant from the lower face of *Imġarsag*, is in line with the front gate. Though only one corner of the former has as yet been uncovered, it suffices to show that its construction was similar to the one in front of the *ziggurrat*.

The southeast wall, which contained the principal gate of the temple, exhibits the same general characteristic features as the fragment of wall from the time of Gudea, which De Sarzec discovered beneath the Seleucidan palace at Tellô, with the exception that the wall around *Ekur* was constructed entirely of unbaked material, while the much less imposing one of the temple of Ningirsu consisted of baked bricks. To judge from the excavated southeast section, the interior face of the wall at Nippur, into which a number of store-rooms were built, was plain and without any ornamentation, while the monotony of the long exterior surface was relieved by a series of panels.[1] On an average these panels measured about 16 feet in width, and were separated from each other by shallow buttresses projecting one foot from the wall, and 9 to 10 feet wide. The gate, which occupied nearly the centre of this wall, was a very elaborate affair, considering that its plan and general disposition, similar to that of the city gates of the Assyrian kings discovered at Khorsabâd and Nineveh, go back to the time of Sargon of Agade.[2] It was 52 feet long and nearly as wide, and was

[1] Comp. the zinctype, p. 470, above, and "Ekur, the Temple of Bêl" (restored) below.

[2] Traces of a crude brick pavement of the period prior to Ur-Gur were discovered at the bottom of the gate walls. In the same proportion as the

flanked on each side by a pair of tower-like bastions, still preserved to a considerable height. They projected sixteen feet towards the northwest and about nine feet towards the southeast. Like the wall itself, which was 26 feet thick, including the storage vaults of the inner court, the front faces of these towers were panelled. A kind of vestibule marked the entrance of the gate on both sides. By means of three stepped recesses projecting from each tower these vestibules (14 feet wide) narrowed into the passageway proper, which measured only 6 feet in width. In the middle of the gate this passage opened into a long gallery, probably serving as a guard-room. The door of the gate which closed the opening towards the outer court swung in the direction of the eastern section of this gallery, as a socket in dolerite imbedded in baked bricks allowed us to infer. This stone, though inscribed with the common legend of Ur-Gur, did not seem to lie in its original position, but apparently had been used over and over, the last time by Ashurbânapal, at the level of whose pavement it was found.

The remains of *Imgur-Marduk* were deeply hidden below the ruins of later constructions. As regards *Nîmit-Marduk*, the outer wall of the temple, we find the case somewhat different. To a considerable extent the course of the ancient rampart could still be recognized and traced through a series of low ridges lying on the northwest and northeast (II) limits of Nuffar. Seen from the top of Bint el-Amîr, they formed two almost straight lines (more or less interrupted by gaps) which originally must have met at an obtuse angle in the north (comp. the plan of the ruins, p. 305). In the course of the third expedition Haynes had driven two tun-

floor of the gate was raised by the gradually accumulating dirt and débris, the door-socket was carried higher and higher, so that Ashurbânapal's entrance lies about six feet above that of Ur-Gur, a fact in entire accord with the difference of altitude observed between the pavements of the two monarchs within the temple enclosure.

nels through the northeastern ridge (near III), thereby ascertaining that both Narâm-Sin and Ur-Gur, whose bricks at some places lie directly upon each other, had done work on the outer wall. His deductions, however, with regard to its original size and construction, turned out to be erroneous, as accidentally he had struck a kind of large buttress, through which his tunnels ran obliquely. At the committee's request, he had resumed his excavation there in the fall of 1899, in order to search for the northeast city gate, the original position of which seemed to be indicated by an especially large gap near the middle of the ridge. Soon after my arrival at the ruins in 1900, I placed a large force, divided into a number of small gangs, along the whole line, with the intention of tracing the course of the entire wall. The examination of the northern section was completed within seven weeks; that of the eastern will require considerably more time and work to obtain a full insight into the meaning of the many fragmentary walls which sometimes run alongside and sometimes above, and sometimes overlap each other. Owing to the heavy mass of ruins, particularly of the Parthian period, under which these remains are buried, they cannot be exposed and understood fully without subjecting to a critical examination the whole group of mounds adjoining them in the direction of the temple. It may be safely asserted that extensive excavations in this section of the ruins will yield important results. For, aside from very large tablets which trial trenches brought to light, we have reason to believe that the buildings which occupied this site stood in a closer relation to the sanctuary, in all probability representing the palace of the *patesis* of Nippur and the houses of the higher class of priests and temple officers serving immediately under them.

The excavations conducted along the outer face of *Nîmit-Marduk* yielded several interesting objects. At the base of the pre-Sargonic and Sargonic walls we gathered a large quantity of baked terra-cotta balls, about 1¼ to 1½ inches in diameter, and a few small stone eggs. Both balls and eggs had previously been classified under the general title of playthings, but in view of the peculiar place where they mostly occurred, this explanation can no longer be maintained. There is little doubt in my mind but that they are to be regarded as missiles thrown by the slingers of hostile armies attacking the city. As stones could not be obtained in the alluvial soil of Babylonia, clay was turned into war material as it served many other purposes. The marble eggs may have originally belonged to foreign invaders, notably the Elamites, who brought them from their mountainous districts, or they were thrown by certain Babylonian warriors of one of the petty states near the Arabian desert who could afford this luxury.[1] The other weapons employed in the battles around the walls of the temple, according to our discoveries, were arrows, spears, axes and clubs, the heads of the first-mentioned three weapons being made of copper; those of the clubs of stone, especially porphyry and granite. In one case we came upon the twisted remains of a quiver. The wooden parts of the receptacle had decayed long ago, but its copper fastenings, consisting of a round, thin plate with two corroded arrowheads attached to it, a narrow copper strap and a nail of the same metal, were still preserved.

The excavations tracing the base of *Nîmit-Marduk* revealed also some of the means to which the besieged inhabitants sometimes resorted in order to protect themselves against attacks from without. In case of necessity they seized any heavy object upon which they could lay their hands, and hurled it down upon the heads of the storming enemies, as was shown by the stone weights, mortars in dolerite, broken statues and reliefs, stone pestles, etc., unearthed along the outer face of the wall. We here found some of the oldest fragments of sculptures discovered at Nuffar, *e. g.*, several

[1] Comp. p. 242, above.

portions of a large stele in limestone, adorned with human figures, similar in design to those which are depicted on a small bas-relief from Tellô representing the meeting of the two chiefs.[1] It was natural that in the débris which had

Pre-Sargonic Bas-Relief in Limestone

accumulated on both sides of the rampart we should find many broken terra-cotta figurines of gods and goddesses. And it was entirely in accord with what we observed in other parts of the mounds that here and there in the slopes of the ruined wall late Arabic tombs were met with. But it was entirely unexpected to find that the pre-Sargonic burials (ash-beds, urns and drains), which at low levels we had previously traced outside of the inner wall of the post-Sargonic period, extended even slightly beyond *Nîmit-Marduk* in the neighborhood of the temple.

As the northeast section of the outer wall confined a large

[1] Comp. p. 250, above.

open court, there was no difficulty in carefully examining the whole structure by means of two long trenches following its course on either side.[1] We soon found that originally a series of small rooms was built against the inner face of the rampart. Three of them opened into a long corridor which ran along the wall (No. 11). Two, exhibiting no entrance at all, seemed to have served as store-rooms, accessible only from above. Some could be identified only from insignificant traces, while still others had disappeared so completely that their former existence could only be inferred from certain indications in the soil. To the northwest of the five preserved chambers was a peculiar receptacle in the shape of a jar made of three different materials (No. 10). A round terra-cotta plate, thickly covered with bitumen, represented the bottom. The lower part of its side consisted of bitumen, while the upper part was unbaked clay coated inside and outside with a thin layer of bitumen. Evidently this receptacle had been a kind of a safe inserted in the floor of a room, the walls of which had decayed long ago. The man who devised this unique specimen of a small "cistern" had probably intended to construct it entirely of bitumen on a foundation of terra-cotta, but finding that his material was not sufficient, he substituted clay, and used only as much bitumen as was absolutely necessary to exclude the humidity from the interior of the vessel. The relative age and purpose of this vase could be determined by the aid of seven fragments of cuneiform tablets lying within it, and also of a few others picked up at about the same level in the loose earth of the neighborhood. A shopkeeper of some sort, who lived at the time of the dynasty of Ur (about 2600 B. C.), had kept his account books in this jar. Similar tablet jars were repeatedly found in other parts of the ruins.[2]

[1] Comp. the zinctype illustrating the "Northwestern Section of the Northeastern City Wall," p. 498, below. The numbers placed in parenthesis above refer to it.

[2] Comp. my remarks in connection with the temple library below.

Our excavations along the northwest section of *Nîmit-Marduk* had shown that in the first half of the third millennium a row of magazines, booths, and closets occupied the space along the inner face of the long wall. In one case a room had been built even into the latter. Our continued explorations in that neighborhood confirmed this result in all particulars. Near the northern extremity of the large enclosure we uncovered a small fireplace with ashes on its top and around its base (No. 9). It was a very simple affair, being merely a hard clay platform surrounded by a row of burned bricks set on edge. A much more elaborate concern (No. 8) was discovered a little to the north of it. Our Arabs identified it at once as a large oven of the same type as is used

Old Babylonian Baking Furnace. About 2300 B. C.

to-day in the large native restaurants of Baghdad, Hilla, and other places of the lower Euphrates and Tigris valleys, or employed in connection with the burning of pottery. This is another striking illustration of the tenacity with which ancient Babylonian customs are preserved even by the present population of 'Irâq el-'Arabî.

This peculiar brick structure, which combined the characteristic features of a kiln and of a kitchen furnace, was about 13 feet long, a little over 7 feet wide, and nearly 4 feet high.

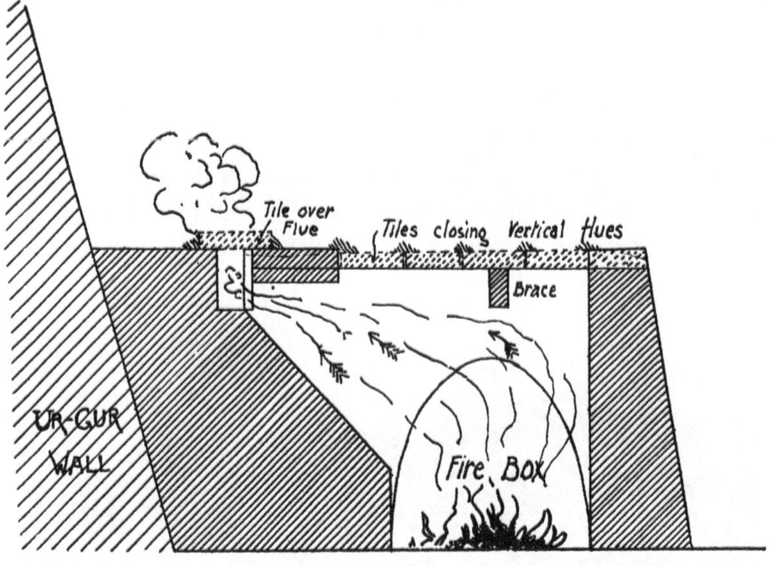

Section of a Babylonian Baking Furnace in Use (Time of Abraham)

It was built against Ur-Gur's wall, and consisted of crude bricks, which, in consequence of their constant exposure to the intense heat, had completely turned red. As the interesting fireplace stood on a somewhat higher level than the curious tablet jar described above (p. 488), it probably is not quite as ancient, and must be ascribed to the time of the kings of (N)isin or to the first dynasty of Babylon, — in round numbers, to about 2400 or 2300 B. C. Its upper surface showed a kind of panelled work, while there was an arched opening at one of its two shorter sides, that towards the northwest. The outside appearance of the whole structure was not unlike a large box such as is used everywhere at the present day to ship birds and other living animals.

Upon closer examination, the furnace was found to be composed of a series of seven (originally nine) arches rising parallel to a southeast solid wall which terminated the whole structure, and alternately joined to one another by fragments of bricks in order to keep the single arches intact. The vertical flues thereby formed descended into the vaulted fire-box, which was about 2½ feet wide, nearly as high, and ran lengthwise through the whole kiln. But they also communicated with a horizontal flue of the same length near the top of the structure close to the rampart. The accompanying cross-section of the restored building, drawn by Fisher, will convey a tolerably clear idea of the manner in which the building was heated, the necessary draft obtained, and the smoke discharged from the interior. The draft was regulated by means of tiles placed over the longitudinal flue, or removed from the same.

The upper surface of this oven now appears worn off at the edges and otherwise damaged, but originally it was entirely level. The pots containing the food to be cooked were put over the open spaces between the single arches. Whenever they did not cover the entire space the remaining openings were closed by bricks, several of which were found *in situ*. In case pottery was to be burned, all the available space was filled with different kinds of earthen vessels. Low dishes were piled on the top of each other, their sticking together being prevented by small terra-cotta stilts of precisely the same form as those used in the china manufactories of Europe and America to-day. They were gathered in large quantities at various parts and levels of the ruins.[1]

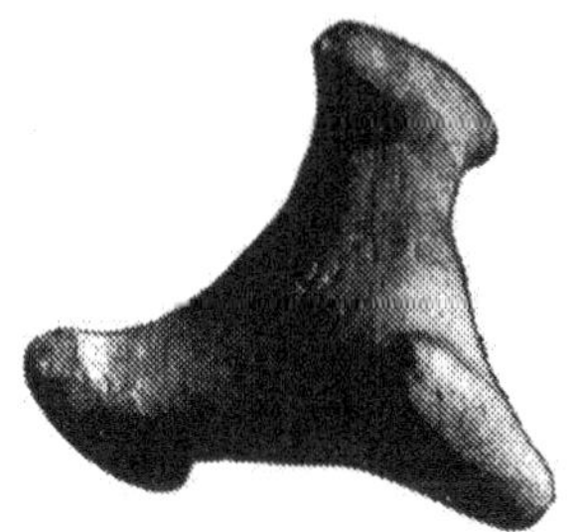

Babylonian Stilt. About 2300 B. C.

Many enamelled dishes of the Parthian period were brought

[1] Comp. p. 313, above.

to light which exhibit those stilt-marks very plainly inside and outside. In order to save fuel, to concentrate the heat, and to secure an even burning of the pottery, the structure doubtless was roofed over.

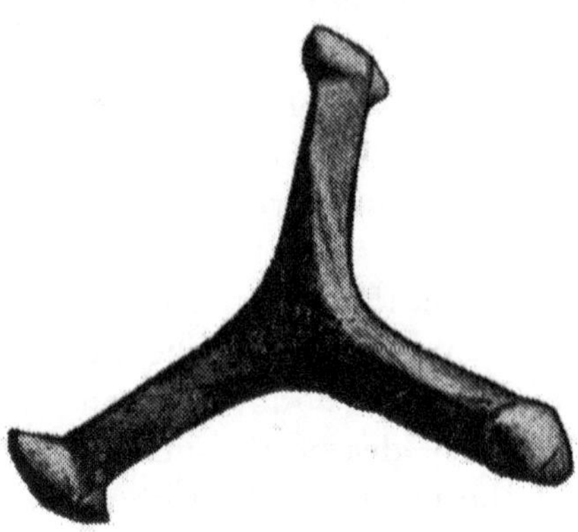

Stilt used in Modern China Manufactories
From Trenton, N. J.

After this brief review of the principal discoveries made in connection with our tracing the inner face of the great enclosing wall, we turn our attention to the construction of the wall itself. The long narrow ridge (II–III, on the plan of the ruins, p. 305), which conceals the remains of the frequently repaired rampart to the north of the temple, varies considerably in height. At some places it stands only a few feet above the plain, while at others it rises to more than twenty feet above the same. Its average height may be regarded as about twelve to fifteen feet. The comparative steepness of the ridge, the absence of extensive traces of later (post-Babylonian) settlements on its top, and the noteworthy fact that the excavations at the highest points of the ruined structure did not disclose the remains of specially fortified bastions or high towers at these places would indicate that at the time of its latest restoration *Nîmit-Marduk* cannot have been less than twenty-five feet high, and possibly was somewhat higher.

The question arises at once, why is it that certain parts of the ancient rampart are preserved almost in their original height, while others have been reduced considerably, and still other large sections of the northwest, northeast and southeast walls have disappeared completely. It is not difficult to give a correct answer. A careful examination of the large adobes which characterize all the true Parthian buildings at Nippur revealed the fact that they were made of clay previously worked. It is generally known among the present inhabitants of 'Irâq el-'Arabî that the clay of old mud houses refashioned into bricks furnishes a much more tenacious and lasting building material than the clay taken directly from the soil. We have ample evidence to show that the early Babylonian builders had acquired the same knowledge by experience. There can be no doubt, therefore, that the enormous mass of clay required for the construction of the huge fortress erected on the temple mound, and for the extensive Parthian settlements on the site of the library, on the mounds to the east of the temple, and on the west side of the Chebar, was principally obtained from the abandoned outer walls of the ancient city. This theory was fully corroborated by our excavations in the wide gap of the northeast wall, marked III on the plan of the ruins (p. 305). While searching there for the possible remains of one of the former city gates, we came upon a very large hollow or depression in the ground filled with mud washings and drift sand from the desert. It proved to be one of the clay beds worked by the brick-makers of the post-Babylonian period, who, after having torn down a section of about 360 feet from the old rampart, penetrated to a considerable depth into the soil below and around it.

In descending somewhat deeper into the ground than the Parthian clay diggers before us had done, we disclosed the ruins of a pre-Sargonic gate, or more exactly, part of its substructure and stepped ascent. It lay four to eight feet below the present level of the plain, which at this point is considerably higher than elsewhere in the vicinity of Nuffar. The structure, as it now stands, is entirely isolated. But while excavating we observed a mass of worked clay, largely disintegrated adobes, and a number of bricks of Narâm-Sin scattered through the loose earth in its immediate neighborhood. These, with certain inferences to be drawn from a fragment of the same king's wall about 175 feet to the northwest of it, and several other considerations, lead us to the conclusion that at all the different periods of Nippur's varied history the northeast gate of the city must have been situated at about the same place. Hence it follows that *Nîmit-Marduk* ran in the form of a great bastion or bulwark around the gate, giving to it additional strength and architectural prominence.

From the illustration facing this page we can recognize without difficulty that the original gate consisted of three divisions, a central roadway (1) for the use of beasts and vehicles, and two elevated passageways (2 and 3) for the people. There have remained only insignificant traces of the main division and of the left sidewalk — practically nothing beyond a few courses of burned bricks sufficient to determine the general plan and disposition of the gate, while the right or northwest passageway was found in a tolerably fair state of preservation. The central road was about 12 feet wide, or nearly three times as wide as each sidewalk. The pavements, steps, and supporting walls were built of that primitive type of bricks which constitutes one of the most characteristic features of the pre-Sargonic age. These bricks, however, exhibiting, as they do, two distinct moulds, represent two different periods. This becomes evident from the fact that they occur separately in the two constructions of the right passageway (5 and 6) which lie above each other, and most assuredly were built with a considerable interval of time between them. The older bricks are more rudely fashioned than the later ones, and only occasionally show a thumb impression. At the same time they are somewhat less in length and width and more emphatically convex than the more modern bricks.[1]

[1] The average dimensions of the earlier bricks are 8½ by 5½ by 2½ inches, those of the later ones 11 by 7½ by 2 inches.

Ruins of the Pre-Sargonic Gate in the Northeast Wall of Nippur

The foundation of this once doubtless imposing structure was laid five to six feet below the foot of the central division. It consisted of stamped earth mixed with potsherds and fragments of bricks. In order to prevent the waters of the moat,[1] which ran parallel to the northeast wall of the city, from gradually washing the earth away, the outer edge of this road-bed (4) was cased with large rude blocks of gypsum laid in bitumen to a height of more than two feet. The main road leading over this foundation from the bridge of the moat to the temple enclosure sloped gradually but perceptibly upward while passing through the gate. It was paved with the later kind of pre-Sargonic bricks, likewise laid in bitumen. They were arranged in a peculiar manner, somewhat similar to those which formed the walls of the arched tunnel in the lower strata of the *ziggurrat* (comp. p. 400). The two sidewalks were provided with low balustrades, about one foot high. They were elevated above the central path and reached by a flight of eight steps, the topmost of which lay six feet higher than the road reserved for animals. This difference in altitude naturally grew less as the three passageways approached the end of the gate, where possibly they entered the sacred precincts at the same level. It is interesting to observe that the preserved right staircase already exhibits the same stepped recesses which are characteristic of later Babylonian gates. In consequence of this

[1] Apart from the peculiar casing of the foundation of the road, which otherwise cannot be explained satisfactorily, the former existence of a moat follows with certainty from another fact. We discovered a number of drains in our excavations along the wall, which emerged from the rubbish around the temple, passed beneath the city wall, and continued their sloping course a little outside the latter until they suddenly terminated abruptly in the open plain. It is very evident that they must have discharged their contents into an open watercourse or ditch, which probably branched off from the Chebar near the beginning of the northwest wall, followed the entire course of *Nîmit-Marduk*, and ran back into the great canal somewhere to the south of the sanctuary.

peculiarity the horizontal passageway starting at the head of the stair is about half a foot narrower than the lowest step. Another remarkable feature of this pre-Sargonic ascent is to be seen in the tapering of the steps with regard to their depth, every higher step being smaller in width of tread than the next one below.[1]

Apart from certain necessary repairs made by later hands along the top of the dwarf walls on either side of the right passageway and at the edge of the lower steps, the entire body of this elevated sidewalk was built exclusively of the smaller kind of pre-Sargonic bricks. Its inner face adjoining the central road had a very distinct batter or slope (easily to be recognized in the illustration opposite page 494), while its outer face was perfectly vertical. It would seem reasonable to assume that the cause of this difference in construction is due to the fact that the inner face was exposed to view, while the outer face was built against the mud bricks of the city wall. As the present length of the sidewalk, which on the whole is identical with what it originally was, is a little over 35 feet, the great bastion of the city wall through which the road passed must have had approximately the same thickness.

The three divisions of the earliest gate ran in a straight line from the moat to the enclosure. But at a subsequent, though still pre-Sargonic period, a remarkable change took place, doubtless in connection with a rebuilding of the walls, and a slight altering of their course. As we shall see later, this assertion can be proved positively with regard to Nâram-

1 I took the following measurements of the width of tread of the different steps constituting the lower stair. The lowest step measured 39 cm., the second 33 cm., the third and fourth 29 cm., the fifth 25 cm., the sixth 23 cm.; the seventh, again being deeper, measured 37.5 cm. A similar observation was made with regard to the upper stair. The lowest step measured 37 cm., the second 35 cm., the third 33 cm., the fourth 29 cm., the fifth and sixth 23 cm., the seventh 22 cm.

Sin's line of fortifications, which ran nearly perpendicular to the axis of the upper flight of stairs. This second staircase lies directly over a section of the earlier sidewalk, which it crossed at a slight angle. It started at a distance of nearly fourteen feet from the upper edge of the lower stair, leading in eight or nine steps to another corridor. As previously remarked, this later structure was composed solely of the larger kind of pre-Sargonic bricks. The time which elapsed between the erection of the two staircases is unknown. However, the period cannot have been very short; it probably embraced several hundred years, for the second elevated path lies three and a half feet above the former. Doubtless it was built because the débris accumulated at the base of the wall and in the open court behind it had grown to such a height as to necessitate a change in the level of the road. At the time of Narâm-Sin the roadbed again must have been raised considerably; for the lowest traces of his ruined wall[1] are four and a half feet above the upper pre-Sargonic sidewalk, while those of Ur-Gur's rampart, which followed a slightly different course from that of Narâm-Sin, lie even six feet higher. From this circumstance alone it follows that Ur-Gur and Narâm-Sin cannot have lived in close proximity to one another, as was asserted by Lehmann and others, who endeavored to reduce the 3200 years quoted by Nabonidos to 2200 years.

A thorough examination of the long ridge to the northwest of the pre-Sargonic gate (No. 6, p. 498) enabled us to form a tolerably clear idea of the original size and character of *Nîmit-Marduk*. As only the lower parts of the wall are preserved, the details which we ascertained apply exclusively to the structures of Narâm-Sin (No. 3) and Ur-Gur (No. 1). Neither earlier nor later remains could be determined with certainty. The general trend of the ridge is from northwest

[1] The base of an excellently preserved perpendicular water-conduit draining the wall of Nâram-Sin.

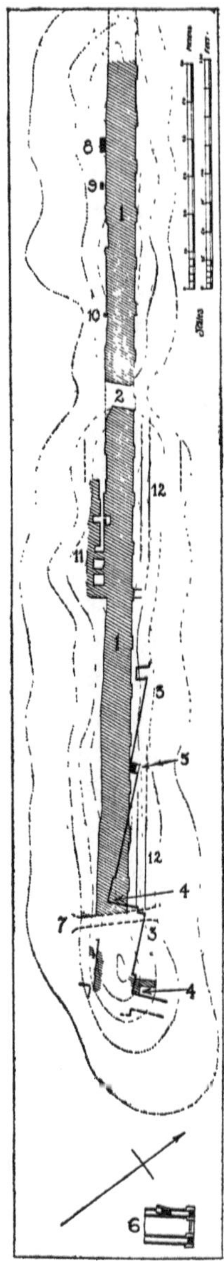

Northwestern Section of the Northeastern City Wall *by Fisher*

to southeast, and fairly represents the direction of Ur-Gur's rampart. Apart from their fragmentary height, the excavated portions are in almost perfect condition. Though uninscribed, the crude bricks of which they are composed in size, color, and texture are identical with those in the centre of the *ziggurrat*, and therefore may safely be ascribed to the great royal builder from Ur (about 2700 B. C.). The exposed northwest section is a little over 750 feet long and 25½ feet thick. Its exterior is effectively broken up by eighteen[1] buttresses, which average in width eleven feet,[2] and project two feet from the face of the wall. The spaces or panels between them, as a rule, measure almost thirty feet. The inside surface of the structure is not nearly so well preserved as the exterior, but there is evidence that buttresses were also used to some extent, similar to those on the outside. Both faces of the wall were covered with a thin plaster of clay which protected the sloping[3] sides against storm and rain. The highest part of Ur-Gur's ruined

[1] We found only seventeen, but the eighteenth can be restored with certainty. It stood in the deep cut (marked No. 2 in the zinctype), through which the latest inhabitants passed out of the ruined enclosure into the open plain.

[2] The second from the pre-Sargonic gate is an exceptionally wide buttress, which measures 13⅔ feet in width.

[3] The slope or batter of the wall was in the proportion of 1 to 3.

structure measured nine feet, and was covered with a mass of disintegrated adobes. Its base rested on a foundation of clay laid up *en masse* (No. 12), which extended seven feet beyond the outer face of the wall and was nearly six feet high,[1] with practically the same slope as the latter.

The remains of Narâm-Sin's wall (about 3750 B. C.) are very insignificant compared with those of Ur-Gur's. The reason is very apparent. A glance upon Fisher's accompanying sketch shows that Narâm-Sin's wall (No. 3) met Ur-Gur's in an angle of 10° 30′. The last-mentioned king therefore, in modifying the plan of the earlier ruler, was forced to raze the old wall in order to prevent the enemy from using it as a base of operation against his new rampart. Consequently Narâm-Sin's structure is preserved only where it lies beneath the wall of Ur-Gur, who, as far as possible, utilized it as a foundation for his own bulwark. From the fact that the axis of the upper sidewalk of the pre-Sargonic gate (No. 6), previously described, is perpendicular to the line of Narâm-Sin's fortification restored, we infer that Sargon's famous son built his wall according to the plan of one of his predecessors. The course of this wall, however, differed essentially from that of the earliest rampart[2] and from that of the time of Ur-Gur, both of which practically followed the same general trend. All attempts on the part of the architects to fix the inner face of Narâm-Sin's enclosing wall have been unsuccessful, so that, Haynes' previous assertions[3] to the contrary, we still are in absolute ignorance of

[1] It descended, therefore, to the level of the present plain, which lies somewhat above that of Ur-Gur's time. This indicates that the ground on which the foundation was laid had previously been raised. It is very probable that an earlier wall, afterwards partly covered by Ur-Gur's foundation, once occupied the same site.

[2] Which must have been perpendicular to the axis of the lower sidewalk of the pre-Sargonic gate.

[3] Reproduced in Hilprecht, "The Bab. Exp. of the U. of Pa.," series A, vol. i, part 2, pp. 20, *seq.*

its original thickness. From the excavations carried on at the extreme southeast end of the ridge, it seems to follow that some parts, possibly representing bastions, must have been at least 40 feet thick.

The fragment of wall laid bare (No. 3) is nearly 300 feet long. Its building material was enormous crude bricks made of well-worked clay mixed with chopped straw. These adobes are exceedingly tough in texture, regular in form, and measure 19 inches square by 3 inches. Many of them are stamped with Narâm-Sin's well-known legend[1] upon their lower faces. Our excavations did not reveal any traces of buttresses and panels on the outer face of the wall. The sole attempt at relieving the monotony of the structure seems to have consisted in the use of heavy return angles (Nos. 4 and 5 in the above sketch), similar to those which characterize the long pre-Sargonic wall disclosed by the fourth expedition on the west side of the Shatt en-Nîl. In one of these angles (No. 5) is a fine water-conduit of baked bricks laid in bitumen and still rising to a height of 5¾ feet. It is in such an excellent state of preservation that we scarcely can realize that it was constructed nearly six thousand years ago. The lower part of this drain is a solid base, a little over 6 feet wide, 8 feet deep, and 2 feet high, covered on its top with a heavy layer of bitumen. The only evidence of a former batter of the wall is found in the two sides of the conduit (which is 4 feet 8 inches deep), each course of brick receding slightly from that below it.[2] In 1895 Haynes unearthed a large number of terra-cotta cones and water spouts at the base of the small section of wall examined by him.[3] None, however, were discovered five years later when we subjected the whole ridge to a most careful examination. The reason

[1] Comp. p. 388.

[2] Most measurements given and certain architectural details stated in my sketch above were obtained from Fisher's report on the outer wall.

[3] Comp. pp. 424, *seq.*, above.

for this seemingly strange circumstance can only be that Haynes accidentally had struck an architecturally prominent part of the wall (No. 7), a bastion well drained and ornamented with parapets, which flanked the great northeast gate of the city.

7. Two theories had been advanced with regard to the extensive building remains discovered in the upper strata of Bint el-Amîr. Peters regarded them as the ruins of the temple of Bêl according to its latest reconstruction by a Persian king living about 500 B. C., and dedicating the sacred enclosure to a new religion (p. 329, *seq.*). The present writer from the very beginning interpreted the vast structure as an entirely new creation of an even later period, which stood in no historical relation to the Babylonian sanctuary beneath it. He believed that it was a fortified Parthian palace built around the *ziggurrat* as a citadel on the site of the ancient temple (pp. 327, 364, 373, *seq.*). The former was convinced that the huge enclosing walls and the two round towers protecting them originated with Ur-Gur (about 2700 B. C.).[1] The writer declared them to form an inseparable part of the Parthian construction built 2500 years later than the time assigned to them by Peters.

In sketching the work of the four Philadelphia expeditions at Nuffar, I repeatedly took occasion to indicate that it is impossible to reconcile Peters' view with all the facts brought to light by our various excavations. The crude bricks characterizing the latest edifice are different from those which we meet in the Babylonian and Persian strata. And with but few exceptions,[2] the antiquities gathered in its rooms point unmistakably to the Hellenistic and Roman periods as the real time of their construction and occupancy.

[1] Comp. Peters' "Nippur," vol. ii, pp. 148, *seqq.*, esp. pp. 157, *seq.*

[2] Stray antiquities belonging to different periods of Babylonian history which occur occasionally in the upper strata of all the mounds of Nuffar. Comp. pp. 340, note 1, 366, *seq.*, 372.

I refer briefly to the numerous coins of the Arsacide kings (about 250 B. C. to 226 A. D.) found in the *débris* filling those chambers, in the bricks of their walls, and in the mortar which united them (p. 327). Or I mention the peculiar class of terra-cotta figurines and the fine enamelled lamp with the head of Medusa, described above (pp. 330, *seq.*), the graceful small flasks, vases, and other vessels in glass, the exceedingly thin and fragile bowls in terra-cotta (p. 288), the fragments of cornices in limestone with their Greek and Roman designs (comp. p. 366), the Rhodian jar handle with the Greek inscription (p. 366), and many other equally instructive antiquities which cannot be considered in this connection. The evidence already submitted is conclusive, and shows that the building under consideration belongs to that period which we generally call Parthian, — a period characterized by the welding together of classical and Oriental elements and the subsequent rising of a short-lived new civilization and art. This period lasted about four to five hundred years, and represents the last flaring and flashing of a great light, once illuminating the whole world, before its final extinction.

Two new important proofs were adduced in connection with the work of our latest expedition to substantiate and to supplement those general conclusions at which I practically had arrived in the course of our first campaign.[1] The complete removal of the large fortification tower opposite the entrance of the *ziggurrat* (p. 444) revealed the interesting fact that it stood directly over the ruined gate of the Babylonian temple (p. 483). More than this, a stray cuneiform tablet of the firm of Murashû Sons, dated in the reign of Darius II (423–405 B. C.), was discovered in its foundation. It had evidently been placed there as a talisman[2] by those

[1] Comp. Peters' "Nippur," vol. ii, p. 118, with the passages quoted on the preceding page.

[2] Comp. pp. 154, *seq.*, 168, 233, *seq.*, 367.

who erected the first fortified palace on the site of the ancient temple. Consequently the banking-house of Murashû Sons, situated on the western side of the Chebar, must have been in ruins for some time previous to the building of that palace. Hence it follows that the latter cannot be older than the second half of the fourth century, when cuneiform writing no longer was understood by the mass of the people, and under the influence of a foreign power that new civilization, to which I referred above, began to be grafted upon the native Babylonian. This leads us to the period of the Seleucidan rulers as the earliest possible time when the first fortress was constructed on the temple mound of Nuffar. To this period must be ascribed all the remains marked I on the plan of the "Parthian Palace built over the Ruins of the Temple of Bêl," which appears below.[1] They are comparatively insignificant, consisting only of a few rooms and two round towers, one of which was incorporated with the second fortress. But, as the two architects observed correctly, they can easily be distinguished from the other buildings by the size and quality of their bricks,[2] the greater depth of their level,[3] and the direction of their walls, the later walls crossing the earlier ones at an angle of 8° 10′. "A line drawn through the centres of the two earlier towers is parallel to the walls of the various groups of rooms of that period; and similarly a line through the centres of the two larger towers [forming part of the inner wall] is parallel to the rooms of the second palace,"[4] and — we may add — also to the principal façades of the ancient *ziggurrat*.

[1] In the chapter "On the Topography of Ancient Nippur."

[2] The earlier bricks measure 12½ by 12½ by 6 inches, and contain less potsherds than the later bricks, which are almost cubical, measuring 12½ by 11⅝ by 9 inches.

[3] The remains of the older fortress lie six to eight feet below the rooms of the later palace.

[4] Quoted from Geere's report.

No satisfactory reason has as yet been found to explain why the builders of the earlier fortress deviated from the direction fixed thousands of years before by the architects of the Babylonian temple. The difference of bricks used in the two fortresses can very distinctly be seen in the illustration facing p. 444. The other principal results obtained in the course of our fourth campaign with regard to the large complex covering the temple mound are incorporated in a subsequent chapter, " On the Topography of Ancient Nippur." In this place it may suffice to state a second important reason for assigning its construction to the Parthian rulers of the country.

Toward the end of November, 1899, an unusually interesting tomb was disclosed in the ruins to the south of Bint el-Amîr (comp. p. 444). It was situated beneath the mud floor of one of the rooms[1] built into the top of the outer enclosing wall of the fortress, and consisted of burned bricks generally placed on their edges. This funeral chamber was reached by a flight of steps of irregular height and tread, constructed of the same material. Both the tomb proper and the stairway leading to it were arched over.[2] When discovered, the entrance way was closed with bricks loosely laid on the steps and some pieces of a large slab, which seem to have belonged together originally[3] and formed the cover stone for the whole stairway. The walls and the poorly constructed ceiling were laid in clay mortar coated with bitumen

[1] Marked No. 3 on the plan of the " Parthian Palace, built over the Ruins of the Temple of Bêl," p. 559, below.

[2] Comp. the illustration, p. 512, below, which represents two similar arched tombs of the same period excavated in the southeastern slope of the library mound.

[3] As the writer was not present when the tomb was opened, he gathered the facts from the reports of Haynes and Geere. The latter remarks: " It is to be supposed that in raising this slab on some later occasion — probably when the second burial took place — it was broken, whereupon the tomb was closed with its fragments and bricks in the manner indicated."

and plastered with a stucco of mud. The floor of the tomb was paved with two layers of baked bricks, so that dampness was effectively excluded from the room.

This vaulted funeral chamber was ten feet long, eight feet wide, and a little over five feet high, while the room above it measured almost twelve feet square. " Entering the cell a gruesome sight was before us. Side by side upon the floor lay two adult skeletons of more than average size." Both were considerably injured by pieces of plaster which had fallen from the roof. The one farthest from the door (II, p. 506), had suffered most. The skull was completely broken, and many of the larger bones had been pressed out of their original position and lay buried in dust and débris. The better preserved (I) had been placed in a wooden coffin, which, with the exception of a few half-decomposed fragments, had long since "crumbled away and mingled its reddish brown ashes with the gray ashes of the grave-clothes and the decayed tissues of the body." By means of these relics and a number of iron and bronze nails, which evidently had held the boards together, it was comparatively easy to trace the outlines[1] of the entire coffin. Two iron bands (1), slightly projecting beyond the long sides of the coffin, at either end of it, had been fastened as a support to the bottom of the box. To the ends of these bars silver rings (2), now badly corroded, had been attached as handles for the purpose of lifting and carrying the coffin.

Fortunately this tomb had not been rifled in ancient times, like so many others of the same general period in various parts of the ruins. We therefore found all the less perishable objects deposited with the two bodies, as far as they had not been damaged and displaced by the falling stucco, exactly where they originally had been laid. Evidently the men[2] buried there had been persons of high rank

[1] Indicated by dotted lines in the accompanying zinctype.

[2] Geere writes, "Judging by the clothes, bones and skulls, I should say that there can be no doubt that the bodies were those of males."

in the service of the Parthian princes who ruled the country. Near each skull lay a square sheet of beaten gold (3) "almost large enough to cover the exposed portion of the face," and a scalloped band[1] of the same metal (3), which once encircled the brow. Two barrel-shaped gold beads (4), possibly used in connection with cords ending in tassels to hold the garment in place, were found near the

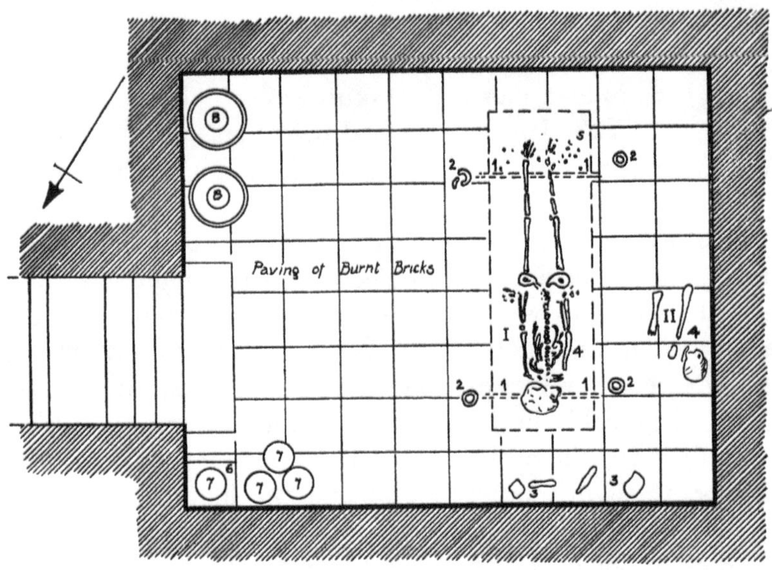

Plan of Tomb of Two High Officers from the Parthian Palace. First Century A. D.

waist of each body. Around the ankles (5) of the better-preserved skeleton, and at intervals along the legs, lay forty-eight small gold buttons provided with ears, and twelve larger rosettes, which apparently had served as ornaments of the outer garment. Two heavy gold buckles with thick wedge-shaped gold latchets, taken from the floor at the feet, were the gems of the collection. They doubtless repre-

[1] Each band is about twelve to thirteen inches long, and over an inch wide.

sented some sort of sandal fastenings. Each buckle was adorned with a well-executed head of a lion in high relief, richly enamelled with turquoise and set with rubies. A small gold ring,[1] the use of which is unknown, and a beautiful gold coin (lying near the head) completed this remarkable collection.

" The body lay at full length in a natural position on its back," with the head turned toward the southeast. From remaining traces of clothing, Geere was inclined to infer " that the man had worn a cotton shirt and what looked like a leather over-shirt, reaching as far as the knees." In accordance with the general custom, food and drink were deposited with the two corpses. The former was originally contained in four terra-cotta dishes (7) placed on a small brick shelf (6) and on the floor in the north corner of the chamber.[2] The latter was provided for in two large jars (8). They stood near the eastern corner, and were partly damaged by the fallen plaster.

Every object contained in this unique Parthian tomb, which may serve as a representative example of many similar graves, is most instructive. But our chief interest centres in the gold coin, which enables us to date this burial with greater accuracy than usual. It shows the head of a Roman emperor, surrounded by the Latin inscription TI(BERIUS) CÆSAR DIVI AUG(USTI) F(ILIUS) AUGUSTUS, by which it is proved conclusively that the two high officers buried there cannot have died before Emperor Tiberius (14–37 A. D.); that consequently the palace must have been inhabited at least as late as the first century of our own era. Other antiquities discovered in the débris

[1] Resembling a heavy earring more than anything else. Similar rings, generally occurring in pairs, were found repeatedly in Parthian coffins containing bodies of women.

[2] When discovered, nothing but " some light grayish powder " indicated the former contents of the dishes.

of the palace make it very probable that the fortress was kept in repair even in the century following.

After this brief review of the principal results obtained by the fourth expedition in connection with its work on the temple mound, we occupy ourselves for a few minutes with the large triangular hill to the south of the latter. As previously stated (p. 445), the exploration of this much neglected part of the ruins, strongly urged by the present writer, led to a unique result, which not without reason has been pronounced one of the most far-reaching Assyriological discoveries of the whole last century — the locating and partial excavating of the famous temple library and priest school of Nippur.[1]

The excavation of this vast site (IV on the plan of the ruins, p. 305) began at its northwest extremity, where the depression separating it from the temple complex proper is covered by a series of low elevations. It was about the middle of October, 1899, when Haynes dug a trench at this place to water level. As it yielded nothing but late graves and a few stray cuneiform tablets, the workmen were soon afterwards withdrawn, to be replaced by a larger force a month later. Trenches were now opened at different places along the three sides of the mound. By the middle of December fragmentary tablets were discovered in large quantities, and at the beginning of January, 1900, complete specimens came forth abundantly. For about two months and a half more the search was continued, until on March 19, for reasons given above (pp. 445, *seq.*), I suspended the excavations in this part of the ruins entirely, in order to devote all my time and attention to the many purely scientific problems of the expedition, for which the assistance of the architects was constantly required.

[1] Comp. my first communication to Professor Kittel of Leipzig, published in *Literarisches Centralblatt*, 1900, nos. 19, 20; and "The Sunday School Times," Philadelphia, May 5, 1900, pp. 275, *seq.*

Northeast Wing of the Temple Library and Priest-School of Nippur

Haynes unfortunately seems to have taken no particular interest in the extensive building remains prior to my arrival, or in the precious documents buried within them, beyond saving and counting them as they were gathered day after day. He did not ask Fisher and Geere, who then stood under his direct control as field director, to superintend the excavations in the temple library,[1] nor did he order the different walls and rooms exposed by him to be measured and surveyed. Consequently our knowledge as to how and precisely where the tablets were found is extremely limited. As I must depend almost exclusively on Haynes' official entries and records for this important question, I deem it necessary to submit a specimen of my only written source of information for the time prior to my arrival when most of the tablets were taken out of the ground. I quote literally from his diary.

"*Jan. 16, 1900:* 30 sound tablets of promise from a low level in 'Tablet Hill.'[2] Many large fine fragments of tablets, 1 pentagonal prism, 7¾ inches long; its five sides from 1 to 2⅙ inches wide. An hour after dark last evening one of our workmen's huts burned down so quickly that nothing was saved and the occupants barely escaped with their lives. By vigorous efforts the neighboring houses were saved.

"*Jan. 17, 1900:* 28 sound tablets from low level from 'Tablet Hill.' Very many large and fine fragments of tablets, 2 prisms and half a prism also from a low level. The tablets are covered with 18, 20, and 24 feet of débris, so that it requires a good deal of time to secure them, quite unlike Tel-Loh, where the accumulations are slight.

[1] Except one day in February, when Fisher was requested to show a visitor how tablets were excavated. To this fortunate circumstance I owe my knowledge as to tablets lying on the shelves of the library.

[2] I cannot even find out in which section of the large mound he unearthed these particular tablets. Nor is the slightest indication given by him as to whether he worked in a room, or found the tablets in the loose earth, or in both.

"*Jan. 18, 1900:* 33 sound tablets from a low level on 'Tablet Hill.' A multitude of imperfect tablets on 'Tablet Hill.' Three most beautiful days! And the nights with full moon are days in shadow, the air soft and balmy.

"*Jan. 19, 1900:* 49 sound tablets all from low level 'Tablet Hill.' Many fine fragments of tablets."

After an inspection of all the unearthed buildings and an examination of a sufficient number of representative tablets and fragments, I could declare positively at the beginning of March that we had discovered the temple library of ancient Nippur, and the most important of all the earlier Babylonian schools, where about the time of Abraham the younger generations were instructed in the art of tablet writing and in the wisdom of the god Nabû. Upon the basis of Haynes' scanty notes; Geere's drawings and reports on the buildings; my own investigations and brief excavations, and an examination of the more intelligent Arab foremen who previously supervised the laborers in the trenches, I present the following general picture.

The mound containing the remains of the educational quarter of the city rises to an average height of twenty to twenty-six feet above the level of the present plain, and covers an area of about thirteen acres. In other words, it occupies about the sixth part of the entire site included in the vast temple complex of Bêl on the northeast side of the Chebar. Only about the twelfth part of this library mound has thus far been satisfactorily examined with regard to the ruins lying above the plain level. The upper layer is easily distinguished from those below by the extensive remains of Parthian buildings constructed of the same kind of large unbaked brick which characterizes the two excavated palaces on the temple ruins and on the west bank of the Shatt en-Nîl. No important traces of Jewish and early Arabic settlements were disclosed in this particular mound. Parthian and Sassanian graves abound in the slopes of the entire hill. They

Vaulted Family Tombs of the Parthian Period, Southeastern Slope of the Library Mound

were not unfrequently found even in the central part of the ruins, where they are sometimes accompanied by terra-cotta drains and wells [1] descending far into the lower strata.

Altogether about four hundred tombs, coffins and burial urns of different sizes and shapes were opened in the course of the sixteen weeks during which excavations were carried on in "Tablet Hill." The two vaulted brick tombs seen in the illustration facing this page evidently represented family vaults, for the one contained six, the other two skeletons. Unfortunately both were rifled in ancient times, since they could easily be reached by robbers, situated, as they were, directly on a public street, whence a narrow inclined paved way led to the door of each tomb.

More than four thousand cuneiform tablets had been discovered in the upper twenty feet of accumulated débris at Mound IV during our excavations of 1889 and 1890.[2] They included several hundred contract tablets and temple lists written at the time of the Assyrian, Chaldean, and Persian rulers (about 700–400 B. C.), a few fragments of neo-Babylonian hymns, letters and syllabaries, a considerable number of business documents, dated in the reigns of the kings of the first dynasty of Babylon (about 2300–2100 B. C.), and more than twenty-five hundred literary fragments of the third pre-Christian millennium generally half effaced or otherwise damaged. I consequently had reached the conclusion that either there were two distinct libraries buried in "Tablet Hill,"—an earlier more important, and a later comparatively insignificant one lying on the top of the former,—or the mound concealed the remains of but one library continuously occupied and repeatedly restored, which contained documents of many periods in the same rooms. For apart from other considerations, the lists of Cassite

[1] Comp. nos. 4 and 5 on the plan of the "Northeast Portion of the Temple Library at Nippur," on p. 523, and the illustration facing p. 362, above.

[2] Comp. pp. 309, *seqq.*, and 341, *seq.*

names and words known from the Qoyunjuk collection, which Ashurbânapal's scribes doubtless had copied at Nippur, proved sufficiently that occasional additions were made to the tablets of the earlier library in the long interval of fifteen or sixteen hundred years which elapsed between the reign of Hammurabi and that of the last great Assyrian monarch. The fact that by far more ancient documents were unearthed than tablets written in the neo-Babylonian script was in entire accord with what we know of the two great periods to be distinguished in the history of Nippur.

In the earlier days, when the sanctuary of Bêl formed the great religious centre of the country, the library and school of the city naturally flourished and received greater attention than in the centuries following the government of Hammurabi, when Marduk of Babylon and his cult were extolled at the expense of the venerable temple of "the father of the gods" on the banks of the Chebar. While Bêl of Nippur decreased, "the Bêl of Babylon"[1] increased in power and influence upon the religious life of the united country. Even the brief renaissance of the older cult under the Cassite sway did not change very essentially those new conditions which had been the natural result of great historical events in the valleys of the Euphrates and the Tigris. It was but an artificial and short-lived revival of a fast disappearing worship, ceasing again when the national uprising under the native house of Pashe in the twelfth century led to the overthrow of that foreign dynasty which had been its strongest advocate and principal supporter.

When, in 1899, the excavations were resumed in "Tablet Hill," two large sections were excavated in the eastern and western parts of the mound respectively. Both yielded large quantities of exclusively ancient tablets at practically the same low level, and only single tablets or small nests of old-Babylonian and neo-Babylonian documents mixed in

[1] Comp. p. 459, note 3, above.

the upper strata. From this general result it became evident that the library doubtless continued to exist in some form or another at the old site through the last two thousand years of Babylonian history, but it also followed that the large mass of tablets was already covered under rubbish at the close of the third millennium. The period in which the older library fell into disuse could be fixed even more accurately. A small jar of baked case tablets dated in the reigns of members of the first dynasty of Babylon was unearthed at a higher level than the body of those ancient "clay books." This seemed to indicate that the tablet-filled rooms and corridors beneath it were in ruins before Hammurabi ascended the throne of Babylon, and, more than this, that there must have been a sudden break in the continuity of the history of the temple library of Nippur. How can this apparently natural inference be substantiated by other facts?

It is impossible to assume that the burying of those thousands of tablets was the result of an ordinary though specially disastrous conflagration. The peculiar condition in which the larger part of the contents of the library was found speaks decidedly against it. The tablets occurred in a stratum from one foot to four feet thick at an average depth of twenty to twenty-four feet below the surface. They frequently were badly mutilated and chipped off, and lay in all possible positions on the floor of the ruined chambers, upon low fragmentary clay ledges extending along the walls, and in the rubbish that filled the corridors and open courts of the vast building. In some of the rooms which produced especially large numbers of tablets, they were found in clusters, "interlacing, overlapping, lying flatwise, edgewise, endwise, two, three, four deep,"[1] so that it was very apparent

[1] This is the only statement in Haynes' diary which attempts to throw any light upon the position in which the tablets were found "in one of the rooms" (Feb. 16, 1900).

that they had been stored upon wooden shelves,[1] whence they were precipitated when the roof collapsed and the walls cracked and fell.

If the destruction of the library had been due to an unfortunate accident, by far more tablets would have been discovered on the clay ledges, where they occurred only sporadically, and the corridors and courts would have been comparatively free from them. Moreover, the priests doubtless would have searched the rooms and extracted the most valuable and complete texts from the débris as soon as the heat would allow, preparatory to rebuilding the entire complex. The mere fact that the library unmistakably was allowed to lie in ruins for a considerable length of time points to a great national calamity from which the entire city and the country as a whole likewise suffered for years. We are thus led to a conclusion similar to that at which we arrived when we examined the results of our excavations at the temple mound.[2] The breaking and scattering of so many thousands of priceless documents of the past was an act of gross vandalism on the part of the Elamitic warriors, who invaded and devastated the Babylonian plain about the middle of the third millennium and played such terrible havoc with the archives and works of art in the court of the *ziggurrat*.

It is not generally known that at the time just mentioned legal documents and important income and expense lists of the temple, in whatever ruins they have been found, were commonly burnt into terra-cotta, while the contemporaneous scientific productions, as a rule, were inscribed upon unbaked clay. The reason for this scarcely accidental peculiarity is easily understood by considering that in case of litigation, everything depended upon the careful preservation of the original and unaltered legal document. It was different with the other class of tablets. Com-

[1] Comp. pp. 342, *seq.*, above. [2] Comp. pp. 380, *seqq.*, above.

pared with the price of fuel necessary to bake the "manuscript," the time and labor required for re-writing a damaged tablet was an insignificant matter to every scribe, since clay was to be had abundantly throughout the country. As nearly the whole of the excavated material from the ancient library is literary and scientific in its character, the tablets, with but few exceptions, are unbaked. They consequently have suffered not only from the hands of the Elamites, but also from the humidity of the soil to which they were exposed for more than four thousand years; from the varying atmospheric conditions after their ultimate rescue; and from the unavoidable effects of long transportation by land and sea. The difficulties of the decipherer are thereby increased enormously, and it will require more than ordinary patience to overcome them and to force those half-effaced crumbling tablets to surrender their long-guarded secrets to our own generation.

There is, however, one circumstance which to a certain degree will reconcile us to the ruthless procedure of those revengeful mountaineers into whose quiet valleys and villages the Babylonian rulers so often had carried death and destruction in the name and "in the strength of the god Bêl." Mutilated and damaged as these tablets are, when fully deciphered and interpreted they will afford us a first accurate estimate of the remarkable height of Babylonian civilization, and of the religious conception and scientific accomplishments of a great nation at a period prior to the time when Abraham left his ancestral home in Ur of the Chaldees. They will impart to us knowledge of a fixed early period which the better-preserved copies of the royal library of Nineveh did not convey, and which probably for a long time to come we should have been unable to obtain, had the temple library of Nippur not been destroyed by the Elamite hordes. For those fragile "clay books," as often as injured or broken in the library and schoolrooms of

Nippur, would have been re-copied by the scribes in the developed form of the script of a later period, and in the case of Sumerian texts frequently translated into the Semitic dialect of the country, which would have made it difficult and often impossible for us to determine with any degree of certainty whether the contents of those copies were already known in the third millennium, or to what period of Babylonian history they actually belonged.

The question may be raised, How did those earlier tablets which we found in the rooms and rubbish of the upper strata come to form part of the later library? After the expulsion of the Elamites, when normal conditions began to prevail again in Shumer and Akkad, the priests of Nippur returned to their former quarters and rebuilt their schools and libraries at the place previously occupied. In levelling the ground they necessarily came upon many of the texts of the ruined library. Other earlier tablets, however, must have been added at a much later period as the result of regular excavations, as is shown by the following instance.

Soon after my arrival at Nuffar in 1900, an important jar in terra-cotta was unearthed in the upper strata of the southwestern wing of the library. It contained about twenty inscribed objects, mostly clay tablets, which constituted a veritable small Babylonian museum, the earliest of its kind known to us. These antiquities, already more or less fragmentary when deposited in the jar, are equally remarkable for the long period which they cover and the great variety of the contents of their inscriptions. They had apparently been collected by a neo-Babylonian priest or some other person connected with the temple library. For there is evidence at our disposal to show that at the time of Nabonidos (556–539 B.C.), whom we may style the royal archæologist on the throne of Shumer and Akkad, wider circles among his subjects began to interest themselves in archæological work. There were persons who not only followed the king's excavations of half-forgotten sites with great attention in general, but who were eager to profit by them, and even to imitate the example of their ruler. To illustrate by a new example this remarkable spirit of scientific investigation fostered especially in the Babylonian priest-schools, I refer briefly to a fine object in half-baked clay, several years ago acquired by me for the University of Pennsylvania. On the front it bears an old-Babylonian legend in raised characters reading backwards, while a label in neo-Babylonian writing is inscribed on the other side. To my astonishment, the antiquity proved to be nothing less than an excellent squeeze or impression of an inscription of Sargon of Agade[1] prepared by a scribe whose name is identical with that of several scribes occurring on contract tablets of the British Museum dated in the reign of Nabonidos. The label informs us that the object is a "squeeze" or "mould" (*zîpu*) of an inscribed stone, "which Nabûzêrlîshir, the scribe, saw in the palace of King Narâm-Sin at Agade."

Squeeze of an Inscription of Sargon I. (3800 B. C.)
Taken by a Babylonian scribe of the sixth century B. C.

But to return to the interesting jar from the library mound of Nuffar: the owner, or curator, of the little mu-

[1] It consists of five lines, reading (1) Shargâni-shar-âli (2) the powerful (3) king (4) of the subjects (5) of Bêl. This inscription is identical with lines 1, 3, 4, 7, 8 of the same ruler's legend from Nippur, published in Hilprecht, "The Bab. Exp. of the U. of Pa.," series A, vol. i, part 1, no. 2.

seum of Babylonian originals must have obtained his specimens by purchase or through personal excavations carried on in the ruined buildings of Bêl's city. He doubtless lived in the sixth century, about the time of King Nabonidos, and was a man well versed in the ancient literature of his nation and deeply interested in the past history of Nippur. This follows from the fact that his vase was found in the neo-Babylonian stratum of "Tablet Hill," and from the

Large Fragment of a Clay Tablet containing the Plan of Nippur and its Environments

circumstance that the latest antiquity of his collection is dated in the government of Sinsharishkun, the last representative of the Assyrian dynasty (about 615 B. C.).

Every object contained in this vase is a choice specimen, and evidently was appreciated as such by the collector himself, who had spared no pains to secure as many representative pieces as possible. The first antiquity of my

Babylonian colleague which I examined was the fragment of a large tablet with the plan of houses, canals, roads, gardens, etc. I could well realize the delight he must have felt in acquiring this specimen. For even before having cleaned it, I recognized that it represented a section of the ground plan of the environments of Nippur, — a subjective view soon afterwards confirmed by discovering that the ideogram of "the city of Bêl," *En-lil-ki*, *i. e.*, Nippur, was written in the middle of the fragment. The next piece I picked up was a somewhat damaged brick stamp of Bur-Sin of Ur (about 2600 B. C.), the only one of this ruler thus far excavated at Nuffar. The third was a well preserved black stone tablet (about 2700 B. C.) with the Sumerian inscription: "To Bêl, the king of the lands, his king, Ur-Gur, the powerful champion, king of Ur, king of Shumer and Akkad, has built the wall of Nippur." The fourth was a tablet containing most welcome information as to the number of temples and shrines once existing at Nippur, and the names of the gods and goddesses worshipped in them. The fifth bore the name and titles of Sargon of Agade (3800 B. C.), at whose time it had been inscribed. The next two antiquities represent the first contract tablets dated according to the reigns of members of the Pashe Dynasty, the one being a tablet dated "in the fifth year of Marduk-na-di-in-akh-khi, king of the world (*shar kishshati*)," a contemporary of Tiglath-pileser I. (about 1100 B. C.), the other being dated "in the tenth year of Adad-apal-iddina,[1] the king" (about 1060 B. C.), father-in-law of the Assyrian king Ashurbêlkala. The eighth and ninth tablets are of chronological importance for the final period of the Assyrian empire, as both of them mention certain years of "Ashuretililâni, king of Assyria," and Sinsharishkun in connection with loans and payments of interest. The tenth contains an interesting astronomical

[1] Written (without the determinative for man) *ilu*IM–TUR-USH–SE-*na*. It was previously known that this monarch built at Nippur.

observation concerning Virgo and Scorpion, closing with the words, "thus the calculation" (*ki-a-am ne-pi-shu*), etc., etc.

This remarkable collection of mostly fragmentary tablets illustrates the high esteem in which those ancient texts, as historical sources, were held by the learned priests, and the methodical manner in which they were gathered and preserved in the latest temple library of Nippur; while at the same time it serves as a good example of the variety of subjects treated in the "clay books" of the Babylonian archives.

According to the results already obtained, there can be no doubt that the whole area occupied by the large triangular mound was included in the temple library and school of the city. The real Babylonian buildings, as far as excavated, may naturally be divided into a northeast and a southwest section. An enormous barrier of unexplored débris, "pierced only by one large tunnel and a few branch tunnels,"[1] lies at present between the two quarters. The ground plan of the entire complex can therefore not yet be determined. Both wings consist of a number of chambers, corridors, fragmentary walls, streets, etc., found at the same low level as stated above (p. 512). Both were constructed of crude bricks of the same size, and otherwise present the same general characteristics. For reasons previously set forth (p. 513), they must be ascribed to the third pre-Christian millennium. Apart from other considerations, we know from the remains of burnt brick structures lying immediately above the earlier rooms, and at least in part following their lines, that the library was rebuilt after its destruction by the Elamites, and probably continuously occupied during all the subsequent periods of Babylonian history.

My present sketch of architectural details deals exclu-

[1] Words and sentences placed in quotation marks on this and the following pages are extracts from Geere's report on the architectural features of the temple library.

sively with the lowest building remains. As it is extremely difficult to distinguish wet crude bricks laid in mud mortar from the earth and rubbish around them, the Arab workmen could not always avoid injuring them or cutting them away entirely. Consequently it often was impossible to ascertain the original thickness and direction of the walls with any degree of certainty. In accordance with what is generally known as a characteristic feature of Babylonian architecture, we observed that "the walls of chambers are frequently not made at right angles to one another." In some cases, especially in the southwest section, extremely narrow openings are to be seen. Being too narrow, and otherwise unsuitable for passageways, and sometimes terminating abruptly, they may have been used as recesses for storing tablets and other objects.

The excavated part of the southwest wing of the large complex comprises forty-four rooms and galleries, more or less connected with each other; the northeast section about forty. The various chambers differ greatly as to their dimensions, varying, as they do, from 3⅔ by 9 feet to 14 by 25 feet. The average thickness of the walls being only 2½ to 3 feet, it is safe to assume that the houses had but one story. We nowhere discovered traces to indicate how the rooms were originally lighted, nor how they were roofed. "The roofing probably was by means of wooden beams which supported flat roofs of matting and mud, similar to those constructed in the country at the present day." If ever there were windows in the rooms, they must have been very small and high up near the ceiling. The explored sections are not large enough to show whether the halls and chambers were grouped around open courts and constituted one enormous building, or, as seems more probable, belonged to separate houses which formed one organic whole, but were divided into single quarters by narrow streets and covered passageways. In not a single case was any trace of pavement observed. We must therefore presume that the rooms consisted only of earth, well trodden, covered with reed or palm mats over which rugs were doubtless often spread. In a like manner the walls were kept entirely bare, no attempt being made at relieving their dull faces with any kind of decoration. "We saw no sign of paint and no remains of plastering, not even of mud plaster."

These early Babylonians, who excelled all other ancient nations of the same period in their lofty religious conceptions, in the depth of their sentiment and in the scientific character of their investigations, did not suffer anything in their schoolrooms that would tend to distract the minds of the pupils and to interfere with their proper occupation. The temple library of ancient Nippur was eminently a place of study and a seat of learning, where the attention of all those who assembled for work was concentrated upon but one subject, — the infusing or acquiring of knowledge. In accordance with an ancient Oriental custom even now universally prevailing in the East — in the great Mohammedan university of Cairo as well as in the small village schools of Asia Minor — we should imagine the Babylonian students of the time of Abraham being seated on the floor with crossed legs, respectfully listening to the discourses of the priests, asking questions, practising writing and calculating on clay tablets, or committing to memory the contents of representative cuneiform texts by repeating them in a moderately loud voice.

The "books" required for instruction, reference and general reading as a rule were unbaked clay tablets stored on shelves, or sometimes deposited in jars. The shelves were made either of wood, — as ordinarily was the case also in the business houses on the western side of the Chebar, — or of clay, for which rooms Nos. 1–3 on the accompanying plan of the "Northeast Portion of the Temple Library" offer appropriate examples. These clay ledges were built up in crude bricks to a height of nearly twenty inches from the apparent floor level, and on an average were about one and a half feet wide. Two of the rooms (Nos. 1

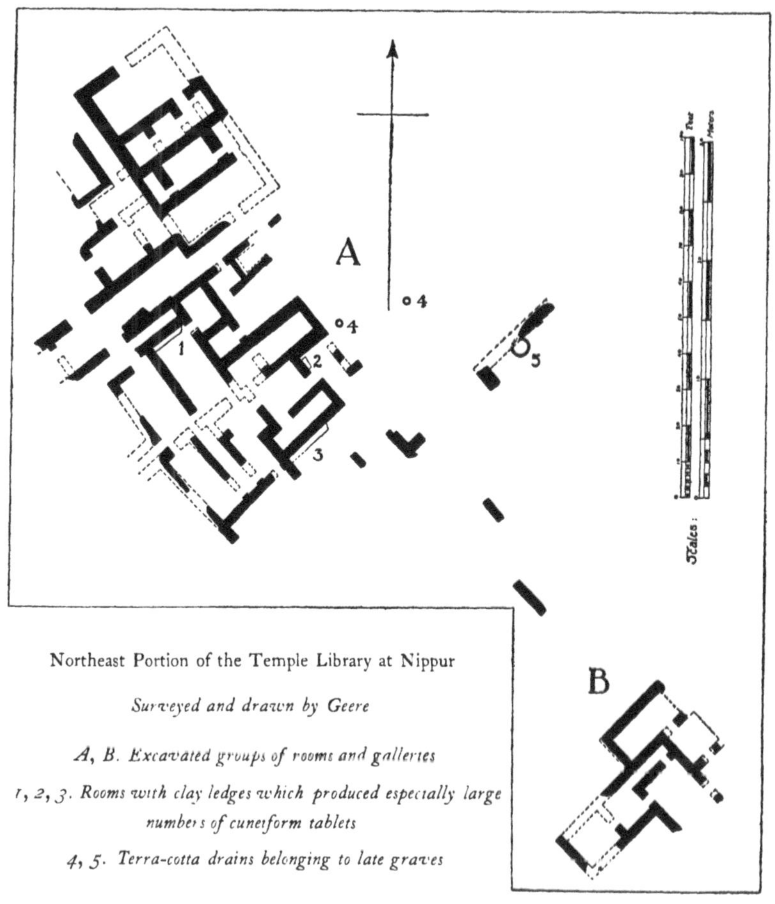

Northeast Portion of the Temple Library at Nippur

Surveyed and drawn by Geere

A, B. Excavated groups of rooms and galleries

1, 2, 3. Rooms with clay ledges which produced especially large numbers of cuneiform tablets

4, 5. Terra-cotta drains belonging to late graves

and 3), yielded tablets and fragments by the thousands, and are among the largest thus far excavated in "Tablet Hill." To preserve the fragile "books" from dampness, the clay shelves were probably covered with matting or with a coating of bitumen. According to the report of the architects, traces of the last-mentioned material seem to have been disclosed on the ledge of the large hall (No. 1).

To judge from the contents of more than twenty-four thousand tablets hurriedly examined, it is almost certain that the vast complex of houses buried under the triangular mound was used by the Babylonians for at least two distinct purposes. Though literary tablets in small numbers occurred almost everywhere in the hill, the large mass of them was found within a comparatively small radius in and around the central rooms of the northeast portion. On the other hand, there was not a single business document unearthed in that general neighborhood, while more than one thousand dated contracts, account lists, and letters came from the southwest rooms of the mound. It would therefore seem natural to conclude that in view of the doubtless large traffic carried on by boats on the Chebar, the business and administrative department of the temple was established on the bank of "the great canal," and the educational department — the school and the technical library — in the rooms nearest to the temple. Tablets were doubtless frequently taken out of the one section and placed temporarily in the other, while certain works of reference seem to have been deposited in both.

The character of the northeast wing as a combined library and school was determined immediately after an examination of the contents of the unearthed tablets and fragments. There is a large number of rudely fashioned specimens inscribed in such a naïve and clumsy manner with old-Babylonian characters, that it seems impossible to regard them as anything else but the first awkward attempts at writing by unskilled hands, — so-called school exercises. Those who attended a class evidently had to bring their writing material with them, receiving instruction not only in inscribing and reading cuneiform tablets, but also in shaping them properly, for not a few of the round and rectangular tablets were uninscribed. The contents of these interesting "scraps" of clay from a Babylonian "waste basket" are as unique and manifold as their forms are peculiar. They enable us to study the methods of writing and reading, and the way in which a foreign language (Sumerian) was taught at Nippur in the third pre-Christian millennium.

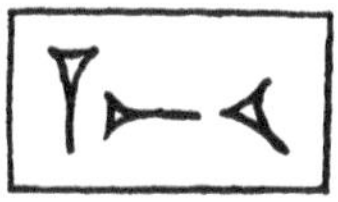

The very first lesson in writing that the children received is brought vividly before us. I refer to several large tablets comparatively neatly inscribed. They contain the three simple elements of which cuneiform signs are generally composed, in the order here given and repeated again and again over three columns. Or I mention a much smaller table showing nothing but the last given wedge dozens of times inscribed in horizontal lines upon the clay. When the first difficulties had been mastered by the student, he had to put those three elements together and make real cuneiform signs. As we do in our Assyrian and Babylonian classes to-day, the easiest and most simple characters were selected first. The pupil was then told to group them together in different ways, generally without regard to their meaning, simply for the sake of fixing them firmly in mind. There are a good many specimens preserved which illustrate this "second step" in the study of Babylonian writing. We have, *e. g.*, a large fragment with two identical columns, in which every line begins with the sign *ba:* 1. *ba-a*, 2. *ba-mu*, 3. *ba-ba-mu*, 4. *ba-ni*, 5. *ba-ni-ni*, 6. *ba-ni-a*, 7. *ba-ni-mu*, etc. Another fragment deals with more difficult characters placed alongside each other in a similar manner: 1. *za-an-tur*, 2. *za-an-tur-tur*, 3. *za-an-ka*, 4. *za-an-ka-ka*, 5. *za-an-ka-a*, 6. *za-an-ka-mu*. A fragment of the easier sort of exercises offers, 1. *an-ni-si*, 2. *an-ni-su*, 3. *an-ni-mu*, etc. A fourth one is of additional value, because it contains no less than four mistakes in a comparatively small space. Let me correct the exercises of this young Babylonian who lived prior to Abraham and transliterate what he has to say: 1. *shi-ni*, 2. *shi-ni-mu*, 3. *shi-ni-da-a*, 4. *shi-tur*, 5. *shi-tur-tur*. It would be interesting to know how such apparent carelessness or stupidity was dealt with by the professors in the great Bêl college and university of Calneh.

But it is impossible for me to go through the whole prescribed "college" course, which possibly even at those early times lasted three years, as it did in the days of Daniel (Dan. 1:4, 5). After the student had been well drilled in writing and reading the simple and more complicated cuneiform signs, he began to write words and proper names. At the same time lists were placed before him from which to study all the difficult ideographic values which the Sumerians associated with their numerous characters. These syllabaries and lexicographical lists are of the utmost importance for our own scientific investigations, and will greatly help us in extending and deepening our knowledge of the Sumerian language. I remember having seen hundreds of them among the tablets which I cleaned and examined in Nuffar and Constantinople.[1] Even in their outside appearance, as a rule they are easily distinguished from tablets dealing with other subjects. They generally are long but very narrow, rounded on the left edge and also at the upper or lower end, or both at the same time. The right side, on the contrary, is always flat, as if cut off a large tablet, which while wet was divided into several pieces.[2]

There are also grammatical exercises, exhibiting how the student was instructed in analyzing Sumerian verbal forms, in joining the personal pronouns to different substantives,

[1] Owing to their long delay in reaching Philadelphia, those tablets which were presented by His Majesty the Sultan to the writer have not as yet been unpacked.

[2] Comp. two similar specimens from Jôkha, published in Hilprecht, "The Bab. Exp. of the U. of Pa.," series A, vol. i, part 1, pl. viii, nos. 18 and 19.

in forming entire sentences, in translating from the Sumerian into the Semitic dialect of Babylonia and *vice versa*. His preparations look pretty much like those of the modern student who excerpts all the words unknown to him from Caesar's "Gallic Wars" or Xenophon's *Anabasis* for his work in the class room.

Special attention was paid to counting and calculating, as will be illustrated below by a few examples. Even instruction in drawing, and surveying lessons were offered. There are a few tablets which contain exercises in drawing horizontal and inclined parallel lines, zigzag lines, lines arranged in squares, lozenge forms, latticework and other geometrical figures.

The course in art led gradually up to free-hand drawing from nature, and probably included also lessons in clay modelling and in glyptics and sculpture (seal cylinders, bas-reliefs and statues). Several fragments of unbaked tablets exhibited portions of animals and trees more or less skilfully incised in clay. One bird was executed very poorly. A lioness, two harnessed horses and a chariot — the latter two pieces doubtless from the upper strata — showed decided talents on the part of those who drew them. Ground plans of fields, gardens, canals, houses, etc., were found more commonly. As according to my knowledge the horse appears in Babylonia first shortly before the middle of the second millennium, without hesitation we can fix the date of the drawing of those harnessed horses as being about a thousand years later than the school exercises previously treated. That art in general was greatly esteemed and cultivated by the priests of Nippur may be inferred from the considerable number of clay figurines, terra-cotta reliefs and even fragments of sculpture (the head of a negro, etc.) discovered in the ruins of the temple library. Apart from several new mythological representations of the earlier time which need a fuller discussion in another place, I refer briefly to two fine identical reliefs of the later period made from different moulds and exhibiting a hog,[1] the animal sacred to the god Ninib,[2] son of Bêl; or to an exquisitely modelled buffalo[3] walking slowly and heavily, and holding his mouth and nose upward in a manner characteristic of these animals. There is another well executed bas-relief[4] which shows Bêltis adorned with a long robe. In her left hand the goddess has the same symbol which we often see with Bêl,[5] while with her right hand she leads a richly dressed worshipper to her shrine. Lastly I mention a much earlier terra-cotta relief depicting a somewhat poetical pastoral scene. A shepherd playing the lute has attracted the attention of his dog, who is evidently accompanying his master's music by his melodious howlings, and another unknown animal (sheep?) is likewise listening attentively. (See opposite page.) The whole scene reminds us of certain favorite subjects of the classical artists.

Bêltis leading a Worshipper

The general character and wide scope of the temple library of Nippur has been illustrated to a certain degree by the tablets contained in the jar mentioned above (pp. 518, *seqq.*) and by my remarks on the work in the Babylonian classroom. The technical "books" on the shelves gave all the necessary information on the subjects treated in the school.

1 Comp. Hilprecht, *l. c.*, vol. ix, pl. xiii, no. 28.
2 Comp. Zimmern in *K. A. T.*[3], p. 410.
3 Comp. Hilprecht, *l. c.*, vol. ix, pl. xiii, no. 27.
4 Preserved in two or three copies made from different moulds.
5 Comp. Hilprecht, *l. c.*, vol. ix, pl. xii, no. 25.

But they also included more scientific works, tablets for religious edification, and "books" of reference. To the first-mentioned class belong the many mathematical, astronomical, medical, historical and linguistic tablets recovered; to the second the hymns and prayers, omens and incantations, mythological and astrological texts. Among the books of reference I classify the lists of dates giving the names of kings and the principal event for every year, the multiplication tables, the lists of the different measures of length and capacity, the lists of synonyms, geographical lists of mountains and countries, stones, plants, objects made of wood, etc. It must be borne in mind that thus far only about the twelfth part of the entire library complex has been excavated, and, though it would be useless to speculate as to the exact number of tablets once contained in the temple library, it is certain that whole classes of texts, only sporadically represented among our present collections, must still lie buried somewhere in the large triangular mound to the south of the temple. During our latest campaign we struck principally the rooms in which the mathematical, astronomical (see p. 530), astrological, linguistic, grammatical and certain religious texts had been stored. This fact alone proves that the library was arranged according to subjects and classified according to scientific principles.

Lutanist surrounded by Animals

In consequence of the unscrupulous proceedings of the barbarous Elamites we can say very little as to the manner in which the single tablets were arranged on the shelves. But there is hope that we may find some better-preserved rooms in the course of our next expedition. From the catch-lines and colophons frequently occurring at the end of tablets we can infer with safety that there were works which consisted of several "volumes," sometimes even of a whole series of tablets. They doubtless were kept together on the same shelf.

Hundreds of very large crumbling tablets, mostly religious and mythological in character, have not yet been

Astronomical Tablet from the Temple Library

deciphered. They need careful repairing before they can be handled with safety. From a mere glance at Bezold's "Catalogue of Cuneiform Tablets in the Kouyunjik Collection of the British Museum"[1] (five volumes), we learn that Ashurbânapal's scribes copied chiefly religious, astronomical and astrological texts for the royal library in Nineveh from the originals at Nippur. Representative tablets of the classes mentioned must therefore have existed at Bêl's temple even in those later days, though the large body of the earlier library had been buried in the ruins beneath their feet for more than fifteen hundred years. With the limited

[1] Comp., *e. g.*, K. 7787, K. 8668, K. 10826 ; Sm. 1117 ; 80–7–19, 64 ; Bu. 88–5–12, 11, etc.

space here at my disposal it is impossible to give examples even of those branches of Babylonian literature which are written on tablets already examined.

In order to illustrate by one example the important rôle which arithmetic played, I call attention to the fact that about 2300 B. C. the temple library owned a complete set of multiplication tables from 1 to at least 1350. The mere circumstance that they existed, sometimes in several copies, speaks volumes for the height of that ancient civilization. They doubtless were used constantly in connection with astronomical calculations, somewhat according to the manner of our logarithmic tables. Among the texts of this class which attracted my attention are the multiplication tables 2 × 1, 3 × 1, 4 × 1, 5 × 1 (two copies), 6 × 1, 8 × 1, 9 × 1, 12 × 1 (two copies), 24 × 1, 25 × 1, 40 × 1, 60 × 1, 90 × 1, 450 × 1, 750 × 1, 1000 × 1, 1350 × 1. As a rule they contain the multiplications of all the consecutive numbers from 1 to 19, followed by those of the tens from 20 to 50. At the end of most of the tablets we find a catch-line. Thus, *e. g.*, the multiplication table 750 × 1 has the catch-line "720 × 1 = 720," thereby indicating that all the multiplication tablets from 720 to 750 (probably even to 780) were classified in the library as one series, known under the name "Series 720 × 1."

Multiplication Table
1 × 6 = 6

There are three different ways in which these tables are written. The following abbreviated specimens may serve as examples: —

5 *a–du*[1]	1	5	or	1	90	or	25	1	25
a—du	2	10		2	180		25	2	50
a—du	3	15		3	270		25	3	75
a—du	4	20, etc.,		4	360, etc.,		25	4	100, etc.
a—du	19	95		19	1710		25	19	475
a—du	20	100		20	1800		25	20	500
a—du	30	150		30	2700		25	30	750
a—du	40	200		40	3600		25	40	1000
a—du	50	250		50	4500		25	50	1250

Concerning the character of the business and administrative department established in the "library," where contracts were executed, orders given out, income and expense lists kept, etc., I have to add little to what has been previously stated (p. 524). A number of letters were found intact. The envelopes sealed and addressed more than four thousand years ago, immediately before the city was conquered and looted, were still unbroken. While writing these lines one of those ancient epistles of the time of Amraphel (Gen. 14) lies unopened before me. It is 3¼ inches long, 2¼ inches wide, and 1¾ inches thick. One and the same seal cylinder had been rolled eleven times over the six sides of the clay envelope before it was baked with the document within. It bears the simple address, "To Lushtamar." Though sometimes curious to know the contents of the letter, I do not care to break the fine envelope and to intrude upon Mr. Lushtamar's personal affairs and secrets, as long as the thousands of mutilated literary tablets from the library require all my attention.

At the beginning of our fourth campaign a long peculiar wall had been disclosed below the level of the desert on the west side of the Shatt en-Nîl (pp. 440, 447). It ran roughly parallel to the south slope of the ridge marked VI on the plan of the ruins (p. 305). Haynes traced it for 489 feet, but having found no opening in the wall, abandoned

[1] *Adû*, literally meaning "time," is the common expression also for "times" in this class of tablets.

it after a few weeks without being able to fix its age and purpose. After my arrival at the ruins in March, 1900, we resumed the excavations at this place, and having followed the wall its entire length, I succeeded in ascertaining its real nature. Geere surveyed the entire structure, and prepared[1] the accompanying diagram, which may help to illustrate the principal features of the explored section.

Except at one point where a complete gap 22 feet wide occurs (between Nos. 2 and 3), the original direction of the wall could be traced without difficulty for about 590 feet, though sometimes only by means of a few courses of bricks still lying *in situ*. Towards the east it ran almost as far as the bed of the Chebar. Towards the west it cannot have extended much farther than is indicated on the diagram, because the boundary of the mound, which doubtless stood in a certain relation to the wall, turns northward at the point where the latter practically ceases. The original height of the structure must remain unknown. In its present ruinous state it varies from two courses of bricks to thirty-nine, or from six and a half inches to eleven feet four inches. In a like manner the thickness of the wall is not uniform. This peculiarity, however, is not the result of subsequent causes, but goes back to the original builders of the wall, who planned and executed it in such

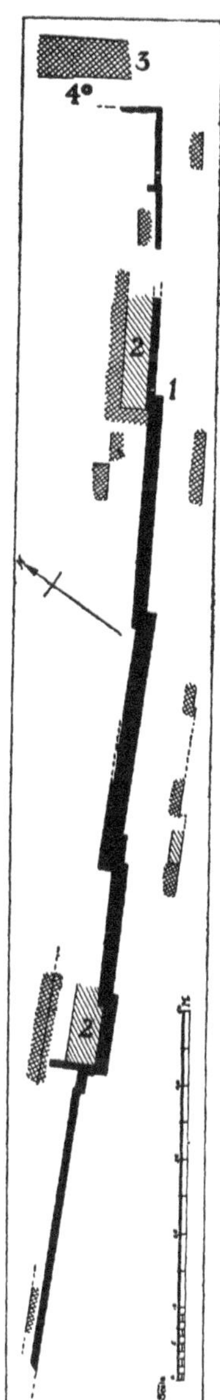

Facing Wall of a Pre-Sargonic Cemetery

[1] Words and sentences in quotation marks are extracts from Geere's report on this wall.

a manner as to have the central part the strongest, and the sections flanking it on both sides successively decreasing in thickness.

Another characteristic feature of this structure is the remarkable fact "that the various sections of the wall are not built in a straight line or from a uniform level." The lowest course of bricks in some places lies about six feet below the average level of the present plain, in others five and a half, in still others only four and a half. In other words, there is a decided difference of from six to eighteen inches between the levels of the lowest courses of bricks. It is very evident, therefore, that the builder of the wall did not dig or level a special foundation for it, but placed his bricks directly on the undulating surface of the ancient plain.

What was the purpose of this wall? We remember that everywhere in the lowest thirty feet of the ruins, even on the west side of the canal, Haynes had discovered nothing but ashes, bits of charcoal, an occasional decayed bone, lumps of clay worked by the hand, crude and baked plano-convex bricks, etc., mixed with earth and sand, and a complete tomb of the general period of Narâm-Sin (comp. pp. 419, *seq.*). Our excavations immediately behind and before the wall led to a similar result. We did not excavate enough to reveal an intact burial vase, but we found sufficient evidence to show that the western half of Nippur, like the eastern section grouped around the *ziggurrat* (pp. 434, *seqq.*), consisted largely of pre-Sargonic burials. Everywhere we came upon traces of cremation, such as ashes and earth mixed, small pieces of charred wood, potsherds, fragmentary walls and pavements of funeral chambers.[1] The portable results accordingly were but few, consisting chiefly

[1] The places marked Nos. 2 in the diagram represent pavements of baked bricks. Remains of cross-walls meeting the long wall at right angles are seen near the two ends of the latter.

of three fragments of pre-Sargonic cuneiform tablets, a clay impression of an early type of seal cylinder, a fragmentary cylinder in soapstone from the interior of a mud brick, a few terra-cotta figurines (toys), the fragment of a large alabaster bead, two copper tubes partly filled with an unknown white substance (handles?), two fragments of a copper arm ring, an entire pre-Sargonic terra-cotta cup, and a few pieces of stone vessels of the same early period.

In continuing our search for possible building remains at both ends of the long wall, we unearthed the fragment of a crude brick wall, 18½ feet thick (No. 3), near the west bank of the Shatt en-Nîl and the remains of a burned brick pavement coated with bitumen close by.[1] Under the latter were a bell-shaped drain (No. 4) and fragments of a second smaller one to the west of it. At the opposite (west) end of the wall we discovered a pre-Sargonic well built of brick,[2] laid in herring-bone fashion. In accordance with the ordinary form of the earliest Babylonian wells, it was considerably narrower at the top[3] than near the bottom. We commenced clearing it of the rubbish with which it was choked up, when at a depth of over eight feet we were stopped in our progress by the water of the spring rains. "The top of the well itself was almost upon a level with the bottom of the drain at the east end of the wall," — a circumstance sufficiently explaining why the baked bricks of the drain pavement are of somewhat more recent date than those of the well at the west end.

There can be no doubt that the long wall was a regular

[1] The bricks being slightly smaller in size than those of Sargon I., and Narâm-Sin, indicate a period of construction not very far remote from the governments of the two rulers.

[2] These doubtless pre-Sargonic bricks are of a peculiar type. Averaging 11¼ by 7⅝ by 3¾ inches in size, they are nearly flat on the top, but have a slight furrow along the one long edge.

[3] Three feet one inch internal and nearly six feet external diameter.

facing or boundary wall, — a huge buttress of the same kind as repeatedly excavated by Koldewey at the edges of the vast cemeteries of Surghul and El-Hibba (pp. 285, *seq.*). It supported the light masses of ashes and dust of the fire necropolis of Nippur, which otherwise would have been blown into the plain or washed away by the rains of the winter. In view of the characteristic form and size of its yellow bricks, which are similar to those found in the lowest strata of a section of *Nîmit-Marduk*, to the east of the temple,[1] we can state positively that this buttress belongs to a period immediately preceding Sargon I. When the cemetery rose higher and higher, its facing wall did not prove strong enough to bear the additional pressure. "The burned bricks were therefore overlaid by large crude bricks," completely imbedding the old wall and extending considerably beyond the exterior face of the latter, into the plain, as indicated by the cross-lines in the diagram above. In many cases it was extremely difficult and often impossible to ascertain the thickness[2] of this additional wall, as the material of which it consisted had "been subjected to a process of infiltration and compression for so many centuries that the débris at the foot of the mound was practically a homogeneous mass." This much, however, was learned with certainty, that the bottom course of the outer crude brick wall was laid at a higher level than the upper courses of the remaining inner burned brick wall, thus illus-

[1] The average size of the well-baked bricks from the cemetery wall was 13¼ to 13½ inches square by 3¼ inches thick, while the corresponding bricks from the lower strata of *Nîmit-Marduk* measured only 11½ inches square by 2⅞ inches thick. The latter evidently were somewhat older than the former. Apart from their color we noticed another characteristic feature of both classes of bricks. They were not entirely flat, but slightly raised at their longer edges.

[2] Outside the central section of the burned brick wall, which required strengthening most, the crude brick wall was from 22 to 28 feet thick, while at its east end it was not quite 19 feet.

trating that the constant mud washings from the mound and the burials gradually taking place along the base of the wall, had changed the contour of the ground to such an extent that they threatened to efface the boundary line between the necropolis and the plain entirely.

There are several other interesting features to be observed in connection with this burned brick wall, which attract our attention. I refer briefly to the fact that at its thickest part the remains of a staircase, by which the cemetery could be ascended from the south, seem to have been discovered; furthermore that patchings and repairings of the wall could be traced at several points without difficulty; or that an opening[1] (No. 1) to give exit to the percolating rain water was found in the eastern section of the wall six and a half feet above the level of the brick pavement (No. 2). But it is beyond the scope of this book to discuss strictly technical questions which are of value chiefly to the architect.

On May 11, 1900, the most successful campaign thus far conducted at Nuffar terminated. Excavations having been suspended, the *meftûl* was sealed, Arab guards were appointed, shaikhs and workmen rewarded, and the antiquities transported to six large boats moored in the swamps. Accompanied by the workmen from Hilla, their wives and children, and blessed by thronging crowds of 'Afej, who had assembled to bid us farewell, eagerly inquiring as to the time of our next return, we departed with a strange feeling of sadness and pleasure from the crumbling walls of *Duranki*, "the link of heaven and earth," which Ninib's doleful birds, croaking and dashing about, still seem to guard against every profane intruder.

As far as time and work would permit, we always made it a rule to explore and survey the neighboring ruins, with a view of placing the information thus obtained at the disposal of some other American or European expedition.

[1] An opening 3½ inches wide and 16 inches high.

During the Easter week I decided to extend our excursions considerably farther to the south and to examine especially the low mounds of *Abû Hatab* and *Fâra*, where, since the days of Loftus, antiquities had constantly been excavated and sold by the Arabs. No trustworthy account of either of these ruins was yet at our disposal. In fact, there was not one modern map which indicated even their general situation,[1] because they lie outside the ordinary track taken by Babylonian explorers. It is true some travellers had been in that neighborhood before, two of them even paying a hurried visit to the low site of Fâra, but nobody thus far had been able to ascertain anything definite with regard to their age and importance. Having previously gathered all the necessary information from several members of the tribes camping along the Shatt el-Kâr, the present writer, accompanied by Haynes, Geere, and half-a-dozen trusted Arabs, left Nuffar one day in April shortly after sunset to examine that whole district. We crossed the Khôr el-'Afej in two long narrow boats (*turrâdas*), and entered the great canal on the opposite side of the swamps, descending the latter in our primitive means of conveyance. The white blossoms of the caper shrub (Babyl. *sikhlu*),[2] growing abundantly along the embankments of the Shatt el-Kâr and the smaller canals, filled the air with their strong aroma. Nothing but the occasional cry of an unknown water-bird, disturbed in his rest by our swiftly gliding boats, interrupted the impressive stillness of that beautiful Babylonian night. At a place nearly opposite the two ruins we halted. Stretched on the ground or in the bottom of our boats we awaited the first rays of the sun that we might proceed with our archæological mission.

1 The only attempt made by the earlier travellers at locating Fâra is found on Loftus' map.

2 The proof for this identification will be found in Hilprecht, "The Bab. Exp. of the U. of Pa.," series A, vol. x, Introduction.

Our First Expedition to the Ruins of Abû Hatab and Fâra

Illustrating 'Afej warriors and boatmen, native canoes (turrâdas) and punting poles (mer dî)

As the results of this exploration tour will be published in another place, I confine myself to a general statement. Both ruins were well worth the pains we had taken in examining and surveying them. Abû Hatab, considerably smaller than Fâra, is also the less remarkable of the two. Several half-effaced bricks and a little excavating in one of the rooms, easily to be traced in the early morning hours, convinced me that the site was occupied as late as the third pre-Christian millennium. Fâra, a few miles to the south of it, is a very extensive but low ruin of the utmost importance. Everywhere the characteristic pre-Sargonic bricks, wells, and drains peep out of the ground and excite the curiosity of the explorer. The higher elevation of the mounds is at the southern end, but some of our most valuable antiquities obtained from there were discovered two feet below the surface in a depression near the centre of the ruin. Like Nuffar and all such other pre-Sargonic ruins of the country with which I am personally acquainted, it contains thousands of burial urns, funeral chambers, pieces of charred wood, masses of potsherds, clearly indicating that a very extensive fire necropolis was connected with the ancient city buried there, which doubtless played an important rôle in the religious life and the early history of the Sumerian people. If vigorously attacked with the spade and subjected to a strictly methodical examination, which, however, should not cease before the end of five to ten consecutive years, it probably will yield as important results as Nuffar and Tellô. The accompanying exquisite head of a Markhur goat[1] (p. 540) of about the time of Ur-Ninâ (4000 B. C.), and an even better-preserved larger head of the same animal (two thirds life size), were excavated at Fâra, together with a pre-Sargonic sword in copper, a fine marble lamp in the shape of a bird, several complete stone vases, a very archaic seal cylinder, a

[1] Comp. Helm and Hilprecht in *Verhandlungen der Berliner anthropologischen Gesellschaft*, Feb. 16, 1901, pp. 157, *seqq.*

number of pre-Sargonic clay tablets, and about sixty incised plates of mother-of-pearl,[1] representing warriors, animals, handicraftsmen, pastoral and mythological scenes, rosettes, etc., in the style of the earliest monuments of Nuffar and Tellô. These antiquities prove that considerable treasures of art must lie concealed in those low and insignificant-looking mounds which date back to a time when Sargon I. was not yet born.

Markhur Goat in Copper
From Fâra, about 4000 B. C.

B. ON THE TOPOGRAPHY OF ANCIENT NIPPUR.

In the previous pages an attempt was made to sketch historically the archæological work carried on by the University of Pennsylvania in Babylonia since 1889. In order to complete the picture and to obtain a clearer conception of

[1] Comp. pp. 252, *seq.*, 474, *seq.*

the contents of the ruins of Nuffar as far as explored, it will only be necessary to summarize the principal results obtained by the four expeditions, to place them in their mutual relations, and to consider them in a coherent manner from a topographical point of view. To avoid undesirable repetitions, constant references will be made to what has been submitted before. The chapter necessarily must be brief, especially as the new facts, which by their very nature were excluded from the previous history, will be easily understood in the light of my former expositions.

The ruins of ancient Nippur (comp. pp. 160, *seq.*, 305, *seqq.*) are divided by the dry bed of the Shatt en-Nîl (Chebar) into an eastern and western section. Both are nearly equal in size, each covering an area of about ninety acres of land (p. 305). The western half represents the remains of the city proper, the eastern half the large complex of the temple of Bêl, generally known by the name of *Ekur* (pp. 464, *seq.*). Twenty-one different strata can be distinguished in the mass of débris which constitutes the present site of Nuffar. It should be understood, however, that these twenty-one layers, marking as many different phases in the history of Bêl's renowned city, by no means occur in every section of the ruins. In some places the remains of the second millennium rest immediately on the top of pre-Sargonic Nippur, in others the two are separated by ten to fifteen feet of rubbish, in still others the earliest remains appear almost on the surface. At first sight, therefore, it would seem evident that certain parts of Nippur must have been in ruins for centuries, while others were occupied by houses continually. To a certain degree this view is doubtless correct. But we must not forget that our knowledge on this question will always remain more or less defective. For on the other hand we know positively that earlier building remains were frequently razed to the ground by later generations, often enough for no other reason than to obtain building material, worked clay (pp. 493, *seq.*), as well as baked bricks (pp. 373, *seq.*, 376, *seq.*, 389), for their own constructions in the easiest and cheapest manner possible.

Apart from Bint el-Amîr, which is considerably higher than the rest of the ruins (pp. 160, *seq.*), the mounds of Nuffar on an average rise thirty to seventy feet above the present plain and the ruins descend from one to twenty feet below it. The twenty-one strata or historical periods represented by these ruins may naturally be grouped together under three different headings briefly designated in the following sketch as the Sumerian period, the Semitic Babylonian period and the post-Babylonian period.

a. In the earliest (Sumerian) stratum we recognize six phases of historical development by means of the different kinds of bricks employed. The first is characterized by the entire absence of baked bricks, and the exclusive use of adobes. The other five are easily distinguished according to the different forms and sizes of baked bricks subsequently adopted. The earliest bricks are very small, flat on the lower

Pre-Sargonic Bricks in their Historical Development

and strongly rounded on the upper side, which generally also bears a thumb-mark. They look more like rubble or quarry stones, in imitation of which they were made (Gen. 11 : 3) than the artificial products of man (p. 251). Gradually they grow larger in size and flatter at the same time.

The thumb-mark [1] begins to disappear, and one, two or more longitudinal streaks made with the index finger or by drawing a reed leaf over the clay [2] come into use, first with a thumb-mark (comp. the third brick in the above illustration), later without the same. None of all the pre-Sargonic bricks thus far excavated at Nuffar bears an inscription.[3] Wells and drains are the earliest constructions for which these baked bricks were required. According to the results furnished by our excavations, the bricks are generally laid in a peculiar manner in those ancient wells. The architects call it herring-bone fashion. The upper and lower three rows of bricks seen in the accompanying cut are especially indicative of the principle followed by the first builders in "the land of Shinar." It is interesting to observe that the sign used in Babylonian writing for "brick" originally represents a section of such a well in which the bricks are laid in herring-bone fashion.

Section of a Pre-Sargonic Well. Bricks laid in Herring-bone Fashion

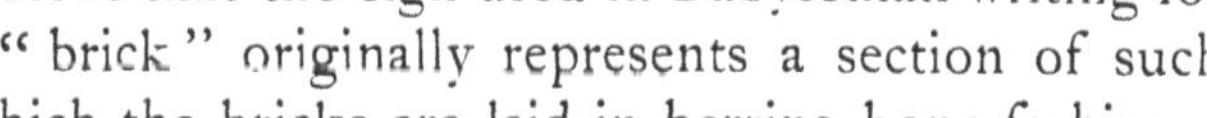

The Sumerian stratum extending from the virgin soil to a point about five to ten feet above the ancient plain level is

[1] Sometimes two and even four such marks occur.

[2] The fibre and form of the leaf are clearly recognized on a number of bricks now in the archæological museum of the U. of Pa.

[3] The case is somewhat different at Tellô ; comp. p. 251.

twenty to thirty-five feet high in the temple mound, where the pavement of Sargon and Narâm-Sin forms an important boundary line. It is characterized by scattered ashes mixed with earth or well-defined ash-beds greatly varying in size, bits of charcoal, an occasional bone, innumerable potsherds often colored red or blackened from exposure to fire, many cracked jars found in different positions, a few of them in a tolerable, some even in a fine state of preservation, thousands of thick fragments of small vases, dishes and pointed cups, broken weapons, damaged seal cylinders, personal ornaments in stone, shell, copper and silver, frequent drains, wells, and abundant remains of ruined chambers built of adobes, exceptionally also of plano-convex baked bricks (comp. especially p. 456, note 2). In other words, wherever we reached this lowest stratum at Nuffar we came upon extensive traces of pre-Sargonic burials, so that we cannot avoid the conclusion that the sacred ground around the temple of Enlil and certain districts even on the west side of the Chebar were largely used as a cemetery, or, more exactly, as a fire necropolis (pp. 456, *seq.*), by the earliest population of the country. Apart from the court and general neighborhood of the temple, we excavated funeral vases and other remains illustrating the praxis of cremating the dead in various other parts of the ruins, especially in the mounds to the south and east of Bint el-Amîr (p. 479), along the foot of the outer wall (p. 487), and in the long ridge marked by the numbers VI and VIII on the plan of the ruins (p. 305; comp. pp. 419, *seq.*)

A small *ziggurrat* (p. 453), the foundation of the north-east city gate (pp. 493, *seqq.*), and partly explored building remains in the mounds to the east and west of the temple proper are the only witnesses of a pre-Sargonic "city of the living" so far discovered in our excavations at Nippur. In view of the enormous amount of rubbish covering the earliest strata this result will not surprise us. Small as the unearthed remains are, they suffice to show that in pre-Sargonic times the city had nearly the same extent as in the days of Ur-Gur (about 2700 B. C.) or Kadashman-Turgu (about 1350 B. C.). But how much of the ground was reserved for the dead and how much for the living cannot be ascertained for many years to come. The numerous single pre-Sargonic bricks, the remains of walls and other early constructions already excavated, together with several hundred inscribed clay tablets (pp. 388, 403, *seqq.*), objects of art (pp. 383, *seq.*, 474, *seq.*) and other antiquities (*e. g.*, pp. 485, *seqq.*) of the same ancient period, and the frequent references to Nippur in the earliest inscriptions from other ruins, allow us to infer that the earliest city must already have had a comparatively large population.

The period of transition from the earliest chapter of Babylonian history to the age of Sargon and Narâm-Sin, the so-called sixth pre-Ṣargonic period, is closely connected at Nuffar with the appearance of the first square bricks made in a rectangular mould. In general it probably coincides with the time of Entemena of Lagash (p. 251). Bricks of this period have been found *in situ* in large numbers at low levels on both sides of the Shatt en-Nîl (p. 535). Though still uninscribed, they are readily distinguished from other later bricks by their yellow color and the circumstance that the edge of the upper surface is somewhat higher than its central portion.

b. The line of demarcation between the Sumerian and Semitic periods in the history of Babylonia cannot be drawn very sharply. Doubtless centuries of commercial intercourse and peaceful intermingling between the early inhabitants of the country and the neighboring Semitic tribes preceded the final conquest of the Sumerians and the subsequent amalgamation of the two races. Even after the former had lost their political independence, in many regards no perceptible change seems at first to have taken place in the life of the people. The foreign invaders remained in the fertile plain and became the docile pupils of the subdued nation. They learned how to cultivate the soil and to dig new canals, how to fortify cities and to erect lofty temples. They adopted and further developed the system of writing which they found in the country, and they made themselves acquainted with the literary and artistic products, and the religious and cosmological ideas of their new subjects. At the time of Sargon and Narâm-Sin, the Semitic element is firmly established throughout the land and in complete possession of the ancient Sumerian civilization, which was successfully directed into new channels, and thus stagnation was prevented. The votive objects and seal cylinders from the period of the Sargon dynasty represent the best epoch and the highest development of ancient Babylonian art, while the inscribed tablets and monuments "are characterized by an exquisite style of writing."

In the western portion of the ruins of Nippur the change from the old *régime* to the new one is scarcely visible. Burials were made there for some time afterwards (pp. 419, *seq.*), as they had been before. But in the course of time, they ceased altogether, and the site of the ancient cemetery was occupied by great business houses and the bazaars of the city (pp. 413, *seqq.*). The 30,000 contracts and account lists excavated from numerous houses along the bank of the Chebar enable us to trace one settlement above another from the fourth millennium down to the time of Artaxerxes and Darius, at the end of the fifth century.

A more abrupt and radical change took place in the eastern half of the city. The burial ground around the *ziggurrat* was levelled, the sacred enclosure extended, and the whole temple court provided with a solid pavement and surrounded with high walls. No cremation was henceforth permitted and no funeral urn deposited anywhere within the precincts of Bêl's sanctuary at Nippur. The city became "a pure place like Eridu" (p. 467), and the temple an exclusive place of worship for the living. It preserved this character for over 3000 years, until Babylonia's independence was lost, and another people with another religion, which did not know of the ancient gods of the country, established itself for a few centuries on the ruined site of Bêl's venerable city.

Notwithstanding the almost continuous occupation of the city during this long period of Babylonian history, nine strata can be distinguished more or less accurately in the temple court. Six of these do not offer any difficulty at all, as they are separated from each other by brick pavements (pp. 376, *seqq.*, 475, *seq.*). The other three overlap the next lower ones to a certain degree in the excavated southeast section of the sacred enclosure, but are recognized more clearly in other parts of the ruins. The débris representing these different strata, with their nearly 3500 years of history (from about 3800 to 350 B. C.), and including the pavement of Narâm-Sin, measures only 17 to 19 feet in the temple court. As we saw above (p. 391), this comparatively small accumulation of rubbish within such a long period finds its natural explanation in the double fact that a considerable part of the court in front of the stage-tower and temple must always have been unoccupied (p. 376), and that every ruler who laid a new pavement necessarily razed the crumbling buildings of his predecessors around the *ziggurrat*, in order to secure an even surface (p. 388) and a solid foundation for his own constructions.

The six periods easily determined by fragmentary pavements of baked or unbaked brick in the temple court are the following: 1. Sargon and Narâm-Sin, about 3750 B. C. (pp. 388, *seqq.*, 497, *seqq.*); 2. Lugalsurzu, about 3500 B. C. (p. 475, *seq.*); 3. Ur-Gur and his dynasty, about 2700 B. C. (pp. 378, *seqq.*, 383, *seqq.*); 4. Ur-Ninib of (N)isin, about 2500 B. C. (pp. 378, 380, *seq.*); 5. Kadashman-

Turgu of the Cassite dynasty, about 1350 B. C. (pp. 376, *seqq.*); 6. Ashurbânapal, king of Assyria, 668–626 B. C. (p. 376). Besides the names here mentioned, other members of the same dynasties have left us traces of their activity in Nippur through fragmentary walls, wells and houses containing their inscribed bricks, or in the shape of votive offerings bearing their names and titles. In the zinctype facing this page I confine myself to indicating only those five pavements which could be traced more or less through the whole excavated temple court, or at least through the larger part of it.

The three periods referred to above as being less clearly defined are, 1. the first dynasty of Babylon,[1] about 2200 B. C. (comp. pp. 480, *seqq.*); 2. the dynasty of Pashe,[2] about 1100 B. C., and 3. the neo-Babylonian and Persian period. They are represented by ruined buildings or inscribed documents found in limited numbers in their respective strata.

According to the evidence furnished by the trenches, the temple complex as a whole presented very much the same picture during all the different periods of its long and interesting history. Of course the stage tower gradually grew larger, and the temple at its side, consequently (p. 472) somewhat smaller in the latter half of the second millennium. The number of chapels, shrines and other houses connected with the cult of Bêl and his large retinue of minor gods doubtless also varied at different times, since Nippur, as the seat of "the kingdom of the four regions of the world," more than any other city in the country reflected the politi-

[1] Including Rîm-Sin of Larsa, whose inscriptions occur in the same general stratum. For the present, comp. p. 408, and Hilprecht, "The Bab. Exp. of the U. of Pa.," series A, vol. 1, part 2, no. 128.

[2] Represented by several fragmentary boundary stones only in part published (comp. Hilprecht, *l. c.*, part 1, pl. 27, no. 80, and pl. *XII*, nos. 32, *seq.*), a fine unpublished boundary stone of Nebuchadrezzar I. with six columns of writing, and a few dated documents (p. 519).

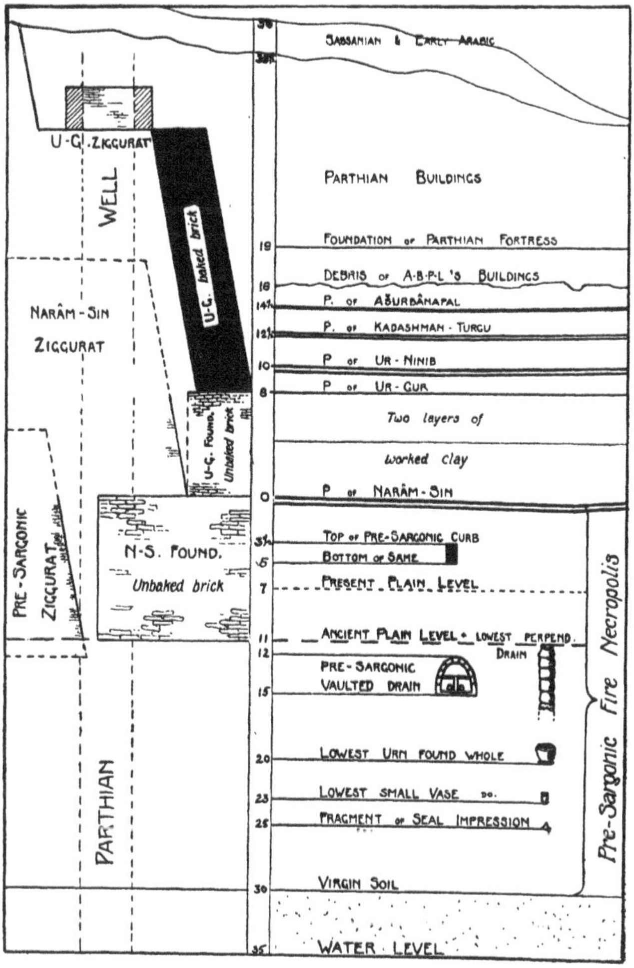

Section of the Stage-Tower and the Adjoining Southeast Court

Restored and designed by Hilprecht, drawn by Fisher

A-B-P-L. Ashurbânapal. N-S. Narâm-Sin. U-G. Ur-Gur. P. Pavement. ■. *Baked Brick.* =. *Pavement of two layers of bricks. Measurements given in feet.*

cal ups and downs of Babylonia. We know even now on the basis of our latest excavations that the outer wall of the temple constructed by Narâm-Sin followed a slightly different course from that of Ur-Gur and all the subsequent rulers (pp. 497, *seqq.*). And it is likewise certain that the temple library of the period antedating the Elamitic invasion was more important and probably also of greater extent than that of the time of Ashurbânapal (pp. 511, *seqq.*). But notwithstanding these and other distinctive features which the temple presented in different centuries, and which easily could be multiplied, the general plan and disposition of the sanctuary changed but little. In accordance with the conservative character of the Babylonian religion, the space enclosed by the walls *Imgur-Marduk* and *Nîmit-Marduk*, or whatever their former names may have been, remained nearly stationary, and the principal buildings erected upon it practically occupied the same position at the time of Sargon I. and in the days of Artaxerxes I. and Darius II.

Roughly speaking, the entire area covered with the ruins of the temple complex (comp. the plan on page 305) forms a trapezoid, the longest side of which runs parallel with the northeast bank of the Chebar. By disregarding the triangular library mound in the south, which never seems to have been included in the walled territory, we obtain a parallelogram with nearly equal sides, each measuring about 2700 feet. Except on the southwest side, where the waters of the great canal, probably lined by a dam or quay, afforded a sufficient protection, this large space was enclosed by a huge wall 25 to 40 feet thick (pp. 498, *seqq.*), and at least 25 feet high (p. 492). Since the government of Ur-Gur this so-called outer wall of the city was adorned with buttresses (p. 498), while at all times, as far as we can determine at present, it was strengthened by a number of well-drained bastions (pp. 494, 496, 503), and by a deep moat which ran along its entire base (p. 495), forming a regular navigable canal on the southeast side, where the principal entrance of the temple must be looked for. A large gate was discovered also in the middle of the northeast wall, through which the main road from the east passed behind the *ziggurrat*, leading to a bridge over the Chebar into the city proper (pp. 493, *seqq.*).

The northwest half of this fortified enclosure consisted of a large open court, along the northeast edge of which tradesmen and handicraftsmen had their shops (pp. 488, *seq.*), and of a group of substantial buildings near the canal which probably represent the outhouses, servants' quarters and magazines of the temple. The mounds between the *ziggurrat* and the Chebar, and between the temple and the northeast wall, have not yet been examined sufficiently to enable us to ascertain their contents with any degree of certainty. A plausible theory with regard to the possible character of the doubtless imposing building which lies buried under the enormous mass of débris in the east corner of the outer wall was formulated on p. 485, above.

The accompanying zinctype, prepared by Mr. Fisher on the basis of my interpretation of the excavated ruins (p. 552), may serve as a supplement to my previous discussion (pp. 368, *seqq.*, 469, *seqq.*, 477, *seqq.*). Viewed in the light of a first attempt on our part to restore the principal features of the most renowned sanctuary of Babylonia in accordance with real facts, this sketch will help the reader to gain a clearer conception of the general plan and disposition of the temple of Bêl during the last three thousand years of its remarkable history. A complete list of measurements of all the examined building remains, photographs and accurate drawings illustrating the necessary architectural details, my reasons for assuming a *ziggurrat* of five stages, and a full treatment of all such other questions as by their technical nature had to be excluded from the present pages, will be found in a special monograph entitled "Ekur, the Temple of Bêl at Nippur." For the present it may suffice to repeat that the

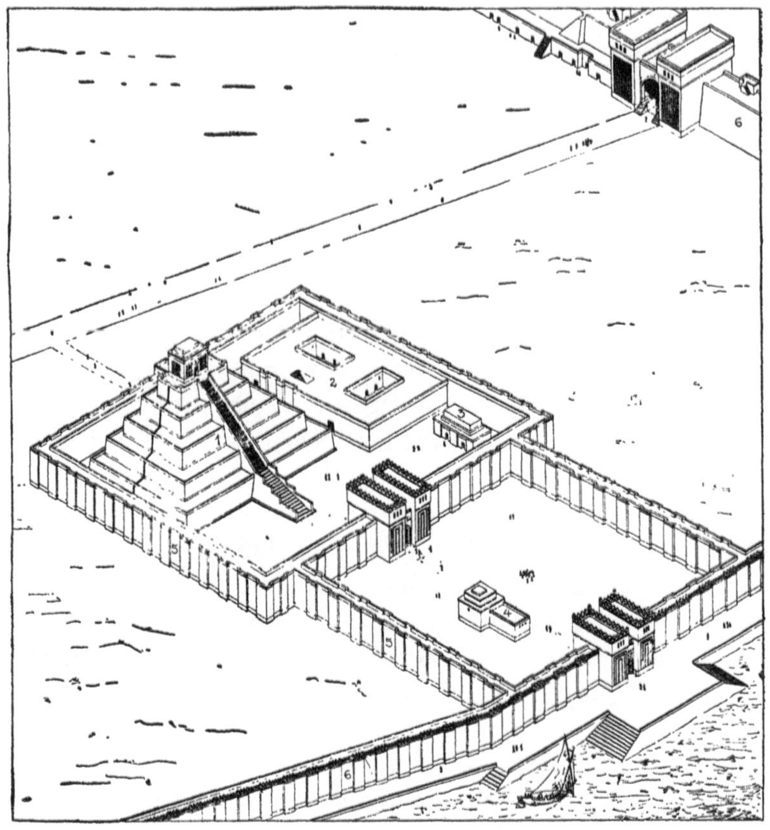

Ekur, the Temple of Bêl at Nippur

First attempt at a restoration by Hilprecht and Fisher

1. Stage-tower with shrine on the top. 2. The temple proper. 3. "House for honey, cream and wine." 4. "Place of the delight of Bur-Sin." 5. Inner wall (Imgur-Marduk). 6. Outer wall (Nîmit-Marduk).

temple proper consisted of two courts (pp. 478, *seq.*) and to emphasize that the exact size of the inner court containing the stage-tower and the house of Bêl at its side cannot be given, before the Parthian fortress covering the Babylonian ruins has been removed completely. As the latter construction, however, on the whole followed the outline of the older enclosure pretty accurately, the measurements quoted in connection with the Parthian fortress can be used in a general way also to restore the dimensions of the inner court of the ancient temple beneath it. The *ziggurrat*, the most conspicuous part of the whole complex, rose highest and was largest at the time of Ashurbânapal. It then covered an area forming a rectangular parallelogram, the two sides of which measured 190 and 128 feet respectively. The outer temple court, probably studded with the chapels of all the different gods worshipped at Nippur (p. 480), appears to have been nearly square, each side being about 260 feet long.

c. Babylonia's independence was lost forever when the Persian ruler removed the golden image of Marduk from his famous sanctuary on the Euphrates. At the end of the fourth century it seemed for a little while as if the ancient cult would be revived with even greater magnificence than at the time of Hammurabi and Nebuchadrezzar. The ruined stages of *Etemenanki*, which the destroyer of Jerusalem "had raised like a mountain" in honor of Bêl, were torn down by foreign soldiers to secure a solid foundation for the more sumptuous structure of their own king.[1] Alexander the

[1] In consequence of this historical fact travellers and explorers have hitherto searched in vain for the remains of the "tower of Babel." Nothing but the lowest foundations of the famous structure will ever be discovered. For modern Arab brick-diggers completed the work of demolition which Alexander's soldiers had begun 2000 years ago. In connection with their pernicious digging they discovered the building records of Nabopolassar and Nebuchadrezzar in their original niches. A fine bomb-shaped clay cone of the first-mentioned monarch and fragments of three duplicate cylinders of his son were obtained from them more than twelve years ago for the Archæological Museum of the U. of Pa. The place where the stage-tower once stood can be recognized even now with absolute certainty from the peculiar form of the depression which the extracted bricks have left in the soil. The Arabs call it *eṣ-ṣaḥan*, "the bowl." Unlike the stage-tower of Nippur the ground-plan of *Etemenanki* seems to have formed a square. A curious depression extending from the centre of its southeast side marks the entrance of the ancient tower of Babylon, in the same way as that of Nippur is indicated in

Great had returned from India to Babylon, with the intention of residing in this city, as the metropolis of his vast empire. Inspired with new and ambitious plans, the execution of which should establish the glory of his name among the nations forever, he was about to rebuild "the tower of Babel" and "to cause its summit to rival the heavens" again, when suddenly he was carried away by an untimely death in the vigor of his manhood. One involuntarily thinks of Gen. 11 : 5 (and 8): "And the Lord came down to see the city and the tower which the children of men builded." Proclaimed as a god in Egypt, Alexander shared the fate of the supreme god of his capital on the Euphrates. Not far from "the sepulchral mound of Bêl" (pp. 459, *seqq.*), which his soldiers had razed to the ground, the unconquered hero succumbed to the Babylonian fever in the palace of Nebuchadrezzar.

The enormous empire which the great Macedonian had founded was divided among his principal generals. Seleucia on the Tigris took the place of Babylon under the new dynasty. Insignificant traces of this period have been discovered also at Nippur. But the rich province was soon lost by Alexander's heirs to more powerful invaders. About a hundred years after the great king's death we find the Parthians in possession of the entire country, erecting their castles and palaces with ancient material on all the important ruins of Shumer and Akkad (pp. 159, 226, *seqq.*, 368, *seq.*). The stage-tower of Nippur was remodelled for military purposes (pp. 501, *seq.*), and a strongly fortified palace arose on the site of the temple of Bêl (see p. 555).

the light-shaded centre of the ground-plan of the "Parthian Palace built over the Ruins of the Temple of Bêl" (p. 559, below). The peculiar depression marking the ancient site of the "tower of Babel" is reproduced accurately in the topographical map of "Tell Amran," published by the German Orient Society. Comp. also Bruno Meissner, *Von Babylon nach den Ruinen von Hîra und Huarnaq*, Leipzig, 1901, p. 1.

For the last time a certain prosperity pervades the country, and all the mounds of Nippur are covered with flourishing Parthian settlements (pp. 309, 313, 327, *seqq.*, 334, *seqq.*, 366, *seqq.*, 423, *seqq.*). But compared with the ancient civilization and wealth of the people, the period of the Parthian rule is a period of deterioration and decay. The resting places of the dead begin to occur side by side with the residences of the living.[1] The city of Bêl rapidly becomes again what it had been at the beginning of its long and varied history — a vast cemetery.

With the rise of the Sassanian dynasty (A. D. 226–643) the importance of the city is gone. The magnificent palace grouped around the *ziggurrat* as a citadel lies in ruins; no imposing new building is henceforth erected within the

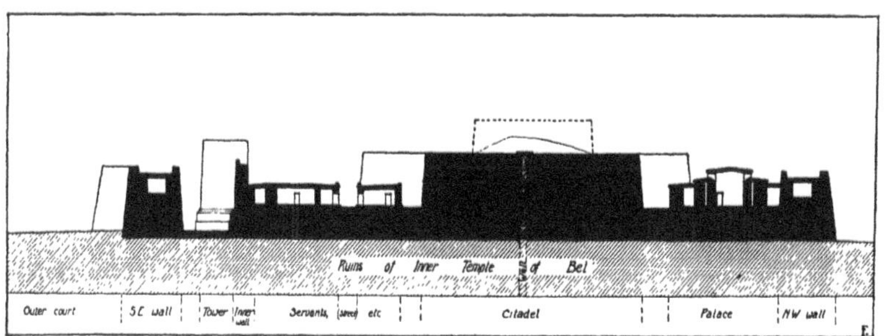

Section through the Parthian Fortress covering the Temple of Bêl, looking southwest

Restored and drawn by Fisher

precincts of ancient Nippur. Of course small mud houses and insignificant shops continue to occupy the most prominent parts of the high-towering ruins for centuries longer. A great number of Hebrew, Mandean and Syriac bowls (pp. 326, 337, 447, *seq.*), the wooden box of a Jewish scribe

[1] We excavated hundreds of tombs from the four hundred years when the Arsacide dynasty held sway over Babylonia (about 250 B. C. to A. D. 226) in the slopes of the mounds and under the floors of the houses of the later inhabitants.

containing his pen-holder and inkstand and a little scrap of crumbling parchment inscribed with a few Hebrew characters, large quantities of late pottery and several rotten bags filled with Kûfic silver and copper coins were gathered by our different expeditions in the upper stratum of Nuffar. All these antiquities show that the city existed in some form or other even as late as the early Arabic period, and that the Jewish element was strongly represented among its inhabitants. About A. D. 1000 or soon afterwards the site must have been abandoned definitely. Arabic historians occasionally refer to it. But the latest inscribed antiquities thus far excavated are thin silver coins of Mervân ibn Mohammed, the last 'Omayyade caliph (744–749), and others of the first 'Abbâside caliphs of Baghdad, among them Hârûn ar-Rashîd (786–809 A. D.), the well-known contemporary of Charlemagne, and several of his less famous successors in the ninth century.[1]

In examining the post-Babylonian ruins of Nuffar, which represent about twelve hundred years of strange history, we distinguished six different periods. Two of them, however, can be recognized with certainty only in the large temple area. Beginning at the surface of the mounds, we first come upon the extensive remains of the early Arabic period, easily determined by low mud houses containing vessels and potsherds, Hebrew Mandean and Syriac incantation bowls, Kûfic coins, shallow graves, etc. (pp. 313, 337). Next we reach the numerous Sassanian burials, characterized by certain forms of coffins and different kinds of pottery drains which often descend far into the real Babylonian strata below, by rude seals badly engraved with human figures, animals, plants and the like (p. 326), and by many minor antiquities. The layers then following are filled with the

[1] According to information from Halil Bey, Director of the Imperial Ottoman Museum, who at my request kindly examined all our excavated Arabic coins, as far as they had then been cleaned.

typical objects of the Hellenistic and Roman age (pp. 330, *seq.*), including a number of vaulted tombs and other graves. They represent three different periods of occupancy during the Parthian rule (pp. 331, *seq.*, 365, *seq.*). A huge Parthian fortress covers the ruins of the temple of Bêl. The doors of the excavated houses and corridors had been walled up from below once or twice, as can still be recognized from the central column of the débris seen in the frontispiece and the illustration facing p. 453. "All of the doors, as we found them, were at least five to six feet and a half above the proper level of the floors." The later inhabitants of Nippur very evidently experienced something similar to that which Nebuchadrezzar describes in connection with his palace and the street of procession at Babylon. The streets and passageways, which originally were on a level with the floors of the rooms, "filled up with débris and mud washed down from the walls and rooms of the houses." It consequently became necessary for the inhabitants "to descend from the street level to the house doors by steps," which still exist in the case of two of the doors directly in front of the *ziggurrat*. This circumstance doubtless rendered the rooms comparatively cool during the summer. But during the rainy season these *serdâbs*[1] often enough must have looked more like cisterns than human habitations. Those who occupied them were therefore forced from time to "time to fill up the houses within to the level of the street, block up the old doorways and cut new ones, build an addition on the walls, and raise the roofs" correspondingly.[2]

Some six to eight feet below the rooms of the last Parthian palace there were remains of an earlier post-Babylonian fortress, which probably belonged to the Seleucidan period (about 320–250 A. D.). As previously stated (pp. 503, *seq.*), apart from the greater depth of their level, these ruins can be distinguished easily from those lying above

[1] Comp. p. 225, above. [2] Comp. Peters, "Nippur," pp. 155, *seq.*

them by the different quality and the smaller size of their bricks and by the direction of their walls.[1] Arsacide coins, commonly found in the upper layers (p. 327), are wholly absent from these lower rooms.

It will have become apparent from our brief sketch of the post-Babylonian history of Nippur that the only building remains deserving our special attention in this connection are those of the Parthian period. They occur practically on all the prominent mounds of the ancient city, and many years more of methodical excavation are therefore required in the upper strata of Nuffar before we shall be able to understand the topography of this last important settlement in the least adequately. All that we can do at present is to illustrate the general character of the larger buildings of this period by the example of the two Parthian palaces already excavated. Their plan and disposition were ascertained chiefly through the labors of the fourth expedition.

The more imposing of the two structures occupies the central part of the temple area. A glance at the plan opposite this page will convince us that the Parthian fortress, like the Babylonian temple beneath it, consisted of two courts. They did not communicate with one another, except perhaps by means of a large staircase, the remains of which seem to have perished. The southeast court not being explored yet, we confine ourselves to setting forth the principal features of the great palace grouped around the remodelled *ziggurrat*. The huge building comprised an area no doubt intended to be rectangular. The entire space was surrounded by a double wall of colossal proportions. It varied considerably in thickness, and was about 560 feet long on its southeast side. The north corner of this vast enclosure has not yet been determined, while its west corner was found to be washed away by the action of rain water

[1] Indicated by the number I in cut on opposite page.

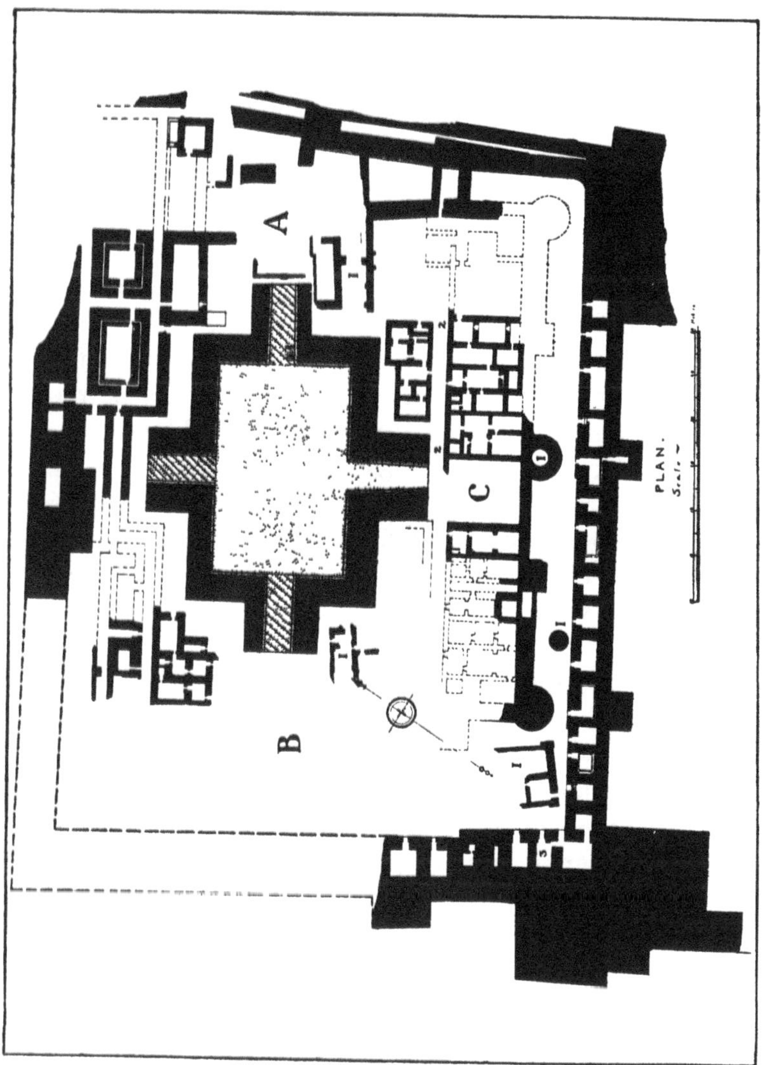

Parthian Palace built over the Ruins of the Temple of Bēl

Restored by Hilprecht, surveyed and drawn by Fisher and Geere

I. Remains of an earlier, probably Seleucidan building, about 300 B. C. The rest represents the remains of a Parthian palace, grouped around the ziggurrat as a citadel (about 250 B. C. to 200 A. D.). A. Public reception rooms and private apartments for the prince and his officers (partly unexcavated). B. Harem (largely unexcavated). C. Domestic quarters, store-rooms, barracks, etc. 1 (on the ziggurrat). The only well of the palace. 2. Street separating the palace proper from the domestic quarters. 3. Room with a tomb beneath.

cutting a deep gulley into the ruins. The bricks generally used in all the constructions of the fortress are large, almost square blocks of adobe (pp. 334, 365, 503).

The southeast side has been examined more carefully than the rest of the building. The ruined outer wall, when excavated, still rose to the height of over sixty feet and was more than thirty feet thick at its top, and almost forty feet at its base, which besides was cased with baked bricks taken from various earlier ruins. This wall was strengthened by two huge buttresses at the corners, and by two smaller ones erected at equal distances between the former. Along the summit of three of the outer walls was a series of rooms at uneven distances and of different sizes. Most of them, entered by doors from the enclosed yard below, apparently served as barracks for the soldiers. Others were accessible only from above, and must have been used as prisons or magazines. The outer northeast wall in reality consisted of two separate walls, the space between them being filled in with mud and débris.

Along the inner face of the southeast wall ran a corridor or passageway over twenty-four feet wide. Beyond it was an inner wall relieved by two buttresses and (probably) three solid round towers, each of which was about thirty feet in diameter and crowned with a parapet. The large open space thus strongly fortified was occupied with a great many rooms and corridors, more or less connected with each other and evidently forming an organic whole. They were generally stuccoed with a plaster, and frequently tinted in green, pink, and yellow colors. Several of them had a window or ventilator of baked bricks high up in one of the walls, while drainage was often effected by an opening under the threshold of the door or through the solid wall of the house. In one case a large perforated vase was sunk below the floor of stamped earth in the north corner of the room.

The north section of the vast complex was set apart for a number of fine large rooms. Two of them,[1] surrounded on all sides by spacious corridors, were composed of double walls with an air space between them, scarcely wide enough to admit of the passage of an adult. Similar passageways ran around a few other rooms in the southeast wall of the fortress.[2] The size of these chambers and the greater care with which the whole quarter evidently had been planned and constructed suggested their use as public reception halls adjoined by the private chambers of the prince or governor and his officers. As practically only a narrow room or corridor connected this wing of the palace with the west section, which to a large extent is still unexplored, we may assume with a reasonable degree of probability that the latter was reserved for the harem. No regular gate having been found in the south and east parts of the enclosure, it follows almost with certainty that the principal entrance of the castle must exist somewhere near the unexcavated north corner of the large structure.

From many characteristic objects discovered (pp. 330, 365) we know that the kitchens, storerooms, servants' quarters, etc., were located in the southeast section of the building. A narrow street running parallel with the principal façade of the stage-tower separated them from the palace proper. In the middle of this unpaved street was a well-made gutter of burned bricks, into which the drains of the adjoining rooms discharged their contents.

Out of the midst of all these chambers and corridors rose the stage-tower as an almost impregnable bulwark. It served as a citadel, on the top of which the garrison and inhabitants of the palace would find refuge even after the lower parts of the fortress had fallen into the hands of the enemy. The infinite toil with which the only well of the whole

[1] They measure 28 by 41 and 21 by 22½ feet respectively.

[2] Indicated in the cut, p. 559. Comp. p. 246.

enclosure must have been cut through the core of the *ziggurrat* to the water level, and the great care manifested in enlarging and strengthening the Babylonian stage-tower by four irregular buttresses, projecting like so many gigantic wings from the centres of the four sides, indicated sufficiently what strategic importance the Parthian rulers attached to this part of their palace. The peculiar cruciform shape of the massive building was originally suggested by the ancient entrance or causeway of the tower (on its south-east side). The first buttress-like additions to the *ziggurrat* accordingly were not much wider than the latter. As they were built of the same kind of bricks which characterizes the remains of the earlier castle,[1] they must belong to the Seleucidan period. Under the Parthian rulers these arms, like the rest of the structure, were broadened considerably.[2] At the same time the ruined stages were trimmed and overbuilt with large crude bricks, thus making an immense platform rising no less than twenty-five to thirty feet above the rest of the fortress. A second stage rose like a huge watch-tower from the centre of the first. To judge from the height of Bint el-Amîr as we first saw it, this cannot have been lower than twenty feet. Both stages were naturally surrounded by a parapet to afford the besieged garrison sufficient protection against the weapons of its enemies. In times of peace this elevated gallery, with its superb view over the endless plains, must have been a favorite place of rest for the residents of the palace, where they enjoyed a fresh breeze and doubtless spent their nights during the hottest months of the year.

The fortified palace with which we have occupied ourselves cannot be considered as typical for the architecture of the Parthian period; for the size and general plan of

[1] Marked *I* in the cut, p. 559.

[2] They were from 45 to 63 feet wide, and projected 30 to 50 feet into the court from the Babylonian tower.

the vast structure were largely determined by the ruined tower and walls of the Babylonian temple beneath. It was different with regard to the much smaller palace on the west

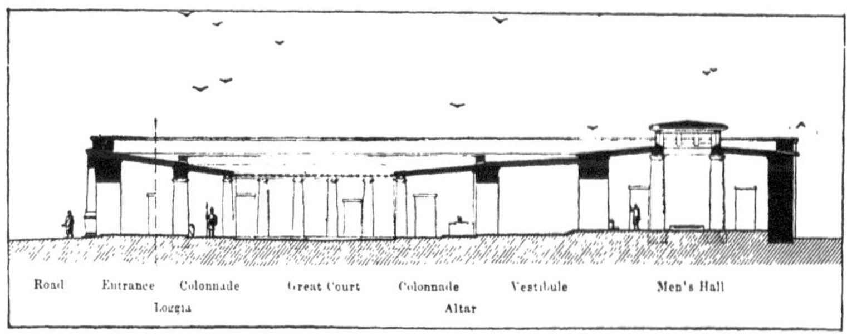

Section through the Small Parthian Palace on West Side of the Chebar, looking Northeast

Restored and drawn by Fisher

side of the Chebar, which belongs to the third or second century preceding our era. The material of which it consists is mostly crude brick, of size, shape and texture similar to that forming the core of the fortress on the opposite bank of the canal. To speak more exactly, the adobes of the west palace are in size between the bricks of the earlier and those of the later fortress, their average dimensions being 12 by 12 by 7¼ inches. Like the latter they are made of clay obtained from the breaking up of older material. That the smaller building cannot be older than the date just assigned to it, and possibly is somewhat younger, follows with necessity from a small thick copper coin discovered in one of the bricks. Much corroded as it was, it could be assigned with a reasonable degree of certainty to one of the rulers of the Arsacide dynasty. A number of stone seals engraved with animals — among them an agate ring showing a fish, — which were taken from the floor level in different parts of the building, afforded additional proof to my theory as to the late origin of the structure.

The absolutely un-Babylonian character of the palace

becomes evident also from an examination of its ground-plan and a study of its architectural details. The clear and regular division of the entire building, the methodical grouping of its rooms around two open courts, the liberal employment of columns as a decorative element, a certain refinement and beauty with regard to proportion, the very apparent aiming at unity, with due consideration of convenience, are characteristic features of the ancient Greek houses on Delos rather than of those known from ancient Babylonia. The building was intended to be square, each side measuring about 170 feet.[1] Its foundation was laid upon the ruins of the early city more than forty-two feet above the level of the plain. In accordance with a well-known Babylonian custom, its four corners pointed approximately to the four cardinal points. As the house stood upon the outskirts of a mound bordering the Shatt en-Nîl,[2] the east corner of the structure is almost completely washed away.

There can be little doubt that the building had but one entrance, which was situated nearly in the centre of the northwest façade. It consisted of an elaborately finished doorway and porch, reached by two steps from the street. As there is undeniable evidence that the southwest and southeast sides of the palace were originally broken up by a system of shallow buttresses, we may assume that the exterior surface of the badly damaged northwest wall was decorated with similar panels or recessings. The northeast side, however, which faced the river, seems to have been left without any ornamentation. "The pilasters on either side of the doorway and the columns of the courtyards were stuccoed,"[3] while the rest of the building was covered with a mud plaster.

[1] More exactly the northwest side measured 174, the northeast 168⅔, the southwest 170, the southeast 172¾ feet.

[2] Comp. the plan of the ruins on p. 305.

[3] The quotations in this and the following lines are from Fisher's and Geere's report on the building.

The walls of the house varied in thickness from three feet to eight feet and a half. From fragments of pavements found in some of the rooms we may infer that the floors of the principal apartments at least were of baked brick. In the construction of steps, pillars, thresholds, fireplaces, beds and the like the same material was used, while the open courtyards were paved with unbaked bricks. The floor of the bathroom was covered with bitumen. As the many charred pieces of wood indicated sufficiently, the roof of the building consisted of palm logs, matting and earth. "We may safely assert that there was no second story to the building." The doors were made of mulberry or tamarisk wood and swung on door-sockets of stone, baked brick, or cement. In the case of quite a number of the rooms, rugs or curtains seem to have taken the place of doors. Owing to the destruction of the house by fire and its farther devastation by rain and later inhabitants who used the ruins of the once imposing structure as a quarry and graveyard, we know little or nothing "as to the methods of decoration adopted by the builders for the interior of the palace." It was probably plastered and painted according to the manner of the more ambitious structure on the other side of the Chebar.

A word remains to be said about the courts and columns. The larger courtyard (4)[1] measured nearly 64 by 70 feet, the smaller (21) was about 28 feet square. "The central part of the former was probably open to the sky, to give light and fresh air to the rooms, while columns, placed at nearly even distances from one another, served to support a roof over the adjoining gallery or colonnade which surrounded it." There were four round columns on each side of the principal courtyard and a square one at each angle. They were built of baked bricks especially made for the purpose, and must have been at least fifty courses, or 12½ feet, high.

[1] Comp. the cut, p. 567.

The lower parts of twelve of them were still standing (comp. the illustration facing p. 340). The circular columns were 2 feet 9 inches in diameter at the base, and 2 feet 1 inch at the fiftieth course of bricks. From the first to the seventeenth course, *i. e.*, during the first third of the entire height, the diameter remained nearly constant; after that it gradually diminished. Certain fragments of curiously moulded bricks found near the courtyard proved that these tapering brick columns also had capitals. As Babylonian imitations of Doric columns, they naturally had no regular base, but rested upon burnt brick foundations eleven courses deep, which were completely hidden in the soil. "Between these square foundations ran an edging, or curbing, of the same material, but only two courses deep."

All the other characteristic features of the interesting building can be studied best in connection with the accompanying plan. We observe that the little palace is divided into two almost equal parts, the northeast half reserved for the public functions of the men, and the southwest half for the family life proper. From the entrance lobby (1) two doors open off, the one towards the west leading through a small anteroom (8) and a long corridor (9) to the servants' quarters (10–15) and harem (16, *seqq.*); the other towards the east through a similar anteroom (2), the main vestibule (3), and the colonnade into the large courtyard (4), flanked by a number of rooms. It will be noticed that the vestibule is not situated exactly in the middle with reference to the courtyard. In leaving the latter and continuing our way towards the southeast, we first pass an altar on our left (5), and next enter the two largest halls of the whole building (6 and 7). They are connected with one another by a large doorway which generally was closed by a double door, as two sockets found *in situ* on either side of the entrance and fragments of iron hinges and nails plainly indicated. One step edged with burned bricks leads from the colonnade to the *atrium* (6), and three steps from the latter into the assembly hall proper (7).

The harem could be reached from the colonnade directly

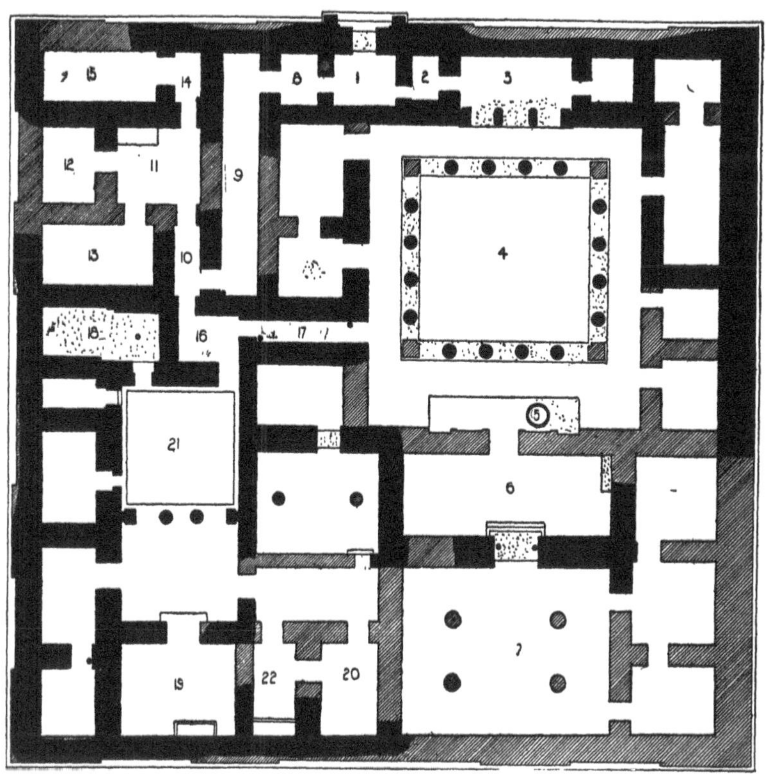

Plan of a Small Parthian Palace at Nippur, about 250 B. C.

Discovered in 1889, and excavated completely in 1900. About thirty-six rooms and halls grouped around open courts. Entrance on the north-west side. Surveyed by Fisher and Geere · drawn by the former.

by a narrow passageway (17), either end of which was closed by a door.[1] A kind of anteroom (16) formed a connecting link between the men's quarters, the servants' rooms and the section reserved for the women. Thus the

1 This was ascertained from two door-sockets found *in situ*.

private apartments of the family were securely shut off from the rest of the building. The general plan and arrangement of this section do not require special interpretation, as they are similar to those of the northeast half of the palace. The elevated constructions built against the southeast wall in rooms 19 and 22 probably are places for reclining and rest (so-called beds). The floor of the bathroom (18) was paved with bitumen, with a border of brickwork coated with the same material, and laid in such a way as to drain perfectly towards the opening shown in the plan. The kitchen and storerooms were naturally situated in the servants' quarters. The former (11) was easily identified by its hearth; the latter were characterized by large jars, abundant ashes, and quantities of charred barley and other seeds.

TURKISH GLEANINGS AT ABÛ HABBA, UNDER SCHEIL AND BEDRY BEY.

The recent awakening of archæological interest in Turkey, and the gradual appreciation of the literary and artistic monuments of the past on the part of the Mohammedan population, are closely connected with the period of reform and progress inaugurated by Sultan 'Abdul Hamîd in different departments of the public administration. For not only was the army reorganized after European patterns, large tracts of fallow land acquired by the crown and rapidly changed into flourishing estates (the so-called *arâzî-i-senîye*), railroads constructed and the many natural resources of the country opened and developed, but the public schools were increased, technical colleges and a university established, daily papers appeared and — something formerly entirely unknown in the Ottoman empire — illustrated journals were published, and even a great national museum was founded. The man called upon to carry out the ideas of his sovereign in the field of archæology was Hamdy Bey, son of Edhem

Pasha, a former Grand Vizier. Richly endowed with natural gifts and liberally educated in the congenial atmosphere of France, where his pronounced personal inclinations found ample nourishment in the *Ecole des Beaux Arts* and in the studios of great painters, he had subsequently entered the service of his own government and gathered considerable experience in prominent positions. Appointed director of foreign affairs in the vilayet of Baghdad under the famous Midhat Pasha, he had afterwards won the favor of 'Abdul 'Azîz and become introducer of ambassadors, and for a short while even governor of Pera, the European quarter of Constantinople. He had participated in the expedition against the refractory 'Afej tribes of Babylonia and had seen active military life in the Turkish war against Russia. Hamdy Bey being well versed in the general questions of archæology and not unfamiliar with the most prominent ruins of Western Asia, and widely known for his deep sense of honor and his frank and chivalrous manners, at the same time possessing firmness of character and a rare understanding for the tasks of his mission, it would have been difficult to find a better equipped man as director-general of the Imperial Museum in the whole Ottoman empire.

The beginnings of the Turkish archæological museum go back to the middle of the last century. Fethi Ahmed Pasha, grand-master of the artillery, then gathered a number of stray antiquities in a room and in the court of the ancient church of St. Irene. Twenty-five years later, when Dr. Déthier was in charge of these modest collections, they were transferred by an imperial *irade* to the quaint little palace of Tshinili Kiosk, one of the best types of early Turkish architecture and faïence work in existence. But the subsequent rapid development and phenomenal growth of this embryonic museum into a great archæological storehouse of international reputation is almost entirely due to the energetic measures and wise administration of Hamdy Bey, who has been its real soul and characteristic central figure. No sooner was he entrusted with the management of the archæological affairs of his country (1881), than the antiquated and detrimental laws of excavations, under which a national Ottoman museum could not prosper, were radically changed and remodelled.[1] The spacious subterranean vaults of Tshinili Kiosk were carefully searched and long-forgotten monuments rediscovered.[2] System and order began soon to prevail, where formerly nothing was accessible to science. Small as the annual sum proved to be which was placed at Hamdy Bey's disposal for meeting the current expenses and for realizing the many new projects constantly cherished by his active mind, the lofty terrace of the old seraglio with its superb view on the Golden Horn presented an entirely different picture at the close of the nineteenth century. Out of the midst of luxuriant gardens and pleasing alleys adorned with Greek and Roman statues, bas-reliefs, pillars, and tombstones, there rise three magnificent fire-proof buildings filled with rich archæological treasures open for public inspection, while close by the museum we notice the School of Fine Arts, with its three sections of architecture, sculpture and painting, created to propagate knowledge and love of art and archæology among younger generations.

One cannot but admire the courage and determination of this single man, who, in the face of numerous obstacles thrown in his way by his own countrymen, by dissatisfied explorers

[1] Compare above. A translation of the present Turkish law on Archæological Excavations is given in Appendix D of John P. Peters' "Nippur, or Explorations and Adventures on the Euphrates," New York, 1897, vol. i, pp. 303–309. Recently, however, there have again been made certain changes with regard to the relations between the government and private landowners.

[2] Unfortunately the monument known as "Sennacherib Constantinople" was not among these antiquities. Comp. Hilprecht, *Sanherib Constantinopel*, in *Zeitschrift für Assyriologie*, vol. xiii, pp. 322–325, and p. 211, above.

and foreign diplomats, was able to accomplish this gigantic task within the short period of twenty years, — a fact even more remarkable when we consider that the inner consolidation of the whole department kept pace with the external growth and development. New sections were created, more officers appointed, a well-equipped library was added, and

The Imperial Ottoman Museum at Constantinople

This building contains a representative collection of ancient sarcophagi, and the Babylonian, Assyrian, Egyptian, and early Turkish antiquities.

competent specialists were invited to classify and catalogue the various collections.[1] In order to protect the more exposed monuments carved in the rocks of mountain passes,

[1] Among them the two brothers of Hamdy Bey, the late Ghalib Bey and Halil Bey, Director of the Imperial Ottoman Museum, for Oriental coins and Moslem antiquities; Prof. André Joubin, of Paris, for classical and Byzantine antiquities; Prof. V. Scheil, of Paris, for the Egyptian monuments; Consul J. H. Mordtmann for South-Arabian and Palmyrene antiquities; and Prof. Hilprecht, of the University of Pennsylvania, for the Assyrian and Babylonian collections.

built in modern bridges and houses, or accidentally found in the ground by the natives, special regulations were drafted,[1] and orders were issued to the officials in the provinces to report new antiquities and to look after their preservation. There is scarcely a branch of archæology which did not profit in some way by these and similar measures which originated in the brain of Hamdy Bey. The inscribed bas-relief of Narâm-Sin discovered in 1892, near Diarbekr, the fine alabaster slab of Bêl-Harrân-bêl-usur from Tell Abta (1894), and the important stele of Nabonidos unearthed by the brick-diggers of Bâbil (1895) indicate some of the more prominent monuments which hereby were saved for Assyriology.

Apart from the numerous antiquities received as gifts, purchased from dealers, and obtained through the personal interest and watchfulness of local governors, the Ottoman Museum drew its principal collections from its own excavations and from the trenches of European and American expeditions in Western Asia. The first tentative Turkish diggings at Nebî Yûnus,[2] undertaken more to satisfy curiosity and to secure hidden treasures than to serve the cause of archæology, were soon followed by the serious exploration of the temple of Hecate at Legina, by Hamdy Bey's and Osgan Effendi's scientific mission to the snowy summit of Nimrûd Dagh,[3] by the former's famous discovery in the

[1] At the request of Hamdy Bey the present writer was commissioned to report to the Ottoman Minister of Public Instruction as to the best manner of protecting the Babylonian and Assyrian relics and mounds. The report was submitted in 1894, and action was soon afterwards taken in accordance with the recommendations. Comp. pp. 68, *seq.*; and Hilprecht, *Türkische Bestrebungen auf dem Gebiete der Assyriologie*, in *Kölnische Zeitung*, second supplement of the Sunday edition, March 8, 1896; also Hilprecht, "Recent Researches in Bible Lands," Philadelphia, 1896, pp. 81–93.

[2] Comp. p. 211, above.

[3] Comp. Hamdy Bey and Osgan Effendi, *Le Tumulus de Nemroud-Dagh*, Constantinople, 1883.

royal necropolis of Sidon,[1] by Scheil's and Bedry Bey's gleanings at Abû Habba, and by Makridi Bey's recent researches at Bostân esh-Shaikh.[2] The new spirit of progress and enlightenment which emanated from the palace and which found an eloquent herald in the halls of the Imperial Museum is best characterized by the unique fact that several years ago a young officer of the Turkish army submitted an essay on the Sumerian question to the present writer for criticism. Though leniently to be judged as to its real merits, this manuscript speaks volumes for the far-reaching influence which the cuneiform collections at Stambul exercised as an educational factor upon the minds of intelligent Moslems. No wonder that it was the Sultan himself who became the originator of the first Turkish archæological expedition to Babylonia. Deeply interested in the epoch-making results of the French and American explorers by which the Imperial Museum had been greatly enriched, His Majesty placed a special sum of money out of his private purse at the disposal of Hamdy Bey for methodical excavations at a Babylonian ruin.

Immediately after Rassam's departure from Baghdad in 1882, Arab diggers, encouraged by unscrupulous landowners and antiquity dealers, had commenced their clandestine operations at most of the places where their former employer had successfully excavated. For several years Abû Habba and Dêr, El-Birs and Babylon, thus became the principal sources from which European and American museums were supplied with archæological contraband. Only a few of these monuments were confiscated and reached the

[1] Comp. Hamdy Bey and Th. Reinach, *Une Nécropole royale à Sidon, Fouilles de Hamdy Bey*, Paris, 1896.

[2] A few miles from Saïda (Sidon). Comp. Hilprecht, in "The Sunday School Times," vol. 43, p. 621 (Sept. 28, 1901), and in *Deutsche Literaturzeitung*, Nov. 30, 1901, pp. 3030, *seq.*, and in "Sunday School Times," Dec. 21, 1901, p. 857.

Ottoman Museum. Abû Habba, as was well known to the authorities in Constantinople, proved an especially rich and almost inexhaustible mine for the illegal traffic. It was therefore decided to apply the imperial fund to a renewed examination of the ruins of Sippar, especially as brief but successful excavations had been conducted there previously (1889) by the Civil Cabinet under the control of the governor of Baghdad.[1] The carrying out of this scientific project was entrusted to Father Scheil, a young and energetic French Assyriologist, who had rendered valuable services to the Stambul museum in connection with the organization of the Egyptian and Babylonian sections, and to Bedry Bey, a well-known Turkish commissioner, who had gained no small experience in the trenches of Tellô and Nuffar. In the beginning of 1894 this Ottoman commission reached the place of its destination. Strongly supported by the officials of the vilayet, and confining their work chiefly to a search for inscribed monuments, the two men were able to execute their task satisfactorily in the brief space of two months, at the end of which their limited means were exhausted. No complete report of these excavations having yet appeared, we can only sketch the principal results obtained on the basis of Scheil's notes published in Maspéro's journal,[2] and

[1] Most of the antiquities discovered were lost to the museum in Constantinople. Among the few which were sent are the interesting archaic stone fragment published in Hilprecht, "Old Babylonian Inscriptions, chiefly from Nippur," part 1, Philadelphia, 1893, plates vi–viii (comp. also, Scheil in *Recueil de Travaux relatifs à la Philologie et à l'Archéologie égyptiennes et assyriennes*, vol. xxii (1900), pp. 29, *seqq.*), and the brick from a well constructed by Nebuchadrezzar, published *ibidem*, part 2, Philadelphia, 1896, pl. 70.

[2] Comp. *Recueil de Travaux relatif à la Philologie et à l'Archéologie égyptiennes et assyriennes*, vol. xvi (1894), pp. 90–92, 184, *seqq.*, vol. xvii (1895), pp. 184, *seqq.*, and the following numbers of the same journal. According to a communication from Prof. Scheil, a book on his work at Abû Habba will appear in the course of 1892 in Cairo, under the title *Une saison*

in accordance with my own personal knowledge of the collections of the Imperial Museum.

Among the objects of mere archæological interest a number of rude clay animals sitting on their hind legs, and on an average about one foot high, attract our attention. There is, *e. g.*, one which represents a monkey, another a dog, a third a bear, while others are modelled so poorly that it is difficult to say what animals are intended by them. Apparently they belong to the earlier period of Babylonian history and must be regarded as votive offerings, like a neo-Babylonian dog in the same material and from the same ruins, which bears a dedication of two lines of cuneiform inscription to the goddess Gula. Small terra-cotta figurines and bas-reliefs, including images of Shamash and his consort, and the mask of an ugly demon, several utensils and weapons in bronze, the common beads, seal cylinders, stone weights, and other minor antiquities as they are generally found in Babylonian ruins, complete the collection. There are also a few bricks of King Bur-Sin II., Kurigalzu, Shamash-shum-ukîn and Nebuchadrezzar II. But the most important part of the recovered antiquities are nearly seven hundred clay tablets, complete or fragmentary, most of them letters and contracts dated in the reigns of rulers of the first Babylonian dynasty, especially Samsu-ilûna, the son and successor of Hammurabi. Some of the inscriptions are of a literary character and belonged originally to the famous temple library of Sippara. We notice several syllabaries and lists of cuneiform signs, school exercises on round tablets, proverbs, incantations, hymns and two fragments of historical interest. The one reveals to us the name of a new member of the third dynasty of Ur, Idin-Dagân (about 2500 B. C.), the other contains in chronological order a

de fouilles à Sippar (with plates, numerous vignettes and a plan of the ruins), and forming vol. 1 of *Mémoires de l' Institut français d' Archéologie orientale du Caire.*

number of dates from the time of Hammurabi and Samsu-ilûna,[1] by means of which the single years of their governments were officially designated and known to the people.

Unfortunately, most of the letters discovered contain, according to Scheil, only accounts. But nevertheless there are many among them which bring before our eyes scenes from the daily lives of the ancient Babylonians in such a realistic manner that human conditions and circumstances may seem to have changed but little during the past four thousand years. For example, an official, stationed in a small village, Dûr-Sin, complains to his father that it is impossible to procure anything fit to eat, and begs him, therefore, to buy with the accompanying piece of money some food, and send it to him. But let the writer of this epistle speak for himself: "To my father from Zimri-eramma. May the gods Shamash and Marduk keep thee alive forever. May all go well with thee. I write thee to inquire after thy health. Please let me know how it goes with thee. I am stationed in Dûr-Sin, on the canal Bîtimsikirim. Where I live there is no food which I am able to eat. Here is the third part of a shekel, which I have sealed up, and forward unto thee. Send me for this money fresh fish and other food to eat."

Another letter, addressed to a female by the name of Bibeya, reads as follows: "To Bibeya from Gimil-Marduk: May Shamash and Marduk grant thee, for my sake, to live forever. I write this in order to inquire after thy health. Let me know how it goes with thee. I am now settled in Babylon, but I am in great anxiety, because I have not seen thee. Send news when thou wilt come, that I may rejoice at it. Come at the month of Arakhsamna [November-

[1] Recently published by Scheil in *Textes Élamites-Sémitiques* (forming vol. ii. of De Morgan's *Délégation en Perse, Mémoires*), series 1, Paris, 1900, p. 83, note 1; and by Lindl in *Beiträge zur Assyriologie*, vol. iv, part 3 (Leipzig, 1901), pp. 341, *seqq.*

December]. Mayest thou, for my sake, live forever." It is clear that this letter was not written to a mother, sister, daughter, or any other relative, because, according to Babylonian custom, relationship is generally indicated by a word placed in apposition after the name of the person to whom the letter is addressed. Therefore we can scarcely be wrong in regarding this clay tablet as a specimen of an ancient Babylonian love-letter of the time of Abraham.

Finally, there may be mentioned a small round tablet of the same period, and from the same ruins, which contains, in the Babylonian style, a parallel passage to Daniel 12 : 3 : " They that be wise shall shine as the brightness of the firmament." It has but three lines of inscription written in Sumerian, the old sacred language of that country : —

1 *Sha*[1] *muntila*
2 *ki namdupsara-ka*
3 *u-gim ğena-e*

That is, " Whoever distinguishes himself at the place of tablet-writing [in other words, at the school or university of the Babylonians] shall shine as the day.[2] "

[1] Semitism for Sumerian *galu*.

[2] For the above sketch comp. Hilprecht, " Recent Researches in Bible Lands," Philadelphia, 1896, pp. 81–86.

GORGIAS REPRINTS IN ARCHAEOLOGY

1. Austen Henry Layard, *Nineveh and Its Remains: an account of a visit to the Chaldean Christians of Kurdistan, and the Yezidis, or devil-worshipers; and an inquiry into the manners and arts of the ancient Assyrians*, vols. 2 (2001, based on the 1850 5th edition).
2. Austen Henry Layard, *Discoveries in the Ruins of Nineveh and Babylon; With Travels in Armenia Kurdistan and the Desert...* (2002, based on the 1853 edition).
3. George Smith. *Assyrian Discoveries: An Account of Explorations and Discoveries on the Site of Nineveh, During 1873 and 1874* (2002, based on the 1876 edition).
4. A. Henry Rhind, *Thebes, Its Tombs and Their Tenants, Ancient and Present, including a record of excavations in the Necropolis* (2002, based on the 1862 edition).
5. H. V. Hilprecht, *Explorations in Bible Lands During the 19th Century* (2002, based on the 1903 edition).

www.ingramcontent.com/pod-product-compliance
Lightning Source LLC
Chambersburg PA
CBHW030827310726
48980CB00006B/675/J
* 9 7 8 1 9 3 1 9 5 6 5 1 2 *